Synthajoy

Edward Cadence was a brilliant man, and a dedicated scientist. He had invented Sensitape, a means of recording the thoughts and emotions of great musicians, religious figures, etc. so that others could experience at first-hand just what it was like to play a magnificent concerto, or to slip peacefully toward an untroubled death with the sure expectation that Heaven lies waiting. And he had added Sexitape, whereby people whose sex lives weren't completely satisfying could experience everything that the most compatible couple in the world felt together.

For all this he was given the Nobel Prize, became enormously wealthy and famous. But finally he set to work on the ultimate application of his experiments: Synthajoy.

And when the enormity of this dehumanising process became clear, he was murdered.

The Steel Crocodile

In answer to an unanswerable future, science has created Bohn, the omnipotent computer whose flashing circuits and messianic pronouncements dictate what tomorrow will – or will not – be.

But Matthew Oliver is flesh and blood and full of questions – not nearly as certain as the machine he's appointed to serve.

And the right hand of science seldom knows what the left hand is doing …

Ascendancies

Into a future where a depleted fuel supply had the world spiralling down into grinding poverty and constant war came … Moondrift. Mysterious white flakes of alien matter that was the perfect fuel – clean powerful, dependable.

But the aliens – or whatever they were – who sent Moondrift seemed to demand a heavy ransom in return. After each Moondrift comes an eerie sound, as pure as a children's choir, heard all over the world. It mesmerises all who hear it with its beauty – and when it is ended, certain people have simply disappeared without warning, never to be seen again.

This is the story of one who disappeared …

Also by D. G. Compton

Katherine Mortenhoe

The Continuous Katherine Mortenhoe (1974)
Windows (1979)

Other Novels

The Quality of Mercy (1965)
Farewell, Earth's Bliss (1966)
The Silent Multitude (1967)
Synthajoy (1968)
The Palace (1969)
Chronocules (1970) (aka Hot Wireless Sets, Aspirin Tablets, the Sandpaper Slides of Used Matchboxes, and Something that Might have been Castor Oil)
The Steel Crocodile (1970) (aka The Electric Crocodile)
The Missionaries (1972)
A Usual Lunacy (1978)
Ascendancies (1980)
Scudder's Game (1988)
Nomansland (1993)
Justice City (1994)
Back of Town Blues (1996)

D. G. Compton
SF GATEWAY OMNIBUS

SYNTHAJOY
THE STEEL CROCODILE
ASCENDANCIES

GOLLANCZ
LONDON

First published in Great Britain in 2014 by
Gollancz
An imprint of the Orion Publishing Group
Orion House, 5 Upper St Martin's Lane,
London WC2H 9EA

An Hachette UK Company

A CIP catalogue record for this book is available from the British Library

ISBN 978 0 575 11810 2

1 3 5 7 9 10 8 6 4 2

Typeset by Jouve (UK), Milton Keynes

Printed and bound by CPI Group (UK) Ltd, Croydon, CR0 4YY

The Orion Publishing Group's policy is to use papers that are natural, renewable and recyclable products and made from wood grown in sustainable forests. The logging and manufacturing processes are expected to conform to the environmental regulations of the country of origin.

www.orionbooks.co.uk
www.gollancz.co.uk

CONTENTS

ENTER THE SF GATEWAY . . .

Towards the end of 2011, in conjunction with the celebration of fifty years of coherent, continuous science fiction and fantasy publishing, Gollancz launched the SF Gateway.

Over a decade after launching the landmark SF Masterworks series, we realised that the realities of commercial publishing are such that even the Masterworks could only ever scratch the surface of an author's career. Vast troves of classic SF and Fantasy were almost certainly destined never again to see print. Until very recently, this meant that anyone interested in reading any of those books would have been confined to scouring second-hand bookshops. The advent of digital publishing changed that paradigm for ever.

Embracing the future even as we honour the past, Gollancz launched the SF Gateway with a view to utilising the technology that now exists to make available, for the first time, the entire backlists of an incredibly wide range of classic and modern SF and fantasy authors. Our plan, at its simplest, was – and still is! – to use this technology to build on the success of the SF and Fantasy Masterworks series and to go even further.

The SF Gateway was designed to be the new home of classic Science Fiction and fantasy – the most comprehensive electronic library of classic SFF titles ever assembled. The programme has been extremely well received and we've been very happy with the results. So happy, in fact, that we've decided to complete the circle and return a selection of our titles to print, in these omnibus editions.

We hope you enjoy this selection. And we hope that you'll want to explore more of the classic SF and fantasy we have available. These are wonderful books you're holding in your hand, but you'll find much, much more … through the SF Gateway.

www.sfgateway.com

INTRODUCTION

from The Encyclopedia of Science Fiction

David Guy Compton (Born 1930) is a UK author, born of parents who were both in the theatre; he lived for some time in the USA after 1981. Compton's novels are almost always set in the Near Future, and present a moral dilemma within that arena: the future is very clearly used in his work as a device of perspective, with the result that his tales bring contemporary trends into focus that is both clear and intimate. Most of the interest transparently inherent in these novels lies in their exposure of personal relationships and the behaviour of people under stress; minor characters are observed with humour which frequently arises from class differences. Endings are ambiguous or deliberately inconclusive. Later novels are increasingly varied in the narrative techniques deployed, but do not significantly depart from the humane focus of his early work. Compton's rare public utterances confirm the impression that he is not interested in the staple concerns of Genre SF.

Compton's first SF novel was *The Quality of Mercy* (1965), in which conspirators conceive it will be appropriate to commit genocide, using a biological weapon, to combat Overpopulation. Further novels followed rapidly, including the impressive *The Silent Multitude* (1967), in which a space-borne fungus has begun to end civilization. In a crumbling cathedral in a small, infested English city, the Dean and two companions begin to face – but very movingly are incapable of grasping – the fact that the world is ending, moment by moment and inch by inch, around them; that the future they cannot grasp has no room for them, or any other mere human. Further titles include *Farewell, Earth's Bliss* (1966), which dramatizes the plight of social misfits transported to Mars; *Synthajoy* (1968) (see below); *The Steel Crocodile* (1970) (see below); *Chronocules* (1970), a Time-Travel story whose UK title, *Hot Wireless Sets, Aspirin Tablets, the Sandpaper Sides of Used Matchboxes, and Something that Might have been Castor Oil*, may not have been a selling point, though the author must clearly be admired for suggesting it; and *The Missionaries* (1972), which describes the efforts of some evangelizing aliens with a good deal of social comedy.

Compton's strengths as a writer are also displayed in the much admired Katherine Mortenhoe series comprising *The Continuous Katherine Mortenhoe* (1974) and *Windows* (1979). A woman in her forties is given four weeks to live. A reporter with eyes replaced by television cameras has the job of watching her decline for the entertainment of a pain-starved public in a world where illness is almost unknown. The reporter sees one of the transmissions and realizes (perhaps a little late in the game) that the camera cannot tell the truth; the recorded film is without mind and therefore without compassion. The second volume depicts the consequences of the reporter's decision to opt for the oxymoron of literal blindness; neither character in the end is allowed to escape into solitude. *The Continuous Katherine Mortenhoe* was filmed as *La Mort en Direct* (1979). Later work includes *Ascendancies* (1980) (see below); and *Ragnarok* (1991) with John Gribbin which also shows Compton's grasp of character depiction; its near-future plot – in which a scientist brings on a Nuclear Winter in an attempt to enforce disarmament – owes much to his collaborator's grasp of scientific process. But *Nomansland* (1993), and the Alec Jordan series of Near Future policiers comprising *Justice City* (1994) and *Back of Town Blues* (1996), increasingly demonstrate his recapture of the perceptive humanity with which, in earlier books, he so eloquently anatomized the near future. In 2007 he was honoured by SFWA as Author Emeritus, a category of that organization's array of Grand Master Awards; the presentation went some way to recognizing his stature as a humanist author capable of grappling with the future. His readers, though there are not as many as he deserves, remain intense advocates of his high worth.

Synthajoy (1968), the first tale to be presented here, is a complex novel that gained Compton wider notice, particularly in America. A surgeon and an electronics engineer develop a tape machine to record and minutely play back human brain activity, the individual's actual and unique emotional experiences. These, taken from people with outstanding professional abilities, are to be marketed so that members of the general public may know what it really 'feels like' to be a brilliant orchestral conductor or champion cross-country runner. Such a machine of course offers less benevolent possibilities, and Compton's story intimately charts the moral destruction of its narrator, the wife of the machine's inventor. Compton does not precisely describe today's virtual reality devices, but the analogies are clear.

The Steel Crocodile (1970) may be Compton's most intricately sustained and successful single tale. It is set in the Near Future, where an unnamed authority has become fearful of the threat of uncontrolled technological advance, and creates a Computer monitor to ward off potential excesses. The lives and careers of those involved in its creation are compellingly recounted, and the punchline is so bedded into the intimate wisdom of the narrative that it comes as a shock, though it perhaps should not: if we allow a preternaturally advanced technology watch over us (Compton asks), who then shall watch the watcher? Forty years ago, that question may have seemed melodramatic. Today it is no longer so.

The last novel here included is more recent. Also more light-hearted. In *Ascendancies* (1980), manna-like free energy begins to fall from space like glittering dust, but there is no free lunch, and somehow an ominous energy-exchange is put into effect, as humans begin mysteriously to disappear. Further side-effects include unexpected displacements, both physical and in the domestic psyches whose traumas have always inspired his best work. It is a mark of Compton's calm prescient vision that the three novels presented here read like reports from the front. He was there before us, telling us how the future was going to feel at home; this omnibus gives us a chance to catch up.

For a more detailed version of the above, see D. G. Compton's author entry in *The Encyclopedia of Science Fiction*: http://sf-encyclopedia.com/entry/compton_d_g

Some terms above are capitalised when they would not normally be so rendered; this indicates that the terms represent discrete entries in *The Encyclopedia of Science Fiction*.

SYNTHAJOY

DAY 25

Mrs Craig has just asked me yet again to remember that she is a nurse, and to address her as such. I wonder if it is simply small-minded for me to persist in calling her my wardress.

We returned from today's tape therapy five minutes ago. She evidently imagines that she has to lead me everywhere, as if I were either very old or an idiot. Unless it's simply that she's so foolish she obeys the letter of her training even with patients who would be much better helped by the spirit. Now she's helping me tidy my room. As I watch her I know that I'm right to call her my wardress. No woman who wasn't a wardress would want to make the folds of a curtain as regular as corrugated iron. She's doing it now, tugging at the hems one after another … She tears off lavatory paper in just the same way – a neat sharp tweak that separates it straight along the perforated edge. The pieces of paper Mrs Craig offers me, folded in two, are as neat and as sharp as envelopes. We know a lot about each other's habits, she and I: I am her charge and she is my wardress.

She tidies my room really so well and so quickly that there's nothing left for me to do at all. It's the same with all of my life now – either from a lack of imagination or a malicious need to destroy me, she's taken over my every department. I find myself left without will or energy. Doctor would say this is a result of my personality break-up, that it started months ago, long before I came to this place. But I know different. I know the will and the energy that I had the day before. No, on the very day that. The very day that. I know it's the result of having Mrs Craig for a wardress. And a wardress for Mrs Craig. That's not a silly thing to say – Mrs Craigs are essential to most of us, but they don't have to be so noticeably wardress.

She's seen now that I'm watching her in the plastic mirror.

'Do you like your hair hanging all over your face, Mrs Cadence?'

That's her way of pretending that she wants me to make a decision for myself. I don't answer.

'It's the way Doctor puts on the headset, Mrs Cadence. It upsets all your good work. And it really isn't necessary, not with these new units. I'll speak to him about it.'

Her ideas of how to flatter me into doing things are quite childish. I may be in her charge, but that doesn't make me either paranoid or half-witted.

'There are things about this place that have to be resisted, Mrs C.' Don't call me that. 'I don't agree with every aspect of your treatment. I shall speak to Doctor again about having you moved into a ward. This single room is doing you no good. No good at all.'

She goes to the door. What she doesn't know – though she must really – is that dignity and self-respect can be entirely interior and that I intend to hang on to these whatever may be done to me. To her I must look like just another sulking psychotic.

'I think you're wrong, Mrs Craig.' I don't know why I'm bothering, why I'm calling her Mrs Craig even. 'Surely the reason for my being here is so that I may come to terms with myself and what I have done? I doubt if I'd get on with that half as well in the friendly atmosphere of a ward.'

I wish I hadn't chosen my words so carefully, hadn't wanted so badly to show her.

'It's not that I like being alone in here. It's just that I believe it's good for me. And so did the judge.'

I don't hear her reply. Now that her hand's on the doorknob I'm soon going to be left alone again. I shake my hair back from my face and look at myself in the mirror. I try to see from my reflection's eyes what my reflection is thinking. Nothing shows.

'The tapes should be doing that for you, Mrs Cadence. For the rest of the time you'd find you were helped by a more normal social life.'

'But haven't you read reports of the trial?' Allowing a note of hysteria. Not able to keep it out. 'All about how I hate Sensitape? Can't you see how much more valuable my salvation would be if I arrived at it on my own?'

'Some diseases are hard to cure by an act of the mind alone, Mrs Cadence.'

'The past isn't a disease, Mrs Craig. To talk of curing it is ridiculous.'

I can't read her eyes either. With subtle people one seldom can.

'The past doesn't exist, Mrs Cadence. Only our different ideas of it.'

Not a bad exit line. And afterward the door is neither more shut nor less. Which I say to myself by way of reassurance since it seems in fact to be more shut than any other door I've ever seen. And in my mind, because of the guilt which is there – what guilt, what particular guilt is this? – the door shuts unfairly, separating off past happiness, leaving on my side of it only past sorrow.

There are other concepts of time, Wardress. Sometimes it is seen as a fixed landscape through which we move, so that the past and the future all exist at once … She does everything knowingly; why has she decided to try to take the past away from me? All the past, that is, before the murder. She's not likely to be doubting the reality of that. The eyes in the plastic mirror tell me nothing. Indeed, they feed back into my own, canceling thought. I go to the door and, because I am calm and sensible, I open it. The corridor is pleasant, carefully domestic. They got the scale right. Of course they well, of course of course

Oh my poor dear dead darling.

I remember how slow the bus was all the way along from the Tottenham Court Road. The trees hiding all but the highest roofs of the zoo and a distant giraffe, I sat on the top of the bus and watched their pale, tiny leaves, so out of place in the seasonless city. If spring belongs anywhere it is in the crocus shop windows, and in the women's clothes. A sour thought, from present experience. Back then the leaves were young and delicate, the sky was cloudless, and I was three bus stops away from Tony.

'Thea. Thea, my dear … My little love –'

I'd jumped from the bus while it was still moving, nearly broken my ankle, run between the amiable people and hung myself up around his neck. Nobody minded how ridiculous it was, me at thirty-one still like a schoolgirl, nobody on the whole pavement. Baker Street was golden. We moved on another plane, and everyone who saw us.

'We're going to the park,' Tony said. 'I've brought you a present.'

It was silly. It was a tin opener and a tin of frankfurter sausages.

The buildings were so clear that afternoon, so tall, so exquisitely detailed. I stopped Tony in front of a blank shop window, trying to see in his reflection the ordinariness other people must see. The reflection was even more marvelous than the reality. He was easier than usual. He took off his hat to it. Then we walked on. A side road gave us a glimpse of a cobbled mews and expensive houses with window boxes. There were daffodils, and some kind of blue flowers, and a cheerful car in front with a spotted perspex roof. The bricks of the house were earth red, the cobbles brown. None of it was real. As we watched a man in a green fake baize apron came out with a watering can and began to water the ground floor window boxes. He disturbed a cat from one and she moved onto the top of the car. Only we saw all this, and it was ours. We went toward the park, humbled.

We held hands.

'Theary, Theary, I have a Theary and I love my Theary.'

I didn't ask him what his theory was. It would have involved some comic mathematical formula and would have reminded us of his work. So silk thin was our happiness.

'In fact,' he said, 'my love is entirely Theatrical.'

His name was Tony Stech (not quite English, you see) and he regarded puns as the apostles must have regarded the tongues of flame.

At the crossing there wasn't a car in sight. The road stretched as clear as a triumphal route right along to Lancaster Gate. We went over the road and into the park. I wish I could remember what we said to each other – there was nothing capable of being talked about. There must have been words, though, helping to build an isolation, communication between us that preserved and enlarged what was ours, our happiness, our suspension. I can remember no effort in finding things to say to Tony. We may even have made plans, but I doubt it. Dogs passed, and people who smiled at us, and once a brewer's dray with polished horses practicing for the parade. Enormous, they flourished themselves like banners. Their brasses caught at the sunlight, the wheels behind them spun silver, the driver cheerfully self-conscious in his fancy dress waved at us as he went by. We waved back, extended by the contact.

Tony found us a bench by the canal, sat me down and opened the tin of sausages. He fed them to me, shiny little things that tasted of salt and herbs and not much else. But they snapped satisfactorily and between us we ate the whole tin. I can experience their feel even now, and the feel of the bench against my back, and the feel of the sharp unlit air that was different from any other day's, and the feel of being with Tony and in him and a part of him. The frankfurter sausages of that particular day too – no other food has ever been so deeply involved in the totality of experience. The totality of experience, jargon words, worked to death by Edward in his Sensitape handouts – but everything he said and did had been a Sensitape handout, had been for seven years – but even so I know of no other. We lived inside out, our souls and our senses indissoluble. This is probably what being in love means. This is probably what made it possible for us to be happy.

Houses showed, cream-painted and regular, through the trees, fine rich houses with fine blank windows. In my mind they were unattainable – also undesirable – though through Edward's money, Sensitape money, I could easily have encompassed any one of them. While I was with Tony neither the past, nor the real present, nor the future existed. Doctor is wrong. If my personality ever disintegrated it was then, more than a year ago. More recent months have in fact seen a coming together.

Tony poured the saline solution that had contained the sausages onto the grass, and threw the tin into a litter basket. He insisted that I keep the tin opener. He said he was giving me the key to his heart, so for the sake of his joke I tried to put it down the front of my dress. In the end it went into my handbag. He had the sense of humor of a much uglier man.

We did usual things. They were there to be done, each one a personal magic. Mostly we walked. Walked. Lovers do walk. There were birds to be fed, and the pointless race up over the bridge and down the other side which Tony won, and my silly shoes to be laughed at, and the page of newspaper that we picked up and read for omens, and buttoned children who thought we were mad because we were not sane, and the final slope of damp bald grass not to be minded as we lay on it and got our breaths back and watched the sky through the tiny leaves (why is it always spring in fairy stories?), and didn't need to kiss or make love at all.

At four o'clock Tony took me to a café for tea. Time was running out, had been from the moment I got off the bus. The place laid on a special tea for men out with other men's wives, weak, with dry yellow scones and a dusty slab of cake. The men never noticed and the wives were too polite to. But it was quiet, and respectable, with a spinning wheel in one corner and a respectability that was catching. It helped us back into the necessary constraint. I had to be in Richmond by six, when Edward's first private patient arrived. The constraint worked so well that I remember Tony asked me when he'd see me again. Memory safe now and not able to hurt, I remember my answer and what followed.

'At the conference tomorrow morning,' I said. 'Had you forgotten?'

'No, I meant *see* you.' Poor Tony, he was embarrassed. 'See you alone.'

'What's the conference going to be about?' I said, not answering him.

'Hasn't Edward told you?'

This was the important conversation. This was the one that could be remembered.

'A new process, he told me. And he gave me a list of the important people attending.'

'And he didn't say what the process was?'

He hadn't told me because I hadn't wanted to be told. I'd had more than enough of new processes. Now Tony would tell me if I didn't stop him, and then it would be time for my train out to Richmond. I gathered together my gloves and my handbag. My face could wait for later, for the cold summing-up on the train home. Already we were running out of isolation.

'Actually he did tell me. I suppose I tried to forget.'

Tony, so distant, didn't see my lie. He put his hand across the table and onto mine, a gesture as much a part of the Spinning Wheel as its red gingham curtains or the genuine beam.

'You don't approve,' he said.

'What's the use, Tony? You don't stop technical progress by not approving of it.'

'There will be medical advantages, you know. With Synthajoy we'll be able to analyze deficiences in –'

'Don't go on, Tony.' Aching. Bleak. 'You show the whole thing up so.'

'Show it up?'

I couldn't bear him pretending he didn't understand. I took my hand away, began to put my gloves on. Fine black leather, hand-stitched. Possessions were mattering a lot by then – they were all Edward gave me.

'We're a part of the entertainment industry now, Tony. We'd better face it.'

'That's not true. You oversimpilfy, Thea. Edward's clinic does very fine work.'

'And the Governor's Wife? Does she do very fine work?'

'You do what you can. The clinic is the one decent bit of Sensitape left. Without you it wouldn't function.'

'The clinic is a face-saver.'

I knew I wasn't being fair, not fair in the way I was blaming Tony. To stand up to Edward would have needed an equivalent ruthlessness. And even then, it wasn't Edward who needed standing up to, but twenty million Sensitape users. That sort of strength would have made Tony different, a fanatic, a man whom I could never, warned by Edward, have loved.

'Leave it, shall we, Tony? It's not worth quarreling about. We're all caught up in the same thing – you should tell me not to be so bloody self-righteous.'

'Years ago – three years ago – when you were showing me the Richmond house for the first time, I told you then what was going to happen. Do you remember?'

'I prefer to remember that afternoon for something else you told me.'

'It does worry me, Thea. It worries me sick.'

'Tony – stay in your laboratory. Edward's shoulders are broad enough for all of us.'

I stood up. He helped me into my coat. The dishonesty of what I had just said closed the subject, closed almost any subject. Otherwise he'd have told me again about the tigers and crocodiles, and the cage it was my responsibility to build against them. I've always thought it a nonsense, this in the world but separate from it, but I loved Tony far too much ever to argue.

Loved him too much ... This love then, does it make morality irrelevant? Does body take over, and soul, leaving conscience safely tucked away in the mind? I don't like to think of my knowledge of right and wrong being situated entirely in my mind. It's my mind that Doctor treats each afternoon with guilt – yet he doesn't reach me, not the part of me capable of love. Love deeper than conscience? I know what Pastor Mannheim would have said. The trouble is, I don't know how he would have justified it.

The corridor has a carpet – I chose a lot here in the Kingston; did I choose that carpet? – and a comfortable unstylish cupboard with a vase of flowers on it. Have the daffodils come from a hothouse or do they mean that outside it's spring? The Superintendent seems capable of knowing the importance of truth in such a matter. I can't tell from the few times I have met him how he would use that importance, though. The cupboard is slim against the wall so that nothing interrupts the full width of the carpet: it spoils the domestic effect, this clearway for trolleys. Still, the attempt is appreciated. Peace of mind, however evilly used, is a welcome gift. In the Kingston we give in almost without noticing. Dungeons and thumb-screws, while easier to fight, would be infinitely worse.

A warder is coming down the corridor. With his neat white coat and his glasses he might perfectly well be a young doctor, even a superior barber. That's probably a comb sticking up out of his top pocket. He looks at the strip of me he can see between the door and the jamb, and he smiles. Encouragingly. He sees a door painted ivory white, and the dark strip of an old woman with wild hair. He knows that the woman isn't old – he knows every single thing about her. He protects her from society and society from her. Feels himself a universal benefactor, smiles at her again. She makes a face at him – perhaps the poor thing sees him as a warder – and closes the door.

Synthajoy … I suppose that was the first time I had heard the word. And I let it slide. Not wanting to know. And I gave the meeting next morning a miss for the same reason. And in the afternoon it was all. In the afternoon it was. In the afternoon it

I like this room.

I like my room. I dare to like it because I know they haven't got any circuits capable of making me like it. With me they're at a disadvantage: Edward and I worked together so closely that I know everything he achieved, everything he planned to achieve. It was his work on prison reform that won him the Prize. This room is what it seems to be, and nothing more. And, most important, Sensitape has been found to have no post-experiential effect whatsoever. Their only hope is to establish a habit of feeling by long repetition. They subject me to Guilt – sorry, Criminal Responsibility – so that in the end I will need it like a drug. They. They do … I must avoid thinking of *me* and *them*; it's the beginning of a psychosis they'd love to foster.

I suppose I ought to be able to remember a time when I was in love with Edward. Perhaps I can. And even he with me – in his own way. That's a sour qualification, the patronizing dig of every aggrieved wife with not enough to be aggrieved about. Edward was in love with me, up to and even after the time when I stopped being in love with him.

Wasn't he?

Young Dr Teddy Cadence. (He quickly ironed out the Teddy.) He'd been fascinated by the patterns of the electroencephalograph ever since his first days at medical school. No doubt they were all he talked about on our first date. I remember little of the occasion except the pain in my guts. There was a mild form of dysentery going around the hospital at the time – if he hadn't been considered a catch by the other young nurses I'd never have accepted his invitation. I have an impression of his mouth as he talked, and of his hands explaining things. Dr Cadence used his hands a lot in those days – it was a habit he dealt with as he became more momentous. My only other recollection is of the sound made by the cistern in the Ladies'. The water fell from a great height, arriving with a thump. Rather Victorian and, oh Lord, I needed it. I don't even remember very clearly where the dance was being held. The old Royal, I think, the tall hotel near Paddington that was pulled down to make room for the thruway. So Edward talked about the electroencephalograph and I thought about how soon I would need to get back to that cistern.

The evening can't have been a success, but I got asked out again all the same. He said afterward it was my anxious expression – he'd thought at the time that it showed a serious mind, an earnest attempt to grapple with what he was propounding. He didn't often just talk; mostly he had some theory to batter you with. He wasn't the only one, of course – the hospital was full of young doctors and the young doctors were all full of theories. We nurses put up with the latter for the sake of the former. I don't think any of us sensed that Dr Cadence was different from the others. I know I didn't, not that first evening. But he was handsome, and he wore his clothes well, and information from the teaching side said he would pass his examinations easily, distinctions all around, so I received that second invitation with a considerable sense of triumph. If I'd managed so to bewitch him when my attention was, to say the least, divided, what marvellous progress I would be able to make this next time. I might even be able to hear what he was saying. And perhaps even understand it.

'It's a question of electrical nano-wavelengths, you see, Miss Springfield.'

Springfield. I can see him and hear him precisely. He had a beautifully shaped voice even then – perhaps his later work on it made it too beautiful. Thea Springfield.

'It's a question of electrical nano-wavelengths, you see, Miss Springfield.'

I'd forgotten all about Thea Springfield. It has needed the name in his voice, young, to remind me. I've been making the mistake of remembering past events clearly and then placing myself in them as I am now, thirty-two, tired, deadened by experience that should not be mistaken for wisdom. Experience is like lead, a lead for which the philosophers' stone really exists. Twelve years ago I possessed neither, neither gold nor the base metal from which gold may be made. Twelve years ago I had hardly begun.

'I know about electrical nano-wavelengths, Dr Cadence.' She really did. 'They're the impulses the brain emits all the time it's working. They form patterns we can record and measure and analyse.'

'Measure? You call it measure, Miss Springfield?'

Such scorn. I'd quite forgotten the ways she learned later of dealing with it.

This was Thea Springfield's second date, the one that's supposed to be so important. And she'd thought she was doing well.

'I've seen the encephalograph at work, Dr Cadence. Our professor analyzed some of the graphs for us.'

'And what did he tell you? "*At this point, ladies and gentlemen, the patient opened his eyes.*" (It was a good imitation.) "*At this point he closed them. At this point he went to sleep. And here, ladies and gentlemen, is the reading for an epileptic fit.*" Is that what you call measurement?'

'He showed us other things too. When the patient became angry, for instance.' So eager.

'That's not measurement, Miss Springfield. I look at your dress, I perceive that it is blue. I go further – I say it is dark blue. Have I in any way measured the quality of blueness that your dress possesses?'

Her main thought at this point was pleasure that he'd noticed her dress. To cover this she sought words that would show she was intelligent.

'Aren't colours subjective, Dr Cadence? I mean, doesn't each person have his own idea of what they are? Like greeny blue or bluey green, for instance.'

'I do know what subjective means, Miss Springfield.'

She didn't find his manners insufferable. He was Dr Cadence, and he'd asked her out to dinner. I expect she fiddled with her knife and fork, and cursed herself for being gauche.

'Actually, Miss Springfield, you've accidentally put your finger on the big fault in my analogy.' She brightened, in spite of the accidentally. 'Although colours do in fact exist as light waves easily measurable with present-day instruments, the electrical nano-waves emitted by the brain are never likely to be so easily systematised. The machine sensitive enough, subtle enough to measure these would need to be as sensitive and subtle as the brain that was emitting them.'

At future meetings, parties and student sociables, Thea Springfield was to hear this preamble many times. Otherwise it would never have remained so word-perfect.

'Perhaps then brain waves are in fact to some extent – using your own word, Miss Springfield – subjective. Existing only in relation to the brain that emits them.' He leaned forward, his tie trailing unheeded in his food. 'Or in relation to another brain perhaps, Miss Springfield?'

The lift in his voice told her that something was expected of her. She tried to be sober and sensible and adult.

'Your tie's in your gravy, Dr Cadence,' she said.

I wonder why he persevered with her, a third year psychiatric nurse who could so monumentally miss so monumental a point. Later on, as young Mrs Cadence, she looked back and decided that it must have been the blue dress after all. My present perspective offers a second, more flattering reason. He didn't bore her. She was the only one of all the nurses who unconsciously recognised his potential – not the potential in his theory, the potential in him. A man who has recognised his own potential likes his woman to recognize it also. So it wasn't the blue dress, or the breasts it showed to such fine advantage. Ultimately it was her perceptiveness that won her Dr Cadence for a husband.

But she was looking for love. Just as, not all that much later, she would be looking for Regent's Park with Tony. It's not tragic that she, that I, should have had to look so hard, not even surprising. Thea Springfield drifted into love too naturally, too easily, too much without pain. Every day was a marvel. The excitement of being alive overwhelmed thought, so that she moved in a state of heightened unconsciousness, of gloriously unheeded revelation. And everything went right for her. Even sex. Until of course

Now that the wardress is gone I'll see to my hair. It's not important that I should avoid looking mad – with my presumed kind of madness and with my known background of self-discipline, the maddest thing I could do would be to avoid looking mad. In all I must be careful to do whatever I do for its own sake and nothing else. To consider its effect on the received ideas of Doctor or Mrs Craig is obviously idiotic. I sit here doing my hair because brushing my hair, feeling the tug, scratching my ear wth the coarse brush bristles, I sit here tilting my head against the pull, because watching the dark hair flow like water, rush in a shining torrent, separate at the rock of my shoulder and pour on down the front of my hospital dress, down almost to my waist, I sit here doing my hair because … because I am not yet ready to think of Thea Springfield and sex. There's too much in the way.

Dr X and his wife's appointment was for seven-thirty in the evening. I remember the time so precisely because they were late. He worked at a hospital over on the other side of town and hadn't been able to get away as early as he'd expected. Edward and I hadn't yet moved out to Richmond of course – we were still using the consulting room provided by the hospital. Edward wasn't even a consultant then, merely one of the hospital's team of psychiatrists. They worked him hard. But he'd got me off the wards as his assistant by then, and neither of us minded the work.

I'd been in the outer office catching up on paperwork, case histories to be duplicated and the file to be brought up to date. After seven the hospital quieted down. I liked working there, being contained by its power – in the evenings this power was somehow more apparent: the stillness of the enormous building, and the small noises, expressed it more personally to me than the obvious activity of the days. I worked at my neat files, the strength of the hospital humming in the silence. At seven-thirty I buzzed Edward to warn him to expect Dr X and his wife. There was no answer, so I went through to see if he was still there. His room had its own door onto the corridor; sometimes patients preferred to leave without running the gauntlet of me.

He had on a Sensitape headset, the new lightweight unit Tony had recently perfected. He appeared to be asleep – Sensitape subjects always do. The tape was turning slowly, an advanced relaxation tape we had recorded some months earlier, from a Yoga expert.

I turned the volume down very slowly. It was almost sad to see how peaceful he was. I loved him then, married love, a structure seven years deep and still only on the edge of self-awareness. Around point two on the dial he roused.

'What's the time?' he said. 'Are they here?'

'Not yet,' I said. 'Something must have held them up.'

He took my hand and squeezed it.

'I was only showing off. No side effects, my mind instantly as sharp as a razor.'

'You feel better now? Not tired?'

'I've been wondering, Thea, about habituation dangers. To have the day's jangle so completely smoothed; it's an effect I could easily become hooked on. Would that be a bad thing?'

'It shows you how, Edward. Then in time you don't need it.'

This was Sensitape dogma. Necessary in those days when Edward did more than nod at morality in passing. If patients experienced the prescribed emotional state often enough they had something to build on, to work toward on their own account. He drew my hand up and rubbed the side of his face with it.

'It's marvelous, Thea. An emotional state it took Grainger forty years to achieve – now I can plug into it just like that.'

'Of course it's marvelous. But it's not for you to say so.'

'I don't see why not. Sensitape is like a painting. For the artist a painting grows, makes itself almost, so that really all the artist is entitled to feel is a sort of gratitude.' He looked up at me, suddenly concerned. 'I'm not noticeably conceited, Thea, am I?'

I told him he wasn't. As he moved about the room getting ready I thought about it. I watched him take out the sherry. No, he wasn't conceited – he was too ambitious to be conceited. Ambitious for his machine, I thought, not for himself. He fetched his white coat from the back of the door and I helped him put it on.

'Formalization,' he said, apologizing. 'This interview's got to be impersonal. Wearing my uniform will help.'

Was it then love, me so aware of his imperfections that he had to apologize for them? Tony in Regent's Park was without imperfections. Tony in Regent's Park simply was. We both heard a knock on the door of the outside office. I went to let Dr X and his wife in, Edward briefly calling me back.

'This is going to be important, Thea. Listen in on the intercom, will you?

Better still, record the whole meeting. I don't want there to be any misunderstandings.'

I left him nervously straightening the furniture. The consulting room was comfortable precisely to the scale laid down by the hospital management committee. No desk for the psychiatrist to hide behind – it had been decided that desks gave a fatal employer/applicant, headmaster/malcontent atmosphere. The room had dusty orange wallpaper, a sage green carpet, a coffee table and several not too low armchairs. Our particular coffee table had a finely produced volume on Egyptian archaeology and – as a really domestic touch – a copy of *Radio Times*. The medical machinery was hidden in something that might have been a hi-fi cabinet – the intercom, the hypnophone, Sensitape, the various recorders for voice, blood pressure, respiration and so on. The final effect was perhaps of the waiting room to a not very prosperous airline.

And my room? The Single Occupancy Ward over my shoulder as I brush my hair in the mirror? I know too much to be able to find it as pleasant as I should. It's hardly more than painted scenery to me, for I know the spec, behind it and the squabbling behind the spec. 'We're not running a luxury hotel, Mr Chairman,' and the painstaking explanations. I can remember the battle fought for the window seat, for the washbasin's fancy taps. It gives them a tenuous hold; things could so easily be taken away. No, not taken. Voted.

Dr X was large and scrubbed, analysis of his audition tapes killing forever the notion that big men are undersexed. His wife looked more conventionally bedworthy, long-legged and plump and slightly greasy. I look through a today-shaped hole, of course.

I showed them into Edward's office, returned to mine and switched on the intercom. I loaded the recorder with a fresh spool. I've listened to the conversation that followed many times. Of the four of us present it was Dr X who would forget it first, his memory cut short by death.

I had missed the first few words.

Edward. … good of you both to come. Please sit down. Make yourself at home – this is going to take some time so you'd better be comfortable.

Dr X. I'm afraid we're rather late. My wife made me have some supper after coming off the ward. Otherwise we'd have been here sooner.

Mrs X. Well, Dr Cadence, you know how it is … important interview this – no use coming to it on an empty stomach.

There's an Australian inflection here. So it's to be a Commonwealth effort. How suitable.

Edward. You believe in feeding the body, Mrs X.

(She makes an indeterminate noise, not knowing how to take him.) No, I mean it. Women who take food seriously are often the most wholehearted sexual partners.

Dr X. Is that a statistical fact, Dr Cadence?

Edward. Inspired intuition, Dr X. Often more valuable than whole pages of statistics.

Dr X. I'll remember that, Dr Cadence.

I'd learned something. Up till then I'd always felt a sense of humor to be a great help in bed. Dr X. got fine results without it.

Edward. Sherry for you both?

(The glasses clink.)

The first thing I really must do is congratulate you on the results of all your preliminary auditions. As I'm sure you've been told, they were quite outstanding.

Mrs X. It's how we were made, Dr Cadence. We fitted, right from the very first time.

Isn't that nice. I wonder if it's hindsight that makes me detect a come-hither even then? Certainly there's no audible sign from Edward that he noticed anything.

Edward. It places you two in a very responsible position, Mrs X. No doubt you realize this.

Dr X. (clears his throat) All this 'Mrs X' and 'Dr X' – it seems a bit like a spy story. Couldn't we get down to names? I'm –

Edward. Please. I don't know your name, and I don't want to. I consider it vital that to everybody involved in this project – even myself – you should both remain anonymous.

Dr X. We were told that our names wouldn't appear on the tape sleeve. That seemed reasonable. It was just that –

Mrs X. I'm sure Dr Cadence is right, dear. If nobody, but nobody knows our names, then if they ever get out then we'll know who to blame, won't we?

Edward. They must not get out, Mrs X. Apart from questions of medical etiquette, this measure also is for your own protection. Public opinion on our project is bound to be divided. There will be sections of the community, people with uncritically traditional minds, who will sling all the mud they can gather. We must do everything we can, Dr X, to protect you and your wife from such attacks.

(There is an awkward pause. Obviously the X's have been so busy congratulating themselves that they've never thought of this. Edward lets it sink in, then continues.)

Edward. I was talking about your responsible position. You've already said this was an important interview. Why important? Important for whom?

Mrs X. Important for humanity, of course.

Edward. You answer off the top of your head, Mrs X. You really have thought about what you're doing? You're convinced that it is right?

Dr X. She understands completely, Dr Cadence. (His voice becomes incantatory.) Helping sexually disturbed or inadequate people to experience the pleasures of fully shared copulation – the successful heterosexual event, I mean – will be a major step toward curing them. A major step toward the elimination of sexual neuroses in society.

(What he offers is a close paraphrase of the handout circulated by Edward around the profession in his search for audition subjects. Edward must be noticing the similarity, for he sighs. I can imagine him reminding himself that Dr X and his wife have been chosen for their sexual rather than their intellectual prowess.)

Edward. I have an agreement here for you both to sign.
(Rustle of Agreement.)
Briefly, it establishes that the patent in Sensitape 57 – a method of recording psycho-electric brain activity for the purpose of subsequent playback into another individual, who will then experience the emotion and sensation as they were recorded – reposes in myself. As do all rights in any such tapes as you or your wife may make. Also there is a pledge that you both preserve your anonymity for a minimum period of fifty years.

Dr X. That sounds reasonable. We want nothing out of it for ourselves. Nothing at all.

Edward. But before you sign it I want you both to think very carefully. You must be absolutely convinced that what you are doing is right. Morally right.

Mrs X. We have thought about it, Dr Cadence. The advancement of medical research, it's a moral duty we all have.

(Again the slick phrase. They don't understand how carefully Edward is choosing his words.)

Edward. For an initial period, determinable at my discretion but no longer than twenty years, any Sensitape 57 tapes of yours that I may preserve will be used exclusively by accredited students and for the treatment of certain psychiatric conditions that have failed to respond to more conventional methods. We are not peddling cheap thrills. During that initial period whatever royalties are paid for the use of such tapes will be devoted to financing further research into the development of Sensitape 57 techniques.

Dr X. Where do we sign?

Edward. It's a serious step, Dr X. If you would rather consult a solictor before signing I will quite understand.

Dr X. I told you, we want nothing out of it. If ever anything wasn't right, it'd be for us to take money for an opportunity like this.

Mrs X. Prostitution, that's what it'd be.

Dr X. So if we don't want anything, then we can't be diddled. It's as simple as that.

(Poor scrubbed young man. And his hot wife. Innocents, both of them. I can't blame him – at that time I'd been married to Edward for seven years and I still believed in his devotion to the advancement of medical research.)

Edward. In that case I shall send for my secretary to witness your signatures. As soon as you have both signed, fold the sheet over where marked. That way neither she nor I will know your identities. The contract will be then placed in a sealed envelope in my personal safe. You understand?

(A pause in which presumably they nod.)

Edward. (loud) Thea – could you come in please?

Thea. At once, Dr Cadence.

My own voice. I've been electronically there all the time. Present. Involved. Unavoidably responsible. Believing in him should not have been enough. An excuse comes to mind, that of the guard in the concentration camp: what could I have done? What notice would they have taken of me? But I ought at least to have doubted. I ought not to have had to wait for the more superficial horrors that came later. The merely electronic grubbiness of the recording session.

I looked down on the recording van from the window of Dr X's flat. The block, one of a small group, was in a development area where vehicles were not normally allowed., but we had produced a good cover story for the Residents' Association. The van was lettered B.B.C., Edward and I were interviewers, Tony was the B.B.C. engineer. Dr X was taking part in a proposed sound feature about the hospital where he worked. All perfectly plausible, nothing to connect it with the Sexitape that would finally be produced. *Dr X* – I still think of him as that, even though I did finally, after he was dead, find out his real name.

The van stood on the large rectangular lawn in the centre of the three-storey block. There was a dark pond and beside it a laburnum tree shifting its kite tails in the moonlight. The window in the side of the van shone an electric bright square onto the sage-colored grass. Down there I could imagine Tony Stech overhauling his circuits. For this recording two simultaneous tracks had to be used – he'd built a special control unit for the job. I called him Tony Stech in those days, both names in order to distance, in order never to have to take us seriously. Tony Stech.

Above the flat roofs of the building across the court the city sky was faintly orange. And it flashed occasionally.

Inside the bedroom the lights were discreet. I don't know why I was there. I certainly needn't have been. Two thick shiny cables, contrasting vividly with the pink beige bedroom carpet, lay across the floor to the window. They moved secretly as Edward adjusted the headset panel. Dr and Mrs X were already in their night clothes and I offered to help them with their headsets. They didn't need help, not after their preliminary auditions. They were sitting on the edge of the bed and it was evident through his pyjamas that Dr X had an

Do the specifics matter?

It's nearly teatime. After my daily session with Doctor my wardress always leaves me for half an hour or so, then brings my tea. Perhaps I am supposed to need the interval in order to recover from what Doctor has done to me. This is ridiculous, of course, for what he does makes no impression at all. He feeds me guilt when I have been borne down by guilt for too many years. Later my wardress feeds me with bread and butter and cake and tea (sedated). If only she fed me with gingerbread then there might be material for a joke. Something to do with Gingerbread and Guilt. My wardress would appreciate a joke – it would show a change in my attitude of mind … Everybody watches you, so very soon you watch yourself. Even if you were not egocentric to begin with, a fortnight in here would make you so. I wonder if I began watching myself before coming here, or after. Just before, I think. Up to then I had always watched others. Now I watch myself. I watch myself putting the table ready for my tea when my wardress brings it. I sneak a glance at myself, colorless old woman, in the unbreakable mirror.

Everything here is unbreakable, moulded, blunt, harmless. Obliquely this fact cheers me: perhaps one day they contemplate doing something to me positive enough to make me want to kill myself. And I won't be able to.

Oh look, I was right. Here's tea. Goody.

'You may put the tray there, Wardress.'

I know what it is. I speak to her as if she behaved as I'm always afraid she will. And she rarely does. She's rarely brisk, or sensible, or heavily maternal. In fact, she's probably a very intelligent woman. So I shouldn't talk to her the way I do at all.

'I wonder if you'd like to start taking a daily paper, Mrs Cadence? It might bring you out of yourself a little.'

'I thought Doctor had forbidden it.'

'I can always say I thought he meant only at the beginning. When there were still reports of the trial to upset you.'

'Not very responsible of you to go against Doctor's orders.'

'I see you more than he does. Besides, I'm a woman.'

How right she is. Like me, she squats to pee. I'd like to believe there's nothing more to it than that. But the power of our shared sex is often overwhelming. So I separate her off by calling her my wardress.

'You can bring me what you like, of course. I can't possibly stop you.'

'You know damn well you can, Mrs Cadence. You can tell on me to Doctor.'

So down to earth. (I wonder if even the 'damn' was calculated.) It leaves me nothing to dramatise. And it shows that in some small way she's willing to put herself in my power. I shall be trustworthy and at the same time incorruptible. I shall let her bring the paper and I shall not read it.

'I'd never tell on you. At least you're slightly more on my side than Doctor is.'

'You're always trying to convince yourself of things that aren't true, Mrs Cadence. We're all on your side in the Kingston.'

Rumpetty tumpetty. One, two, three, four. Off we go now. The same dear old jingle.

'It doesn't always seem so, Nurse. Not from where I'm standing.'

'Perhaps not. But your treatment, for example – don't you find the tape is helping you?'

'To discuss a patient's treatment with her is against the rules.'

'But –'

'You forget that my husband set this place up. I probably know more about the Kingston even than you do.'

I cannot bear confidences. Not with my wardress. We've got to face each other for a long time to come. Distance between us is essential.

She fiddles awkwardly with the teapot. It's almost as if I had physically hurt her. I can imagine that in different circumstances she'd be an attractive woman. The way she does her hair softens the square shape of her face. And her brown eyes often contradict the professional line of her mouth. Just now they're worried. She looks down at the teapot, then up at me. Now that I'm officially psychotic I can stare at people without myself feeling any embarrassment. It's a sour pleasure, one of the few left. My stare disconcerts her, for I suspect that she knows my real mental condition only too well. She's probably even realised that I am aware of the contents of the teapot.

'You're wrong not to trust me, Mrs Cadence.' She pulls the folds of her overall, herself, together. 'But that's your loss. Come and drink up your tea now, while it's hot.'

'I don't feel like tea today.' A little game with her. They feed and water me perfectly adequately at their own convenience. 'In fact, I don't think I'll have anything, thank you.'

'I'll take it away then.'

'You do that.'

'It interests me, Mrs Cadence.' She still hasn't picked up the tray. 'I'd like to know why you so often pretend irrational behaviour.'

She will persist in dealing so directly with me. It pushes me further and further off.

'I wouldn't call this irrational. People don't always want tea at teatime. Sometimes they may prefer coffee instead.'

Will she offer coffee? She picks up the tray and starts for the door. I see now that it's a situation she can perfectly well deal with in another way later on. Just give me a pill. So much less dignified, to have to meet her eyes and take it.

'Bring the tray back, please. I'll drink the tea, now that you've brought it.'

I pour the tea out for myself, thin and golden and faintly musty. The room is close-carpetted, its corners rounded for ease of sweeping. The door won't slam on account of air so excellently contained. There is bread and butter, a small pot of jam, and two round coconut cakes on a plastic plate. There is a linen tray-cloth – such an odd attempt at the homey, so very out of date.

My wardress doesn't bother to watch me drink the tea. She goes out, obeying her instructions not to make the patients feel awkward about their meals. If I'm not sedated by the time she returns for the tray, there are plenty of pills. For what purpose would I have gained an extra ten minutes of awareness? I expect they know best; no doubt the half hour prescribed for me between treatment and tea is the most that is good for me. I drink two cups. Tomorrow's return will be my new day. I eat my bread and butter without jam, and then one of the cakes. My comfort lies in knowing precisely what they are doing to me. The drug creeps in like a mist. So that I can't

DAY 26

The sound of the doors of the treatment room flapping shut behind me comes as a slight shock. So the day's treatment is already over. This is my first gulp of reality. Why don't I receive it with joy? Or at least enthusiasm. Enthusiasm. I must muster enthusiasm.

My wardress leads me by the hand as if we were both girls. Curiously sympathetic, I come near to giving in. But the association is wrong, of someone whose name I won't remember. It leads down a hot school corridor to a situation I can't remember. Only the corridor, glass on one side looking over a patch of grass with a lily pond to tennis courts, three boys and a girl playing a sort of mixed doubles, and the resonance of bare tiles and walls and the smell of gym shoes and someone's scent, and this cool soft corridor smells carefully of nothing. It's comfortable not to be able to remember.

'I've brought you a newspaper as I said I would.' Bold on account of the close fit of the doors behind us. 'There's been an accident on the Manchester Monorail. There's nothing like a good healthy interest in disasters.'

'Thank you.'

'I've also spoken to Doctor about moving you into a shared ward. He's going to put it to the Committee.'

Edward chose every single member of the Committee. How deeply responsible they'll feel.

'Doctor's being more reasonable, Mrs Cadence. He let me put your headset on. You'll find your hair is quite undisturbed today.'

'You always do what you say you will.'

'Of course I do. If you've had any training at all you'll know for yourself how important to the patient it is.'

'We present each other with problems, Mrs Craig. You're afraid I know too much so you pretend to treat me as an equal. For myself, I'm not sure if you know everything, or nothing at all.'

'So you pretend to treat me as an inferior. It's quite understandable.'

An error, to be so knowing. She'll worry about it afterward, realising that I won.

'There's a concert in a few days' time, Mrs Cadence.' She opens the door into my room. 'If you'd like to go to it I'll ask Doctor. I'm sure it could be arranged.'

'You know I can't stand music. It breaks my heart.'

'I know you have an irrational fear of it.'

'Not fear. Inadequacy.'

I close the door behind us myself. She doesn't suggest that my differentiation was false. Thank God such simplifications are over between us.

'It's a neurotic symptom, Mrs Cadence. I believe you will find you have grown out of it.'

'Paul Cassavetes hasn't grown out of it.'

'You're being melodramatic. He's a very old man.'

'He was a very great musician.'

Which is why he was a natural candidate..

She's a mind reader. 'Which is why he was a natural candidate,' she tells me.

A Sensitape 57 made by him would have been of historic value.

'A Sensitape 57 made by him would have been of historic value.'

She tells me that too. She's read the book.

'He's a great man, Mrs Craig. He made his choice. He has something none of you will ever understand about.'

'Shouting is unsuitable, Mrs Cadence. Unsuitable for you, I mean.'

She's wrong, of course. For me in some situations there is only shouting. In others, bullets, so some say.

'Edward hounded him. He'll never play again.'

'Dr Cadence pursued a vision.'

'And the effect of Edward's vision on Paul?'

'Like the effect of your vision on Edward, perhaps.'

She calls him Edward for neatness of phrase, which is offensive. Her theory – a polite word for hope – is that what she thinks I did to Edward may have cured my hatred for what he did to Paul. But for me to have killed Edward would have cured nothing. So many things I ought to have done, ought today to feel differently. Now she reads into my silence God knows what.

'I'll tidy your room, Mrs Cadence. I've left the paper on the end of the bed for you to have a look at.'

Three-pronged. To help her or to read the paper – either would show a weakening. While to do neither would be childish.

'Did you ever meet my husband, Mrs Craig?'

'I heard him lecture on several occasions.'

Small talk. The last thing she must have expected.

'People used to say he lectured very well. I knew him too intimately to be able to judge.'

'He lectured brilliantly.' Tweak, tweak, tweak on the curtains. 'His timing was faultless. He seemed to know exactly when he was going over and when he wasn't. He must have had a sort of thermometer with which he constantly took the mental temperature of the audience.'

'That's interesting. So he was good with groups. He was quite hopeless with individuals.'

She'll have to allow some level of criticism. She takes her time, fills in by picking up clothes and putting them away.

'You'll agree that he was a great champion of the individual, Mrs Cadence. Nobody who wasn't could ever have invented Sensitape.'

Cant. The hand-out again. I lose interest.

I stare at myself in the mirror, at the hair my wardress has been careful not to mess. This, of course, is Edward's great achievement; he brought all the implications of Sensitape down to the simple concern as to whether it would mess up a person's hair or not. He helped us to get our priorities right. He gave us the means by which to preserve mental stability. Now we concentrate on our hair.

'I'll just go and get your tea, Mrs Cadence.'

She must be used to losing me somewhere in mid-flow. To losing all her patients.

'Mrs Craig, at the moment do you have other people you're … looking after?'

'Good gracious yes, Mrs Cadence. Five others. Staggered consciousness periods, of course. You're not the only pebble on the beach by any means.'

A comfort? Or a warning? Or just another of her exit lines …

Eyes staring into eyes staring into eyes staring into eyes. With brain at one end of the exchange to give it an extra nudge. Interesting to imagine uncertainty as to which end. Me looking at myself or myself looking at me. But I'm not there yet. Acoustically the effect would produce a crescendo feeding on itself. They shut me into my own system of feed-back weeks ago. But I can still look away. It's as simple as that. I can still win.

Neat wash basin, neat taps, neat paper towel. And a neat plastic foam mat to catch the drips. Edward didn't invent the Sensitapes. The vision may have been his, but the actual process of invention was Tony's. If the two hadn't come together the thing would never have happened. If Tony's father hadn't died so opportunely.

Old Jacob Stech was no maestro Cassavates. Edward's patient, he'd been admitted to hospital in the final stages of UDW – Uncompensated Death Wish, a terminal condition prevalent in those days. So common that we in the trade simply knew it by its initials. Like TB or VD or MS it was in fact a complex condition needing diagnostic subheadings. On his admission card Jacob Stech was described as Archetypal. Archetypal UDW. He was indeed archetypal, an archetypal old man – old Jew, to be more precise.

He was a bed patient of course, since by the time he came into our care he was too weak to be kept up and about. He stayed cheerfully in the end bed of Ward K and watched, with us, the course of his Archetypal UDW. And, like us, he was in no doubt as to the final outcome. We got him eating again fairly quickly – his former starvation had been rather from neglect than from intent. When you've decided to die eating becomes pointless. But he gave in to our persuasions out of innate courtesy, and dutifully gained weight. When his son came to visit him, the young man was delighted.

Edward took Tony to his office after his visit The same office that modernized would be used four years later by Dr X and his wife.

'Mr Stech, I judge you to be a man who would like to be told the truth. In my opinion close relatives have a right to know these things, especially when the patient himself so obviously knows. Your father is very sick. With medical science at its present stage he will die within a matter of weeks.'

'I don't understand. Since coming here he looks so much better.'

'We're feeding him up, Mr Stech. In this way his body fights his mind. But we have found that the body never wins in these cases. Our technique is to prolong the struggle as long as possible in the hope that something external may happen to change the mind. It's an inadequate treatment, and in my experience it almost never works.'

'Last time I came you told me he'd made up his mind to die. There must be some reason for this. He's always seemed so happy.'

'In Archetypal UDW there are never any discernible reasons for the decision – this is what gives it its "A" classification. The others, the neurotic conditions, are much more easy to deal with.'

'I suppose it's a sort of short circuit, Doctor. So that life becomes the reason for death.'

I remember Edward looking up sharply from his papers, then across at me. The familiar conversation had taken a new turning.

'Exactly so, Mr Stech. And a malaise as deep as that is inaccessible to any of our present techniques. Shock treatment, hypnosis, narcosis, nothing reaches far enough in.'

'Then my father is going to die.'

'That is so.'

Stripped of technicalities, the words were violent. Tony weathered them, frail-looking though he was in the days before he had found a center. I'd seen him and his father together – there was a feeling between them my hospital experience had already shown me to be peculiarly Jewish. It certainly wasn't callousness that gave Tony his strength.

'Let me understand you properly, Doctor.' The occasion forced a formality on him. 'You are not trying to say that my father will finally commit suicide?'

'Not as we at present understand the word. One day he will simply cease to live. All we can say is that there is a determination quite separate from the mind. With our present equipment we cannot touch it. We cannot even detect its presence. His body is as fit as yours or mine. And so, as far as we can tell, is his mind.'

The office was not as grand, not as insidious as it came to be later. Desk, upright chairs, examination couch, five instructions on the wall, three filing cabinets and an unobtrusive table behind the door holding teacups and an electric kettle. If it was a room that made not enough effort to be nice, it was at least a room without a devious, psychiatric purpose. The subtle rooms existed even then, of course, in the suites of private consultants where you paid for what you got. Tony Stech stared at the burnished floor of our little office, moved one foot along a join in the linoleum.

'Perhaps the world has got to be too much for him. Poor old man … The papers say UDW rates are mounting.'

'Statistics are difficult. But it's safe to say that there's been a marked increase in the first three months of this year alone.'

Tony Stech was silent. I was to find out later how fervently he believed in life – UDW to him was utterly shocking, utterly inconceivable. He believed in life … how else can I describe the passion with which he took, turned over in his hands, tried to undertstand, every experience the world offered him?

'It shows you how close we still are to the primitive,' he said at last. 'Natives have been doing this sort of thing for centuries.'

'You must come and visit your father whenever you like, Mr Stech.' Edward stood up. He was admittedly overworked. 'You can see we're doing our best for him. He's quite contented, and I'm sure your visits cheer him up.'

'How long will it be?'

'Two weeks. Three at the most.'

'I'll call every day.' He began putting on his gloves, for it was cold outside, had been snowing. 'I suppose I ought to thank you, Doctor, for being so frank with me.'

'Not at all. My name is Cadence. Any time you want to, come and have a talk with me.'

Again silence. Edward glanced unobtrusively at his watch.

'Is my father right, Dr Cadence? Is the world really such a rotten place to be alive in?'

'I'd hardly be a doctor if I believed that. Now, if you don't mind …'

They turned. Tony Stech saw me, probably for the first time.

'And thank you, nurse. My father has already told me of you in his letters. We both appreciate your kindness very much.'

And I, officially Mrs Cadence, no longer mere Thea, still couldn't find enough voice to answer. I nodded up and down and smiled excessively, as if to a deaf person. He didn't smile back. Why should he; there was nothing for him to smile at. He made something almost a little bow to Edward, and went out. His slowly fading footsteps kept him in the room with us just that much longer.

'An interesting young man,' Edward said. 'A powerful personality. What does the file say about his job, Thea? I wonder what he does for a living.'

The file was reticent. His job was the same as that of his father – shopkeeper. Then the telephone rang, calling Edward away. And Sister sent word, wanting me to help with a shock therapy. The feeling of strangeness and yet of recognition that had been in the office was gone, and even very quickly forgotten.

At that time there was still an excellent chance that Tony might have escaped, might have missed his share in the glory, might never have come to love Dr Cadence's wife and ultimately be loved by her in return, might never have been destroyed by what he had helped to make. Which of course is melodramatic nonsense. Tony was never destroyed. He was killed. Never destroyed.

Seventeen days later it became clear that Jacob Stech was ready to die. During the afternoon the sight retreated from his eyes, not blindness but rather the choice not to see. It was a bitter evening, snow piled against ward windows as I went around drawing the curtains. To me, never ill in my life, insulated by my own vitality, the brightness of the ward was reassuring. I arranged to do night duty. The old man would die in the lost hours between two and four. His son had been that morning, had probably known. An obscure selfishness made me not call him, almost as if I wanted the death all for myself.

The windows in the double doors at the end of the darkened ward glowed a dull yellow, two small discs of light. The patients had all settled by eleven, a barbiturate calm, close, storm-heavy, immovable. I'd accepted his refusal of the tiny pale cylinders without comment. Now I stood at the foot of his bed and watched his light sleep, and its contentment. Expecting him to wake, maybe I brought it about. He frowned, and opened his eyes. He saw very clearly.

'I tell you,' he said, 'we people manage to do two big things. We make our children and we give them space. It's my big consolation.'

'More than just that, Mr Stech. Surely.'

Not understanding, I shouldn't have spoken. After that I don't know why he bothered.

'We have a saying, nurse. We say that dying makes a space for the new life, for the new life that's waiting.'

I think I kept silent. He smiled, sorry for me.

'You're thinking that's what's wrong all the time. All the time too much coming in, and not enough spaces, not enough going out. Not enough dying. But that's not it. That's not it at all.' He held his hands out to me, cupped a little, elbows close to his sides. 'The night is a long time for you. So maybe you wouldn't mind talking a little?'

'Of course not. I'd be very glad to.'

'Then sit down here, close beside me, so I don't have to shout. Oh, I know nothing wakes those who sleep here in the hospital. All the same, the middle of the night is for being close, and for whispering like children.'

I sat by the head of his bed, took his hand. Even then I think I realized who was comforting whom.

'You see, nurse, God could provide. God could provide so easily. What is quantity? I ask you, when you are God, what is quantity?'

Trying to enter his world, I mentioned the Christian parable of loaves and fishes.

'I know it. Don't I know it? When you are God – twice times two, it doesn't matter. Quantity, quality – they're for people doing sums. Adding things up. Deciding. All this eating, working, sleeping. Making love ... You understand what I'm saying?'

Footsteps passed in the corridor, growing and fading with dream-like slowness. He allowed the dream to complete itself.

'All this interests me, nurse, knowing that I will soon die.'

The words confused me. A shopkeeper, a dealer, a doer of sums ... why was he not afraid? He spoke of God lightly, as if a metaphor, not as a refuge and protector. And besides, the unknown was always frightening. Unless of course the known was worse.

'What I mean, nurse, is that I examine this knowledge. I try to remember when it came, and how. In my shop the days are very much the same. How do I know when I have had enough of them? But then one day I do know, and my dinner is there for me, and I say to Tony, "No dinner for me today, Tony." And he thinks I am ill and in the end he sends for the doctor.'

'He was quite right to, Mr Stech. You were ill. You still are.'

'Do I feel ill? Do I look ill? Don't I know best if I am ill or not?'

'Your mind is ill.' I wanted to reach him. 'Or perhaps your spirit.'

'It's not me that's ill. No part of me at all.'

I thought them the words of his sickness. Now that I perhaps understand them a little better, are they only the words of my own sickness? I recognized him as a happy man, but denied him a right to this happiness. I thought him happy because he was dying. I know now he was dying because he was happy – dying for the sake of his happiness, if you like. Thea Cadence then and Thea Cadence now.

'What about your son?' I said. 'Doesn't he still need you?'

'You go see him, my girl. After I am gone you go see if my son still needs me. Tony will go up, all the way. Tony needs nobody.'

The dim light above his bed left shadows under his eyebrows, so that I almost missed the sharp movement of his eyes as he looked sideways at me. I wondered if he was wanting me to correct him. I looked away, at the motionless white bedrails down to the end of the ward and the two yellow dials. I was young and I denied him my honesty.

'Not true, of course.' He corrected himself instead, sadly. 'We are put in this world to need people, and my God we do. Tony needs in a different way, is all. You go see him. He'll tell you.'

It's understandable, this feeling that all my life has been spent in hospitals, but quite false. In fact I can clearly remember holidays, and journeys. And after Sensitape was a success, hardly a sight of a hospital for three whole years. And the journeys, their reasons – conferences, consultations, holidays – quite forgotten in the joy of mechanical progress. I can call it nothing else, just an acute pleasure in being propelled along the ground at great speed, in seeing people for whom I could by no stretch of the imagination be held responsible, and places that were, decorative or ugly, gloriously irrelevant. This progress had to be mechanical, for nothing else would have been separate enough, fast enough. I remember a trip to Bristol, a meeting at the neurological centre there, and the tour around Wales afterward, the hills we roared up and the uncontainable views like clouds streaming by.

Edward drove very well. He didn't do everything well – I was never besotted enough to think that – but he had a great mechanical competence, getting the best out of whatever machine he was presented with. In his hands the various cars did all that the makers said they would, and more, from the old Austin up through the Rovers and Lancias to the big Chev-Bentley of his tycoon years. That was the car I wrapped around a Keep Left sign on the night of

Travelling. An activity magnificent in its own right. Never merely a means of getting there. Travelling. A means of not being where you were before. A period during which nothing is expected of you.

To understand – is it inevitably to judge? Is it inevitable that I should sour past joy by declaring its reasons to be unworthy? Unworthy? There I go again. What is this sanctimonious word? It comforts, for it assumes in the first place worth, and then the possibility of regaining it. It also feeds and is fed by luxurious guilt, which – as Doctor well knows each time he gives it me – is wholly destructive. And I really believed my treatments weren't affecting me.

Better to go back to Tony. And Tony's need.

I got his address from the file and went to see him that same morning, as soon as I had eaten some breakfast after coming off duty. His father had died at two fifty-seven, the death I had been so eager to be in at. I'm glad now to say that his dignity denied all possibility of trespass. I learned nothing and felt nothing and should not have expected either. His body was taken away for postmortem examination. As I left the office after consulting the file I saw UDW penciled in on the death certificate in Edward's neat handwriting.

Stech and Son turned out to be a radio and television shop, covering the more expensive end of the trade. I hesitated outside, shuffling my feet in the thawing slush of the night's snowfall and shading my eyes to see the goods in the window, the color TV sets, video tape recorders, cameras, wrist radios, hi-fis. Jacob Stech had liked a lot of light – it was one of those shops one dreaded to enter. Its deathly fluorescence beamed out onto the dirty snow. My eyes hurt, their pupils unable to contract enough. And only a minute before I had found the grey light of the morning depressing. I went in, my skin prickly. The shop was warm and in spite of the lights I began to feel better.

'Miss?'

After eighteen hours on duty too. Well, I was very young. All of twenty-four or so.

'May I see Mr Stech, please?'

'Mr Stech senior is not available, Miss. Was it food mixers or washing machines?'

I saw the man's point. No one except a representative would enter a shop like that at ten past nine on a dirty morning.

'It's Mr Tony Stech I want to see. I'm from the hospital. It's about his father.'

'Mr Stech senior has been away for a long time, you know. In his absence the shop is my responsibility.'

He wasn't stupid. He just hadn't listened. He raised his eyebrows encouragingly and waited for me to sell him a food mixer.

'May I see Mr Tony Stech please? My name is Cadence. I'm from the hospital. I have news of his father.'

'Mr Tony Stech?' A pause. Nobody ever asked for Mr Tony. 'Just wait here, please. I'll see if he's available.'

The triteness of the delays, the utter triteness of the man who caused them, is much clearer in my mind than my eventual interview with Tony. I remember the electric colour of the manager's skin and the workings of a sectional demonstration shaver on a shelf by his head. I remember his fiercely bitten nails, how they surprised me, revolted me, and how he hid them quickly under the lapels of his jacket. So many things I remember to blur my first real sight of Tony.

I remember his room, tangled, chaotic, cathode ray tubes and ranks of aluminum casings. There was the smell of electricity I was to come to know so well, of hot transformers. A workbench littered with minute instruments. A lathe in one corner. His room should have showed me at once the part Tony was going to play in the plans of my husband.

Tony himself was doing sums in the corner of a homemade diagram. He didn't look up.

'So he's dead,' he said.

'Early this morning.'

'Peacefully, in his sleep.'

'Not in his sleep, but very peacefully.'

He was staring down at his sums, his pen no longer moving. His stillness held menace.

'You're the nurse from the hospital. You must see a lot of bereavement. It can't really still give you a thrill.'

No answer seemed possible. I wondered whom he was wanting to hurt, and why.

'What have you come for? Somebody could have telephoned. Your name's the same as that doctor I spoke to. I suppose you're married.'

I nodded. It was as if he was trying to find something to blame me for.

'He said you were kind.' Tony looked up at me, the hardest eyes I had ever seen. 'You were kind for five weeks, and then he died. You – and your husband – you did nothing for him. Less than nothing.'

'What was needed was a reason for him to go on living. I don't think we had one.'

'What was needed, nurse, was a reason for not dying. Women give birth astride a grave – our only disease is life – we read Spinoza but we manage. Or most of us do.'

'Many don't, Mr Stech. In this country half a million last year. Now that the psychological possibility exists people are making use of it.'

'And all you do is offer kindness.'

He shouted, the room giving back nothing at all. Totally insulated, a room you couldn't hurt yourself in. A padded cell. He got up awkwardly and turned away.

'I'd much rather have been told over the telephone,' he said.

'Your father asked me to come and see you.'

That wasn't the reason I was there. Nurses receive too many deathbed requests to be able to obey them all. I was there because I was cold, and already dead, and he was Jewish, and I wanted to see how Jews kept warm and alive.

'I can't be bothered with manners, nurse. He was an old man, and an innocent man, and where he is now he would much rather you had kept away.'

'He said I was to ask you if you needed any help.'

'Now you've asked.' He stayed with his back to me. 'Thank you for calling.'

'Suppose we could have cured him, Mr Stech, do you think we should have?' He turned to me, incredulous, then deeply angry. I went on. 'Must there never be a time when a man may simply choose to die? Do we have to attack him with mechanisms? Aren't we right just to offer them kindness?'

His answer stretched far into the future. It shaped his death.

'That, nurse, is an attitude of mind, an attitude of mind that I will fight with everything I possess. I believe in life, Mrs Cadence. In the pain of staying alive.'

I envied him. He could say these things and still not sound grandiloquent.

'Half a million UDW's this year, two million next – it's beguiling, this final permissiveness, this admission that life as we have made it is not worth the bother. And it's not true, Mrs Cadence. UDW is not a noble civilized device – it's a squalid social evil. It rots minds just as leprosy rots bodies. I shall fight it, Mrs Cadence, in any way I can. You might say I've received the call. I believe in too much. You and your husband must keep away from me.'

We didn't keep away. Between them Edward and he for their different reasons developed a machine that reduced UDW mortalities from a peak of three and a half million to last year's figure of I believe seventeen. Thus Edward oozled Sensitape in under the banner of Tony's idealism.

I'm supposed to be reading the newspaper. My wardress mentioned a monorail disaster. Added some quick cliché about an interest in disasters being healthy. Healthy, no – normal, yes. Thea Cadence's thoughts on Being Interested in Disasters: fondling other people's disasters will make you appreciate your own. And there's a mawkish sentiment for you. The Auntie Thea Column – Count your blessings while you've got 'em, or fate may come and spank your Pompom Circle Dance, Pomp and Circumstance, Round the Mulberry Bush, Here Comes Everybody as somebody once called him. And if I don't look away, what then? I seem to have been carrying on the same argument for seven years.

'Cassavetes is a great man. He has something none of you will ever understand about.'

'Shouting is unsuitable, Mrs Cadence. Shouting is unsuitable.'

'He's a great man, Edward. He has something none of us will –'

'He's an hysteric, my dear. There's also a touch of senile dementia.'

'He's a great man, Tony. He has something –'

'He has the prejudices of his generation, darling. A tragic romanticism.'

'But Tony –'

'I agree that Edward shouldn't have pressed him. It was a mistake, and Edward's genuinely sorry for it. But –'

Perhaps lovers are always generous to wives' absent husbands. It was so easy, talking in the sun, or above the noise of a pub or theater foyer, so easy for someone with a belief, even a belief in Sensitape. But Tony hadn't been with Edward on that last visit to Paul Cassavetes, and I had.

'They have a right to buy this with money, Dr Cadence?'

'Nobody wants you to make up your mind at once, Mr Cassavetes.' Edward was sorting through a pile of music, his mind apparently only half on what he was saying. 'The musical experience would of course be far more complete than anything ever known before.'

'You do not answer my question.'

'The money isn't important, Mr Cassavetes.' Gentle. So casual. 'Everybody has money – a price tag is either convenient or inconvenient. In this matter money is irrelevant.'

'That I do not see. You are asking me to sell my soul.'

'Rather to give your soul away, Mr Cassavetes.'

It was a room that in all its hundreds of years could never have known an equal sophistry. Three high, uncurtained windows, sunlight between their half-closed shutters standing in long white-gold columns across the floor, its centuries of polish calm and grave, dust moving slowly to and fro and around and down, as if in some ancient passepied to remembered music. A piano, and a cello leaning on a chair. Shelves of music and small stone sculptures. Spaces of grey-green shadow, caught from the garden, carried precious far back to the distant door with the shining brass finger plate.

Edward looked as fine as ever. He had positioned himself easily by the end of the piano, his feeling for the vertical line of his light suit against the coffin bulk of the instrument quite instinctive. The absence of anything to sit on worried me, and I wished I hadn't been brought. I moved to the mantelpiece, then dared not lean on it. Edward stood motionless, completely restful. Nothing external about him could justify the strange impression of agressiveness he gave.

'My soul is my own, Dr Cadence. One thing not for giving away. Another is this that I feel, that I know, when I play.'

'Your greatest strength is Beethoven …' As if the old man hadn't spoken. 'I suggest something popular. The *Moonlight Sonata*, perhaps. Issue the Sensitape and the record together. To hear what you hear, Mr Cassavetes. To know what you know. Or perhaps you think ordinary humanity is not worthy.'

'You pretend to serve humanity, you doctors. Your real hope is to be God.'

'Thea my dear, tell Mr Cassavetes about Sensitape. My wife has worked with the apparatus since its inception. She'll tell you anything you want to know.'

'I want to know nothing.'

'Thea, tell Mr Cassavetes about Joel Fossom.'

Idiotically I had begun to tremble as soon as my name was mentioned. In the cool room I sweated.

'Oh yes … Joel Fossom. I'm sure you've heard of him, Mr Cassavetes. The painter, you know. Such a high reputation. He's the man who painted that beautiful Crucifixion. He's one of the few artists today who work from a genuine Christian conviction. He –'

'You don't have to sell Joel Fossom, my dear. Just tell Mr Cassavetes about him and Sensitape.'

Quiet. Quieter than ever. He was using my fear of him as a demonstration. I didn't realize at that time that I feared him. I thought instead that I was a foolish, scatterbrained woman. And that Paul Cassavetes was obstinate and wrong.

'Oh yes ... Sensitape. You see, Joel Fossom was working on a painting. We made a recording of the creative process. It turned out to be –'

'I am sorry, Mrs Cadence, but I have already told your husband. I want to know nothing.'

'Like Fossom, you too are an old man.' Edward spoke as from a long way off. 'You have a unique gift.'

'And it shall die with me.' Painfully vehement. He allowed a long pause. 'As is the nature of unique gifts.'

He was a small man, thick and broad, with thick broad hands, and below his bald head veined temples and heavy, almost eyebrowless frontal ridges. He had the sort of strength that Edward would coldly wear away with gentleness. Already his eyes in their old brown hollows were too bright for comfort. Edward's voice retired still further, every word like glass.

'You have many charitable interests, Mr Cassavetes. A half million pound fee could mean a great deal.'

'You are a visitor in my house, Dr Cadence. But if you continue to –'

'Donated anonymously, Mr Cassavetes. Nobody but us three need ever know.'

'I shall never feed your need for power, Dr Cadence. Will you please go now.'

'Certainly. It was very good of you to see us.' Still no movement. 'When may we call again?'

The old man had half-risen from the piano stool. He sat again, where he was safe. The room was huge around him.

'No doubt you will call again. I shall give instructions for you not to be admitted.'

'Just as you wish.' Nine quick paces to the door, me following, inadequate. 'At your age I'm sure you're entitled to some small self-indulgence.'

Cassavetes said nothing. He seemed to have stopped listening.

'My need for power. Your need to be inviolate. Other outside needs we can only guess at. You might say it's a conflict beyond any resolution.'

The force of will he turned on the hunched figure at the keyboard was monstrous.

'You must understand, Mr Cassavetes, you have to *want* to make this recording. Any shade of reluctance will come through clearly. So we're all entirely in your hands when it comes down to it.'

'Dr Cadence, your talk is like a sickness.' The old man muttered to himself for several seconds, unheard. 'I must have nothing to do with you ever again. Your talk is evil. Sin. I have no words for my horror at what you are doing.'

'What I do is to enrich human life.'

'What you do is to ...'

The strength of his voice failed. He sat very straight, showing a sudden surprise in his eyes. Then he fell off the stool – in a detectable way no longer human – onto the tiny polished blocks of the floor. Edward looked at me. A sensitivity in him – he was always immensely sensitive – suggested to him that I might prefer to be the first to go to the old man. I shook my head, for I couldn't move, either to him or blessedly away out of the room to call servants. Call servants – or his wife. Christ, his wife.

'Here's your tea, Mrs Cadence. I've brought honey today, seeing you didn't fancy yesterday's jam.'

Edward squatted beside the old man, first neatly tucking up his trouser legs. One old square hand was flung out, lying palm up in the strip of sunlight from the centre of the three, grasping minutely at nothing. Motes whirled above it, agitated.

'He's not dead. Send for his wife, will you, Thea?'

I suppose I must have done.

'Are you all right, Mrs Cadence? I've brought you your tea.'

My impression of the room is continuous, with his wife now in it. But her husband had been moved, composed now, Edward's jacket rolled up for a slight pillow.

'Cerebral hemorrhage, Mrs Cassavetes. A stroke. For the moment his right side appears to be affected.'

'Affected? What do you mean, Dr Cadence?'

'Paralyzed. I suggest that you send for his regular physician immediately.'

'Tea, Mrs Cadence ...? My goodness, you're miles away, aren't you?'

'You two – what have you done to him?'

'You must keep calm, Mrs Cassavetes. Quite possibly there is no lasting damage whatsoever. Modern electronic reeducation techniques work wonders. With the patient's cooperation a complete recovery is often possible. We'll keep in touch. A Sensitape made by him would be of historic value.'

The old woman very silent, very stiff, not with pride but with the pain of what had been done. The sunlight surely moving as I watched it, so long we stood and waited for the paramedics and their trolley. No one could cause another person's stroke. I told myself that. Strokes were caused by –

'I shall have to send for Doctor if you go on like this, Mrs Cadence.'

Soon finished now, Wardress. It is necessary, however, to remember how they carried him away, carried away what Edward had made, what I had made, what an old man's blood had made, carried away the face already lopsided, the good side shaking with what we probably believed was palsy. But I suspected then, as I know for certain now, that it might very well be laughter. He's still alive, trundling around his beautiful garden and feeding the goldfish. He teaches a lot. For me in here that's a fine thing to be able to remember.

'It's a fine thing to be able to remember, Mrs Craig.'

'You're not thinking of losing your memory, are you?'

'You misunderstand me.'

'You've been miles away. I can hardly be expected to follow you.'

How she disciplines me. How easily I could spill out of the shape of the present, running idly down uncertain corridors.

'I live a lot on memories at the moment, Mrs Craig.'

'Memories of what really happened?'

'Of course.'

'Tea, Mrs Cadence. And I've brought honey instead of jam.'

She means something. I prod the honey suspiciously.

'Bread and honey? Homely comfort? Knowing what's what? Is that why you've brought me honey?'

'We're not trying to get at you. You didn't seem to like the jam, that's all.'

Jam or honey? – and what nice cakes on such pretty china. Edward's mother managed talk about such things for most of a long afternoon. And Thea Springfield panting along behind, astonished that this was the form the exam should be taking, too young to detect the performance learned for the sake of a son who liked to operate within the system, too young to be insulted by it.

'Have you had a chance to look at the paper yet, Mrs Cadence?'

'I'm afraid not.' No need for remembering to entail bad manners. 'But it was kind of you to bring it.'

'Not kind at all. I have very good reasons.'

'You said you thought contact with the outside world would be good for me.'

'More specific reasons, Mrs Cadence.'

'Tell me what you mean.'

'There are other things than monorail disasters in a newspaper.'

I don't want to know. Whatever it is you're trying to tell me, Wardress, willing me to discover, I don't want to know it. My relationship to the knowledge I already have is far too precarious.

'Perhaps I'll look at it later. After I've had my tea.'

'I'm sure you can imagine, Mrs Cadence, how careful my briefing was for this case. The proceedings against you, for instance, were not to be brought up by me in any way at all. They were to be dealt with by Doctor under tape therapy.'

'To disregard clinical instructions, Mrs Craig, is to risk your whole career.'

'I never would, Mrs Cadence. Believe me, I've checked the paper carefully for any reference to *your* case. There isn't one. I'll take the paper away when I come for the tea things.'

Your case … Why the emphasis? What other case would be likely to interest me? Surely she knows the extent of my egocentricity? I smile at my wardress and she goes out quietly.

Nothing on the front page except the disaster. Photographs of twisted steel, lists of the dead and injured, a message from the Queen, a visit from the Prime Minister. Back page – all sports. What paper is this? I don't remember any sports in the paper Edward had. Must I go through this one column by column? I can't hold it still, can't manage it, can't turn the pages. The huge, noisy pages.

It is extraordinary to watch my hands. They smooth and fold, now so neat and expert, so accomplished that they act without mind, without my volition. The paper is put away. As I said before – whatever it is, I don't want to know. Hope is like a fever, a heat engendered by battle, and it leaves a deadly chill behind it. My arms ache. My hands tingle and creak. I don't want to know. Suddenly I'm so tired I could cry. No longer with even the energy to pour tea and find rest.

I hope my wardress comes back soon. My nurse.

Mrs Cadence senior poured tea with little difficulty. I hid in my admiration of how well she poured tea.

'Milk and sugar, Miss Springfield?'

'Thank you.'

Edward told me later what a capable woman Rachel his mother was, how even before sexual intercourse with his father she had laid down the terms on which she would accept motherhood. The career she was building for herself – she was a social statistician – would be interrupted for a bare ten months, three months before the child's birth and seven months after. And so it had happened. She was a woman of her time, aware of her child's needs (hence the seven months' mother-love), and also aware of her own. Grading the easing of the physical bond between herself and her son carefully, she delayed full-time work till he was three years old and capable of relating to the larger unit of the nursery school. During these three years she resisted instinctive nest building – she and her husband had lives of their own to lead, outside the material confines of an elaborate home. For their son a centre was needed, a home territory. Nothing more.

It would not have been fair to say that Edward married me because I would be useful to him. But that he allowed himself to fall in love with me for this reason I have little doubt. And with my very different background – Rachel researched this background most carefully – he reasoned that care must be taken if I were not to be put off. He didn't realize, never realized, how helplessly I doted on him.

The steps his mother took as part of fulfilling her motherly duty were all her own idea. That was the great thing about Rachel – you never had to tell her what to do. She could be relied upon to find out for herself. Her responsibilities hadn't ended at seven months. They occupied her intelligent concern up to the day she tidily died.

'Edward tells me you haven't any brothers or sisters, Miss Springfield.'

'I'm afraid not.' Thea Springfield felt this to be vaguely improper. 'My mother couldn't,' she explained. 'There was a blood incompatibility.'

'So sensible of your parents not to turn to AID. Compound families seldom seem to be successful.' No doubt the relevant statistic appeared in her mind and was dismissed as socially unsuitable. 'Do have a biscuit, Miss Springfield,' she said. She watched the girl with a kindly expression. Edward was on duty, so Thea Springfield was facing the ordeal on her own. Rachel had already commented on this, putting Miss Springfield at her ease with a reminiscence about her own first meeting with her future mother-in-law. Which was back before the second world war.

'Edward also is an only child, you know. My husband and I were always going to have more – three is probably the ideal number. Then he was killed in one of the early supersonics.'

'It must have been dreadful for you.'

'It's a long time ago now, my dear.'

I think it must have been Mrs Rachel Cadence who started my uncertainty in the presence of other women. Her motives were obscure. No more or less than men, women judge you, dominate you, flatter you, compete with you. But unlike men, their motives are unfathomable. My wardress, if I understood her motives I could deal with her entirely. Even allow friendship. Mrs X, to have understood her motives earlier would have enabled me to save the whole structure of my life. The similarities between me and other women, our clothes, the reasons for our bodies, the hinges of our minds, have always seemed to me, since Mrs Rachel Cadence, like tricks. Mirrors reflecting what isn't there.

'More tea, Miss Springfield?' Then the dainty teapot (bought specially, as was whispered later that day in a postcoital confidence) was suddenly set down with a firm, sensible gesture. 'You know, this is all very silly. Edward talks of you as Thea. I think of you as Thea. It's an unusual and beautiful name. So the sooner I start calling you by it the better. Don't you think so?'

'Yes. Please do. Yes, of course.' Her mind twittering at the thought that she might now be asked to call this woman 'mother.' She needn't have worried.

'You call me Rachel, my dear. Edward does. They all called their mothers by their given names at the school he went to.'

Bourgeois criticism was disarmed. And the girl's mind too confused to extend that criticism to the Cadence family's chic choice of school.

'Thank you. I will.' She couldn't bear to. 'Edward tells me' – seeking wildly – 'that you haven't been in this flat very long.'

'I move around a lot. My work often takes me to America. It's never seemed worth keeping up a permanent home anywhere.'

'How funny that must be. My parents have lived in the same house all their married life.'

'It's a very valuable ability. Western society needs a stable element. I think my own ancestors must have been nomadic.'

To Thea Springfield this attitude of mind was quite new. This habit of relating even the smallest personal act outward to society, and then backward and forward to the past and the future, gave the girl an uneasy feeling of continuity, of being infinitely responsible. The Springfields, on the other hand, were very finitely responsible. Professor Springfield was responsible to his head of department, to his daughter, and to his wife. Mrs Springfield was responsible to her position. And Thea Springfield was responsible to … to an impersonal thing called Suffering Humanity. Hence the profession of nursing.

'Edward's restlessness is more directed than mine, Thea. He's very ambitious – though I'm sure I don't have to tell you that, my dear. It's difficult for me to remember that another woman now probably knows him even better than I do.'

'But that's not true.' Thinking reassurance was needed. 'You and I know him differently, that's all.'

Her sudden blush at the unintended double meaning was ignored. Rachel had decided it was not helpful for her to be aware that her son and this girl were sleeping together.

'Anyway, Thea, ambitious is not really the right word. Single-minded would be better. He pursues a vision. It won't make him easy to live with, I'm afraid.'

'I think it's marvellous.' Deb word. 'I shall do everything I can to help him.'

'I'm sure you will, my dear. He tells me you plan to get married.'

'At the beginning of August, we thought. Just a registry office – nothing grand or fancy.'

It sounded modern and sensible. She had no idea then what it meant. The formica-topped desk and the bland satin-bronze clock. The sad air of a necessary legal formality.

At least, it seems sad to me now as I look back on it. For Thea Springfield it was as magical as everything else that year. A girl in love. Doubled. Astonished at how unaware her last few grown-up years had been. Astonished at the inadequacy of every earlier experience, the poor sort of interest earlier men had aroused in her, the poor sensible indifference to the ugliness of their private bodies nursing had given her, squashy organs obviously meant to be guts and only hung outside as a rather poor joke. A girl in love, finding beauty. Incredible, where Thea Springfield could find beauty. My memories of her are so vivid, they point the painful differences between us, what our eyes see, what our hands feel, what our minds know. Each morning Mrs Cadence puts clothes onto the unscrubbable staleness of skin, try not to touch herself, not to look. Thea Springfield retained her man's sweat on her, too romantic to wash it off.

I'm at my wash basin now, there to externalize a psychological cleansing. Knowing what I do, I still do it. The thermotap insults me even more than usual – why shouldn't I scald myself if I happen to be careless? Are there to be no penalties for inefficiency? Lather between my fingers, and disgusting sliding. Rinse off and dry. As I hang up the towel my wardress returns.

'Still not drunk your tea, Mrs Cadence?'

'I meant to. Will you pour it for me?'

She does so, hands me the cup and I drink.

'You've been crying, Mrs Cadence.'

'Not crying. Only washing my face.'

'Do you think you could live like this for quite a long time, Mrs Cadence?'

'All my life.' What a strange question.

'Doctor asked me to tell you he wasn't satisfied with the progress of the treatment.'

'Tell him to try another tape. This one is too generalised.'

'I don't think he was asking for advice.'

'Give it to him all the same. The guilt needs to be more specific. Jealousy-oriented?'

'Not guilt, Mrs Cadence. Contrition. It's a contrition tape.'

I suspect fine differences not my own of being artificial, put in to confuse me. Besides, her hands are gathering up the paper, feeling its untidiness, deducing perhaps that it has been opened and read. She's not going to comment.

'More tea? Before I take it away?'

'Please. The dose is calculated on a basis of two cups, I believe.'

She stares thoughtfully. She won't be needled.

'I wonder if the tape really is wrong for you. Or perhaps you simply choose to think it's guilt because that's what you feel you can deal with.'

'You shouldn't be suggesting that. Doctor wouldn't like it. Poor man. I'm knowing enough as it is. And I expect he's doing his best.'

She pours the tea while I walk, disjointed, around the room. Before contrition there must be guilt. Obviously. And before both, motive. She knows this as well as I do.

'I'll be in again soon, Mrs Cadence, to see how you're doing.'

So many of her remarks have the same rhythm. They're the same remarks really, only with different words. If I've read the paper, whatever it says needs space in which to do its work. And Doctor says he isn't satisfied with the progress of the treatment.

DAY 27

'How are you feeling, Mrs Cadence?'

This is which minute of which hour of which day? And which repetition of that disgusting question?

'I asked you how you were feeling, Mrs Cadence.'

'Guilty, Doctor'

'No need to shout, Mrs Cadence.'

'I feel like shouting.'

'And I feel like slapping you for shouting.'

'Do so. Go on as you have begun.'

The room jolts. He's hit me. Hit my face. Quite hard.

We both know where we stand.

'What was I supposed to say?'

'You're very agressive today, Mrs Cadence.'

'It's the treatment working. It's what guilt does to you.'

'Contrition, Mrs Cadence. It's what contrition does to you.'

'You're a liar.'

'Another slap would put us one all. I'm learning how you work, Mrs Cadence.'

'Tell me why you say my name so often.'

'To reassure you.'

'Another lie.'

'To remind you.'

'I wish I needed reminding.'

'I'm glad you don't.   Mrs Cadence.'

Such a pause he hopes as one could grow old in. I use it merely to remove the headset in. Technical progress has slowed – it's the same model I fitted on Dr X five years ago. But later refinements would hardly be necessary in the Kingston. Five years ago, fitted on Dr X and his wife. His tame vagina. Which is what wife means.

'I'm in heat, Doctor.'

'A complication.'

'Wouldn't you masturbate in me?'

'An original request.'

'You have a sense of humour.'

'The humour lay in your choice of words, Mrs Cadence.'

'Loveless sex – mutual stimulation – I've been a nurse. I possess the vocabulary.'

'You're whipping up hate, Mrs Cadence. You're wanting the normal to sound nauseous.'

'How puritanical of you, Doctor. What's nauseous in … in what I said?'

'To me, nothing. To you, so much that you couldn't say it again.'

The door opens. It's my wardress come.

'Wardress, the stepped-up treatment's wonderful. I've been telling Doctor I'm in heat.'

'How very theatrical of you.'

'It's what you put in the tea, Wardress. There's a nineteen day backlash.'

I don't care how many pretenses I spoil. I like to see them controlling their faces. Tells me nothing about the accuracy of my date guess, though.

'The patient is ready to go back to her room now, Nurse.'

'At once, Doctor.'

'Hadn't you better come with us, Doctor, just in case?'

'You know Nurse's training, Mrs Cadence.'

'I ought to. I received it myself.'

'A long time ago, Mrs Cadence. You haven't kept it up as Nurse has.'

'But the insane have the strength of ten. You've read the stories.'

'Which don't apply to you, Mrs Cadence, for you're not insane.'

The treatment room has a rooflight, with variable transparency glass. It's fully clear now, a high blue sky filled with hawks and small hand-saws. But I don't bother – we're all professionals here, in our own particular ways.

'Come along now, Mrs Cadence. Up you get. We mustn't waste Doctor's time. He's a very busy man.'

There's an importance in not going out in style. Along the corridor meekly (different flowers today, tulips), she knows me too well to think I'm beaten, then into my room and the door is closed. I never see other patients. My wardress talks of putting me in with others, but that's likely to be her joke. The Kingston's a huge building but it never breathes in the night like other buildings.

'I've just had an amusing idea, Wardress. The Kingston has been abandoned and taken over by two of the medical staff. I'm the only patient left, and you and Doctor daren't let me out to tell on you.'

'Why don't we kill you?'

'Medical staffs are like that. They hate simple answers. Besides, then they'd have nobody. Nobody to look after. Nobody to torture.'

'You should write a play about it.'

Busily she tidies nothing. Doctor is right – she's hard muscled, mind and body. I wonder how Mr Craig managed.

'Are you a widow, Mrs Craig?'

'What makes you think that? My husband's very much alive.'

'Do you worship him with your body?' Ho ho.

'I was married in a registry office. The issue wasn't mentioned.'

'So was I. On the fourth of August. With mimosa. But it still applied.'

'Worship is too one-sided. I've tried to understand him. We've both tried to understand each other.'

'Christ. How serious-minded of you both.'

'I thought yours was a serious-minded question.'

'It's a big place, America.'

She doesn't recognize the allusion. Flummoxed for once.

'I'll get you your tea.'

The normal, he said. The normal.

Normal.

Edward and I had gone down to the van to watch the dials of normality. It was hot and passionate for us out in the recording van. Tony was absorbed in his levels, and he left us nothing to do but watch. All engineer inside his headphones, not normal at all. I saw a needle jump, and counted nine times. And a sort of floating one.

'He's counting her ribs,' I said to Edward.

'Wrong register,' he said. Then he caught my eye and laughed. 'But it's an interesting interpretation.'

The reels spun, and a gauge somewhere ticked imperturbably. The van generator gave a discreet cough.

'I think he's gone to sleep,' I said.

'Not with that pulse reading.' Reverence in his voice.

A CR tube gave off a pattern like an angry porcupine.

'Tactile excitation, reading nine.'

'His or hers?'

'His on this side, hers on that.' Edward gestured.

I wrote HIS and HERS on bits of sticky tape and pasted them onto the polished instrument facings. The porcupine was HERS. It was followed by a respiration seizure, forty-three seconds. Tony concentrated on his knobs and switches, navigating a now familiar sea. He'd been in charge of the auditions, learning all the time. The machinery emitted a small electric whoop.

'Peaking beyond twelve,' said Edward. 'His turn now.'

The tactile register on his side scribbled complicatedly, filling HIS screen with a dazzling concentration of rockets. HER porcupine became restless too.

'Blood pressure up,' said Edward. 'And he's closed his eyes.'

The tubes signaled to each other frantically across the van. His audiometer climbed to five.

'From her speech signal that can't have been more than a very faint whisper. Interesting example of heightened perception. Normally he'd hardly have heard it.'

'They are rather close to each other,' I said mildly.

Edward ignored me.

'Look, Thea – she's telling him to stop it.'

'How sweet.'

HER porcupine had calmed to a rolling swell. HIS rockets burst brighter than ever. Both audiometers rose and fell. Dr X and his wife were addressing each other in low speech signals. My legs were beginning to ache. Too much standing – this was overtime, after a full day in the hospital. I pulled out a hinged seat and perched on it. speach signals continued, perception evaluators showing very little cerebration. No abstract concepts, apparently.

'We'll edit some of this out,' Edward said, 'if we find it drags on playback.'

There was sudden activity on every tube and dial in the place. Mercury leaped up gauges, needles spun, screens gave off pulsing psychedelia.

'Oh look,' Edward murmured softly. 'They're kissing.'

As the kiss continued, respiration was resumed around it. The twin tapes slid smoothly on, down the guides, past units, and up to the receiving reels – bland brown ribbons now bearing the finest ardour Britain could muster. It irritated me that the charged and passionate reels should look so exactly like the calm empty ones. This was foolish, of course – a calm brain looks no different from an excited one. Emotion is of the electric soul.

The kiss merged into something else, hard to identify. Different readings for HIS and HERS, no pattern at all that I could discern. Edward's eye, however, was more skilled. He slapped one of the HERS dials triumphantly.

'That proves it,' he cried. 'I obtained an identical reading last month from a nursing mother. Mammary stimulation – it must be.'

He photographed the screen excitedly.

'Another breakthrough,' I said.

'One day they'll all be cataloged, Thea. Think of that.'

A bank of insulators began to buzz, bringing overload relays into circuit. Tony juggled adroitly with the compensating switches.

'I hope the resistances can take it,' he said, not looking up.

'They did on the trial runs, Tony. I shouldn't worry.'

'People have a habit of saving their best for the final performance. Just our luck if they blew something.'

'Do what you can, boy. A retake at this stage would be very troublesome.'

'You can say that again.'

I wondered if it was my imagination, or if the interior of the van was really becoming rapidly hotter. I suspected that my growing dizziness was attributable to other causes, to my secret raid on Dr X's whiskey. I'd thought I might need help to contain my frustrations. All the same, the machinery was evidently excited on its own account. The feedback whoops became more frequent. Indicator needles flicked like windshield wipers. And the CR patterns came on top of each other faster than the eye could register, filling the van with an eerie radiance. And the warmth was neither imagination nor whiskey – at that moment the thermostatically controlled cooling fan whined into action.

Even a positron will creak, if pushed beyond certain limits.

'Aha,' said Edward. 'Penetration.' And he made a note of the exact microsecond.

Nature's orchestra. The noises increased and held, a raucous chuckling sound interspersed with piercing whistles. The van leaped about on its springs, windows rattling, sides bulging outward. Well, it should have done. Edward raised his eyebrows speculatively, watching meter after meter climb into its red sector. Perhaps the three of us were in great danger. Tony tore off his jacket, the sweat gathering in rows along his forehead. He returned to the battle. And the two tapes, HIS and HERS, recorded dutifully the magnetic intimacies of fervour.

There is a point beyond which crescendos become meaningless. They move beyond known dimensions, beyond experience. Tick chuckle whoop whine into a world of moving lights and heat and timelessness, only the dial pacing the excitation torrent from the room above. I saw the poor clock had opted out, its face obscured with heavy condensation. I began to laugh, and roll about.

'For God's sake, Thea, control yourself.'

'It's so funny, Edward ...'

'Nothing remotely funny. Your thinking so is a clear denial symptom.'

'Clickle, tickle, chuckle, snuckle, wheeeee ...'

'You're quite hysterical, my dear.'

'Blow for half time, Edward. Half time and change ends.'

'Keep still, Thea. You'll break something.'

'Ninety-nine, a hundred. Change ends.'

'Schoolgirl rudery. This is a serious scientific experiment. I believe you're drunk, Thea. What a disgusting state to be in at a time like this.'

I was past speech. I rocked helplessly and the van rocked with me. A switch fell off the wall and dangled, smoldering. Tony leaned sweatily over his indicators, as fast and as secret as a poker player. Edward smoothed his hair, a sure sign of near collapse. Whatever havoc Dr X and his wife might cause, they were obviously quite unconcerned. I tried blowing on various tubes to cool them.

Outside there was moonlight. A grassy court surrounded by the pale fronts of houses in which no doubt other similar electrical excitations were passing unrecorded. Similar but lesser. Nice people, too nice, perhaps. But Dr X and his wife – hell, they weren't nice at all. And I was drunk enough to find it amusing.

There had to be an end, even for Dr and Mrs X. The needles stuck against their stops, the relays screamed like elephants, and a final blue haze poured from the apparatus labeled HIS. (No reflection on HERS, as it turned out. Merely a faulty winding.) The seconds passed. Tony gave up, turned away.

'They can't still –'

'They bloody can, boy.'

Even ends have ends. At last the counters sank, the screens came to gentle satisfied curves, the relays purred, the generator cleared its throat. Suddenly my head was throbbing louder than anything in the place.

'Keep 'em turning, Tony. We're not losing signal, are we?'

'Plenty there, though God knows why. These resistances were never designed to –'

'I don't care a damn about that. Getting the next few minutes is absolutely vital. Their complete lack of postcoital depression was one of the big things in their favor. It's one thing to peak beyond twelve, quite another to …'

The post-coital depression was all mine. I climbed stiffly out of the van and was sick on the grass. A dim yellow light above me showed around the curtains of the Xs' bedroom. I imagined their warm contentment and was sick again.

This room is for me to be alone in. They leave me here with myself, leave me to disgust myself into some different state. Contrition, they call it, and deny me any mortification save another's electric guilt. And they offer comfort as an insult. I wonder what poor psychopath they taped, what man's intensity of suffering they took and wrapped up neatly on a plastic reel. He believed in guilt and gave them what they wanted with delight. I hadn't felt this quality of demonic joy before – until today. Doctor must have been filtering off the edge of it. It's a therapeutic triumph that comes near to unhinging me. Another time and it may. I wonder what else they have in reserve along in the treatment room.

My bedroom has a carpet with a pattern of small roses on it – completely washable, in case I should disgrace myself. I know about the carpet because I chose it. Edward said the women's wing should be basically feminine and gave me a free hand. I could do no more than choose things I liked and trust to their basic femininity; curtains, light fittings, chair covers, bedspread, pictures, furniture, wallpaper, not the washbasin, that was standard. My taste has changed little in the three years since. The rooms I made were pretty – I find this one pretty now. I wish to God I didn't.

If admissions of guilt are what is wanted, I'll say it at once. All this, the whole hellish structure, is my fault. After meeting Tony I could have held my tongue. I could have altered the fate of the human race. And that's not kidding.

'You ought to go, Edward,' I said. 'You ought to go and see young Mr Stech. The son of our latest UDW. Apparently he's the electronics king of West London,' I said. 'He's invented a 3-D video tape that really works.'

'You know how I hate 3-D TV, Thea. Why the hell should I be interested in a machine to record it?'

'I talked to the shop manager. He says Stech has made a special meter for measuring nano-waves. He says it's more sensitive than anything known before.'

Edward stopped what he was doing.

'But that's marvellous, darling. He'll be able to help me with my –'

'He says he'd like to try. I haven't told him much – you know how I get things muddled. I thought you'd rather go along and explain for yourself.'

I was always an efficient sort of person, not in the least liable to get things muddled. But Edward needed the myth of a poor weak woman and in those days I loved him enough to be willing to connive at it. No, in spite of Mrs Craig I must speak the truth. I worshipped him. With my mind and with my soul and with my

'Oh, and by the way, Edward, Stech has an obsession about curing UDW. Tell him you're working on that and he'll be your slave forever.'

'And so I am. If my idea ever works out UDW will be one of the first conditions I tackle.'

I didn't go with him to the radio shop. I was on duty at the hospital that afternoon, so when the night staff finally came on I hurried home to hear how Tony and he had got on. I remember banging in at the front door and the emptiness that the flat flung back at me. At that moment I really did see the sort of life I was to have, the succession of empty rooms I would enter hopefully, the sort of life that being married to a man with a vision would entail. And I didn't mind. Ever since I had known him Edward had been searching. He had hoped for help from my father and had been patronizingly offered research facilities he wasn't trained to make use of. He had hoped for help from the hospital authorities and had received nothing but angry incomprehension. The committees of several scientific bodies had listened to him in a kindly manner, offering nothing except warm invitations for him to address their members. Now Edward was no longer searching. And the responsibility for this change was mine. I felt proud. The Thea Cadence of that period – Thea Cadence, B.C., Before Cynicism – was proud.

I looked up Tony's father in the telephone and rang the shop. I counted the rings. At fifty I gave up. The place was obviously empty, the shop staff gone home long ago, Edward and Tony on their way back to the flat. They'd have supper and go on talking far into the night. I pictured the wife whose self-effacing devotion would help the vision to become reality. I began to cook the supper, preparing for a guest. I was twenty-three.

At nine o'clock, still alone, I had an idea and rang the hospital. I'd stared between the curtains down the slushy street so often that the houses and lamps had become unrecognizable. The girl on Reception was wonderful, pretending not to know who I was, not to notice how bright I was being. Yes, she said, Dr Cadence had come in three hours ago. With another gentleman. They'd gone through to the lab block. She'd ring through to them if I wanted. No, I said. If Dr Cadence was busy it didn't matter.

I ate my first spoiled supper. Already the self-effacing devotion was wearing thin. At eleven I woke with a start, my head on a carefully cleared space on the table. With the edge off my tiredness – I'd been on duty since six that morning – I became angry. I walked to the hospital slowly, through streets with piles of snow wet-hardened in the gutters: an avenging angel, dark and hooded, through the city jungle. He should have phoned. He should have said he would be late. He should have phoned.

Nobody importuned me. I was too formidable.

Across the hospital forecourt and up the stretcher ramp. I noticed Edward's car neatly parked among those of the night staff. He should have phoned me. No man ought to treat a wife like that. Even a hotel manager would demand more consideration. Ritual thoughts. Ritual comfort.

'They're in the lab block, Mrs Cadence. Would you like me to –?'

I was past, the double doors flapping slowly shut behind me. I knew which laboratory to go to. On the door: EKG. AUTHORISED PERSONS ONLY. Inside the lights were so bright I had to shade my eyes.

'Ah, Thea. I was wondering when you'd turn up. You've met Tony Stech, I think.'

You should have phoned. But I didn't say it.

The place was in chaos. Unrolled graph strips were draped everywhere. Cables hung about the room, control boxes turned back to front, their insides half dismantled. Tony Stech lay on one of the treatment couches, shirtless, electrodes and pads and gauges taped to his chest and temples. He raised his head.

'How d'you do,' he said. Then he returned his gaze to the ceiling.

'I'm glad you're here, Thea. You can make yourself useful.'

I stood quite still, my hand on the door behind me.

'What if the Director comes?' I said.

'He's out of town. I'm not a complete fool. Now, see this?' He picked up an unfamiliar metal box that trailed cables, a sector of glass let into its upper side. 'I can't be in two places at once,' he said. 'You watch this while I apply the stimulus.'

'What stimulus?'

'Loud noises. Auditory stimulus, level ten. We're dead scientific in here, woman.'

From Tony Stech there came something that might have been a suppressed giggle. I was the outsider. I approached the metal box. Behind the glass sector I saw a strip of brilliant green light.

'It won't bite you.'

He thrust it at me and I took it. The box was warm and vibrated slightly. Edward moved away, stepping over furls of paper. He spoke to me as he went.

'Look at the glass squarely and you see a number. What is it?'

Two figures were projected onto the glass. I was gratified that they had appeared for me.

'Seventeen,' I said.

'Rotate the knob on the right till you see the number ten. That gives us enough to play with either way.'

'Either way ...' It wasn't a question. I was too absorbed in making the numbers change. In having fun.

'Plus or minus, you fool. We're not sure which way it'll go.'

I found ten. It was next door to eleven. I was a success. Looking up, I saw Edward standing beside Tony Stech. He seemed younger than I remembered, and more alive.

'In a minute I shall apply the stimulus. I want you to notice any change, either in the number or in the position of the green light. Any change at all. You understand?'

I nodded. It was a night when great things happened. I had a mind above such things as burned potatoes. Edward stooped, and cupped his mouth to Tony's ear.

'YAAAH.'

Auditory stimulus, level ten. I flinched, but held fast. We were dead scientific.

'Well? What was the reading?'

'No change.'

'Well try again.'

Louder this time, but I was ready for it.

'YAAAAAAAAAAAAAAH.'

Pause.

'I think the green light may have swelled a little.'

Tony Stech raised himself on his elbows.

'Knob on the left,' he said. 'Turn it fully clockwise. We'll try again.'

I did as I was told. Tony lay back and they tried again. The ten remained, and the green line never wavered. Tony sat up and started peeling connections off himself, while Edward consulted various graphs.

'I don't understand it, Tony. The reaction's there all right. The pen has swooped all over the place.'

'Purely quantitative. What my meter's after is a qualitative reading. From what you've said there ought to be a qualitative change as well.'

'Very tiny.'

'Christ, Edward, that thing goes down to a power of minus twenty.'

'But you heard what my wife said. It's not registering, and that's that.'

They checked leads and terminals, the argument continuing all the time. I put my metal box down and wandered idly around the room. I was a failure. Perhaps there'd been a reaction after all, and I'd missed it. I knew I dared not ask for a replay. Perhaps it was a failure of faith on my part – if I'd believed in a reaction strongly enough it might have happened. It was so important for Edward, his frustration lay like a weight on the whole room.

'For God's sake don't touch anything.'

I made myself as small as possible. I wouldn't have dreamed of touching anything.

'We might try a smoke box,' Tony muttered. 'You can measure a single electron in a smoke box.'

'I went into that eighteen months ago. Apparently there's a location difficulty.'

'Yes … Yes, there would be.'

I watched them run down. The checks they made were obviously pointless, confirming certainty with still further certainty. They slowed, lost impetus, and finally returned to the treatment couch where they perched side by side and stared at the surrounding litter. I wasn't there.

'We've had these machines for forty years.' Edward pounded the couch with his palm. 'Forty years and we still can't measure the impulses, let alone reproduce them.'

'What about the Russians? I thought –'

'Crude. Hit or miss. Sticking electrodes in on a trial and error basis. Twenty years ago the results looked spectacular. Rage, laughter, that sort of thing. But there was no grounding of measurement. It petered out, as a lot of these flashy results do.'

He paused, looked up at the clock. It was after midnight.

'I've said it a thousand times. Before we can induce even the simplest emotion it's essential to know precisely how that emotion is made up. The shape of the change involved. Its quality is what we need to know.'

'I'm sure it can be done, Edward. It's a problem of isolation more than anything. You'll just have to leave me to work on it.'

'Once we understand the changes, then we can reproduce them. There are all sorts of conditions against which this is our only hope. UDW, for example.'

'You know my feelings about that, Edward. I'd do a lot to get that beaten.'

His sincerity was embarrassing. Sincerity usually is, God help us. And the way Edward was using it.

'Design me a machine, Tony, that will measure the entire range of electrical activity in the human brain and I can promise you a cure within months.'

Next day Tony Stech would put his shop on the market. With the capital thus gained he would equip a laboratory, and eighteen months later the first Sensitape would be made. Twenty-seven thousand pounds the experimental period must have cost him.

Tony Stech put on his vest and shirt. He looked around for his coat.

'Christ, what a mess.' I really believe he'd only just seen it. 'We'd better start clearing up.'

After my failure with the meter, neither of them had taken the slightest notice of me, except to tell me not to touch. I didn't mind. Those who will one day alter fundamentally the shape of human life had a right to proper nourishment. I was Edward's proper nourishment.

'Have you tried,' I said, 'feeding a reaction straight from one person into another?'

Edward found me indistinct and kind of hard to focus on.

'What would be the point of that?' he said.

'It was only an idea.'

'Mrs Cadence may have something, Edward. If it did nothing else, it'd provide a useful check on our apparatus. If even another human brain failed to pick anything up, then we'd know there was something more fundamentally wrong.'

'More fundamentally wrong?'

'Couldn't it be that the electrodes we're using, or the cables even, simply aren't capable of carrying the type of current involved? The impedance could be wrong. Anything.'

Edward looked from me to him and back again.

'That's not a bad idea, Thea. Not a bad idea at all.'

Science is a great leveller.

They put me on the treatment couch and Tony beside it, wired to me with encephalograph contacts. Quite soon I slept. Edward let me, knowing that I'd been up for nearly twenty hours. Each time they were ready for an experiment they woke me up. As Tony and I were so close to each other the stimulus applied to him couldn't be auditory for I would have heard it almost as well as he. Instead Edward would stick a pin in the back of Tony's hand. He was bad at pain, leaping and writhing while I felt nothing. Nothing except an overpowering weariness. When they woke me up for the last time it was half past five and I had to be ready to relieve the night staff on my ward at six. Edward had decided that the cable they were using was too heavy, that the current was being swallowed before it reached me. Tony rang a friend who might be able to help them about low resistance metals. The time was twenty to six in the morning and the friend was uncooperative. Tony banged down the receiver. He and Edward had been working all night and were hardly sane.

'What now?' he said. I was washed and was trying to do my face in the side of a stainless steel sterilizing cabinet.

'Try again later. You must learn patience. I've been at this thing for five years already.'

'But we're so near –'

'Near? Near to what, for God's sake? We're no nearer to anything than I was five years ago.'

Edward's dedication was above the illusions that mere enthusiasm needs. He started tidying the laboratory. Tony watched.

'I tell you what. I'll bodge up an amplifier. Boost the signal and we're bound to get something.'

'I went into amplifier characteristics years ago. Nobody could guarantee me the lack of distortion I need. Any measurements would be worthless.'

My reflection in the sterilizing cabinet bulged grotesquely. But it reminded me suddenly of the clothes I was wearing. The clothes in which I had hoped to entertain a guest to supper.

'Edward – I'm very sorry, darling, but you'll have to drive me home for my uniform. I'm bound to be late. Perhaps you could have a word with Sister.'

'Come on, then.' Edward never argued where hospital discipline was involved. 'If we hurry we may make it. I dislike asking favors of the ward staff. You know that.'

He paused in the doorway.

'Sort this mess out, will you, Tony? I'll get back as soon as I can. I'll be out of a job if the place isn't in full working order by eight-thirty.'

He took my arm and rushed me down the corridor. The lab door bounced open again behind us.

'I've had an idea,' Tony called after us. 'These video tapes I work with. I never measure the signals – simply record them. What goes into the machine comes out unchanged. The distortions cancel. I think this measurement theory of yours is a dead end.'

A dead end. Edward kept going, across Reception and down the ramp to the car park. Outside the hospital it was still as dark as night. He opened the car door and helped me in. By the courtesy light I saw he was smiling. I slid across and he climbed in beside me. Later I would learn to drive for myself. He started the engine, reversed briskly, swung out into the road.

'It's funny,' he said, 'how for years you can miss the obvious. This Tony of yours is quite a discovery. What he said just now makes sense.'

He got me home in seven minutes, into my uniform and back to the hospital just as six was striking. And he sent some pills along later to keep me going. What really kept me going was to know what an attentive husband I had.

There's Criminal Responsibility for you. That Tony of mine, he'd said … And the first CR of all, not to have pushed Edward under a bus before it was too late. Poor earnest Doctor along in the treatment room, pumping me full of psychopathic guilt when a simple comparison with the indigenous brain waves would tell him he was wasting his time. He goes on the court bailiff's historic terminology, I suppose. Not guilty, I told him. NOT GUILTY. And detectably meant it. But I shall not tell him he's wasting his time when he moves on – if he ever does – to contrition.

Anyway, perhaps what I feel is not contrition. Perhaps it's only regret.

I stare at the door, willing my wardress to arrive through it with my tea. She does so.

'I'm glad you've come, Mrs Craig. I want to apologize for my bad behaviour after treatment.'

'I've known a great deal worse. As I'm sure you have yourself, Mrs Cadence.'

'And for that reason, if nothing else, I ought to know better'

'Your position is very difficult, Mrs Cadence. Believe me, I do understand.'

The silence beyond the still half-open door. Passages and other doors, and I can't remember the way through them to mine..

'Mrs Craig, how will I get out of here?' Out through the thundering silence?

'It's a decision for the Home Secretary. You know that. And he's advised by the Committee. And the Committee is advised by Doctor.'

'You said he wasn't pleased with the progress of the treatment.'

'Slow, he said. Too slow.'

'But that was yesterday. How about today? I know so little. What does he expect?'

'You should ask him yourself, Mrs Cadence.'

'This guilt he's applying, it seems to –'

'Contrition, Mrs Cadence.'

'I tell you, guilt. Guilt.'

She's staring at the side of my face. Why should she stare so?

'You told me the rule yourself, Mrs Cadence. Treatment not to be discussed with patients.'

She closes the door behind her with one foot, goes to the table and puts down the tea-tray. The hand she holds out withers me, its touch dry and cold. I move unobtrusively to the mirror, wanting to see what it is about my face that made her stare. The reflection I see is an outline into which I quickly pour back my unmindful identity. The cheek she stared at is clean, reasonably unwrinkled.

It's odd how long it takes me to remember Doctor's slap. And then only as an outsider would, seeing the red mark linger.

'You haven't brought me another newspaper.'

'I don't like wasting my time. You never read yesterday's.'

'How d'you know I never read yesterday's?'

I pitch my voice carefully, giving nothing away. She doesn't look at my cheek at all.

'I'm sorry. I've been told so little it was silly of me to interfere.'

'Yesterday made me too tired to want to begin it all again. There was something about the trial, wasn't there?'

'Which trial?'

'There's only been one trial.'

'I … told you. It was silly of me to interfere.'

She speaks with such kindness. Her warmth of course is entirely professional. I wish I could batter through it.

'Will I ever get out of here, Mrs Craig?'

'Usually when patients ask that question I make a comforting noise.'

'You mean I won't.'

'I mean I don't know. I'm told really very little.'

'When they took away UDW they took away everything.'

'You jump about, Mrs Cadence. And I dislike cynicism more than almost anything.'

'They took away a last hope of dignity. And it's no jump at all.'

'You'll be released, Mrs Cadence, when you have become habituated to contrition. The terms of your sentence are quite specific.'

'You're right to hate cynicism. I hated it at first, when I found I'd been loving it.'

An elliptical remark, conceited of me, but she fields it easily enough.

'The trouble with cynicism is that people really do seem to enjoy it. That seems to me a sin. Pour your own tea, will you?'

Nothing will really get through to her, not ill manners, not pathos, and now not even an attack upon her sacred Dr Cadence. She stands over the tea-tray and watches me – not looks at, watches. I hardly ever see her sitting down. And – even for the sake of Mr Craig – the idea of her supine is unthinkable.

As she goes out I speak to her back.

'In the opinion of the trial I'm dead and buried. Exhumation may uncover a lot of ugliness, but it doesn't help the corpse. If I get out of here I want to be myself renewed, not just dusted and put back in the window.'

Her wariness is more than professional. She seems almost afraid, using the door as an escape, closing it firmly on all knowledge of me. Yet in fact she must take me with her – we are by now too involved for her to be so compartmental – just as I retain her here with me. So many things I ought to tell her, so many explanations. But blasphemy, my real reason for being here, is never capable of explanation. Inexcusableness is built in. Gods are gods, men are men; to justify blasphemy is to question this necessary order.

Besides myself now and Thea Springfield, there is another identity I can remember. There is Thea Cadence, B.C., the woman who worshipped Dr Cadence before everyone else did. And even after. Her eyes saw very nearly the things I see, but saw them so differently.

I'd just put through an outside call, a woman who wouldn't give her name. This must have been about a year after the Sexitape recording. The day before Pastor Mannheim. As I was breaking my connection I'd caught her first question, 'Is this line private?' and Edward's reply, 'My secretary never listens in to patients' calls.' Her voice was vaguely familiar – as a psychiatrist he had patients who rang him at all hours. I returned to my typewriter; although an assistant had been engaged I still had to do some envelope addressing to help cope with the orders for Sexitape 57 that were coming in from medical institutions all over the world. The woman's anxiety amused me – if only she knew how little time I had for listening in. I typed half an address and then the internal phone rang.

'May I speak to Dr Cadence, please? This is the secretary to the Management Committee.'

'I'm afraid Dr Cadence is occupied with a patient. Can I help?'

'It concerns the meeting he attended yesterday. The Chairman is awaiting his decision.'

'I'll mention it to him as soon as he's free. Get him to ring you.'

'His reply will need to be in writing. But he knows all about it.'

And the man rang off.

His abruptness was strange – relations with the Kingston's Management Committee were usually friendly, effusive even. I made a note, finished the address and took another envelope. The indicator buzzed as Edward finished his call. I spoke to him on the intercom.

'I've had a call from On High,' I said.

'Oh Lord, yes. I was forgetting.'

'The committee seems to want a decision of some kind from you. In writing, so the little bureaucrat said.'

'Come through, will you, Thea? I like to see you when I'm dictating. Hell – I just like to see you.'

Pleased to hear him so cheerful in spite of everything, I went through. His room hadn't received its final restyling then, it was still basically an office, but smoother than it had been at the time of old Jacob Stech's death, with a plastic-topped desk and a leather swivel chair. A Sensitape machine stood beside the examination couch. The desk lamp was the latest thing, variable intensity.

'These women.' He indicated the telephone. 'She sees me tomorrow morning anyway. She could perfectly well have waited.'

'From what I heard of her she sounded quite calm. Not like some of them.'

'Calm? She's always calm. She'd be better for a storm or two.'

He changed his position, making it clear that he was also changing the subject. He rarely told me even as much as this; I felt honored.

'This memo, Thea – in your very best typing please. Layout, everything as formal and official as possible.'

I sat down with pad and pencil and waited.

'"To the Chairman of the Hospital Management Committee. Sir" – then a capitalized heading underlined ... REF. YOUR DEMAND FOR THE RESIGNATION OF SELF. New paragraph. "After careful consideration of the arguments advanced by the Committee I have come to the conclusion that –"'

'Resignation?' I couldn't help myself. Why hadn't he told me? 'They can't be serious.'

'Deadly serious. And secretaries should be seen and not heard. "After careful consideration of the arguments advanced I have come to the conclusion that it would be –"'

'But, Edward, you should have discussed this with me. You can't just –'

'"... I have come to the conclusion that it would be in the interests neither of the hospital nor of the advancement of medical science as a whole for me to tender –" no, "for me to presume to tender my resignation from membership of your staff." Have you got that?'

I nodded meekly. He smiled at me, arranged his fingertips in a mocking gable.

'"The discredit you claim is to my mind both transitory and greatly exaggerated. I am confident that any examination of the true state of affairs –" I suppose to underline *true* might look insulting. A pity ... "any examination of the true state of affairs will show myself to have behaved at all times with complete propriety. I deny categorically all accusations of unprofessional conduct and would welcome an official inquiry into my financial affairs –" no, we've had *affairs* already. "Into my financial ..."'

'Financial arrangements?'

'*Arrangements* will do very nicely. Just the right squalid tone. "The committee will understand that any resignation on my part at this stage would amount to an admission of guilt." Full stop. No signing off – just a space for my signature, and then all the official letters and professional clap-trap you can think of. How many idiots sit on that committee, Thea?'

'Seven, I think.'

'Then I'll need eight copies. One for the file, of course.'

I stood up and walked towards the door. If all he wanted was a secretary, that was all I'd give him.

'Now for God's sake don't get on your high horse, darling. You say I should have discussed it with you. In fact there was nothing to discuss. In my mind there was never any question at all of resigning. And if there had been, it would have been my decision, my affair, nothing to bother you with.'

But I'm your wife, I thought.

'How on earth did it happen?' I said. 'What's biting them?' Also, he was my husband.

'An article in the *Lancet*. Some Jeremiah carrying on about professional etiquette.'

'To do with money? I don't understand.'

'Sexitape, Thea – it's selling well. The suggestion is that I must be lining my own pocket.'

'But that's ridiculous.'

'Not so ridiculous. I quite easily could be. The whole system's open to any number of fiddles. The X's contract says that royalties must be devoted to the development of Sensitape. I might easily argue that the development of Sensitape would be advanced by us having a new house or a new car or something. If I wanted money that badly there'd be no difficulty at all. In fact, between you and me, I framed the contract with that possibility in mind.'

'But your salary's more than enough to live on. Not to mention mine. Why on earth should you want more?'

He'd never wanted money, possessions, things. He knew and I knew, so it wasn't a question worth answering. Suddenly he looked up at me, apparently forgetting the whole business. He looked up at me as most wives would pray to be looked at by their husbands. Not up and down, assessing meat, but in my eyes. In my eyes, asking me, disregarding the familiarities of eight years, asking me.

'You're a very beautiful woman, Thea.'

'Please don't.'

'Why not? It needn't … imply anything.'

'But it does, Edward. You know it does.'

'We're civilised people. We can choose which implications to ignore. For the sake of –'

'Will they sack you, Edward?' I had to stop him. 'Now that you've refused to resign, will they sack you?'

'I'm sorry, Thea. You must see it as a sophisticated form of nagging. But your need to be appreciated is even more deep-seated. You're lost without it.'

'I asked you a question, Edward.'

Anger. Running to his desk, leaning over him, needing him, rejecting him. Flushed cheeks, quickened pulse, suppressed tears. Sexual despair. A year of it.

'Will they sack you, I said.'

'I doubt it.' Always the psychiatrist. Always willing to go along just so far with a patient. 'That's why I've suggested the face-saver of an official inquiry. They know I'd fight – and they know the publicity would do them no good at all. This hospital has a reputation for progressiveness, Thea. And on the psycho-neurological side they have nobody to thank but me. Sexitape has great popular appeal. Think what the press could do with my dismissal. They'd never dare.'

The light on his desk was turned down low. Beyond this silenced room the corridors and wards were bright, endlessly demanding. His confidence was more than anybody had a right to.

'You would go on working here,' I said, 'knowing how they've tried to get rid of you?'

'People in offices get out of touch.' So tolerant. 'They get frightened. A man who has nothing but his job is always afraid of losing it.'

'And you have your vision.' A challenge. Dangerously near to scorn.

'Thea – the whole future of Sensitape depends on the unique research facilities this hospital has to offer.'

And the future of Sensitape is the only thing that really matters to you? Even though I was Thea Cadence B.C. then I didn't ask the question because I feared the answer. It would probably be yes and I feared it.

'So long you've worked here, Edward – and they still thought you'd go like a lamb. They really should have known you better.'

'See to those eight copies, will you, darling?' He pushed back his chair, the ordeal of me survived. 'I've got one more patient to see, and then we'll call it a day.'

'It wouldn't make much difference, would it? If they did sack you, I mean?'

'Tony has his laboratory, God bless him. We'd manage somehow. Might have to live on your salary for a bit.'

'Wouldn't they sack me as well?'

'Not a chance. Good nurses are rare. Even rarer than beautiful ones.' He called to me as I was going out through the door. 'Thea – let's go out somewhere tonight. It seems like years since we went out together.'

I looked at him doubtfully.

'No strings,' he said, spreading his hands in Tony's Jewish way. 'A nice evening, then separate beds. No strings at all. And no reproaches.'

The offer itself was a reproach, yet I couldn't refuse it. While he saw his patient I finished the typing, his memo and the rest of the envelopes. Then we drove home, dressed ourselves up, went out to a night club. Waiting for him at home was a stack of results Tony wanted analysing. And this on top of his hospital work and the business side of Sensitape. He'd get up early, analyse them in the morning. Watching himself carefully he'd cut his sleep requirements down to four hours. And still he'd have rogered me two or three times a week if I'd been willing.

He was working on that too, but so far the medications he had tried were useless. Either they had no effect at all, or they doped me down to the level of a warm corpse.

'Good band,' he said. Conversationally. 'Thank God we've grown out of those everlasting groups.'

'I suppose they made identification easier, of individual musicians, I mean.' Nobody could say I wasn't doing my best. 'Nowadays we're back on the band leaders. They tend to be older men but maybe we're older too.'

'Thea, forgive me. Forgive me if you can.'

'Forgive you?' Quaking. 'What for?'

'I've turned you into a media anthropologist. No crime could be worse. As penance I swear to recite a thousand Hail Freuds every morning before breakfast.'

I suppose he must have been trying too, but it didn't seem like it, He seemed happy and foolish, uncomplicatedly jollying along a prickly girlfriend. He made me laugh. It was the nonsense he talked, and his distinguished air, and the beautiful way he wore his clothes.

A German woman came onto the tiny stage and sang a mordant song

So your cookie gets her cancer and your whole world tumbles,
Wein' nicht, honeybabe – that's just the way the cookie crumbles.

Edward laughed and I was drunk enough to join him. Schoolboy stuff, but her accent helped. Not exactly a thigh-slapper.

Such little things would never trouble you
If they'd only give you back your dear old UDW.

Edward laughed some more. The German woman then did a sketch with a man wearing old-fashioned acoustic headphones, the flex from which led up under the front of her skirt. It was all very decadent and topical – and couldn't have been more apt if they'd laid it on specially for Edward's benefit. As they were taking their bow he leaned over and spoke in my ear.

'They'd as soon try to sack the Archbishop of Canterbury,' he said.

His meaning escaped me so I laughed again brightly and forgot it in the next second, my subconscious filing it deceitfully away for future disquiet. I laughed, and drank the champagne Edward poured for me. I was warm, I was in a crowd of happy people, and my husband – meaning it – had said I was beautiful. And he was beautiful too. Beautiful in his – I remember thinking the words very clearly, repeating them round and round the lights and the cold feel of the champagne glass and the unladylike trickle of sweat down the front of my bra – beautiful in his dedication to humanity.

He pulled back my chair, guided me to the foyer, where he settled me while he fetched my cape. My shoes were chicly transparent, with a pattern of small gold stars. A porter brought our car around to the door. The night was clear and cold, the hospital no more than something out of a bad film

I had once seen. Edward drove carefully. I put my hand on his knee and moved it up the inside of his thigh.

'No strings,' he said.

'No strings,' I agreed, letting my hand continue.

'You'll make me have an accident,' he said.

At that point I must have gone to sleep. I didn't wake till next morning. I think he engineered the whole thing. In the mood I was in that evening, relaxed, full of love, I might easily have been cured of my … my little trouble. And by then he had other plans. He'd had his phone call. He'd –

'Back again, Mrs Cadence. Hope I didn't make you jump. Two tablets for you, from Doctor. Take them with a little milk. Don't bother with the tea – it'll be stone cold by now anyway.'

At least my shaming exhibition has brought about new knowledge between us, and a new degree of honesty.

DAY 28

The three of us were talking about UDW. On a picnic somewhere. Talking about UDW.

'You can see what society is, Tony. Haven't people a right to opt out if they want to?'

'Society isn't life, Thea. It never has been. The one goes on in spite of the other – life goes on inside, Thea, so does awareness. Growth is always possible. If there are any sins, denying that is one of them. Sin. Deep sin.'

Someone else had told me that. What an odd coincidence.

Tony's eyes were wide apart, frighteningly intense. The angle of his head, as if listening, a frown creasing his forehead. The sunlight casting long shadows down from the left. And the lower part of his face lit with a curiously rippling green light off the river. Then, the moment gone, Edward behind me laughing easily, myself turning away to fuss with the food for the picnic, impatient, hardly having noticed, never imagining the vividness with which the picture would come back to me. Tony squatted with his arms on his knees, and in front of us willows, a cornfield, the possibility of belief.

Someone else had told me that, too.

'You're coming around now, Mrs Cadence. No more treatment for today. We've had a good session. Soon be your teatime.'

Behind Tony's voice the noise of insects. And the smell of hot grass. I remember my eyes were sore after so much driving.

'Take my handkerchief, Mrs Cadence. Now relax. Cry some more if you want to.'

Possibilities die. Cold. So cold.

'I'm all right, Doctor. Thank you.'

'I'm sorry if the treatment seems cruel, Mrs Cadence. Sometimes emotional pain is necessary to –'

'It's not the treatment, Doctor. Honestly, it hardly touches me.'

'It touches you more than you think. I'm on the outside, you know. I see a lot.'

'Doctor, you puzzle me.' He waits, his face mildly questioning. 'You trained under my husband, I think?'

'That's right. My last three years.'

'Edward used to talk a lot about truthfulness. The need for a psychiatrist to match his mood to that of his patient and yet at the same time maintain a basic truthfulness.'

He reaches to cloud the rooflight above me, seeing that the light is bright in my face.

'My work here is rather different, Mrs Cadence. After leaving your husband I did a further course. I specialized in penal psychiatry. That may sound ugly, but it's not really. The only difference is that in penal psychiatry we have a known end to which we are always working.'

'That must make things easy for you.'

'A great deal more difficult. Society lays down what it wants, and it's up to us to provide permanent results. Sentences are of necessity simplistic. Sometimes they need interpretation.'

I wonder if I could possibly assume the personality he offers me, this image of a disintegrated mind, for the purposes of my sentence. It's a refinement I hadn't thought of. It makes reaching the real him even harder.

'Doctor, this guilt you're feeding me with –'

'Accepted Criminal Responsibility, Mrs Cadence. Leading to Contrition.'

'I'm no stranger to guilt. I'm also very experienced in Sensitape reactions. I'd hardly be likely to make a mistake in such –'

'I suggest that you're practicing a psychological substitution, Mrs Cadence. Refusing to accept an unpleasant reality. You know Court Instructions. You don't imagine we'd go against them so blatantly, do you?'

'Doctor – I've been familiar with guilt for most of my life. You can't imagine I wouldn't know the difference.'

'You honestly think we're disregarding Court Instructions?'

'But I know what guilt feels like.'

'In which case we'd hardly bother to feed you with it.'

He's made the window above me gray. It shines indifferently on me, on Doctor, and on the vast clinical tape machine beside my couch. At least the machine is neutral. I control rising hysteria.

'Please don't treat me like a fool, Doctor. Of course I know – we both know – that my taped experience has to be focused. But I also know, as you must, that the focus on that tape is entirely paranoia. It's guilt, which can be pleasurable, leading to Life Incarceration'

'I'm sorry. It's clear to me that you're substituting. It can happen with a patient who is strong-minded enough. Court Instructions specified Criminal Responsibility. If you like I can show you the reference number on the tape sleeve.'

He smiles. He speaks so gently, to destroy me. He looks at me with such sad understanding. Perhaps yesterday never happened. Was there yesterday?

'I am not paranoid, Doctor. Ask my wardress to come now, please. You and I, we're wasting our time.'

'Mrs Craig will be here soon, Mrs Cadence. And you must know that conversations of this nature are never a waste of time. We make minute changes in the stimuli – it's all very much trial and error, of course – and we note the results. We're working on you only for your own good, you see.'

His words bring up ghosts, crowd the room with faces. The air becames heavy with grieving faces, priests and noblemen, inquisitors, camp commandants and unnumbered saddened hating fathers. It's no hallucination. They gather, more and more smiling and nodding, stacking the centuries closely into the space around us. He has their face and they have his. They blossom, multiply. And all at once there's only Doctor. And nothing I can say to him.

'Mrs Cadence, turn back to me. Look at me, Mrs Cadence. Nurse has come. Sit up now, Mrs Cadence. Nurse is here. You said you wanted her to come. Remember?'

I don't have to go back. I can stay on the river bank.

They can make me walk, and go through doors, and stand, and sit, but they can't get me back if I don't want to. The river bank was sun-warm, in days when I was never tired. We'd driven out from London, attended the conference and driven on. I was Thea Cadence, B.C., before Dr X, before Paul Cassavetes, before Pastor Mannheim, Thea Cadence out for the day with the young inventors of Sensitape. Relaxatape 09, we called it, since that was all we could make it do. In those days we gave all our tapes development numbers. The adventure had just begun.

'How about there? That field there, beside the river. That looks like a good place.'

'Pull in then, darling. We'll have a look.'

We'd been seeking a good place for the last half hour. Cars behind us tended to herd us on. This time Edward ignored them, braked, and turned off onto the shoulder. The next driver accelerated angrily to fill the gap. Edward switched off.

'We're here now,' he said, 'whether we like it or not'

The grass we carried our picnic across was dry and tussocky, with fresh, fly-covered cowpats. The three of us pretending not to mind the cows in the far corner under the trees. We crossed that field, and the next, till the noise of the road became inaudible. Following the river along, we came to a lock with white metal railings. The river must be one of the routes maintained by the Leisure Ministry. We laid out our picnic near to the trim white railings; they were exquisite among the rough grass and daisies and buttercups. As we sat down, accidentally we were all suddenly silent, hearing the country sounds, river and insects, and the cry of a small dark bird that paddled quickly away across the water. I said it was a dabchick, Tony said a moorhen; they were both no more than words. Then we were silent again. A tractor passed behind the distant hedgerow, towing something we couldn't see that made a rhythmic creaking. Tony picked a single stem of grass, spread the dusty pattern of seeds between finger and thumb.

'Just show them one of these,' he said. 'You'd think that would cure them.'

We knew what he was talking about. Edward slapped a fly off the back of his hand.

'You can't win, Tony. The association would be with man's alienation from the natural world. Not spoken, of course. Probably not even conscious. But there all the same.'

'Morbid.' Tony peered at the grains in his hand, angry, thinking perhaps of his father. 'Christ, Edward, how much longer before we get the thing beaten?'

'You're like a soldier hurrying to get to the battlefield before he has the proper weapons. I shouldn't worry – this particular war will wait as long as you like.'

Tony looked up sharply, worried by such callousness. It surprised me that he still wasn't used to Edward, to the scientific detachment my husband had been forced to cultivate. I interrupted before he could reply, changing the area of the discussion.

'You can see what society is, Tony. Haven't people a right to opt out if they want to?'

'Society isn't life, Thea. It never has been. The one goes on in spite of the other – life goes on inside, Thea, so does awareness. Growth is always possible. If there are any sins, denying that is one of them. Sin. Deep sin.'

At this point the film sticks, is reluctant to go on. I urge it past the wavering green light on Tony's face and Edward's easy laughter. Thea Cadence opens the picnic box, defensively absorbed in the movement of her fingers. Someone else has told her that. But the moment passes.

After eating we lay back on the ground, watching the sky. We talked about nothing, about Tony's landlady, about the shop to go to for pimentos. Something about the rough stalks of the grass pressing against my back and sides reminded me of my body. I brought my hands down from behind my head, and then sat up. I hadn't been thinking of Tony – if I glanced first at him it was the purest accident.

'Let's walk down river as far as the next lock,' I said.

'Let's not,' said Edward.

'But it's pretty. And there seems to be a sort of island.'

'You go, my dear. You're the one with all the energy.'

Tony was watching, ready to jump up and be gallant. I stayed sitting where I was, shoulders up around my ears. A silly thing, but I'd very much wanted Edward to come with me.

'It's too hot,' I said. 'I can't really be bothered.'

There had to be things that didn't matter, after five years. Tony settled on Edward.

'I was going to tell you about the extension I'm planning for the lab,' he said.

'No shop.' Edward scratched. The flies seemed to like him more than us. We should have brought some repellent.

'But we're three obsessionalists,' said Tony. 'If we don't talk shop, what do we talk?'

'Obsessionalists ...? I suppose so.' He scratched again. 'But we ought to fight against it. To have an obsession is to be dangerously limited.'

'Since my father's death the tape's given me something to live for, Edward. I wouldn't say that made me limited.'

'It makes you exclude, Tony. It must. You ask Thea how much of life I exclude as inessential.' He paused. 'I exclude her for a start,' he said.

'Nonsense, darling. Of course you don't.'

The grasses rattled faintly as he laughed. They hid his face, so deep he lay among them.

'See how indignant she is, Tony. She dislikes being classed among the inessentials.'

Tony was silent. Perhaps he remembered his father's and mother's different talk together.

'I tell her, Tony. I'm a rotten awful husband. But at least she's quite free, not even tied by children. I'd never stop her if she wanted to leave me.'

'You wait.' I sounded bright. 'You wait till the day I take you up on that.'

He rolled over suddenly, caught hold of my foot and pulled me down to where he was lying. My skirt rucked up and thistles scratched the backs of my thighs. He pulled me down till he could put his arm around my hips. He held very tight. We laughed and pretended it was all a game. I remember he bit my stomach, and it was all foolish and a little degrading, and I let him because I thought he was telling me he hadn't meant a word of it. And telling Tony too, of course.

We stopped wrestling to watch a stylish small white motor yacht go by on the river. It nosed in till its bow actuated the electric eye. Then the gate closed behind and it slowly dropped out of sight. The music from its radio faded, and the tick of its echo-sounder. We watched the top of its mast edge out, its engines echoing in the dripping hollows of the lock. Whoever was on board kept out of sight – they might have been asleep, or dead, or making love. The boat appeared beyond the lock and glided away, high among the water into long dark lines. It stayed in sight between the willows for a long time, gleaming blue and white and chromium.

Afraid of firing the grass after so many weeks of dry weather, Edward burned our rubbish in the middle of the upper lock gate, closed now after the passage of the boat. He leaned on the rail and held his lighter to the paper cups and plates and packaging. A gentle wind blew pieces against the raised base of the railing. They lodged there and as the fire burned he pushed them into it with his foot. Below him the lock gate was dark and slimed, white water fountaining through the vents. A curl of burned paper lifted over the edge and hung silvery gray for seconds till the cold river air caught it and drew it down out of sight. Edward burned the paper carefully, well, leaning on the rail with unconsidered grace, as preoccupied with the simple process as he might have been with the most complex. I smiled as I watched him, thinking how little my parents must have understood to let me marry a man so far outside their framework. They'd asked me if he loved me, and I'd told them he did. He loved me still, his love my only path through the frightening private world he now inhabited.

'Are we ready, Thea? It's time we were making a start.'

We picked our way back to the car. Tony was quiet, watching Edward as he walked on ahead, talking all the time about the traffic we could expect, and his plans for avoiding it. All the way back in the car the scratches on the backs of my legs hurt against the material of my skirt. I remember a place near Cambridge where –

'Don't leave me, Nurse. Please don't leave me.'

'I have to, Mrs Cadence. I'm expected in the kitchen for your tea.'

'Later. Please go later.'

'But Mrs Cadence –'

Her hand is warm and dry. I try to hurt her, squeezing it so hard.

'He never loved me, Nurse. Do you understand how a man like that cheats? He can't help it – to get what he needs he has to pretend he's a part of the human animal. He's a part of nothing.'

'You're talking about your husband? I really don't think you ought –'

'He cheated me of simplicity. He made love disgustingly, and I didn't know.'

'We know about the sex recording session. Dr Cadence should have realized what a deep impression it would make on you. We admit that he should not have let you be –'

'I'm not talking about the recording session.'

'You'll upset the other patients, making a noise like that.'

We've been through this before, been through the idea of the other patients. I only know that I never see them, never hear them. Do they see and hear me?

'I'm not talking about the recording session.'

'We do agree that you shouldn't have attended it. That it upset you seriously – as it would many people. It's an explanation for much of what's happened since. An explanation – not an excuse, Mrs Cadence.'

'I am not talking about the recording session.'

'You may not like to admit it, but all the same I think you are.'

'I'm talking about a whole way of life, Nurse. The whole nine years in which I was a young woman.'

'Self-pity never gets anyone anywhere. At thirty-two you're still a young woman.'

If only she were like Doctor. At least his not meaning well makes him accessible. All her sympathy and I still can't reach her. But she can't leave me, not for as long as I've got her hand.

'Nurse – I don't expect you'll want to hear, but I'm going to tell you about the first time we slept together. Edward and me. It's only words – we know what they mean, it can't do any harm to say them.'

'If you're sure you want to.'

Professional gentleness. I shouldn't let it affect me, but it chokes me up.

'We were both students, he in the last year of his psychiatry course. I was nearer to my finals by three months. I'd gone on to specialize in mental nursing. Medical students did it all the time, of course. Mate, I mean. As uncomplicatedly as rabbits. But without rabbit-type families. No doubt they still do, in spite of Sexitape ...'

Not I, of course, but Thea Springfield. Will I be able to tell you, without corn, dear Nurse, that Edward Cadence and Thea Springfield were different? Different from most students and – although she didn't know it – different from each other? It's important, this separation they shared that she saw as a bond and that Edward knew was a means. It's important that for their different reasons they'd neither of them slept around; it was important to Thea Springfield at any rate. Shall I have to begin, dear Nurse, by telling you about that Thea, her background, the hats she wore, the words she wrote down to look up later in her dictionary? And what can I begin to tell you about him? He was distant, almost brusque till he felt he had his companion's interest. Then he changed so that you could warm your hands at him, at his enthusiasm and vitality. She felt this almost painfully, having so little of either. Of course, he could switch himself off again just as quickly. It was his sensitive soul, she thought.

'He was very charming, you know, Nurse ...'

And she has removed her hand so quietly that I never felt it go. I still have the sensation of her fingers in mine, the bunch of them and one nail sticking into me a little. They have thickness, and blood in them, still her warmth although the rest of her has gone. I keep hold of the pattern of her hand for as long as it can resist the reasonable fact that she has gone. I can't blame her. I'd wandered off myself. And I could never have told her anything so that she'd understand.

I have to remember the terms themselves, before I can begin. Thea Springfield was in love, unclouded, with limitless perceptions of joy. (How could I ever have said that to my wardress?) She and Edward both took the same free afternoon when they both should have been working, and they both went to the zoo instead. She knew that the day might end with them naked together.

It rained as soon as they arrived so they took refuge in a restaurant where they sat overlooking the seals who preferred wet weather. One wall of the restaurant was an aquarium containing a sunken Spanish galleon in which – so the waiter told them – an octopus lived. The room was dimly lit, with a foliage ceiling real enough for her to imagine spiders. A shocking pink parrot perched glumly on a piece of bamboo. Edward bought them each an expensive fizzy drink imported from Africa – though reputedly native it appeared to have been modelled on Coca-Cola. Which is what the need for a world market does to you, he said wisely. The restaurant became increasingly crowded as more people were driven in by the rain. Finally the noise and the pushing drove him and Thea out. They made inadequate hats for themselves out of paper napkins.

With lovers' luck no sooner had everyone back in the restaurant ordered lengthy things to eat and drink than the rain stopped and the sun shone brilliantly.

I remember nothing about the zoo itself except the vivid shadows cages made on the gleaming wet paths. And the feel of Edward's fingers between mine. It was an afternoon spent in unspoken anticipation of the evening.

Edward had a flat of his own, four furnished rooms with central heating. As a qualified doctor, his grant was generous. The day progressed quietly and logically toward his bed. Even so, the moment still came when dinner was finished, lights were lowered, and the first conclusive move had to be made. They'd been sitting in his big armchair for some time, still keeping to safe paths. Then Edward eased away, back into his corner.

'Well?' he said.

'Well ...' she said, trying to sound practical. He stopped her.

'Bedtime,' he said.

Three sufficient, insufficient words and the paths were no longer needed. They were together, safe, in a dark forest. He kissed her for comfort. In the bedroom she let him undress her.

'I love you,' she said.

'I know.'

'Do you love me?'

She dared that even.

'Never ask a man that when the pupils of his eyes are huge and deep. He'll say anything. Besides, you know the answer.'

'I can't see your eyes.'

'Because your own are similarly affected.'

'I wish red wasn't the colour of passion. It's all wrong. I wish our blood was golden.'

'Precious and incorruptible ... Yes, the myth-makers slipped up badly there.'

Gently he placed her hands for her to take off his clothes. It didn't matter that she was clumsy. Ritual was important, a solemn way through the forest. She felt suddenly very special. The surface of her body seemed to radiate its nakedness and she hid it under the bedclothes. She heard his feet pad round to the other side, and then he climbed in. It was easy to turn to him, to feel the cold sheet lifted off by his arm and by the breadth of his body. The forest was set with bright flowers, making it easy to slip out of self, to lose mind in the dark spaces between the trees, to be safe, a part of something larger.

I lie, of course. This is Thea Cadence, old, looking back, seeking a beguiling metaphor. Thea Springfield, young, certainly felt she glowed, but she wasn't making fancy phrases. She was familiar with penis and vagina, foreskin, clitoris, orgasm. They were textbook, nurses' manual, names for human bits and pieces. Even the prosey dead hand that described what they were doing as heterosexual coitus wasn't worth a girlish giggle. It was Edward's love that mattered. He'd take care of her.

Her orgasm was small. This first time she derived her deepest satisfaction from his.

They lay still, and she thought he had gone to sleep. The smell of him filled her with strange pity. Suddenly he laughed.

'Edward? Is something wrong?' She had the quick fear that she had failed in some way.

'Nothing at all. It's just that I'm happy.'

But she felt there was something else.

'And I've been waiting for you to ask again.'

'Ask what? What should I ask you?'

'My eyes are golden now, golden with contentment. And I love you.'

She remembered her question. Which in fact he hadn't answered.

'I don't think that's very nice.' She'd wondered how lovers – real in-love lovers – would talk to each other. Afterwards. 'Almost as if you had tried me out first.'

'If we hadn't matched, then all the love in the world wouldn't have made a good marriage.'

'We did match … didn't we?'

'You have a marvellous eye for essentials, Thea. It's even made you pass over my proposal.'

She lay quite still, terrified. Joyful. She hadn't noticed it.

'Marry you …?'

'Please, Thea. We've known each other nearly two years. If you love me, please marry me. I'll make you happy. Marry me, Thea. I love you so much.'

'I love you too, Edward.'

And the bloody shitty no-good bastard cheated her. Cheated her all the bloody shitty no-good way.

CAMERA ONE ON WITNESS 27. SUNLIGHT EFFECT
THROUGH CIRCULAR WINDOW BEHIND.
WITNESS 11.
Your worship, he never loved her.
JUDGE.
And who are you?
WITNESS 11.
Their grocer, your worship.
DEFENSE COUNSEL.
Just tell the court, in your own words, exactly what happened.
WITNESS 11.
What happened when, Miss?
DEFENSE COUNSEL.
Don't call me Miss. I am counsel for the defense.
Just tell the court what happened on the occasions when he didn't love her.
WITNESS 11.
But he never loved her.
DEFENSE COUNSEL.
Then tell the court what happened never.
CAMERA ONE MOVES IN. WITNESS SMOOTHS HIS FOUR
STRANDS OF HAIR ACROSS HIS SHINING BALD HEAD.
CAMERA WATCHES FOR DAZZLE.
WITNESS 11.
The way he always carried her basket, your worship. He never fooled me for
a moment. When he scruffled her hair – never more than a performance.
And she never noticed his eyes; to me they were as cold as a cash register.
And his smile, like packets of detergent.
DEFENSE COUNSEL.
You were telling the court what never happened.
WITNESS 11.
He never lit up, your worship.
JUDGE.
Never lit up?
DEFENSE COUNSEL.
Never lit up?
JUDGE.
Never lit?
WITNESS 11.
Not once, ma'am. Not in seven years of groceries.
COMMOTION IN COURT.
CAMERA TWO ON PROSECUTION COUNSEL AS SHE RISES.
PROSECUTION COUNSEL.

Acting on instructions from the Crown, your worship, and in the face of the overwhelming weight of evidence presented by the defense, I beg leave to state that Her Majesty's prosecution withdraws its case.

FURTHER COMMOTION.

JUDGE.

About time too, in my opinion, Mrs Wilberforce.

PROSECUTION COUNSEL.

Furthermore, damages to the figure of seventeen thousand pounds are offered to the defendant in consideration of her wrongful arrest.

QUICK CUT TO CAMERA ONE.

DEFENSE COUNSEL POWDERS HER NOSE.

DEFENSE COUNSEL.

May I suggest, your worship, that while mere money is very nice and my learned friend's offer at least provides a basis for negotiation, what is needed is not so much recompense as a lasting token of national gratitude.

PROSECUTION COUNSEL.

I was coming to that, your worship. In addition we suggest that a medal be struck, a special award in recognition of Mrs Cadence's outstanding services to mankind. With one minor qualification.

DEFENSE COUNSEL.

Shame. Withdraw.

PROSECUTION COUNSEL.

The Crown appends the comment that in the opinion of Her Majesty's counsellors it is to be regretted only that Mrs Cadence did not see where her duty lay some twelve years earlier.

CAMERA TWO PANS R. CENTRES ON THE DOCK.

MRS CADENCE.

Your worship, may I speak?

JUDGE.

Madam, anything you may have to say will be of the liveliest interest to us.

MRS CADENCE.

Your worship, ladies of the jury – I am a woman.

PROLONGED APPLAUSE FROM ALL PARTS OF THE COURTROOM. MRS CADENCE.

In earlier days a woman's duty lay first to her husband. Even today, even after the Married Woman's Supremacy Act of 1988, some shreds of this feeling remain in most women, to be fostered treacherously by their menfolk. I married young, my mother told me nothing. Brainwashed from the very first moment of meeting my husband, how else could I act? For enlightenment finally to penetrate took twelve long years. The Court has already before it evidence of the chain of circumstances that

showed me where my duty really lay. This duty once seen, your
worship, it was done. And with dispatch.
THE NOBILITY OF HER DELIVERY CASTS A HUSH OF AWE
OVER THE COURTROOM. THE JUDGE
CLEARS HER THROAT.
JUDGE.
Mrs Cadence, the case against you is withdrawn and you are hereby
discharged without a stain upon your character. The Crown further
admits wrongful arrest on any charges, be it of first, second, third,
fourth, or fifth degree murder, and promises compensation at a
figure to be agreed upon out of court. In addition, at a special
investiture to be held this afternoon, Her Majesty the Queen has
graciously consented to invest you with the order of –

What might she have been invested with? What suitable order could they have devised? Not that it matters, of course. The real trial was quite a different matter.

Behind the witnesses there was a small window, and three feet beyond the window a mottled grey-brown wall. The courtroom was quite sunless, and yet not in the least cool since the judges who attended it all suffered from the idea of drafts. My judge was a small man, made ugly perhaps by his many years of understanding and administering the law. He brought a small Sensitape with him and during all recesses he stayed where he was, one contact pressed to his left temple, his eyes closed. With the volume high enough I suppose he might have got something out of it. I've no idea what tape he used, but it seemed to help him. By the end of a long sitting he would be thoroughly ragged.

'The witness is doing his best to answer, Mr Vincent-Clarke. We would all be very pleased if you could refrain from harrying him.'

Or again –

'The facts speak for themselves, Mr Siemens. You would make a more favourable impression if you let them.'

Mr Siemens was my counsel. He maintained a brisk confidence in the case's outcome right up to the moment of the verdict. Even on the limited evidence I gave him he seemed certain of an acquittal. Yet he was a subtle man – he must have been aware of the pressures against him. When a national figure, a national hero, is murdered the case can't be allowed to slip away into decent obscurity. If not me, then some other murderer would have to be found. The police had their reputation to think of. The nation had its pride. Not only had I to be found guilty, but also for the right reasons. For myself, I just didn't care.

'Mr Bowden, you are a taxi driver?'

'That's right.'

'On the night of June 3rd, this year, you took a fare out to an address in Wimbledon?'

'That's right'

'Please tell the court what happened then.'

Mr Bowden had a pale face, and pale eyes behind contact lenses. He wasn't a good witness – he wanted too obviously to please.

'I'd dropped my fare in Wimbledon. I'd decided to make it my last. I was on my way back home across Putney Common. The time was just after eleven-thirty.'

'How can you be so sure of the time, Mr Bowden?'

'I was going home. I reckoned on getting back before midnight. I live in one of the new Highgate Estates. With the theatre traffic over I could easily make it through the West End in half an hour.'

'So you can swear to the time being eleven-thirty.'

'That's right. Give or take a few minutes. Halfway across the Common I was hailed by a woman. I wasn't showing my light and I was in two minds whether to stop. In the end I did. The woman asked me if I'd take her to Richmond. A house on the Green, she said.'

'You don't remember the exact address?'

'She may not have given it to me. It's not a large green. She may just have said, "A house on the Green." I don't remember.'

'You took her there.'

'It wasn't far out of my way. I could pick up the thru-way in Chiswick. I dropped her off on the Green at eleven-forty.'

'You didn't see where she went.'

'My mind was on my bed. It'd been a long day.'

'But you're willing to swear that you dropped her off at eleven-forty.'

'That's right.'

'I draw the jury's attention to the fact that Mrs Cadence's call to the Richmond Police Station came through at eleven-forty-seven. Also I would like to remind the jury of the relevant passage in Mrs Cadence's statement, made that same night to the police. I quote: "I came home by taxi from Putney Heath. As soon as I realized what had happened I phoned the police."'

Mr Siemens closed his folder noisily. No doubt his intendon was to give the impression that he had proved something. Mr Bowden fidgeted.

'Can I go now?'

'Just one more thing from me, Mr Bowden. After that I expect the prosecuting counsel will want to have a word with you. Mr Bowden, am I right in saying that you cannot positively identify Mrs Cadence as the woman you took from Putney Common to Richmond Green on the night of June 3rd?'

'That's right. It was dark, and I was tired. Besides, one fare's very like another.'

'You cannot positively identify her by her voice either?'

'She hardly said three words to me. Just "Richmond Green" and then "Thank you" at the other end.'

'So you cannot positively identify her. On the other hand, can you positively say that the woman in question was *not* Mrs Cadence?'

'How could I? I hardly noticed her. I just took her where she wanted to go.'

I didn't remember him – why the hell should he remember me? It was a complete fluke that we'd got hold of him at all. Now Mr Vincent-Clarke was on his feet, slowly removing his spectacles. Everything was drama to him, even removing his spectacles.

'Mr Bowden, you seem to remember very little about this mysterious fare of yours.'

'That's right.'

'Yet you say she hardly spoke three words to you. And you tell us what those words were.'

'I meant she said what fares usually say. I didn't mean that those were her exact words, only the sort of thing she might have said.'

'You're under oath, Mr Bowden. When you tell us exactly what she said, we believe you. Now you tell us those mightn't have been her words at all.'

'That's the sort of thing she said. I mean, she wasn't chatty.'

I couldn't share Mr Vincent-Clarke's evident opinion of his own virtuosity. The driver's evidence was so inconclusive I couldn't see why he bothered.

'You remember that she wasn't chatty.'

'It's the other way around. If she had been chatty, then I'd've remembered.'

'But you might have forgotten. Even if she'd been chatty, you still might have forgotten.'

'I don't remember what the fuck she said. I don't see why it matters.'

The judge became agitated, about to complain at the witness for swearing, I suppose. Mr Vincent-Clarke cut in quickly, not wishing a defense witness to gain the jury's sympathy.

'You're an intelligent man, Mr Bowden. You know quite well why it matters. Mrs Cadence has a fine speaking voice – exceptionally fine and well-modulated.'

Except when drunk. I have to be honest.

'If she had spoken more than a very few words you'd have been likely to recognize her voice easily next time you heard it.'

'Is that a question?'

He'd got Mr Bowden angry. Perhaps on purpose.

'You've said that one fare is very like another, Mr Bowden. May I suggest that in a taxi driver's life one day is very like another?'

'You may suggest what you like.'

'And your reply to that suggestion?'

'I remember nights when I'm out after twelve. It's a sort of deadline for me. I remember that Friday because I didn't get home till twelve-twenty. And I remember why.'

'Friday, did you say, Mr Bowden?'

'I meant Thursday.'

'Which did you really mean, Mr Bowden? Thursday or Friday?'

'When I picked her up it was Thursday. When I got home it was Friday.'

'Thank you, Mr Bowden. No further questions.'

Bowden had covered his slip of the tongue very neatly. As far as I could judge he was telling the truth, for what it was worth. Mr Siemens waived his right to a further examination, and the taxi driver stood down.

The purpose of all this, of course, was slightly squalid. Bed-linen evidence suggested that Edward had been shot very soon after sexual intercourse. If I had arrived home at eleven-forty and rung the police less than seven minutes later, then it was very unlikely to have been with me. (There were other reasons also, of which the court was only partially aware.) And if not me, then there must have been someone else. And the strong possibility that I might have seen her. I admitted seeing nobody, so the prosecution's contention was that I had in fact got home considerably earlier than I claimed, early enough to have been available for Edward's pleasure. So Mr Bowden's evidence might have been quite useful.

All this was merely chipping at the outer edges. Like me, Mr Siemens knew perfectly well where the core of the argument lay. The prosecution – and the nation – wanted a verdict for fifth degree murder: murder while the balance of the mind is disturbed. This and a suitable plea for mercy. With no real evidence on either side, the case hinged on this insanity and on its causes. With the motive established and the psychological capability, the lack of real evidence against me wouldn't seem too important. The result was exactly the sort of psychological muckraking that the public loved.

Mr Siemens was disappointed when I declined to take any part in it.

Mr Vincent-Clarke did his best, however.

'Thank you for sparing us your time, Dr Mbleble. You are a consultant psychiatrist at the Kingston Hostel originally set up by Dr Cadence?'

'That is my present position. Yes.'

Dr Mbleble was very large and black and gleaming.

'You knew Dr Cadence well?'

'Very well indeed. We worked together in the Fairbairn Hospital and later I assisted him in his Richmond Clinic.'

'You would discuss patients' case histories together? That sort of thing?'

'Certainly. We were colleagues – and also close friends.'

That was an exaggeration. Edward had never had a close friend in his life – only people who served his vision. But Mr Vincent-Clarke was satisfied. He leaned forward, paused, and then relaxed again. When his question finally came it was thrown off with studied casualness.

'Did he ever discuss his wife with you, Dr Mbleble?'

'Many times. He was very worried about her.'

'Would you say he had good reason for his worry?'

'Certainly. His wife's mental condition was not good. In the last years of their marriage she suffered a severe sexual block.'

'How severe?'

'Intercourse was quite impossible for her. Uncontrollable nausea would set in.'

The court observed me with new interest, the woman for whom intercourse was quite impossible. I stared back at them. In my mind I composed tomorrow's headlines.

SICK OF SEX
Pornotape Queen boggles

'Did you and Dr Cadence arrive at any conclusions as to how the block had come about?'

'It is by no means unusual in people of both sexes who are subjected to the sort of repressive puritanism Mrs Cadence was brought up under.'

'And the precise effects of such a block, Dr Mbleble?'

'If you dam a river, Mr Vincent-Clarke, the river does not cease to exist. It builds up, increases pressure, finally finds some other way out. Repressed sexuality can be productive of great artistic creativity. It can also produce blind destructiveness. Besides many other dramatic psychological disturbances. The sexual may not be our only drive, Mr Vincent-Clarke, but it is certainly one of the more important.'

You might say that we live in an age of enlightenment. The gleaming doctor was able to go on to explain my mind's agony and my body's deprivation in excellent detail, without any thought that either I or the public at large might suffer some slight embarrassment.

'... Mrs Cadence's case is undoubtedly one that would have benefited at once from treatment with the Sexitape, limited frequency, female edition. Unfortunately, as sometimes happens, her early conditioning was so powerful that areas of her psyche in fact did not want to be cured. She refused the Sexitape treatment categorically. In the circumstances there was nothing that either Dr Cadence or myself could do.'

Observe the poor crazy woman, the woman who didn't want to be cured.

In the circumstances there was nothing that anybody could do, not even

Tony. And Christ, he tried hard enough. I listened to Mbleble's voice roll musically on, comforted by my own private knowledge of how mistaken he was. Mr Siemens, faced with my refusal to discuss the subject (which fitted perfectly with the rest of my neurotic behaviour, of course), had decided against calling a rival medical expert. If juries get muddled they tend to lean toward a psychological explanation rather than away from it. Mr Siemens preferred to rely on cross-examination to make his few points.

'Dr Mbleble – would it be true to say that until the last three or four years Mrs Cadence's sex life had been completely normal?'

'To the best of my knowledge, yes. As far as any norm exists, that is.'

'At any rate, Dr Cadence never mentioned any earlier disturbance?'

'That is correct. And he probably would have. Our later discussions of her condition were very thorough.'

Dr Mbleble had come out to meet my man halfway. He must feel very confident.

'Is it usual, Doctor, for such a block to occur for the reasons you describe after a long period of normality?'

'No. It is most unusual.'

'This vomiting – is it not a symbol of moral distaste? Disgust even?'

'Certainly. A splendid symbol. Crude, but splendid.'

'Disgust for what, Doctor?'

'Disgust for the sexual process, Mr Siemens.'

'Could it not rather have been disgust for the person of Dr Cadence?'

I'd thought of this argument myself, but dismissed it as glib.

'That is possible, Mr Siemens.'

'In that case the river you were speaking of needn't have been dammed at all. The sexual drive could simply have found a perfectly normal outlet with some other partner.'

'Certainly. All the same –'

'And if Mrs Cadence herself understood this – and I remind you that she has considerable psychiatric training – if Mrs Cadence understood this then she would also understand that the Sexitape treatment would be useless.'

'But she did not understand this, Mr Siemens. We tried repeatedly to discuss the matter with her. She understood nothing.'

'Would she have been able to admit to anybody that her husband disgusted her? Bearing in mind that she loved him, would she have told you, knowing that you would be bound to pass the information on?'

Dr Mbleble inclined his head to one side, leaning forward slightly, patiently willing to explain.

'It's her love that makes the whole thing so much more dangerous, Mr Siemens. Her disgust with sex left her no primordial outlet for her love. Therefore –'

'You are evading the question, Doctor. I had put it to you that Mrs Cadence might not have felt disgust for sex at all, and you had agreed with me.'

'But –'

'And you had agreed with me.'

The judge's voice started up, creaking like a slow audio tape.

'Counsel must not bully the witness.'

'But, your worship –'

The rest of Mr Siemens' reply was lost in the general laughter. Dr Mbleble was six feet seven, with neck and shoulders like a big black bull. He could have crushed Mr Siemens' head in one broad hand.

I wondered if perhaps Dr Mbleble was right – perhaps my upbringing really had crippled me. Not that it mattered. Even so, the fun they were having was still offensive. This was my life they were picking to pieces. Me. And they could take time off to laugh at the antics of a huge shaven-headed black man and a little white man in a fuzzy white wig.

'Dr Mbleble – total sexual repression such as you claim Mrs Cadence was suffering from is a serious affliction, is it not?'

'Certainly. But this is more than just a wild claim, you know. Both Dr Cadence and I had come to the conclusion that –'

'Please answer my questions, Doctor. A person suffering from such an affliction is liable to show symptoms of mental stress, is she not?'

'Probable. But not invariable.'

'Did Mrs Cadence display any such symptoms? And if so, could you please describe them to the court?'

'Certainly. She was irritable.'

'She was irritable.'

'She was often depressed.'

'Often depressed.'

'At other times she showed an almost irrational cheerfulness.'

'Irrational cheerfulness.'

'You asked me for symptoms, Mr Siemens. Every one of these is typical.'

Mr Siemens met his anger with a small deprecatory smile.

'I must admit to displaying all those symptoms myself, Dr Mbleble. My wife will be astonished to learn what they prove me to be suffering from.'

Again the laughter. Ominously polite, Dr Mbleble waited until it had subsided.

'The defendant also suffered a complete mental breakdown on one occasion, Mr Siemens. Some eighteen months ago. State of total amnesia.'

'Ah yes – I'm glad you reminded me of that, Doctor. That would be just after the suicide of her husband's partner, Mr Stech.'

'To connect the events is deceptive, Mr Siemens. Stable personalities do not suffer total breakdown on the suicide of a business associate, or even of a friend.'

'Of a close friend, Dr Mbleble?'

The implication was clear enough. It shattered me – I had had no idea at all that Mr Siemens would use it, that it existed in his mind even. I searched the negro doctor's face, finding to my relief only careful surprise. Of course, I thought, of course Edward wouldn't have told him. Not out of the suggestion of a personal inadequacy – simply because he wouldn't have bothered. It wasn't significant enough, not by then.

Dr Mbleble shrugged his shoulders.

'We have no proof that any such outlet was psychologically possible,' he said.

'But if there were, Doctor – and you certainly have no proof to the contrary – would there not then be sufficient grounds for the breakdown you described, quite apart from any deep psychological disorder ...?'

'Certainly there would. However, I must repeat that –'

'Thank you, Doctor. No further questions.'

Mr Siemens was very pleased with his progress. For myself, I was so angry I could have wept. I had intentionally told him nothing about my relationship with Tony – he'd come up with the whole thing on his own account. And even then, however obvious it was, he should have let it lie. He had no right to trespass and trample; none of them had. God, how I could have done with a breakdown at that moment. Just for the fun of it. To be able to stand up and scream and pound the shelf and vomit on the floor and show them I was all they wanted to prove me and more. To scream and roll my eyes, shouting 'Sex! Aaargh! Sex!' and delightfully horrify them. But I sat on, puritanically docile, my face calm, my hands folded meekly over the cause of all the trouble. Fun was beyond me. My awareness of body, of flesh, was such that I dared not move.

Of course Mr Vincent-Clarke could not let the doctor go without a further picking at my genitalia. He had to undo the misguidedly good work my Mr Siemens had done. He led Dr Mbleble through several other case histories, all outwardly similar to mine, and all ending in sudden violence. He was able to prove that –

'Mrs Cadence – Doctor slapped your face yesterday, didn't he?'

Mrs Craig. Nurse. She's come back.

'What did you say, Nurse? I wasn't listening. I'm sorry – I didn't hear you come in.'

'I've brought you your tea, Mrs Cadence. You wouldn't have any lunch so there's a poached egg as well.'

'How kind of you. Perhaps that's what's wrong with me – perhaps I'm just very hungry.'

For her sake it seems necessary to simplify. This afternoon I'm sorry for her. She looks so worried as she puts the tray down.

'You were talking about Doctor slapping my face, Nurse.'

She jumps. Obviously she'd hoped I really hadn't heard her after all.

'I was wondering if he did it because you were violent, Mrs Cadence.'

'As I remember it, Nurse, I shouted at him. Loud but not at all violent. Perhaps he thought I'd disturb the other patients.'

'The treatment room is soundproofed, Mrs Cadence.'

'What did you tell me that for? Frankly I'd rather not know.'

'I was only reminding you. I thought you would know, your husband having specified it.'

That's true. Clearly I'd been able to avoid knowing. Dear me. What a pity.

'Was this only yesterday, Nurse? I'd have thought it was much longer ago than that.'

'Doctor shouldn't slap you. I'll speak to him about it.'

'I'd prefer you not to. Today he was kind to me. I find that much more disturbing.'

'Your egg will get cold very quickly, Mrs Cadence.'

A piece of buttered toast, and on it the neat round of eggwhite and the marvellously yellow yolk. Cut gently, turn the knife, and watch the yolk bleed down onto the dull buttery surface of the toast. Twist the pepper grinder, brown flakes in a light shower, and add salt. Instantly the salt crusts over. For me poached egg on toast is a delicate childhood ecstasy, a fleshy delight, a blending of texture and flavor, of present and past. My fork prongs through the egg-white are held in the softened toast. I lift and and eat.

'The paper I brought you wasn't about the trial, Mrs Cadence.'

Pay attention. Concentrate on the toast. The egg, salt, pepper, and the butter.

'There's an item about someone the papers call Mrs X. She's suing Sensitape for a lot of money. There seems to be a missing agreement involved. It's all most sensational.'

Egg. Toast. The edges still crunchy.

'I thought you'd be interested. That's all.'

My simplification was correct. I was indeed hungry. This food makes me feel much better.

'Am I to have tablets again, Mrs Craig? Or does the tea contain the necessary?'

'Tablets.'

'I'm glad you've told me. I'll be able to enjoy the tea a lot more now I know.'

'And it's twenty-eight days you've been here, Mrs Cadence. Not nineteen.'

'Thank you, Mrs Craig.' I go on eating, go on smiling. 'Thank you for telling me.'

'I want to help you in any way I can.'

Then why, in God's name why chip nine days out of my life and show them to me, gloating? Why drag me back to what I have blessedly forgotten with your vulgar talk of Mrs X? Why tell me the noises I make under treatment are so animal that they must be soundproofed out of general existence? Why tie me so tightly to reason when what is obviously needed to get me out of here is complete insanity?

'I'm sure you do, Mrs Craig. It's very kind of you.'

'You don't believe me.'

'Indeed I do. You want to help me. You'd have to be a monster not to.'

'I have plans, Mrs Cadence. You must trust me.'

Pause.

'Have you ever heard of Synthajoy, Nurse?'

'No. What is it?'

'No, I thought you wouldn't have.'

Tea. If I tilt the teapot gently enough the tea swells out of the spout, round and smooth, not spilling, held firm by surface tension. Exquisite. One degree of tilt more and it breaks, runs down the spout onto the tray cloth where it spreads as quickly as an opened hand. Destructive of me – tea stains are the very devil. Ultrasonics useless, chemicals are needed, extra work for all concerned. If they're wise they'll make me put up with a stained traycloth.

She's gone. Thank God she's tactful at least in the easy things.

Was my upbringing really as puritanical as they say? My father the Professor, Thea Springfield's father, was Arnold really so narrow, so repressive? Thea Springfield's mother, did she really hold the views she said she did? Or did she merely utter them, expecting nobody – least of all her daughter – to believe in them?

'Eat your crusts now, Thea dear. Millions are starving, dear.' For this was 1966. 'I hate to see you be so fussy.' For Thea Springfield with no front teeth the crusts of toast were torture. Being only small she didn't think of telling her mother to eat them herself. She would never think such a thought, not then or later. Through love though, never repression.

'We live in the lucky half of the world, dear. We should always remember it.'

The lucky half of the world looked nice – without the understanding that coins have two sides *lucky* was meaningless. Sunday afternoon tea in Daddy's study; pine panelled, with angular metal lamps, and hundreds of books, and a huge view of the garden and the house next door. Thea liked the house next door; it had a spiral staircase. Daddy said of course it wasn't spiral at all, it was a helix. Spirals got bigger or littler, like the spring in Thea's clock. And anyway, the wretched thing wasn't very practical. Remember what happened when one of next door's party guests had to go up it drunk. Something in the frank way he and Mummy said *drunk* made it sound very naughty and exciting. The house next door took on the aura of the people who lived in it – naughty and exciting. Daddy sat very comfortable in his study's leather chair. When Thea climbed on his knee he would bounce her, saying not too rough or the leather would split. It often split in Thea's nightmares. Daddy was allowed to have his high tea on his desk. Sometimes Mummy and Thea ate with him. This scene rather than any of the others because of the poached egg, of course.

'They're broadcasting a teach-in on Vietnam tonight, Pammy. Open-ended.'

'Don't forget we're half-expecting John and Carol. They said they'd come if they could get a baby-sitter.'

'Damn. Well, we'll make them listen. Do them good.'

'Don't be dishonest, Arnold. You know how you show off if people come. You'd never dream of shutting up and listening to the radio.'

Egg. Huge. As large as Thea's hand almost. And crust easily dealt with if sucked a bit first.

'The moral is, Pammy, that we ought to get out of town. Disengage. Knowing our limitations – my limitations, if you like – we ought to get out. Gain ourselves space to think.'

'And your job? We're commuter-belt people. Where is there space to think within a hundred miles of London? Besides, Thea's just settled in at her school. You love your school, don't you, Thea?'

'What I like most about you, Pammy, is that you give me good reasons for doing the weak things I do do. But I still hope John and Carol won't come.'

Thea drank her hot milk. On Sunday she was allowed soap flakes in her bath to make bubbles. She had a submarine that would sail around out of sight under them. It wound up with a key and there was a cork for the keyhole. The cork fitted very tightly.

'Will your diet allow you another piece of toast, Arnold?'

'Of course it will. If there's one thing I hate, it's diet bores.'

'Not to mention how-I-gave-up-smoking bores. And of course people who –'

'All right, all right … I know I'm over-critical.' He laughed easily. 'It's a reaction against the permissive age we live in.'

Thea Springfield thought a lot about her parents' conversations. If they often went on at her – 'going on at you' was a precious new phrase learned at school – at least they went on at each other just as much. And it was all, they told her, only because of loving each other and wanting each other to be good. Even in those days she understood this good to be different from the more specific good that was the opposite of naughty.

She glanced sideways at the Sunday paper on the coffee table beside her. She was sitting up to the low table on a stool, her legs fitting neatly under it.

She knew the paper had a picture of one of the poor hungry babies in it. She ate her egg on toast, every crumb.

And sex? Well, in later years the word that came up most was respect, respect for herself and for the boy she might want to enjoy it with. Sleeping around was inadvisable. A bad thing. But in the end it had to be up to her. No rules existed; it was all up to her.

I suppose it might be called repressive. It certainly wasn't like the guidance Edward got from Rachel. She advised him to have a bit whenever he could. Facts had to be faced, she said. It was the male way, the male prerogative. He told me this himself, laughing, lying, considering it nonsense.

'Here you are now, Mrs Cadence. I've brought you your tablets. I can't find Doctor at the moment but I shall certainly have a serious talk with him later.'

I never poured the tea out. And now it's cold. Certainly Pammy and Arnold never allowed Thea Springfield to let her tea grow cold.

But the egg was in every way delicious.

DAY 29

It's good to feel so comfortable when walking. Supported and warm all over. It must be the effect of the dream I was having. The walls of the corridor were luminous, and curved slightly – as if I was walking around the inside of a long white balloon. Only not so, for the other wall of the corridor curved outwards, outwards and away. Also the corridor should get rapidly narrower, and stop. But it didn't, not even behind me, behind my companion who was supporting me, is supporting me, not even when I turn suddenly to grasp it. So the curve I see is the curve of my eyeball, the curve of the inside of my head. The curve I take with me, part of the dream I was having.

Dream? What dream was that? Mine is a dreamless sleep, the sleep brought by the tablets. And nothing is colder than my awakening. The corridor is hard, and the hand hard on my arm, and the pair of double doors that grow and grow and grow. And then part silently.

'I'm afraid the patient is up around ninety percent today, Doctor.'

'Are you sure, Nurse?'

'Quite sure. Approaching a hundred. Stiffened noticeably as we came along the passage.'

'Can't be helped. We'll just have to increase the dosage.'

He turns to me. I can see he's doubtful.

'Good afternoon, Mrs Cadence. Time for your treatment. Are you ready?'

'Please tell me my percentage for the rest of the twenty-four hours, Doctor.'

'Between thirty-five and forty.'

My God, that's barely human. Makes sense, though. It's all they need for Able To Eat.

'We keep you low, Mrs Cadence. It rests the brain. And of course it makes nursing so much easier.'

And any periods of consciousness that much more intense. And the tape's suggestions that much more persuasive.

'Are you ready, Mrs Cadence?'

I sit on the couch and they fit the headset. Mrs Craig makes an ostentatious fuss not to disturb my hair. Doctor tightens the screw and the electrodes move in, pricking slightly. I lie on the couch, cold to the backs of my legs. Doctor sees that the rooflight dazzles me and he dims the glass. I stare up at the white glow. I wait.

My mind-brain-memory complex offers me pictures and sounds. Pictures and sounds. Offers me Mr Siemens.

'Can you think of anyone else who could have been in your Richmond house that evening, Mrs Cadence?'

'Nobody at all. I've thought and thought.'

'And nothing was disturbed, you say?'

'I do understand how important these questions are, Mr Siemens. I only wish I could give you more helpful answers.'

I can't remember why I lied. The first lie, and the covering up to the police, it can't have been prompted by pride. Not dignity either. Was there an instinctive wish to preserve the Cadence myth? And the later lies? I'd had plenty of time for second thoughts. I wonder if I really believed I was pursuing a course of heroism. I knew damn well who had been in the house that night. I tidied up after her. Was it expiation? Or vengeance? Or did I actually tell the truth? All I can remember now is

'It's time to begin now, Mrs Cadence.'

Pain?

As long as I resist, pain. A huge frozen lake that cracks from shore to shore. Echoing cliffs, pressure of starlight. Finding words to describe it helps. It comes in waves, flashing like an ax. Bites deep. And if I stop resisting

Somewhere Doctor is telling me, I think it must be Doctor, is telling me to, telling me. It's as if he

Crying again. And from the feel of my mouth, for a long time. A weight beyond endurance, squeezing out groans and moos and gross bubblings. Nobody should see me like this, hear me like this, nobody.

'Do you remember anything, Mrs Cadence?'

'These questions are important, Mr Siemens. I wish I could give you more helpful answers.'

'I'm talking about your treatment, Mrs Cadence. I want you to try to remember.'

I must cut my nails. They've made my palms bleed.

'I'm sorry about your hands, Mrs Cadence. I didn't notice till it was too late. I should have inserted pads.'

'My God, Doctor, how many stechs were you using?'

'Maximum. I thought it was time.'

'You've gone beyond memory, Doctor. Perhaps it's an effect you're not familiar with.'

'Tell me.'

He knows. He knows the mind can be pushed beyond sensation, beyond thought, memory, pain, guilt, beyond humanity. He knows damn well.

'It's all in Edward's book, Doctor. Look it up. Under Blanket Stimulation Effect, if I remember right.'

'Nurse tells me she thinks I act unethically, Mrs Cadence.'

'Does she?'

'Have you been complaining about me, Mrs Cadence? She says I slapped your face, Mrs Cadence.'

'You like saying my name.'

'My intention is to give you a sense of identity.'

'We've been through this before.'

'You might not have remembered.'

'I didn't tell her about my face. She saw for herself.'

'There's nothing I'd like better than to be taken off your case, Mrs Cadence. You still have rights, you know. You have only to put in a formal application.'

'If I were going somewhere it might be worth it. But I'm not.'

Strangely enough it's the sort of wriggle that satisfies him. His mouth remains serious. I never see his features as components of a whole, rather as separate items. Thus I have no real idea what he looks like. But his mouth definitely remains serious. Not tight enough to be sadistic or relaxed enough to be simply pleased. So I deduce from this, and from his silence, a level of negative satisfaction.

And I really don't want him replaced. The programme allows me half an hour a day and he takes up commendably little of it. Another man might try analysis, suggestion therapy, anything to pare off a few more minutes of my life. My half hour. My search.

Now he sits quiet, content to wait for Mrs Craig's arrival.

It was the day after I had sent around the copies of Edward's memo laying out his reasons for refusing to resign. The morning after our visit to the night club. Edward was busy down on outpatients and Tony was waiting in my office until he should be free. I remember magnificent Dr Mbleble stopping in for a few minutes and then hurrying off. He had a schizo under a variant of the anti-UDW tape and he was interested to go and check progress. That left Tony and me alone.

I'd known Tony for five years now – we should have been old friends. Yet in fact I was finding him increasingly difficult to talk to. I hid behind the pretense of a lot of work to do. I really did have plenty of work, but I'd have put it on one side if the relationship had been easier. He passed the time perched on the corner of my desk, rereading the report he had brought to discuss with Edward. Suddenly he spoke.

'Any reaction from the Management Committee?' he said.

'Not yet.'

'I suppose it's a bit of a facer for them. Nobody likes a bluff to be called, especially a committee.'

'They'll be having another meeting this afternoon. We'll hear after that.'

I wasn't really attending. My mind was on the case history in front of me. It took some seconds for what he was saying to connect. I looked up.

'He told you about it, did he?'

'Days ago. As soon as he received their letter.'

I wondered how this letter had got to him without my seeing it. Personal messenger, I decided. My curiosity must have showed.

'I expect he didn't want you to worry,' Tony said. I wished he wouldn't mediate. There was no need. 'He obviously likes to settle anything difficult in his own way.'

'He's quite right, of course.' I typed a few words. 'It would have worried me a lot.'

Too often the things I said to Tony were obscure. Keep it simple. There was no way of refuting his unspoken concern. Silence would have been as bad.

'There's no chance at all that they'll sack him,' Tony said. 'They'll just set up this inquiry as a face-saver.'

'A lot more paperwork for all of us.' I was glad of the new topic. 'Invoices, balance sheets, cash appropriations. Sometimes I wonder how we get any real work done at all.'

'You were trained as a nurse, Thea. It seems a waste that you should end up as just another secretary.'

'My training comes in useful', I indicated the file of case histories, 'dealing with this lot.'

'All the same, it's people you should be working with, not pieces of paper.'

The outside telephone rang.

'People,' I said, and picked up the receiver.

It was the woman who had called the day before. Again she wouldn't give her name. When I told her Dr Cadence wasn't available she said she'd ring again. She seemed calmer than on the last occasion. Again I thought I knew her voice but couldn't put a name or a face to it. I ought to have. After all, I'd known her well enough. But in a different context.

As I was finishing an orderly put his head around the door.

'Urgent,' he said. 'I'm looking for Dr Cadence.'

'He'll be on his way up from outpatients by now, John. I'd wait here if I were you. You'll only miss him somewhere on the way.'

'It's very urgent, Mrs Cadence.' He looked doubtfully at Tony. 'I'm from Ward S.'

'You know Mr Stech, don't you, John? He's the technical half of Sensitape.'

'I've seen you around of course, sir. But I wasn't sure. Glad to meet you, Mr Stech.'

They shook hands. John was edgy. He couldn't sit down.

'Ward S, you said?' I tried to remember. 'Is that where Pastor Mannheim –'

'I don't think there's much time, Mrs Cadence.'

'Sister should have rung down if it's as urgent as that.'

John glanced awkwardly at Tony.

'We understand Dr Cadence is in a … a difficult situation. The exchange girls listen. Sister wanted to be sure nothing went wrong.'

There was something he wasn't saying. They didn't want word getting out.

'What could go wrong?' Tony said. 'The Pastor agreed to this recording. Surely the authorities wouldn't –'

'I don't know, sir. Sister just didn't think it worth risking.'

'She's probably right,' I said. 'You ward staff often have a much better idea of what's going on than we do.'

Edward burst into the room, followed by the chaplain. That made five of us in my tiny cluttered office.

'Damn,' Edward said. 'Damn, damn, damn. This couldn't possibly have happened at a worse time. I met the chaplain on my way up. He tells me the Pastor's dying.'

John straightened his tie. Already Edward was a great man.

'I'm from Ward S, sir. Sister thinks there's still time if we hurry.'

'Haven't you heard, man? Emergency Committee meeting this morning. I'm suspended pending the findings of the special inquiry. They've bloody well suspended me.'

The chaplain coughed like a man of the world.

'Notification of your suspension, Dr Cadence – has it yet reached you?'

'I heard it from one of the messengers, Chaplain. There's no doubt it's true enough.'

'My point, Dr Cadence, is that you have not yet received official notification.'

'That'll take hours yet. It's got to go through the typing pool.'

'Surely, Edward, you can't consider yourself suspended on the mere word of one of the messengers?'

Edward stared at him. John moved to the door.

'There's no time to lose, sir. If –?'

'Chaplain, you have a magnificently Jesuitical mind.'

'You do the Order an injustice, Doctor. However, there are occasions when I feel –'

'Your beautiful prevarication will have to be lost, Chaplain. Lost among the intrusions of modern life. Stay here, will you, while I go and organize things?' He turned to me. 'Get the consulting room ready, Nurse. I'm going to have the Pastor brought down here.'

'But, Dr Cadence –'

'Discretion, Nurse. We're less likely to be disturbed in my own private room. And if we are, then we can lock the door. And argue afterward.'

He hurried away, giving John instructions as he went. I led the chaplain through into Edward's room and sat him down in a corner where he'd be out of the way. I turned up the heating. Tony helped me to prepare the Sensitape machine, thread a new twelve-inch spool and connect the recording headset. He went over the machine for me, checking levels, cleaning the recording heads, testing the monitor, while I moved the treatment couch out of the way. Then we waited. The room was very hot now, and the chaplain expertly made light conversation.

Edward came back.

'They're bringing Pastor Mannheim down on a trolley. I thought it best to keep out of sight. He's being taken to the Intensive Care section, if anybody asks.'

The outside phone rang in my office. I went through and answered it, recognizing at once the woman who had called earlier.

'It's for you, Dr Cadence. Outside call from a patient.'

'Tell them I'm busy. Tell them to call later.'

'She says it's important.'

'What I am doing is also important. Tell her to call again later.'

'She called while you were down on outpatients. I think you ought to speak to her.'

Obstinacy on my part? Was I curious? Edward came through, grabbed the phone angrily out of my hand.

'Dr Cadence speaking. What I am engaged in at the moment, madam, is a matter of life and death. If you could please –'

He stopped and listened for several seconds, his face registering nothing at all.

'I see.'

Two careful words. His eyes met mine and he smiled, made an exasperated face.

'Yes indeed. I'll ... attend to it. At the time you suggested. Certainly. And thank you for calling.' He rang off. 'What an insistent female.' I took the phone from him and he turned back into his office.

A lover. Nobody else would have known, only his wife. An explanation of the night before, the way I had been bought off with fine food, with champagne and dancing. Bought off and then left.

I remained standing by the phone throughout the conversation. It was perfectly reasonable, perfectly natural that he should find a sexual outlet somewhere else, now that I had become so … unsuitable. I tried to pretend I didn't mind. But for his last night's indifference I might have succeeded. But that he'd just been bored, hadn't bothered, just hadn't bothered, this made me very angry. Satisfied elsewhere, he'd bought me off. Just hadn't bothered. Being angry made me feel better. More a person.

I heard the door of his office open, a murmur of voices, and the soft clang as some part of a trolley jolted on the door frame. I went through into the next room.

'Ah, Nurse. Help me prepare the patient, will you?' We were always formal when on duty. But the way out it now gave only angered me still further. 'Over here now, hold his head. Come along now.'

Then I saw the old man on the trolley.

Pastor Mannheim was fully conscious. He was consumed beyond pain now, his eyes piercingly aware. He saw me and smiled, and made the faint rasping that was all the speech left him. I took his hand and shook it gravely – I'd discovered on my visits to the ward that he preferred the stiff Germanic greeting. With his formality became dignity, completely unassuming. His hand returned my grip with surprising strength. Then I moved away to pick up the headset. The stylized things I might have said were quite unnecessary.

After passing the headset to Edward I leaned forward and lifted the Pastor's head an inch clear of his pillow. Edward fitted the casing delicately. I could feel him holding his breath. Against the old man's face my hands were fat coarse-textured lumps. I took them away as soon as I could, their greasy heat would corrode his skull, and hid them below the edge of the trolley. I can still see his eyes, and his gray lips smiling from within.

'Pastor Mannheim, we have the hospital chaplain here.' Edward pitched his voice accurately, neither brisk nor over-reverent. 'Perhaps you would care to …?'

The old man acquiesced politely, though whether for his own sake or for the chaplain's I couldn't guess. I fetched a chair, set it beside the head of the trolley, and then moved back out of the way. The trolley smelled faintly of metal and of the lubrication on the wheel bearings.

Tony had started the machine. Reflected light off the spools turned in a slow pattern on the opposite wall. Tony checked his gauges, made a note of the starting time. Edward had seated himself behind his desk, watchful but quite relaxed. The spools revolved in complete silence. Stillness settled over us, shaped us so that soon the spool made the only movement in the room. And the only sounds were hospital sounds from beyond the passage door, loud footsteps down the passage, the whine of a lift. I became aware that Edward was trying to attract my attention. He nodded toward the door, made a turning motion in the air with his right hand. I walked to the door and locked it. Without being told I went through into my office and locked that outer door as well.

My office seemed hardly to be real. I straightened its two chairs and removed both the internal and external telephone receivers from their cradles. The dialling tone buzzed loudly. Returning to the next room I was halted in the doorway, coming on the scene as if for the first time. And suddenly I remembered a white piano, night club cheerful.

... Such little things would never trouble you

If they'd only give you back your dear old UDW.

There was nothing world-shaking about the scene here in Edward's consulting room. Gray daylight, people untidily grouped, a tawdry aluminum trolley. And the reflections turning on one wall like a Christmas decoration, the chaplain leaning forward slowly, placing his head close to the dying man's lips.

He stayed for a long time, then sat back.

'Could this all be a bit more normal?' His voice came out slightly too loud. 'He knows it will be difficult, but couldn't you all talk, or something? He liked the ward, it was always so alive.'

And in my head the Marlene Dietrich accent –

Wein' night, honeybabe, that's just the way the cookie crumbles.

And Edward laughing.

Edward who now had sat up straight, put his elbows on his desk and taken his pen out. The things he did to remind himself of his position. He cleared his throat. Regretted it. Covered his mouth and spoke.

'Tony – I should have asked before, what on earth are you doing here anyway? I thought you were going to be busy at the lab all day.'

'I've been analyzing CR tube readings on Blayne and Gerrard and that other man – those musicians we taped last year. Before the Cassavetes episode. I think I've hit on a common factor.'

'Slow them down, did you? See a lot more in slow motion.'

'Matter of fact I filmed them. Compared them frame by frame.'

'Well, Tony, that's wonderful. What have you got to show me?'

'It's all a bit complicated. You see ...'

Like a job interview, careful question and careful answer. Not much to do with the grumbling humanity of Ward S, with what the pastor wanted. And even this ran down fairly quickly.

'It's getting stuffy,' I said. 'I'll see to the air conditioning.'

Tony eyed his guages and mumbled something to Edward, something about preparing a back-up reel. I adjusted the conditioning unit and went back to my position by the open door into my office. I needed an escape route, the possibiliy of one. I watched Tony, not a medical person, unused to death, a technician. And we, weren't we the ones unused to life? I became much concerned with the idea that somebody was about to knock loudly on the door.

'Hush a minute, please,' said the chaplain. 'He's trying to say something.'

The pastor's lips quivered like a moth's wings, shaping his breath into an unheard whisper. It must have been a prayer, for the chaplain said 'Amen.' The old man's fingertips moved uncertainly on the white hospital sheet. He and the chaplain held a painful, silent conversation. After a while the chaplain raised his eyes to where I was standing.

'He wants to speak to you, Nurse.'

I shivered. It was mediumistic, like being named in a seance. The bones had fallen, pointing at me.

'He would like you to accept his blessing.' Three steps to the side of the trolley. 'He knows you aren't a Christian – he hopes you might value his blessing all the same.'

I stooped down – I would not kneel alas – and felt the impossible weight of his hands on my head, put there by the chaplain. Real. A real old man, real faith, real death. I tried to hear what he was saying, sibilants and a faint ticking in the hollow of his mouth. Everything would be different if only I could hear. Like the dreamed revelation never quite regained. Everything would be explained. It's four years now, and I still try to hear sometimes.

He finished his blessing and died. Looking in his face I saw it. I put my hands up to my own head, felt his hands and the huge hands of the chaplain covering them.

'He's dead, Chaplain.'

'Yes … Yes. Well …'

'I shall be interested to see,' said Edward, 'how much of the specifically spiritual flavour comes over. Keep it running, Tony. The activity fades slowly.'

The chaplain put Pastor Mannheim's hands together on his chest.

'Dr Cadence – if the experience wasn't spiritual it wasn't anything. Sometimes I wonder if you experts have the faintest idea what you're doing.'

'At least we're always seeking. We keep open minds. There's nothing we'd ever say we're certain about.'

'The scientific approach. Yes …' The chaplain watched himself interlock his fingers. 'I believe the human mind needs certainty. We're making tiny certainties all the time. Often false.'

They were both of them manufacturing words to fill out the decent interval. The tape reels spun and on the dials the waves faded.

'Anyway,' Edward said, 'the pastor's death should be a model to us all. Personal confidence, a mind at peace, and a concern for others. It ought to be quite invaluable.'

'Nobody need ever die unhappy or frightened again,' Tony offered, more to his spools than to us in the room with him. 'Mystical reconciliation … it's frightening to have such a powerful experience almost literally in one's hand.'

The chaplain was staring down at the dead man. He might have been praying. The room was painfully the same, painfully undiminished. Edward put his pen back in his pocket

'If the chaplain's right, Tony, then uses for this tape may be rather more limited than we'd hoped. If the Christian elements are too strong they may war with indigenous agnostic or atheistic patterns. We may have to make a humanist recording as well, for example. Compatibility is going to be our problem.'

It always was. I went back to my doorway.

'I'll ring for John,' I said. 'The pastor's body should be taken back to Ward S as soon as possible. If we can avoid getting awkward questions asked, then so much the better.'

I rang the ward, then unlocked both doors. Tony checked the monitor for negative signal, switched off and began winding back. Edward loosened the headset, eased it out from under the dead man's head.

White hair spilled onto the thin trolley pillow. I remember the moment with sadness, my distaste for Edward, the squalor of our lives. Not in their details but in their aspirations, that was where the squalor lay. Human detail is always squalid. Aspirations don't have to be.

My bedroom. My Individual Ward. Myself alone in it, the door shut. Carried here, or brought here like a goat on a string. Either way I had hidden in my head, sparing Doctor and sparing Mrs Craig. The woman is becoming excessive. She genuinely wants to help me, but has no idea at all how. Nobody had ever known, except perhaps Edward, who had other priorities. Nobody could have known – I keep the necessary data to myself. I'm forced to the dreary conclusion that I must just like to suffer. It's no use telling my wardress that – she'll only see it as another defense to be brought down. Never a face value to anything, not in the world of psychiatric nursing.

Yet I'm calmer today. CR at saturation levels, laced with shame, has clearly changed something. Yesterday is even harder to remember than was yesterday's yesterday. And tomorrow's yesterday seems scarcely to be happening. I'm amused by words, rather than by their meaning. Games. I'm calmer and more rational. That much was obvious in the way I dealt with Doctor.

Shame, though. That really is evil.

Now I've remembered something funny. A hoot. I really must tell Mrs Craig.

It can be funny mainly because it happened Before Cynicism but After Innocence, a narrow time-frame in which Edward could no longer shock me.

It's like another word game, amusing on the level money can be if considered separate from the life that uses it. After Innocence – that means after Tony's death. Exactly how long after I don't remember. A few months – it doesn't matter. There certainly wasn't long between it and … and my coming here.

Edward was working harder than ever. Mornings at the hospital, two afternoons a week teaching, running the Richmond Clinic, managing Sensitape Ltd, and also somehow fitting in his affair with Mrs X. It was Thursday, when he spent the whole afternoon and evening in the Clinic. He made a point of finishing on these days at eight – to spend some time with me, he said, though we both knew he physically needed the free time if he was to keep going. The last patient on this particular day had been a depressive. I remember this because I'd handed Edward the wrong treatment tape and he'd been angry. The last patient of a long day – I didn't blame him for being irritable.

I'd seen the patient out and was on my way upstairs (we lived over the shop)to ask our housekeeper to serve dinner at once, when the doorbell rang. I remember looking down the stairs and across the magnificent entrance hall to the closed face of the door. The glory of it all, the chandelier, the Louis XIV furniture, the gleaming black and white tiles, and the misery it dressed up.

Then I went back downstairs to see who was ringing.

Two men, quiet, smoothly dressed. Hindsight makes me say too smoothly dressed.

'Could Dr Cadence spare us a few minutes, please?'

'The clinic is closed, gentlemen. If you'd care to make an appointment I –'

'This isn't a medical matter, Nurse. Purely business.' Somehow they were both in the hall, the front door closed behind them. 'If you'll just give Dr Cadence my card, Nurse, I'm sure he'll see us.'

'Dr Cadence has just finished an exceptionally long day. He's tired.'

'Only a few minutes, Nurse. Show him my card. I'm sure he'll see us.'

Jasper Thomson Pheeney. I.M.S.

'I.M.S.?'

'International Medicraft Supplies. Suppliers to the Royal Family.'

His companion sniggered.

'Mrs Cadence – I've just checked. The tape is definitely not just CR.'

Oh God, not you, Mrs Craig. Not you and tea. Not just when I was trying to get my timing right.

'His card said I.M.S., Mrs Craig. How was I to know it was a bad joke?'

'Mrs Cadence, you must listen to me. Doctor's disregarding court instructions. The tape sleeve certainly is cataloged as Criminal Responsibility but I've just been trying it. There may well be CR in it but they've topped it up with something else. I'm not an expert but I think it's Shame. It's not listed in my handbook but I know they sometimes use it.'

Of course they do. But it won't be in my handbook either. The Treatments Handbook Edward gave me.

'The things found under stones are etiolated, Mrs Craig. Etiolated. It's a beautiful word.'

She puts the tray down on my bedside table to give her emotions greater freedom.

'But court instructions said –'

'Has it never occurred to you that court instructions specify only what should be in a treatment? Never what shouldn't?

'That's disgraceful. It couldn't happen. Not in this country.'

I allow a short pause. Derisive, I hope.

'I was telling you my about these two smooth men who called on my husband. The name of one of them was J T Pheeney. Jasper Thomson. The other I only ever heard called Bunk. He had a scar.'

'Mrs Cadence – you must listen. It'll be a mistake. I'll speak to Doctor about it. It's sure to be some sort of mistake.'

Her strong hot hands are clasped and sweating. Poor Mrs Craig. She's only a simple harassed nanny after all.

'Mrs Craig, please humour me. Please listen to my story. I'm insane, Mrs Craig, so please humour me,'

'You're saner than most, Mrs Cadence, holding out against what I've just experienced.' So earnest. 'I believe you're innocent. The jury was wrong. And whatever the Court's verdict was, I believe it was wrong.'

I have to shut her up. I scream. Several times. Then I stop.

'Sit down and listen. Just for once do something I want. Just listen to me.' She stares. Perhaps I really am insane. I bring my voice down almost to a whisper. I'm a ham at heart. 'Please listen to my story, Nurse.'

She sits on a chintz-covered chair. The silence in the room after my shouting is very pleasant. I enjoy it. Then I too sit down. Busy, busy, busy. All this standing up and sitting down.

'I took the business card that the J T Pheeney man gave me back into the consulting room. Edward was under the Relaxatape so I turned it down and roused him. He removed the headset. As I handed him the card I felt the two men come into the room behind me. "If you don't mind, Dr Cadence.Just a short talk. We won't keep you any longer than is necessary." Have you guessed who they were, Nurse?'

She stares blankly. I wonder if she's even been listening.

'They were gangsters, Nurse. Real gangsters. I was going to leave the room but the one with the scar called Bunk produced a tiny gun – he said it was disposable – and the Pheeney one said I must stay. They didn't want me to call the police, I think. Edward said he wanted me to stay as well, so I stayed.'

'What were the two men after?'

'Don't hurry me, Nurse. First the Pheeney one searched the room for hidden microphones. He had a little detector of some sort. They were both highly mechanised. Then he carefully arranged the patient's chair opposite Edward and made himself comfortable. The Bunk one was still showing off his gun. A hit man, I suppose he'd be called.'

'And this is a funny story, Mrs Cadence?'

'It really is funny. Hilarious. Like a vintage spy film. Pheeney started the conversation. He said his company had been following the development of Sensitape with great interest. Edward asked him exactly what his company did. "You have my card, Dr Cadence. International Medicraft Supplies. It's perfectly genuine."

' "I've never heard of it," Edward said.

' "We don't operate in your area, that's all. The supplies we handle are more … more old-fashioned." The hit man sniggered.

'I put two and two together. Edward had already done the sum.

' "In that case," he said, "you've probably heard that I'm soon going to put all of you out of business."

' "Which is precisely why we're here tonight, Dr Cadence." '

I should have been an actress. I do the voices so well. Nurse's eyes are popping.

'But he did,' she said. 'Put them out of business, I mean. True drug addiction has ceased to exist.'

'Hush, Nurse. Wait and see.

' "Experiments have been held back by the recent death of my technical adviser," Edward said. "However, preliminary results show that we should have no difficulty in producing a series of tapes giving the whole range of drug effects, from pot to cocaine and main-line heroin."

'Pheeney nodded sympathetically.

' "So our information has it," he said. "And believe me, it's welcome news."

'Edward sighed. I honestly think he was bored, Nurse. He didn't find the smoothy gangster performance as amusing as I did.

' "Please come to the point, Mr – er – Finsey. There must be one."

' "As we understand it, Dr Cadence, you do not claim to cure addiction. You merely switch the addicts from our product to yours. And the name is Pheeney."

' "And my product is totally harmless. There is no physical deterioration and addicts will be able to lead relatively normal lives. The moral slur will be removed from addiction and the whole of society will be healthier."

' "And the addicts will live longer."

' "Certainly they will. With their damaging need satisfied they will otherwise be fairly normal citizens." '

Nurse shifted her bum. 'He was a man of vision, Mrs Cadence. It's all turned out just as he said.'

'At this point, Nurse, Pheeney became more relaxed than ever. I guessed we were coming to the crux.

'"That sounds like good business, Doctor. Big business. Business we want a share in."

'"Good business, Mr – er – Heaney, but not big. The mark-up on the machines is small, and the tapes – as you know – are just about everlasting."

'Bunk sniggered. It seemed his only noise. His more articulate colleague lit himself a cigarette to spin out the theatricals.

'"Pheeney, Doctor. The name is Pheeney. And our information has it that a very small change in tape composition would … improve the situation. We have decided therefore that the tapes you make will wear out. Wear out as quickly as we say they will."

'Edward cut short an exposition that Pheeney must have been looking forward to for days.

'"I think I understand you, Mr – er – Pheeney. Your organization wishes to act as sole distributors for addiction tapes. And to boost business you suggest a built-in instability of some kind."

'"We have the contacts and the organization. You have the product."

'"And the commission you require will be large?"

'"Not unreasonable. Fifty percent of retail, our directors thought."'

'I think you're making up this whole affair, Mrs Cadence.'

Poor Nurse, she's way out of her league. The things Edward got up to put him out of everybody's league.

'The tea's getting cold, Nurse. Would you pour us some, please? You can have the cup – I'll get my tooth mug.'

'If you're just trying to prove you're mad, Mrs Cadence, then –'

'I'm in the Kingston. Once you're in the Kingston you don't need to prove anything.'

She seems to find Bitterness and Despair more suitable than Bitterness and Jokes, so I go haggardly to get my tooth mug and I hold it out for her to fill. She does so, watching.

Red nose time again.

'Edward frowned at the offer Pheeney'd made. He drummed his fingers on the desk. Pheeney's style of performance was catching.

'"And if I don't agree, Mr – er – forgive me, Pleaney, was it? The usual unpleasantness, I suppose?"

'"Scientific equipment is very vulnerable, Doctor. So are scientists."

'"So I really have no alternative, Mr – er – was it really Pleaney? You didn't say."

'Poor Pheeney. He did so want to be taken seriously.'

'So what happened?' Nurse is hurrying me along. My timing must be off. 'Dr Cadence never agreed, did he?"

'Of course he didn't, Nurse. Of course he didn't.'

Wait for it. Now then – 'He offered twenty-five percent and settled for forty.'

I believe I've embarrassed her.

'That's the punch line, Nurse. Why aren't you laughing?'

'I'm sorry, Mrs Cadence, but I don't believe it.'

'Pheeney produced a contract which Edward signed. I witnessed his signature as I had done on a previous contractual occasion. The document nominated I.M.S. as sole distributors of anti-addiction tapes on a sales commission of forty percent, less agency fees. I checked later – I.M.S. really did exist. They were listed as holding an agency for a harmless sleeping pill, Panadorm. So the contract Edward signed was perfectly legal.'

'Dr Cadence must have had his reasons.'

Of course he had. He wanted a quiet life. And if he eased tape prices up the company would soon be back more or less where he'd started. He could easily do this – as a recent Nobel prize winner he could do anything. Sensitape had changed the face of society. He was a national hero, cabaret fodder. Up with the Archbishop of Canterbury. But I'm sorry for Nanny, poor faltering Nanny.

'His reasons were quite clear,' I told her. 'Any trouble from the strong men of the I.M.S. organization and the development of anti-addiction tapes might have been held up almost indefinitely. It was a risk he dared not take.'

He explained it to me very carefully after his visitors had left. As a doctor he had felt obliged to make the deal. The other Sensitape directors would object, but it was a small price to pay for the permanent end of illegal international drug trafficking. Instead of trying to beat him the traffickers had sensibly joined him. Together they would work toward a happier mankind, even if for rather different motives.

True, but neither here nor there. I don't know why he bothered to try to fool me. He was certainly too intelligent to be fooling himself. And it wasn't the money. Psychiatric research got all the proceeds. It still does. He wanted a quiet life.

Mrs Craig hasn't poured her tea. What a pity. And she had the cup and saucer too.

She tells me, 'I'm afraid your story really isn't very funny, Mrs Cadence.' Of course it isn't. 'Great men have to make difficult decisions.' Edward was great all right. 'And it's easy for other people to criticise them afterward. But –'

'I never criticise him. You might as well criticize Stonehenge. I try to find out about him, that's all.'

'Did you kill him?'

'I was importantly involved with him for over twelve years. Then he importantly died.'

'Being in the Kingston may have taught you to be evasive. But surely not to be pretentious as well?'

Wow. You're tougher-minded than I thought. Thank God I have the edge on you. I'm cleverer.

'Tell me, Mrs Cadence. Did you kill him?'

Also I cannot be bullied. Twenty-nine days in this place and help that is offered as questions with one-word answers is more than I can bear. It should be easy to say yes or no, to nod or shake my head, but that's something not even Mr Siemens expected of me. His job was to prove that I was sane, and he failed. Mrs Craig came in here this afternoon believing in me. I've footled with her and she's still willing to make the effort. I stand up, walk around her, go to the mirror, stare at the reflection in it. I knew the answer to her question once. Now, though, I stare at the woman in the mirror. I'm tired, and I need her to tell me what to say, and she won't even meet my eyes.

They'll have to feed her up if they're ever going to let her out of here.

She's the woman Edward Cadence never loved.

'You remember Tony Stech, Nurse? My husband's partner – the man who committed suicide?'

'I've heard a lot about him. I never met him.'

It's no use telling her. It's just so pathetic to go around assuring people that you did after all once arouse love in a man. Or was it pity? Search, Thea Cadence. Search.

'Mrs Cadence, you must help me. I took a risk to find out what I did this afternoon. But you're like talking into cotton wool – nothing comes back. I know now that the tape you've been under is damaging. But you must help me. I've got to decide what to do.'

Search. Drive her out. Get your priorities right.

'If Doctor is disregarding court instructions, then he must have a reason. Did he know you before you came here? Can you think of any reason why he should want to discredit you?'

Search.

At first I suppose there can be no doubt that all Tony felt was a mild sort of pity for me. He had a sympathetic nature. He must have felt pity for hundreds of people.

'You hinted, Mrs Cadence, at two levels of court instructions. Have you any proof that there are two? If so, they should be exposed. Please, Mrs Cadence, this opting out helps nobody.'

But in my case his pity was complicated by his admiration for Edward.

'Will you listen to what I'm saying, Mrs Cadence.'

No.

'If it goes on, that tape will destroy you. You know that?'

Tony loved me. He believed it was wrong, but he still loved me.

'I shall be back later with your tablets. I very much want you to be more cooperative.'

Shut the door behind you. Shut the door behind you. Get out and shut the door behind you.

It started in the most ordinary way imaginable. In any society patterns must recur and recur. The three of us – by then it was usually the three of us – had to attend a Sensitape board meeting at the factory in Teddington, near the television studios. At that time, still only six months or so after the Sexitape recording and before it was released on the general market, Sensitape 57 as a commercial enterprise wasn't doing very well. The reproducing equipment was expensive, the range of tapes limited, and as yet only a few Sensitape parlours were in operation. Edward had of course weathered the hospital's attempt to make him resign; since the accountants who investigated his affairs could find no evidence at all of fund misappropriation, medical opinion in general was now firmly on his side. Public opinion was less predictable, swinging in response to press coverage which was equally undecided.

We drove out along the Hammersmith thruway. It was raining and the atmosphere in the car was uneasy. Edward was silent, hiding behind his driving. I sat beside him, staring out at the ends of houses cut off thirty years ago by the road engineers, the temporary buttresses and cement rendering now decorated with posters and huge graffiti. DEATH TO ALL JEWS and FEED STARVING INDIA. A fine drizzle was falling, and I found myself hating the townscape which was all I knew. Lamp posts flicked by, and barn-high road signs. I was alone, afraid of Tony and totally isolated from Edward by the civility which was now all we offered each other. Without even sex, all we had in common was an interest in Sensitape.

Tony sat hunched sideways in the back seat, all knees and elbows. He had nothing to say and wisely said it. This was unusual for Tony – mostly he had a flow of heavy jokes that were endearing in their awfulness – and his silence depressed me still further. In his silence I was able to sense his thoughts – or what I imagined his thoughts to be – and they frightened me. They threatened contact. I watched the traffic signs and the heavy wet leaves of plane trees lining the road.

We drove through Teddington, past the big black church and the fashionable pubs. It was the time of year for geraniums. We turned right, along beside the river till we came to the Sensitape building. Edward parked the car among those of the other directors – we were a little late – and ran round in the rain to open the door on my side for me. He avoided my eyes. We went into the foyer and straight up to the board room. The meeting had been delayed for our arrival.

We listened to the company secretary's report: the six months' trading figures poor, profits on sales to the Health Service unsatisfactory, no chance of increasing prices while the present government was in power, laboratory costs mounting, new equipment needed, insufficient capital for an all-out promotion drive. And so on. I occupied my time observing the other members of the board, businessmen, a phenomenon I had only recently come into contact with. Everything about them fascinated me, the way they worked, what they thought, the faces they made. Merchants, with merchants' x-ray eyes.

Now Edward was on his feet. I had no idea what he would say. Business stuff.

'I should like first of all to thank Mr Wheeler for the conciseness of his report, and for its accuracy. To my mind he has neither minimized the seriousness of the situation nor exaggerated it. By making a few cuts it would be possible for the company to continue trading more or less as at present. Certain sections are at the moment overstaffed, and a balance sheet such as we can show today should ensure our having no difficulty with the unions about redundancies.'

The thing about Edward was that he managed to be believed by both sides. In fact, he managed everything. Everything except the stuff I needed. So I was the unreasonable one, certainly unreasonable in that I still loved him.

'However, ladies and gentlemen, none of this should be necessary. I am happy to be able to tell you that I believe I have the immediate answer to our problems. Mr Scrutton – could Statistics please give us a breakdown on the broad types issued so far?'

Mr Scrutton was young, square-jawed, manly. Already with merchant's eyes.

'Expressed as percentages of total sales, Dr Cadence, the Goof Benson tape alone accounted for nearly half the market.' (This was pre-IMS, by the way) 'The explanation here seems to be that it attracted the jazz club organizers who saw a way of increasing membership by installing a machine. Also the screamer chosen made considerable impact.'

I remember that screamer. It made my toes curl. *Really Live It With Goof Benson*, the posters said.

Mr Scrutton spoke with little expression, but warmly enough. He might have been discussing the fortunes of some distant cousin.

'On the other hand, Tune In To Great Minds has made only very slight progress. The Poet's Ethos, The Mind Of A Painting, and Mysticism For All, together only take up eight percent of the total market. Classical Music has done rather better, with twenty-three, more or less equally distributed between the three virtuosos involved. The biggest single seller after Benson has been the simple Relaxatape at twenty-two.'

He smiled at me meaninglessly. I was the chairman's wife.

'Shall I cover the medical side as well, sir?'

'No need, Mr Scrutton. It's on the retail entertainment side that this firm has to expand or die.'

Mr Scrutton sat down; he had spoken without notes, and attended politely to what the chairman had to say.

'From what Statistics have given us, ladies and gentlemen, it's obvious that Sensitape is missing out on the mass market. Not that we really needed Statistics to tell us that. Certainly Mr Benson's tape has broken new ground, but the royalty paid to jazz musicians is very high, and anyway I doubt if further issues in that field would do very much. It's new machines that we need to sell, new machines for the home, and new machines in a chain of parlors right across the country. In order to do this our tapes must offer an experience intensely desirable to the majority of consumers. This is a consumer durable, ladies and gentlemen, one nearly as expensive as a motor car. The incentive to buy must be very high indeed.'

Edward was offering the statutory amount of gab. Directors like to arrive at the chairman's conclusion long before he does so himself, in order that they may have time to think about it and decide their own attitudes. Edward gave them what they wanted. He ground on for another ten minutes. Then he arrived.

'We must remember that we are not in this business only to make money. We are here to enrich human life, to heal the sick, to extend the experiential potential of the meagrest member of society. Until our appeal is universal, until we can offer personal fulfillment to everyone, we are failing in our human duty.'

He held up the fingers of one hand, ticked them off.

'Basic human requirements – air, drink, food, sunlight, purpose, companionship. The first four of these are not within Sensitape's province. The last two have many facets, the most important being sex. It is in the fields of purpose and companionship – which in general may be equated with importance – that Sexitape can play a vital part.'

He'd slipped the word in casually enough, but not one of the directors had missed it. Their attitudes already safely decided, they waited eagerly for a chance to give tongue.

'Sexitape is my own private property, ladies and gentlemen. I have come to the conclusion that society at large should be able to benefit from it. Therefore I propose licensing it to Sensitape for immediate commercial use. Obtaining a Medical Council certificate will present no difficulty – its efficiency has been tested clinically in literally thousands of cases.'

As he paused for breath Legal Department was on her feet at once, asking to inspect the copyright agreement in respect to Sexitape. Public Relations was shouting his head off about Company Image and Pressure Group Diplomacy. Sales murmured something about Questions of Censorship, but I think only I heard him. Research and Development asked prickly questions about side effects – he'd had nothing to do with Sexitape and was obviously determined to be awkward. To use Sexitape under clinical observation, he said, was very different from flinging it out for any Tom, Dick or Harry to dabble in. Besides (the clincher) what about the Protection of Minors?

Edward dealt with the questions and objections patiently, one by one. He'd never have started if he hadn't known he could. He also wisely involved everybody in the project, handing out jobs to make them all feel needed. Legal Department was instructed to check carefully on the Obscene Publications Act. Public Relations was handed a list of archbishops, chief constables and television personalities whom Edward had already approached privately and found to be sympathetic. Sales was asked to get together with Promotions and decide on the agency best fitted to handle this new development. And Research and Development was pacified with an extensive program of Graded Response Experiments to ascertain the best level for general issue. Edward was able to assure him, as a psychologist, that to anyone not yet sexually developed the Sexitape brain patterns would be meaningless.

Finally the meeting broke up. Outside the board room Edward paused, glanced at his watch – never registered the time it said, I'm sure – and smiled at me as if at someone else's child.

'I shan't be coming home yet, Thea. No point in you hanging around. Take the car. I can easily get a lift in with young Scrutton or somebody.'

'You know I hate driving on the thruway.'

'Ask Tony to drive you then. I know he wants to go straight back, once he's had a short chat with Research and Development.'

'I wish you'd come, Edward.' A million other wives, a million other pleas not to be pushed to infidelity. 'I don't mind waiting till you've finished.'

'Nonsense, dear.' Another echo. 'There's so much to see to I shall be ages. You go off with Tony. It'd only worry me, knowing you were having to wait around somewhere.'

I walked slowly away down the carpeted corridor to the lift. If I wanted to I could now feel that the decision had been taken for me, that whatever I let happen now would comfortably not be my fault. I left word for Tony in the Research Department two floors below and then went on down to Reception.

'It's stopped raining, Mrs Cadence. I think it's going to turn out nice after all.'

All a part of the conspiracy.

Across the foyer, through the automatic doors, and out to the car. I climbed in and sat. Tiny pebbles of rain on its polished bonnet glistened in the sunlight. Public Relations came out to the car next to Edward's and drove away. He had Edward's list sticking out of his pocket and he didn't see me. His tyres made dark stripes on the already drying pavement. A huge scenery van passed on its way to the studios just down the road. Behind Sensitape on the river a pleasure steamer approached with a small jazz band. Thick shadows sat under Sensitape's ornamental cherry trees planted along the edge of Sensitape's grass. Inside me nothing happened at all. I loved Edward.

'Edward says I'm to drive you back into town.'

'I know.'

Tony climbed in, adjusted the seat. He was shorter than Edward.

'I hear you're thinking of buying a house in Richmond.'

'Edward's going to open a clinic. He needs a smart address.'

'Expensive place, Richmond.'

A remark needing no answer, the implied criticism slightly insulting. I sat as thin as I could, my leg well away from the drive selector. Tony drove slowly out onto the road. We gathered speed, the stiff shadows of the trees clicked under us as we passed, like a stick along a fence.

'I'll take you to the flat,' Tony said.

'No, not there.' An immoral proposal? Or did I just not want to be left there alone? 'I don't feel like going home, Tony. It's … the weather's too nice for stuffing indoors.'

'Where then?' So minimal. Hypersensitive, it seemed to me to be all that remained sayable perhaps.

'I tell you what, Tony. You're not in a hurry to get back, are you? Why don't we have a look at the house in Richmond, the one Edward's going to buy? I love empty houses. It's not far out of the way. I've got the key – we were supposed to give it back to the agent this morning on our way out but somehow there wasn't time.' Babble. 'Will you come, Tony? I'd love to know what you think of it. I've told Edward it's too large. He says he'll get a housekeeper. I suppose he knows what he's doing.'

'He knows what he's doing all right. I've never met anyone who knew better.'

A flat tone of voice, indicating nothing. I knew he'd come.

'It's one of those high white houses overlooking the Green. Regency. A scheduled ancient monument, so the agent said. Edward's determined to do the thing in style.'

'I'm sure he's right. It's what private patients like. It makes them feel they're getting their money's worth.'

Tony didn't approve of private patients. We talked about it along the thruway as far as the sign for Richmond, a general issue, safe. Once on the road through Chiswick the conversation became more particular. I altered it myself – the morning's board meeting had worried me.

'When you started out with Sensitape, Tony, did you think where it would all lead?'

'Does one ever think like that? I was working on a cure for UDW. By the time we'd found it I was committed.'

'Do you wish you'd backed out?'

'There's no answer to that. We can't choose where to stop, what to discover and what's better left unknown.'

'Wouldn't you say Sensitape has gone too far?'

'I haven't given it much thought. I'm an engineer, not a philosopher.'

Traffic was heavy. We had to wait at the Mortlake roundabout for some minutes.

'My father used to say we'd become a nation of spectators, Tony. I visited him and Mummy a few weeks ago, the first time for years. They're in a gimcrack duplex, with a Sensitape as big as a battleship. It all seemed so sadly unsuitable, somehow.'

'You're falling into the trap of thinking that what Sensitape offers is secondhand. It's not. What happens inside your head really does happen. There's a range of experience most people hadn't even dreamed of.'

Oh Lord, not the handout.

'You know it's wrong, Tony. I'm sure you do.'

'Wrong? What is "wrong"? It's your puritan upbringing, Thea. We've grown out of ideas like right and wrong.'

I didn't answer. The cant words that year were 'enriching' and 'impoverishing.' Tony didn't believe it any more than I did. Only a part of truth. A dangerous part. Tony stamped on the kick-down and shot forward into the line of traffic.

'There are too many people, Thea. Congested living breeds neurosis – take the terrifying logicality of UDW, for example. Isn't anything that keeps men sane and happy in their environment "good"? Sensitape gives every sign of being able to do just that.'

We were coming into Richmond, the Twickenham stadium away on our right. The road was lined with residential blocks forty stories high, and behind them countless others patterned the surrounding grassland. It was luxury living, proportioned and angled with subtlety, far different from the way the millions further out managed. The aspirations stacked here had a sort of chance. I remembered that in the middle ages, the dark ages, men had fattened pigs in boxes, getting box-shaped pigs.

'You realise he won't be home till late this evening.' The first words after a long silence. 'Your husband, I mean. He probably won't be home till the early hours.'

'He works too hard.' Please, Tony. Pretend with me. 'I often tell him about it. Half an hour's Relaxatape and he reckons he rested. It's complete nonsense, of course.'

'He won't be working late today, Thea. And you know it.'

'Puritanism from you too, Tony?'

'Common humanity.' He spun the wheel and we turned onto the access road leading round the Green. 'Some wives wouldn't mind. You do.'

'I've no right to mind. It's not as if –'

He interrupted me.

'You must tell me which of these bloody palaces it is. I'll drop you and find somewhere to park the car.'

'Halfway along. The black door with the fanlight.'

He dropped me. I leaned in at the window.

'You'll come back? You won't just go off and leave me?'

'How could I? It's your car.'

There was a wrought iron gate and a short path up to the front door. On the steps up to the porch I turned and looked back – the car was already out of sight. I unlocked the door, pushed it open, shuddered slightly. I'd said I liked empty houses. Facing alone the life that would be mine in this one was another matter.

The hall was airy and brightly lit from a glass dome high above the staircase, its calm certainty protected by an expensive invisible screen. The contained air pressed against this screen, ready to spill its assurance, pour it past my face, lose it among cars and Do Not Walk On The Grass. I dared not break it. The door began to swing shut again. Another woman would enter through that screen as if down through the surface of a lake. It would close behind her and the world on the other side would be cool and welcoming. I stood on the step and the door closed in my face. I was not more shut out than I had been when it was open.

I rested my forehead on its smooth surface, told myself I was carrying sensitivity to the point of madness.

So I went in and stood firmly in the middle of the hall. The door, now behind me, swung shut again. I'd made a fuss about really very little. To be haunted by the future was singularly unproductive, not as if anything could be done about it. I went up the stairs, making a clatter on the bare treads. Were they marble? As I climbed toward the glass dome the air became warmer.

I wandered in a practical way through the upstairs rooms, checking on cupboards and electric light points. There was a pleasant attic. If we had a housekeeper as Edward wanted then she could have a flat up there and be completely self-contained. The view across the treetops on the Green was pleasant – even the distant housing blocks had a cheerful grace about them. I looked down at the pavement, saw Tony's untidy mass of hair among the Richmond homburgs and American peaked caps. I watched him open the gate and walk up the path till he was out of sight under the curved roof of the porch. He'd come as he said he would.

'I'm glad it's you, Thea. I had the sudden horrid feeling that I'd come to the wrong house.'

'Come on in, Tony. I feel overawed, alone in all this grandness.'

I stood back to let him in, then closed the door. He talked through what might have been a moment of constraint.

'I found a place in the Karstak by the station. Very lucky really … So this is the place Edward has chosen for the centre of his empire. Government House. Let's hope some of this dignity rubs off. It's a fine building … How will you feel, Thea, being mistress of all this?'

'It's nothing to do with me, Tony. I'm just the parlour-maid.'

'Governor's Wife, my dear. You stick up for your rights.' He wandered into the big room on the right, the one Edward had earmarked for Reception. 'What's left of them.'

He frightened me.

'Governor's Wife, Tony? What d'you mean?'

'Power.' He went ahead of me, through the double doors into the room beyond. I heard his voice echoing against the bare walls. I said I didn't know what he meant. 'To control Sensitape is to control peace and war. I mean that, Thea. I've given the subject a lot of thought.' He reappeared in the doorway. 'Sensitape will make him rich, of course. But that's nothing to the cultural power Sensitape will bring.'

I'd never dared to explore risky stuff like that.

'Why have you helped him, Tony?'

'I'll go on helping him. The usual reasons exist. If I don't help him someone else will. Scientific advance continues independently of the individual. And so on. And so on. Probably the real fact is that I enjoy the sense of vicarious triumph.'

The floorboards narrowed in a steep perspective under his feet. Behind him on the far wall a mirror in ornate plaster above the fireplace showed me his back view, a nameless someone. This mirror gave me a strangely new, outside view of him. Unlike Edward, he was a man who needed an identity. At the moment he gained this from my husband.

'You know who his mistress is, of course?'

We shared lines of thought. He merely spoke the end of his.

'No, Tony, I don't want to.'

'Mrs Malinder. Only we're supposed to think of her as Mrs X. I'm surprised you didn't guess long ago.'

'I could have. Without a name or a face she was less real.'

'It's the done thing, Governors having mistresses, I mean.'

'I wish you hadn't told me. I asked you not to.'

He came toward me. The cornice above his head was covered with a deep plaster moulding of oak leaves and ivy and bunches of grapes. He took my hands.

'The business partner. The husband's best friend. The unregarded wife. It's traditional.'

I looked away, at the long shutters neatly folded by the windows.

'But at least you needn't be alone any more, Thea. Governor's Wife is a pretty lonely job.' He lowered my hands down to my sides. 'You'd better show me the house and get it over with. These rooms have seen too much – they're too old and experienced for my liking.'

I showed him the small salon and the big salon, the dining room, the study, the automated kitchen quarters. Behind the house there was a small rectangle of ancient paved garden, an overgrown lily pond and a catalpa tree. He had little to say about it all, the house where my husband and I were going to live. Often I caught him watching me instead of admiring the fine big rooms. Could it really have been no more than pity?

We went out into the tiny garden, blue-green shadows smelling of ferns. He hadn't touched me since releasing my hands in the main drawing room. Nothing had been said about our new relationship. He found a stick and stirred the rusty pond water.

'You'll never leave him,' he said.

'Are you asking me to?'

'He doesn't love you.'

'That's not so important. Not if you –'

'You see what I mean, Thea.'

He'd stopped me in time. Words have separate existences that needlessly explicate the things they describe. He poked deeper into the pond, releasing a stream of bubbles.

'Has Edward told you about me, Tony?'

'Told me about you? Hardly ever mentions you. What should he have told me?'

I knew he'd been discussing my sexual difficulties with his colleagues at the hospital, with the Nigerian sexologist in particular. I wouldn't have been at all surprised if he had spread the news more widely. Women have women talk. Why shouldn't men have theirs? No doubt his reticence was partly to do with Mrs X – she made my inadequacies not matter to him.

'What should he have told me, Thea?'

'Oh, I don't know. That I'm demanding and possessive. That I nag. That I don't understand him. All the usual sort of things.'

'If he had I'd have told him he was a bloody liar.'

Perhaps I should have warned Tony about … myself. But my disgust was for Edward, for his work, his obsession, for what it had made our life into. Tony's nature was different, and I would be different too.

'We've been leading very separate lives for some time now, Tony. He'd have been perfectly justified in complaining about me.'

'Mrs Malinder came to the lab one day to fetch him while I was there. They weren't very pretty together. It wasn't that they were open about their interest in each other. It seemed more that with them sex was being used as a cover for something else. Something truly reprehensible. Edward's no fool. Since that evening the only conversations we've had have been strictly to do with Sensitape.'

He thrust his stick right down into the water and let it go. We watched it rise up again, then fall over sideways. He turned away.

'What's happening, Tony? What's happening to the world?'

'All you can do, Thea, is have faith in life, in your own strength. Build a cage for yourself to keep the crocodiles and tigers out. Inside that cage you can find everything. We're alive, Thea. The past is gone and the future hasn't happened. This moment – each individual this moment for the rest of our lives – is unique and marvellous. we must live it as such.'

I suppose he was being sententious. He had that tendency. As he spoke I found myself apologizing for him. At least he's got something to say, I thought. And my question too had been sententious. Without words now, we stood at the green bottom of a high brick well, an irregularly angular patch of blue sky far above us, chimneys and barred windows, and closer the startling shiny leaves of the catalpa. The traffic sounds were dulled and distant. If any moment in my life would be unique and marvelous it was this, and at the same time peculiarly continuous before and behind.

'It's getting late,' Tony said. 'We must go and have some lunch.'

The restaurant was on the point of closing, but expensive enough for the waiters not to stand over us or start clearing up before we had finished. Unlike Edward, who exacted good service as his right, Tony won it by his

'Mrs Cadence, I've brought you your tablets.'

Oh God. Not Nanny again.

'Do you know, Nurse, that if Edward had lived a few months longer you'd be addressing me now as Lady Cadence?'

'No. No, I didn't.'

'Wouldn't that have been shit, Nurse? A knighthood for *him?* Every day I thank God he died when he did.'

That's thrown her. She came in full to bursting. Tony loved me, you ponderous blob. Not for what I had suffered but selfishly for what we could share with each other. He loved me.

'I've been thinking about your situation, Mrs Cadence. I was wrong to expect cooperation from you. Your treatment here must have … had an effect.'

'If you mean it's made me bloody-minded, you're damn right.'

'Do you want to get out of here, Mrs Cadence?'

Do I? There's a Sensitape fortune waiting for me. My husband is dead and also my lover. The crocodiles and tigers are as loud as ever. Do I want to get out of here?

I asked her something else. 'Your life, Nurse, do you celebrate every moment of it? Is every moment unique, marvellous?'

She didn't answer me, either. 'In here people die, my dear. The Kingston is the outside world, ten times larger. You'll preserve nothing staying here. Nothing at all.'

Often I made the mistake of trying to leave her behind. I don't want to be met and equalled – it disquiets me. I should have known they'd never put a fool in charge of so significant a prisoner. Excuse me – *patient*.

'Just give me the tablets, Nurse. Do your job and give me the tablets.'

'Your husband's death was a national tragedy. I think we should have distrusted such an easy uncomplicated answer.'

The tablets stick in my throat, burn unfelt into the epithelium. Why shouldn't a great man be killed for an easy, uncomplicated reason? Swallow, and swallow again. A vapour of aluminum and stale urine rises, incense of contemporary forgiveness. Swallow again, for the negative ecstasy of cessation. More practically, for a blessed relief from the pressure of Nurse's good intentions.

Now she stands watching me. Soon she'll have to put me to bed, woman indifferent to woman. Is she basically as indifferent to my person as she is to my flesh? Is her interest rather in an abstraction, in justice? As Tony's was in the abstraction of pity? Or might have been. Or did he love and does she … I stand for so many things. The truth about Mrs C. Not enough of me that is me for me to know.

DAY 30

Still in bed? Not got up and dressed and potted and propelled along the corridor? It's a funny thing, but I'd forgotten what beds feel like. The tablets are holding me less and less. Yet I shouldn't be in bed, not if the clock is right and the time really is four-thirty.

They could easily be cheating me, of course.

Stretch. Feet down to where the sheets are cool. Like the freedom it was when Edward gave us separate beds. And the poor man meant it as a reproach. I don't mind, although I ought to, that they might make the clock lie to me. Before I came here I'd have minded – to know the time was to know the shape of life and to be in control of it. That's one illusion, one tyranny the tablets relieve. Perhaps my treatment is still to come and the clock is simply meant to fool me. I can't imagine for what reason but it doesn't worry me.

I feel loved, lying here. The sheets love me. The Kingston, Mrs Craig, Doctor, the High Court judge, each one loves me. I should never have doubted it. In his own way Edward even. There's not room in any great man for everything. George Washington managed it, fitted in a treasured wife – I wonder who else has. That makes George Washington the greater man, but I am the wife Edward Cadence chose and perhaps I just wasn't up to it. This room is a benediction. I shall ask them to allow me the transcendence of this bed again. To avoid searching, that is the gift. To exist solely in the peace of the body. No shadows. Nothing to be remembered and not to be remembered, to be forgotten and to become unforgotten.

'Mrs Cadence.'

A nest of my choosing. Pretty curtains, gentleness in the air.

'Mrs Cadence.'

A man. He wears a white coat. Curiously bright, his face flickering like the flame of a candle. Doctor. One of them. Doctor.

'Are you awake, Mrs Cadence?'

'I was thinking how very like a candle you are, Doctor. The longer she stands the shorter she grows.'

'Mrs Cadence, you won't be having your period of treatment today. There's been a slight accident along in the treatment room.'

'Ninny Nanny Netticoat, in a white petticoat … It would have been nice to have children. Never room in Edward's life for children. He used to say he was my child but it wasn't true. He was a cliff I'd never climb.'

'Nothing serious, you understand, but the tape has been damaged. The contrition tape.'

'Did George George Washington have children? He wrote such beautiful letters.'

'Don't cry, Mrs Cadence. You know we'll look after you.'

Cry? I hardly knew it. My body cries, not my mind. It's my body that's mad, Doctor. My body.

'You said there'd been an accident, Doctor.'

'Good. I wasn't sure you were listening to me. There's been an accident in the treatment room and the contrition tape has been damaged.'

'Contrition tape?'

'The one we've been treating you with.'

'I see.' Why not? 'And you say there's been an accident.'

'I've sent for replacement from the Central Library but it won't be here in time for today's session. Nurse Craig has suggested that you might like to read the newspaper to pass the time.'

'Pass the time.'

'I'm beginning to agree with her. Isolation works both ways: it helps you to come to terms with yourself but it also hinders the creation of a social integrity.'

A cold wind. A shrivelling blast of former realities. I remember now.

'Would it not be truer to say, Doctor, that isolation helps to destroy the self, so that it no longer needs to be bothered with? That we gain most of our ideas of what we are from other people's faces?'

'It's interesting, Mrs Cadence, to observe how suddenly the drug effect drops away.'

I've never seen him outside the treatment room before. He's always been the extensor of some electro-therapeutic complex. He still is, operating me now by remote control.

'An accident, you said?'

'Three times.'

'And Mrs Craig?'

'I'll be sending her along in a minute. It hardly seems worth while, getting you up and dressing you.' He pauses to let me feel his disapproval. 'Mrs Craig is taking a great deal of interest in your case. I hope her reasons are suitable to her profession.'

'We're not lesbians, if that's what you mean. Neither have I bribed her.'

He laughs and pats my cheek. If he ever does that again I'll –

'You could only offer promises, my dear. The disposition of your fortune awaits our decision on your progress. Which is all the more reason for getting better as quickly as possible.'

'I like your "getting better," Doctor. A charming choice of phrase.'

'A humble and contrite heart, Mrs Cadence. It opens many doors.'

I wait for another of his little laughs. Sadists are like pornographers, faulty in artistic judgment, their prose style terrible. 'These people are mine,' an Auschwitz guard once remarked with noble simplicity, just to prove the rule. My father used to read the trials aloud when I was old enough, saying it could happen again, and I never believed him.

But I overdramatize. Doctor doesn't laugh. He goes out quietly, without effect.

I know there's a proof of Tony's love. There's a scene that evades me. It's sickly to be so constantly concerned that he might only have been sorry for me. He had no reason. Edward wasn't cruel. And I had no children for him to disregard. Hunger, thirst, cold – I suffered none of these. So where does this mawkish assumption come from, the assumption that I must have been pitiable? That I was functionally a victim? If it had showed, then he couldn't have pitied me. Nobody could.

We had spent the afternoon together in his flat. Sensitape royalties were at last bringing him a decent living so that he had been able to move from the small rooms over the lab that had been his home for seven years since selling up after his father's death. His new flat was the first floor of a big house on the Boltons in Kensington. The day after moving in he had rung me at the clinic to say it now took forty-three paces to go from the sitting room window, out across the landing and down the passage to the bathroom. That was a long way. And thirty-seven paces from the bed to the refrigerator in the kitchen. The space he inhabited meant a lot to him. He considered himself now almost a landowner.

I'd got lunch for us both. The day before, after our visit to Regent's Park, he'd bought me a bottle of scent and he kept sniffing me to make sure I was wearing it. Still shy – two years after we had looked over the empty house in Richmond – he liked an excuse before he would touch me, liked an excuse to laugh off his inclinations. Halfway through the meal he became serious for a moment.

'When did you last cook – I mean *really* cook – a proper meal, Thea?'

'Not for years. Not since the early days with Edward. It'd be so false. So artificial. Back-to-nature fiends are always such phonies.'

'Don't you think you miss something?'

'Of course I do. I miss getting my fingers puddled peeling potatoes. I miss saturating my hair in the rancid smell of frying.'

'You'd laugh at me if I talked of the old-fashioned joys of actually making something. You're such a child of your age, Thea. But I'm sure it's basic, the pleasure of being really involved in the food your man eats.'

I remember laughing, just as he said I would.

'Do-it-yourself's gone out. We saw through it years ago.' After lunch he settled down to read a scientific paper that had come by the two o'clock post. I sat with him in the controlled atmosphere of the living room while kitchen electronics disposed of the dirty dishes and garbage. Once Eskimo women had softened their husbands' shoes every morning by chewing them. Was it really their gain that the shoes were now synthetic, unaffected by snow or freezing? Love was so cerebral now, and the brief effects of skin on skin. And once Edward had succeeded in isolating them, those would be available as a magnetic tape. I became aware that although Tony still had the pamphlet held up in front of his face he was no longer reading it. Outside the window was a big chestnut tree in the railed garden around the church. Over the top of his paper he seemed to be observing its solid mass against the towers of Drayton Gardens beyond. He moved his head slowly from side to side, concentrating. He was haggard these days. His nerves were bad and he was often depressed. The factory psychiatrist had tried in vain to talk to him about it. It hurt me how little even I could do to help.

'You weren't at this morning's meeting,' he said.

'Too many meetings. The Governor's Wife suffered a vapour.'

'Then you missed Edward's report on the new process.'

'Too many new processes. The Governor's Wife preferred to nurse her poor head on a chaise longue in the garden.'

'Pity.' He closed one eye, moved his head again, lined up the window frame and the edge of the tree and a particular tower's lift shaft. 'It's a development you ought to know about.'

'Why ought I? I don't find the awfulness of things amusing any more. Not since us.'

'Know thine enemy. That's why.'

'Such a lovely afternoon, Tony. Don't spoil it.'

He threw the pamphlet across onto the sofa and looked at his watch.

'I've got to be in Teddington by four. Are you coming?'

'What a horrible idea. Must you go?'

'Governor's official invitation. Actually it's my work that will be on test so of course I've got to be there.'

'Tell me about it, Tony. I know you must.'

He'd waited till now, till the last minute, to tell me. Usually we discussed everything as soon as it happened. What he had to say now would be unpleasant. He'd been worrying about it all through lunch. He leaned back in his chair and closed his eyes, as if to pretend it was not he himself speaking.

'For three years,' he said, 'Edward has been photographing, analysing, cataloging. Identifying patterns. Till a few months ago I thought this was just another example of his methodical nature. After a while, though, it showed that too much Sensitape exposure leads to a general dulling.' He opened his eyes. 'That's one little gem we haven't published. Had you heard?'

I nodded. Edward had passed a sheaf of receptivity graphs across to me during breakfast a few weeks earlier. They weren't significant, he said. There wasn't an absolute – these things were entirely relative.

'As usual, Thea, I was underestimating him. He now has film of more than seven hundred clearly defined CR responses. He knows the emotions they indicate, and he asked me some months ago to work on a modulator sensitive enough to reproduce them artificially. I've been reasonably successful. That's what this morning's meeting was about – giving a report on the results so far.'

'I'll never understand the sort of work you're willing to do. What were these results?'

'Roughly what might have been expected. My modulator does the job, but not so convincingly. There's a loss of definition I can't seem to attribute. It seems there are still a few things that the human brain is better at.'

'I expect you're working on it.'

I must have sounded very bitter. He got up and crossed the room to where I was sitting. Like Edward, he was a man whose work was his life, but in his case the outcome of this work was inconsistent with everything he believed most deeply. This dichotomy I found bewildering. I liked things to fit.

He squatted on the floor beside me.

'These reports are all the same – they leave out the most significant aspects. Today's were typical. No mention at all was made of the real purpose in Edward's mind.'

'You're obviously appalled, Tony. Why the hell don't you do something about it?'

'I sometimes feel that he and I are parts of the same man. A sense of common identity – I felt it that very first time he came to visit me, when I was still in that little room behind the shop. In some disgusting way he completes me. That's why I do nothing against him.'

'You were telling me' – I couldn't bear the truth of what he had just said – 'about the real reason for all this research.'

'Edward's aim is to create new pleasures, not merely reproduce the old.'

He let this sink in.

'By combining patterns from different tapes, superimposing them, electronically distorting them, computing complex sequences for them, he intends to produce new, higher forms of experience. We've been working for weeks now blending mystical ecstasy with certain musical elements and compatible extracts from Sexitape. This afternoon we'll be making the first clinical test.'

It was logical, of course. It grew out of our society as organically as the concentration camps had grown out of Nazi Germany. It was unreasonable to be uncomfortable with Tony's dichotomy. Separate existences go on in all of us, the social and the individual. Denying the social motivations, the shared needs, I left myself truncated, terribly alone. However many of us there were who did deny, we were still in this totally instinctive world – the freaks, the sports, the odd ones out, the enemy.

'Poor Tony,' I said. 'Don't look so solemn. I still love you.'

'There'll soon be a substitute for that too.'

'Never. I'll never let there be.'

He kissed me. I pressed the back of his head with my hand – for just that once I felt more powerful than he.

We took the train out to Teddington station, then walked slowly through the shopping centre to the riverside. The day was hot, the sun standing behind a fine haze under which the exhausted air circulated and recirculated. There wasn't a breath of wind, the flags and mobile advertisements hung motionless. We passed a Sensitape 57 parlour, its door tight shut against the weather. It was offering the Art Appreciation tape, plus spoken commentary and framed reproductions of the pictures, on hire for a bargain twenty new pounds weekly. With art schools springing up like supermarts it had probably been doing a good trade. The receptionist had obviously seen Tony's photograph in some company journal, for she recognized him, came out and waved. She was charming. She was part of Sensitape in a way I could never be.

We went on down the walkway to the crowded river esplanade. The water was dotted with scooters and tiny high-performance sailboats. Tony walked ahead of me, clearing a way through all the people. Brought out by the heat of the sun like flies, I thought. Inexcusably. We entered Sensitape by the side entrance, staff only. Building was going on, an extension to the main block on fine gold-flecked concrete pillars. The contractors were sinking foundations with a sonic drill. A pump droned shrilly, lifting out the river water that continually seeped in.

Inside Sensitape there was a prepared hush. They were proud of the soundproofing, promised working conditions better than any others in the district. The lift took us up to Research and Development where Edward was waiting. His persona for the afternoon was to be doctor – he wore his white coat, complete with stethoscope. He wasn't the first great man to have enjoyed dressing up.

'You don't look too good, Tony. It's the weather, maybe. I see you've brought Thea.'

It was a pointless comment. We went to most places together.

'I'm glad, of course. I'd like her to be present. Come on then, into the E.T. room. Quick as you like.'

Small and fussy. Did I say great?

The Experimental Treatment room had one window wall shielded with green Venetian blinds, making the place like a cave where the only light came through deep water. Another wall was taken up with low computer consoles and control equipment for the various test machines. There was the usual treatment couch, more chairs than seemed necessary, and a bank of tightly directional lights in the mirror ceiling. Edward began by going over the room carefully, looking for listening devices.

'Industrial espionage,' he said. 'It'll seem melodramatic to you, but I'd rather not take unnecessary risks.'

He used the sort of detector he had first seen in Mr Pheeney's hand the year before. He was quick to adopt any new gadgets that came to his notice. He'd bought a gun like Bunk's as well, I knew.

Finally he was satisfied.

'Now, Tony, the cover story here is very simple. A complaint tape came in yesterday – flutter and interference like tiny sparks of light, so the customer says. It's the third complaint of this nature in the last month. I have the tape here. If anyone asks, you're here, Tony, to help me analyse the trouble and deduce its cause.'

He turned to me.

'I expect Tony has told you the actual nature of this experiment. If it comes off it'll be our greatest achievement.'

'It'll come off, Edward. Your experiments always do.'

'I'm glad you have such faith in me, Thea.'

He put the complaints tape on the shelf above the tape deck and took down another. He showed me the sleeve: Animal Reactions: Cat, Test Conditions I & II. Just in case someone was nosey. The tape inside it would at the moment be blank

'Looks uninteresting enough. Well, Thea – would you care to be the first ever? I think I shall call it Synthajoy.'

I backed away.

The first successful commercial replay tape had been seven years before, a simple relaxation experience. We'd called it Relaxatape 09. We thought it would cure UDW straight off. I remember how we passed the big awkward headset eagerly from one to another, our first acceptance of total submission to an outside wave source. And we the first people ever to experience it. I remember Edward tried it first, then me, and then Tony. It was enormously exciting. As a cure for UDW it turned out to be only the first stage. But seven years ago it was enormously exciting.

'Well, Thea? Are you caught up on one of your principles again?'

'Just frightened, Edward. I'd rather not.'

'I suppose I ought to insist. You ought to be made to aspire to higher things. But I'm not going to bother.'

I hate these rooms with mirror ceilings. In my training days lecture rooms often had them so that we students could all properly see the patient. I have my own dream picture of what I look like from above, recumbent, really quite appealing, and I don't want it challenged. Edward turned away and fitted the tape from the cat test sleeve onto the tape deck.

'Lie down, will you, Tony? I'll operate and Thea can observe and take notes. Not that I'm expecting very much external to happen. That arrangement all right with you, Tony?'

'Absolutely, Dr Cadence.' Formal with the moment's importance. 'And I appreciate the opportunity to –'

'Something to tell your children, eh?' Both of them glanced at me. For their different reasons. 'A new experience, Thea. A blending of synthetic delights. Are you sure you don't want to be the first to know what it's all about?'

I shook my head, went to the window, bent the slats of the blind apart with two fingers. I was looking down onto the construction work, the soil flying away beneath the drill and the quick bright people beyond as they hurried to and fro on the esplanade. Sunlight flashed off the river like pins. Their brilliance made the scene more real. Behind me I could hear preparations going on, the slight creak of the couch as Tony lay down on it, quiet conversation between the two men. The colors and movements of the world outside were quite silent, so that I saw one existence and heard another. And belonged to neither. I let the blind slats flip back together, bringing abrupt darkness. I closed my eyes. The voices behind me came louder.

'... fifteen minutes, I thought. Enough for you to make a fair judgment.'

'Build-up will be slow, of course. Don't hurry me out of it if all seems to be going well.'

'I'm hoping for visual images, Tony. Try to remember them. Hey Tony – look at my hands. I hadn't realized I was so het up.'

Pause. Then Edward again.

'I plan to analyse thousands of reactions, Tony. Once we can associate a particular picture with a particular wave pattern, then we'll be able to –'

'I'm trying to relax, Edward.'

'Here – I'll help you fit the headset.'

'You're no good, man. You're as tense as I am.'

'Thea – come over here and fix this headset for me. I can't make it expand enough.'

He had to call me twice. Then I went and fitted the headset around Tony's thick hair. I wound in the needle electrodes and inserted the temporal pads. Under the helmet-like contraption Tony was unrecognisable. It wasn't Tony – just another face, another patient, another subject. I heard Edward running water at the sink in the corner, washing his hands. Then the roar of the hot air as he dried them.

'All ready, Thea? Just check the levels for me, will you?'

I crossed to the tape deck, took the monitor, pressed it against my temple and tested the signal peaks. Nothing but a mild blur.

'Levels well below saturation, Doctor.'

Edward came across the room to the treatment couch, dangling his dried hands, his sleeves still rolled up. He took Tony's pulse. Tony smiled up at us.

'The patient appears to be alive, Doctor. Make a note of that, will you, Nurse? The day and the time.'

Admittedly not a time to be funny, but I loved Tony, heavy jokes included. So I obediently entered the details on my data sheet. Edward threaded the spool, pressed it home and spun it a couple of times with his finger.

'Amplitude of four, I think we agreed on?'

'Amplitude of four.'

'Good luck, Tony. You're off into unknown waters.'

And he started the tape.

Familiar as I was with subjects' reactions under Sensitape, I suppose this time I had expected something special. Of course nothing special happened. Tony closed his eyes, began breathing very slowly. After a few seconds his face relaxed into a gentle smile. The tensions faded.

'Reaching you, is it?' Edward said.

Tony frowned, his eyes still closed, and shook his head, as if shooing a fly in his sleep. We watched him in complete silence for several minutes. I looked away, at the bright spools revolving at their different speeds. Silence stood like a fourth person in the room with us.

'I hope we do have a record of the starting time, Thea.' I didn't bother to answer. 'Look at him … Gone on the strangest journey man has ever known. This is a great moment. Thea? You do realize that?'

'For a Governor's Wife I'm afraid I have a very poor sense of occasion.'

'This Governor's Wife joke of yours and his. It's very troublesome.' Again I didn't bother to answer. 'You've always been against Sensitape, haven't you, Thea? Right from the very beginning.'

A remark as stupid as that could have only one purpose – to bait me.

'If I'd thought about it properly, Edward, I would have been. Not that it would have made any difference.'

'People's needs, Thea, they're not an absolute laid down by gods or philosophers. We're stacked high and we're going to be stacked higher. Unnatural conditions produce unnatural compulsions. The world must be dealt with as it is, not as you'd like it to be. If we can't change the conditions, at least we can do our best to satisfy the needs.'

After a string like that, what could I say?

'What you're doing to Tony there – can you justify that as satisfying a need?'

‘Of course I can. The need for innovation. It’s as potent as the need for power, or for sex.’

Against his rationalizations I could only range a deep, instinctive repugnance. We had talked this way before. We would always talk this way. It was our differences that made it possible for me still, at this moment, to love him. To love him as one animal and Tony as another. And to respect them both. Parts of a whole, perhaps, but emotionally separate.

He watched my decision to end the useless dialectics, and wouldn’t accept it.

‘You were happy enough till Sexitape, Thea. We must face these objections for what they are, signs of a profound sexual immaturity.’

‘Don’t bully me, Edward. Isn’t this supposed to be your great moment? Don’t spoil it.’

‘My God, Thea – back in the sixties they were going around with stop watches and tape measures. Was that better? Was that less an invasion of the individual?’

‘It’s meaning too much to you, Edward. You should apply some of this Freudian analysis to yourself.’

So cold. So cold together. Is it really honest of me to maintain there was also love?

At least I shut him up. He turned back to Tony and leaned over the couch, staring into his face as if to find external proofs of success or failure. The time was four-thirty-two. The tape had been running just over three minutes. I timed Tony’s pulse at sixty and wrote the figure in the four minute space. Slow, but not dangerously so. Edward had moved away and was checking levels on the monitor. He raised the amplitude half a degree, made sure I had noted the change.

‘It’s time we had a talk about Mrs X, Thea.’

‘I don’t see why.’

‘She’s an ambitious woman.’ He needed to. Captive, I could only endure. ‘Ambitious for money. She sees her association with me as a way of getting it. For my part, I see the relationship as a way of keeping her quiet. I intend to keep her travelling hopefully for as long as possible.’

A course that had its compensations.

‘She reckons she’s chipping away at my resolve. Sexitape sales have gone to her head and she wants me to tear up the old contract. Do you think I should?’

‘Why ask me?’

‘You’re my conscience. You must know that.’

If I was his conscience then he should have tried harder to fool me. Always I’d believed that whatever the worst was, I knew it. His words made me uneasy.

'It's modern to be sensible about these things, Edward. Your wife fails you, so you take a mistress. An accepted, modern reaction. But isn't it plain sadism to discuss the new woman with the old?'

'But I'm not discussing Mrs X with you. I'm talking about business morals.'

'And for God's sake stop calling her Mrs X. You make her sound like some passé divorcee. You must know her name – why not use it?'

We both looked across at Tony. My raised voice hadn't shifted him. He was far away on a strange journey. Dials were registering alpha-plus activity.

'Mrs Cadence ...' Voices. 'Mrs Cadence, are you dreaming? Are you having a bad dream?'

Peace. Not voices. I just want peace in which to remember. I open my eyes and see ... Edward standing over me, trying to explain about calling her Mrs X. My unfaithful husband who I had thought was dead.

'Mrs Cadence – Doctor has sent me to ask if you want to get up or not. Are you all right, Mrs Cadence?'

Edward? It can't be. Why should Doctor send Edward? What sort of doctor would ever be foolish enough to send Edward?

'You've been having a bad dream, that's what it is. Come along now, Mrs Cadence. All over now.'

Leaning over me. Hands on my shoulders. Husband Cadence calling his wife Mrs Cadence, like in the Austin books.

'You've been in bed quite long enough, Mrs Cadence. I'm going to get you up. It's selfishness really, saving me a bedpan. You don't mind, do you?'

Mind? He's gentle, why should I mind?

'Shall you dress yourself, or don't you think it's worth the bother?'

'Dress me. Please dress me.'

'Doctor's been in. I can see that. I wonder what he's been saying.'

'He wasn't unkind. I don't think so ... Was it you who talked about Mrs X or was it he?'

'I told you about her a couple of days ago. How she's suing Sensitape for three years of royalties.'

'Dress me. Please dress me.'

'Stand up then. Help me slide your pyjamas down.'

I'm not ashamed in front of him. I brought him a lot of contentment once. I'd forgotten the feel of his hands on my thighs. Step out of the trousers. Meekly leave him to undo the jacket fastening. He used to like the rituals. Please handle me gently, Edward.

'Arms out, now. That's right ... I'm sure Doctor told you about the damaged tape. I worked it so that it looked like an accident – tipped over the contact fluid. Now he'll have to order a replacement.'

Edward, is there never anything in your mind but work?

'Is there never anything in your mind but work?'

'I'll be able to get a look at the order form. He'll have to order the tape by its proper catalogue number. Then I'll know for certain if last time was only a mistake. Arms up now, and I'll slip your dress over your head for you.'

Try me, Edward. Try me. I won't fail. Throw the dress away. Try me …

'Please try me.'

'Lucky I was able to catch you, Mrs Cadence. Staggering about like that. The change in your routine has upset you more than I realized. Sit down and wrap this around you. My goodness, how you're shivering.'

… shivering. Laid out under the quilt in my hospital dress. Utter depression weighing on my forehead. A sense of uncleanness. I have a vague impression of Nurse being here yet the room appears to be empty. Grey light through the frosted glass of the window – I never ordered frosted glass for the bedroom windows. I never thought how the real world would need to be excluded.

Real world? I never thought how –

Dear God, how the existence, the idea even of Mrs X broods over me, crushes my eyebrows down onto my eyes. Nurse told me yesterday – was it yesterday? – told me Mrs X was suing, told me that nobody could find that contract. I hope she succeeds. She'll be a very rich woman. Her thrills are curling the hair of millions, frigid bitches, wives of unmen, virgins, the unmateably hideous. She deserves it. Her husband would have deserved it too, if his bits had deserved anything other than instant cremation. Cheap bitterness, Thea. But a blood test after the car smash said he must have been seriously drunk. Dr X drunk? Never. He'd been so innocent. So true. Never drunk. And after Sexitape so seriously drunk he died. Bitterness is reasonable. And his name wasn't X, it was Malinder.

'I was wanting to know, Thea, if you thought I should tear up the old contract and give Mrs Malinder a share in Sexitape.'

'I have no opinion. The name alone puts me off. You might have called it something a little more dignified.'

'It buys us dignity, Thea. We have a fine house, universal respect. We get known as benefactors of humanity.'

Sometimes it was hard to tell if Edward wanted to be taken straight or not. He had that in common with many great orators, his dialogue read very badly.

'I shall give her nothing,' he said. 'She's grasping, deceitful, with her brain between her legs. She's everything you are not, Thea.'

I shall give her nothing – thus spake the Lord. He rogered her for the same reason. Tony had been right. Power.

'Thank you for the compliment, Edward.'

'I watch you a lot, my dear. You consistently underestimate yourself. I've always known how much I need you. And the higher we go, the more I'll need you. If a psychiatrist doesn't know his own weaknesses, nobody does.'

I was needed by Tony. Our mutual need built happiness, airy towers, celebration.

The time was four-thirty-four. I wrote it on my data sheet, then took up Tony's wrist to record his pulse. The tape had been running for five minutes and the dials, which had been kind of hyper, were calm. I changed my grip, not able to find his pulse. He had none. I tried once more to be certain. After that I crossed to the tape deck and switched him off.

'What the hell did you do that for?'

'You've killed him,' I said.

The real and the image on the mirrored ceiling were equal. Face up, face down, both pale, surrounded by doubled improbable apparatus, two heads in identical helmets, two white shirts, two known bodies. And two white-coated doctors, head to head, hair almost touching. Edward switched on the searing lights over the couch. He had never looked so tall.

'There's always a measure of risk in these things.' He was calm, his hands busy. 'We knew alien patterns might set up a dangerous period resonance. A moment or two on the cardio-meter and we'll soon get him back again.'

The machine gliding over on its huge castors.

'I've brought you a pick-me-up, Mrs Cadence. I told Doctor how you were. He said, take one of these. He said you were having a difficult time.'

Don't touch me. You make me sick.

'Take this, Mrs Cadence. Yours is only an artificial depression. I know how it feels like – we're made to experience one during Sensitape training. But of course, you know that.'

'Don't touch me.'

'I wasn't going to, my dear. Here are your tablets. Mephelmidone, if you like to know what we're giving you.'

'You talk and talk and talk. We put him on the cardiometer, got his heart working. But –'

'It's supposed to take the patient's mind off things to chat happily. Most patients are too polite to say how irritating it is.'

'For God's sake, Nurse. He was dead. Dead. Killed. Murdered. Tweaking his heart into action with electric shocks wasn't going to help him. Edward injected something. I should have asked him not to.'

'Once a patient of mine died under treatment. You can't help feeling guilty.'

'But this was Tony Stech, Nurse. Tony Stech.'

'I think you're confused, Mrs Cadence. Mr Stech's death was accidental. I read the coroner's verdict.'

How can she be so stupid?

'Of course it was accidental. What would have happened to Sensitape sales if someone had actually died while under? You have to admire Edward's quick thinking – the injection he gave Tony was of a common barbiturate. The cardiometer pumped it around. Do you see now? He was found in his bed at home next morning. Suicide was rumoured but there was no motive, such a successful man, and he hadn't left a note. Accident made more sense. Nothing to do with Sensitape. A simple overdose. He hadn't been sleeping well and he'd miscounted. A tragic accident. So sad.' 'You're suggesting that Dr Cadence murdered his partner?'

Am I? I wish I were.

'I thought so at the time, Nurse. Just for a few seconds.

' "You've murdered him," I said.

'"Murdered him?" he said. "What on earth for?"

'He looked at me, genuinely interested.

' "Because he was your lover?" he said.

'Then he laughed. Not a lot, but he laughed. And I knew he hadn't murdered Tony, and I wished he had. I wished he'd cared enough to.'

'Then you think this was an accident, Mrs Cadence? An accident during some failed experiment?'

'It's ancient history, Nurse. It doesn't matter. Synthajoy. Edward was going to call it Synthajoy. But we can only accept so much joy, Nurse. Tony Stech was given too much. It killed him.'

Poor woman. She's afraid I really am raving.

'It was a beautiful way to go, Nurse. I shouldn't grieve for him.'

I grieve. When my shame allows it, I grieve …

She puts the tablets and the glass of water down on the table. She stands watching me, not knowing if she should smile, if a smile would look nervous. I remember that feeling; easy attitude, mild expression, pulse racing, muscles ready for the attack that so seldom came. And one's mind trying to find something peaceable, totally neutral to say. And at the same time not too idiotic.

'Why don't we make your bed, Mrs Cadence? It looks in an awful mess.'

Good for you. I couldn't have done better.

'All right.' Guarded. Keeping her in suspense. 'All right. I don't mind.'

We strip the bed down to the mattress. Remake it, foam insulator, sheets, overlay, quilt, each smoothed neatly onto the magnetic sides of the mattress. The occupation is supposed to keep my interest while she works out her next move. I enjoy the job, I enjoy doing something after all these weeks. Stoop a few times and I'm short of breath. No use trying to run away in my present condition – I wouldn't make it to the end of the corridor. She's around the other side of the bed watching me, uncertain, kindly. Yet she revolted me for some reason when she first came in. Perhaps I am a little odd after all. She's well-meaning, quite a fine looking woman, managing a difficult situation better than I'd ever have done. And she's concerned for truth even to the extent of risking her job for it.

'Mrs Cadence – your husband said Mr Stech was your lover –'

'That's right. Edward didn't care. He laughed.'

'Was it true?'

A brave question for her to ask. And hard for me to answer.

'True? We loved each other. Which was more important than physical details.'

'And you say Mr Stech died as a result of your husband's experiment.'

Motive enough, which the court failed to find. She's deciding I was guilty.

'It was an accident, Nurse. I couldn't consciously blame, couldn't hate. But I did stop loving him. His coldness did that, his detachment. It wasn't scientific, Nurse, it was insane.'

'And the death was arranged to look like suicide? You didn't mind?'

'You don't understand what he had been to me. I didn't mind anything after that.'

The things we talk about over the beds. Woman talk indeed. She still thinks I was guilty.

'It doesn't matter, you know, Nurse. Court Instructions should be obeyed, guilty or not.'

'Of course.' Too quick. Intellect only. 'Of course they should.' And she goes away to tug at the curtains.

How clear my mind is. I think of Par Bay, where the china clay river in spate pours a white path out across the sea for miles, cutting the clear bay water in two. Without this river, without my treatment, without my shame, the sea is whole, unclouded. I dare see anything. I dare see the day

the day I went to the committal of Rachel Cadence's ashes.

A formality necessary even to the sensible mother of Edward Cadence after the anatomy students had finished with her. Edward of course was indifferent, much too busy, so I went alone. He suggested I take in a show afterwards, in case I was depressed. In case I was depressed.

'Well, Mrs Cadence, I really can't do much until I've seen Doctor's order form for the new tape. We need proof, you see. Otherwise he might say it was just a mistake.'

'Don't bother, Nurse. The verdict was necessary. A national hero shouldn't have a scheming mistress. Much tidier to blame the unbalanced wife, poor thing. A political verdict, Nurse – you'll never be allowed to challenge it.'

'I don't want you to tell me anything, Mrs Cadence. I don't want to challenge anything. If I find an irregularity it is my duty to report it. I know nothing more and I want to know nothing more. Our rule book – it's the one strength we civil servants have.'

She's tidied everything there is to be tidied. She'll be off now to the kitchen. Teatime.

'Teatime, Mrs Cadence. I'll be off now to the kitchen.'

Thank God.

Rachel's ashes were committed at three-thirty in the afternoon. Which is to say that they were given to me in a sort of plastic tobacco jar at the end of a short memorial meeting. The Head of her Statistics Department read a short report on her behalf, someone else explained the great favor she had done the world by giving it her son, and the chief of some surgical department announced to mild applause that already a blind man had been made to see by the gift of her one good eye. Apart from these three gentlemen I was the only member of the general public present. One crematorium official, and the rest of the hall filled with newspapermen. It was the silly season, so somebody told me.

Then they gave me the jar. I smiled at the cameras as I accepted it. On behalf, of course, of my husband, whose duties unfortunately kept him away. His ceaseless service to humanity. I found I was expected to make a short speech, so I made one. I said all the things about my deceased mother-in-law that a Governor's Wife would say. In point of fact I'd hardly seen her in the last seven years. She'd rung up after the public inquiry into Edward's affairs to congratulate him on the satisfactory outcome – in the anxious weeks before she had remained conspicuously silent. She had her position to consider. Her death, of a single catastrophic brain haemorrhage, had been similarly tidy. The reporters taped my speech and in one case it made the front page of the evening edition.

DEATH OF CADENCE MATRIARCH
Mrs Cadence tributes Mrs Cadence.

More applause, then organ music switched on as we went out between the classical pillars of the crematorium. Simple, dignified, and very reasonably priced. The way she had specified. I tried different ways of carrying my tobacco jar – it tended to seem either a trophy or something I was slightly ashamed of. I stood on the crematorium steps and chatted with the dean of the ashes' university department who had known them so much better than I. We posed in the afternoon sun for some colour photographs.

'The bereaved Mrs Cadence, sweetly solemn, wore silver-gray crylene, her lemon-yellow shoes and shoulder bag providing discreet contrast. Lightly made-up, her face held a tranquil sadness. Her hat was a structure of metallic flakes that shimmered like the skin of a snake as she moved her head. The total effect

was forward-looking, the keynote that would surely have pleased the deceased, well-known for her progressive views.'

If things had turned out differently I might even have started a fashion for gray and yellow committals.

As soon as I could get away I hurried to the crematorium Karstak, stuffing the jar into my shoulder bag as I went. I wasn't, as Edward had suggested I might be, in the least depressed. If anything I was cheered – it was one of my days for finding awfulness amusing. But his mention of taking in a show made it perfectly clear that my presence at home that evening was not desired. Mrs X – I preferred calling her that, it made her seem ridiculous – had been taking up more and more of his time in the months since Tony's death. I tried not to intrude on their privacy.

I drove in to Battersea and left the car, Edward's vast Chev-Bentley, in the underground car park there. I walked slowly back across the river, over the new Albert Bridge. I stopped, primitive, in the exact middle, leaned on the rail and looked down into the water. I believe I thought of nothing, just water slipping by in my head. A tug passed underneath, pumiced deck, spirals of white ropes, and a glimpse through a deck-light of engines. Into its wake I dropped the jar of Rachel's ashes. It floated, remaining in sight till my eyes ached with watching it and the silver water danced like anesthesia. I walked on, took a bus into the West End.

The titles of the plays were not encouraging, neither were the photographs outside the theatres. From an agency I learned that stalls were available for that evening in two of them, boxes in another three, no seat at less than thirty-five new pounds. The non-plays being presented in the fringe non-theatres were all booked till the autumn. I could try queueing for a gallery seat if I hurried. I've never belonged to the esoteric group of live theatergoers and on that particular day the prospect of observing them in action for two or three hours repelled me.

Unwilling to go home, I wandered about the gaudy streets at a complete loose end. My cheerfulness ebbed rapidly. On impulse I turned into the Sensitape parlour then on the corner of St Martin's Lane and Long Acre. I had never been in such a place before. I was so ready to be shocked it might well have been a brothel. The tone of the reception area was that of a small private hotel. I picked up a list of the tapes available.

'Good afternoon. You have something in mind perhaps, madam?'

'No. I – er – I just thought I'd see what you've got.'

'A very wide range. All recent tapes. In some parlours the tapes are played to death, you know. We aim to give only the finest definition. All our tapes are replaced after twenty playings.'

This I knew to be nonsense. Except for the special addictive tapes, Sensitape kept full frequency response virtually indefinitely. I looked down the list.

'This is madam's first visit, perhaps?'

'Well …'

'Prices are laid out clearly. The experience lasts from half an hour to forty-five minutes. Replays for seventy percent of the original fee. Both cubicles and private sensing rooms are available. We don't provide group sensing rooms here – we find our customers prefer to pay the small additional fee and enjoy complete privacy. Refreshments can be served after sensing. We are fully licensed and have an arrangement for light meals with the restaurant next door. All experiences are confidential and the superior quality of the equipment is guaranteed.'

I looked at the receptionist, trying to find a person behind it all. Sensi-drunk, to coin a word.

'We're slack at the moment, madam. Perhaps you would like to see a cubicle and a sensing room before making your choice.'

'That would be best. I like to know what I'm letting myself in for.'

A little laugh. In new situations I'm bad at knowing on what level to operate. I followed the receptionist through and was shown a carpeted cubicle eight by four, containing nothing but a couch and a Sensitape machine. The place was air conditioned and had variable intensity lights. It was one of a dozen sound-proofed cubicles arranged around a small central foyer with leather seats and a tiny fountain.

The sensing rooms were on the next floor down. The one I saw was twice the size of a cubicle, and better swept. As well as the couch and the machine there were indoor plants, an aquarium with tropical fish, a table laid out with that week's magazines, and a comfortable chair – in case clients wanted a friend to sit with them. A shower was available as an optional extra. Sweating sometimes took place under the more intense experiences.

I chose the room, but did without the shower. I was not reckoning on one of the more intense experiences.

'You're not a journalist by any chance, are you, madam? We offer special terms to journalists.'

'No. No, I'm afraid I'm not a journalist.'

'Between you and me, madam, that's a bit of a relief. It's dying down now, of course, but at the beginning we did receive a certain amount of adverse publicity. Turning the nation into sensi-slaves – I'm sure you remember the sort of thing. Public opinion was too strong, of course. It's only the reactionary oddballs who are still against us. Only the reactionary oddballs.'

The words seemed to give the receptionist satisfaction. They were repeated several times. The worst thing in the world was to be a reactionary oddball.

I chose a musical tape – Beldik conducting Brahms' second symphony. I remembered Edward's excitement when he finally persuaded Beldik to cooperate. Fifty percent of all royalties it cost us, but the prestige gained was enormous.

The receptionist circuited the record player in, synchronized it with the tape machine and tried to help me into the headset.

'Thank you – I can do it.'

'You've fitted one of these before. I can see that, madam.'

'I'm a nurse, you see.'

The receptionist didn't comment. She took my hat – a hundred and seventy new pounds of it – put it carefully on the table and went out. If I wanted to pretend, in my Vega suit and my Baretti shoes, that I was only a nurse, that was up to me. I started the tape and the record player.

To buy (with money) what Beldik had recorded (for money) was to compound a moral felony. The music lived in him as in a noble palace, echoing down the generations of his sensibility, lit by his intellect, fired by his passion. It didn't matter that the palace was being let out to a thirty bob visitor. It didn't matter that somewhere in the design of the Beldik palace there had to be a flaw. He knew the music's subtlest changes, shared himself with it, loved it as I felt it loved him. Some people say the truth loves them. Without a doubt music loves Klaus Beldik. To experience the tape was to trespass on that love, on that act of love.

I had gone into the parlour expecting to be shocked. By squalid conditions, I suppose. Or by the blank-faced customers staggering out. In the event I saw no customers and found no squalid conditions. But I was shocked nonetheless. I was appalled.

The receptionist tried to press a card into my hand as I passed her, hoped I had had a satisfactory time, suggested that I recommend the place to my friends, offered me a glass of something before I left. As I went out the words were still being voided.

I was too appalled to do anything but get away, stumble away down the road past the theatres and shops. Appalled and angry. I found myself in Trafalgar Square, the sun low, catching rainbows in the huge fountains. All my theoretical objections, my appeals to Edward, were nothing. I talked always about something I had not myself experienced, declaring it in theory to be an evil. In theory. Now the thing had entered my soul and I knew.

Just a reactionary oddball.

I must have made a sad show of myself. I think I ran about staring into people's faces. I talked to some of them, shouting to make myself heard above the fountains and the swirling pigeons and the traffic. Mrs Craig would have loved it. I remember an Indian woman with a little boy who gazed up at Nelson and took no notice of me at all. I told her she should die rather than let her country get this thing. She must go home, implore the politicians to keep it out whatever happened. She was polite to me. I told her it was better to starve than to die of the soul's degradation. She took her little boy's arm and moved politely away.

Just a reactionary oddball.

My loneliness that evening seemed total, terrifying, worse than the worst insanity. I've no idea for how long I stumbled from group to group among the fountains and the litter baskets and the great stone plinths of the lions. The poor mad woman. Somebody really ought to do something for her. And probably I was mad. In the end a policeman came and asked me if I needed any help. He asked for my name and address and said he would arrange for a car to take me home. If he connected my name with the great Dr Cadence he gave no sign.

I was calm by then, but even less balanced. I waited quietly by him while he called up Headquarters. I spoke to him soberly, and said I was sorry I had made such a fool of myself. I knew him as one of the enemy. I remember with great clarity the two of us standing together and talking sensibly about all the foreigners who were in London at this time of year. We were waiting for the police car to come. I asked him if I could go to the lavatory and we crossed the road together to a public convenience. As there were two entrances he positioned himself centrally between them. I left my conspicuous hat in the cubicle and went out in the middle of a group of four other women, my shoes carried in my hand to make myself that much shorter. The crowds were so thick that the policeman never saw me. I hoped the lavatory attendant got the hat – it would have fetched fifty, even secondhand.

In the first shop I came to I bought myself a new suit – a horrible flowered affair that made me look fat and forty – and a new red velvet hat. Then, my bright yellow shoulder bag packed in the parcel with my Vega crylene suit, I went out into the streets a new woman.

London was hellish, the chicken to Sensitape's egg, impossible to tell which had come first. I thought of farmers with their rented Sensitapes, and fishermen, and foresters. There was nowhere I could go to get away. So I decided to take the policeman's advice and go home. I wasn't thinking of Edward then, or of Mrs X. I was thinking of Tony, how glad I was for him to be dead and out of it. I'd avoided his funeral. Dead was dead.

It was his car that reminded me first of Edward. It would. I'd taken a bus along the Embankment and across Chelsea bridge. Then I'd walked through the park to where I'd left the Chev-Bentley. Everything about the huge vehicle reminded me of Edward; it was the sort of machine he so instinctively made his own. I disliked the car and was afraid of it.

The corollary was clear enough.

I thought of the successful, unprotesting body of Mrs X. I thought of how near Edward now was to perfecting Synthajoy, how Tony's death had if you like done no more than show him the way. I'll admit this was the moment when the shameful idea of murder first came into my mind as a serious possibility.

The sun had set and the streets were lit by moon-coloured neon. I set out for Richmond, the accident happening as I was just coming up out of Wandsworth. I've no idea why the accident occurred, for the road was quite deserted, clear in both directions. Suddenly there was a Keep Left sign on an island in front of me and I was driving directly into it. I doubt if I even applied the brakes. The sign approached and steadily entered the front of the car. The windshield crazed over and I suppose there must have been some noise. The car's chassis was built on a principle of graded resistance, so that I was able to scramble out unhurt, reach back in for my parcel and walk slowly away. The pavements were deserted, the shops unmoved, and the flats above the shops. When I looked back after about a hundred yards a motorist coming up the hill had stopped and was climbing out to investigate. I kept on walking. Some time later a police car passed me, going fast. I unpacked my handbag and had a few drinks in a pub. I hadn't eaten since before the committal.

I don't know. Perhaps I had hoped to get away with killing the car instead of its owner. Get away with in relation to my own internal police force, at that moment very active. After the accident I felt calm and eternal. I had several measures of brandy in the pub, watched telly for a bit, and then started walking again. I have no memory of how long I walked, or in what direction. I must have been drunk. The first thing I do remember is feeling tired and hailing a taxi.

I let myself into the house with my latchkey. Mrs X Mrs Malinder Mrs X Mrs Mrs was coming down the stairs. She looked almost beautiful against the fine marble sweep of the staircase. I thought of myself in my fat and forty suit and my bright yellow accessories all wrong.

She sees Mrs Cadence coming toward her across the jewelled hall. She thinks *What a sight, poor thing* and steps graciously to one side, allowing Mrs Cadence room to pass. Against her smooth belly beneath her gown she still feels the pounding, the slap of sweat on sweat. At will she can mock it or find magnificence in it. She moves on down the hall, a piece of paper held unobtrusively in one gloved hand, her handbag in the other. She fetches her stole. The car Edward has bought her is parked just outside. She drives away into the star-shot night.

Mrs Cadence has plodded upstairs in her red velvet hat. She finds her husband naked in his room, shot four times in the chest and quite dead. So Mrs Malinder has done the job for her, she thinks, with a mixture of relief and resentment. The wall safe is open, its contents spilled out onto the floor. She doesn't have to go through the papers to know which one will be missing. She rings for the police from the telephone by the bed, then replaces all the papers in the safe and closes it. Mrs Malinder has style. Mrs Cadence, not to be outdone, determines to achieve the only sort of style now left to her.

'Tea up, Mrs Cadence. Settled down now, have you?'

'How promptly you come, Nurse. Right on cue.'

'That's nice. You mean you were ready for me.'

'I have a little silent film I run through in my head. Or I used to during the trial. Before the treatment started.'

'You're looking better, I must say.'

'They never found the gun, Nurse. She took it away in her handbag. I must have brushed against it as we passed on the stairs.'

'I've told you, Mrs Cadence, I don't want to know anything.'

'I suppose I needed all this, the verdict, the treatment, as a sort of atonement. Which is a shameful joy.'

'I've poured out your tea, Mrs Cadence. Why don't you drink it?'

Which I do. It tastes nasty this time, stronger, but I feel it hit me hard and quick. So that I barely have time to

DAY 31

'I've given your Mrs Craig a few days' leave, Mrs Cadence. You're so much better I think you can perfectly well make your way back to your room on your own.'

The shapes unmerge. They separate and become the treatment room. *My* Mrs Craig? That's an odd one. Still Doctor looks as bland and uncontroversial as ever. He's been giving me my treatment. It was the same treatment but he's right when he says it's made me better. Or, to put it more accurately, I will be better the moment I choose to take on the responsibilities of being better. He's been feeding me the shame again, but my day off has helped me come to terms with it.

'Do you think, Doctor, that I'm better enough for you to tell me what's happening about Sexitape? I understand this Mrs X may sue.'

'The case comes up at the end of the week, Mrs Cadence. Four years' back royalties are being claimed for herself and her late husband. The defense seems to be based on an agreement that can't be found.'

He must really believe I'm better, telling me this.

'I was there when the agreement was signed, Doctor. I witnessed the signatures.'

'But you are in the Kingston, Mrs Cadence. Your testimony will be of little value.'

Thank God for that. I want her to succeed. Success is the greatest punishment. A murderess lives with her crime. I want nothing to happen to her that could possibly count as atonement. Success and more success. How clear everything now is.

'Headset off now, Mrs Cadence. Time you went back to your room and tidied up.'

'You've really given Mrs Craig the day off?'

'Several. She deserves a holiday. I'll drop in myself later on and see how you're doing. May even bring you your tea. Then we could share a cup.'

Mrs Craig's gone. Found out for certain about the tape and said something. I wonder exactly what Doctor's reaction has been. Amusing if she turned up in the room next to mine, undergoing treatment. Not that we'd ever meet, even if she was there.

'Last time we met, Mrs Cadence, you asked me about George Washington's children. I looked it up for you. He married a widow, apparently. They had no children of their own, but he was devoted to hers. Was it his mythical truthfulness that interested you?'

'His letters to his wife. Have you never read his letters to his wife? He managed to be a great man, Doctor, and also a loving husband.'

'I follow your line of thought and arrive at Dr Cadence. You'll remember that I knew him quite well.' Remember? Have I seen you before I came to this place then? 'You probably never guessed at the time how intensely I disliked him. He was neither mad enough to be great nor sane enough to be big.' I don't remember him but I bet this isn't the first time he's said that. 'Dr Cadence was riding for a fall. For a man in his position he had too little charm. In many ways it's a good thing he died when he did. The pioneering work is done. At least he's in the Abbey now.'

'This isn't the hospital common room, Doctor. You're talking to his wife.'

And what about Synthajoy? Is the world never to have Synthajoy?

'On your feet now, Mrs Cadence. That's right … There's no harm in giving you an outside point of view. It's often helpful.'

'And what about Synthajoy? Don't you really think it's a good thing he died with that uncompleted?'

'It's a word I'm not familiar with, Mrs Cadence.'

Thank God for that. I wonder if I do remember him. Or why I should so definitely have forgotten him.

'Remind me, Doctor' – on my way to the door – 'remind me when we met.'

'I imagine you were too much in love to notice. I was at a conference on the final design stages of the Kingston. Mr Stech was there as well.'

'I remember you perfectly.' I do too. 'Your name is … Harvey. With an "a". '

The doors of the treatment room slap shut behind me. I see the Kingston's conference table, and my own hands gathering folds of curtain stuff. There's a clip of chair designs I've just passed around, and samples of carpeting. Tony watches me across the table. And Dr Harvey, unmemorable except for his awareness of us which I disregard. He talks about … he talks about colours, full of new Japanese theory of wavelength significance in the treatment of mental disorders.

'Do you want help along to your room after all, Mrs Cadence? Or were you just thinking?'

'Just remembering, Dr Harvey. It's a long time ago.'

'It must seem so.' Watching me as I walk away to my room. 'All of three years.'

After the meeting Edward stayed on. He always left me to go home with Tony. I know he assumed we were sleeping together. In fact, more than a year after that morning in Richmond, I still hadn't risked it. We'd never even talked about it, Tony and I – his attitude was nonmedical, instinctive, tender. I believed that when the time was right my body would be right also.

That afternoon I suddenly knew the time *was* right.

We drove back into London in Tony's car. To him cars were antagonists, needing to be placated. He hadn't yet moved to the Boltons, and we went to the laboratory he rented, with the three rooms over. When we arrived his assistant had been turning a tiny nylon insulator and was busy collecting up the swarf. Tony told him to pack up, take the rest of the day off. I smiled bravely. Whether accurate or not, the three of us knew what that implied. Tony and me standing together, within an almost tangible aura of sexuality. The assistant dusted off his coat, hung it by the door and went away. Tony turned the key in the lock behind him. By now I was over by the foot of the stairs and he threaded his way between the benches and the stacks of equipment till he reached me. He switched off the lights. We were left with daylight, grey and full of shadows. London in November.

'You're a lovely Goy,' he said.

'And you're' – grasping the nettle – 'a lovely circumcised Jew.'

'Any objections?'

'Not if you haven't.'

We went upstairs to the bedroom. And I must must must remember.

I remember he kept up a soft flow of talk, telling me how he loved me, what it was of me he loved, the years when he'd had to keep his love hidden. I remember how even around our kissing he made gentle nonsense noises. He seemed to think I would be afraid, and for reasons he didn't know about perhaps I should have been. But I was safe with him, and confident. He left me for a moment to go and draw the curtains. He thought I would be afraid of the light. Even the movement of his arm was an exquisite pain, his shoulder muscles, the creases of his shirt, his strong legs. I was safe with him, needing him. We undressed solemnly, like children, and lay together on top of the bed.

I have to remember his hands on my breasts, mine touching the strange scars of his circumcision. Kissing me, legs over mine, his weight pressing me down. And, oh God, my stomach knotting, bitterness in my mouth, face wrenched away, the labour of getting his body off mine, heaving, stumbling, hurrying to kneel by the lavatory pan. I tried to kick the door shut behind me, but he came in and knelt by my side. I wanted him never to see me again. I wanted to hide from him, from the whole world. And I wanted him never to leave me.

We knelt naked, side by side in front of the lavatory with its tipped-up seat. He stroked my hair, and when the retching had stopped he kissed my teary cheeks and my eyes. His softness was beautiful, if nothing else was.

'I didn't know,' over and over, 'I didn't know what it had done to you.'

I flushed the pan and we stood up. He wiped my lips very earnestly. I hid my face in the hollow of his shoulder, smooth and smelling of skin.

'I didn't know, my darling. I didn't know …'

I rinsed out my mouth, tried not to look at myself in the mirror. I caught sight of his expression as he stood behind me, compassion and love. He suggested some brandy, was going for some into the tiny sitting room. I caught hold of his hand as he passed.

'No, Thea, there's no need … I didn't know, darling. I didn't understand.'

'Come back to bed, Tony.'

'No, my love. I shouldn't have made you go through that. I should have known.'

'Please, Tony. Please come.'

My shivering stopped quickly under the bedclothes. He was there for me, timelessly and complete, my lover, companion, dearest friend. A guide to cleave to in the darkest storm. It wasn't patience, it wasn't pity. It wasn't watchful, considered, doing its sums. I have to say this – it was love. It was at the same time simple and infinitely complex. It was happiness.

Together, there, that evening, Tony and I defeated all that Edward, the essential Edward, had done to me.

And now Tony's dead.

Doctor Harvey has said I should tidy my room. It doesn't look too bad. Just straighten the bed, fold my pyjamas, jerk the curtains out of respect to Nurse's memory. Observe a minute's silence even.

Yesterday's withdrawal of the treatment (for which I can thank her alone) has changed my life. As has the sense she gave me of not being alone. No longer them and me, the sane realism of them and us. An acceptance of myself. After thirty days in here I can look at the extent of my injuries, and the way Tony loved me in spite of them. Thirty days lost before I could again examine the circumstances of Edward's murder.

And thirty-one days before I could wonder at my perversity in concealing them. Had I needed, demanded, enjoyed my suffering? And for what squalid reason? There's nothing more tedious, more corrosive than shame, wallowed-in shame, vainglorious. Oh God, how boring I am.

I promise not to wave my stump ever again.

You know, I've decided my hair's a mannerism, a cliché like going mad in white linen. Fancy Mrs Craig putting up with it. I must see about getting it done – perfectly possible to have a hairdresser come to the Kingston. A new face. It's not as if I were poor … A new face. I'm an urban creature, I love remote faces, faces distanced by the danger of their numbers. The countryside I stare at out of car windows. I perch precariously on blades of grass, sensible of my daring. I love townscapes that don't ask anything of me, and faces.

Yes, I shall order a hairdresser. It's in the regulations. And it's not as if I were poor. In fact, I'm very rich. I'm the Sensitape heiress.

'Do you know something, Doctor? Make me contrite and I'm the Sensi-tape heiress.'

'Quite right, Mrs Cadence. The head of a great company. A position with advantages and responsibilities.'

'Don't be so pompous, Doctor.' Put the tea-tray down, man. Don't just stand there with it. 'If I choose, the advantages can be mine and the responsibilities all left to the Board.'

'I doubt if that will be your way. Tea on the table here, is it?'

He talks as if he believes I'm going to get out of here. 'I think you ought to know, Doctor, that yesterday's missed treatment has made a lot of difference.'

'It has?'

'It's let out a lot of things you were hoping to block.'

'Milk and sugar?'

'How English of you, using tea to hide behind. Yes, it's allowed me to remember about love.'

'I've brought two cups. You don't mind if I serve myself?'

Social chitchat? Doctor Harvey must must be trying to establish a new relationship. At least the tea can't be drugged. Is he afraid of me now?

'I want to tell you the truth about the murder. Something I've told nobody.'

'That would certainly be a help, Mrs Cadence.'

He's retreating already. Behind a polite interest, behind professionalism. He's come to do my hair really. Shame is not contrition but maybe shame will do.

I tell him the story of the film. It's easier that way.

'"She sees Mrs Cadence coming toward her up the gleaming staircase. (That's me – I'm Mrs Cadence.) She thinks *What a sight, poor thing* (which is fair enough) and steps graciously to one side, allowing Mrs Cadence room to pass. Against her smooth belly beneath her gown she still feels the pounding, the slap of sweat on sweat. At will she can despise it or find magnificence in it." You're following me?'

'You ought to have been a writer, Mrs Cadence.'

'"She moves on down the stairs, a piece of paper held unobtrusively in one gloved hand, her handbag in the other. She fetches her stole. The car Edward had bought her is just outside. She drives away into the star-shot night."'

'Flowery. But I know what you mean.'

'Do you know what the piece of paper is, Doctor?'

'Please go on. I'm sure it all comes clear in the end.'

'"Mrs Cadence has plodded upstairs in her red velvet hat. (She bought the hat as part of her disguise after escaping from the policeman.) She finds her husband naked in his room, shot four times in the chest and quite dead. (That's Dr Cadence, of course.) So Mrs Malinder has done the job for her, she thinks, with a mixture of relief and resentment. The wall safe is open, its contents spilled out onto the floor. She doesn't have to go through the papers to know which one will be missing."'

'Ah. Now I see.'

He's not believing me. I only tell it this way to make it possible. But the truth is inconvenient, so obviously he draws back from it.

'"She rings for the police from the telephone by the bed, then replaces all the papers in the safe and closes it. Mrs Malinder has style. Mrs Cadence, not to be outdone, determines to achieve the only sort of style now left to her."'

'Mrs Malinder?'

'You know who she is, Doctor. You must.'

He drinks his tea, demonstrating his steady hand. My hand is going like a sex vibrator. How capable some men are of calculation.

'Why have you told me this, Mrs Cadence?'

'I've only just been allowed to remember it.'

'Not an answer. Why have you told me this?'

'Nurse. Mrs Craig. She will ...' What was I going to say? 'She believes in me.'

'We all believe in you. As we do in Nelson's Column.'

Always barriers. It's word-play time again. He may have told the truth about Mrs Craig's day off. Why did I mention her? Now I'm stuck with not giving her away.

'I've always thought of Mrs Craig as an ... ally, Doctor. A friend. She's helped me a lot in these last few days.'

'Mrs Craig is a very good nurse. She does what she's told.'

Dropping away under me.

'Procedures at the Kingston have changed. We've become more efficient. Rather more efficient.'

Dropping away.

An impression of the room running down the room like wax. Dropping away fast. And myself left impossibly high and alone on a singing pinnacle, wind in my ears, the countries of the room running out below me.

Doctor is down there, far away and small and shouting. His words arrive tiny and clear.

'This Mrs Malinder – as she passed you on the stairs, didn't she say anything to you?'

'To me?'

As tiny as he, as far away from my mind.

'A bit melodramatic, this sibylline silence as you pass.'

'She said

She said we really ought to have got together ages ago. She called me "my dear."'

An outrageous thing. Why should I ever have got together with her?

'What then? What did you say?'

'I said nothing. She looked surprised. She said he'd told her I was being quite civilised. Civilised. She said she hoped we weren't going to have a sordid quarrel.'

'And did you have a sordid quarrel?'

'Certainly not. I told her the word civilised held different meanings for different people. Then I went on up.'

'You swept by.'

A duologue from which I can keep myself separate. Just word play, meaning very little.

'The stairs are very elegant. They demanded it. She called after me. She said, "He's in his room. I shouldn't go in there." She's an Australian, you know. But not very. I paused. "Why shouldn't I?" She turned and went on down. She closed the outside door after herself very quietly.'

'No stole?'

'Stole? Certainly there was a stole. I'm sorry if I left it out.'

'And no piece of paper?'

'She had a chic little handbag.'

'And you went up to your husband in spite of what she said.'

'He was on the bed in his room, quite naked. I've never seen anything as disgusting as his condition in all my life. And me a nurse.'

'And you a nurse.'

'He was just as she'd left him.'

'The comforts of central heating.'

'He was just as she'd left him.'

'So you shot him.'

'He was just as she'd left him.'

'Spent.'

His tiny face smiles, and his tiny words curve up and drop into my hands like pebbles.

'He opened his eyes and saw me and didn't move. Didn't care. The safe was untouched. His crumpled foreskin crept with life of its own. He was sleepy and contented. He said, "My God, Thea, we're selling a million of that every month. And believe me, we're giving good value."'

'And you shot him.'

'I mightn't have. He said, "Don't look at me like that, Thea. It's not my fault her husband got killed in a car smash." He meant that otherwise he wouldn't have had his fun with her.'

'He resented your frigidity so you shot him.'

'He said that. He said, "No use being pi, Thea. Tony served you well and often before he died."'

He shouldn't have said that. I'd forgotten. I wonder where my treatment found it.

'And so you shot him.'

That's why I'm so ashamed. So ashamed.

'I'd wrecked Edward's car, Doctor, but I never told him ... The gun he had bought after Bunk and Pheeney, he kept it in the drawer by his bed. I took it out of the drawer and he said, "You're not going to shoot me with that thing," and I did.'

'Because of Tony.'

Please let me stop now. The pinnacle has melted away. He was so dead. To shoot a naked man makes holes you can see. They were hard to bear, hard to keep away from. I'd seen plenty of dead people, but now with the blood I was seeing Thea Cadence dead. Please let me stop now. Please.

'Because of Tony.' Who is this relentless Doctor Harvey?

Or find me my pinnacle again.

'Because of Tony.'

'Because of everything. Can't you see that? Because of the committal, because of Sensitape, because of the receptionist, because of Mrs Malinder, because he'd never loved me –'

'Because of Tony.'

'If you like.'

No, that's not true. Not even if I'd like.

'I killed him because I hated him. And I hated him because I hated myself.'

'Oh, the melodrama.'

'It's true.'

Or not. Or maybe.

Alternatively I got the taxi man to leave me at the edge of Kew Green. His driving had suggested that he was eager to get rid of me. The street lights on the green were dim and far apart but the moon was bright. Edward's house was eighth along on the left, and in darkness, but as I opened its wrought-iron garden gate a light came on inside the interior reception area, shining out through the semi-circular fanlight above the door. I stepped quickly forward, into the shadows cast by the porch, close beside the house. The door latch clicked minutely. It was the vilest of coincidences. At this time of night the only person who could possibly be leaving Edward's house was Mrs Malinder.

She opened the door, paused in the porch, presumably for her eyes to adjust to the darkness, then closed the door, went down the three stone steps and along the path to the gate, which I had left open. I remember that clearly. She'd left the light in the reception area burning. A proprietary gesture? I'd soon be back from my show and I'd know that she'd been there? Why bother? Equally, why had I hidden? What had been the point?

Her car was clearly quite close. I listened as she reached it, got in, and drove away. She may have been wearing a stole but I never saw it. When the night was silent again I got my house key out of my handbag and went inside. The staircase was indeed elegant.

Doctor Harvey empties his teacup and puts it back on the tray. He hopes he is godlike. It's terrible to come back now to how much the muscles of my face and throat ache from crying. And degrading to have to get up from my knees on the floor.

He's too tactful to help me. Too tactful even to notice.

'We'll have you out of here in no time at all now, Mrs Cadence. A day or two on the contrition tape and you'll be as right as rain. I'll get Mrs Craig to fix it. We'll give you a spell before your rest.'

Spell. What an apt word.

'Isn't it Mrs Craig's day off, Doctor?'

'Only in a manner of speaking.'

'Establish an ally and then withhold her?'

'I was afraid with your training that you might have guessed. Every smallest detail of your stay here has been intentional. But you know that now.'

I hear the tigers and the crocodiles roaring. Crocodiles must roar, or Tony wouldn't have said they did. All you read about is the musky smell. Or is it musty?

'She says you were very hard to get through to. It's a rare quality. You have a very strong mind, Mrs Cadence.'

'She told me she was my friend.'

'But, Mrs Cadence, she was – she still is – your ...'

'All right. Please don't say it. We all operate within a framework, and within her framework she is my friend. What my framework needs is a framework inside it. A cage, Tony called it. Far enough inside, and you're outside. Or does that sound too tricky?'

I play with words as Doctor Harvey does. And for the same reasons.

'How many of the things you've told me are true, Doctor? What, for example, about Mrs Malinder suing Sensitape?'

'Perfectly true. The case comes up at the end of the week.'

'I'm the only person who knows about the agreement. Will I be able to give evidence?'

'Doubtful. Your release from the Kingston needs three expert opinions. And that takes time. Why not pay her off? I'm sure the firm can well afford it.'

I'm damned if I will. Cheap little gold-digger. To connive at her success would be perverted.

'I destroyed the agreement myself, Doctor. Like the disposable gun, down the kitchen garbage unit. I made Mrs X so guilty that I even believed in it myself. You don't want to know me.'

'And then you simultaneously protected her and became heroic.'

There's a word for you. *Heroic*. Poor Mrs X.

Edward. *Sherry for you both?*
(The glasses clink.)
The first thing I suppose I ought to do is congratulate you on the results of all your preliminary auditions. As I'm sure you've been told, they were quite outstanding.

Mrs X. *It's how we were made, Dr Cadence. We fitted, right from the very first time.*

Edward. *It places you two in a very responsible position, Mrs X. No doubt you realize this … I have an agreement here for you both to sign.*
(Rustle of Agreement.)
Briefly, it establishes that the patent in this method of recording psycho-electric brain waves for the purpose of subsequent play-back …

Dr. X. *Where do we sign?*

Edward. *Before you sign anything I want you to be absolutely certain that what you're doing is right … If you want to consult a solicitor before signing I shall quite understand.*

Dr. X. *I told you, we want nothing out of it. If ever anything wasn't right it would for us to take money for an opportunity like this.*

Mrs X. *Prostitution. That's what it would be.*

Poor righteous Mrs X. Doctor stands up.

'Well, well, well. I must go and see about laying on some contrition. Hardly more than a formality, of course. Also I must tell Mrs Craig the good news. She'll be so pleased.'

He goes to the door.

I shall call him back. I need to tell him that it doesn't matter if poor righteous Mrs X somehow gets her hands on the actual contract. It speaks specifically of Sensitape 57 – it's probably where it's always been, stored in my office safe here at the Kingston, along with the audio tape – and it's worthless to her. The money-earning Sexitape trademark name came months later and Edward registered it separately. And Mr Siemens tells me that once my contrition is legally established I will be allowed to benefit from my crime. Furthermore, in addition to that, I'm sure I can piece together enough from Edward's notes, and Tony's, to complete the development of Synthajoy. Imagine the fun. Synthajoy and I, the two of us, dancing together, hand in hand.

I shall annihilate righteous Mrs X and then, out of the goodness of my heart, I'll give her half a million new pounds as a comforter, which she will take because she's only human.

And so am I. You don't want to know me.

THE STEEL CROCODILE

ONE

Gryphon turned on the high-frequency jammer. Before being taken over by the university, his office had been used by an insurance company, and therefore had been fully wired. Gryphon had ripped out the equipment as soon as he'd moved in, and bought himself a bug jammer. It stood on his desk now, neither obtrusive nor in any way concealed. Matthew recognized it from the advertisements, and also because it was the model recommended in the previous month's bulletin from the Civil Liberties Committee. Matthew wasn't himself a member of the C.L.C., but he was on their mailing list on account of his work.

'Were you followed on your way here?' Matthew nodded. 'So?'

'So I did what you said.' Matthew felt grubby. He'd never had a tail before. He was a sociologist, an ethnologist, not an alienee. Not that he had anything against alienees – some of his best friends were ... But if working at the Colindale meant that he was no longer to be trusted, then he'd refuse the job while there was still time.

'It worked?'

'Not at first. I didn't believe in your radio homer, so I did a lot of running up and down stairs and hiding in doorways. I might have saved my energy.'

'Where was it?'

'In my coat collar. Silly little thing on a pin. I expect it was stuck there while I was in the washroom at the Ministry.'

'They must have thought you very innocent, Matthew. They have much craftier ways with the old hands.'

'Innocent? Don't you mean naïve?'

Of course he was naïve. He needed naïveté in his work; it helped him to remain outside, separate from the problems he studied. Abigail didn't agree with him, of course – her tutor had preached total commitment, the discovery of truths-from-within: far truer truths, Abigail said, than his overall ones. Abigail ... even to remember her name comforted him. He wished she were with him at that moment. He functioned so much better with her around.

'And this pin,' Gryphon was saying. 'When you found it, did you do what I suggested?'

'I did not. What about the feelings of the next man – being followed all across London for no reason at all?'

'He'd probably be used to it. Most people are.'

'It's all wrong, Gryphon. The very fact of being followed – it made me feel guilty at once.'

'Isn't that one of the points? Besides, with my letter in your pocket they'd have said you *were* guilty.'

'That's what I mean. I'd rather you left me out.'

Gryphon's room was cool, with reversible wall panels in green and black, white bookshelves and racks for microfilm. The picture on the back wall was responding to the harsh city sunlight with a range of metallic yellows and grays. The window overlooked St Paul's, the dome below them sharply striped with the shadow of the narrow Senate House. The University had come there as part of the European Save-the-Cities campaign, populating the voided towers with thirty thousand undergraduates. Matthew looked down at them, not ant-like, too still, too controlled by their fear and by an awareness of its potential. He wondered irrelevantly if Paul, Abigail's brother, was among them. He remembered his own College years, his and Gryphon's, in the days before the students had really tried their strength. Even then he had avoided the tear gas and the batons, and so had Gryphon. They had pretended to be apolitical, too absorbed in their studies. Perhaps they had been wise beyond their age after all.

'Well?' said Gryphon. 'What did you do with it then?'

'The pin? I'd gone into a gents to search for it, so I flushed it down the pan.' Matthew shivered. 'There you are. Being watched. Scuttling. Hiding in lavatories. Looking for electronic pins. It's ridiculous – and slightly disgusting.'

'I wonder what its range was. Amusing if your tail is running after it along the course of some sewer.'

Gryphon wasn't answering him. Matthew turned back from the window.

'You're not answering me.'

'Don't let's be too naïve. You're here, therefore –'

'I'm here to tell you I've decided to turn down the job at the Colindale Institute.'

'You made that decision thirty seconds ago. I watched you make it.'

Always so right. Always the harder, clearer mind. So why stil a junior lecturer? Matthew, on the other hand, had been consultant on half a dozen major resettlements, was author of as many books, retained by three of the nine industrial giants … It seemed an impressive record.

'And I hope to watch you unmake it.' Gryphon pinched the bridge of his nose as if he still wore glasses. 'Why did you come, Matthew? And why did you throw your tail as I asked you to?'

'It's the moral duty of' – Gryphon was laughing at him but he battled on – 'of everybody to make tailing as difficult as possible. Or we'd be back where evasion on its own was proof of guilt. And you know how the Public Prosecutor –'

'That battle's been won, Matthew. We can thank the student body for that, if not much else.' He sorted through his papers and found a booklet which Matthew recognized: *Physical Surveillance and the Free Citizen*, issued by the C.L.C. 'There's another one coming out next week on Audio Surveillance,' Gryphon said, 'and there's nothing the Public Prosecutor can do about it. The citizen has a right to protect himself. I want you to become a spy, Matthew.'

No pause, no change of tone. Was it a compliment, considering him too intelligent to be softened up first? Or an insult, knowing him too stupid to need any finesse at all ...? Gryphon wasn't smiling.

'Matthew, I want you to accept the job at the Colindale Institute, and I want you to tell me what work is really being done there.'

'You want me in jail for life?'

'Reformative custody ... and it might be worth it' – Gryphon sounded tired – 'if you got the information out to me first.'

Matthew wondered what Gryphon's first name was. Five years at University, twelve years since, and he was still Gryphon. Matthew decided it was a mannerism, and became irritated.

'Your paranoia shows, Gryphon. That's why you're still a junior lecturer.'

'Your wife, Matthew, is a remarkable woman.'

It was a remark that Matthew couldn't resent, for its implication was correct. He had never spoken like that to Gryphon before in his life, and he should have. Abigail was making him grow up.

'She'll agree with me about the Colindale. Surveillance, distrust, secrecy ... there's plenty of useful work I can do without all that. If being head of the Social Study Department means being watched and having my letters monitored, then I don't want it.'

'You could write in code. There are plenty of good coders on the market.'

Gryphon wasn't missing his point. Indeed, he was making it even more forcibly.

'I don't need the money.'

'None of us does. We're vocationalists – sorry, dirty word.'

'And I'm not interested in the status.'

'You are, but not very. Probably not enough.'

'So I shall find another job. Take some time off even. Cultivate my own garden. Abigail would like that.'

They had a cottage in Wales. Abigail would like that. Their chance to discover if their better life was no more than a Thoreau fantasy. Gryphon sighed.

'When I heard they'd offered you a job at the Colindale I thought they'd made a mistake. I still do.' He was rolling a microfilm to and fro on his desk, watching it closely. 'Their first, their only mistake in a very long time. Which is why we must, must, must take advantage of it.'

'We?'

'You and I. This isn't a C.L.C. matter. Far too indefinite. I need first-hand evidence before I can put it to the Committee.'

'I'm not a member.'

'Nobody ever is.'

'But I'm really not.'

Matthew knew he was being willed to involve himself, to ask the question. Once he did so he was past halfway to accepting the answer, accepting its intellectual necessity. Gryphon wouldn't be bothering otherwise. A cloud covered the sun, and the picture on the back wall shifted to orange and blue.

'You'll have to tell me what's going on.' Done for. 'After all, what possible erosion could come from the Colindale? It's one of the most enlightened projects ever thought of.'

'I look for pattern, Matthew, and when I don't find one I get suspicious. You believe in pattern, and so do I. It's possible, of course, that my sample just isn't big enough.'

'Computers?'

'I've tried, of course. Not even remote associations emerge. Nothing. Just a list of isolated facts.'

'Tell me.' Putting himself up to his neck, and beyond.

Gryphon clipped the microfilm into his desk viewer. It contained a list of names, with symbols beside each. He spun the reel, letters flicking shapelessly by. The striking of the Cathedral clock passed unnoticed.

'Ten thousand students over the last four years', Gryphon said, 'analyzed by age, sex, race, income, political, religious and integrative criteria. The four years of the Colindale Institute. Ten thousand examination results, ten thousand theses, ten thousand decisions on further education, ten thousand first year grant appropriations, ten thousand second year appropriations. And no pattern.' He spun the reel back again. 'Examination results, thesis subject, social relevance, political bias, even sex – nothing makes a discernible pattern.' He stopped the reel, enlarged a single name, translated the code for Matthew. 'Danderson, female, twenty-three, unmarried, Nordic, fifth degree affluent, Communist, Buddhist, integrative index 01. Examination results, par for her year, disappointing on previous record. Thesis subject, virus caging in the S.17 group. Rating, 90 – that's very good. Further education, naturally. First year appropriation, five hundred marks. Second year appropriation, nil.' He sat back. 'Which makes Miss. Danderson an excellent example of what is worrying me.'

Matthew stared at the row of Astran coordinates. In view of the rating, five hundred a year was niggardly. And why the sudden cutoff?

'Any explanation given? Subject duplication?'

'I expect so. It's a usual one. No way of checking, of course.'

'What makes you think the decision came from the Colindale? Why not the Appropriations Board?'

'The Board exists on a political basis. A sample as big as this ought to reflect that fact, even allowing for overcompensations.'

'So you want me to find out why Miss Danderson was discouraged.'

'And four thousand like her, Matthew. A forty percent cutoff, and no pattern.'

Matthew frowned. To make the issue one of academic freedom was unfair, attacking him where he was least protected.

'I gather your figures deal only with the physical sciences.'

'Three months' work. Not possible to include Arts or Social Sciences, even if the information were available to me. But I'm confident from what members of the staff have told me that there's the same lack of pattern.'

Of course there was a pattern. There must be. Group decisions threw up patterns. A lot depended on the subtlety of the scanning.

'I've been using the Friedmann 5000,' Gryphon said. 'Loops, parallel scanning, the lot.'

'I still don't see why you think the decisions are originating in the Colindale.'

'Perhaps they don't. Perhaps it's just coincidence that the pre-Colindale appropriations were quite childishly predictable ... Somebody has to make the decisions, Matthew. Whether they are right or wrong depends on the criteria.'

'And you want me to find out the criteria as well.'

'You'll probably be working on them.'

Gryphon was a member of the central C.L.C. – Matthew knew this and had always tried not to know it. Not to act upon such knowledge was an explicit admission of approval. And Matthew neither approved nor disapproved. He was a sociologist. He hunched his shoulders against the choices being forced on him.

'If we decide to use anything you tell us, Matthew, the leak will immediately become obvious. You'll be the first one to come under suspicion.'

'You're only saying that to make the whole thing a point of honor to me.'

'Intellectual honor.'

At first Matthew had been keen to go to the Colindale. It was a considerable honor to have been invited there. The computer resources of the Institute had been set up to coordinate and interrelate research findings throughout the whole European Community. By pooling the scientific resources of the member nations it minimized waste and moved competition out onto the larger, inter-powerbloc scale. Also it made its data stores and cross-referencing capability available to thousands of universities, research groups, and individual scientists. In the terms of its charter it was not a decision-making organization. If it was being used as such, then people should be told. Centers of power needed watching.

'I must talk it over with Abigail.'

'I wouldn't. She'll only push you even further than you want to go.' Gryphon paused. 'One other thing. I hear there are other people interested in the Colindale. People even less constitutional than we. I should like us to get in first, simply as a matter of saving lives.'

'Other people?'

'A group. Bombs, guns, the usual paraphernalia of militancy. So don't dawdle, there's a good fellow.'

Abigail was in the garden. A city garden, a Kensington garden, not a very large garden, not even very beautiful. Nevertheless, only money brought such things. The garden was money. Claiming to be uninterested in money, Matthew stood at the top of the iron steps down to the lawn and watched his wife playing with the cat. The sunlight made her dress very yellow against the green grass. The room behind him was high and cool, with elegant plaster work and old-fashioned calm. Had the day-long leisure of the pre-industrial rich really been as desperate as people said today, perhaps in order to excuse their present desperation?

Abigail existed to disprove them all. She was not in the least afraid of inactivity, of the small preoccupation, and she felt no moral qualms. She was filled by whatever she did. Now, playing with the cat, she shared its rightness, its energy, its precise adjustments ... He went down the staircase to her, his hand trailing in the honeysuckle that had grown up around the cast-iron supports of the rail.

'Tell me what you think of Gryphon,' he said.

'Come and sit down and get grass stains on your trousers.'

The cat crouched, glaring at Matthew's feet as they approached, then was off through the bushes and over the wall.

'You're very beautiful this evening.'

'So are you.'

She looked up at him and he kissed her, stooping, his hands on her breasts.

'No –'

'Whyever not?'

Her bright brown eyes looked up over his shoulder, at the upstairs windows of the house next door, just showing above the garden wall. He moved his hands up and held the curves of her skull in them, containing her thoughts in them, her mind.

'You once said you'd gladly keep house for me in a bus shelter even.'

'So I would.'

'Fat lot of cuddling we'd get in a bus shelter.'

But he loved her unfashionable modesty.

She was silent. He knew, not through his fingers, that her thoughts were on the material wealth surrounding them. She disliked it, used it, disliked herself for using it, enjoyed it, feared it so that sometimes it almost stood between them. They'd never come anywhere near to the bus shelter, the shack that she obscurely felt would have ennobled them, and she blamed him for this easy success, this cheerful failure to be poor. A Roman Catholic, her attitudes were strangely puritanical. Yet she knew about poverty. All her life till she had met him she had been poor. He moved his fingers through her hair, close against the hard white bone.

'I love you more than yesterday,' he said.

They lay on the grass, just their hands touching. The sun was lowering, and Matthew half-dosed his eyes against its brilliance on the white stucco of the house behind them. There was a recent cherry tree, its stippled, shining bark exuding reddish anemones of resin. The garden itself was old and tired, with dusty figs growing against the south wall, nectarines, and a pear tree long barren. The woodwork of the greenhouse sagged: if Matthew repaired it technology would dictate extruded aluminum and anti-filter sheeting. So he left the dulled white paint to gather mold, and the glass to cloud over. The garden might have been claustrophobic, preserved falsely, feeding on itself. Instead it formed a starting point and a safe return.

'I'm taking the Colindale job. It'll mean moving house in a few days.'

'Is that all it'll mean?' She leaned up on one elbow. 'The work sounds so abstract. Your hold on reality is flimsy enough at the best of times.'

'Plenty of studies have been done on closed academic communities. I'm sure they'll be watching out.'

'I feel uneasy, Matthew. That's all.'

'Besides, it looks as if I shall be having a strong outside interest.' He stood up. 'Let's go indoors so that I can kiss you.'

They went up the curving staircase and in at the French windows. He kissed her. They stood together for so long that their shadow had time to move on the soft carpet within the room. He told her about what Gryphon had asked him to do. He repeated the question he had asked earlier.

'Tell me what you think of Gryphon.'

'I'd rather tell him to his face. He's a bore.' She smiled. 'I suppose what I have most against him are the short cuts in his conversation. The more right they are, the more insulting. People should be allowed to progress at their own tempo.'

'That's funny. I find his assumptions of my intelligence flattering.'

'They're not meant to be. He only makes them to prove how even more intelligent he himself must be.'

'That's very uncharitable of you, love.'

'He's arrogant, Matthew. I can't stand arrogance.' She turned away from him. He thought how small she looked. 'But you must do what he wants you to.'

'If I'm found out it'll finish me.'

'Good.' She turned back to him. 'Finish you for what? For all this?' She indicated the room, the garden, the town car, the long-haul car, the holidays, the space. 'For all this?'

'It might mean jail.'

'I'd wait for you.'

'You romanticize.'

'God loves me. We're never tested beyond our strength.'

Matthew thought of the millions in mental hospitals. God loved them too. Unfathomably.

'I'll take you out to see our new house in the morning,' he said.

She walked away, went downstairs to prepare his dinner. It wasn't that he needed to guard her faith. Years ago he'd lost the conceit that it depended on his protection, on the things he said or left unsaid. It existed in spite of, or perhaps because of … The front doorbell rang and he went to see who was there.

'Police.' Two men in slacks and bright shirts. 'We're looking for a Dr Oliver. Matthew Oliver.'

Matthew was wary. 'I am he,' he said.

'Will you hear that?' said the fatter of the two men. 'The verb *to be* governing the dear old nominative after all these years.'

'You wanted to speak to me?'

'Detective Inspector Kahn, that's I. Sergeant Wilson, that's he too. I reckon.'

Matthew had obviously started badly. The guilt he already felt had made for a bad beginning. He tried to do better.

'Please come in, Inspector.'

'That's nice. If you don't ask, we push – so where are you?'

The two policemen entered. They stared at the staircase curving up under a glass cupola. Matthew knew he should ask them for their identification warrants. He wanted to avoid being difficult.

'They tell me you write books. Get all this writing books?'

'It helps.' He refused to sound apologetic. 'I also work for a government planning agency. And for one or two business corporations.'

'The man, Sergeant Wilson, is a vocationalist. Holy, holy …'

'Perhaps he can't help it.'

They walked, trailing Matthew, through into the living room. Kahn lit a cigarette and threw the match on the carpet.

'Name of Edmund Gryphon mean anything to you?'

'I know him very well. We were at College together.'

'You were at College with ten thousand, but you know Edmund Gryphon.'

'We shared a room. We had a lot in common.'

'Had ...?'

'Have. We still have a lot in common.'

'You said *had*.'

'He's a physicist. We work in different fields. I haven't seen so much of him latety.'

'Then have you a lot in common or haven't you?'

'We think with similar techniques.' He was pleased to have avoided saying they thought in similar ways. Words could be dangerous. 'It's a question of minds, Inspector.'

'Which I wouldn't know about.'

Matthew decided he was wasting his time. 'What's Dr Gryphon supposed to have done?'

The police sergeant had been looking along the bookshelves. He flipped out a C.L.C. pamphlet, *Aspects of Censorship*, and held it up for Kahn to see. The inspector sat down, made himself offensively comfortable.

'And you haven't seen so much of him lately.'

'Not for a month or two. I was with him this afternoon, though.'

'Wise man. University porter, half a dozen students, they all saw you.'

'I'm not surprised. My visit wasn't secret in any way.'

'Yet you threw your tail.'

'Of course.'

'He knows his rights, Sergeant. You and me must watch ourselves.'

Naturally the interview was being recorded, probably from the sergeant's shirt pocket. The balance between legality and intimidation was very nice. Matthew asked for the policemen's warrant cards and was shown them. His wife came up from the ground floor.

'Visitors, Matthew? I thought I heard the doorbell.' He made the introductions,

'Shall I go or stay?'

'You can please yourself.' Kahn had not risen. Abigail led Matthew over to the couch and sat him down beside her. The sergeant was still prowling, looking now in the music chest beside the harpsichord.

'I asked you what Dr Gryphon was supposed to have done,' Matthew said.

'Illegal, you mean? Nothing, as far as I know. Perhaps you know better.' Kahn tossed cigarette ash in the direction of the fireplace. In that room his shirt was the greater offense. 'This visit of yours – tell us why you made it.'

'I'm leaving Central London in a few days ...' Matthew had had time to work this one out. 'Taking up a new job out in Colindale. I thought I'd have a chat with him before I went.'

'A chat ... What about?'

'Nothing in particular.' He saw he'd never get away with just that. 'We talked about' – improvising – 'some of his students' results. They were sociologically interesting.'

'Tell me.'

'It's the relation of background to performance, Inspector. Plus variants such as leisure activities, ethical positions, integration/alienation quotients, and so on. There seems to be a clear connection between these and –'

'You could keep that up all day, Dr Oliver.'

'I don't understand you.'

'True or not, you could keep that spiel up all day. It's your field. You could keep it up all day.'

Abigail's hand tightened on his, her anger like an electric current. He felt none himself, only an intense depression. For her sake he defended himself.

'You asked me a question, Inspector Kahn. I was doing my best to answer it.'

'So you talked about whatever it is you vocationalists talk about.'

'There's no need to sneer. Isn't the police force classed as a vocation, in view of the hours you work?'

'The police force, Dr Oliver, provides a legitimate outlet for men with a warped or immoderate need to excercise power. Warped or immoderate, the words were.'

Matthew's words, the words he had written. A tag like that would have gone the rounds. Theory at the time of writing: now observable fact. 'You don't like the police force, Dr Oliver.'

'Would you want to be liked?'

Inspector Kahn was amused. He showed his amusement loudly, for a long time, longer than was credible. At last he subsided.

'So you talked about students' records. On a visit to tell him goodbye.'

'We have a common interest in techniques of statistical analysis.'

'And then you shot him.'

Even Sergeant Wilson was still, caught at the window, etched into by the sun behind him. Matthew could hear the sound of the house around him. His perception altered, narrowed to a policeman's colored shirt collar, driving Abigail away, denying her hand in his, leaving him alone with Gryphon's death.

'Shot Gryphon?'

'Records show you with a license for a laser pistol, Dr Oliver.'

'That's right. I … In case there was any more civil unrest I thought –'

'No bullet, no ballistics. No ballistics, no proof. And you the last person to see Dr Gryphon alive.'

'Except the murderer.' Abigail was on her feet. 'I shall issue a formal complaint. You have no right to interrogate my husband without –'

'Emergency regulations have a way of lingering on, Mrs Oliver. If parliaments are frightened enough.'

She faltered, looked back at Matthew. Her vulnerability restored him. The policeman had spoken the truth; for her sake if for nothing else he wished it were not so.

'Don't worry, love. They still need to be able to prove more than just the opportunity ... I have a laser, Inspector, because they can be tuned down till they only burn. I'm not good with guns and I didn't want to kill anybody.'

'They can also be tuned up till they go straight through and take a piece out of the chair behind.'

'I know that.'

Matthew wouldn't be shocked again, refused the picture of Gryphon held up in his seat by flesh welded to the chairback.

'But not by me.'

He and Abigail stood in the open doorway and watched the police car till it turned the corner at the end of the tall street. Shadow from the low sun lay in a precise roofline across the houses opposite. There were plane trees with heavy, summer-dark leaves. And aching pavements. The rich were very silent, and kept safely within walls.

'Do you still want me to go to the Colindale?'

Abigail didn't answer. He felt that, without outward sign, she was crying. Her grief was always like this, an inward bleeding. He put one arm around her and let her rest her head on his chest. He looked out above her at the street.

'That was a silly question. I'm sorry.' He pressed his chin down into her hair. 'There have always been bullying policemen, and suspicion, and hiding around corners. I suppose they're necessary. We've just got spoiled, and let our sensitivities become unbalanced.'

He heard himself trying to sound wise. But she didn't move away from him in disgust. Perhaps she didn't mind. Or hadn't been listening. Or had even found what he said true ... If his protection was to be worth anything she needed to respect him. But to retain that respect he must now expose her to the Kahn and the Wilson, and expose her again. For they were what Gryphon's job for him at the Colindale was about. He drew her gently into the house and closed the front door.

'Poor old Gryphon.' He did not grieve for Gryphon, only for the idea of someone dying. 'I wonder what he did to get himself killed.'

'Been right on one level and wrong on every possible other.'

So casual?

'It's funny how you never liked him.'

'I'm sorry he's dead. Desperately, desperately sorry. I feel –'

'You'll ask for prayers to be said for him at Mass?' He looked at her, sensed something he did not understand, perhaps anger. 'That's not sarcasm, Abigail. I just wasn't sure that prayers could be said for non-Catholics. Officially, I mean.'

'I expect the truth is that he was killed for his moderation?' She smiled brightly. 'It's the usual reason nowadays. I doubt if the authorities would want him dead.'

She was describing the entire failure of the C.L.C. Its sanity had made it acceptable, had made its reactions able to be predicted, able to be absorbed. Matthew walked away, back into the living room. Society evolved. Perhaps man was too multifold ever to control its direction.

'We'd better eat,' he said.

Inspector Kahn had never seriously suspected him of killing Gryphon. The visit had been purely routine, to be cheered up in the only way Kahn knew. If he'd needed a target, the space of Matthew's life supplied him with one. He earned five hundred a month; he had never known to the slightest degree what had once been called hardship; above the basic twenty he only worked the hours he cared to work. But he felt deprived. Possibly he bucked social pressures and worked forty hours or even fifty. Possibly his wife thought he was crazy. Possibly his flat was forty up. Possibly there was no Wide Open Door Group working in his housing unit. Possibly there was and he hated it, being a born recluse … Whatever the causes, he could never win. Matthew went over to the harpsichord and sat down at it, sliding his knees under the keyboard.

He struggled with Scarlatti while Abigail finished getting the dinner ready. He wondered if he liked the music, or only his own dexterity. Whichever it was, it overlaid the evening's unpleasantness, made him excited and happy. He chose the stamping, more rowdy sonatas, torrents that he tried to catch at as they flowed past him. When Abigail came up with the food he was wide open.

'Abigail love, what can I ever do to deserve you?'

'Just love me.'

Such replies were hard to credit. It would be easy to attribute them to fear, or fake naïveté. But her presence took away from him his nagging need to analyze. He put his arms around her thighs as she stood beside him holding plates.

'I do.'

'Then we're all right.'

But as he hugged her he knew perfectly well that things were never as simple as that.

During the meal they talked about the Colindale, and the people Matthew would be working with. He knew most of them only from the work they had done, always of particular distinction. Even his future assistant, Margaret Pelham, had been unavailable on his previous visits. But he knew her work very well, and admired the habits of mind it showed. He had met the principal, of course, a psychiatrist called Chester Billon. The interviews had been long and detailed and very tiring.

'It's an odd name, Matthew. Is he American? And what's a psychiatrist doing in charge of the Colindale?'

'I'm not quite sure. He's one of these physiological psychiatrists. Got there via chemistry and microbiology. And I doubt if he's American. He doesn't sound like one.'

'I don't like physiological psychiatrists. They use large hammers for very small nails.'

'They get more done than the analysts.'

'Perhaps that's why I don't like them.'

They laughed, spinning a shield around themselves, secure in the love they would make later.

TWO

For Abigail the police car was unimportant, and the policemen – but for the news they brought – hardly real. Edmund was dead. Incomplete, years too soon. The moment she had recognized the nature of Kahn's bullying it had ceased to bother her. The questions had gone on and on, around and around, offering no threat in the face of Matthew's innocence. Now they had stopped. She stood beside Matthew and watched the car out of sight. She had loved Edmund. Not as she had loved him once – not any more in love with him – but with a sad love, as for a cripple. It was through him that she had met Matthew, in the years when Edmund was coldly denying her everything but hope. Loving her from behind bars, chopping at her hands if she put them through, but never sending her away. And through him she had met Matthew.

'Do you still want me to go to the Colindale?'

She found it hard to connect Matthew's words and discover their meaning. Edmund was dead, his soul already judged. Over the last few years she had seen him infrequently – at University functions when she had gone with her brother, a few dinner parties, a sailing weekend arranged by Matthew among the Greek Islands. On these occasions the echoing coldness in him had repelled her remembering how it had once hurt. He shouldn't have died so. He should have been given time.

'That was a silly question. I'm sorry.'

Long ago she had told Matthew what she had once felt for Edmund. He couldn't have forgotten. It must be that he didn't know what to say, was embarrassed, jealous even. She couldn't go on listening. Edmund, whom she had failed to get through to, was dead. And God was merciful … Then the front door was closed and she was alone in the hall with Matthew.

'Poor old Gryphon. I wonder what he did, to get himself killed.'

'Been right on one level and wrong on every possible other.'

'It's funny how you never liked him.'

She had been willing to discuss the subject in a way that Matthew found easiest. But not at the price of denying the past, denying her responsibility.

'I'm sorry he's dead, Matthew. Desperately, desperately sorry. I feel –'

'You'll ask for prayers to be said for him at Mass?' So he didn't want to know. He always moved off into the mechanics of her faith when he needed distance. 'That's not sarcasm, Abigail. I just wasn't sure that prayers could be said for non-Catholics. Officially, I mean.'

Sarcasm? Perhaps there was something she hadn't heard … She felt so far from Matthew that it frightened her. If he was jealous without cause he must battle with it by himself. They knew too much about each other: reassurances would be insulting. She chose a remark completely neutral.

'I expect the truth is that he was killed for his moderation. It's the usual reason nowadays. I doubt if the authorities would want him dead.'

She turned away in the direction of the staircase down to the kitchen: Behind her Matthew said, 'We'd better eat,' not having noticed.

She went downstairs and chopped onions angrily. Above her Matthew began to play Scarlatti, also with anger. His clatter made the ceiling buzz. She concentrated on what she was doing, the texture of the onions, the way the rings separated, the rim of each circle sharp against the next, each crisp squeak of her knife. The bitter, milky vapor stung her eyes. Actuality. There, at that moment, physical actuality. The onions browned, and the pizza dough rose among olives and peppers and slivers of anchovy. And Matthew's body, folded over the harpsichord when she took plates up, lived and breathed and moved. She loved him. It was so lucid, so simple. And through him she experienced the other half, the man-ness of God.

As she stood beside him where he sat at the harpsichord he asked her what he could do to deserve her, offered her phrases, formal thought.

'Just love me.' She said the words, feeling their inadequacy to be their strength. He put his arm around her thighs. Mind stopped getting in the way between spirit and body. And the love they made after the evening had shaped to it, was a unification.

Dear Saint Joseph and Saint Anne,
Find me a husband as quick as you can.

It was a childish prayer, but she was grateful to have had it answered in Matthew.

The coffee bar was austere yet vivid, Vasarely out of Bauhaus. She had walked there, even run a little, humming with the excitement of sunshine and coming change. Always she climbed out of sleep slowly, not really in the day till ten thirty or eleven. Matthew had long been up and away, snatching moments, submerging them, she thought, with devoted activity. Even when she was dressed and out of the house the streets came to her only gradually, the bookstalls, the exhibitions, the students, the occasional town cars. The thrill of living could only be accommodated bit by bit. And now the smoky coffee bar, eleven fifteen.

'Abby, you're early. Come and sit down.'

'I ran.'

'Ran? It's the over-forties who run. What the hell are you proving?'

Her brother pushed back a chair with his foot and she sat down. He was soberly dressed, carefully shaved, pale as if from sleeplessness. He wouldn't welcome being fussed.

'Give us a cigarette.' He offered the packet. 'Thrown any good bombs lately?'

'That was in your day. Students don't throw bombs any more. They're too intelligent, too afraid of chaos.'

'Oh Paul, not one of your gloom mornings. What's wrong with being afraid of chaos?'

'Nothing.' He lit her cigarette, then poured coffee for both of them while the machine checked his student's card against the account 'I thought we might talk about the summer vac,' he said.

'Matthew's just taking up this new appointment. I don't expect we'll be having one.'

'Don't vocationalists ever rest?'

Abigail wondered what was wrong, why he wanted to spoil her morning.

'You're not stupid, Paul. That sort of sneering doesn't suit you.'

'I mean it. A man should exist in himself, not only through his work.'

'I'm not going to justify Matthew to you. If –'

'Drink your coffee, sis.' He was seven years younger than she. Far enough away for them to get on well together. 'I know I'm being runtish. It's because I want something.'

She would have liked to take his hands, it was that sort of morning, to offer him anything she had. He wouldn't appreciate it.

'I don't know what I can give you except money, Paul. You know there's always plenty of that.'

'Bless you, Abby.'

'Then it is money?'

'There's a summer project a group of us wants to do in the African Federation.' He pushed an ashtray across for her. 'We're avoiding Student Council backing in order to have a freer hand. Travel's cheap enough and food's no problem. It's the beads we'll have to give the natives that'll come expensive.'

There was no need for him to tell her all this. And if he was driven to give explanations they ought to be good ones. She knew from her own training that there were bribery allocations – called fieldwork easement funds – available from many organizations other than the Student Council. If he wanted to have a good time while in Africa he should say so.

'What is this project?' she asked.

'The uses made of superstition in regional merchandizing.' He laughed. 'It's red hot. The Student Council are the only people who would touch it; they're not afraid of the merchandisers. But they'd pin us down in a dozen ways.'

'Like making you hand over your findings to the C.L.C.?'

'I don't think that would worry us.'

'Wouldn't it? I thought the C.L.C. was impotent, wishy-washy liberal – a tool in the hands of the authorities.'

'It exists.' He shrugged his shoulders. 'It must do some good, I suppose.'

Even this guarded admission was new. For years he had done nothing but shout militancy; if he had at last recognized the realities of student power she was delighted. The lesson of the last disorders was that such immense power frightened not only its victims but its possessors. European society had come near to collapse. Now the student body as a whole was wiser, with a longer perspective, concerned to work as a leaven through their whole lives rather than only during their years at University. If Paul had come around to this view she could forgive him anything. She got out her check book.

'Ten thousand do you?'

'The group will be very grateful.' Again a wrong note.

'Paul – something's not going on, is it?'

'Of course something's going on. We're going to split the whole racket wide open, the obscene, religio-sexual confidence trick that's being played on unsophisticated millions, stroking their pitiful new wealth away from them. We're going to mount the same investigation as the merchandisers mounted, analyzing folk myths, fetishes, tribal symbolisms. And we're going to show the direct relationship, the disgusting relationship between these and each successful merchandising operation. We're going to expose the European merchandising ethic for what it really is. And that of the other power-blocs as well.'

She knew that this tirade was an evasion of her question. But at least his anger was genuine. She made the check out for fifteen thousand and handed it across. He read her neat, left-handed writing.

'Getting a little vulgar with our riches, aren't we?' But he took the check and put it in his shirt pocket. 'So the old man's got a new job … and I use the term affectionately. I know he's not really old – only forty to your twenty-nine. And what's eleven years?'

'Now you've got your money, can't you be a bit nicer? These digs at Matthew are so tedious.'

'Of course. It's how young you feel that counts. And Matthew feels like a ten-year-old.' She wondered if he was meaning to be obscene. He laughed, lit two more cigarettes and passed one across. 'I'm sorry, sis. You married him, so perhaps he isn't the dead weight he seems to be. Just don't be bent into his shape, Abby. That's all.'

'I'm my own shape, Paul. You know that.'

He laughed again, embarrassed. In the pause that followed Abigail looked away, around the coffee bar. There were a few students, but it was filled mainly with older men and women, presumably lecturers. She guessed that Paul had chosen it as the most respectable of the University bars. On another day Edmund might have been among them. She drew on her cigarette, coping With the recollection that Edmund was dead.

'Sad about Edmund Gryphon,' she said abruptly.

'You might not have heard. Frankly I funked telling you.'

'Funked telling me? But –'

'Do me a favor. I may have been only a child, but I wasn't blind.' To her surprise he took her hand and squeezed it. 'Who told you? On the tell, was it?'

She decided this was a question she could get away with not answering. She was suddenly angry with herself for having remembered, angry with Edmund for having got himself killed, angry with herself again for minding so much. And Paul, it was surprising that he should concern himself for her. So little that Paul did seemed to add up.

'All a long time ago,' she said. 'You mustn't worry.'

'Who's worrying? I'd say I was sorry, only what good's being sorry? Most sorts of being sorry.'

The reference to confession lay between them like a sword on the table. Neither of them dared take it up. It was only lately that conversation with Paul had become like this, with so much they didn't talk about.

'Heard from Mum and Dad recently?' he said.

'Mum phoned last week. She was full of Dad's Retirement Counselor. Plans for this and plans for that. It may be good sociology, but it sounded pretty horrible to me.'

'That's it. Horrible. The application of mechanical techniques when everything else has broken down. That we have a science of sociology at all is an open admission that the world we have made for ourselves is basically rotten.'

He was talking nonsense. Such nonsense that she hardly thought about it. She had wanted to talk about how they could help, not wallow in slick nihilism.

'You should change courses,' she said sharply, 'if you really feel that way about it.'

The house was still empty when she got back. Matthew would be collecting her at two, so there might be time to wash her hair. She leaned at the top of the stairs overlooking the garden and decided that the walk home deserved a cigarette. Her talk with Paul had dragged on pointlessly: she had learned that he was leaving for Africa on Saturday by the eleven o'clock plane and that he'd be away six weeks or more. In return she had told him unimportant things about the Colindale … Yet he was her brother, and they had once understood each other.

The cigarette took her whole attention. The feel of the stub, the cupping of the smoke behind her tongue, the different ways to inhale and exhale, the steady, delicate erosion of the white paper, the gray droppings that crumbled hygienically to dust. She stubbed out fifteen full minutes of her life on the underside of the iron handrail.

If Matthew was coming for her at two, then she'd better go and change into clothes more suitable for the Colindale. She founded all her mental pictures of the place on the name of its director, Chester Billon. Vaguely she imagined a dusty street with tethering posts, cowboy country with the uneasy addition of laboratory blocks and computer centers. Matthew would have a broad-brimmed hat and be magnificent in his bearded six foot two. And she ... Somehow, although in these imaginings she was always there, she never really existed. Then she realized what was wrong: the cowboy's name had been Dillon anyway, not Billon. Something came into her mind from the linguistics course: d/b transfers were very common ... or wasn't that d/th? *Bad* in German, *bath* in English. *Pfad* in German, *path* in English ...

What a lot people had tried to teach her. And then given her a degree. In spite of that she still had a good mind when she cared to use it. Matthew would arrive soon, so she'd better wash her face. This she did, drying it vigorously on a *genuine* towel Mum had sent her for her birthday. *Genuine* was the latest trade word for *old-fashioned*. A few years ago *traditional* had been more common ... One could see the progression and ought, with luck, to be able to predict the next step. She heard Matthew calling from just inside the front door.

'I must just put on some lipstick. And brush my hair.'

'It's two o'clock. Have you eaten?'

'Coffee with Paul. And I'd better change my skirt.'

'Abigail, it's two o'clock.'

But she heard him go into the kitchen and she knew he'd be getting her something that she'd have to eat. And suddenly she was hungry.

She took off her skirt and went downstairs with several other skirts over her arm. Matthew was frying bacon and reconstituting bread for a sandwich. She laid the skirts out on the kitchen table.

'Which one shall I wear, Matthew?'

She could see him make an effort.

'The red one's very pretty.'

'For the Colindale Institute? Not too saucy?'

'Please, Abigail – it's five past two.'

She held the red skirt up against herself, refusing to be hurried.

'When did you tell them we'd be there?'

'It's myself I told, not them. And I told you too, days ago. I told you I wanted to leave sharp at two.'

'Don't be so pettish.'

'Pettish?'

'Pettish, pettish, pettish.'

Matthew suddenly put down the slice mold, and the bowl of breadmix. He took the skirts, scrumpled them into a large ball, and threw them down the waste chute. It was, for him, an incredible gesture. After that, anything might happen. Afraid and penitent, she retreated from him, holding the one remaining skirt tightly behind her. He advanced.

'There are,' he said, 'many more things in life than self-imposed punctuality.'

Behind them the bacon smoked in the pan, and eventually they turned to move it.

As always, sleep was a natural part of their lovemaking. And the slow return at his side, the warmth of him, the smell of sexuality, the bony hardness of his chest. He moved, and looked down the sides of his nose at her.

'I'm sorry I threw your skirts away, love. Doing a thing like that … it's –'

'It was funny really.' He mustn't make a drama out of it. She stretched. 'What's the time?'

'Who cares?'

But she knew he did care. There was suppressed tension in his arm under her head. She craned up to see the clock.

'Matthew – it's half past three.'

'Like the gentleman said, who cares?'

'We can't spend our whole lives in bed, Matthew.'

The suburb of Colindale had tried to come to terms with the motorway by throwing up huge blocks of flats. There was a heliport as well, and a big new Catholic church. Quick-growing elms had been planted, now ten years old. But below the striding motorway too much old building remained, ribbon development along meaningless roads. The roundabout at ground level had a thatched motel, a bowling alley and a covered swimming pool, their neon flickering even in the brilliant June sunlight. A small factory was being torn down and a larger one put up in its place. The road was constricted, undergoing reconstruction. Abigail realized how much the stasis of Central London was untypical of life.

She felt warm and full. She had spent much of the journey praying, as always, for a baby. For the four years of their marriage they had shied away from the mechanisms that might help them, the implants, the impregnations. She had even avoided the indignity of being properly examined. She preferred to trust in God and Matthew.

He moved the town car smoothly across the traffic lanes and headed out past a hypnotic succession of maisonettes, their black and white frontages flicking past almost audibly. They represented the poverty that Abigail had been brought up in, and she felt as if she were coming home. Her parents still lived like that, as boisterous as their surroundings. But if this was home, then what was the Kensington house she shared with Matthew? And the Colindale Institute that must now be so near, what would that be?

Matthew drove on past a shopping complex and a self-service battery station. A hundred or so batteries were on charge in open-fronted racks. She glanced across at their own charge gauge – the car had been in all night, had a good thirty hours left. Matthew sat silently beside her, all his attention on the crowded traffic lanes. She edged closer to him, put her hand between his legs, looked out of the car windows with new courage.

The Colindale Institute was dark blue and white, a political coloring: Switzerland, small enough for no one to fear, center of the Federal European government. The flags of the member nations curled idly above the entrance gates. On either side were wide strips of lawn with a token fence of white posts and nylon cord.

'That's a relief,' she said. 'I was afraid they'd all be security conscious, with a high wall and guard dogs.'

'The wall is there, all right. Thirty feet high, they tell me. It's just that you can't see it. Improves the psychological effect.'

They waited in front of the barrier while the guard checked their passes in the scanner. Abigail looked sideways at the clear sunlit air above the grass. There were birds on the ground, some of them searching for beetles, some of them dead. She saw the little notices that might have said *Keep off the grass*. They were warnings about the force-field fence. The passes tallied and the barrier in front of them rose automatically. Matthew drove through and stopped, waiting till the passes were returned to him by the guard.

'That barrier,' he said. 'It's armored to withstand the latest two-meter laser. There's an electronic scanner under the driveway. Also aerial radar coverage and full televisual monitoring.' He turned sideways on the seat to face her. 'I want you to know exactly what you're going into, Abigail. This isn't the Ministry. It's all very discreet, very pretty, very velvet gloved. But it's efficient.' He turned back and started the car. 'German equipment, most of it. Needless to say.'

They drove along an informal, tree-lined avenue, glimpsing varied blue and white buildings through the leaves, graveled courtyards, fountains, flights of mosaic steps that made pleasing patterns against crisp grass edges. Abigail saw many small street lamps. It was a place where people were encouraged to walk slowly and talk. Matthew drew up at a corner, looking down two short roads of low residential blocks. The buildings contrived both dignity and grace.

'Well?' he said, 'That out there and this in here. It's an evil contrast.'

She stared around her, gnawing what was left of her fingernails. There was something about such planned serenity that made her perversely uncomfortable.

'Will I ever be allowed out of here?' she said.

'Any time you like. Remembering that the tail goes along too.'

'The tail?'

'We all have tails. Yours is to be a Mrs Foster. I haven't met her yet, but I hear she's very charming.'

'You really are trying to put me off, aren't you?' She pointed at the blocks of apartments. 'Will we live in one of those?'

'Good Lord, no. That's Technicians Grade I and Junior Programmers. In this place grades are observed most carefully. Department Heads get detached houses in noble seclusion up behind the library. They're very nice, I promise you.'

Abigail got out of the car. There was a comfortable scent of grass and sun-hot brickwork. Three young women hurried chattering out of a doorway, trotted to the end of the road and went over a stile into the field beyond. One of them vaulted it. They wore white shorts and were probably going to play tennis. Abigail walked around to Matthew's side of the car, testing the ground, testing the feel of the place.

'Do you yourself want to come here, Matthew?'

'That's not the point.'

'It's a large part of it.'

'I'm less impressionable than you. I can only say that the work interested me from the very beginning. And now there's what Gryphon asked me to do as well ...'

'Then we'll come.'

She ran around to her side of the car and climbed in. Decisions for her were always very easy. Things happened.

'We'll find out how adaptable we are. It'll be fun.' Matthew didn't start the car. He stayed staring at the road in front.

'I wonder if everybody who comes to work here has the same doubts,' he said.

'The academics won't. All they ever ask is to be left in peace to get on with their work. For them this sort of place is just about perfect.'

It was all a great adventure. Force-field fences, scanners, television monitoring – the first camera she saw she'd put her tongue out at. But she wouldn't dare. She wanted him to drive on. She wanted to see their new house.

'Perhaps it's because I've always kept myself so uninvolved. Politically uninvolved, I mean.' He was answering a question in his own head. 'Yet I'd have expected my connection with Gryphon to rule me out from the start.'

'You're good at your work. Perhaps they're just reckoning on keeping an extra sharp eye on you.'

'Yes.' He started the car. 'That's what I'm afraid of.'

They went first to the Computer Center because that was where the director was probably to be found, and Matthew said it would be civil to pay their respects before going on to look at the house. Abigail was impatient. The thought of a new house, paint to be put on, curtains to be altered, excited her. Now the rest of the afternoon would go on polite nothings with Chester Billon. She was mistaken.

They had hardly sat down to wait by the reception desk before he came out to them, festooned with computer tape. He wore a white coat over very correct suit and shirt and tie.

'Fools kept you waiting? New faces, I suppose. Won't happen again. Mrs Oliver? Delighted. Moving in tomorrow, I hear.' He talked through her protest 'Won't have to do a thing. Our men work wonders. Field where human hands and human judgment are irreplaceable.'

He began to tidy his loops of tape. Abigail saw how big he was, almost as big as Matthew, with big thick-fingered hands and a big face. He was clean-shaven, had tangled eyebrows and a scar down his forehead that he had never bothered to get masked. His boxer's features and army officer's mannerism contrasted oddly with his reputed brilliance. His hair was glossy gray, consultant smooth. When he moved he moved, and when he stood still he really stood still. Abigail felt her husband getting ready to say something. Too late.

'Must get back. Thing's making sense for once.' Billon started back in the direction he had come. 'Twenty-two hours a day and there's still never enough computer time. You'll excuse me.' The door closed behind him. Reopened. 'Forgive me. No manners. Obsessive paranoia, treatable with two grains of mardil. Only then what?' He leaned on the door handle. 'Start work nine thirty Monday. Know where to find your house? Good. Mrs Oliver, forgive me. Computer time is precious.' He hesitated, then quickly walked the length of the corridor back to where they were standing. He leaned forward. 'And if either of you ever thinks I look at you a bit oddly, blame the plastics industry.' He opened his eyes very wide, rolled them, and then tapped the left eyeball with his pen. It made a crisp, billiard-like noise. 'False,' he said neutrally.

The interior of the house was beautiful. The outside wall fronting on the library cloisters had worried Abigail, totally blank except for the door and a pattern of air-conditioner vents. But, once inside, she saw that the blankness made sense. The whole house looked inward to a small central garden with a deep, blue-gray pool. A tall pine tree grew out of this garden in the middle of the house, the ground beneath it soft with brown decades of needles.

As she walked quietly from room to room – Matthew had encouraged her to go on in alone, busy himself doing something to the car – Abigail felt the house fit together about her. Whatever the Colindale might do outside, in here she felt safe. It wasn't like a house at all: more like a nest.

'It's not like a house, Matthew – it's more like a nest.'

Matthew's reply from out in the sunlight was indistinct. She progressed further into the house, finding a study with floor-to-ceiling booksheves. So the last head of Matthew's department had also been sentimental about books … Sentimental. The fir tree was sentimental. The whole house was sentimental. Which was why she liked it so much, being a sentimental person. She sat down on the kitchen window seat and slid back the glass. There was a smell of pine needles. So she was a sentimental person. Sentimental. By now the word was quite meaningless. Sentimental mental center, mental centimeter center … She lit a cigarette.

Matthew was a success. It always worried her how he managed it. The people who gave him commercial consultancies and departments at the Colindale, what did they see in him? If they simply saw a brilliant talent, wouldn't they be afraid of it? Wouldn't they need a willingness to compromise? So whom was Matthew fooling – her, or everybody else?

She frowned at the idea of Matthew deceiving people. He would be capable of it, of course, but would find it hard to see the necessity … Except that Gryphon had shown him the necessity, and had made him accept the position almost of a secret agent. And now Gryphon was dead. And it was all sensational, and silly, and very wasteful.

She finished her cigarette and put the stub carefully down the sink waste pipe. Then she went around the house the other way, till she reached the front door. The ground plan interconnected, and offered two ways of getting anywhere – three, if she went across the garden. She stood at the inner end of the entrance hall thinking that it was the first house she had seen that really didn't need furniture to dress it out. Its spaces were adequate, requiring only movement to complete them. She seemed to have been alone in the house for a very long time. She ran out into the wide air of the cloisters. The car was in the road beyond, but no Matthew.

His absence left a painful gap in the fabric. For a second she stood rabbit still, the tense calm of the Colindale like a weight against her face. The pillars of the arcade framed diminishing squares of sunlight on the mosaic pavement to right and left. She had lived alone, traveled alone, worked alone, made her own life for years before she met Matthew. She wasn't a child.

Then he came around the side of the house, talking to a stranger, and it was all suddenly very ordinary. She turned and he saw her, he stopped talking, the other man saw her, she walked calmly toward them, everybody smiled, everything moved on, happened all in the same moment.

'There you are, Matthew. You were a long time, I was looking for you.' There was a tiny pause. Uncharacteristically, she felt obliged to go on. 'I love the house, Matthew. It feels so safe … Just like a nest.'

She had thought the words so clearly. Almost as if she had already said them many times before.

'Abigail, this is Dr Mozart. Dr Mozart, this is my wife, Abigail.'

'How do you do.' He was German, and Jewish, in his thirties, and accustomed to being found attractive by other men's wives. She judged him to have been married, but almost certainly by now divorced.

'My father christened me Wolfgang, but spared me Amadeus. He was a man of shaky convictions …'

He used English as if he despised it. She shook hands silently. Dr Mozart was looking puckish.

'In any event my father was right, of course. I grew up tone deaf. To me all loud music is Wagner, all soft music Papa Haydn.'

His humility was false. In a minute he would let drop that he played the forty-nine fugues, only not very well. Still with nothing to say, she waited for Matthew to rescue her.

'Dr Mozart has been telling me about my predecessor. Henderson.' Matthew was speaking harshly. She could tell that he was going to shock her. 'Henderson was burned to death in his motor car, Abigail. It wasn't an accident.'

Two messengers now had brought news of violence. Violence off-stage. She wondered if the convention would continue to be observed. The tell reports of Henderson's death had implied a car crash. The director, if no one else, should have told them the truth. Dr Mozart was looking not at her, but at Matthew. He made a small modifying gesture.

THREE

'Don't wait for me. It sounds as if the air-conditioner filter needs clearing. I ought to take a look. You go on in.'

She left him to tinker. He stooped, unscrewed the filter unit under the dash, gave it a couple of turns, and tapped out the saturated crystals on the grass beside the car. Cement dust, burnt rubber, carbon dioxide, bacteria, urban effluent – it was a wonder anybody dared breathe undoctored air at all. From inside the house he heard Abigail calling that she liked it, that it was like a nest. He smiled. A revived housing concept, as old as sensate life. Perhaps his *People in Glass Houses* had helped after all.

'Peace shall reign within your ramparts, and prosperity within your palaces,' he called. He attended Mass quite as often as she did.

When he had replaced the filter unit he closed the car door and turned to the house. He had sent her on ahead because she would prefer to make her first exploration alone. It would, if he knew her, deserve a cigarette. He stepped back a few paces to see the outline of the house separate from the cloisters along its front wall. It was one of a dozen or so, homes of departmental heads, around a large grassy quadrangle. The blankness of its outside walls could be said to make it into a nest, a fortress. It could also be called a prison, a trap.

He walked on the grass down the side of the house and around the back. Three narrow strips of clerestory window nine or ten feet up, lighting what he thought must be the back wall of the living room. Nothing else. Of course, justification was easy enough: the view from this side of the house was hideous: a high-speed train-way humping over elevated roads, some factory blocks, a big unexplained plastic dome, and as far as the horizon green fungoid rooftops, semi-detached. But windows that kept the view out also kept the people in. He frowned. One hour in the Colindale and he was already getting a persecution complex.

'Stay where you are, please. Tell me who you are, and what you are doing.'

Matthew turned. A man was standing some ten yards away, his hands in the large patch pockets of his jacket.

'My name is Oliver.' Matthew made the spare words sound as insolent as possible. 'And I'm looking at my house.'

'Dr Oliver? May I see your identification, please?'

Casual clothes, no hat, hardly a security guard. Unless they wore plain clothes at the Colindale.

'Here you are.'

The man took the card and examined it long-sightedly.

'My dear Dr Oliver … well met by moonlight. I am Dr Mozart. Spectroscopy. Welcome to the Institute.' His hand was cold and damp, as if from holding something metallic. Matthew wondered if everybody there was supposed to carry a gun. 'We are edgy, Dr Oliver. You were not expected until tomorrow.'

Matthew understood this to be an apology, all the apology he would get.

'My wife's in the house,' he said. 'We're just having a look around.'

'A man such as you will have a beautiful wife. I look forward to meeting her.'

Very precise English, used for a very German brand of flattery. Dr Mozart patted his back, became confidential, would have put his arm around his shoulders if he could have reached.

'I did not mean to offend you … You and I, Dr Oliver, we represent the European predicament. We must work together – for life itself we must work together. Yet I find you stuffy and you find me brash. And whatever we are, when we meet we become more so.' He looked earnestly up into Matthew's face, and then burst out laughing. 'If we stand here much longer we shall become pure grotesques. So take me to meet your wife.'

He led Matthew back in the direction of the cloisters. Planning to spare Abigail, Matthew began to make excuses.

'We're in a bit of a rush, actually. The director has sprung tomorrow's move on us, and we really ought to get back to –'

'Did you know,' said Dr Mozart, casually, 'that Professor Henderson was murdered?'

'Murdered?' Matthew kept on walking, British to the core. 'No. No, I didn't.'

'Oh dear. Then perhaps I should have kept the cat in the bag, out of respect to the director.' Irrelevantly Matthew wondered if his companion would ever learn that his English was let down by his use of cliché. 'But it's too late now … Yes, an incendiary bomb in the car. A few yards down the road, by the tennis courts.'

Too cheerful about his indiscretion for it to have been accidental. Matthew wondered why. Why a lot of things.

'No, I hadn't heard. How very unpleasant'

'In the midst of life we are in death, Dr Oliver.'

They came up into the shadow of the cloisters. Abigail ran toward them.

'There you are, Matthew. You were a long time. I was looking for you.' He detected hysteria. She was usually silent in the presence of strangers. 'I love the house, Matthew. It feels so safe … just like a nest.'

'Abigail, this is Dr Mozart.' He made the introduction to give her time. 'Dr Mozart, this is my wife, Abigail.'

Abigail was shaking hands, and wilting under the halitosis blast of his charm. Matthew had to tell her. He ignored the words, simply waited for a gap in them.

'Dr Mozart has been telling me about my predecessor. Henderson. Henderson was burned to death in his motor car, Abigail. It wasn't an accident.'

She had to know while there was still time to back out. The director had lied by omission. Had he done so in case Matthew might otherwise be frightened off? What opinion must the director have of him? Dr Mozart made a small modifying gesture.

'What you say is not completely accurate, Dr Oliver. An element of accident did exist. The car belonged to Professor Billon and nobody could have known that Henderson would borrow it. The implication is obvious.'

Dr Mozart shrugged, his elbows bent in by his sides, his hands together, turned forward at the wrists.

'An unpleasant subject, Mrs Oliver. But at least it suggests that your husband is himself not in any particular danger. Anyone attacking the Colindale project would go for the head, not the arms.'

'Then what exactly is the Colindale project?'

As it was nearly seven o'clock they had been lucky to catch Professor Billon. He was in his private office at the computer center. A faddish room, showing the Harley Street-acquired taste of its owner. Practically nothing expressed its function. Even the windows were *jeus d'-esprit*, three huge blown-up color slides of eyes which the evening sunlight projected askew onto the opposite wall. And behind the professor's desk a tall sculpture of polished aluminum and spun glass netting which revolved, catching the light

'The Colindale project? My dear Oliver, I went over it very carefully with you. Non-political. Belonging to the European Federation. Financed by the central government. Collects scientific information, catalogs and freely disseminates it. Peaceful. Aimed solely at improving the welfare of humanity. Widest possible terms of reference.'

'If it's all so peaceful' – Matthew controlled his increasing irritation – 'why the hell did somebody try to kill you a few weeks ago?'

'Some people are more afraid of peacefulness than of anything else. Witness the fate of Christ. Not that I make a comparison.'

'And why weren't we told about it? Right from the start?'

The director smiled with a frankness that Matthew suspected of being professional.

'You've guessed already. The only answer I can give will be unsatisfactory.' He got up from his mesh chair and walked to the center window. He stared out through the eye's iris at the blue strip of grass and a blue generating station. 'Buddha's eye,' he said. 'The eye of the soul. Of truth. Salutary reminder.' He turned back into the room. 'Information detrimental to national security, Official Secrets Regulations cast a wide net. Perhaps too wide. However.'

'Is that all you can tell us?' said Abigail.

'Until you are sworn in. Pedantic, but there you are. I'm glad you came to me instead of going to some newspaper friend in the outside world. It looks well.'

Matthew gazed steadily at him across beams of colored light.

'Then there'll be other things you've kept from me about the Institute?'

'Thousands.' Billon smiled again. 'But nothing material. I believe.'

The director had not asked him how he had heard about Henderson's death. Perhaps he knew. Perhaps the whole episode had been a squalid test of probity. And its result had looked well.

'Well, well. Getting late. I recommend the canteen. One thing I demanded was good food. At canteen prices. Geneva can afford it and the staff deserves it. Hardly anybody eats out or in their quarters.'

'We shall,' said Abigail. 'Mostly eat at home, I mean.'

'What a way to live,' she said on their way home in the car. 'I bet the cook's a computer. They'd disembody your brains altogether if they could.'

'That man Mozart did mention tennis courts.'

'How nice.'

'Abigail love, you know perfectly well bodies are becoming more and more of a social embarrassment.'

They drove on in silence. Helicopters idled overhead on their different airways to and fro. There were trains and buses and cars, movement instead of activity. Matthew turned off the North Circular and entered the approach to the Central London checkpoint.

'We're not so holy ourselves,' he said. 'When did we last sweat?'

'*Mea culpa, mea culpa* ... We see everything, we admit everything – it's obscene the way we live on ourselves, enjoying a sort of mutual stimulation.' She covered her face with her hands. 'No, I don't mean that. But we've lost balance. There's too much time for thinking.'

He hadn't realized she was so serious. He tried to play it down.

'Thinking is to be encouraged,' he said. 'It takes up so little space. Uses so few amenities.'

'Please, Matthew, don't just be bitter. It's too easy.'

He braked at the checkpoint, waited for the scanner to register his resident's sticker and let them through. By another entrance the driver of a neat gray town car was arguing with the attendant over his visitor's pass. Matthew had thought he knew all the passes – resident's pass, even day pass, odd day pass, weekend pass, midweek pass – but this man's was of a bright yellow color he had never seen before. The light changed and Matthew drove on into Central London.

'It's ludicrous,' Abigail said suddenly, 'to long as I do for ordinary, old-fashioned pain. For men who are dirty, and swear, and fight in anger. For the real issue to be survival.'

'Not ludicrous at all. There are still places where you could find that sort of life.'

'And waiting lists a mile long of people who want to go to them.'

'With our qualifications, love, we could get there easily.'

And with their qualifications the whole thing was made pointless. You couldn't put on simple issues like a coat – at least he couldn't. She was so much younger, of course ... The thought worried him.

'At least one doesn't have to go to the think-tank extremes of the Colindale,' he said.

For a long time she didn't answer. They talked of other things, of his morning spent tidying up at the Ministry, of her meeting with Paul in the coffee bar. She told him of the money she had given her brother. He approved.

'Anything that keeps him busy, gets him out of the country for a bit. He's not being taken up enough by his work. Either he's in the wrong course or it's the fault of his teachers. I'll have a word with Gryph –'

But Gryphon was dead. It was shocking how easily one forgot.

'Have you realized what Gryphon's death means?' he said suddenly. They were finishing supper.

'All sorts of things. What in particular?'

'It means I don't have a contact with the C.L.C. any more. Whatever I may find out about the Colindale, there's nobody to tell.'

'Don't you know any other executive members?'

'You talk as if there were an official list. I only knew about Gryphon because he happened to be a very old friend.'

The C.L.C. was supposed to be illegal. As a power in society it was thus more credible. Everybody played this game, even if with varying degrees of sophistication. The executives guarded their identities. Even the printing presses were officially secret.

'Surely the government knows who they are?'

'They'd never admit it.'

'Not even to you?'

She started collecting the dirty plates. Matthew lit a cigarette and considered. He had often worked closely with the Minister for Social Planning. There was friendship of a sort between them.

'I might try Beeston. I'll need to think of a good excuse.'

'Easy. A private survey you're doing. Patterns of divergence in the executive classes.' She went down to the kitchen, calling over her shoulder, 'Why not ring him now?'

'And have Billon know within ten minutes that I'm trying to contact the C.L.C? Don't be naïve.'

He had a sudden thought and went over to the window. A neat gray town car, familiar, was parked a few doors down on the left. And in it the man who had been arguing at the checkpoint. Abigail came up from the kitchen, saw he was smoking.

'Don't I get a cigarette?' she said.

He handed her one. There was a whole box on the table – why didn't she get one for herself? Anyway, she smoked far too much.

'Thank you.' She lit it. 'I smoke too much,' she said contentedly.

Too much? Why? On what grounds? Moral, or financial? With the health risk beaten what else was there? People who were orally fixated liked to smoke. It helped them and did no harm whatsoever.

'Yes, you do,' he said, staring resentfully out at the gray town car.

The gun in his pocket made the whole outing seem basically frivolous. He ran down the front steps of his house and crossed the pavement to his car. The street was deserted, his tail apparently reading a newspaper. Matthew aimed the laser and burned holes in both front tires of the gray car, so that the bonnet end subsided abruptly. Then he ducked into his own car and drove away. He should offer the idea to *Physical Surveillance and the Free Citizen*. Except that most free citizens weren't allowed laser guns.

Two streets away he turned into a multi-story Karstak, relic of the time before the new University, when Central London hadn't yet been made a Limited Traffic Zone. He was planning to get rid of his car; a radio call from his tail would have half the police in London looking for it. He took the lift up to the fifteenth floor and parked in close to the shaft. The upper stories were silent, lined with last year's models nobody knew what to do with. The big Italian manufacturers' lobby had forced through safety legislation in Geneva that made eighty percent of not-new cars illegal. Which was good for business and gave many urban Karstaks a temporary usefulness.

Matthew took the lift down again to the ground floor, and slipped unobtrusively into the nearest underground station. He was enjoying himself. If he was to be treated like a criminal he might as well behave like one.

Out of University hours the trains were infrequent, and by the time he reached Whitehall it was nearly nine o'clock. If Sir William were in, at least he would be certain to have finished dinner.

The Minister's roof garden was high enough to be still warmed by the last of the evening sun. Long shadows lay across the gravel. There was a pond, with lilies and fat golden carp. Matthew stood in the doorway and looked down at the Minister, sprawled virile on a traditional cane chaise longue.

'My dear Matthew, I do hope you haven't been kept waiting. I'm afraid I've only just got back from the studios.'

'Then I won't trouble you, Sir William. You'll want to eat.'

'Nonsense. Sit down … They fed me as if I was a visiting Chinese diplomat.' Matthew smiled politely. 'That's why I'm so late. I … I don't suppose you saw the transmission?'

Matthew sat down on the low parapet surrounding the lily pond.

'I don't think I've looked at the tell for weeks,' he said.

'Wise man. I was softening 'em up for some new Movement Incentives. We've got to drive 'em up into the Highlands somehow, you know … They tell me it went quite well.'

Obviously Sir William had not yet changed his clothes. He was still wearing the informal sweater everybody loved. And his hair was tousled.

'But then, of course, they would. They stroke me and I purr. Vanity, vanity, all is … I don't suppose this is altogether a social visit, eh, Matthew?'

'You're quite right, Sir William. I'm afraid I want something.'

'It can't be money … And it can't be influence because you know I haven't any.' He waved aside Matthew's protest. 'You've come to me for information, Matthew Oliver. Information you can't get anywhere else.'

'You're quite right, Sir William.' Despicable. No man should work on another's mechanisms so crudely. Worse, there might be in it something of the connivance of stooge and principal in a bad double act. 'And the information I need will be hard for even you to give me without bending the rules a little.'

'Rules, Matthew, are for the obedience of fools and the guidance of wise men. Place me somewhere between the two extremes' – the Minister held up a mocking finger – 'and hope.'

Matthew looked away, watched the silent, indifferent fish. All through his life people in authority had liked him. He wished they hadn't. Somewhere there must be a basic dishonesty in him. If he had ever presented himself truthfully to these captains of society they would have loathed him. He agreed with scarcely a thought in their heads, and frankly considered himself superior to any of them. Which made his sycophancy particularly disgusting.

'As you know, sir, I've accepted a position at the Colindale Institute as head of the Social Studies Department. Possibly because they wouldn't get men otherwise, they allow department heads a certain amount of time for their own work. The project I'm engaged on is a study of the patterns of divergence in the executive groups.'

'That sounds interesting.' Thanks to Abigail. 'Can I take it the Government will get a look before you publish?'

'Of course.' A thoroughly safe promise.

'Can't you feel the rules beginning to flex a little, Matthew? I'm sure I can.'

The Minister was coy. Matthew should have been nauseated, but made allowances. For what he could not say.

'Of course, divergence takes many forms, Sir William. Political, sexual, religious, behavioral, social-relational, interpersonal-relational, and so on ...' The Minister loved long words. 'Most of these are checkable from existing records. I still have my ministry pass card to the Paris data store. There is one field, though – perhaps the most important – that is not available to me.'

'Ministerial divergences – is that what you're looking for? I could give you a letter to Security. I haven't seen the files myself, and I don't want to.' Sir William was adept at saying one thing and meaning the opposite. 'But, for research purposes they might be –'

'Thank you, Sir William, but I'm afraid that's too specialized a sample to be of much use.' Matthew took a breath. 'I was thinking of the secret societies, and the C.L.C. in particular.'

The Minister went carefully blank.

'But my dear fellow, the C.L.C. is an illegal organization. Nobody knows its members.'

'I realize that's the official position.' Matthew dabbled his fingers in the pond. Fish darted away, hid under lily pads. 'All the same, it is widely believed that –'

'Widely believed? I don't like your implication, Matthew. Widely believed by whom?'

'That the Government is well aware of the exact membership of the C.L.C. but chooses to take no action. There are, after all, good sociological reasons for permitting such organizations.'

Sir William hoisted himself abruptly to his feet. Behind him the cane chair creaked and settled. He paced, his soft soles making scarcely a sound on the gravel.

'You are suggesting a cynicism in the Government, Matthew, that –'

'Not cynicism, Sir William. Sophistication.' But he knew he had lost out.

'Cynicism, Matthew. The cynical manipulation of motives. My God – you're in the wrong bloc, Matthew. That isn't what democratic government's about.'

'Then you're saying' – give him one more chance – 'you're saying that nobody in the Government knows the names of the C.L.C. executives?'

'If we did, we'd arrest them. You can't make a mockery of the law; either a thing's illegal or it isn't. Dammit, Matthew, I thought you were a man of honor.'

Matthew moved his hand gently to and fro in the water, said nothing, resisted a mild impulse to make excuses for himself. More than anything else, intellectual dishonesty depressed him. The Minister was working himself up.

'Sociologists as ministers – that's what some people want. Did y'know that? I'd like to show them you. You're like those bloody psychologists who tell us about God: Oh yes, He's a good thing. We see a definite psychic need for Him … I'm sorry, Matthew. I seem to have lost my temper. But you assume a sort of doublethink that just won't do. Not in democratic government.'

Matthew looked up, realized that to Sir William he was not, and never had been, a person. He was the dark, shiny, two-inch lens of a television camera.

When he reached home the gray town car was still in position, but its occupant made no attempt to speak to him. Matthew found a note pushed through the letter box. It was a bill for two car tires, six hundred marks. It cheered him up, and he wrote the check immediately.

FOUR

Abigail came up from the kitchen. Matthew was standing by one of the high windows at the front of the house, looking down into the street. He was withdrawn, and did not seem to notice her arrival. He was smoking. His hair stuck out in tufts where he had been ruffling it. She tried to reach him.

'Don't I get a cigarette?' she said.

He held his packet out to her and continued to stare out of the window. She was hurt by this disregard for one of heir love rituals: the placing of the cigarette between her lips, his two fingers against her cheek steadying the flame, the smoky kiss that so often followed. She tried to remember what they had been talking about before she went down with the dirty dishes. He had called her naïve, and her mind had retorted by skipping away into other matters, the new house, the repellant Dr Mozart. She remembered now that they had been working out a method of contacting the C.L.C. She felt ashamed, and took a cigarette from the offered packet.

'Thank you.' She lit it, and tried a second time to make contact. 'I smoke too much,' she said.

'Yes, you do.'

A silence in the room while she grappled with that one: hurt not by its abrupt truth, but by its conflict with the hundred other times he had denied the fact, and so convincingly. Did he really need his mind to be three-quarters preoccupied before he could be honest with her in little things?

'We were followed back from the Colindale,' Matthew said. 'The man's sitting in a car outside.'

She joined him at the window, saw a man sitting in a gray car reading a newspaper.

'Are you sure, Matthew?'

'Of course I'm sure. I remember seeing him hanging around the guard house.'

'Then what are you going to do about the Minister? You can't go and see him, not with that man watching. If you can't use the telephone either, then what –'

'I'll think of something.'

And only two days before life had been concerned with Matthew's work, with the church, with keeping up with the technical journals, with infrequent visits to her parents, with occasional films and plays and concerts.

*

The first stage of Matthew's scheme worked very well. She watched from the window as he drove away, leaving the tail car disabled. The man in it did not even get out. She saw him speaking into his radio handset, and a few minutes later another car arrived. The two flat tires were replaced by the spares from both cars and then the second car drove away again. Just because she had been inside the Colindale Institute she was apparently to be watched day and night. They were children, trying to make their little activities seem important. She went out to the gray car and leaned in through the open side window.

'Good evening,' she said.

'Evening, Mrs Oliver.'

'Why are you here?'

'I'm here to keep an eye on you, Mrs Oliver.'

It was disappointing that he should remain so unabashed.

'Why are you keeping an eye on me?'

'Orders.'

'And that's all you know?'

'More than that'd only be trouble to me.'

'Do you often have to watch perfectly innocent people?'

'Innocent's a big word.' He scratched his cheek. 'But I expect so.'

'And that's the way you serve society?'

'I hadn't thought about it. I don't see why not. It's a job in a growth profession – aren't many of them left.'

Through the open front door behind her she could hear the telephone ringing.

'Aren't you afraid I might shoot you, attack you in some way?'

'Doesn't often happen. Besides, your husband went off with the only gun.'

'We might have another. Without a license.' The man shook his head.

'Not you.' He was civil, but indifferent. He would push her off a cliff in exactly the same tone of voice. 'We scanned the house, room by room. While you were out. No explosive, no propellants … and you're not the sort to come right out and poke me. Isn't that your telephone?'

She did not answer. She was furious that their house should have been grubbed around in by men like that Kahn.

'I suppose that's under powers left over from the last emergency,' she said finally.

'I could quote you the subsection, Mrs Oliver.'

He arranged himself more comfortably in his seat and again scratched his cheek. The Nevershave hormone treatment had been recent, and she could see it still itched.

'Anyway, you ought to be glad to have me here.' The telephone stopped ringing. 'After all, you say you're innocent, and as long as I'm here I say you're innocent. That's two of us saying you're innocent. Could come in useful.'

She had offered him a questionnaire and he had obligingly filled it in. She now knew how he worked. The knowledge gave her little satisfaction. The telephone began to ring again and she used it as an excuse to turn back to the house.

'And Mrs Oliver …' He had leaned across the car and was looking up at her. 'Thanks for the company, Mrs Oliver.'

'Why not come in and put your feet up?'

'Very kind of you, ma'am. Only I mustn't leave my radio.'

Had he really completely missed her sarcasm? In the doorway she stopped.

'Have they caught my husband yet?'

'His car's been found on the fifteenth floor of the Sloane Square Karstak. Perhaps that's him trying to ring you.'

She closed the front door and hurried to the telephone. If it was Matthew then her not answering would have worried him badly. She switched in the receiver.

'Hullo? Abby?' It was her brother. 'Got you out of the bath, have I?'

'No. I was just … busy.'

'I'm off in the morning, Abby. Been going around the family saying goodbye.'

'You mean you've rung Mum and Dad?'

'I've been to see them. And Grandpa.'

'What's going on? Are you afraid you won't be coming back?'

'I'll ignore that. Tell me instead how you enjoyed your trip out to Colindale. Pick up any good bits of scandal?'

'If I had I wouldn't tell you. They're very security minded out at the Institute.'

'Which means you think the phone is bugged.'

It hadn't occurred to her. Her reticence, the half-truth about why she had been so long answering, it was her instinctive reaction to an unknown situation.

'I saw the house we're going to have,' she said. 'And met the director.'

'And Matthew's job? Has he been told much about that yet?'

'He knows about his job. He's known for weeks.'

'And he's taking it?'

'Why shouldn't he?'

'No reason. Not if you don't know of one.' He was behaving very oddly.

'Are you drunk, Paul?'

'I doubt it.' He seemed to pull himself together. 'Anyway, I really rang to tell you about Grandpa. He's very low. You might care to go and cheer him up.'

'Did he ask for me?'

'Not in so many words. It's just this dreary business of being alive. It's getting him down.'

'Grandpa? But he loves life.'

'That's not the way I read him.'

Her brother's words made her ashamed. She had not been to visit her grandfather in more than a year, had thought of him perhaps three times in all those months. The immediate world took so much of her attention. She urged Paul off the line so that she could ring the Estate.

She looked up the number in the directory, feeling guilty that she did not know it as she knew the numbers of friends. She rang the Estate warden. He said her grandfather might have gone to bed; in the circumstances it wasn't wise to call his flat. She asked how the old man was. Very fit. Very fit indeed. Not walking so much, of course, but very fit. Perhaps he was telling her what he thought she wanted to hear. She said she'd visit her grandfather in the morning, and the warden said not before ten. He seemed unenthusiastic.

When she had rung off she stood by the telephone and said two short prayers, the first for Grandpa and the second for forgiveness of her own neglect. Then she was cheerful again.

Matthew came in shortly after ten, laughing at a bill for tires stuck through the door. She was glad to have him safely back, so she laughed as well – although she didn't really see the joke. Two policemen had been waiting by his car in the Karstak, but they'd had to let him go. There was nothing they could charge him with, and the C.L.C. was very active against arbitrary arrest.

He told her about his meeting with the Minister – although he made a great show of believing the worst of everybody, Sir William's dishonesty had surprised and upset him. They tried to think of other ways of contacting the Committee, but came up with nothing. Before going up to bed they drew the curtains and looked down into the street. The gray town car had been replaced by a red one. Night shift. They could see a tweed elbow resting on the sill of the window on the driver's side.

The Colindale removal men arrived at eight thirty next morning. Abigail, still in bed, had forgotten it was the day of their move; she had other things on her mind, especially Grandpa. But the foreman wasn't worried: his men brought in a large number of plastic crates which they began filling at once with random articles. Abigail took Matthew out into the garden.

'You must stop them. That's not the way to pack things. They'll rattle about in the van and get chipped to pieces.'

'I expect the men know what they're doing.' That was always his reaction.

'If you don't stop them, then I will.'

He went up the stairs into the house with the patient air of someone humoring a lunatic.

'Wouldn't some of those things be better wrapped in newspaper?' he said mildly.

'Waste of time, sir. We seal these crates and pump 'em full of gas. The gas solidifies in five minutes and there you are. It's not really a gas, of course: it's a sort of vaporized polystyrene. Breaks off clean as a whistle at the other end.'

'Very ingenious.' Matthew turned away.

It was far too early in the day for her to be able to endure Matthew being right and tactfully not saying so. She banged off into the kitchen and started taking the previous night's dishes out of the machine. But she had forgotten even to start it, and they were still dirty. She went back to bed. Yet the house was her job – if she didn't do that she didn't do anything.

'Abigail, didn't you say you were going to see your grandfather at ten? You'll need some breakfast first. I'll see to it.'

If only she could believe that the reproach implicit in everything he did at these times was in her own head and not in his. It was possible to be just too good, to be just too loving ...

The old people's Estate was just outside the restricted traffic area, close to Richmond Park. Small blocks of flats linked by covered travelators, a shopping complex, a church, a sports and social center. A surgery with tiny hospital attached lay a little to one side, among trees. At eleven thirty in the morning the Estate was busy. Power tools buzzed in the workshop, several men and women were cutting the grass and weeding the flower beds, others were repainting the doors of the church. And there was a steady flow of the chairborn to and from the shops. Abigail sat in the car at the gate for some minutes and watched. Theoretically nothing was lacking. She went to the church to find the warden.

'I told you the truth, Mrs Oliver.' Father Carter was immediately defensive. 'Your grandfather is very fit indeed.'

'I'd have preferred you to tell me he was happy.'

'I have two duties, my child. One to the old people here and one to their relatives in the outside world. It would have been wrong of me to give you unnecessary worry.'

'Unnecessary? How can I help if you don't tell me the truth?'

The priest shook his head. He motioned for her to sit down. The room they were in was a recent addition, and still smelled of new wood.

'Your grandfather is in a terminal depression. Now only God can help him.'

He began explaining what was meant by *terminal depression*. If he'd done his homework he'd have known that she had a degree in Social Geriatrics. She checked her impatience. How many old people had he in his care? And how many relatives would each old person have?

'... It's as if there were a clock inside each of us. Science ignores that clock. Science works on the principle that the purpose of life is life. You and I know that this is not so.' He smiled gently, staring into her face, making sure that he was understood. 'For your grandfather the clock has run down. Yet he cannot die. So ...'

Her grandfather's flat was on the ground floor, with full-length windows overlooking a lawn and dovecote and a dark line of fir trees, the hills of Richmond Park beyond. She paused by his front door and watched the doves circling. Two landed untidily on the dovecote and went inside. A few white feathers drifted down in the still air. There was a smell of mown grass. She rang the doorbell and entered without waiting. Grandpa was watching the tell.

'Mornin', Grandpa.' She flattened her accent without noticing. 'Got the kettle on, have you?'

He didn't answer. The film was a documentary, a study of post-industrial France.

'Have you got the kettle on, I said.'

'Didn't know when you was coming.'

He remained motionless, a well-filled bundle of clothes.

'Never mind, Grandpa. I'll do it.'

She went into his kitchen, filled the built-in kettle and switched it on. Behind her the tell spoke of leisure fulfillment.

'What else is on?' she called, and got no response.

There was an old-fashioned teapot, and tea in a caddy. The details were good; the kitchen looked out onto a busy concourse. Grandpa had been there for six years and had things the way he liked them. Nothing clinical.

'How many spoons, Grandpa?'

'Four.'

She made the tea and found a packet of biscuits. The old man was exactly as she had left him.

'What're you doing with yourself these days, Grand-par?'

'Bloody nothing.'

'I thought you'd got a job in the bakery.'

'Job? Nowt but a sop for an old fool. Packed it in.'

'Somebody has to do it. The Estate can't afford to pay staff.'

'Let 'em find someone else then. I've had my lot.'

She poured him a cup of tea, spooned in the sugar she knew he liked. She was familiar with his condition from casework. If he'd been younger his depression could have been lifted with E.C.T. or a leucotomy. In his case the only answer was total sedation till death supervened. But all these facts applied to casework patients, not to her grandfather.

'Matthew's taking a new job, Grandpa. We're moving out to Colindale.'

'The rubbish these people talk.' He was watching the tell. 'Every day more and more rubbish.'

'Why not try another channel?'

'They're all the same. If it's not this it's music. Or that's what they call it. Or else jokes that don't make sense. And folks laughing like hyenas.'

He had been born before the first world war – what could he possibly make of contemporary mass media? There were plans for a special old people's channel, but it wouldn't come in Grandpa's time. She tried again.

'I hear Paul's been out to see you. Did he tell you about his trip to Africa?'

'There's another one. Either he's mad or I am.'

'He's young, Grandpa. But he means well. You shouldn't –'

'Then I don't want to hear. It's time I was dead, that's what.'

'You don't mean that.'

He needed to be told that he didn't mean it. He needed to believe that he didn't mean it.

'Yes, I do. I mean it.'

'God loves you, Grandpa. He'll take you when it's the right time.'

'You've been talking to Father Carter. Just wait till you're my age. Then you'll know …' He came near to spying more, but the habit of faith held him back. 'There's five feet of plastic tubing in my guts, Abigail. God knows what else beside. I wish they'd never …'

Again he stopped short. He wished what he daren't wish. Prodding him was cruel: he was far too censored, too unprepared. Father Carter had been right. She was worse than useless, she was getting in the way.

'I'll go now, Grandpa.'

An ordinary room, simple, not at all modern. Furniture and pictures she recognized from Grandma's lifetime. Sitting, uncomprehending, in the middle of it all, Grandpa. Abigail closed the door quietly and leaned against the wall outside. She would arrange with Father Carter to come more often – though whether for her grandfather's peace of mind or her own was unclear.

Matthew and Abigail stood side by side for the swearing-in ceremony, their right hands raised. Matthew felt foolish, and also uneasy. He didn't share his wife's deep reverence for oaths as such: he believed in a personal morality that might have to overrule them all. But he hoped it wouldn't need to. When the ceremony was finished the director shook hands with them and motioned them back into their seats.

'Work begins Monday morning. So you'll have a little time for settling in over the weekend. Very pleased to have you both here at the Colindale.' His smile stopped abruptly. 'Now. Have to start with a telling-off. Last night you took a little trip, I hear.'

'I went to see the Minister for Social Planning. I –'

'Destination doesn't concern me.'

'It was just a friendly visit. He and I have worked together on –'

'Doesn't concern me. But you evaded surveillance. Bad impression. Irresponsible.'

Matthew felt himself getting angry. It confused his thoughts and made his eyes difficult to focus. He heard Abigail shift warningly in her chair beside him.

'I make a point of evading surveillance,' he said. 'I thought everybody did. It's a basic human right.'

'Here at the Colindale we put up with our tails,' said the director. 'Make life easy for them. Anything else would be ridiculous. They work for the Government, so do we. Besides, they protect us. In three ways.' Fingers held up for counting. 'One, from attack. Two, from suspicion. Three, from subversion. So we give them all the help we can.'

It made a crooked sort of sense. Always assuming that nobody could ever be trusted. And who was he, Matthew, to become self-righteous?

'I'm sorry, sir. It's a new idea – takes getting used to.' But he couldn't resist a dig. 'You see, in all my other jobs the boss has trusted me.'

The director appeared not to notice.

'Good. Good. No surveillance at all within Institute boundaries, of course. Must arrange for you to meet your tails. Decent people, as far as the job lets them ...'

'Now that we've been sworn in,' said Abigail, astonishing Matthew, who hardly ever got a word out of her in company, 'now that we've been sworn in, Professor, can you tell us more about the Colindale project?'

'Of course. Start with a conducted tour. Just had a memo from Geneva. About a thing called spouse participation. Treat us all like children, you know.'

The director got up from his desk.

'Start in here. Not much, only a printoff console. If I'm kept waiting late for a result I may slip in here for a kip. Let the machine wake me. No keyboard. I leave programming to the programmers. Even the new Astran would take more time to master than I can spare.'

He led the way out of his office. Matthew followed, an arm protectively around Abigail. The door at the end of the corridor was a single transparent sheet that slid up at their approach. Billon walked toward it, still talking.

'It's a science of its own, programming the new as sociative complexes. Almost like working with live matter.'

Beyond the door was the main computer room. Matthew had worked in computer centers before. The blank, gray-white cabinets, the glare of the anti-glare lighting, the coolness, the outward calm that masked an inner hysteria of machine and intellect – he was familiar with it all. But the computer center at the Colindale was different, for it was almost completely silent. Apart from the occasional high scream of tape over reading heads and the distant rustle of the six Bohn teleprinters, there was nothing but a huge pressure of silence. It stopped Matthew in the doorway, his arm closer around his wife. Nobody spoke. Service engineers trod carefully between the bland metal surfaces, rubber shoes on rubber floor, their white coats tight about them, It was a place he did not wish to enter, bitter smelling, anti-human.

'The data processors work ninety minute shifts,' murmured Chester Billon. 'It's all they can stand.'

He walked away down a side aisle, ran his hand jauntily along the sides of the cabinets, patted the flank of the one at the end. His manner denied any threat in the appetite of the machine he commanded. Matthew followed reluctantly, Abigail close behind him.

'Chat isn't encouraged. We'll go through to Data Reception.'

The door at the far end opened, letting in a gust of activity. The area beyond was large, crowded with desks and argumentation. Sheets of blue teletype were scattered on every surface, people in groups passing them to and fro, arguing over them, smoking, drinking coffee or chocolate from the automat in one corner.

'The human touch, and not nearly as chaotic as it looks.' The director's sentences were expanding with his enthusiasm. 'Here we're divided up into sections according to subject. Which accounts for most of the noise. Subject barriers vaguer with every day that passes. Could get all this done by computer as well, but I don't. I believe the interplay of human minds at this level is useful, produces more surprises. Which are what we're after.'

Matthew caught his wife's inquiring glance and unobtrusively shrugged his shoulders. Not unobtrusively enough.

'What's going on, Mrs Oliver, is really very simple. Data comes in from all over Europe on thirty teleprinters, each offering stacking facilities up to a hundred. So the line's practically never engaged. The data is streamed roughly by those people over there. Classified according to subject, I mean. Then it goes around to the groups who hash out the final streaming. Anything particularly awkward or interesting goes to the department heads. That's the part of your job I described last week, Oliver. Every item that finally gets into the data store is the department head's responsibility. So that's Data Reception.'

He surged across to the automat and handed out coffee.

'I said we were after surprises. I meant it. Computers capable of learned responses are nothing new. But this one surprises us every day. Bohn can't have known what they were cooking. We've tried off-beat streaming, even downright perversity. Stretching the machine simply forces it to dig deeper. You see, you might say we've programmed it to trust us. So it rejects practically nothing. Spots the association even if it takes three minutes to do so. Which at ten million scanning operations per second is quite something.'

He picked up a sheet of teletype and read the first few lines.

'Seismographic analysis.' He shrugged his shoulders and put the sheet down again. 'Myself, I know nothing about everything. Except perhaps brain physiology. And then only what sort of hammer to hit it with.'

Matthew recognized his defensiveness, resulting no doubt from public distrust of 'pill psychology.' He distrusted it himself, for reasons part ethical and part woolly theological. But Billon himself he was beginning to like. It was interesting that in his sixties, at the height of a successful career in medicine, he had chosen to leave it for the Colindale. Matthew didn't doubt that there was some very good reason.

'So that's Data Reception.' They gulped their coffee, obviously off again. 'Astran programmers are in the room over there. They put the streamed data onto ten-track magnetic tape. You have to believe in them, because what they do works.'

He glanced at his watch.

'These people will be working till three. Two shifts, eight till three and three till ten. That way we just about keep up. By the way' – he turned to Matthew – 'did you notice the lack of printout clatter? The Bohn 507 does it photographically. Television-type scanning on sensitized paper. Thousand lines per second. Without it we'd be output-bound. Mechanical printing had gone as far as it could.'

He started herding them across the room toward the far door.

'Data output is fully automatic, emergency panels in the basement. Random access, of course – no more of the waiting around you get with tapes or disk storage. It's available twenty-two hours out of the twenty-four. The Bohn needs two hours daily for servicing. The engineers run check programs, watching for weaknesses. Perhaps I'd better explain data output, Mrs Oliver.' He didn't wait for her to answer. 'We offer five services. A, you can ask for a specific data unit. B, you can ask for a transcript of a specific paper. That's where the quick printout comes in. C, you can mention a specific paper and ask for everything in that field. You then get a list of primary associations, authors, dates, comprehensive titles. If that is not enough you can ask the Bohn, D, to cast its net wider, bringing in the secondary associations, possibly three hundred or more. Lastly, you can ask for data simply by subject, in which case you may end up with a list several hundred yards long. In this case the computer will enter into a dialogue with you, and try to establish what it is you really need to know. And all by phoning in, using basic Astran from the handbook, two hundred symbols, no problem.'

Abigail had known all this months ago. Advertising material from the Colindale Data Rental Service had come to Matthew through the post. They were out of Data Reception now, going down a passage lined with doors.

'What are all these?' asked Matthew, hoping to distract.

'Offices, staff amenities, door to the classified wing ...' Billon gestured vaguely. 'Classified wing?'

'For department heads to get on with their own projects. When they've time. Computer facilities. Nothing very interesting.' He turned back to Abigail, relentlessly continued his exposition. 'Bohn facilities are available on a rental basis to any individual or organization in the European Federation. We install a small teleprinter plus printout, and you use it as you would a telephone. The Bohn will even correct your Astran for you as you go along. The secret is huge storage capacity – on the molecular level, in fact. Four years' use and still not at ten percent of capacity. Data Reception feeds in maybe a thousand new data items a day. And the Bohn thinks up increasingly subtle methods of inter-relating them. We never really know what we're sitting on.

He broke off, as if feeling he had – incredibly – said enough. He stopped Matthew and Abigail outside a door marked PROGRAM STORE.

'Program Store,' he said unnecessarily. Matthew wondered who wanted to be shown racks of magnetic tapes. Billon opened the door and obliged them to look inside. 'Upward of ten thousand different programs.' He glanced at his watch again. 'Life wasn't always as easy as it is now. Scientists, programmers, systems analysts, took us months to make the thing work. Months of trial and error, checking miles of tape to find perhaps one tiny mistake. Now we've got diagnostic programs, do the job for us.'

He ushered them out. Matthew was feeling impatient. He'd been shown nothing new so far, certainly nothing to warrant all the secrecy, all the security precautions. If Abigail could be pressing, so could he.

'And this is really all there is to the Colindale project?'

'Not precisely ...' The director looked at his watch, this time as a performance. 'It's nearly two. Promised my wife I'd be home for lunch. What say we meet again this evening? Around six?'

It might be a genuine excuse. Matthew couldn't see that anything was gained by it – then or at six, he'd have to be told sooner or later. So he contained his irritation.

'So you see,' said Dr Mozart, leaning against the sitting room doorjamb, 'there's someone in the Colindale who wants to kill the director. What interests me is what he's waiting for. One attempt, and then a three-week gap. War of nerves, do you think?'

Abigail wasn't interested. She was busy turning up curtains for the living room and she found Dr Mozart a bore. If he was going to make a habit of popping in then she'd have to get Matthew to ask him not to. She wondered if – horrors – there was a Mrs Dr Mozart.

'Or simply lack of opportunity.' Matthew's voice showed that he too wasn't very interested. In Dr Mozart.

'But the director is not a careful man. There are opportunities every minute of the day.'

'Is that why you carry a gun around, Dr Mozart? Is everyone supposed to?'

'My name is Wolfgang. Please call me Wolf. And I shall call you Matthew.'

'I was asking you about your gun.'

'And I was evading you.' He stretched his arms and yawned. Abigail bent lower over her curtain, bonding the hem with neat dabs of adhesive. Matthew hadn't told her anything about a gun.

'I might play a game with you,' the German went on, 'and ask you what gun. And then you would be embarrassed, because you are the sort of man whom deceit embarrasses. So I shall trust you instead.'

'You're a security man?'

Dr Mozart spread his hands in friendly admission.

'I trust you because you come after the bomb incident. For a second ill-wisher to get past screening is beyond belief.'

'Perhaps it's not as difficult as you think.' Matthew was having a perverse sort of fun, and Abigail wished he wouldn't. She felt her ears prickling, hoped the blush didn't show. 'I dislike spies,' Matthew said. 'I dislike security, and everything to do with it. I'm a scientist. So if trusting me means asking me to help, please don't.'

He sounded so righteous, he would have fooled Saint Michael. But silence would have been far more dignified. She finished her curtain and looked up. He was sorting books onto the bookshelf, placing them according to subject and author. So tidy.

'I wouldn't dream of asking you to help. As an amateur you'd be far too inept.'

'Then what are you really here for?'

'I go everywhere, laugh and talk with everybody. People don't like me too much, but I have no wife and might be lonely, so they open their homes to me. I see and hear a lot … I'm here to offer you help, Matthew. Just in case you might ever need it.'

'You, help me? What with?'

'Help you to stay alive.'

Abigail began measuring another curtain. Boys' talk, men's talk, security, guns, staying alive … She told herself they needed danger, manufactured it out of nothing at all.

'You see, Matthew, it is just possible that Henderson's death was not after all an accident.'

'But you told me it was. You described the circumstances.'

'Circumstances that could be interpreted in one other way. I'm surprised you haven't thought of it yourself. But you're not a suspicious person. You see, there *was* somebody who knew Henderson was going to borrow the director's car.'

'The director himself?'

'The director himself.'

Abigail reached for the tube of adhesive. From what she had seen of Chester Billon he was certainly capable of ... But it was getting more like a spy story with every minute.

'Why should the director have wanted to kill John Henderson?' she said.

The two men looked at her with surprise, as if they had forgotten she was there.

'Honestly, Mrs Oliver, I don't know.' At least he hadn't got around to calling her Abigail.

'And even if he had, why should he want to kill Matthew as well?' She wanted to make the whole thing seem ridiculous. It was ridiculous ... 'Unless, of course, you think he's planning to kill off all the leading sociologists who come here.'

'I think Matthew should be careful, Mrs Oliver. That's all.'

The German took himself so seriously. Unless, to be fair, it was the situation he took seriously. A man had died. And somebody, probably still in the Colindale at that moment had killed him ... All her denials broke down and she was frightened. Matthew picked up another pile of books.

'Does the director know you're an agent?' he said.

'I hope not.'

'What can you tell me about the Colindale project?'

'It's dangerous.'

'Nothing else?'

'That's the director's job.'

'I see.'

Matthew was alone in the garden, prodding the pool to see how deep it was. As she hung the sitting room curtains she watched him move the stick vaguely about in the shallow water.

'The Minister has water lilies and carp. I wonder if we'll be here long enough to bother.'

She saw him as a man for acres, not lily ponds. For storms and tempests, not petty intrigue, who killed whom. A cottage on an island, a field of potatoes, windblown hens pecking in the mud, Matthew coming up from his boat swinging a string of fish.

'If you went fishing in the sea off an island,' she called, 'what sort would you come back with?'

'Mackerel ... if I had a motor or didn't mind rowing like hell.' He put down his stick, came to the window, and leaned in. 'But the islands are getting terribly crowded,' he said.

'There must be one somewhere.'

'You read that survey of the Orkneys.'

What was the use of him catching up with her so quickly, if he then crushed her? She lowered her arms from the curtain rail.

'You were very good at lying to the German,' she said.

'Only by inference. Besides, I'm keeping an open mind. I've got to find out just what the Colindale project is before I decide what to do about it.'

'Perhaps' – she couldn't keep up her bitterness – 'perhaps that's what Henderson said to *his* wife.'

'I love you, Abigail.' He hugged her through the window. 'I'm not going to get myself killed.'

His hands were on her shoulder blades, shaping them. He wanted to make love. It would be their first lovemaking in the new house. Dimly she heard the clock in the room behind her begin to strike. His hands paused, and then continued. She laughed into his ear.

'I've lost you,' she said. 'Tell me what you think you ought to be doing.'

'Wasn't that six?'

'I expect so.'

'That's when the director's expecting us.'

She'd had enough of the director, of the computer center, of the Colindale. It was all so grubby somehow.

'You go. I've had enough of the computer center for one day. You can tell me all about it when you get back.'

She smoothed his hair, but he still looked like a tufted guinea pig. She did not tell him to be careful – if he needed to be told then telling was a waste of time. He knew what life for her would be without him. He must simply get on with what had to be done.

After they had argued and he had finally gone alone, she drifted about the house for half an hour or so, doing nothing, waiting for him to come back. The rooms were without associations – except as dead man's shoes – and the sameness of their views of the central garden began to oppress her. They needed a past and a future that were identifiably hers and Matthew's. Then the broken bits of polystyrene from the packing cases caught her eye and she spent nearly an hour clearing them up. Finishing in the bedroom, she lay down on the piled blankets on the bed and felt that she deserved a cigarette. After that she leaped up and purged the bedroom, stuffed everything into cupboards and drawers, and made the bed. Then she cooked some porridge because she felt hungry.

It wasn't until daylight began to fail that she realized it was late, and that Matthew had been gone a very long time. The guns and incendiary bombs she had ridiculed suddenly became real, and she rang the director's office. Getting no reply, she rang Reception. Professor Billon was busy and in no circumstances could be disturbed. The receptionist had no idea where Dr Oliver might be – except that she was sure he had not left the building. She offered to ring around all the offices, but there were a large number and it would take time. She mentioned that she went off duty at ten. Abigail told her not to bother.

Her panic increased when she called Dr Mozart's apartment and got no answer. There were hundreds of reasons why Matthew should have been delayed – his having come to harm in some way being the least probable. Obviously the least probable. But the emptiness in the house was becoming hard to bear. She went out, disjointed by anxiety, into the dusk to look for him.

She walked down past shadowy doorways and groups of trees and dim courtyards; already she felt better, a little foolish so that she almost turned back. But – fear apart – there was no reason why she shouldn't visit her husband where he worked ... Rounding a corner, she saw the low bulk of the computer center, lights spilling from it across the gray-blue evening. Its normality comforted her further, and she entered the foyer feeling totally in command. The place already had a night look about it, each feature unnaturally clear and still. The burred glass floor was now lighted from beneath, and she crossed it briskly to the reception desk, feeling as if people were looking up her skirt. She showed her pass.

'I want to see my husband.'

The receptionist was now the night porter. It was a few minutes past ten, and he'd only just come on duty. He was sorting out his keys and checking his two-way radio. He looked briefly on a chart to see if Dr Oliver was still in the building.

'You know where his office is, Mrs Oliver?' He let her pass without waiting for an answer. 'I've booked you in for ten five, Mrs Oliver. If you're hoping for computer time, there ain't none. Reserved solid by Professor Furneau.'

Abigail liked his assumption that she was working there. She found herself wishing that she *had* been wanting computer time. Not to spoil the illusion, she thanked him and walked quickly away. Her University days had been fun, and the period afterward with the L.C.C ... Once out of sight she returned to reality and paused, considering what she should do next. Of course she had no idea at all where Matthew's office might be – if indeed he had yet been allocated one. She suspected not, otherwise the girl on the phone would have suggested ringing it. She decided to follow the route – the only one she knew – that the director had shown them that morning. If the director was busy, he was probably either in his office or the computer room itself. And she'd probably find Matthew with him.

Professor Billon's office was deserted and in darkness, except for the beginnings of moonlight through the three eye-shaped windows. She crossed it, and went out into the corridor that led to the computer room. The corridor itself was also unlighted. But, film-like, as if projected onto the full-width glass door at the corridor's end, Abigail saw the computer room, unbelievably chaotic, in minute and brilliant detail. The room was crowded with people. Several of the console cabinets were open, their circuit blocks pulled out in units on the floor. Folded printout sheets lay around in concertina piles, and ribbons of magnetic tape were being trodden underfoot. An assistant was going around trying to rescue them and put them up for rewind. There were also quantities of books and microfilm, and a film projector.

As Abigail approached the glass door it began to rise automatically, letting out an unpleasant murmur of controlled human hysteria. Then an awareness of her presence in the doorway spread slowly around the huge room, and the murmur dwindled down to silence. People became still, interrupted in what they were doing, fixed staring at her. Desperately she sought a familiar face, found the director and, rather in the background, Dr Mozart. There was no sign of Matthew.

'Who are you?' From a man in a white coat she didn't know. 'What are you doing here?'

She felt trapped in the surrounding silence, unable to reply. Professor Billon came toward her, stepping over curls of brownish tape.

'It's all right, Furneau. This is Mrs Oliver. I expect she's looking for her husband.'

There was a gigantic smoothness about him, filling the whole doorway so that she could see nothing around it.

'That's right, isn't it, Mrs Oliver?' She nodded, still dumb. He smiled. 'I was busy. Sent him to have a chat with his assistant.' He pointed back in the direction she had come. 'Along to the other end of the passage. Turn right. Third door on the left.'

She turned and walked away. The glass door closed behind her, shutting off the huge uncomfortable silence. Behind the door people would be getting on with what they had been doing. She realized that somehow she had created a crisis, and that the director had averted it. As if she had stumbled on some obscene ritual and should be grateful to him for sparing everybody's embarrassment.

At the end of the passage she hesitated, always uncertain in matters of left and right. Finally she turned the wrong way, and went through a pair of blank double doors into another passage, thickly carpeted. She counted doors. The third had the name Z. MALLALIEU on it. The initial seemed absurdly sinister. She knocked firmly and went in.

An old man was working in a brilliant cone of light, his head bent over piles of books on the desk. He was alone.

'I'm so sorry. I must have got the wrong …' She began to withdraw.

'Don't go.' The man looked up and she saw that, although white-haired, he was young, scarcely thirty. He scuffled some books out of sight and came quickly around the side of his desk. 'Don't go, I said.'

She would have turned and run, but he had the flat of his hand on the door and was closing it behind her.

'Come into the light so that I may see you.'

She wasn't imagining it: his voice, his physical presence, everything about him was threatening. The Colindale was peopled with madmen. His white hair moved in the darkness, nodding her forward. She walked to the desk, uncomfortably aware of her body, the mechanics of ankles and knees and hip joints as she moved. She didn't know what to do with her arms.

'I'm sorry I interrupted you. I was looking for somebody. My husband. I –'

'Your husband? In the classified wing? Forgive me if I don't believe you.'

Her fear turned to weary irritation. A classified wing, a cone of light, a white-haired young man with Z for an initial and a too-carefully modulated voice … It was cops and robbers again. She leaned on the desk.

'I don't really care if you believe me or not. My name is Oliver. My husband is the new head of sociology. I've just come from the director. He'll identify me, if you really think it necessary.'

She looked down at her hands, almost colorless in the painful light. Then across the surface of the desk, waiting for the young man to reply. She saw the books he had been trying to push out of sight. One of them was a well-used copy of the Holy Bible. And beside it, in Latin, *Apologia pro Vita Sua.*

FIVE

Matthew needn't have worried about being late for his six o'clock appointment with Professor Billon. The director was too busy even to notice his arrival. There were a dozen or so other people in the office, all grouped tensely around the printoff console opposite the windows. It was delivering a list of references, the sheet of sensitized paper streaming from it in a steady blue torrent. In front of the console a metal trough caught the paper so that it folded neatly to and fro. From a slot in the bottom of the trough Professor Billon was drawing out the paper in his own time, and reading the list loudly and clearly. Matthew waited in the background, unwilling to interrupt.

'Heissenger, wave theory, MW 7012x. Hill S., sub-a polarity, NP 5576. Hindl, transformer design, MF 10012k. Holt, low temperature flux, KV 99dll. Hummelmann, sub-a density variants, NP 4070 …'

The scientists around the console were making notes. Occasionally one of them would ask the director to re-peat a title or a reference number.

'… Lowther, beam cutoff characteristics, MW 0019. Loxton, cathode retention, CR 237Q. Mansen G., aging theory, three parts, G 6672, 3 and 4. Mansen, J., petroleum catalysts, CO 79009. Mansen L., refraction indices, LW 9292x …' The director paused. 'Any surprises yet? Buhler? Johnson?'

'The Hill S., NP 5576.' An old man, bearded. 'I must reread it, of course. An interesting paper, from what I remember, but I cannot see the connection. Not with the Naples discovery.'

'Good, Buhler. Good.' Billon returned to his list 'Maque, reentry speeds, BM 60079. Markheim K., critical masses …'

Matthew thought he understood what was happening. Each scientist spotted anything that was in his or her field and made a note of the reference. Presumably the list was being delivered in response to a particular stimulus. But what stimulus, and with what purpose?

'Morgenstern, Moebius extensions, QP 17d. Mort, graduated responses, SS 42 –'

'Professor Billon, sir. Excuse me, sir.' A young man who might have been a rugger coach. 'Don't you think Boney's flipping his lid, sir?'

'Unlikely.' The list continued to flow from the printout slot by Billon's head. 'What makes you think so, Furneau?'

'That's the fifth SS classification he's come up with. It's not my field, sir, but what can Strategic Studies possibly have to do with the Naples discovery?'

'You should have more faith in the Bohn.' Billon turned to a man with spectacles and untidy red hair. 'Coombe-Watkins, you're our strategist.'

'The five papers in question all have to do with nuclear attack from satellite. I don't remember the details, but –'

'Then the connection is clear.' Buhler again, excited. 'I have at least a dozen papers relating to nuclear warheads.'

'Which accounts,' said Professor Billon, 'for the sequence's high priority rating. And justifies my calling you all out at this time on a Saturday.' He looked around the group. 'It seems as if some of us are in for a working weekend.' His one seeing eye passed Matthew, and then returned to him. 'My dear Oliver, I didn't hear you come in.'

'I knocked, Professor. When nobody answered, I ...' Everybody turned to stare at him. 'You were obviously busy, so I decided to wait until ...'

'Of course. Of course. Should have sent word for you not to come. The Bohn put out a high priority rating, so, I ... But you don't know what I'm talking about.' He covered his eyes for a moment, exasperated. 'No time now. See you Monday morning, nine thirty.'

Apparently Matthew was dismissed. He turned to go, angry at being treated like an office boy.

'Sorry to do this. Oliver. Bit of a panic.' Matthew looked back in time to catch the director's most professional smile. 'Your assistant's in her office. Why not go and get acquainted? Save time on Monday.'

Matthew went out, closing the door behind him. The Colindale project was as far from being explained as it had ever been. He controlled his irritation – at least the latest delay was genuine enough. He was tempted to go straight home to Abigail. But the director had suggested he should get acquainted with Miss Pelham, and he supposed he had no alternative.

He knew his assistant only by the work she had published. Steady and dutiful, it left him unprepared for the spectacularness of its originator. Margaret Pelham concealed both her intellect and her humanity behind an enormous tangle of bleached yellow hair and an amount of makeup that Matthew had previously associated only with ballet dancers. Her eyebrows were plucked bare, and she had sequins at the outer corners of her eyes. With stick arms and legs she looked – put at its most charitable – like a worn-out fashion model. If she'd got past Chester Billon with her appearance so against her, then her work must be really outstanding. Unless the director had a weakness for worn-out fashion models.

'You're Dr Oliver? How super. I'm Maggie. And am I glad to see you – the last few weeks have been bloody hell, since poor John was killed.' She kicked a large filing cabinet. 'Full of problems,' she said. 'I've done my best, but I bet I've let through dozens of things that ought to be coded under something utterly different. Medical, topographical, God knows ... Luckily old Boney does his best to sort it all out, poor thing.'

'I see.'

Matthew felt very old. But at least he didn't have to ask who 'old Boney' was.

'You know, I saw you about the Institute yesterday, and I thought to myself, I bet that's him. The craggy, distinguished look. And sexy, to boot.'

Matthew cleared his throat. Discipline, the establishment of authority, never came easily to him, even at the best of times.

'The thing is,' she continued, 'you don't have to worry. Not about me. It's my anti-social-worker's act. I learned it around the Buildings, and I'm afraid it's stuck.'

'The Buildings?'

'The Hampstead dropouts, you know. The community they've got there – it's smart to call it the Buildings. I did a study for my thesis.'

'I've read it.'

'Have you? How super ... I've read all yours, of course. Mutual admiration soc. Shall we get on with some work?'

They got on with some work. As she explained Institute procedures her extravagant mannerism faded. Codings, classifications, internal distribution routines – she had the ability to make everything clear the first time through. She was friendly, and humorous, and easy to get on with. But the only possible relationship with her would have to be to do with work. Outside that the smoke screen went down, the distancing act. For himself Matthew was relieved. He enjoyed the company of women, but he was married to Abigail: in the Ministry it hadn't always been easy to explain the unfashionable difference. But he couldn't help wondering what had happened to Maggie to make her so defensive.

When he thought he properly understood the basic system, she fetched a file of doubtful codings and they went through it together. The work was fascinating: new data from all over Europe, much of it controversial. At this stage he didn't have to worry about statistical accuracy. The Bohn would check all figures against material already stored and send him back a list of discrepancies. Dealing with this list would be one of his first jobs each morning. And the Bohn was giving this service to all the other seventeen department heads at the same time. Besides dealing with incoming queries from more than three million subscribers.

Impressive as this was, there was obviously more to the Colindale project than just this. Otherwise, why the strict, almost pathological secrecy? And why the scene he had witnessed so recently in the director's office?

'What does the director mean,' he asked suddenly, 'when he says that the Bohn puts out a high priority rating?'

'It's a way the computer has of judging the importance of supplied data.'

'Judging the importance? Surely that's not a job for a computer?'

Maggie looked at him sideways.

'Boney isn't an ordinary computer. I thought you knew that'

'I know it's associative. I know its capacity for observing relationships is unusually subtle. All the same –'

'You must ask C.B. He'll fill you in.'

Her sudden reserve was uncharacteristic. He sat back, puzzled. She held up a warning hand, five gold-painted fingernails.

'All right. So there're things I can't tell you. The director likes to do things in his own way.'

'You might tell me just one thing. Has any of this any connection with Henderson's death?'

She shook her head.

'There's too much I don't know. For one thing, I'm only an assistant. I don't get in to the conferences. John's death upset me – we'd worked together for three years. Nothing very sexual, you know, just that he was fun, and a wonderful man to work with. But questions weren't encouraged, never are at the Colindale. As for *why* he died – once again, I can only tell you to ask the director.'

She paused, needing to say more but uncertain of the right words.

'The Colindale's a strange place. Frightened of itself. Not quite sane ... I think you need to be not quite sane yourself in order to bear it.' She laughed, reverted to the act. 'Sane? I mean, pet, who *is* sane these days? Who'd want to be? I ask you.'

He left it there. She had referred to more than just the place and the people. There was a third element she had grasped at, and then drawn back. He didn't press her because in a way he understood what she meant. Sitting beside Abigail the previous day he had shuddered as he entered the gates.

'I must get back to my wife,' he said. 'She's been expecting me for hours.'

'Boney may be big and fast.' She couldn't leave it. 'But he's still only a computer. He doesn't create, you see; he only shuffles the possibilities. He spots relationships and serves them up. That's not being creative.'

Matthew wondered whom she was trying to convince. There had to be some human capability that computers could not duplicate or exceed. A frontier must exist. She looked across at him, possibly sharing his thoughts, and smiled ruefully.

'You'll see what I mean. When you start working with the Bohn yourself, you'll see what I mean.' She watched him get up and go to the door. 'It runs away with you,' she said. 'It's important to keep a sense of proportion. Remember that there are limitations.'

She was going to say something more, but the telephone rang. Matthew began to edge out through the door. The conversation had taken on a disturbing quality of controlled panic. He reminded himself that Maggie must have been grossly overworked since the death of Henderson. And her fears played too easily on his own …

As he was going she called him back.

'It's your wife. She's along in the classified wing, with Mallalieu. Go and rescue her at once. She shouldn't be there, and certainly not with him. Of all the department heads, he's the maddest. He's so mad it's not funny.'

They walked back to their house together. Abigail fitted under his shoulder, and he shortened his stride so that they walked in step. The sky was pale with the lights from the surrounding motorways, brighter than the moonlight; the courtyards and colored pavements lit at neat intervals by street lamps. The distant rush of traffic emphasized their isolation. They passed two men in white coats arguing over calculations on the back of an envelope. Matthew sighed. So much about the Colindale was right.

Abigail described what she had seen in the computer room.

'What was happening, Matthew? I've never seen a computer in such a mess.'

'I have. I remember a day once at the Ministry … Something goes wrong. Your program doesn't give the sort of answer you expect, and you blame the computer. Just occasionally it *is* the computer that's wrong, but more often it's your program, or your expectation. It can take all night to get things sorted.'

'So they've run into some kind of trouble?'

'It happens. Nothing to worry about, of course. It's only the pressure on computer time that makes people get so desperate. And at least they don't have to pay for time here as they would in any commercial computer center.'

They walked on. Abigail began talking about Zacharie Mallalieu.

'Anyway, Matthew, why have a classified wing? I think they just enjoy making things mysterious.'

'The director told us. It's where department heads get on with their own private projects. That's why it's out of bounds to staff.'

'But Mallalieu's an economist. Even if he was reading this Bible, why should he want so much to hide it?'

'Perhaps he makes a great thing of being a rationalist.'

He knew this was no explanation. Rationalists read Bibles, if only for the purpose of explaining them away.

'But he was so odd, Matthew. Terribly suspicious. For a long time he didn't even believe I was who I said I was.'

'I wouldn't worry about it. My Miss Pelham says he's quite mad. Outside economics, of course.'

He distracted her, told her about Maggie – omitting what she had said about the Colindale. Its closeness to his own feeling worried him. He tried Abigail's trick of dropping the whole thing out of his mind. He ran with her, sat her on a low wall, kissed her, ignored her protests. They hurried home and made cocoa in bowls, the mugs still hidden somewhere under one of the various piles in the kitchen. They went to bed. He thrust the cold hand of the Institute back till he no longer felt it.

Sunday morning they idled about the house till it was time for eleven o'clock Mass. They sorted out the kitchen and hung the bedroom curtains. Matthew spent a long time moving the harpsichord around the sitting room till he found the right place for it. The move had disturbed the tune of the upper octaves, and a further half-hour was taken up with the electronic sound-wave matcher. They finally left for church with little time to spare. At the gate they were delayed while their tails were fetched and introduced.

As promised, Mrs Foster was charming. Somebody's aunt, but with muscles, and a laser gun in her handbag. Matthew's tail was called Wilkinson. Not the man who had followed them home the previous Friday; of a better class altogether. He was shabby and thoughtful, and might easily have been an intellectual alienee, one of the thousands of middle-aged dropouts who chose to live on the social services. His car was suitable to such a man, an old model, only barely brought up to the new safety requirements. His front was perfect, giving him a reason to be anywhere at any time, idle and contented.

Since Matthew and Abigail were going out together, and were not going to separate, only one tail was needed. Mr Wilkinson and Mrs Foster tossed, and Mr Wilkinson won. Mrs Foster accompanied the Olivers to church.

The Catholic church in Colindale was new, a white, circular building with darkly colored windows. Matthew and Abigail were among the last in, and the service had already begun. Matthew walked behind his wife, not genuflecting when she did, fearing ritualized gesture, not crossing himself before the Gospel. He went to church always hoping to be gusted into complete participation. But he gave the responses for their beauty of language and joined in the prayers for the history of human aspiration that they represented. He kept himself warily separate, preferring to draw his comfort parasitically from that of Abigail. If he prayed on his own – to a God he hardly believed in – it was for understanding. He knew this was the wrong way around: faith should come first, and then understanding. He also knew that for as long as he approached the Church because it was observably a good thing, he would get nowhere. But –

He stood up so that Abigail could pass him and go to receive the wafer. Afterwards he found his joy in hers.

After the slanting purple light of the church, the road in Colindale was like a tawdry amusement arcade, with flashing signs and slot machine people. He stood beside her and let the crowd jostle past, shading his eyes. He wanted to protect her from the contrast. A young man came up to them. He was small and thick-chested – would probably have been a hunchback but for prenatal corrective treatment. He had the hunchback's sharpness of eye and manner.

'Excuse me. Aren't you Dr Oliver? My name is Andrew Scarfe.' He was the sort of young man who expected to shake hands. 'I work at the Colindale, Dr Oliver. Systems analysis.'

Matthew introduced him to Abigail. They stood on the pavement thinking of things to say.

'It's our first time at this church,' said Abigail. 'We enjoyed the service very much.'

'I come every Sunday. The priest's very good, I think. I like his delivery, and the way he doesn't hustle the responses.'

'And the organist's not bad. And the layout's good – everybody gets such a good view of the altar.'

This sort of in-group familiarity made Matthew uneasy. Mechanical, irreverent somehow. He wondered what young Scarfe had really come to talk about. Unless he simply wanted to strike up a friendship with fellow-Catholics.

'Can we give you a lift back?' he said.

'No thanks. I've got my own wagon. Besides, the tail wouldn't like it. He might think I was trying to dodge him.'

Matthew frowned. He had been forgetting the ways of the Colindale.

'Perhaps we could give you some lunch,' said Abigail, evidently not realizing that Andrew Scarfe was one to like regularity in his life. No cooking had been done so far, and they would expect to eat lunch around three.

'No thank you, Mrs Oliver. My flat-mate always does the Sunday lunch. It's one of her few domesticities. Though it often needs half the afternoon to tidy up after her. I believe she's your assistant, sir. Margaret Pelham. Strange woman – I'm afraid we don't get on all that well. Don't misunderstand me, sir. I'm sure she's a wonderful person to work with. Good at her job and all that.'

Matthew distrusted such eagerness to say the right thing. If he had to choose between Scarfe and Maggie, he'd choose Maggie every time. The young man's openness was too wide-eyed. Nobody could be as simple, as genuine, as Scarfe appeared to be.

The crowd outside the church was thinning. Along the street a procession with placards could be seen approaching, middle-aged alienees demanding the vote back, ALIENATION NO CRIME, said the placards. And PENSIONERS NOT OUTCASTS. The suburban Sunday strollers paused to stare. It was an orderly, pathetically orderly demonstration, heralded by neither drums nor loudspeakers.

'By the way, Dr Oliver,' – Scarfe cocked his head and looked up at Matthew, eyes keen and bird black – 'if you ever want any help with Astran I'll be only too glad to oblige.'

'That's very kind.' Matthew was watching the procession. 'All the same, I don't think –'

'I'll lend you a book. Bring it around one evening.'

'Thank you, Mr Scarfe. Actually, I doubt if I shall be doing much programming myself.'

'Still, it'll be a help at least to know how it works. Short for Associative Transliteration, of course.'

Of course. Who did the lad think he was talking to? Matthew pulled himself up, wondered why he was being so intolerant. He settled, ashamed, on Scarfe's slight deformity. In young people physical perfection was so universal, and deviation so ringed about with psychological implications, that it made him distinctly uneasy.

'Very kind of you, Mr Scarfe. Come around any time you like.'

At that moment Scarfe's tail arrived, asking if he could get back to the Colindale fairly soon as his wife was expecting him for an early lunch. A charmingly domestic touch.

'He must be very lonely,' said Matthew, watching the two of them walk away in friendly conversation.

'From what you told me about Miss Pelham she doesn't sound the easiest person to share with. Though he struck me as not being very keen on women at the best of times.'

'Perhaps they're not very keen on him. Anyway, he's stuck with it – Billon mixes the sexes as a matter of policy. He says it makes relationships less dependent on love or sex. They work together, so they should live together. As laid down in his quartering register.'

Abigail took his hand. 'The man's a fool,' she said.

The procession had nearly reached them. As they watched it was overtaken by three police cars, which turned across in front of it and stopped. The marchers stopped also, and waited meekly. Policemen from the three cars went through the ranks taking names and addresses, checking identity cards. Nobody ran, or struggled, or even protested: there were two more cars and a large closed van waiting at the rear of the procession. People in general had little sympathy with alienees and their conditional pensions – being alienated was no more than an excuse for being bone idle. The idea that work was a good thing in itself lingered tenaciously, no matter how much the experts told people it was out of date.

After its members had been counted and listed, the procession was allowed to go on its way. This it did, though more from pride than from conviction or continuing hope of success. Pensions were conditional, conditional on too many things. The machinery of government was orderly and discreet.

Matthew and Abigail watched the people march by, men and women in their thirties and forties, some of them extravagantly dressed, some of them merely seedy. The purpose of their demonstration was oddly out of character; usually alienees took no interest at all in the democractic process. This untypical political interest suggested outside influence, either from the East or from the Americas. Which explained the police intervention. Usually alienees demonstrated against compulsory education for their children or in favor of better housing.

Matthew waited, saddened, for Mrs Foster to ease her car out of the crush. The scene he and Abigail had witnessed was part of the real world; their lives at both the Colindale and in their Kensington house were totally disconnected, out of touch. Viewed like that, there was no doubt little to choose between the two. They drove home in front of Mrs Foster, the car's air conditioner cooling the sweat on their hands and faces.

On their return they found an assortment of Sunday newspapers waiting on the doorstep, further signs of Colindale efficiency. The afternoon was hot and still, and they lunched by the pool in their central garden. The fir tree smelled rich and dark. They half expected Dr Mozart to pop in, and were very glad when he didn't. The papers remained where Matthew had put them, on the floor just inside the front door. That afternoon he and Abigail were happier to talk about what came into their heads. If anything did.

Around six o'clock Matthew went in to try out the newly-tuned harpsichord. He felt very hot, and chose to play Couperin. After, a few minutes Abigail spoke to him from the garden, not raising her voice, so that he hardly heard.

'Grandpa's lived too long,' she said.

She might have been talking to herself. He went on playing. She had been to see the old man on Saturday morning. He blamed himself for not having asked her about her visit – it had been crowded out by the move, by the Colindale. No doubt she had been waiting for him to ask.

'Did you hear me, Matthew?'

He stopped playing. With even cancer controlled, what was there left to die of?

'I wasn't sure if you meant me to,' he said.

'I've been thinking, Matthew. I've decided he belongs with us.'

She came into the sitting room. He got up and went to her, put his hands on her shoulders.

'He'd only feel he was being a bother.'

'We wouldn't let him.'

'We couldn't help it. The three generation family just doesn't work any more.'

'We could make it work.'

Matthew would have liked things to be different. He would have liked the old man to be able to feel he had a place with them, a place where he was respected for his age and wisdom. But the two, age and wisdom, no longer went together. The tradition of respect, even of usefulness, had died.

'It can't be done, love. It's thirty years too late. He'd feel he was out of touch, nothing but an old fool, an object for our pity. You see, we don't *need* him. Anything else is so artificial.'

'But everyone's worked so hard to keep him alive, Matthew.'

To which there was no answer.

Monday morning was overcast, and it looked as if there might be rain. Matthew decided it would stay dry until lunch time and went to the computer center without his coat. He frequently made such decisions and they were frequently wrong. In the last two hundred yards of his walk rain began to fall heavily. He ran, and then stood under the awning shaking water off his jacket. The wet paving stones smelled of his childhood, of the first hot summer he remembered, and of the rain he had stood in, soaking his hair and face, the day that the heat had lifted.

'Dr Oliver, the director wants to see you at once.'

'I'm not late, am I?'

He hated to be late.

'Not at all. He just left word that he'd like some time with you before the conference.'

'Conference?'

The girl behind the desk stared at him without expression, as if his question had been in bad taste.

'Please go through at once, Dr Oliver.'

The director's office was dim, except for a lamp over his desk. Professor Billon was talking on two telephones at once. Matthew sat down and waited. He saw for the first time that the pupils of the three eye windows were sensitized so that they dilated and contracted in response to the light outside. At that moment they were very wide. Expensive toys, and quite pointless, they irritated Matthew's puritanical soul. He tried not to listen to the director's two conversations. In any case, they made little sense. Finally they ended.

'You wanted to see me, sir.'

Something to say after a long pause during which the director stared at him, his mind apprently far elsewhere.

'Seems I've got to throw you in at the deep end, Oliver.' He frowned, his tangled eyebrows concealing his eyes. 'Unless you've already worked everything out from the little charade you walked in on day before yesterday.'

'I'm afraid not.'

'At least you know there's more in the Colindale project than meets the eye. Has to be. You'll see why in a minute.' Professor Billon sighed and shifted in his seat, grumbling to himself inaudibly. Then his voice surfaced. 'The Bohn is a remarkable device, Oliver, More remarkable than its designers imagine. It extrapolates. Is in fact a product of its own extrapolations. Extrapolates on a sufficiently wide base to appear creative. Human creativity works by selection, sorting through the individual's memory store and selecting items that interrelate unexpectedly, amusingly, interestingly, profitably. It is the subtlety of this selection process, the criteria it employs, that determines the creative ability of each individual person.' He leaned forward across his desk to point his next sentence. 'And the criteria we have given the Bohn are the subtlest we here at the Colindale Institute could devise.'

'You're saying that the Bohn invents.'

'I'm saying that the Bohn perceives relationships and extrapolates logically from them.'

Which was the same thing. This was what Maggie had been trying to tell him on Saturday evening. He hadn't wanted to know then, and he didn't want to know now. Knowledge would force decisions on him, force him to think of Gryphon and what the man had or had not died for … The director sat back and smoothed his already smooth hair.

'So we have a machine that – if you like – invents. Plots future trends. Tells us what will happen *if* … And does all this better than any other person or organization in the world, simply because of the unique supply of data at its disposal. So what do we have, Oliver?'

Matthew waited to be told.

'We have a unique way of carrying every new discovery, every complex of discoveries, to its most imaginative conclusion. And doing so in a matter of minutes. Months, perhaps years before anyone else will arrive at the same point … Saturday evening you walked in on the Bohn at work, Oliver. It was responding to a discovery received that afternoon from a team of scientists in Naples working in the field of electromagnetics. In itself a small item. But to the Bohn it was like the last piece in a gigantic jigsaw puzzle only the machine itself knew about.' He frowned and tapped the desk with the fingers of one hand. One-two-three-four. One-two-three-four. 'No. I choose words badly. I don't want to suggest that the Bohn had known about this puzzle for some time and had been waiting for just the right last piece. What I mean is that its scanning techniques are so rapid and so complex that all the relationships made possible by the Naples discovery were perceived in virtually the same instant. To choose the more meaningful of these was, for the Bohn, a simple matter. You watched the result of this process being delivered. A list of ninety-six different papers, the contents of which – taken together – made up the whole picture. My team has been checking this list for the last thirty-six hours. Soon we go into conference to hear their conclusions and to decide what is to be done.'

'Done?' Here was the crunch, the million dollar question. 'If an invention exists, it exists. What can possibly be "done" about it?'

'I'll tell you a story, Oliver.' the director paused. They were coming to a part of the script that was familiar to him, complete with stage directions. 'In 1933, Oliver, a laboratory was built for the physicist Pyotr Kapitza. For its facade he ordered the head of a crocodile in stone. "The crocodile of science," he said. "The crocodile cannot turn its head. Like science it must always go forward with all-devouring jaws ..."' Again Billon paused. He turned his chair one complete revolution. 'A generally accepted fact, Oliver. But one that we here at the Colindale deny.'

'You mean you try to suppress discoveries of which you do not approve?'

'Suppression is seldom necessary. You can't suppress what hasn't yet been discovered, what only exists in the circuits of the Bohn. Prevention is another matter. Once you know what a particular invention is to be, there are many ways of preventing it. Research is so specialized. The right hand of science so seldom knows what the left hand is up to ... and then, of course, there's money. The administration of research funds. And so on. And so on.'

'You take a lot on yourselves.'

'We have to. Scientists have refused responsibility for their discoveries for far too long. We've left that to the politicians and the philosophers.' He gestured widely, indicating the resultant state of the world. 'We now have machinery for intelligent, imaginative extrapolation. With this as our basis we can, we *must*, accept responsibility. Accept it and exercise it.' He sighed. 'And exercise it secretly. People in a democracy dislike being told what is good for them.'

It had stopped raining. For a moment Matthew's attention was distracted when a ray of sunlight caused the centers of the windows to scrape softly as they contracted. He feared what the director was telling him.

'No delusions of grandeur, Oliver. Every decision is a committee job. Imperfect system. Better than nothing. Better than the free-for-all that has landed us where we are today. I'll give you an example from your own field. Sociology. To do with organ transplants ... You know why they're no longer carried out on people over fifty?'

'The risk's too great. The drugs controlling rejection leave older people too vulnerable.'

'Right. But last summer a thesis on compatability came in from a Bristol student. Extrapolation showed its line to be new. Probable result: trouble-free organ replacement in all age groups. We needed to know what this would imply. The Bohn gave us the percentage increase in average life expectation.

Relating this figure to housing and pension schemes produced a crippling increase in national expenditure. This was set against an index of life fulfillment patterns devised by your predecessor. Even allowing an optimistic increase in productive working life, the deficit was still far more than the European economy could stand. A study of terminal depression rates, together with an estimate of possible drug control in this field, confirmed the conclusion on purely humanitarian grounds.'

'So?'

'So the girl from Bristol didn't get her post-graduate grant and was forced to go into industry.'

So Gryphon had been right. Decision making on this basis would produce no detectable pattern: the criteria were far too wide-ranging and variable. Individual academic freedom sacrificed for the ultimate good of the whole. A dangerous but attractive possibility. If it worked.

'What if the work doesn't come from a helpless undergraduate?' Matthew asked. 'What if it comes from a famous scientist?'

'Who pays, Oliver? Pays for his equipment, his laboratory, his staff, his food even? Where would any scientist, no matter how great, be without Government money? The important thing is not to do it crudely, to shape the direction of research by giving a little money here and taking a little there. And never giving reasons. Existing legislation offers plenty of loopholes.'

Matthew saw that it could be done. Even the private sector of industry was dependent on the Government for subsidies, grants, tax concessions – besides needing the data facilities of the Colindale. It could be done, but would it?

'What does the Government have to say? How did you persuade them to give you such enormous power?'

'But we have no power at all. No real power. Purely an advisory capacity. Politicians, you see, are seldom scientists – they have to believe what we tell them. Apart from anything else, we save them money. The system can be seen to work. And politicians are pragmatists.'

Science in control of itself. The quality of life at last as the deciding factor. And who was better trained to make judgments on the quality of human life than the sociologist, the ethnologist? He would have to come out from behind the protection of his impotence, his power to do more than theorize. He was being taken onto a high mountaintop and being shown the kingdoms of the world.

'Humbleness, Oliver. Above all, humbleness. We need to listen to each other, we need to listen to ourselves, we need to pray.' This was unexpected. Matthew had made his spiritual uncertainty quite clear during the first interview. He shifted awkwardly under the director's steady gaze. 'Pray to anything you like, Oliver. To the good in yourself, if that's all you believe in.'

Professor Billon sat back, his elbows on the arms of his chair, his fingers interlocked under his nose, staring out over them, missing nothing. Behind him the tall sculpture revolved endlessly. The scar on his forehead was unpleasantly clear in the brilliant overhead light. He was considerable. He could talk of humbleness so that Matthew believed him and did not mentally turn away to vomit. He was considerable.

'You needn't stay here at the Colindale, Oliver. After my exposition to senior staff I always give them the chance to leave.'

'Do many take it?'

'None. So far. But there's always a first time.'

The Colindale project. He could refuse. He could betray it to the C.L.C. He could do what Gryphon had asked him to. He could rouse righteous democrats all over Europe … the kingdoms of the world. With Abigail to help him.

'I'd like to stay, sir.'

The director nodded briefly, and blew through his nose onto his knuckles. A sign perhaps, or an expression of satisfaction. He got up and walked to his place beside the central window. The sky behind him had closed over again, hot and heavy.

'Now,' he said. 'Business. Today's crisis. Conference starts in five minutes. You'll pick up most of the form as you go along.'

Summer lightning flickered, momentarily bleaching the room's thick shadows. Both men waited for the thunder. When it didn't come they felt cheated.

'We'll be discussing an electromagnetic shield. A technique for deactivating nuclear warheads. Total immunity. We're shaken out of our mere recommendations, Oliver, out of our memoranda to the Appropriations Board. We've got to *do* something.'

Matthew shook his head, not fully understanding. It sounded thrillerish and improbable, quite outside his field.

'The bloc that first sets up this shield, Oliver, can initiate atomic war and win. You realize what that means?'

There was a second flash of lightning, brighter than the first. Neither man noticed it.

'Don't worry,' said the director. 'Get it sorted out by lunchtime. There are precedents. Thank God.' He walked to the door. 'Conference time, Oliver. After you.'

SIX

The sound of rain on the pool outside their bedroom window was soothing. Abigail curled up in the big bed and was comforted. She felt very alone now that Matthew had gone. The house was not yet his, not yet theirs, not yet solidly inhabited by the two of them. His warmth was still beside her, her shoulder still smelled of sweat from its place close under his arm. Yet he was completely absent: somebody she distantly hoped would reach the computer center without getting wet.

The Colindale should have reminded her of the University. The University buildings had been taller, but similarly thoughtful, expressing the movement of people with a conscious logic of material and mass. The colors had been similarly mannered. The purpose had been similarly to provide an intellectually stimulating environment. Yet for her the two places held nothing in common. The Colindale, adroit, pretty, costly, of noble aspiration, was totally alien. She rolled over in bed and stared at the ceiling. The University had been open, and the Colindale was closed. And in its parts it was closed, one part against the next. In the Colindale even Matthew, when he was away from her, was closed to her.

The first flash of lightning came when her eyes were half shut, and she thought she might have imagined it. The second, brighter, caught her with her face turned toward the window. She sat up in bed, waiting for the thunder. When none came she got out of bed and went to the window. Storms excited her, prickled her skin. The rain had stopped, leaving the air heavily moist and hard to breathe. The garden outside the window seemed tiny, and its four glass walls reflected each other's black surfaces opaquely. It was like looking into a dead aquarium.

She went to the back of the room and stood on a chest to look out of the high strip of window there, seeing an empty expanse of wet grass, the side of the cloisters, and the blank wall of another building. Over to the right were rooftops and motorways, city to the far horizon. She climbed down from the chest and looked for some clothes to put on. She would be sensible, would go out and do some sensible shopping.

It was while she was hunting for a shopping bag in the kitchen cupboards that she found the first of the microphones. It was no thicker than a piece of paper, with hair-thin leads at one corner – just like the illustrations in Matthew's C.L.C. leaflet. Searching carefully, she found four more, two in the sitting room, one in the bathroom, and one in their bedroom. They had not been in position two days earlier, when the house had been unfurnished: somebody must have broken in to fit them, presumably while she and Matthew were at church. She supposed that bugs for the spare rooms and the lavatory would come later.

It was pointless to be angry or disgusted. The hiding places were hardly more than a matter of form. The breach of etiquette was hers for having uncovered them. She sat down and lit a cigarette. People would often break into her home: to approve it, to bug it, to search it, to protect her from herself and Matthew from Matthew. All this would happen, and more, because she was living at the Colindale Institute.

She thought of Gryphon, and his suspicions about the Colindale. She could believe now that his death had been arranged, that there was indeed something needing to be hidden. She would help Matthew to uncover it. She felt closer to Edmund than she had ever been … Suddenly Matthew was unpredictable, his reactions. He claimed to approach every decision from first principles, but he possessed none – nothing but an expedient, humanistic, woolly sort of love. He would understand her hatred of the Colindale, and he might say he shared it.

The telephone rang.

'Mrs Oliver? Main gate here. We have a man who wants to see you. He's dressed like a priest. Says you know him. Name of Hilliard.'

'Father Hilliard? Of course I know him.'

'Regulations say you should come down and identify all visitors personally. Then we issue a day pass.'

Father Hilliard had been one of the priests attached to the new University of St Paul. Abigail had known him well: a very old man even then, vague in his movements, but his mind still clear, with a Jesuitical clarity that she found herself temperamentally unable to appreciate. Years of dealing with undergraduates had given him a professional elusiveness, so that – although he basically never gave an inch – he seemed always to be in a state of agreeable retreat, always willing complacently to admit doubts that to her were inadmissible. She had never been able to discover the exact boundaries of his faith. He would smile, and shift his ground, and tie his questioners in knots that for all their obviousness were irritatingly difficult to unravel. He relied on experience alone to evade the inept sincerity of his young opponents. To her his words were thin things, inadequate, irrelevant to matters that could only be dealt with by faith.

Father Hilliard was the only priest she had known whom she could not respect. She had not seen him now for more than five years. She wondered why he had come to see her, and almost wished he hadn't. Paul never mentioned him; it surprised her that he should still be alive.

She saw him while she was still a long way from the gate, sitting with his feet close together, his hands folded in the lap of his old-fashioned soutane, on a chair the guard had placed for him under the awning outside the guard house. He was tiny and frail, far older than the five years since she had last seen him. Such a helpless old man – it angered her that the machinery of distrust should have kept him waiting there like a supplicant. She thought of asking the guards why they hadn't stripped him and probed in his anus for bombs. Except that the scanner would do the job better, and with at least a show of dignity.

She vouched for him. The guard reluctantly called him *Reverend* and let him through.

'It's refreshing, my child, not to be trusted. I've worn this uniform for too long. I'd quite forgotten what non-acceptance felt like.'

She caught herself suspecting this of being manneredly innocent, and offered him a silent apology. Not that he wouldn't contentedly have agreed with her.

He had arrived on foot from the bus stop, carrying a large black umbrella. She took it from him, it looked so thick and heavy. They walked up slowly under a lowering sky, lit by infrequent flashes of lightning. Father Hilliard said little, saving his breath for the gentle ascent and the occasional short flight of steps. Beside him Abigail felt indecently robust. She identified a few of the buildings for him, and then fell silent. His ascent was single-minded, leaving room for nothing else. She shared his effort.

By the time they reached the house they were both exhausted. She offered him a chair in the unfinished sitting room, and he chose an upright one from which it would be easy to rise. She made him tea as she remembered he liked it, trying not to despise him for all the infantile milk and sugar. If his mind had been infantile too she would never have objected.

'I worry you, my child. I always did. Yet there is more than one way of skinning a cat.'

'Of course, Father.'

'But you are far calmer than I remember you. I like that. You do not pester me with questions. You let an old man take his time. I like that.'

He had that ability of the very old to pay compliments that neither embarrassed nor needed answering. To disclaim his praise would be impolite, an unsuitable criticism. She stood by the window and waited, keeping herself apart. She had hated his cliché about cats.

'You are well, Abigail, and your husband? Your marriage is well, you are happy and strong in your faith?'

These statements, not questions, seemed a necessary grounding, as if he wanted them out of the way as quickly as possible. She allowed him their truth.

'I'm here to speak to you about your brother, my child. You may be able to help me.'

'Paul? He's been to see you?'

'We have talked.' He drank his tea, holding the cup in both hands, looking up at her over the rim. 'Not within the Confessional, you understand. It is possible that he has done this as a way of leaving my hands free – more than that, as a way of demanding that I take some action.'

'I saw him a few days ago.' She still gave nothing. 'He seemed all right then. A little overexcited, but he's like that.'

'Seven years younger than you … You know him well?'

'Not very. He has his own very close circle.'

'I need background, you see … What can you tell me about your parents?'

Her inclination, which she knew was wrong, was to tell him nothing. But Paul had gone to him for advice.

'Father, what did he talk about? If I know that, perhaps I'll be more able to help you.'

'About militancy.' An upward inflection. 'About the Church's definition of a righteous war.'

This shocked her. She thought Paul had moved on from that. Instead his thoughts had simply become secret. She went nearer to the priest and sat down.

'I thought Paul had moved on from that.'

'Moved on?'

'Nobody wins wars. In societies as closely ordered as ours militancy does no more than provide excuse for further repression.'

'That's what you've told him?'

'It's obvious. The only alternative is social disintegration, which we can no longer afford.'

Father Hilliard shifted on his chair and stared into the half-empty teacup. If he didn't continue with the argument it would not be because he agreed with her but rather because he had other things to do than differ. Perhaps he thought her reasoning over-sophisticated, even slick. She felt obliged to press the point.

'There are other methods of resistance,' she said. 'Surely you see that?'

'For you certainly there are.'

The sort of open-ended remark that had always annoyed her. She said nothing, fearing in her bone marrow to be rude.

'I fear this isn't going very well,' said Father Hilliard. 'We'll be safer on the neutral ground of your parents.'

She offered him a second cup of tea and brought in some biscuits. The circumstances were like those of her visit to Grandpa, and with as little communication. Yet Father Hilliard was perfectly capable of understanding, if he would.

'Dad retired a few months ago.' She leaned toward him, forearms on her knees. She saw her thin wrists. 'I don't really know what he thinks about anything. He was very hard on me as a child, and on Mum. Then, when Paul was born, the usual thing – he spoiled him completely. Mum went along, only too glad of the new atmosphere. It's a long time ago now, Father. I promise you I'm being objective.'

The priest nodded tolerantly.

'A resentful man, would you say?'

'He couldn't adjust to the new patterns of work. He'd never learned a trade, so the only virtue work could have was in its length and its arduousness. He found post-industrial attitudes very worrying.' She broke off, aware of sounding too much the sociologist. 'I don't want you to think he didn't care for me. Only that he could never manage to show it.'

'And your mother?'

'A good Catholic wife. Afraid of Dad, very working class, very old-fashioned, very simple.'

'Which your father is not, I take it. Or there wouldn't have been two such intelligent children.' He mumbled a biscuit, dropping crumbs down his black front. 'So your brother's image of a man is of one frustrated, powerful, but never able to realize his potential. Something of a demagogue in the home where it was easy, but impotent elsewhere.'

Abigail disliked this sort of slot machine psychiatry. But she had to admit that this particular analysis was good. If she'd ever made it herself she might have understood Paul more readily. She changed the subject.

'I've been very worried about his retirement,' she said. 'But his counselor has got him really fired up. He's busier than he's ever been before.'

'And Paul knows this?'

'I suppose he does. He'd be blind not to.'

She realized for the first time how much they both resented this, and Paul even more than she. Father Hilliard finished his tea and put the cup down very carefully, as if he were in the habit of breaking things.

'He did well at school, your brother? Pushed on perhaps? Not allowed to choose his own friends?'

'Of course he chose his own friends.' She couldn't allow that. 'I was the one with the unsuitable friends – or so Dad said. Paul always chose the goodies – he had a sort of instinct as to what would please.'

'Meek boys, probably his intellectual inferiors?'

She wanted him to stop. It was unworthy, like fortune-telling after you'd seen the family album and examined the souvenirs in the china cupboard. She filled in by fetching a cigarette for herself and lighting it. Belatedly she offered the priest one, which he took.

'I suppose they might be described like that. Though it doesn't make him seem a very nice person.'

'Nice person?' Father Hilliard concentrated on making his cigarette burn. He seemed to be lacking in suction. 'Come now, my child, morality is overloaded as it is, without making it a basis for choosing our friends.'

She nearly answered as Matthew would have. Matthew made everything a question of morality. The number of times he brushed his teeth in the morning, even that was a success or a failure to meet a self-imposed target. Remembering quirks of Matthew's mind comforted her. The conversation with Father Hilliard had taken her further from him than she had been in years.

'I can imagine circumstances, Father, in which one might choose one's friends immorally. Simply as flatterers, for example.'

'Is it really immoral to need flattery? It's all a question of levels, my child. I tend to reserve morality for all questions of the eternal soul.'

She saw he was almost mocking her, matching her own pomposity. To her relief he began raising himself attentively to his feet. 'Thank you so much for our little talk, my child. It has been very helpful. I must go now. The bus journey is long, but most comfortable, I'm glad to say. Such a change from the buses of my youth. And if I could just use your lavatory before I go?'

She showed him where it was, and blanked down on a sudden mental picture of him using it. Not from disgust, but from sadness, wondering if celibacy finally withered a man's body. Afterward she felt tender toward him, and motherly. In a way that he would least suspect he had reminded her of God's glory. She fetched his umbrella for him and walked with him down to the gate, holding his hand.

'You've been very helpful, my child. The more I can understand your brother the more likely I am to say the right things to him next time he comes.'

'I'm afraid that won't be for some months, Father. He's just gone to Africa on a project.'

'Are you sure, Abigail? He made no mention of it when he saw me yesterday.'

'Yesterday? But he was leaving on Saturday, catching the morning plane.'

'I don't think I'm that muddled ...' He wasn't muddled at all. 'Yesterday *was* Sunday? Yes, he came to the Presbytery yesterday afternoon. Perhaps it was today he was going. Or next Saturday, even.'

'Yes, Father. Perhaps it was.'

But she knew it wasn't. She felt afraid for Paul, afraid of his reasons for setting up such an elaborate deception. Going around the family to say careful goodbyes while all the time he intended to stay in London. She could think of no satisfactory reason, and she was afraid for him ... Beside her the old priest stumbled a little. She supported him, and they continued down to the gate. She handed him his umbrella.

'Goodbye, my child. God bless you.' She tried to listen to him. 'And don't worry about your brother. That he came to me is a good sign. With God's help I shall be able to advise him.'

She stood for a moment, watching Father Hilliard drift uncertainly away, the wind blowing his robe tight against the backs of his thin legs. He paused, perhaps for breath, and waved his umbrella. She waved in return.

As soon as she got back home she rang the University and asked if they could contact her brother. After a delay, the secretary returned to say he was not available. He had gone to Africa on a merchandising project. She expressed surprise that Abigail, his sister, should not have been told. The secretary thought everybody had been.

The conference room at the computer center was circular, like a tiny Roman amphitheater, with five white, deeply-cushioned steps leading down to a low area in the middle which contained a small Bohn keyboard and printoff console. Dark blue telephones lay around on the cushions, and computer-linked doodle pads. The ceiling was a shallow cone of cedarwood, its point a long way off center. Panels of complex prisms were set in the cedarwood, and the patterns of light from them changed continually. It was a room that, although circular, had no obvious focal center.

Matthew and the director were the first in. Billon walked casually down over the cushions and started explaining the facilities available at the computer desk. Matthew followed him, worried to be walking on what looked like white velvet. But their feet left no trace. Another of Billon's expensive toys, showing a delight in technical ingenuity for its own sake. Curiously eighteenth century.

'... Knowledge is power, Oliver. For too long we've regretted that fact. We've said that knowledge is unfortunately power. Reflection of our inadequacy. Our lack of control. In this room we control the head of the crocodile. Close its mouth. Science guiding science. Real power.'

Matthew remembered the director's protestations of humbleness.

'We know it's dangerous, Oliver. Men of good will. That's the answer. You're one. I've got seventeen others. You'll see. Of course it's dangerous. Isn't the alternative more dangerous?'

A phrase occurred to Matthew, coined back in the sixties, increasingly apt in each successive year. *The runaway world.*

'What about the other powerblocs? This may work for Europe, but what about the –'

'A start. Besides, we must be grateful for the curtains. Behind their curtains the East and the Americas may still be hell-bent. But precious little gets through. With care we'll survive the both of them. Quality of life, Oliver. We don't define it, but we know what it means.' Voices were heard approaching. 'All right, Oliver? I'll introduce you.'

The members of the committee began to arrive. Matthew was bombarded with faces and famous names. It intrigued him that he might be considered as distinguished in his field as they were in theirs. A new thought, but not unpleasant. In the end he could only confidently identify the men he had seen before: Dr Mozart, Zacharie Mallalieu, and Professor Buhler. And the rugger man, Furneau. They settled themselves, informally, the director among them, Matthew at his side. If there was a floor, it was held by the austere gray cabinet of the Bohn 507.

'Begin by confirming the findings,' said the director. 'You've had time to check, Buhler?'

'The calculations were simple enough, once I was sure of the direction.' Professor Buhler looked tired and worried. 'The Bohn checked them for me last night. It's the Littgen paper on molecular polarity, of course. Plus the work being done in Sweden on high-gain generators. Taking into account Parden's revised theory on wave frequency and some of the findings of that man in Switzerland whose name I forget.'

'Morgenstern,' someone said unnecessarily. Buhler smiled.

'Thank you,' he said. 'The paper came in a month ago. For myself I would have said it was mostly nonsense. But Furneau let it through, and the Bohn made no fuss, so here we are.' He smoothed his beard. 'Fission would definitely not take place. Theoretically the shield is feasible.'

'Gardner?' said the director.

Gardner turned out to be a woman. Sexual equality at last. Matthew wondered if Gardner thought this a triumph. From her scraped-back hair she might.

'As far as practical considerations are concerned there should be no difficulty at all.' She drew a quick diagram on her doodle pad. It appeared as it was made on all the other pads. Matthew was fascinated. 'Horizontal beaming in the two kilowatt range would blanket an area of ten square miles. Refractive beaming from ground level would need a bit more.' She laid out calculations and Matthew watched the answers come up. 'Three point seven-five kilowatts. Roughly.' She looked around. 'With today's cheap power, what's that to the Defense Department? You could cover all major population centers for around a thousand kilowatts.'

'Side effects?' said the director.

'None at all. Unless Evans has any radio problems.'

'Not that I can think of.' Evans was as Welsh as his name, small and bushy. 'It's the frequency, you see. Far too long. And laid too close. Today's transmitters would go straight through it without even noticing.'

Dr Mozart cleared his throat, straightened his spectacles, made sure that everybody was listening.

'As I see it,' he said, 'there might possibly be some risk of X-ray interference. Clouding of negatives that would result from spillage. This of course would depend on the limits of the beaming. How narrowly could they be defined, Miss Gardner?'

'You underestimate current band limitation techniques.' Gardner appeared to have taken this as a personal insult. 'Spillage is almost unheard of. Down to point o-o-one, at the most.'

'Thank you, Miss Gardner.'

Dr Mozart removed his spectacles and cleaned them unnecessarily, seeming to have made some private point of his own. From the speed with which the director cut in Matthew guessed that the team was not without its internal stresses.

'Then we're agreed. The shield is practicable.' He glanced at Furneau. 'Counter measures?'

'No trouble there, sir. A suitable mask for the warhead could easily be devised. An anti-shield shield. It would mean modifying all existing missiles, of course. Which would inevitably take a bit of time.'

'So,' said the director, 'the bloc first discovering the shield would immediately make war.' He was unself-consciously playing ticktacktoe with himself as he spoke. 'All-out war. Us in the middle. Probably attacked from both sides.'

'Unless we ourselves perfected it first,' said Mallalieu. 'We could then be the aggressors. Both ways, simultaneously.'

'What the hell would we gain by that?' said a man who hadn't spoken before, his name lost to Matthew in the flood of introductions. Mallalieu shrugged his shoulders. 'The possibility exists. Therefore it needs considering.'

The director had stopped doodling. Matthew felt him stiffen.

'Advantages?' he said.

Several people began to speak at once. Matthew wondered if it was a game they played, or if it was for real. Billon nodded to the strategist among them, a man called Felsen, recognizable from the dustcovers of his books.

'Europe possesses over-kill,' Felsen said, 'even against the two opposing blocs at once. Destruction of industrial potential in the East and in the Americas would simplify her position. Less of the G.N.P. would need to be spent on defense. As we have no territorial interests there would be no problem over policing. A massive relief program would need to be mounted, but this would be aimed solely at alleviating immediate distress, and would be of short duration. Our position then established, we could command a permanent lead – especially in the field of scientific control being pioneered here. The outcome could be the greatest happiness of the greatest number.'

He paused. 'As for the economic results of a drastic reduction in world population, I leave that to my friend Mallalieu.'

'The results would be excellent.' Mallalieu drew a square on his pad, then another inside it and another inside that. 'Europe is at the moment largely self-sufficient, but with an inevitably low growth rate. Markets are retracting, and our post-industrial society competes badly with the totalitarian regimes marketing in Africa and India. Although we have largely adjusted to our lack of oil by the provision of cheap electric power, the possibility of favorable import rates for oil would provide room for expansion. There would in general be no difficulty regarding payment for goods supplied to the newly-devastated countries since they have ample resources for settlement in kind. This combination of new markets for consumer goods and new sources of raw material could increase our growth rate tenfold over the first few years. The loss of several hundred million consumers would make little difference.'

The squares inside each other had continued, down to a tiny square dot. Such a mind would be comforted by the tidying of people into consumers. Matthew could keep quiet no longer.

'And the moral issue? The effect on conscience? Professor Billon – each one of us has a view of himself, and of the society in which he lives. We survive by believing ourselves to be right. You may not be able to compute a thing like national conscience, but that doesn't mean it doesn't exist.'

'Of course it exists.'

The director stood up, walked down to the Bohn, and began sorting through a file of storage disks.

'First of all, if the others will forgive me, proof for Dr Oliver that intangibles like national conscience can be usefully computed. Your predecessor, Henderson, did a lot of work in the field.'

He passed up to Matthew a disk with the classification *Indices of Pride, National and Personal. Jan.* 87. Matthew believed it because it was there.

'You see, Oliver, once you have an associative capability you can use it in non-quantitative fields. Anything may be expressed in terms of anything.'

He took the disk back and looked around the rest of the group.

'We were talking about national conscience. I think I can say the national conscience at large need not worry us. Malleable. Easily subject to shaping. Drugs, abreaction, the cruder propagandas. I could deal with it in a matter of weeks.'

He paused. Matthew stared at him, appalled. Suddenly he was every scientist that Matthew had ever feared: passionless, an offerer of facts, not even boastful. It was in him a cause neither for pride nor for shame that he could deal with the national conscience in a matter of weeks – the fact existed. It was like Everest, like the storage disk, there.

'But, Professor –'

'I referred to the national conscience at large, Oliver. This is, as I said, shapable, worthless. But there is another national conscience. We in this conference room. Self-appointed. All the more aware. Whether we like it or not, we are the conscience of the European Federation.'

It was disturbing. But at least it followed. Everything that the director said did that.

'So?'

'So we have developed a method of discussion here. First the practicalities, then the intangibles: pride, love, hate, work incentives, conscience, aesthetics and so on ... No point in taxing our higher centers before it's absolutely necessary.'

He turned to the other members of the group.

'So here we have it. Matter of conscience. Conscience personal to each one of us. Ends that might be beneficial to humanity. Means that could not possibly be. Anybody in favor?'

His tone made it clear that he considered the question to be no more than a formality. Nobody said a word – not even Zacharie Mallalieu. It was not that before they had knowingly been playing an intellectual game, and now they had stopped playing. It was more that they found it necessary to keep morality as a separate issue. And it was only morality that could turn the head of the crocodile.

'Nobody in favor. Possibility ruled out.'

Obviously the meeting was being recorded. Professor Billon glanced across at a man who had not yet contributed.

'Political solution, Blake?'

'Either we all have the dratted shield or none of us does. May we take it that the thing couldn't be kept quiet forever, Furneau?'

'Independent discovery is inevitable, sir. I happen to know that Littgen's work is already duplicated in the Argentine.'

'Then we all have it, and the sooner the better.' Blake was tall and lean and brisk, the image of a successful negotiator. 'International control treaties would be piffle. So the answer is simple. We all have it, we all use it, and we all develop anti-shield shields for our missiles.' He shrugged his shoulders. 'Political solutions tend to be crude. I'm sorry.'

A disapproving fidget ran around the group, like a wind ruffling the feathers of roosting birds.

'A lamentable drain on the Defense Appropriation,' said Mallalieu. 'But I suppose it can't be helped.'

'Come along now, Zack' – this was Dr Mozart, the first time he had spoken in far too long – 'we all know Defense is the great adjuster. Haven't you been worried by the imbalance in the Danish economy caused by that improved bacon yield we got a couple of months ago? Surely all these shields are just what's needed to mop that up?'

Mallalieu shook his head angrily, the white hair flopping like a sparse mop. 'It's easy to see you're no economist, Mozart. I should have thought it was perfectly clear that –

'Then we're all agreed.' The director cut in firmly. 'Blake's solution must be adopted. I'll get the machinery in operation at once. Same procedure as before?' Nobody argued. 'Right. Then we'll have a ten minute break.'

He sat back and closed his eyes. The committee members broke up into groups and began talking about other things, the rest of the morning's work ahead of them. The problem of the nuclear shield, now settled, had no further interest to them. Phone calls were made, and Professor Furneau went for some coffee.

'Is it really as easy as that?' said Matthew, under the general conversation.

Billon shifted, but didn't open his eyes. 'I told you not to worry, Oliver. There's an established procedure. We've done it before. New nerve gas and its counter, for example. Two years ago. We organize a handout in Geneva. Fullest possible details to everybody. Then we develop it neck and neck and nobody either wins or loses. Childish, but there you are. Excuse me.' He reached for a telephone. 'Need a systems analyst. The Bohn will even do the handout, given the right program.'

Matthew stared at the people around him. Gryphon's question was answered – with an answer so big that it made the question unimportant. All the secrecy, all the unpleasant superstructure of the Colindale now made sense. With Gryphon dead and Sir William uncooperative, Matthew now had no immediate way of contacting the C.L.C. He would do nothing to find one.

A technician in a gray overall came in down the white velvet steps. He was the systems analyst Professor Billon had rung for, Andrew Scarfe with a neat folder under one arm. Billon got wearily to his feet and went to join him at the computer console. Scarfe recognized Matthew and waved. Matthew waved back. He was thinking of Abigail, and he was – in a sudden moment of clear-sightedness – fearful.

SEVEN

Abigail faced him across the kitchen. Behind her the machine was beating eggs for omelets.

'I think it's insane. And you accused Gryphon of paranoia.'

'I know all that, love. But isn't the alternative worse?'

'The alternative is education. We're all being taught a new awareness. We can all choose, we can all accept or reject. Science can only do what people let it do. We've rejected nuclear war, haven't we?'

'Of course we haven't. It looks over our shoulders day and night.'

'But it doesn't happen because we don't let it. We've been given free will – we are responsible for ourselves. It may not be comfortable, but it's how we are. The future is between God and each one of us: not something to be shunted off onto a bunch of faceless, soulless experts of whose existence we haven't even been told.'

She saw his incomprehension, and it frightened her. They had been arguing now for ten minutes; the eggs would be like plastic foam.

'But that's how it has to be, Abigail. People's vision is limited. They go for the short-term gain, the immediate benefit. That's the big thing wrong with democracy. And they can't be told about the Colindale for the simple reason that they're so bloody stupid they'd immediately blow it up. Or something.'

'We are responsible for ourselves, Matthew. All we can do is trust in God.'

She watched his bitter reply remain unsaid, and for the wrong reasons: out of respect for her, out of an intellectual understanding of her position, out of a wish not to hurt. She couldn't reach him. She couldn't make him see the sin in relieving people of the basic human agony of self-determination. Before his return her mind had been full of Paul, wanting Matthew's advice. What should she do, knowing that he had lied? What had he really wanted the money for? What was he doing? The questions had gone around and around. Now they were unimportant.

'Abigail, it seems to me that you see God like a father handing his child a box of matches. He tells the child that the matches are dangerous, but he goes on handing them, box after box … I have a feeling that God might be very pleased if some of the matches were taken away.'

She wouldn't listen to him. She wouldn't hear him betraying his intellect, damaging her respect for him, ultimately – through hurt – her love. She turned away and switched off the egg beater. She had never felt less hungry in her life.

'We've always had leaders, Abigail. People who make decisions for us. What's the Pope if he isn't the ultimate responsibility shift?'

She heated a pan, didn't answer.

'You'll say the Pope is guided by God. Why can't we in that conference room be guided by God? On earth peace to men who are God's friends?'

God's friends – who inhabited a devil's trap of secrecy and intrigue. Who murdered each other. Who lied, and carried guns, and sought through all this for an earthly salvation ... But the argument wasn't only in her mind. She was thinking now with her whole body, with her whole life. For her it wasn't a matter of reason, it was a matter of knowledge. Everybody must make their own world, the world they lived in. Everybody.

'Listen to me, Abigail ...'

'I won't listen. You only argue so hard because you know you're wrong.'

'Of all the –' She turned and stared at him, seeing a man she had known and ignored. 'Of all the easy ways out, that is the bloody easiest.'

She cooked omelets and he ate them. Nothing ever put him off looking after his body. She watched him snouting for several minutes.

'I ought to have told you,' she said. 'They've bugged the house.'

'That's nice. That's lovely.' Shoveling food. 'Now the whole place knows how you feel about the project.'

'Don't you mind being spied on? Doesn't the whole outfit make you want to be sick?'

'Of course I mind. It's just that I can see their point of view. With a project as important as this they obviously can't afford to take any –'

'Eat your food, Matthew. Just eat your food.'

He was a stranger. She stood by the sink and waited till it was time for him to go back to the computer center.

'Well?' he said. 'What are you going to do about it?'

He spoke loudly and clearly for the benefit of the microphones. She could have stuck kitchen knives in him. She could have taken his hands and ground them in the waste disposal unit.

'I don't know what I'm going to do about it.'

'That's a change. I thought you always knew.'

'Please, Matthew ...' Suddenly all her hatred had ebbed away.

'I'm sorry. That was cheap ... It's just that I see here the most hopeful thing that has happened in six hundred years of science, and you – you see it as the devil going forth like a raging lion. Yet we both start from the same point.'

'I wonder if we do.'

'Abigail, think of the men who worked on antibiotics. They looked no further than the immediate problem. You might say they were directly responsible for the misery and starvation that followed. If the Colindale had been in charge then, work on population control could have been started at the same time.'

'If the Colindale had been in charge,' she said bleakly, 'wouldn't it have seemed easier simply to suppress the antibiotics? Avoid creating a problem for which at the time there was no solution? Don't you think so?'

Matthew's eyes flickered. She watched him trying to evade. She knew she was wasting her time.

'That's where basic good will comes in,' he said. 'Obviously Billon has chosen his men carefully.'

Abigail fetched his briefcase from the chair by the door.

'You'll have to hurry or you'll be late.'

'You haven't told me what you're going to do.' Thinking of the microphones?

'Nothing for the moment. I promise.'

He went away down the cloisters, paused at the corner to look back. At that distance he was familiar, all of him precious. She ran after him and hugged him, held on to the size of him. What he had told her was so monstrous, so insane that it shifted life off onto a completely different level, a level where neither of them belonged. They were too close to each other; she couldn't have lost him to such a system of ideas. She wanted instead to talk to him about Paul, but that would have made him late for the afternoon's conference, spoiled the punctuality that meant so much. He was edging away even as she hugged him.

When he was finally out of sight she walked back a few paces toward the house, then leaned on a pillar and tried to think what she should do. Do about Paul. The other thing she had put away as unreal, nothing to do with her and Matthew, basically irrelevant. She trusted that the truth of what she believed would come to him in its own good time. But Paul's trouble was immediate.

She was afraid. Father Hilliard interpreted her brother's avoidance of the Confessional as an appeal for practical help. Abigail saw another possibility: actions that Paul was not yet ready to confess. He had lied, he had obtained a large sum of money from her, and he had gone into hiding. And he had asked the priest for a justification of violence … She stared out across the grass at a distant line of trees, pylons and point blocks behind them. The conclusion was obvious. Paul had joined some subversive organization and had contributed her fifteen thousand marks to its funds.

She turned back to the house. If Paul was in hiding she was sure she knew where. There was a vast underground carpark near the University, left over from the time when the buildings had been offices and unlimited cars had been let into Central London. He had often explored there during his first year, fascinated by the total emptiness and silence and lightless desolation. He had described to her corners where for seven years the dust had lain undisturbed by so much as a breath, where there were fungi like trees and shallow lakes of reeking water that stretched beyond the beam of his strongest lamp. The place delighted him almost to the point of perversity. And it was an ideal hiding place. For him, or for a small army.

She found Matthew's flashlight in one of the still unpacked crates. She would go and see her brother at once, and talk to him. At once, before the idea lost urgency or was even thought better of. She must first think of a way of ditching Mrs Foster. She smoked two cigarettes while working out a plan. In the end the simplest seemed the best.

She changed into her most uncharacteristic dress, a pink affair given to her by her mother, and covered it with her rain coat. She chose a hat into which she would be able to stuff her hair. Mrs Foster's number was on the pad by the telephone.

'Mrs Foster? I'm just going in to the University library. St Paul's University. I'll be ready in about half an hour. Meet you at the gate.'

She then drove quickly down to the guard house and parked close outside. She waited with every sign of impatience for ten minutes. After that she went in.

'I really can't wait any longer,' she said, in a charming state of agitation. 'I phoned up my tail simply ages ago, told her exactly where I was going, and when. Look, be a dear and tell her I've gone on.'

The guard looked doubtful.

'It's Mrs Foster. She can't possibly be much longer. She knows where I'm going, to the University library. She'll find me there easily enough. I think it closes at four, so I'm sure she'll understand.'

The library stayed open until at least five thirty. Abigail had hoped she would find the deception a challenge, fun even. She didn't. It was dreary, squalid, and too easy. The guard let her through; he really had no alternative. It wasn't his job to hold up department chiefs or their wives. If the surveillance staff was slack, that was their affair. But he made a note of Mrs Oliver's white raincoat, to show he was aware of his responsibilities.

Abigail wasn't a good fast driver, but she made it somehow to the University. Parking in a prominent position, she ran in to the library and chose a book at random from the shelves. She checked it out and left the University buildings. There was still no sign of Mrs Foster. Paul had told her about the sealed entrances to the carpark – there was one in a side street that had a loose section of shuttering, perhaps used by students needing privacy, and small boys.

The entrance was at the bottom of a ramp between Victorian terraced houses off Cannon Street. Once their ground floors had been rented by importers of jute and by wholesale button agents. Now they were shops, serving the University with microfilm and magnetic tape, anti-bug devices, clothes, TV repairs, gimmicky sports equipment like power-boosted roller skates. Abigail was able to mingle with the shoppers and slip unnoticed down the ramp to the carpark entrance. The shuttering could easily be prised away to make a three-foot gap. It sprang back into place behind her.

At first she thought the place was totally dark. Then she began to see dim patterns of slatted light from ventilators overhead, and cracks around the shuttering at other entrances. When she switched on her flashlight they vanished, adjusted out by her eyes in the new brilliance. A square repetition of beams and pillars, gray undressed concrete, continued as far as she could see. She had expected movement from rats, but there was none: the place was too dead, too inorganic for them to bother to come. There were black rubber tire marks on the plastic floor. She looked for footprints, needing a direction, but the area around the entrance was too scuffed.

Once she had left the entrance it would be difficult to find it again. So she wedged the shuttering open a few inches with a piece of wood, making a broad crack of light, easily identifiable. Then she walked away down a corridor of pillars, quietly, shining her light onto the ground a few feet in front. She wanted to know as little of the place as possible. She found that the corridor of pillars was not straight, but curved away to the left so that one side of it made a wall to conceal the entrance from her. She called her brother's name, but softly, afraid to rouse echoes from surfaces she could not see. It was useless for her to look for Paul. If she moved, and showed a light, and occasionally called his name, he would find her. Providing he wanted to.

She began to hear water dripping. The morning's rain had stopped long ago, but here it would seep on down for hours. She came on a black skin of water and paused, watching it spread, its tiny lip bulging infinitesimally, held back on grains of dust and burnt rubber. She skirted the water, shone her torch on its surface to convince herself it really was the centimeter deep she knew it was. The reflection told her nothing. She walked on.

The sound of the water faded. Darkness pressed against her face and her clothes. The carpark was more than a mile square – it was idiocy to offer herself to be found in such a place. Besides, if Paul knew of it, who else did? If others, would they stand motionless behind pillars and let her pass? Instantly the dark became peopled. She reasoned that they would not want to be discovered, that they would not harm her if she did not see them. She kept the beam of light close, and her head low.

The air was stale and heavy, and sour with smells of cement dust, of dead damp, of long-departed motor cars. She had left the ventilator shafts behind her, and the darkness around was infinite. She didn't know how long she had been underground. She never wore a watch: usually the exact time was of no interest to her. But she realized that the longer she was away the harder it would be to fool Mrs Foster on her return. Suddenly at the very edge of the light from the torch she saw a movement away to the left, the definite movement of a pale hand and a face above it. She had planned what she should do when this happened. She switched off her light and ran to the last pillar she had seen ahead.

'Who's there?' Her back to the pillar, darkness bearing in on her. 'Paul? Is it you?'

'You're a brave woman, Abby.' After a torturing pause. 'It might just as well not have been.'

'I'm here, Paul.'

She switched on her torch and shone it in his direction. He was dressed in black, clothes she had never seen before, with some sort of gun by his right hip.

'Paul – are you on your own?'

'There's a group of which I'm a member. You wouldn't approve.'

'I meant, are you on your own down here?'

She couldn't bear to think of it, being alone for even an hour in that dark place.

'Point the light down, Abby. I can't see a thing.' She did so, and he came nearer. 'I like it here,' he said. 'It appeals to me.'

'I asked if you were on your own.'

'And I didn't answer you.'

She listened for the movement of others, would have been glad to hear it, to have had people to fear rather than emptiness. Nothing moved. She fastened instead on the reality of Paul's shoes in the trembling disk of light. They were dusty, the laces knotted. She didn't want to know about his plans, about the other people in his group, about what her money was to be used for. She simply wanted to get him out.

'We mustn't quarrel, Paul. I came here to help you.'

'I thought Hilliard would have the sense to keep his mouth shut.'

'You should have known he wouldn't. You're lucky he came to me. He might have gone to someone much more awkward. Your tutor, for instance.'

'But he didn't. He came to you, and you remembered this place, and put two and two together, and here you are, saying you want to help. If you really want to help –'

'Please, Paul. Don't stay here. Not in this terrible place. Come with me, and –'

'If you really want to help, Abby, just go away and forget you ever saw me. Would you? For your own sake as well as mine? Please?'

She turned her torch up onto his face. He closed his eyes but didn't try to move away. The light told her nothing, produced a disembodied mask hardly recognizable.

'You were going to Africa, Paul. It's still not too late –'

'For your own sake, sis, just shut up and go away. I mean that.'

She switched off her torch, disliking the melodrama it made of his face. Their voices came back at them at odd angles from the flat sides of the pillars. The place was cold. She closed her eyes, and in the darkness it made no difference. To like being here Paul must be a little mad, she thought.

'I suppose you think all this is exciting and romantic. An exciting plan to set the world to rights.'

'One has to begin somewhere.'

'You're behaving like a ridiculous little fanatic. I thought you'd grown up.'

'Grown up?' He moved away from her, raising his voice. She had the distasteful impression that he was talking to others than just herself. 'Grown up? Perhaps I have. Perhaps it's you who's stuck. It's not enough simply to be well-meaning. There's something beyond the dot – you can go through and come out on the other side.'

'Paul, listen to me –'

'Everything, sis – art, politics, religion, philosophy, everything reduced to a tiny, self-regarding dot. Push a little harder and you come out on the other side.'

'Into anarchy?'

'You have a labeling mind. Tidies everything up. You call it being grown up.'

'Into what, then?'

She heard him come close, felt him in front of her, the pressure of the air he displaced. She thought he might be going to strike her.

'Into anarchy, if that's the only word you have. Into people. Into death and hatred and disease and suffering and injustice and a thousand things we thought we wanted to be without.' She tried to concentrate on the hysteria rather than the words. 'Sweat, Abigail. That old fool's blood and sweat and tears. If he'd added joy to the list he'd have had the whole of life. Except that he wasn't a fool – he knew the respectable Christian mind. Blood and sweat and tears are respectable – joy isn't.'

She would have preferred him to strike her. The words he used were closer, more painful. She shifted her ground.

'You asked Father Hilliard for the definition of a righteous war,' she said quietly. 'I don't believe there is one.'

'It's your way of life, Abby. I can't talk to you. With your reasonable husband and your half-starved soul, I can't tell you anything.'

She let his theatricality pass.

'Please, Paul. Come with me.'

'No.'

She recognized finality. There was nothing more to be said.

'I'll come again. Tomorrow, perhaps.'

'For God's sake don't. It only makes things difficult. You know where I am now, and you know I'm all right. So there's no point.' He lowered his voice. 'And I'm sorry I cheated you over the money.'

She reached for his hand in the darkness, touched it, and felt it drawn away.

'And you can trust me to go away and not say anything?'

'You're my sister.'

'But –'

'And you're more than half with me.'

She denied it.

'I want things to be changed, Paul. But I –'

'You won't betray me, Abby. Come on, now. I'll show you the way back to the entrance.'

He switched on his own flashlight and took her arm. He led her firmly, counting pillars half-aloud as he went. She kept quiet so as not to interrupt him. At the thirty-third pillar he turned right, and from then on he didn't need to count, merely followed the curved line of pillars till they reached the entrance. Still she didn't speak. He paused close to the shuttering, with his hand still tight on her arm.

'Now, sis, there's no need to worry. Nothing's going to happen for some days yet. And anyway, you'll be safe enough when it does.'

'You're telling me this plot you're involved in has something to do with the Colindale?'

'I'm telling you nothing.'

'Stop playing at cops and robbers, Paul. If your group's planning to sabotage the Colindale I can tell you it's quite hopeless. You'll never get through the –'

'Be quiet, Abby. Just be quiet.' He gripped her arm till it hurt. She could see him listening. All that she could hear behind the silence were the distant sounds of the street. 'It's all right. I think they trust me. Just as I trust you. All I can tell you is that you mustn't worry – you'll have plenty of warning. Now you must go.' He began easing back the shuttering for her and peered out. 'It's clear. Go along now. And be careful ...' He helped her through. 'And Abby ... lie for me. If you have to. As you find out about the Colindale you'll see that ours is a good cause.'

He closed the shuttering behind her. The gray daylight hurt her eyes. Her hands were still patterned from the pillar she had leaned against. She walked up the deserted ramp, finding it hard to believe in the crowded darkness behind her, hard to believe that she had spoken to Paul, hard to believe in what he had told her. The opposing pressures of him and Matthew were more than she could bear. They demanded decisions from someone who had happily given up decision-making in favor of her husband, and who even before marriage had been content to let things happen. Prayer and right thinking had always been enough – the rest had been seen to by God.

She took refuge in the immediate, in coping with Mrs Foster. To this end she removed her white coat and hung it over her arm, disclosing the surprising pink dress. She made sure that the library book was still in the coat pocket, just in case Mrs Foster asked.

The foyer outside the University library was as crowded as always. Abigail had to stand around for some minutes before Mrs Foster found her.

'Where have you been?' Abigail got it in first. 'I chose my book ages ago. When there wasn't any sign of you I went up to the canteen for coffee.'

'I looked in the canteen,' said Mrs Foster coldly.

'Well, I was there … such a crowd. Perhaps you missed me on account of this awful dress. And the hat. I *knew* they were a mistake the moment I put them on.'

Certainly Abigail bore no resemblance to the slightly mouse-like person, always hatless, with long dark hair, that Mrs Foster must have been familiar with. Abigail chatted on cheerfully. Even if the woman was unconvinced, there was still nothing she could do about it. Finally they returned to their cars and drove back to the Colindale in very close convoy.

When she got home, Abigail was pleased to find Matthew still not back. She needed time to think. Suddenly hungry, she hydrated a small beef casserole for herself. Necessary decisions crowded in on her. She wanted the Colindale project put an end to quite as much as Paul did, but she could not see that violence was the way. Publicity would in the end be far more effective. If she could get details of the project to some member of the C L.C. committee, she could make the plans of Paul's organization quite unnecessary. Public opinion, as Matthew had admitted, would close the Colindale in a matter of days. The snag was that she didn't know how long she had before the sabotage plan was put into operation.

Then there was Matthew to think of. She poked in the casserole, looking for fat. If Matthew still supported the Colindale project – and she had to admit that this was very probable – then she couldn't tell him anything about Paul: once he knew he would feel obliged to pass the information on to the authorities. For the first time in their marriage she would be forced to tell him less than the truth. It was necessary to contact the C.L.C. without his knowledge, and as soon as possible.

How she was to do this she had no idea. She ate her stew at the kitchen table, staring unhappily out into the garden. She chose not to consider the implications of going against Matthew in a matter as central as this. The sooner the lid blew off the project and he was out of a job, the better.

For Matthew the afternoon was spent in the conference room, going over Bohn extrapolations. Most of these were unexciting, a cheaper substitute for neon, a growth accelerator for conifers, two new applications for laser analysis techniques. But Matthew did have occasion to join with the philosophy group head, Schatten, in opposing a chromosome shift likely to make fetal sex a matter of paternal choice. Its implications were considered too far-reaching for an immediate decision and the paper was put on one side pending a Bohn study of the relevant distribution statistics.

Matthew walked home from the computer center very slowly, dreading any more discussion with Abigail. Around him people were hurrying, turning off into court-yards, running up the short flights of steps between lawns that led to the different residential areas. Zacharie Mallalieu passed him going in the same direction, grunted something supposed to be friendly. Most of the department heads lived around the same large quadrangle; Matthew supposed a social life must exist among them, a coming and going for bridge or cocktails or talking endless shop. He and Abigail would have to decide whether or not they wanted to compete.

Abigail … he couldn't see how the present situation between them was to be ended. For once their basic differences in matters of faith seemed insurmountable. There was no middle ground on which they could meet. Perhaps it was true after all that any structured religion – no matter what – acted as a strong reactionary force, holding back moral and physical progress. This was something he would very much rather not believe.

Therefore he was relieved, when he arrived home, to find a pot of tea waiting for him, and Abigail cheerfully upacking the last two crates of belongings from the old house. If there was constraint between them, it was far less than he had expected. She told him she had been visited that morning by Father Hilliard from the University. The priest was worried about Paul.

'He would be.' Matthew stirred his tea. 'Nobody seems to take the demands of our society into consideration. His tutor, the principal, you, and now this Father Hilliard – none of you seems to have heard of normal adolescent rebellion.' He was glad of something external to talk about.

'But he's twenty-three, Matthew. Hardly adolescent.'

'So he's a bit late getting things sorted out. You must admit society hardly encourages people to grow up nowadays. Anyway, this trip to Africa's just what he needs. Work him hard and keep him out of mischief.'

Her face went blank on him, and she didn't reply. Not that he blamed her; his comment had been off the peg, not even dusted down. He drank his tea meekly, aware of the danger of being forty.

'Matthew, I've got to talk to you about these microphones. Is there really nothing we can do about them?'

'I don't see what.' She would want him to be more indignant. 'Friend Billon will say they're just something more for our protection. We'll get used to them.'

'But there's one in the bedroom. They can even listen to us making love.'

She seemed to be whipping something up, keeping it going. In a way he was grateful to her.

'I doubt if they'll be bothered.'

'I wouldn't be too sure. Who knows what secrets we mightn't whisper to each other in our post-coital stupor.'

'It's no use being bitter, Abigail. If I work at the Colindale I have to accept the limitations it places on me.'

'Exactly.'

He'd walked straight into that one.

'I have to do what I believe is right, Abigail.'

'I don't.'

He didn't care that the microphone listened. There were many other things more important. Besides, each one couldn't be monitored every hour of the day.

'That's true, Abigail. Both of us, we can only do what we believe is right.'

'You'll work here then. Whatever I do?'

'Abigail ...' The situation was unbearable. He reached across the table to take her hands, and she let him. Because they were inert, hardly hers. He squeezed them, trying in vain for some response. 'I have to do what I believe is right,' he said again.

There was a long silence. The kitchen, the rough bark of the fir tree outside the window, the chair he was sitting on, everything seemed unreal. Even her face. Was there really anything in the world more important to him than her?

'I have to, Abigail.' Even as his heart rebelled. 'I have to.'

'Yes.'

Utter helplessness in her one word. This was the confrontation he had dreaded, the confrontation that in honesty could not be avoided. She moved around the table to him, and he felt her go through the motions of putting her arm around his shoulders, her cheek against the side of his head. He was faintly nauseated, but it would have been cruel to draw away.

'We'll sort something out,' he said.

'No.' She ruffled his hair. 'But nothing goes on forever.'

He wanted to ask her again what she intended to do, but he had not the courage. So he hid behind trust that he did not altogether feel.

Without the matters largest in their minds to talk about, they talked trivia with false ease. She told him she had been in to the University library, and then seemed disinclined to show him the books she had brought back. He guessed they would be theological works relevant to her side of the present situation. He countered with the news that Professor Billon had asked them both to dinner some time, to meet his wife. The mouse wife would break his heart, Matthew said. Nonsense, said Abigail, she might be a positive virago. A lot of dominating men became doormats when they entered their own homes. Time was passed imagining the home life of Chester Billon.

A brief spark was struck when they started talking about Abigail's grandfather, but it quickly failed.

'There's a case in point,' Matthew said. 'Wouldn't it be better if the operation that's kept him alive had never been invented?'

'Why not kill off everybody over eighty and be done with it?' said Abigail.

So it was pleasant to have the doorbell ring shortly after dinner. Matthew answered it, and showed in the young systems analyst, Andrew Scarfe. He brought the promised, unwanted Astran Primer. They welcomed him, and gave him coffee.

'It's very good of you,' he said. 'You may not realize it yet, but free evenings in the Colindale are few and far between.'

'Shift work?' said Abigail. 'I thought that was only for Data Reception.'

'Not shift work, Mrs Oliver. I wish it were. No, it's the chief's special project, unpaid overtime. When he gets Dr Oliver going on that you'll hardly see him from one week's end to –'

'Special project?' said Matthew.

'Well, obviously you'll be taking over where Henderson left off. Since his death we've been marking time, more or less. So the sooner you can pick up the threads ...'

He tailed off, seeing Matthew's puzzled expression and misinterpreting it.

'Bugged?' he said, in an efficient whisper.

Matthew nodded, still not understanding.

'I'm sorry. I should have thought.' And he started talking loudly about the tennis club.

The director's special project, so special that not even the camp guards should know about it. Boxes within boxes within boxes. Matthew's first reaction was to be pleasantly intrigued. Then he looked uneasily across at his wife. Whatever the project was, on present form she would be unlikely to approve. Scarfe was still babbling, trying to cover his indiscretion. The principles underlying everything at the Colindale were so rational, so alien to Abigail's nature. He would prefer to avoid anything that might damage their relationship still further.

'By the way, Mrs Oliver, did you know I was up at University with your brother?' Scarfe shifted his thick shoulders to get more comfortable. 'I got to know him quite well. I was in my third year when he was in his first, of course, but we met at the Union. He's an interesting debater.'

'I'm glad to hear it. We've gone our separate ways. He's seven years younger than me, you see.'

Her coldness surprised Matthew. Normally she would have been delighted to talk about Paul with somebody who knew him. There had been a similar freeze earlier in the evening. Yet a subject as uncontroversial as her brother would tide them excellently over the rest of Scarfe's visit. He decided to try to help the young man along.

'Paul's in Africa now,' he said. 'Did you know that?'

'I had heard something. There's a team gone out to study merchandising. Isn't that it?'

And they were off. Social anthropology, one of Matthew's favorite subjects. And Scarfe was agreeably willing to learn. But even as he talked Matthew was aware of Abigail's reserve, and of the occasional efforts she herself made to break through it. Twice he lost the thread of his argument, watching her and wondering what was wrong. At the second blank he gave up.

'I'm sorry, Scarfe. I must be getting tired. It's been a long day.'

'And your first in this sweat shop. I should have thought. I'll be on my way.' The young man stood up. Seated, you forgot how short he was. 'Very good of you to put up with me as long as this, Mrs Oliver. It's been very interesting.'

Abigail smiled and shook hands. She was charming, and invited Scarfe to call again. Matthew recognized the effort it was costing, the set to her jaw that made her almost ugly. At the front door Scarfe drew him out into the quadrangle and lowered his voice. The long summer evening was over, and – incredibly – from somewhere on the Colindale Matthew could hear a nightingale. He could have done without Scarfe's muttering.

'I really am sorry I didn't think before blabbing about the special project. I've been here long enough to know better.'

He was protesting over-much. Matthew felt annoyed.

'As a matter of fact, I haven't been told anything about it. Not yet. So perhaps you were a bit premature.'

'You haven't? That makes it worse than ever. I suppose the chief just hasn't had time to get around to it yet.'

Probably true: the day had been very full. But Matthew, with a jangled evening behind him, was pettish. Besides, he didn't like Scarfe, and he was obviously going to be working with him on the special project, whatever it was.

'It doesn't matter,' he said. 'I've got used to people dropping me hints about my work and then shying away. Perhaps it's intended to make the whole thing more mysterious and interesting.'

'I say, I do hope you don't think I did it on purpose.' Still not able to leave it. 'I mean, why should I?'

'Don't worry. As you said, I'm sure to be told just as soon as the director has time to get around to it.'

Cowardly, taking out on Scarfe his general anger against Life ... Matthew watched him walk away, merging quickly into the gray dusk. The nightingale had stopped singing, and might have been imagined. It had been a gray day, and mist was rising. There was something about the young man that was false. His public school vocabulary, perhaps. That sort of aspiration irritated Matthew very much. He turned and went back into the house.

'What was all that about?' he said to Abigail. 'Why the sudden freeze-up?'

'Do you like that young man?' She was clearing away the coffee cups.

'Why not?' He attacked to avoid being attacked. 'He's friendly, intelligent, not in the least conceited. I expect he hoped his knowing Paul might give him a link with us.'

She shrugged her shoulders, and carried the tray away into the kitchen. It was unfair of him to argue with her rather than with himself. He helped her stack the day's dirty crockery in the machine.

In bed that night they made love because not to do so would have been worse, would have been an admission. They made it quietly, neither having the need to do otherwise. And they pretended to each other that it made things right between them. She lay in her place at his side, his arm around her, her head in the hollow of his neck, and quickly slept. Matthew was wakeful. He regretted the cold dampness against his thigh. He couldn't retreat into sleep as she could. He asked himself again if anything was more important to him than she was. This mess couldn't last. They were dramatizing. In a day or a week or a month they'd come to their senses. He prayed vaguely, knowing neither for what exactly nor to whom. In the Colindale dark a sense of proportion was difficult.

EIGHT

Tuesday morning the sky had cleared, and with it all Abigail's worries. About Matthew, about Paul, about the ominous special project. Nothing stayed complicated in her mind for long: she had the sort of faith that accepted right solutions as inevitable. Thus she saw in Matthew's quietness over tea and bed and then at breakfast proof that her prayers were being answered. He was being helped to do what was right. It might not be easy for him, his niggardly reason might fight all the way, but the outcome was a foregone conclusion. There was no need at all for her to contact the C.L.C. – Matthew would do so himself, if not that same evening then at least within the next day or so. Then none of it, least of all the special project, would matter.

The oath she and Matthew had taken did not worry her; she could dismiss it as merely a civil affair. Ultimately one was responsible only to one's own conscience.

Not even the discovery that her absence at the University the previous afternoon had been used to place microphones in the spare bedrooms and the lavatory – even the lavatory – could depress her. Soon they'd be out of the place for good. Even if they left under escort, on their way to jail – a possibility she didn't really credit, public opinion would be so strongly on their side – even that would be preferable to staying. There would be nobility in suffering jail for such a cause. She thought.

She collected Mrs Foster and went shopping in the complex nearest to the Colindale. The manager was used to Institute executives, and arranged card facilities at once, without reference to the central finance information bureau. Abigail wandered around the shops, buying food and a few clothes. Nothing for the new house – they wouldn't be staying there long enough. She asked Mrs Foster's advice over a new shirt for Matthew. If they had to go about everywhere together there was no point in being polite enemies. The shops were cool and gently lit, and smelled carefully enticing. She realized that she didn't mind the many tell cameras set up between the counters: surveillance was part of the normal shopping background. It only took time, and one could get used to anything.

When she had chosen everything she could possibly think of – the rich had a social duty to spend their money – she went up to the manager's office again to arrange delivery. The complex ran special packing facilities for easy inspection at the Colindale gate. Mrs Foster stayed downstairs choosing herself some stockings.

'Some time this afternoon, Mrs Oliver?' The man was a new generation manager, an individualist liking a rigid framework, running the complex on extended franchise. 'No sooner, I'm afraid. One of the vans is in for a battery overhaul, and I –'

'There's really no hurry. Any time before six or so. I don't start thinking about the evening meal till then.'

'Dr Oliver works late, I expect.'

'Not very. Only by leisure society standards.'

She realized that the man had given Matthew his doctorate. An intelligent guess.

'You know my husband?'

'I've been told about him.'

The reply was carefully significant. She waited while the manager stamped her dockets and returned them to her. She was still bemused from the adroit techniques of the shops below. And now the bright, restless colors of his office.

'I've been instructed, Mrs Oliver, to say that when your husband is ready to make contact I am in a position to help him.'

'Contact?' She was genuinely slow to catch up. Once a difficulty was solved she no longer thought about it.

'With the Committee, Mrs Oliver.' He mistook the slowness of her reaction. 'No need to worry – I've a jammer going just in case. We retail them here, so there's no problem.'

He knew of Matthew's attempt to get in touch with the C.L.C. She wondered how.

'I see ... I didn't think the C.L.C. knew anything about it. Or were you in touch with Dr Gryphon personally?'

'Gryphon?' The man's face was expressive, showed genuine incomprehension. 'Wasn't he the University lecturer murdered a few days ago? No, I didn't know him.'

'I'm just surprised that anybody knew we might want to ... to get in touch.'

'News travels, Mrs Oliver.' He stood up and smiled, selling her his own integrity. 'Now you'd better get back to your Mrs Foster before she starts getting edgy.' He accompanied her to the door. 'Just remember, I can put your husband in touch within a matter of hours ... And thank you for your custom, Mrs Oliver. If there's ever anything you want, please don't hesitate to ask.'

Abigail went downstairs slowly, gathering her thoughts. She wondered who, except Edmund, had known that Matthew might want to contact the C.L.C. From what Matthew had said, Edmund had been playing a personal hunch, working very much on his own. So who else could know? Nobody. Unless of course one considered – assuming that he had been astute enough to see the real reason for Matthew's visit – Sir William Beeston. Not that considering him made any sense. But whatever else Sir William was, he was certainly astute enough for three …

'… I rather fancy these gray ones with the copper thread, Mrs Oliver. But maybe a bit too young … What do you think, Mrs Oliver?'

Abigail focused on the concerned, motherly face of Mrs Foster. It was hard to believe that she carried a gun, and had been trained in unarmed combat.

'I'm sorry. What did you say? I'm afraid my mind was wandering.'

Maggie Pelham repeated what she had just said, a little peevishly. She gave her full attention to whatever she was doing, and naturally she expected Dr Oliver to do the same.

'The last up from Data Reception, Dr Oliver. I've checked all except these three. I'd like you to have a look at them.'

Matthew took the three blue sheets of teletype from her. Tuesday was a day for catching up with data queries, confirming classifications before the material was transliterated and fed into the Bohn. The morning's work had been hard, and made harder by the way his thoughts strayed continually back to Abigail or wandered curiously around the special project mentioned by Scarfe. He stared at the teletype, seeing instead Scarfe's sharp young face and in the background Abigail watching. It came to him suddenly that she had been frightened. The Colindale frightened her, and Scarfe represented the Colindale in its most essential form.

'Maggie, tell me something. Did John Henderson ever talk about a special project, something he was working on with the director?'

'I knew of its existence. He kept stacks of paper locked away in that drawer.'

She indicated one of the filing cabinets, a drawer with a blank label.

'Are they still there?'

'How should I know? I've been far too busy. Anyway, the drawer's locked, honey. I told you.'

Matthew tried the drawer and it opened easily. It was completely empty, folders swinging loosely on the side runners.

'That's funny.' Maggie began to take interest. 'There were masses of stuff in it – sometimes it would hardly close. John used to work on it till all hours. Either here or tucked away in the classified wing. And he always kept the drawer locked – used to make little jokes so I wouldn't feel hurt.'

'This lock – who else has a key?'

'No idea. Come to that, who has John's key?' She paused, and sat down again very slowly. 'Not that there'd be much left of it. Not if he had it on him when, he … died.'

Matthew slid the drawer shut. There were too many things still being kept from him. He found the continued secrecy insulting.

'I'm breaking for lunch.' He clipped the three teletype sheets together. 'These can wait till this afternoon. Then we can start on the backlog.'

He rang the director's office and spoke with his secretary. Professor Billon would be away from the Institute for the whole day. Matthew struggled to keep a sense of proportion, to believe that the director had other things to do than simply to evade and insult Dr Matthew Oliver. He got up and went to the door.

'Walking home, Maggie?'

'Lunching in the canteen.' He saw that she was still upset from talking about Henderson's death. There were other concerns in life than his own. She pulled herself together. 'The young turd I flat with – I daren't use the kitchen except on Sundays when he's out at church. He's the house-proud type, has a dinky little apron.'

'Scarfe? I wouldn't have said he was one of those.'

'Perhaps he isn't. Then again, perhaps he is. He's never tried anything with me, but that don't prove much. Me and him wouldn't mix, love. I mean, would we?'

She flounced away, stridently cheerful, trying a little too hard, even for her.

In the foyer Matthew caught sight of Dr Mozart. He hurried to catch him up; if Professor Billon wasn't available then perhaps the security man could help him. They walked away from the computer center together, along paths thronged with other staff members, some in white coats and some in bright hot weather clothes. Again Matthew was reminded of University scenes, and again there was something wrong. In this case the distant band of rich green turf set with warning notices about the force-field fence.

'It's a lovely day,' said Dr Mozart. 'I trust you are settling in after yesterday's trauma. Usually new boys are brought to the water more gently. I'm glad that you intend to drink.'

Matthew had no time for idiomatic fireworks.

'I want to talk to you,' he said. 'My house is bugged – why didn't you warn me?'

'My dear fellow, a man as intelligent as you should need no such warnings. Also you must remember that I work with the system, not against it. But you should have noticed how I came to pay my respects while you were still moving in. They leave empty houses clean. It makes a better impression on the incoming tenants.'

'You're very cynical.' And untrustworthy? Matthew walked a few paces in silence. 'Tell me, if you're not connected with the security organization within the Institute, to whom are you responsible?'

'Faceless men, Matthew. Faceless men in Geneva …'

'Are you here to find out about Henderson's murder?'

'Not particularly. It interests me, of course. But the indigenous guard force has excellent machinery to deal with that sort of inquiry. I've been here nearly two years now, Matthew. My brief is much more general …' They were walking past a row of glass-fronted laboratories. Dr Mozart covertly watched his reflection. 'You had something you wanted to say to me?'

'I wanted to ask you if you knew anything about a special project. Something the director was hatching with my predecessor.'

'Henderson was one of the group? I suppose I should have guessed.'

'You know about it, then?'

'No details. Even its existence is only a matter of deduction. I got interested in it six or seven weeks ago.' They were walking slowly, and most of the crowd had left them behind. 'As you know, we department heads are supposed to be allowed time for our own work. I wanted to seem willing, so I cooked up a bit of a theory and then tried to book some evening computer time for its development. This proved to be very difficult. One of four people was always ahead of me – Mallalieu, Schatten, Dingle or Blake. And very occasionally, Henderson. Anyway, I finally went to the director to complain. He was most charming. Too charming. Of course I had a right to complain, he said. Of course I had a grievance. He'd see to it that I was fitted in at once. And so he did.' Mozart shrugged his shoulders. 'Such consideration made me suspicious. It wasn't typical. He had something to hide.'

'But you still don't know what sort of work they're doing.'

'An economist, a philosopher-theologian, a politician, a historian and a sociologist … what unites these three with our psychologist director?'

'Many things might.'

'Quite so. So I still have no idea what they are doing. And it's probably none of my business. What makes you so interested?'

Matthew told him about the empty drawer in Henderson's filing cabinet. Mozart was silent as they walked up the path toward the Institute library. They were almost alone, now that they were approaching the higher, more exclusive residential areas. Mozart turned off the path and sat down on the grass under a small group of lime trees. Matthew leaned on a treetrunk beside him, hands in pockets. The sun flickered down through the leaves. They might have been discussing Nietzsche or the Test Match.

'This interests me very much, Matthew … Just let us suppose that this special project had in some way got out of hand, started moving in a direction Henderson did not like. He only has to try to stop it, and there at last we have a motive for his murder.'

'Billon again?'

'It has to be.'

'But you're making far too many assumptions.'

'I find it useful. Theories exist to be refuted. It's their only purpose.'

Matthew withdrew from the discussion. He had been interested in what Mozart knew about the special project, not in refuting his murder theories. He did not have a murder mystery mind.

'The director isn't available,' he said, cutting through whatever his companion was saying, 'but the moment he is I intend to go and see him. He can't refuse to tell me about the project, not if Henderson was so deeply involved in it.'

'I shall be interested to hear what you find out, Matthew.' There was an element here almost of threat. 'But he's away for the day, explaining yesterday's discovery to the Prime Minister and the Chiefs of Staff.'

'Then I'll go to his house this evening, after he's got back.'

Mrs Alice Billon turned out to be no virago, but more of a mouse even than Matthew had feared. He'd walked up to the director's house after his evening meal. He was rather glad to get away: Abigail treated him with curious care, as if he were nine months pregnant with something only she knew about. And she asked him odd questions, mainly about Sir William Beeston, shying away when he tried to find out why she should want to know. They were no longer able to be honest with each other; he was forced to be evasive when she asked him why he was going to see the director.

At the front door of his house he paused, looked back at her, as beautiful to him as ever, dark hair loose on her shoulders, doing simple things about the sitting room; as beautiful and as desirable. But he observed her from the outside, as a stranger. Between them nothing touched. She was as far off, in the low golden light, moving between the balanced shapes of the furniture, as if she had been a projection, a three-dimensional hologram. And he had to do what he believed was right.

He was glad to get away, up the path beyond the quadrangle, through a round white archway with a Spanish wrought-iron gate, to Professor Billon's low white house. Unsurprisingly the director liked beautiful things: there was a jade fountain by the entrance, spilling pale green water into a tiny pool of white and gold mosaic. And sculpture, steel strip and rod, exact upon the paving stones. And when Mrs Billon opened the door, she showed a hall with a huge photo-sensitive mural, shifting from blue to silver in the evening sunlight.

Viewing Mrs Billon against this background, Matthew liked her husband less. It was as if the setting had been chosen to make her cease to exist. Billon himself, Matthew had no doubt, would dominate it with ease.

'You wanted to see the professor? I'm afraid he's not in.'

'I'm sorry I troubled you, Mrs Billon. I thought he'd be back from London by now.'

'Oh, he got back from the meeting two hours ago.' She said the pronoun as if with an upper-case H. 'But he's gone down to the computer center now. I'm alone in the evenings a lot, you see. He often doesn't get back till two or three in the morning.'

It might have been self-pity, but it sounded more like a simple statement of facts. At that moment Matthew had no wish to be caught up in her troubles. He spoke briskly.

'The computer center, you said? Perhaps I can find him there.'

'You may try, of course … but he's always very busy.'

'My name is Oliver, Mrs Billon. I'm the new sociology man.'

'Replacing poor Mr Henderson … Well, I expect it's all right, you going down to the center, I mean. But I wonder if you would be good enough not to suggest that I sent you.' Head on one side, hair retained by old-fashioned pins at all angles. 'Because I didn't, you know.'

'Of course you didn't. There's no need for me to say I came here at all.' He smiled as warmly, as comfortingly, as he knew how. 'I'll be going, then. And I'm sorry I disturbed you.'

She pattered after him to the gate.

'And please, Mr Oliver, do not say definitely that you were *not* here. Chester has a way of getting things out of me – out of one. And lying is so seldom a good thing. Don't you agree?'

Matthew reassured her. What strength she had ever had must have been given away years ago. Chester Billon in his mid-sixties was boundless, undauntable. His wife was an old, old woman. She stayed by the gate, watching him, till he went down the last short flight of steps into the cloisters.

The girl on reception in the computer center said that if Professor Billon wasn't in his office he was probably at the Bohn desk in the classified wing. She looked at Matthew doubtfully. He glanced up at the computer register and saw Schatten's name against the evening period.

'I'm working with Dr Schatten,' he said. 'I believe computer time has been arranged.'

He smiled down at her and she let him through. He never thought about it, but in general he didn't have any trouble with receptionists. Unless they were elderly, ex-service, male.

The director's office was empty. Matthew went through it and along the corridor to the classified wing. He found the Bohn desk there without much difficulty. It was up a short flight of steps, under a transparent dome that overlooked most of the Institute. Only Schatten and Professor Billon were there.

'Dr Oliver, you make a habit of walking in on me unexpectedly.' Matthew drew breath to explain. 'You can be of use, however. Now that you are here. Pre-Christian Palestine, twenty or thirty A.D. Effect sociologically on the Jews of being a subject people? Hmm?'

It sounded a serious question, expecting a serious answer. Matthew was reminded of his schooldays, a waiting silence stretching ahead of him like a long, too brightly lit tunnel. He found words.

'A general hardening of attitudes … a tightening of the internal structure. Also a group shame, I should think. Causing a sort of fierce dignity.'

'Rather as we have in society today?'

'A dangerous analogy. I wouldn't think so. We have this total lack of a unifying element. All we share is a generalized anti-them feeling.' He sat down opposite the two men, now more or less in control. 'I could do you a study, of course, but I've never found that sort of comparison very valuable.'

Billon laughed, short as a cough. 'Very good recovery. Resourceful. Very good indeed.'

Matthew flushed, placed his hands on the arms of his chair, got slowly to his feet.

'Professor Billon, I'm the head of your sociology department, not a little dog doing tricks. Perhaps your purpose is to test my spirit. In that case your object has been achieved: you are now the man I most love to hate. Which I know is a perfectly good and workable relationship.'

He would have gone on longer, but for his awareness of how foolish most people looked when angry. The director waited, tapping his pencil on the plastic surface of the desk. Schatten collected his papers.

'I'll get off to the canteen, then. I could do with a break.' He stopped by Matthew. 'The last few days have been unusually hectic. That's not an excuse, Dr Oliver, merely a statement of fact.'

He smiled, and came near to taking Matthew's arm, near to making some gesture of understanding. Then he went away down the steps. Matthew waited for the director to speak. The glass dome came down to floor level, exposing them on every side to the sky. Behind the director's head, and to one side, Matthew could see the asymmetrical roof of the conference chamber. And above it fine weather clouds in a high, pale sky.

'Sit down, Oliver. We could exchange psychological jargon all night. Contrary to what you may believe, I don't "handle" my staff members. Mutually degrading. I simply react. I can't work with people who are too eager to please.'

Eager to please. The words dropped coldly into Matthew's head and stayed there. Eager to please. They were a crushing indictment: of his life, even of his marriage. He remembered all the ways in which he had shaped himself to Abigail's image. Eager to please. And now that he wasn't, now that he was opposing her, she withdrew from him completely. Was this the real basis of their relationship, his eagerness to please?

'You see, Oliver, to be director here is to be a blind man led by the partially-sighted. They can only proceed at my pace. I need to be convinced that each step is safe and is in the right direction. It may be that I lead. But from behind. Like a wise general.'

Matthew thought of the previous night, his question to himself: Was anything more important to him than Abigail? Than pleasing Abigail, should he have said? If so, then the question answered itself.

'People have been dropping me hints, Professor, about a special project you were working on with Henderson and some others. These hints are embarrrassing. If I am not to work on the project I should like to be told. And if I am to work on it, then I should like to have it explained to me.'

'Reasonable.' Billon felt the need for a change in the relationship and stood up, going to lean his head against the glass of the dome to the right of the desk. 'I had intended to introduce the project to you gradually. It is not easy. But other people talk, of course, so here we are.' His breath laid a mist on the glass and he moved his head. 'My starting point for the project was the accepted theory that any new development, practical or philosophical, needs to wait for its moment in history. For the right mental climate. Examples abound. Da Vinci's discovery of the principles of steam power went unnoticed. The time wasn't right. Philosophical theories change from decade to decade … Look at the arrival of Jesus, followed by Paul, at exactly the right historical, emotional moment. A hundred years earlier, and they'd never have made themselves heard. But the Middle East was ready for them, and even Rome.'

'Which was the point of that extraordinary question you greeted me with?'

'Except that we already know the answer. Or hope we do.'

Matthew was unsurprised. His arrival had annoyed Billon, and Billon had accordingly – to use his own word – reacted. The director turned back to the computer desk.

'Scarfe will be here in a few minutes to do some transliterations for me. Not much time.' He picked up a roll of magnetic tape and tightened it smaller and smaller in his fingers. 'We did a study of the entire Romano-Jewish ethos, Oliver. Plenty of literature, Roman, Greek, Arabic, Egyptian, as well as non-Biblical Jewish texts. We've analyzed the factors governing the phenomenal spread of Christianity, and we think we understand them. We've attempted a similar study of the Buddhist inception, but the sources are less good.' He petered out, frowning perhaps at the inefficiency of the Oriental chroniclers.

'And your reason for all this work?' said Matthew.

'The important thing to remember, Oliver, is that a need for Pauline Christianity had to exist before such teaching could get itself heard. Observably this need exists no longer. Different needs have arisen, to which Pauline Christianity is almost an irritant.'

'You admit then that we do still have spiritual needs?'

The director didn't bother to answer.

'By extrapolating from what we know of the relationship between the Romano-Jewish ethos and Pauline Christianity we can determine the precise quality of spiritual teaching that would satisfy our present day ethos. Extrapolation, Oliver. Extrapolation by association. The special province of the Bohn 507.'

If this was going where Matthew thought it was, he didn't like it.

'And when you have determined this precise quality?'

Professor Billon looked down at his hands, arranged them to touch lightly the keys of the teleprinter. He pattered on them, making no mark.

'Our social balance is precarious, Oliver. Sustained by oblique oppression. Democracy is eroded almost beyond recognition. The established churches have become little more than social clubs. The –'

'All right. We're in a bad way. But how –'

'We're leaderless, Oliver. And needing leadership. Crying out for a relevant messiah.'

'Which the Bohn is going to supply?'

'Determine the exact nature of the need, and then satisfy it.'

Matthew stared at him, finally incredulous. Either the man was mad, or this was some elaborate joke. Some new test of his character.

'You talk a lot about humbleness, Professor. Yet here you are, proposing to supply a messiah, tailor-made, just like any other consumer durable. Humbleness? Is that what you call humbleness?'

He remembered Mrs Billon's use of the capital H. Billon sat down, leaned his face forward on his two clenched fists, looked out under raised eyebrows. It was a characteristic attitude.

'God works through the minds and the consciences of men,' he said. 'You agree? Up to now the provision of great spiritual leaders has been the divine prerogative. Why? Because the minds and the consciences of men have not been sufficiently developed. But if we believe that the present explosion of technology is part of God's plan for the world, then what follows? We have new tools. They can bring about our destruction, or they can help us to our spiritual salvation.'

'And giving people precisely what they want will bring about their spiritual salvation?'

He was indeed talking to a madman.

'Not what they want, Oliver. What they need. And not from a position of superiority – from a position of humble involvement. From understanding. From the ability to correlate many variables. From knowledge that has been given to us by God.'

'So the Bohn is an instrument of God's will?'

'We can make it one. On its own it's nothing. It would be equally a sin either to misuse this potential or to ignore it. We have been given the means of our own salvation.' He paused, then spoke softly, hardly more than a whisper. 'We must use them.'

The sky was stippled with long feathers of pale orange cirrus. The sun had dropped to the top of the generating station, and cast a long shadow on the roofs around them. They seemed alone, supported in its radiance. The only sound was a faint electric hum from the computer desk between them. Matthew stared at his companion, trying to fix his thoughts. Instead he found himself irrelevantly wondering which of the two piercing blue eyes fixed on him was human tissue. One of them was a triumph for the plastics industry. But he had forgotten which.

'It's an interesting argument.' Shying from commitment. He sought a way out, shifted his position, broke the tension. 'Even so, your custom-built messiah still has to be accepted. If he's to offer people what they need instead of what they want, he's going to have to say some very unpopular things. And the enemy is better armed than he was in Christ's day. Won't the battle go to the big battalions?'

'Two points, Oliver. First, faith. In an ultimate good. Second, the harnessing of science to the propagation of that faith. Where I come in. Why I'm in the group at all. Conversion is no new science. Greek writers describe methods of mystical initiation. You should read Plutarch or Pausanius. Remember the conversion of Paul. And that the authorship of the Acts is attributed to Luke – the physician. Conversion techniques are respectable, Oliver. In case you thought otherwise. But the ancients used them pragmatically, not understanding … Under the more emotive name of brain-washing, techniques of conversion are now a well developed science. The brain is a mechanism, Oliver. Pavlov found out how to interfere with its function over seventy years ago. Modern pulse generators do the job even better.' He closed his eyes, perhaps to dissociate himself partially from what he was about to say. 'Given a cause I believed was right, Oliver, I could spread it through Europe within a matter of weeks. I could bring converts to their knees in millions. In itself this is no great achievement. Even Hitler, using the crudest methods, inspired thousands. Genuinely inspired them. But the cause needs to be right; it needs to be a seed that will grow.'

Matthew had done some work himself on drug abreaction and cerebral wave interruptors. He could believe that the director was not making a vain boast. The success of revivalist meetings proved this. What the revivalists lacked – mercifully – was large enough backing, especially in the reinforcement stages. Professor Billon's resources, with the weight of the Colindale behind him, were probably unlimited.

'For the last three months,' the professor went on, 'we have been storing data in the Bohn. Sociological surveys, educational analyses, hospital reports, historical comparisons, political influences, reports from economists, philosphers, theologians, psychiatrists … I won't bore you. Any day now the program for relating all these will be complete. In response to it the Bohn will deliver a precise definition … the canon of a new faith. A spiritual framework to satisfy contemporary needs. The program is uniquely complex. We can only work at it humbly, as men of good will.'

His words ended, but his reasoning continued in Matthew's head. God existed. It was only man's way of reaching Him that changed from century to century. Today human needs were increasingly understood and catered for: sex, companionship, ritual, challenge. If God was anything, He was all of these …

But Matthew still refused to accept what his reason told him. His objections were emotional, irrational, amounting to an almost physical revulsion. They could be related to no objective truth, and he distrusted them. Racists felt just as violently about what they called miscegenation. But his objections, no matter how untrustworthy, were loud in his head, shouting down reason so that he could only cope with them by deferring them, by screening them off, by diverting his thoughts onto more practical, more encompassable matters. He took refuge in the peripheral, in a question sparked off by a sudden recollection of Dr Mozart's face under the flickering green light of the lime trees.

'John Henderson,' he said, 'did he approve of what you are doing?'

'Henderson? He was the mainstay. A great loss.'

'With the project nearly completed? Hadn't he in fact served his purpose?'

'My dear Oliver, the project only really starts when we receive the Bohn's specification. A representative has to be found, for example. There are months of work ahead – interpretation, selection, presentation, so much still to be done.'

Matthew's question had amounted to a near accusation. That Billon should simply not have noticed it seemed a sign of innocence: a murderer would have been more sensitive. Yet the project was of total importance to him. Was it not conceivable that he would have been willing to kill in order to preserve it? Had the director killed John Henderson or had he not? To Matthew this relatively superficial question assumed great significance. He was faced with a decision for which he was morally ill-equipped. So he fixed on the director's guilt or innocence as a safe, easy, externalized deciding factor. Almost like flipping a coin. He would judge the project by the conduct of its chief. He would help no man who could kill coldly, for the sake of an idea.

'Miss Pelham tells me Henderson had papers relating to the project. I can't find them.'

'Naturally. I could hardly leave them there for anybody to read. I got Blake to pick them up for me the day after Henderson died.'

'May I see them?'

'I was going to suggest that myself. You'll find them in the drawer in my office. Bottom right.' He handed over a bunch of keys, a gesture of trust. 'I'd come myself, but I'm expecting Scarfe.'

He stopped Matthew halfway down the steps.

'One thing more. Your wife.'

'My wife?' He felt himself flush. Had their differences been noted down, discussed, passed about the place from hand to hand? 'What about my wife?'

'Only that she's a Catholic. Bound to disapprove. You know your own business, of course. Handle with care, I'd say. Any reason she should be told?'

Matthew went on down the stairs without replying. If it was necessary for him to deceive Abigail, that was a matter between him and her. He was entering into no compact with the director about it.

Abigail had spent the evening in a state of pleasurable anticipation. In her mind there was only one reason why Matthew, after a day of obvious mental indecision, should go to see the director: he was offering his resignation. Which would be accepted. She thanked God devoutly. Matthew would leave the Colindale, they would contact the C.L.C., and the whole evil business would be brought to an end. Without violence. Paul would see how much more effective it was to use public opinion than bombs.

She sat and watched the tell. The house no longer interested her, for they would soon be leaving. Their house in London waited for them, the strands of their old life there to be picked up. Not even the possibility of jail – reformative custody – worried her. God never tested anybody beyond their strength. So she sat and watched the tell, and waited for Matthew's return.

'Well, love – what did he say?'

'Say? What about?'

'When you told him.'

Matthew was carrying a pile of thick plastic folders. He looked at her with genuine incomprehension. Suddenly she felt very sick.

'You didn't tell him.'

'Tell him what?'

'It doesn't matter. Tell him you weren't staying. It doesn't matter.'

It did matter. She got up wearily, and turned off the tell. She would make one last appeal, and after that another, and another last appeal.

'Matthew, what have you been thinking about all day? And last night, when you couldn't sleep?'

'Work. I've been thinking about my work.'

He was striding about the room, trying to hide from her in aimless movement.

'You have a conscience, Matthew. You know the project is wrong. You know it is. Please, love, don't –'

'Project?' He rounded on her, unexpectedly savage. 'What project?'

'Don't be foolish, Matthew. There's only one project. You know quite well what I'm talking about.'

She watched him relax, had no idea why. Most of the previous night's conversation with Andrew Scarfe had passed her by: mention of Paul had sent her off on tracks of her own, recollections of the place where he was hiding, a script of words she would use to tell him what she and Matthew had done. This at a time when she had believed in Matthew, in the essential rightness of his mind. Now she watched him, inexplicably relieved, circle her as if she were a wild animal and place the plastic folders in a drawer which he then locked. He took the key and put it carefully in his pocket. Once there had been trust between them.

'Abigail, please remember that we may be overheard.'

'I don't care. I want to be overheard. I want them to know that everybody isn't as corrupt as they.'

'Darling, be reasonable.' But he came no nearer to her. 'What good will it do to get yourself put away where nobody can hear you?'

'Put away?'

'You know they have the power.'

'And you'd let them?'

'What else could I do?'

He spoke to her patiently, in sadness. Only then did she realize how alone she was.

'You'd stay here working, Matthew, while I was taken away?' It still had to be spelled out. 'You'd do that?'

'Abby ...' He never called her that. Now he came toward her and she backed away. 'Abby, there's no need for you to be taken away. No need at all. If you'd only –'

'But you'd stay here working?'

He turned from her and went to the mantlepiece for a cigarette. He offered her one, which she refused. He lit his own carefully, delaying beyond everything that was possible the moment when he would have to reply.

'Abigail, we all have to do what we believe is right.' His words disgusted her. 'Would you respect me if I betrayed my principles, went against my conscience, just in order to keep you out of jail?'

How could she tell him that conscience was so often the prompting of the devil? That only God's help, which he had never humbled himself enough to ask for, could truly show him right from wrong? She sat down, leaned her face in her hands.

'We're married, Matthew. We don't need to –'

'And what does that mean?' He spoke so fiercely that she recoiled into the corner of her chair. 'Does it mean that I should do only what pleases you? Or that you should sometimes do what pleases me? Where are your marriage vows now, Abigail?'

There was nothing she could say. In three days their relationship had come to this: childish talk of vows and who pleased whom. A weak, degrading, irrelevant word, and applied to the thing she had thought strongest in the whole world. She closed her eyes and prayed for it all to end. But he could not let it rest.

'Abigail, you must promise me. Promise me you will do nothing to endanger the Colindale. For your own sake you must promise me.' For her sake, or for the Colindale? 'Do you hear me?'

She heard him. If she did not promise, the microphones would come and take her away. Or Matthew himself would arrange for her to be removed. She would be silenced either way. She did not blame Matthew; she did not even blame the Colindale.

'I promise.'

She lied. She lied loudly, for the microphones, with every sound of sincerity. Her framework of habitual truth was such that she expected to be believed. She said her lie again, more quietly, for Matthew.

After she had gone to bed, Matthew sat on in the sitting room, trying to read Henderson's notes on the special project. His mind kept returning to Abigail. He'd been pushed far further than he had intended. Perhaps her Catholic faith was the root cause of their present situation: the belief, when pressed, that she had divine authority for what she thought, while he had none. This made for an imbalance of intensity between them. From where she stood the things he did wrong were often sins; from where he stood the things she did wrong were never more than understandable mistakes. So it had always been harder for him to hold out against her, easier simply to give in and please. Billon's word ate in. Each time he had agreed to ideas of hers that basically he thought mistaken, he could at least comfort himself with the certainty that she had arrived at them intelligently, and from the highest motives. Besides, quite often she turned out to have been right after all. In those circumstances no mere idea had been worth endangering their relationship. It had been so much easier to give in and please.

She would keep her promise to do nothing. Knowing her, he was sure of it. Not that there was much she could do, with things the way they were at the Colindale … Not much either of them could do. Still tortured by indecision, he turned back to Henderson's notes. There was a chance they would in some way prove him to have been killed by the director. In that case the coin would have come down tails: both projects would have been shown up for what, perhaps, they were, the children of madness. He sorted through the plastic folders.

The room was gentle, green curtains from floor to ceiling along the inner wall, his harpsichord glowing burnished amber, the chairs metallic gray and white, the whole area dimly blue under the background lighting he had chosen. And the variable tick of the clock slow and calm, defining the aural limits of the space.

Above the corner of the sofa where he sat was a single untapered column of light, clear white for reading. He saw that the folders were dated, and found the one with the latest date, the last one Henderson had been writing in, many of its pages still unused. The notes were mostly in diary form, often quite personal, detailing experiments and developments in chronological order. He turned to the final page. Handwriting neat, steady and unhurried.

Wed. 4th June.

Boney up with some good stuff, but impenetrable. Answering Schatten's query about contemporary attitudes to ideal age of prophet. Offered this a.m. expressions of p.'s optimum age in terms of a 6-language etymology! Makes you think.

Basic concept still bugs me. E.g. sunset = grid = of integers = graph = equation. Equally well, sunset = grid of integers = electrical impulses = sound/music. As CB says, anything can be expressed in terms of anything. Don't altogether get it, but not to worry. It seems to work, so who cares.

NOTE Regional nature of p. worries me. CB says 300 mill Euros are enough for a beginning. I expect he's right NOTE Refer to Boney re. Danish marriage survey – Hinks MG 70791 (I think). Must do before evening session.

Wednesday, the fourth of June. The day Henderson had died. Died, involved up to the last minute in the director's special project. Supporting it. Enthusiastically. Perhaps it had only been a few minutes after writing his notes that he had borrowed the director's car, and driven down past the tennis courts, and died … Matthew let his eyes slip out of focus. The coin had come down heads. He was tired. Also he was committed. He knew, had always known, that Professor Billon was no murderer. The Colindale staff was huge; any one of hundreds could have placed the bomb in the professor's car. Perhaps Mozart himself. Mozart who would be on to him in the morning, wanting to know about the special project. He'd be told nothing, and he wouldn't like it. Matthew was tired. The coin had come down heads, and his prejudices were stirring. He turned back to the beginning of Henderson's notes. He was tired, but he didn't want to go to bed. He didn't want to go to Abigail. In spite of everything, he felt guilty.

NINE

She went through the morning business of getting Matthew off to work. In the middle of the night she had woken, found herself alone, and got up. He had been asleep in the corner of the sofa, surrounded by papers. She had helped him into bed, leaving the papers to be tidied in the morning. Moved by his sleeping, blind-kitten helplessness, she had treated him tenderly, and he had responded, not waking, drawing close to her, curled up in the big bed. She had watched him against the early dawn. Then they had woken together, as on any other morning, staring at the day beyond the curtains. Till, suddenly rigid, he had torn away and hurried into the sitting room, modest in quickly grabbed trousers. There had been no tea in bed. And when she had gone there later, the papers were all tidied and locked away. She went through the morning business of getting him off to the computer center.

When he had finally gone she sat down in the kitchen and lit a cigarette, let reality flood in on her. She knew what must be done, and she knew that she must do it alone, unaided. Everything depended on her being right about Sir William Beeston. She must explain the situation to him in person – sending a message would be far too complicated. She decided to check first with the shop manager to make sure that her guess about Sir William had been right.

If Mrs Foster was surprised to be called out on a second shopping expedition so soon after the first, she made no comment. It was no concern of hers how vocationalists spent their money. They found the manager down on the shop floor, checking stock with one of his assistants. Abigail encouraged him to explain to her the relative merits of different ultrasonic washers, asking him questions till Mrs Foster drifted idly away to a mixer demonstration.

'Yesterday you offered me a certain kind of help.'

'Indeed I did.'

They squatted down to look closely at a turbulence control unit.

'I want you to tell me the name of the person who would receive my message.'

'Nobody has names.'

'But you have met him?'

'On one occasion.'

So it was a man.

'Is it Sir William Beeston?'

'Nobody has names, Mrs Oliver. I told you.'

But the sudden lack of expression on his very mobile face told her what his words denied. He was likable, she thought, but not a very good intermediary. They moved around to the front of the machine.

'Have you a message you wish passed on?'

'No, thank you.'

Caution prompted her to tell such a transparent young man as little as possible. He shrugged, and began explaining to her the control panel of the Mark VII Bendix.

The Minister's secretary said that Sir William was very busy. Abigail replied that she would not be bothering him if the matter was not very urgent, and that her name was Oliver – her husband had worked with the Minister on several important schemes. The secretary checked in the Minister's diary and found that he had a cancellation between twelve thirty and one. Abigail said she'd be there.

One of the advantages of calling on a senior member of the Government was that one was unlikely to be suspected of sedition. Abigail left Mrs Foster firmly outside in the waiting room. It was a personal visit, Matthew having worked with Sir William so many times in the past.

'Mrs Oliver, how good to see you. Do sit down.'

His office was light and airy, cantilevered out over the Thames, giving a view of the new South Bank heliport and the hovercraft landing ramp. The Minister seemed relaxed and cheerful. She looked at him, thinking how she had never liked him, yet now she was to trust him completely. His life seemed to be one long public-relations operation. Yet an act of some kind would be necessary to a man in his double position – it was the stuff of all the best spy histories. Of course he would have put Matthew off the way he had, while he asked around, made sure.

'I expect you know why I'm here, Sir William.' His face carefully showed nothing but a polite interest. 'The shop manager … spoke to me.'

'Shop manager? Forgive me for being slow, Mrs Oliver, but I don't think I –'

She grasped the nettle. 'About the C.L.C., Sir William.' His gaze didn't flicker. 'I think you are a member, Sir William.'

'Nobody belongs to the C.L.C., Mrs Oliver.'

'That's what Edmund Gryphon always said.'

'Gryphon …'

He pushed a cigarette box across the desk to her, killing time while he made up his mind. She took one and he lit it.

'And you say that some shop manager in Colindale gave you my name?'

'Not your name.' No point getting the man into trouble. 'I worked that out from … from internal evidence, if you like.'

'So?'

They could circle around each other for the rest of her half-hour.

'I need someone I can talk to in the strictest confidence, Sir William.'

He sat forward abruptly. 'I am a Cabinet Minister, Mrs Oliver. One of the privileges of my position is an office free from microphones. If you have something confidential to say to me, I can assure you it is quite safe to do so. I tell you this because I think we share a concern for the liberty of the individual in these perilous times.'

She suffered a last-minute panic. She came down to telling herself that he had a kind face when his mask was down.

'You must have the courage to trust your internal evidence, Mrs Oliver. I can give you no proofs – we hardly carry membership cards about with us. You take a risk, of course. But no doubt your husband sent you. I respect Dr Oliver, in spite of what he might have gathered from our last meeting. Anything he has to tell us – to tell me – will receive careful attention. All human relationships come down to this, Mrs Oliver: at some time or another the risk has to be taken, the gesture of trust made …'

The shadows from the window uprights were moving across the floor. She had little time, and a lot to say in it.

When Matthew got home for lunch the house was empty. Fearing for a moment that Abigail had left him, he went into the bedroom and opened the cupboards. Her suitcases were there, and all her clothes. Her brushes were on the dressing table, and her identity card was in the top drawer. Typically, wherever she had gone, she had forgotten to take it. He wondered for how long he could live on the precipice edge. It would be better if he sent her away himself, perhaps to stay with her parents. A break might help them both. He cooked himself some food, miserable to be alone, and returned early to the computer center.

He had cleared all the queries from Data Reception by the time Maggie came in. Work was a way of not thinking. She closed the door and leaned against it, blowing down the front of her dress.

'Stone me, but it's hot. Did you know we put the stopper on climate control as too controversial? Bloody faint-hearted, if you ask me.'

She walked limply across to her desk.

'Still, without the weather, what'd there be left to complain about? Except the Government, of course.' She sat down. 'Maybe that's why they left us the weather.'

Matthew hadn't noticed the heat. He decided he liked Maggie; the limited openness her act allowed her was easy to get on with.

'Maggie, are you happy working here at the Colindale?'

'Happy? Who's happy? What a question.'

'The tails, the secrecy, the microphones, don't they worry you?'

'Haven't you heard the handout?' She closed her eyes and held up a benedictory hand. 'We at the Colindale are privileged to be taking part in uniquely meaningful work. Whatever price we pay for this historic role is amply justified.'

'Professor Billon?'

'None other.'

'And it satisfies you?'

'The hell it satisfies. I like to work for people who trust me.'

'Yet you stay.'

'Just you try leaving.'

They all knew too much. Matthew hadn't thought of that. Abigail was with him, whether either of them liked it or not.

'Look, Matthew, in the official mind there can be only two reasons for not wanting to stay here, for not loving every minute of it. First, political deviation. And second ...'

'Insanity?'

'Well done. You're not as naïve as I thought.'

She laughed, but he didn't join in. Gryphon had called him naïve. The director had said the same thing, in different words. Abigail too, in every aspect of their relationship. It was time he stopped being naïve.

'I surprised myself,' he said.

She laughed again, this time more because it was expected of her than because she thought his reply funny.

'By the way, I've been thinking about my flat-mate. How kinky do you really reckon he is?'

'I don't know enough about him to be able to say.'

'Well, either he's that or he's some dreary sort of agent. I'm sure he pokes in my drawers. And I once caught him reading one of my letters.'

'What sort of letter?'

'Well, that's the point. As it happens, the letter was the purest porn. There's a boy gets a thrill out of writing them to me; they do me no harm, so I let him. Other people's quirks are sad, don't you think? Anyway, there you are. At the time I was furious, accused him of being a spy, threatened to go to C.B., had a grand *crise* ...'

'Why didn't you?'

'Go to C.B.? Well, there's enough spying in this place already. I reckoned I'd frightened Andrew good and proper. Anyway, now I come to think of it I'm bloody glad I didn't tell on him. I bet that letter was making him bust his jockstrap. And I bet he rummages in my panties for the same reason.'

Admittedly it was hard to see what Scarfe, in his central, privileged position, could hope to learn from reading Maggie's letters. But if Mozart could be a spy, then why not Scarfe? And a spy for whom? Come to that, Matthew had no real idea for whom the German was working either … He was beginning to see the extent of his own naïveté.

Maggie was sorting through the litter on her desk. She uncovered the telephone.

'Look at this. Must have come in during lunch.' She tore off the paper that projected from the phonoprint. 'For you, by the look of it.'

Scarfe says program fini. Running this P.M. *CB.*

The director's notes were as telegraphic as his speech. He must be referring to the special project program. Matthew had hoped for longer in which to get used to the idea. He felt slightly sick.

'You don't need to tell me what it's all about. Whenever John got cryptic notes from CB, he always slipped them into the special project drawer. I take it you're now an initiate?' Matthew nodded. 'Good luck to you. All it ever gave John were lines around the eyes and gray hairs from lack of sleep.'

When he got in that evening he found Abigail waiting for him. He had walked up from the center warily, not wanting to meet Dr Mozart. He trusted nobody. The house was cool, air-conditioned. Abigail had pulled down the sunblinds to keep out the glare, and she was standing by the sitting room window, watching a blackbird hunt for worms in the shadow of the fir tree. He kissed the back of her head, and talked about the weather. He didn't ask her where she had been at lunchtime – he felt he no longer had the right. But the question existed, and she answered it.

'I'm sorry I wasn't in at one, Matthew. I felt I just had to get out. Mrs Foster and I went in to the Finchley shopping center.'

'I hope you enjoyed yourself. Did you buy anything?'

'No.'

He believed her. Except as a social duty she seldom made purchases unless they were greatly reduced in a sale, or the result of a long discussion. This wasn't meanness, merely a way of living with their wealth. He could have checked with Mrs Foster about the expedition, but he preferred not to insult Abigail by doing so. It didn't matter where she'd been: he had her promise.

He told her he had to go back to the computer center immediately after dinner and she accepted this, also without question. There was so little left for them to say to each other. How long he could keep it up he didn't know.

She had his food ready, and served it at once. Some people could live lives on a level of domestic efficiency and not much else. They ate in silence, his mind on the coming night's work. He was obscurely afraid of what the Bohn might tell them.

*

Back at the center the receptionist directed him down to the basement. He found the other members of the special project group in a long low room beside the shielded storage banks of the Bohn. Small sounds filtered through the wall, a constant clatter of relays as the machine dealt with incoming queries and with data being fed in from the teleprinters of Data Reception. The room was intended for the use of research teams and was comfortably furnished, recognizing the long sessions that were sometimes necessary before the program ran right. At one end of the room there was a long tropical fish tank, a brilliant microcosm, salutarily uninvolved, silent.

Professor Billon was sitting at one of the three teleprinters, checking a tape against the hand-printed master. Scarfe was beside him, at a large drawing board. As Matthew entered he looked up from a sheet of flow diagrams and penciled calculations, and waved.

'Glad to have you with us.'

Matthew wondered if it was hypersensitive of him to see this remark as an abrogation of the director's position. Certainly Professor Billon was too busy to notice. Scarfe had taken trouble to acquire a necessary technique, and it had won him a place with distinguished men. He wasn't a man to cope wisely with such a situation.

Zacharie Mallalieu sat on one of the couches, reading the day's *Financial Times*. All that could be seen of him was his white hair and his young pale hands. Schatten and Blake were setting out the pieces of a pocket chess set. Dingle, the historian, was filling a large meerschaum pipe. There was a feeling in the air that nobody expected anything to happen for a very long time.

Matthew sat down beside Professor Dingle, put on the cheerful friendliness he used with strangers.

'Looks as if I ought to have brought a pack of cards.'

The older man finished filling his pipe, then dusted shreds of tobacco off the front of his jacket. He spoke carefully, and with great good manners.

'You will be Dr Oliver. My name is Dingle. We were introduced in passing the other day. How do you do.'

Matthew wondered if he should stand up to shake hands. Dingle employed the typical distancing mechanisms of a converger. It often surprised Matthew that people should behave so much as their profession suggested they would.

'Cards are supplied, as a matter of fact. Should any of us care for a game.'

'What could we play?' The evening was fantastic – why not compound the fantasy with a game of cards? He looked around. 'We seem to be the only two not fully occupied.'

'I expect Mallalieu will be glad to join us. Henderson and we used to have some fine old tussles. Been quite at a loose end since the poor fellow's sudden departure.' Dingle leaned slightly closer. 'But I feel I should warn you that friend Mallalieu likes very much to win. It's as if the whole efficacy of a mathematical turn of mind were at stake.'

'Friend Mallalieu also possesses excellent hearing.' The *Financial Times* had not moved a centimeter. 'Five mark ante, just to make the game more interesting?'

'I'm willing,' Matthew said.

Apparently the game was to be poker. Mallalieu folded his paper carefully and put it in his pocket. He rose and, nudging a small table across the floor in front of him with his foot, came to join the other two men. The table legs made an unpleasant noise on the floor. Andrew Scarfe bent lower over his flow diagram and clicked his tongue in loud irritation.

'If we are expected to be here,' Mallalieu said, to no one in particular, 'we can hardly in addition be expected to preserve a monastic silence.' Matthew foresaw an edgy poker game. 'I'm surprised, Oliver, that you did not come better prepared. Every computer session I have attended here has turned out to be a considerable waste of everybody's time.'

'I expect,' said Dingle mildly, 'that Dr Oliver is used to more normal computer operations, employing a large number of technicians. The secrecy of our work here makes that impossible.'

'In other words, Oliver, we're expected to blow the thing's nose for it. And wipe its arse.'

Matthew disliked self-conscious man's talk. But then, he disliked Zacharie Mallalieu. It would be pleasant to take his money from him. Dingle fetched a pack of cards, and began to take out all those under seven. Then he put them on the table and Matthew cut. Mallalieu dealt. Matthew anted the five marks and picked up his hand. Two knaves and three odd cards, ace high. He kept the ace with the knaves and changed two.

'Hmm,' murmured Dingle. 'Drawing to a three.'

'Rubbish,' said Mallalieu. 'Pair and an odd ace. They all do it.'

Cards betrayed people more than any other single activity. Except perhaps driving. The two cards he gave Matthew were ace knave. Dingle changed three, and the dealer one. Matthew, with a good full house, tossed out a ten-mark piece. Dingle folded and Mallalieu, snorting, raised to twenty.

Matthew hesitated. He had no idea how the other two played. He reasoned that he had been placed either with a three or two good pairs. Mallalieu was either filling a straight or a flush, or drawing to two pairs. A further raise should tell him which. He kept the raise at ten. Mallalieu put it up again a full twenty – either bluffing or with five of a kind. Unless he'd matched one of his pairs. Matthew paid the twenty to see him, feeling the money well spent, if only to find out how the other man played.

Mallalieu put down five odd cards, king high. The chat was obviously an integral part of his game. Matthew showed two of his knaves and gathered in a profit of fifty marks.

They played several more hands and Matthew, never a distinguished player, continued to win. He enjoyed cards for their own sake: their precise shape and texture, the excitement of each new hand, the skills of dealing and shuffling, he enjoyed it all. So that, within limits, he had no objection to losing. Mallalieu was different – to put down a hand better than his was to offer him a personal insult. The money was of little significance to any of them. It was the sense of personal success or failure that troubled Zacharie Mallalieu.

At any other time this situation would have made Matthew play to lose. He would have felt no game to be worth anger, tension, unpleasantness, a possible row. But tonight he was a new man. Anyone as small-minded as Mallalieu deserved all he got. So he played hard and tight, and kept on winning. It was one of those nights.

Behind them Professor Billon finished checking the tape. He and Andrew Scarfe muttered together, heads bent over calculations on various bits of paper. Matthew was aware of their activity all the time, as a background to the game. He watched the director take the final tape and move toward the computer desk. Scarfe called him back. The two of them conferred over an Astran service manual.

'I've raised you twenty, Oliver.'

'See you,' said Matthew, not concentrating.

When it was too late he remembered that he held four queens and had intended going up with every mark he possessed. Mallalieu showed four triumphant kings. It was one of those nights.

Finally Billon and Scarfe were satisfied. They mounted the tape on a twenty-four-inch reel – Matthew saw that it barely fitted. He was used to seven-inch reels, with a running time of two or three minutes. The present program might take up to half an hour. Professor Billon was at the computer desk, threading the tape across the heads, clumsy with excitement.

'First run, gentlemen.'

There was a slight rustle of interest.

'Tenth run and I might begin to take some notice,' said Mallalieu, very audibly.

'I raised you five,' Dingle said. The cards were beginning to run his way.

'Five? What sort of raise is that? Either they're worth raising on, or they're not.'

Dingle pursed his lips and said nothing, let his bet stand. The second filling of his pipe had just gone out. Mallalieu, his temper worsening, raised a further twenty and lost again. The chess players, who had looked up at the director's announcement, returned to their game. And the Japanese fantails circled contentedly between their pillars of pink coral.

It was Mallalieu's turn to deal. Meanwhile, the first few cleaning feet of the tape ran through quickly. Then the note changed: there would be a brief ugly scream till the heads reached a stop combination and paused. The sounds from the next room would intensify. Then the tape would rush on again, chattering and shrieking. Matthew had the feeling that if only the noise could be slowed, as on a tape recorder, it would make human sense. He was hearing thought. He was hearing an intellectual process. And to his mind intellectual processes were inseparable from words. Computer logic – anything expressed in terms of anything – frightened him.

'How many are you changing, Oliver?'

Suddenly the monitored, synthetic perfection of their environment nauseated him. The careful lights, and the jibber of the computer. And the people. Scarfe, all brain, studying his flow diagrams as he had on another occasion, all body, studied Maggie Pelham's letter. Billon, quite without movement or apparent emotion. And the other four men, manneredly absorbed in their own irrelevancies.

'Make up your mind, Oliver. How many are you changing?'

'One.'

He didn't even look at his hand. The machine screamed and paused, screamed and paused. Schatten offered his opponent a quiet *Check*. The scene should have been completed with a palm court orchestra playing *The Flight of the Bumblebee*. Badly.

'I've put up ten, Oliver. Are you in?'

He fidgeted with the cards in his hands, but still didn't look at them.

'Raise you fifteen,' he said.

Dingle met this, and Mallalieu upped it fifty. Scarfe got up from his drawing board by the group of teleprinters and joined Professor Billon at the computer. He checked the tape counter to see how far the program had advanced. The tape feed had been badly aligned, and used tape was beginning to spill out across the floor.

Matthew automatically raised a further fifty, and then dragged his mind to look at his cards. Mallalieu must be desperate, putting in raises of fifty … At first Matthew thought he had five odd ones. Then he saw that they could be sorted into a straight – ten knave queen king ace. His blind draw had turned out incredibly well. But he hadn't been attending, and he had no idea what the others had drawn. Mallalieu with his fifty raise, and Dingle quietly meeting even the hundred now needed.

Mallalieu folded his cards into a neat stack, put them facedown on the table, and raised a hundred. Matthew had allowed his attention to wander on the hand that was apparently to be the showdown. Betting blind, not knowing what was against him. Under such circumstances he would normally have got out. But Mallalieu's gross confidence annoyed him. The room's hysteria was infectious.

He tossed out a two hundred note. 'It's a shame to take your money,' he said.

Dingle met the two hundred, and the four subsequent raises – never raised himself, but always kept level. He was staying in, believing he had a good chance of picking up the pieces. Mallalieu ran out of money, and had to borrow. He hadn't looked at his cards since putting them down on the table. Matthew kept his in his hand, needing constant reassurance that he really held what he thought he held. At any moment the knave might turn out to be a queen, or the ace a seven. His cards were nowhere near good enough for the level of the betting. Mallalieu *had* to be bluffing. Dingle he would lose to with pleasure.

Suddenly the note of the computer changed, and the console put out a short blue paper tongue. Scarfe tore it off.

'Error in phase seven,' he translated aloud. 'Loop incompatability. Holding.' He referred to his flow diagram. 'Phase seven ... there's a hierarchic loop, three-level structure. Worked well in isolation.'

'Copy misprint?' said the director.

'We'll have to see. Might be a simple data error. Dr Mallalieu ...?' Scarfe had wound back the tape and was reading it off straight through on the print-out 'Dr Mallalieu, your stage. Stand by, please.'

Mallalieu appeared not to have heard. He was entirely focused down to the act of willing Matthew's cards to be worse than his. Suddenly Matthew felt sorry for the man, that it should really be so important.

'No point in throwing any more money down the drain,' he said. 'I'm running.'

'But you can't run. Not now.'

'I just have.'

'But –'

'As far as I'm concerned the kitty's all yours. Must be upward of two thousand marks.'

He turned away to watch Andrew Scarfe. But out of the corner of his eye he saw Dingle pay to see Mallalieu's hand. And he saw Mallalieu's flush go down to Dingle's four nines. His own hand had been the weakest of the lot. And nobody would ever know. The relief that he felt told him that he had backed down not out of compassion but out of cowardice.

'Dr Mallalieu. Please. I have a list of figures here for you to check.'

The game was interrupted. Dingle gathered the money he had won, and scooped it unobtrusively into his pocket. He and Matthew stared, embarrassed, at the scattered cards on the table, waiting for Mallalieu to return.

'It's a strange game for men like us to choose to play,' he said. 'Which probably explains why none of us is very good at it.'

'Men like us?' said Matthew, preferring speech to silence.

'Not gamblers by nature, I mean. At least, I don't think we are.'

'So we gamble with money, which doesn't really matter.'

'I wonder if you are right. I receive the distinct impression that we have been playing for something far more important than money.' He began refilling his pipe. 'If I were prone to generalizations I would say that with no gambler is money ever more than a tertiary motive. If that even.'

'Nobody likes to lose.'

'You, my dear Oliver, are being intentionally obtuse. Perhaps you are wise.'

A long silence followed, in which the movement of the chess pieces and the background clatter of the relays next door became unnaturally loud. Mallalieu could be heard muttering over his data list … Dingle had been partially right. Matthew *had* offered a remark that was knowingly inadequate. But certainly not out of wisdom.

'I suppose we have to go on playing,' he said at last.

'Sportsmanship demands it. Zacharie is losing – whether we stop or continue must be his decision.'

'And he'll want to go on. So we'll just have to hope that luck changes.'

'Which is egregiously patronizing of you, my dear fellow.'

The *dear fellow* and Dingle's charming smile robbed the retort of its edge, if not of its truth. Matthew collected the cards and began to shuffle. His companion's fusty appearance and turn of phrase sorted badly with the technical chic of the room they were in, with the special project, with the Colindale.

'Tell me,' Matthew said, his eyes on the cards he was shuffling, 'what made you agree to help with this particular project? I'd have thought it out of character.'

'It's perfectly simple. The project won't work.'

'Won't work?'

'Of course not. I look on it as an intellectual exercise and a harmless way of keeping our director happy. But please, never tell Zacharie that. It would mark the end of an indifferently beautiful friendship.'

'Why won't it work?'

'Because it's a logical impossibility. While it might be possible to deduce grass from the needs of a horse, to work the other way is utter nonsense. The ability to deduce a horse from the properties of grass is quite beyond us.'

'But you're saying one can't deduce man from the properties of God, which was never in question. Anyway, this project has nothing to do with God. It's man we're analyzing, not God.'

'We start from different points, my dear Oliver. You see, I believe in God, and you don't.'

The penetration of this remark shocked Matthew into silence. Since his marriage he had believed in God rather in the manner of the Red Queen's advice to Alice that she should believe six incredible things every morning before breakfast. And it had never quite worked. He didn't believe in God; instead, he believed in Abigail, and she believed in God, and that made everything all right.

Mallalieu returned to the table, and they began playing again. But the tension was broken, the hands dull. Scarfe rethreaded the tape – the error had not been in the data but in the copying – and the Bohn continued where it had left off. Scream, pause, scream. Schatten won his game against Blake. Neither player seemed inclined to start a second. The program tape jerked through its last few yards, its end finally rustling down among the coils that moved secretly on the floor around the computer desk. The calculation phase began, the associating and cross-referencing. To fill in, Scarfe found the end of the tape, clipped it into a new spool, and began winding back. The coils were gathered up from the floor, rubbing together like snakes. The rewind rose to a high whine, then cut abruptly as the last few inches flipped, slowing, around and around. Finally the room was left to the faint considering chatter of the relays. The card players laid down their hands.

Professor Billon seated himself by the printout console, rigid, resting no more than he had done throughout the program run.

'Five minutes,' he said. 'Perhaps less.'

Nobody moved. Matthew noticed that Dingle had put his cards face upward, two tens, an eight, a queen, and a king. He couldn't remember if his own hand was better or worse.

'Of course,' offered Andrew Scarfe, his voice abnormally normal, 'it'll be a miracle if it comes through right first time. Much of the flow is pure guesswork – beside straining Astran to its limits. I wouldn't be surprised if all we get is a sound of popping elastic.'

It wasn't a good joke, and nobody even smiled. But the atmosphere relaxed. To try that particular brand of schoolboy risque perhaps Scarfe was public school after all. Thought Matthew.

There was a general stir of activity as the five-minute wait became real, an absurdly long time to remain silent and motionless. Conversations were instituted. Dingle saw his turned-up cards and pushed them into the middle of the table.

'I was folding anyway,' he said.

Mallalieu threw in also. No incentive remained for another deal. Slowly the five minutes passed, then six, then seven. At last, with a faint turning of wheels, paper began to flow from the printout console. Billon switched in the big monitor screen so that everybody could see.

INRELATE FAZ NOTKOM POINSTOP TENPREFIN SM 101 POINSTOP LATERAL KX THOZE FEET IN ANSIENT KAKBKK TENPREFIN SM 101 TIME WALKIN WALKIN WALK BLASS UNKOMPAT AST OBJEKON BIPA AST OBJEKON BIPA 2 SM 101 POINSTOP KAK-BKKKDKEKF KAP FAZ ERROR NOBIPA POINSTOP 1 123 123456 12345678910 1234567891011 12131415 123456789 101112131415161718192021 1234

The printout ran on as far as this before Scarfe could switch it off.

'Slipping into a very simple progression curve,' he said. 'It's the interrelations in the capstan phase. They'd leave a blank series all the way.'

'And the recurrent objection?' asked Professor Billon.

'The whole aesthetics loop is hunting. Or we wouldn't get that breakthrough. But at least we've succeeded with the nationalism block.'

Matthew lost interest. Their language was too private. All that mattered was that something had gone wrong. He wondered how long he would be expected to stay. An error in the capstan phase – what was the capstan phase anyway?

'Gentlemen' – the director stood up – 'gentlemen, this SM 101 reference. Mean anything to any of you?'

Matthew jumped, as if caught talking in class. 'S is a sociology prefix,' he said. 'But I've not seen an SM. At least, I don't think so. I'll check if you like.'

'Would you? We'll get a redefine first, but it seemed consistent.'

The redefinition produced nothing helpful. Matthew went up to his office to look in the classification index. There was no SM listed. Outside his window the night was clear and starlit. He leaned on the windowsill, staring up. Astran demanded a basic humorlessness, yet there was no real reason why KAP FAZ should seem to him so irresistibly funny. The typically British habit of laughing at the natives, maybe.

Back in the basement room he found Scarfe handing around sheets of codified data for checking. Apparently the capstan phase provided the central motivational impulse and was returned to between each associative operation. Thus its interrelations involved all departments. At first glance Matthew could make no sense of his data list at all. He had several hours' work ahead of him.

Abigail spent the evening alone, alternately exultant and appalled. Exultant at the success of her meeting with the Minister: he had promised her a special meeting of the Committee within two days, the publication of a broadsheet within a week at the most. He had shown a reassuring, unhysterical determination; he would get things done. Now that she had started an irreversible process she experienced a pleasant dissociation from it. Already in her mind her visit to the Minister was completely innocent. Her good intentions spilled over onto actual events, transmuting them … until, appalled, she thought of Matthew.

She had betrayed his trust in her; to this the rightness of what she had done was irrelevant. She needed time in which, with God's help, to walk slowly with him till he understood. It was for this reason that she had lied about where she had been. It was in his power to have her taken away, committed to reformative custody, and in the immediacy of his hurt this would seem justified. She needed time. Events towered about them both, a windowless city. If she was taken away that night she would carry with her nothing of him. He would snatch back the past even. If he simply knew that night that she had lied to him, she would go alone. And this she feared far more than jail, far more than anything. She needed time.

At midnight she went to bed – to stay up would be to erect a barrier of significance against his return. Later she was woken by the familiar, four-year-long sound of him brushing his teeth. Instinctively her body opened to him, then closed, suddenly remembering.

'Matthew?'

'It was a long session. I'm sorry.'

Their bathroom door was ajar, letting a narrow strip of light fall across the floor and the bottom of the bed. The strip widened, and was filled by his shadow. Then darkness. She heard him undressing: shoes, socks, the zip of his trousers.

'I hoped I wouldn't disturb you.'

'It doesn't matter. I'm glad you're back.'

He turned back his side of the bedclothes.

'It's a hot night.'

His weight depressed the bed so that she had to prevent herself from rolling toward him.

'I love you, Matthew.'

'My eyes hurt. If this goes on I shall have to see about glasses of some sort.'

'Don't you believe me?'

'It's after two, Abigail.'

'You must believe me.'

'All right. And I love you too. But I can't. Not tonight. I honestly can't.'

'That wasn't what I meant.'

'No. No, I suppose not.'

She listened to him breathing, felt him slowly unwind. Then he slept. A warm summer wind blew across the Colindale, causing the fir tree to scrape soft green needles against the bedroom window.

TEN

At the coffee break next morning Matthew received a call to the director's office. From the look of him, the director had been up all night. He was as sleek as ever, but the sockets of his eyes were gray and the skin at the base of the scar on his forehead was twitching.

'SM 101,' he said. 'Are you sure you've nothing in your index?'

'I've checked several times. There are no SM classifications. None at all. Either the Bohn's mad or this isn't a classification at all.'

The director screwed up his face with the pain of his tiredness.

'I've sent Scarfe back to his quarters. He's done all he can. For the last six hours we've got nowhere.'

'Might I suggest you went home yourself, Professor?'

'I know my resources. There's an answer here somewhere. Couple of hours ago we ran a diagnostic check. Nothing wrong, Oliver. Nothing there to diagnose. This one reference, it's all we have. All there is to show for three months' work. It must mean something.'

'No change in the final printout at all?'

The director gestured in the direction of the console.

'See for yourself. A miracle might have occurred.'

Matthew crossed to the machine. The long hours of the previous night had taught him a lot about its controls. He dialed the repeat sequence.

> FINDEF SM 101 POINSTOP REQ STA2 POINSTOP FINDEF SM 101 POINSTOP REQ STA2 POINSTOP FINDEF 101 SM REQ ST

He stopped the machine and ripped off the piece of paper.

'Request stage two? What's this stage two it's asking for?'

'Well, well ...' The director smiled wryly. 'It's getting impatient. Stage two is the campaign stage. Not even begun on yet. We have to understand the final definition first.'

'What happens if you ask for a redefine?'

'Thing goes wild. All its party tricks. Kings of England, Haydn symphonies, passages from the Revelation of St John the Divine – anything and everything. We had to stop it. Looked like keeping it up all day.'

'And there's nothing wrong with the program ...'

'Of course there's nothing wrong with the program. And yet there must be.

SM 101 – what sort of definition is that? How can the whole thing possibly be brought down to just one series?'

Matthew scrumpled the neat rows of symbols and tossed them down the waste chute.

'I'm afraid I can't help you, sir. I'm sure it's not a classification anywhere on my files.'

He started to move toward the door. Professor Billon called him back.

'You, er … you think I've bitten off more than I can chew?'

'Not at all, sir.' There was too much at stake. The director's entire career might have been directed toward meeting this one challenge. 'There must be other S's. What about Dr Mozart's subject: what about spectroscopy?'

'Thought of that. All SP's.'

'And seismography?'

'Been through every S classification we have. Anyway, what single scientific paper could possibly …?' He tailed off. But he didn't want to be left alone. 'Sit down, Oliver. Time I told you about my dud eye.'

Matthew had a duty to be generous. He sat down in one of the mesh chairs. He might have lived a hundred years since he had sat there beside Abigail, making up his mind if he wanted to work at Colindale. In less than a week his life had been enlarged till he was a different person, a Colindale person. He believed in the director and he believed in the Bohn. He saw the special project as logically, beautifully inevitable. And he accepted it as being larger than himself, larger than himself and Abigail.

'… Student days,' the director was saying. 'I used to go around the closed wards, asking too many questions. Closed wards they had in those days. Felt it my job to stir things up for the regular staff. Far too resigned. Complacent even … Maybe they did it to warn me off and maybe they did not. Might have been quite accidental. Not that it matters.' For once he paused not for effect. He was reliving the moment. 'Somehow the poor woman had got hold of a knife. Interesting tradition, strength of ten men. Sound physiological explanation. Anyway, there you are.' He made a quick slashing movement with his right hand. 'Sorry as hell about it afterward, of course. Made me think. You see, it was all psychoanalysis in those days. And who benefitted? Not who needed it most. Couldn't get near the seriously disturbed. Never claimed to. That woman changed my life. It was she needed help, not the wets afraid of their virility. And to help her, Oliver, some other way was needed. Surgery. Drugs. Unpopular ideas even now. But they work. The brain is just as much a machine as the heart or lungs … Story of my life. Case you've ever wondered how I landed here.'

Matthew had reservations. His eye wandered away to the sculpture revolving in the corner. He had been warned about trying to please.

'The brain may be a machine, sir. But isn't it something else as well? Hasn't it other qualities?'

'Careful here. Only talk about what we know. You refer to the soul: repository of higher emotions, conscience, love, hate, honor, duty, faith … Right?' Matthew nodded. Billon held up fingers, started counting them. 'First thing, as defined, the soul exists. Second thing, we don't know where. Third thing, its nature can be changed. Drugs, applied hysteria, illness, even the simple processes of time – all these can modify the nature of the soul. And all these act on a physiological level. Fifth thing, what then is the soul?' He leaned forward. 'And if you see where that takes us and don't like it, neither do I. Keep an inquiring mind, Oliver. And humbleness. Nothing else will do.'

Matthew was uneasy. In spite of his admiration for the director, there was at the back of his mind a nagging distrust of people who professed humbleness. Perhaps, like children, it should be seen and not heard. The director closed his eyes and leaned back in his chair, his tiredness doubly returned now that his story was finished.

Abigail was enduring a visitor. Wanting nothing more than to be left alone, she was having to be polite to the resident Colindale doctor.

'I'm really very sorry not to have called before, Mrs Oliver. I make this routine call to all newcomers, just so that they'll feel welcome, looked after, you know the sort of thing.'

'Of course, Doctor. Sit down, won't you?'

'Thank you, thank you. Only a fleeting visit.' He looked around the room, saw the harpsichord. 'You are musical, Mrs Oliver? Or is it your husband?'

'I like music. But it's my husband who plays.'

'You have no children?'

'No.'

'You are a practicing Catholic?'

'Yes.'

All this had been in the preliminary written questionnaire. But no doubt he had to find something to talk about. Suddenly she thought how unreasonable it was that the assumption between her and Matthew had always been that she was the barren one.

'If you want any help in that direction you know I'll be only too glad to do what I can.'

'Of course.' She dared a bitter note. 'Perhaps you'd care to talk to my husband.'

The doctor would have to have been a complete fool not to see that this was a subject best left.

'You're settling in well? You've made the house quite delightful … Tell me, how do you like it here at the Colindale?'

'Not very much.' No harm in that much honesty.

'We do our best to make you comfortable. Why don't you like it?'

'Perhaps you do too much. I don't think being comfortable is all that important.'

'A well-ordered life makes you uneasy?'

'It depends on who's ordering it.'

She could spar like this all day. The doctor smiled disarmingly.

'Believe me, Mrs Oliver, I'm not trying to get at you. I simply have a professional concern for your comfort. Yours and your husband's. A move is more disrupting than many people think. *Autre pays autres moeurs* ... Both of you are well?'

'You're right, doctor. The Colindale *is* another country.'

'I think you'll settle down, Mrs Oliver.' He paused, looking for a comforting noise to make. Abigail lit herself a cigarette, unhelpful. Behind her she could feel the mid-morning garden, hot and still. 'There's a very active social life here, Mrs Oliver, which you probably haven't yet come much in contact with. I expect you're suffering from a sense of isolation. It's very common among newcomers. You should get out more. I'll ask the Leisure Counselor to call.'

'Please don't.'

She'd been a Leisure Counselor herself, immediately after leaving L.S.E. In the days when she'd been in love with Edmund. She couldn't face the patter, and the life it would remind her of.

'Not if you don't want me to.' Unconcerned. 'Her number's in the book, should you change your mind.'

'I'm afraid you'll think me very uncooperative, Doctor.'

'Of course not. Most of the people here are sufficiently intelligent and well-adjusted to run their own lives.' He got up. 'Another hot day. Chance for me to sweat off a bit at the tennis courts. Stir up the old circulation.'

He paused on the way to the door.

'I expect you're not yet used to the microphones. Do they worry you?'

'They stand for distrust. That worries me.'

'Distrust, Mrs Oliver?' He smiled down at her, almost as tall as Matthew. 'Don't we all long to know what happens in houses when the doors are shut and the curtains drawn? I'd say it shows a healthy curiosity. I think you're jealous, Mrs Oliver.'

Or guilty. Why didn't he say what he was really thinking?

'Observing a phenomenon changes it, Doctor. Nothing happens in houses when the doors can never be shut and the curtains never drawn.'

The remark came out more violently than she had intended. The doctor seemed not to notice.

'You'll be surprised how quickly you forget all about them.'

'I doubt it.'

She wouldn't be staying that long. He went out into the cloisters, looked at the smooth grass and the other houses generously spaced around the sides of the quadrangle, the trees and the informal shrubberies, and was pleased with what he saw.

'You have my number,' he said, 'should you ever want me. Anxiety states are easily dealt with, you know.'

'I am not suffering from an anxiety state.'

'You might find it cleared up your … other trouble as well. Often a matter of tension, nothing more.' Cheerful to the end. 'Good morning.'

He deserved no medal for noticing she was tense. She went quickly into the house and closed the door. All right. She was tense, she was anxious, she was barren, she was guilty. She lit another cigarette. Also she had an oral fixation. She curled her bitten nails into her palms, hiding them even from herself. If the doctor had been sent to undermine her, he had done a good job. And Matthew soon to be in for lunch.

She rang his office in the computer center. He wasn't there, so she left a message with his assistant, asking him to lunch at the canteen. For wasn't that the purpose of the canteen, to help wives whom the Colindale had turned into screaming neurotics? She went into the kitchen and prayed, leaning against the sink, staring at the taps.

Hail, Mary, full of grace, the Lord is with thee: blessed art thou among women, and blessed is the fruit of thy womb, Jesus. Holy Mary, mother of God, pray for us sinners, now, and at the hour of our death.

Amen.

She prayed the single simple prayer for a long time, not repeating it but listening to its echoes. Then she went down to the canteen, to the public table where nothing could be expected, nothing said.

Early in the afternoon Matthew's routine work was interrupted by Andrew Scarfe. He put his head experimentally around the door.

'Afternoon, Dr Oliver. Afternoon, Maggie. Room for a little one?'

Maggie sighed audibly, and went on checking classifications. She didn't have to be polite to Scarfe; she lived with him. Matthew had wider obligations.

'Come in, Scarfe. I thought you'd been sent home to get some sleep.'

'Sleep? Could you sleep with this thing on your mind?'

'I managed a peaceful six hours.'

'But you're not really involved. I'm supposed to be the computer man. When I close my eyes all I see are compensating loops and differential feedbacks.'

He sat down in stages, like an old man. He certainly looked as if he hadn't slept much. His self-importance of the night before had gone.

'I'm at a complete dead end. I could understand it if the Bohn weren't so specific. Usually when there's something wrong all you get is a load of bunk. But this –' He checked himself, glanced across at Maggie. 'Well, it's something quite new. And I can't even shop around for a second opinion.'

Maggie got up, glad to be able to get out and at the same time register I-know-when-I'm-not-wanted.

'I'll take these down to Data Reception. It's a good thing to show the rest of the group that we are real people in here – people with problems, people who make mistakes. Not like bloody old Boney.'

She went out, taking a bundle of classifications with her. Scarfe turned in his chair to watch her go.

'She doesn't like me.'

'I wouldn't say that . . .'

'I would. She's a bitch. God, how I hate women like that.'

Matthew fiddled with the papers on his desk. He had work to do. And to have a row with Scarfe in his present state would be pointless.

'If I were you I'd try to occupy myself with something else for a day or two. The subconscious grinds on – you'd probably find the thing solved itself if you gave it time.'

'And the director? What's going to happen to him? He's far nearer to breaking up than I am.'

Matthew had seen few signs of disintegration when they'd talked that morning. Perhaps Scarfe needed to prove something.

'Maybe he's stronger than you think. I was with him a few hours ago, and –'

'All you've seen is the act. And he's good at it. But I tell you, the better the act's going the worse he is inside. You should have seen him the first few days after Henderson's death. As bright and busy as a light bulb. And just about as brittle.' He laughed at his own wordplay. He might have been talking about someone he hated. 'If I don't come up with an answer soon, Dr Oliver, he'll just fall to pieces.'

Computers exacted from people a service equal to their own tireless, elusive circuitry. It was the Bohn that drove Scarfe on, not his sense of responsibility to Professor Billon. Matthew had seen computer men before, the same sharp bright talk, the same sleeplessness, the same need to personalize their servitude. And with Scarfe there was something more, some additional tension. He should think himself lucky the Colindale wasn't a commercial concern, where each misrun cost somebody thousands.

'I don't suppose there's anything I could do to help?'

'Do? Just tell me you made a mistake. Tell me there's an SM on your file, a paper about some noble guru living near West Woking with all the answers.' Matthew smiled and shook his head. 'Well, failing that, there's not a thing.'

He started to get up. 'Unless … Well, there is just one thing you could do. Stupid thing, really.'

Matthew waited. With Scarfe it could be anything. The deeply personal things men asked men to do in books. Matthew waited, looking helpful, feeling apprehensive.

'I ought to ring my mother. I wonder if you'd do it for me. Here's the number …' Ring his mother? It might have been a lot worse. 'Just tell her I'll be working late for the next few nights, so I won't be over as I promised.'

'Wouldn't it be better if you rang her yourself?'

'I suppose it would. But, hell, you know what mothers are.' Matthew didn't: his own had left him with an aunt so that she could get on with her career. 'You see, she'll want to know why, and I won't be able to tell her. Then she'll say it's some girl, and why can't I at least be honest with her. Then I'll deny it, and she'll say … and I'll say … and so on and so on. So I'd be very grateful if you'd do that little thing for me.'

Matthew wondered if it was his imagination, or if Scarfe really had said *girl* as if it were a dirty word. If that was the sort of mother he had it was no wonder he'd turned out a little odd. Matthew took the number and dialed. It was his first outside call, and he could imagine the recorders grinding.

'May I speak to Mrs Scarfe, please?'

'Speaking.' Formidable indeed. The one flat word.

'I'm calling from the Colindale, Mrs Scarfe. I have a message from your son. He says he's very sorry, but he'll be working late for the next few nights, so he won't be able to get over as he had promised.'

'I see. Nothing else?'

Matthew raised his eyebrows at Scarfe and the young man shook his head vehemently.

'No, nothing else. Except that he's sorry. It's a very busy time here at the computer center.'

'I see. Tell him I'll be writing.'

She rang off. If that was motherhood, Matthew was glad to be without it.

'She'll be writing,' he said.

'So I heard. You know, I wish she wouldn't. Pages and pages of nag. I feel such a fool if I ever have to go down to the censorship office.' He stood up. 'Anyway, you're a hero. Now I'd better get my nose back to the grindstone … By the way, I'm forgetting what I really came in for. Could I possibly borrow back that Astran primer? There's a couple of points I think I ought to look up.'

'I'm afraid it's at home. I could ring my wife, ask her to bring it down for you.'

'Please don't bother her. There's one in the library. I was only trying to save myself a couple of minutes.'

After he had gone Matthew tried to get back to his work. *Ring my wife, ask her to bring it down for you …* such easy, such proprietary words. Words that lied, words he must stop using. Once she had said that he was the fire, she the fuel. And the desolate present, that too would pass, giving place to a quality of life he could not imagine. He didn't know how long he could continue to burn without her. He didn't believe that everything could founder, not on a ragged lifeless ideal. That evening he would talk to her, try to reach her.

When Maggie came back from Data Reception he filled in his own silence by telling her about the phone call to Scarfe's mother. She stood by the window, thoughtfully picking her nose. A mower hummed by, ridden by one of the groundsmen.

'So *that* was why he came to see you. I thought all the other was a bit put on. Poor little worm – I suppose one ought to feel sorry for him … But it's all too neat. Anyone else would have got themselves cured of her long ago. I reckon she's his excuse.'

'Have you met her?'

'She's never been to the Colindale. But I've seen her letters, pages and pages of them. He shows them around as if he was proud of them.'

Perhaps he was. But, as Maggie said, the whole structure was too neat, too analytically sound.

At about five o'clock Abigail was called by the guard at the gate with the surprising news that a man claiming to be her brother was there. Would she please come down and identify him, so that a day pass could be issued.

He was standing where Father Hilliard had been, under the awning outside the guard house. He was shaved and neatly dressed. He might have been anybody's kid brother taking the evening off to visit his married sister. Too neatly dressed, too much like anybody's kid brother. She greeted him cautiously.

'Paul, this is a surprise.'

'Hi, sis.'

The guard came out of his kiosk and stood between them, Paul outside the Institute confines and Abigail on the inside.

'This your brother, Mrs Oliver?'

'Of course it is.'

She signed the guarantee form for him and the guard made out a pass. As Paul crossed the scanner it emitted an ugly rasping buzz. He pulled a camera with a flash attachment out of his pocket and handed it cheerfully to the guard.

'Sorry. I forgot.'

The guard accepted the camera without comment. 'Your property will be returned to you on your way out, sir.'

He gave Paul a numbered disk and returned to his glass cubicle. Paul walked up the tree-lined avenue behind his sister, whistling Beethoven, leaving her to start whatever conversation there was to be.

'You might have known you wouldn't get away with it.'

'No harm in trying.' He grinned. 'A few feet of film would've been very useful.'

'Is that what you came here for? Use me to get you in so that you could take photographs? Your group must be very simpleminded to think you could get away with that.'

He shrugged his shoulders. 'Talk about it later, shall we?'

'No, Paul, we'll talk about it now. If you're here to make trouble I shan't allow it. This is too important – if necessary I'll hand you over to the guards.'

She looked up, noticed Dr Mozart standing outside one of the laboratories they were passing, and smiled at him. To her relief he made no move, but simply acknowledged her greeting with a formal bow. At that moment a pretty young lab assistant came out of the door behind him and they went off together arm in arm.

'You must be mad, Paul, breezing in like this when you're supposed to be in Africa.'

'Who knows that except you and Matthew?'

'Andrew Scarfe does.'

'Andy? Any old story'll do to keep him happy.'

'And what about Matthew? What are we to say to Matthew?'

'We'll sort that out when we get to it.'

'No, Paul, we'll sort it out now.'

She guided him into a courtyard surrounded with low residential blocks. There were flower beds and a fountain, pigeons standing around in the cool air of its lee. She sat down on a seat close to the fountain and pulled him down beside her. Water pattered agreeably on the stones close to their feet, running away down the cracks between.

'Paul, what are you doing here?'

'Can't a brother visit his big sister?'

'Don't be childish. We both know there has to be a reason.'

'And you're talking to me here because your house is bugged? Is that it? Do they really force you to live like that?'

'Just answer my question.'

He stretched his legs in his permaprest trousers and stared at his permabrite shoes. She had never seen him so outwardly respectable.

'The fact is, Abby, I've come here to warn you. I shouldn't be doing it, and if it ever gets out I'm as good as dead.' It sickened her that she couldn't immediately trust what he said. 'You see, I swung it on the boss that an onsite inspection would be useful. Up to now our plans have been based on hearsay. So here I am.'

'Warn me? What against?'

'Against getting yourself killed this coming Sunday night.'

'But, Paul –'

'I'm not saying any more. Just stay in your house and you'll be safe. Just stay indoors – don't come out, whatever happens.'

She was silent, watching the water splash on the ground in front of her. A pigeon came too near, and wet its feathers.

'You must be mad if you think your people can break in here, Paul. There's the fence to get past, and –'

'Just stay in your house. And Matthew too, if you can make him.'

'What are you planning?'

'A short sharp bang. Nothing more. Nobody injured even – just a short sharp bang.'

'I warned you, Paul. If necessary I'll –'

'Listen, Abby. You won't turn me in; I think you've been here long enough to know just how rotten this place is. Our plans are simple: the night porter at the computer center leaves his desk at one o'clock for a walk around the block. At that time of night the place will be deserted – the maintenance staff doesn't come on till two. So an explosive charge timed to –'

A couple came out of one of the apartment blocks and passed close by. Abigail lit herself a cigarette, passed one to her brother, tried to appear normal.

'You can forget all these plans, Paul. I've been in touch with the C.L.C. Within a week the whole Colindale project will be public property. It won't continue after that. It can't. You know it can't.'

'You have touching faith in the power of public opinion, sis. Me, I don't share it.'

He couldn't be allowed to wreck everything. There must be some way of convincing him. She didn't ask him how he knew so much about the organization of the Colindale – she wasn't interested. She just had to stop him wrecking everything she had risked so much to achieve.

'Anyway,' he went on, 'how the hell did you manage to contact that happy band? House bugged, phone tapped, followed everywhere you go – how the hell did you manage it?'

'Let's say I managed it. I'm not a complete fool, Paul. I got to see you without much difficulty.'

'I don't believe it. Tell me who you met. I don't believe it.'

'A member of the Committee.'

'Who, Abby? We have a list of every lousy member. Tell me who.'

She hesitated. To convince him she would have to trust him. As he was trusting her.

'Sir William Beeston.'

He stared at her. Then he began to laugh. He laughed till the walls around rang with it. He slapped his leg. He took out a handkerchief and mopped his face.

'Billy B.? You can't mean it. You went and told *him* what a naughty place the Colindale was?' He saw her face, and was suddenly serious. 'Abby love, Billy B. is a monster. A genuine, twenty-two carat monster. He's no more a member of the C.L.C. than I am. Whoever put you on to him was conning you all the way. Believe me. I *know*.'

'But of course he'd pretend to be a monster. If he didn't, then …'

But her voice was losing confidence with every word.

'Look, love' – his kindness didn't help – 'who told you he was a Committee member?'

The answer was that nobody had, not even Sir William himself. She must have been marked down by Security as a poor risk – perhaps they'd listened to her conversations with Matthew – so they'd offered her a bait, a chance to betray herself. Which she had taken. The exact progression of her thoughts must have shown in her face. Paul took her hand.

'You should have known it wasn't possible, love. All of you here, they have you just where they want you. You can't move a finger without them knowing. It has to be like that; without it this place wouldn't have lasted a day. It's taken us three years to set up this plan of ours. And even then –'

'What will they do to me, Paul?'

He looked away. She sensed that he was going to lie.

'Do to you, Abby? What can they do? They need Matthew, so they'll just have to put up with you. Keep a very sharp eye on you, of course. But I don't see what else they can do.'

She wanted to believe him. If Matthew stood by her, perhaps he was right. But Matthew was a Colindale man. And there was so little time. She stood up. The doctor's visit that morning now made sense.

'Are you coming up to the house, Paul?' She didn't want to be left alone. 'I'm not expecting Matthew back for another half-hour or so.'

'I'd love to. Besides, it'll look better if you invite me in.'

She threw away her half-smoked cigarette, watching it quench and darken on the damp paving stones. She disliked women who smoked while walking in the street. Paul and she went up together past the library.

As they entered the quadrangle she saw Andrew Scarfe standing uncertainly in the vivid shadow of the cloisters outside her house. She tried to pull her brother back out of sight, but it was too late. Scarfe had spotted them.

'Paul – how very nice to see you.'

'Andy – how are you?'

'Mustn't grumble. But I thought you were in Africa.'

'I had some things to see to. I'm joining the others next week.'

Paul was very smooth, and Scarfe seemed satisfied. Abigail reminded herself that he had no reason not to be. He turned to her.

'I'm very sorry to trouble you, Mrs Oliver, but I wonder if you could dig out that Astran primer I leant your husband. I went for the one in the library, but it seems to be out. As I was just around the corner, I thought –'

'Of course.' She had no alternative. 'Come in. I'll get it for you.'

The house was empty, full of ears. Closing the front door did nothing to shut the Colindale out. She sat the two men down in the sitting room she had so quickly come to hate, and offered them drinks. Paul said he'd like something long, with ice in it. Although air-conditioned, the bus journey out had been cramped and stuffy. While she was at the refrigerator in the kitchen she heard them talking behind her, friendly, easy talk about the University. She delayed her return to them, dreading the social forms. Everything was unreal to her; even the cubes of ice that stuck in their coldness to her fingers were dreamlike, at a great distance. She returned to the sitting room, the floor surprising her at each step.

They chatted for a few minutes. Incredibly Scarfe seemed to notice nothing wrong with her. When he had finished his drink he excused himself and left, taking with him the book he had come for. She returned from the front door and sat down, aware of Paul's eyes following everything she did. There was a quality of sadness in his gaze that she didn't understand. And the microphones waited.

'Well, Paul?'

'Well, Abigail?'

'Matthew will be home soon.'

'It would be simpler if I didn't meet him.'

'I suppose you're right.'

'I'll wait in one of your spare rooms.'

'Wait?'

In a way everything that he said was expected, part of the spiral process of her life. Yet he must not be allowed to hide from Matthew in Matthew's house. There was no reason.

'Just till he goes out again. He works late at the center most evenings, doesn't he?'

'No, Paul. There's no reason.'

'I could keep you company. We might go for a walk. Surely you don't object?'

'I'd rather not have to pretend you weren't here, Paul.'

Inadequate words, admitting their own futility. She had deceived Matthew before, and she would do so again if Paul told her to.

'Well, then, Abby, don't pretend. I've no objection to seeing Matthew. I was thinking of you.' He paused before giving her the explanation she didn't want to hear. 'You see, there might be things I'd tell him that you didn't want me to. You know how tactless I am.'

Blackmail. Between Paul and her, blackmail. He met her incredulity with a regretful smile. She shrank into her chair, sickened.

'After all,' he said, 'I've nothing to hide. It's as I told Andy: at the last minute I had to put off my African trip for a week. I'm going next Monday instead.'

Gryphon dead, Matthew stolen, Sir William a trap, her parents powerless, Paul newly menacing. And the Colindale a cell.

'Don't worry, Abby. I'll look after you. Isn't that what brothers are for?'

'Paul, I've been thinking about what you told me down by the fountain …'

'I had to get you to invite me up here somehow, Abby.'

'Then what –'

He silenced her, pointing at the microphones. Anyway, her question was unnecessary. His story of coming to the Colindale to warn her was so transparent: she would never have believed it had she not wanted to. There could be only one reason for his presence. She had told him his group would never get through the fence, past the guards, and there he was. She could do no more than hope he would fail. For she, who at that moment had the power to betray, to shout into the microphones what she knew, would do nothing, would decide nothing, would be confused, insufficient. She had cultivated subjection according to the canons of her faith. She would be passed over, would pass herself over, in what still had to be a man's world. Ultimately responsibility, even for herself, was not hers.

Matthew came home as usual, shortly after six. He found the house unusually neat, glasses and plates and cutlery drying in the machine, his food ready on the table. Abigail moved calmly around him, made sure he had everything he needed. He felt she was using her attentiveness as a barrier. He couldn't let her.

'Come and sit down, Abigail. I want to talk to you.'

She sat. Composed herself to listen. The things he had to say weren't for an obedient child.

'Abigail, love, look at me.'

She looked at him. She looked at him for no more than a moment. She could feel him reaching out to her, and she couldn't bear it. Events were not hers. She inhabited a timeless gap. If life slipped back a cog and started in a new direction, why, then she would be different, able to –

'Abigail, I know this is a mess.' Seeing her agony, forcing himself not to recoil from it. 'We're both stuck in attitudes. We can't get out of them, and they're driving us further and further apart. The issues are big. I expect we're both willing to die for them. But are we willing to kill? To kill each other?'

She didn't know what he was asking of her. Neither did he. He was simply talking as truthfully as he could, waiting for something to happen between them. Words.

'We make a habit of trying to understand things, my darling. Motives, purposes … No, that's not right. It's I who has tried to understand. You have tried to *know*. But –'

She could stand his pressing in on her no longer. She could not be raped, not even she.

'I had a visit from your Mr Scarfe this afternoon, Matthew.'

'Please don't do this, Abigail.'

'He wanted the Astran primer back. I gave it to him.'

'I love you.'

Not that.

'We had a little chat. He seems nicer than he did the other night. Perhaps you overawed him, Matthew.'

She actually smiled.

'Abigail, I do not want to talk about Andrew Scarfe.' And she, she did not want to talk. 'Our whole lives are in an awful bloody mess, and all you can do is evade, prattle on about the first thing that comes into your head.' She continued to smile. Against such a stretching of the lips he had no weapon. 'We must not be torn apart, my love. We're all we have.'

Weak generalities, all he had left. She didn't move.

'Stay with me this evening, Matthew.'

'Abigail, I can't.'

'Of course you can.' It had been a sudden idea, a test.

'The director is expecting me.' On what other occasions had he not scrapped everything, knowing she would not ask without need? 'No, Abigail, I just can't.'

'Please, Matthew. Don't leave me.'

'Only a very few more evenings, love.' So she closed her face to him, let him run on. 'I wouldn't go if it wasn't really important. But I'll try to get back as early as I can …'

'Your food's getting cold, Matthew. It's not like you to let your food get cold.'

There was nothing more he could do or say. Not then. The next day, perhaps. Or later that night, when he got back from the center. Meanwhile, needing words, avoiding silence as he ate his supper, he played her game and told her about Andrew Scarfe. About the phone call Scarfe had asked him to make to his mother. Oedipus complexes were common territory, a refuge for them both.

She leaned against the front door, listening to Matthew's footsteps fade. She had not asked him again to stay – at heart she was glad of his refusal. For him to stay would have complicated a situation already beyond her. By the time she got back to the kitchen Paul was sitting in Matthew's place, clean cutlery in front of him, waiting to be fed. She did so without comment.

'It's a pity you didn't get Matthew to stay,' he said. 'I'd have enjoyed a chat.'

His crude irony was slightly pathetic.

'Paul, what do you want with me?'

'Want with you?' He held up a finger to remind her they were overheard. 'Just to talk quietly for a couple of hours or so. I don't often get over to see you. And when I go to Africa I'll be away for a long time.'

So they talked. Quietly. For a couple of hours or so. Discussions about Dad's hobbies, about Mum's back, about what could be done for Aunt Nora. Abigail felt she was going quite mad.

When she could stand it no longer she suggested they go for a walk. It was, she said, a beautiful evening. And Paul had amused himself at her expense for long enough. She took him out, away from the microphones, across the quadrangle, up to the open ground by the white wall to the director's house. They sat down, as if to watch the sunset.

'What are you really doing here, Paul?'

'That's a difficult question, Abby. On one level I'm sitting beside you, watching a sunset. On another level I'm battling with a disease called life. On another –'

'You're not sixteen any more, Paul. Do try to grow up.'

'You grow up too, then, Abby. Stop asking questions when you know the answers.'

'It won't do any good, Paul, destroying the computer. They'll only build another. You must fight it with ideas, not bombs.'

'I'm not here to argue. Anyway, it's too late. I've done my job now, and –'

He stopped. She was on to him quickly. Away from the house, with the sky over her and grass under her feet – even a Colindale sky and Colindale grass – she could think again.

'Done your job, Paul? What job was that?'

'It doesn't matter.'

'What job have you done, Paul? You've been with me ever since you arrived. Not out of my sight for a single minute. How could you possibly have …'

Then she remembered. He had asked for ice and she had gone into the kitchen to fetch it. He had been alone in the sitting room with Andrew Scarfe.

'Scarfe? Is he one of your group?'

'Catholics stick together. Always have.'

'I'm a Catholic. And –'

'And look at you sitting here with me, a traitorous saboteur swine.'

'You gave Scarfe something. What was it?'

'Explosives are very compact nowadays.'

And Scarfe had access to any part of the computer at any time. And Scarfe was thorough. She saw now why the book had been forced on Matthew – so that there would be an excuse to call reclaiming it at a time when Scarfe knew Paul would be in the house. The delivery couldn't have taken place anywhere safer. And the talk, the smooth talk about why Paul wasn't in Africa had been simply to fool her. To keep her quiet, to keep her in ignorance for as long as possible. They had used her, her home, her loyalty. And Paul was speaking to her now so gently, so reasonably.

'You see now why it had to be me, Abby. Some newcomer whose right to enter wouldn't be questioned. Somebody making a first visit: no regular would have got away with using that camera to cover him through the scanner at the gate. Andy managed the same trick the day he came here, brought in an incendiary under the cover of a pocket tape recorder. And even then he was damn nearly caught.'

'Then it was Scarfe who killed Henderson.' No longer disgusted, simply dulled and weary, weary of the words.

'Bloody fool, he was told to go for the machine, not the man. He'd have been withdrawn and punished if his cover here hadn't been so perfect. Killing is not our way, Abigail. It won't be our way tonight. I promise you.'

It was a promise he was in no position to make. She distrusted him and she feared him. The sky was darkening as they watched, cloudless and pale to the jagged roof horizon.

'You tricked me, Paul. You used me to –'

'It's up to you then.' He sounded bored, lay back on the grass, his hands behind his head. 'It's up to you. I'm unarmed. The director's wife is in the house behind us. If you called for help she'd be bound to hear. I couldn't stop you. So it's up to you, Abby.'

ELEVEN

Impatience. Matthew could feel it gathering like electricity in the air. It showed in controlled voices, in sudden pointless getting up and sitting down, in vain attempts to attract the attention of the Japanese fantails behind their wall of glass. It beat the air-conditioning, made the basement room profoundly uncomfortable.

But the members of the group, even Mallalieu, contained it, bore with the director's desperate persistence out of compassion if nothing else. They checked the data he asked them to check. They sat with him, one by one, going over each associative complex. They even showed enthusiasm, followed by disappointment, in each new half-hour run of the program. Only Scarfe didn't bother to hide his disenchantment. The checks he made for Professor Billon were cursory, the results tossed insultingly onto his desk, merely humoring an obstinate old fool. It was an unpleasant exhibition which the director chose, with effort, to ignore.

FINDEF SM 101
POINSTOP FINDEF SM 101

And the output never varied.

Abigail hugged her knees and stared down at the neat, sophisticated buildings of the Colindale. Mist was beginning to gather in the hollows. It was merciless of Paul to make the responsibility hers. Merciless but just. She remembered Matthew on decision-making: however much you weighed the advantages and disadvantages, the decision you finally made was intuitive, emotional, the one you had secretly known about all along.

'I shan't interfere,' she said.

Paul rolled on his side and broke off a long stalk of grass to chew.

'Good for you.' He spat pith. 'Not that it matters, of course. The question was academic. I mean, it had no practical application. You see, the charge has a failsafe device. Andy's setting it to go off at five past one, when the porter's out on his rounds. But there's an acoustic trap so that any interference with it before one five will make it detonate there and then. So your gracious permission was hardly needed.' He patted her shoulder. 'Still, it's nice to know where we stand.'

She didn't flinch away. She also was glad to know where they stood.

'Paul – you promised no killing. But Matthew's down at the center now, and he didn't get home last night till after two. There's bound to be others with him.'

'Andy's dealing with that. He's there, and it's part of his job to get everybody out. I meant it, Abby, when I said we want no killing. All I'm here for is to help him get away if it's necessary.'

'But why does it have to be tonight? Why not some other night when there wasn't the same risk?'

'I don't know why. That's Andy's decision. He sent the message to come, so I came.'

'Message? I thought this place was supposed to be proof against messages.'

'We fixed a very simple code. Just a message to his mother saying he would be busy for the next few nights and couldn't get to see her. His mother's been invaluable – she writes interminable letters to him, the sort of personal code that's just about unbreakable.'

A message to his mother, sent by Matthew. And for some good reason. She didn't mind if Matthew was being set up; it would make Scarfe want to keep him alive. She was at a stage where situations could only be dealt with one by one, as they arrived. And she wanted Matthew alive.

The Colindale was dusting over into night, windows losing the buildings around them and existing simply as yellow squares of light. With the sun gone Abigail felt cold, and shivered. Paul helped her up, leaning back with outstretched undergraduate arms, and they walked slowly back together, down to the house.

Paul played Matthew's harpsichord for an hour or more, simple pieces, very badly. Abigail sat in Matthew's corner of the sofa and smoked and watched the clock. When it struck eleven Paul stopped playing.

'If I don't go now I shall miss the last bus.'

'You can't go.' Thinking he meant it. 'You can't leave me alone here.'

'I'll stay the night, sis, if you really want me to. If you're sure Matthew won't mind.' And then she remembered the microphones. About an hour later there were footsteps in the quadrangle, and quiet voices. She recognized Zacharie Mallalieu's. She listened as they passed, expecting to hear Matthew's key in the door. When he didn't come she ran out into the cloisters, called after the small group of men, not caring.

'Your husband, Mrs Oliver?' Their voices came back along the tunnel of no moonlight. 'Your husband, Mrs Oliver? He's stayed behind with the director. He and Scarfe. They looked to be settling in. No point in waiting up for him, Mrs Oliver. I'd go to bed, Mrs Oliver.'

They had no reason to be mocking. It was her imagination. She shut them out, slamming the door.

'There's no need to panic, Abby. Andy'll get him out. There's plenty of time; you really mustn't worry.'

At twelve forty there were more footsteps, and then a sudden loud knocking on the door. She hurried to answer it. Paul came after her, caught her arm.

'Don't open. Find out first who's there.'

'Who is it?' she called.

'Dr Mozart. May I have a word with you, Mrs Oliver?'

'What do you want?'

'Just a word with you, Mrs Oliver.'

His voice was compounded of soothing reassurance. Paul drew her nearer to him.

'Security?' She nodded. 'I thought so. Don't let him in. I'll handle this. Where does Matthew keep his laser?'

He noticed the movement of her eyes toward the bedroom even as her brain was refusing to tell him.

'Mrs Oliver? Let me in, Mrs Oliver. There are things we must talk about.'

'It's nearly one o'clock, Dr Mozart. My husband's not here. Can't we talk in the morning?'

'I'm afraid not. It's a matter of the greatest urgency.'

'Tell me what it is. I'm not letting you in till I know what it is.'

There was a pause, confused muttering on the other side of the door. Paul returned from the bedroom, Matthew's laser in his hand.

'Mrs Oliver, please be sensible. I have guards with me. If you do not open the door we will simply have to burn out the lock. Please be sensible.'

'What do you want with me? How dare you come threatening to break down the door.'

'We have an order for your committal, Mrs Oliver. The doctor's report and the evidence of Sir William Beeston. It will be much better for all concerned if you agree to come peacefully.'

She stared at Paul, suddenly terrified. He moved quickly to the door and turned the light out at the switch there.

'You're early,' he said loudly. 'Storm troopers usually make these raids at two or three. The effect is supposed to be more demoralizing.'

'You must be Mrs Oliver's brother. Talk to her, please. Tell her to be sensible. Resisting committal will only worsen her situation. Tell her –'

'I'll tell her nothing. If you want her, you'll have to come and get her. And I warn you, I'm armed.'

Dimly Abigail watched him take a stool to the door and stand on it, so that he could see through the narrow strip of window above. Outside in the cloisters there was careful movement, and the sound of orders being given. More than anything else, Abigail felt incredulity. Suddenly she was judged insane, fit for reformative custody. The transition from her Kensington life to this had been too abrupt. She was the same person, yet she couldn't be. Paul was whispering at her in the dark.

'... Half an hour. That's all we need. When the charge goes up in the computer center that'll draw them off. We may be able to get you out in the confusion.'

'I don't want to be got out, Paul. What's the use?'

'Once in that lot's hands and you'll sink without a trace, Abby. If you don't care for yourself, then think of Matthew.'

Matthew ... he was still at the computer center. She no longer trusted Scarfe to get him away in time. She no longer trusted anybody.

'Paul – I'm going to ring Matthew and warn him.'

'But, Abby –'

'Don't try to stop me. This may be the last chance I'll ever have of speaking to him.'

'All right. But if you tell him about the charge, for God's sake tell him it's no use trying to defuse it. If he does try, he'll only –'

The cloisters were suddenly illuminated with brilliant greenish light, throwing Paul's head into sharp silhouette against the narrow window. At the same moment the guards moved in quickly to the door. Paul fired down at them, shattering the glass. Return fire cut brief rods of light around him. The guards retreated, one of them wounded. The hall filled with the smell of scorched plaster and brickwork. Paul tried with his gun for the light source, but it was out of range.

In the hush that followed, Abigail stumbled to the telephone in the sitting room and dialed the computer center. The bell at reception rang and continued to ring. The room she was in was strange and hideous. She moved from the phone to switch off the lights, preferring darkness. As she waited there was a further attack on the front door. The hiss of the lasers cracked like whips and there was a brief muffled scream from one of the guards. No killing. Her brother had promised no killing. Events would take control, push her back from stand to stand.

At last the night porter answered. Calmly she asked to be connected with the director's office. Another bell began to ring. From the cloisters silence, and then the clicks of an amplifier being tested.

'Listen in there.' Dr Mozart, his voice huge. 'Mrs Oliver, talk to your brother. Make him see sense. We can get you out with gas any time we want to. Make him see sense.'

The phone rang in the director's office. The time was ten to one. For Abigail life had moved away into fantasy, into classic nightmare. The phone bell rang on steadily in the creeping dark.

'Coffee, Oliver. D'you mind?'

The director did not look up, his belled reflection motionless in the black glass of the dome. Scarfe fussed beside him, urging him on, screwing him tighter. Matthew had tried several times to intervene and each time had been repulsed by tormentor and victim alike. They were locked together, satisfying complimentary needs. Matthew went down the steps and through the double doors into the main part of the building. He was glad to get away.

Data. Data analysis, data response, data association, data looping, data definition, data compensation, data redefinition. Round and round into insanity. And back always to the same conclusion, the output that was wrong and could not be and was and could not be. Matthew cursed himself for being there, for staying when the others had left. The director had not asked him to. But when he and Scarfe had gone up from the basement to the Bohn desk under the blank glass cupola, Matthew had tagged along. He was sure that somehow that night, out of the mutual suffering of the two men – for Scarfe suffered while making the director suffer – a solution to the problem would come. FINDEF SM 101: with repetition even the symbols' meaninglessness sometimes took on meaning. Could that be the point, the whole thing a bad joke? Had the Bohn acquired a tortuous sense of humor? FINDEF SM 101. And Matthew had stayed, gooseberry to a sophisticated coupling, obscenely needed.

As Matthew passed the director's office he heard the telephone ringing. He went in to answer it. In the darkened room moonlight flashed off the slowly revolving sculpture, scattering random flakes. He crossed to the desk and had his hand on the telephone switch when the ringing stopped. It left the room painfully quiet. Against the moon-white grass outside he saw the huge pupils of the three eye windows. Suddenly they were more than a harmless eccentricity. He returned quickly to the corridor and made his way to Data Reception.

He collected three cups of coffee from the machine. The late shift had been gone for nearly three hours, leaving the room unpeopled, falsely still, its unreality heightened by the uncompromising neon. The tables were everywhere littered with blue data sheets. Some of them would be on his desk in the morning, part of an endless process larger than human. The three plastic cups began to burn his fingers.

Professor Billon stared at the coffee as if he didn't recognize it, had forgotten that he had ever asked for it. The pad in front of him was covered with minute, obsessive calculations. He scrubbed the lot and began again.

'Substitution, Scarfe. There's a relationship we're missing somewhere, a progression that the Bohn accepts – but on what level? Suppose we assume faulty conditioning?'

They had assumed faulty conditioning before and before. The words were meaningless scurryings to and fro. The telephone began to ring, a receiver unit without amplifier. The dome was a place for concentration, not to be interrupted. Billon picked up the receiver and laid it down on the desk, taking no further notice of it. A faint rasping sound came from the earpiece, possibly female. He had not looked up from his pad, from his assumption of faulty conditioning.

Scarfe sighed. 'It's five to one,' he said.

Matthew checked, agreed pointlessly that it was five to one. Scarfe got up slowly from the desk and crossed to a low bookshelf by the door. He stooped in front of it, searching. When he straightened and turned back toward them, a plastic-bound manual in his hand, his whole manner had changed. He stood straighter, his deformity more noticeable. Gently, almost caressingly, he spoke the director's name.

The older man didn't respond, continued to draw flow diagrams, boxes with phase numbers neatly printed in each. Scarfe repeated the name, slightly more loudly.

'I'm trying an address substitution, Scarfe. Help me. Don't stand there.'

'But you're wasting your time, Professor.' A long silence. 'I said, you're wasting your time. I have the solution. I have it here in my hand.'

'Go home, Scarfe. You've been at it too long. I can get on quite well without you. Just go home.'

Angry, Scarfe strode across to the desk. Matthew was about to intervene, Scarfe's manner so threatening that he might have struck the professor. Instead he flung the manual he was carrying down on the desk.

'There's your answer.'

Billon touched it uncertainly, straightened it. Matthew edged around behind him, read the title of the manual over his shoulder: *Manual of Basic Control Circuits on the Bohn* 507. *Confidential.*

'Control circuits, Scarfe? There's nothing wrong with the control circuits. Anyway, we're neither of us electronics engineers. What possible good is this to us?'

'We can read, Professor.'

'Far too late for games, man. Just tell us what you're getting at.'

Scarfe leaned forward and pointed with sarcastic patience at the index number on the top right-hand corner of the service manual.

'You see,' he said. 'Paranoia is catching.'

The index number was SM 101.

Matthew refused the implications, looked away at the distorted reflections above them in the curved black glass. Hardest to bear was Scarfe's perverse humanity. Now he was explaining, his arms swelling and dwindling as he gestured, not because explanations were necessary, but because he enjoyed making them.

'You see, Professor, the Bohn has never been given a word for itself. To itself it has no name. Not even a number. Its existence has been so complete that one was never needed. Then we offered it a program for which itself was the only answer. Undefeated, it decided it was the sum of its own circuitry – as expressed in Service Manual 101. Asked to redefine, it resorted to its party tricks, under the impression that a thing *is* what it *does* …'

He lowered his voice, stooped, spoke close in the director's ear, his words a mocking incantation.

'Bow down, Professor. Worship the Cathode Printout, the Random Access, the Loops and Ten-tier Processing. Bow down and worship. And if you are sickened, just remember that the Bohn is what you made it. You and the others, you taught it the basic connections. So if you are sickened – and I believe you are – just remember what it is that sickens you. As I said before, paranoia is catching.'

Matthew drew his attention back from the looming presences all around them. He looked at Scarfe, flushed, triumphant. Then at the bleak figure of Professor Billon, motionless but for the scar twitching on his forehead and his eyelids blinking steadily over the one real and the one plastic eye. He needed a shave. His hair had fallen sideways, disclosing a small bald patch. But he still commanded. He ceded none of his dignity to the upstart, grasping Scarfe. The triumph could offer no glory. Above all, he was not pitiable.

'You've known this for some time,' he said.

'It came to me this afternoon.'

'Playing an unseemly game with me.'

'Waiting for the right moment.'

'No doubt you enjoyed it.' Professor Billon at last turned his head to look at the other man. 'Of course, Scarfe, you hate me. You envy me and you hate me. No doubt it was you who killed John Henderson.'

'Does it matter?'

'It matters to me. Matters to his wife and children.'

'I like your order of priorities. Consistent to the end.'

The director saw his cup of coffee, picked it up and drank it. Matthew wanted to speak, but had nothing to say. He was essentially outside. Scarfe looked at his watch, narrowed his eyes.

'I'm going home.'

'You're a man without responsibilities, Scarfe. Simply a systems analyst. It is I who ought to envy you.'

'If you've any sense, Dr Oliver, you'll come with me. While there's still time.'

To Matthew the threat in his words was meaningless. He stayed by the desk while Scarfe went to the head of the stairs.

'Are you coming?'

'Go on, Oliver.' Billon swirled the last of his coffee around and around in the bottom of his cup. 'Go on, man. There's nothing to be done. Just leave me. Moment of truth and all that. Just leave me.'

Matthew did as he was told. Scarfe was so far ahead that he had to run to catch up. He didn't want the man's company, but neither did he at that moment want to be alone. The computer inhabited the place, the air tasted of it. Their footsteps were louder than was suitable.

'Hang on, Scarfe. What's the blasted rush?'

'I want to get out of here. Don't you?'

Matthew didn't answer. They hurried on down interminable corridors. At last they reached the reception hall. The big clock there showed a minute past one and the porter was getting ready to make his round of the outside of the building.

'Signing out, gentlemen?' A chatty man. 'Glad to see it's not quite as late as it's been the last few nights. You gentlemen work too hard, in my opinion. Enough's enough, that's what I say …'

He registered the time and they signed alongside. He looked slowly down the column, still keeping them.

'Most of the other gentlemen left at midnight, I see. Who's left now, then?'

'Only the director.'

The porter confirmed this carefully.

'That's all right then. He pleases himself when he comes and goes. Fine gentleman … Well, I'm trotting along now, gentlemen, so I'll see you out.'

The three of them walked together across the dimmed glass floor to the entrance.

'By the way, sir, you're Dr Oliver, aren't you?'

'That's right.'

The man had seen the signatures but it made him warm all over to be told he was right. Matthew paused, resisting Scarfe, who was dragging him on.

'Anything the matter?'

'Only a phone call for you, sir. I rang around, but I couldn't find you. Rang your office, rang the director's office, rang the basement, rang the computer room, even rang the upper level desk, sir. Couldn't seem to find you.'

'Who was it? Was it important?'

'I'm trying to remember who it was, sir … Got it wrote down back at the desk. Shall I take a trot back and have a look?'

The desk seemed very far behind them.

'No, don't bother. I expect it was my wife.'

'There you are, sir. Right first time. At first she said it was important, then when I told her I couldn't find you she said not to worry. Said it didn't matter.' They pottered on, arrived at the doors. 'Still, you're going home now, sir, so I expect you'll hear all about it …'

They went through the doors and down the steps. On the path they parted from the porter and walked away, slowing, their eyes becoming accustomed to the moonlight. Behind them the computer center was in darkness, except for the foyer. As they moved further away they were able to see the glow from the glass dome and to make out the figure of Professor Billon. He was sitting exactly as Matthew had seen him last. Something, possibly this sight, started Scarfe talking.

'You know, I nearly didn't tell him. If his favorite word hadn't been humbleness I don't think I ever would have … I suppose you think I'm just another sadistic cripple.'

Matthew thought nothing. There was a bigger conclusion he needed to find.

'He had to be told, of course. You'll see why in a couple of minutes.'

He wasn't yet certain, he couldn't yet see for sure if the mistake was inevitable. The edge between necessary pride and outright delusions of grandeur was narrow. Scarfe caught at his arm.

'Honestly, Dr Oliver, doesn't it terrify you to think of society in the hands of people like yourself?'

Matthew wouldn't argue. It was suddenly possible that his wife had been right.

'At least the rest of the project is sound enough,' he said, hoping to be left that much.

'Do you really think so? The director doesn't. Not now. He's shrewder than you, even if he is madder.'

Matthew stared up at the dome against the sky. It contained whatever trust in himself he could ever have.

'I'm going back,' he said

'I wouldn't, Dr Oliver.'

'I'm not asking for your advice.'

'But I'm giving it. Just wait another two or three minutes.'

Matthew shook him off and ran back the way they had come. Scarfe stared after him till he came into the light from the foyer and vanished inside the building. Perhaps he was better dead. Andrew Scarfe had done his best. And Dr Oliver would make a far more useful scapegoat *in absentio.*

The house was silent. After Dr Mozart's warning about gas they were left to think it over. She waited by the telephone, listening to bells ringing in various parts of the computer center. The clock in the sitting room said five to one – if she kept the porter much longer he would be late going out on his rounds. She would not for anything have his death her doing. She told him it didn't matter. She said it wasn't important.

When she had rung off she stood for a moment in the dark, undecided. Then she went through to where her brother was still standing, watching through the broken window above the door.

'Paul, I can't contact Matthew. I must get out. I must try to get to him.'

'You haven't time. Leave it to Andy.'

'No, Paul. No – I must do what I can.'

'You'll never make it.'

'I will. I can get up onto the roof from the garden. If I'm careful I can drop down the outside wall.'

'It's up to you, then. Just be quick. If I hear them going after you I'll create a diversion out the front here.'

She stood for a second staring up at him, grateful for his unexpected sympathy.

'If you're going, then go.'

She crept away, out into the garden. Under the brilliant moon it was a tiny landscape of extremes, the shadow of the roof lying across it, one side silvered dew and the other side dead, not there. She had never seen how total was the darkness cast by moonlight. She could use that darkness, slip down the shadowed outside wall and not be seen. And there was still time.

Even for her the climb onto the flat-pitched roof was not difficult, window frames and ledges providing ample footholds. Once on the roof she crawled up to its outer edge, using the tall mass of the fir tree to prevent herself from being outlined against the sky. She sat on the edge of the roof and looked down. Everything was still and quiet. From the cloisters Dr Mozart's voice came to her clearly, his English as disdainful as ever.

'Have you not yet made up your mind, Mrs Oliver? You and your brother must know there is nothing to be done. We cannot wait all night, Mrs Oliver. Please come out now, and avoid further trouble. I promise you will both be treated well.'

She turned onto her stomach, her legs hanging over, toes scrabbling at the wall, and let herself slip slowly backward. Her skirt was up around her waist. The edge of the roof hurt her breasts. Then she was hanging by her hands, gathering the courage to drop. She released her hold awkwardly, one hand before the other, twisting her shoulder.

As she fell into the wedge of shadow she was clutched at, surrounded at once by people, by men, by men whose uniforms she could smell. They held her tight. She screamed like a rabbit in a net, and continued to scream till one of the guards got a damp sweating hand over her mouth. She tasted his sweat.

From the front of the house there were confused sounds, banging, shouts, the quick indrawn breath of laser guns, then silence.

The guards led her, surprisingly gentle, around into the brightly lit cloisters. Green light, and a smell of burning wood and brick and flesh. Dr Mozart met her, tried to block her path; but she looked past him to the small group close outside the front door. Two guards, Paul on the ground between them. The scene was like a smart photograph, underexposed, crudely black and white.

'He came out firing, Mrs Oliver. What could we do?'

The diversion he had promised. Because she had screamed … She stepped around the German – he made no real effort to stop her – and went to Paul, experienced a quick flush of hope when she saw he was not dead. But his eyes were. When he turned his head to face her, his eyes were.

'Abby? I want to tell you –'

'I'll fetch a priest.'

'There's not time.' He groped for her hand and held it, his grip very strong. 'I remember learning the act of Resignation at school. But it's gone … Pray for me, Abby.'

'It's not the words that matter, Paul.'

'You'd be surprised, you'd be surprised how much it is the words that matter.'

Then he was still for so long, his eyes so empty, that he might have died. One of the guards walked away, examined scorch marks on the wall around the door. Lights were on around the quadrangle, doors open, people roused and curious. She prayed for him.

'… There are things I want to tell you, Abby.'

'Not me. There's no need to tell me anything.'

'I want to. I want you to forgive me.'

'My forgiveness isn't important.'

'You loved Gryphon and I murdered him.'

'I loved him once …' She was past surprise. 'Not to me, Paul. You don't need my forgiveness.'

'Did the guard hear me? Might as well put the record straight.'

She looked up at the guard high above her. He nodded.

'He heard you.'

'I believed it was right. He knew about us, about the group. I believed it was necessary.' He shuddered briefly. 'I was mistaken.'

The searchlight was turned off. Slowly the moon established squares of gentler light between the pillars. Dr Mozart approached.

'The ambulance is waiting, Mrs Oliver.'

'It won't be necessary. My brother is dying.'

'Not for your brother, Mrs Oliver. The ambulance is not here for your brother.'

Paul released her hand.

'The computer center – you must go while there's still time.'

She shook her head. There could be no time at all.

Professor Billon had risen from the desk and was carefully replacing the service manual in the bookcase. He made no comment on Matthew's return. The air under the dome possessed a curiously dead quality; it was the only part of the building where the incessant activity of the Bohn was inaudible.

'Interesting fellow, Scarfe. Devious, but no fool.' He kept his head down, looked at Matthew from under his eyebrows. 'Strange it should need somebody like that. No way of reckoning the harm we've done, Oliver. The harm I've done.'

'I'm involved, Professor.' Eager for a place. 'If you're throwing guilt around, it's mine as well.'

'You think that's what I'm doing?'

'Aren't you?'

'Self-knowledge, perhaps. I've dealt with enough paranoids. Ought to know the signs.'

His thought processes, rendered even more obscure by truncation, were beyond Matthew, who was there for reassurance.

'Scarfe was saying the whole project was finished. The Colindale project – all of it.'

'Indulge me, Oliver. Will you? Just for a moment?'

He returned to the desk, sat down. He pulled a pad toward himself and started writing. Suddenly he scrubbed the lot.

'Of course the project is finished. Paranoia implicit in every stage. Fed by the tainted, blinkered minds of brilliant lunatics. That sort of thing rubs off, Oliver.'

'I think you're exaggerating, Professor. I –'

'For God's sake, man, if you must be loyal, be loyal to people. Not to ideas. Be loyal to me. Sit down. Help me. Listen to me. Indulge me.'

Matthew sat down beside him, in the chair that had been occupied by Andrew Scarfe. If everything was not to fall about him he needed to find the break, the fault in his line of reasoning, the jump that had made it possible for his work at the Colindale to be the logical extension of his career and beliefs. Where he had gone wrong. Without that break in continuity he was left with nothing.

'We're left with nothing, Oliver. Except our natural resilience. Our inquiring minds. Nothing more.' He turned suddenly sideways in his chair, looked at Matthew as if for the first time. Then he relaxed and leaned back. 'Time I told you about my dud eye,' he said.

Paul was struggling to look at his watch. Abigail eased back his sleeve and read it for him. Beside them Dr Mozart's feet shuffled irritably on the smooth mosaic. The waiting guards were beginning to talk in whispers. The time was five past one.

In the seconds of waiting Paul died. His sister, feeling no difference, seeing no difference, was as aware of the event as if his soul had risen like a white dove from his body and flown away across the slanting moonlight. He was dead, his hand no colder in hers, his head no heavier on her arm. She prayed for God's mercy on him and on Matthew, on herself and on all sinners. She lowered his head to the paving.

When the explosion came, it was disappointing. She had hoped for something more sensational. Dr Mozart was dragging her to her feet. Around them alarm bells were ringing, car engines being started. She stood up slowly.

'It is clear now, Mrs Oliver, why your brother was here. You have a lot to answer for, the three of you.'

'Three of us?'

'Your husband was a part of the plot. I misjudged him. If your brother brought the explosives in, then it was Dr Oliver who took them to the computer center.'

And all she could think of was to tell him that *misjudge* wasn't used like that: you misjudged a man if you thought evil of him when he was really good.

'Where is he now, your husband? You know of course that he cannot possibly escape.'

She knew that Matthew was dead. That he had been in the computer center and that he was now dead. She knew this beyond any possible doubt. Toward Andrew Scarfe she felt nothing. He was unimportant. He would go free, perhaps live to blow up the second Colindale and the third ... Dr Mozart was speaking to her, but she couldn't hear. Firelight began to overpower the livid city glow above the roof of the library. The sky became red and full of smoke. Matthew was dead.

'Will you come this way please, Mrs Oliver?'

Guards came and went, making reports. The fire was under control, would not spread beyond the center itself. No one was able to find the director. He had last been seen by some systems analyst at the upper level Bohn desk.

'Will you come this way please, Mrs Oliver?'

'If I'm to be charged with something I demand' – why not? – 'that my solicitor be present.'

'No charge is necessary. The doctor's report is more than adequate. You're a sick woman, Mrs Oliver.'

They would tell her this. Every day they would tell her she was sick, and she must not believe them. For the rest of her time with them she must resist believing them. She was not sick. She did not believe them. She was not sick.

'My solicitor –'

'This is not a legal matter, Mrs Oliver. You're not a criminal. You have a schizoid personality. Please come this way, Mrs Oliver.'

'I am not sick.'

'Please come this way, Mrs Oliver.'

Mrs Oliver. Wife of Matthew, widow of Matthew. She began to cry. Grief that was long overdue, an inward bleeding, secret. But God loved her and she'd survive. Nobody was tested beyond what he could endure. She let herself be led away down the moonlit cloisters to her novitiate.

ASCENDANCIES

for Virginia

INTRODUCTION

That Tuesday afternoon, as the yellow city electric came silently up the hill, the street was immaculate. Behind their railings the gracious terraces of old, tall-windowed houses were vividly white in the sparkling summer air. Cats basked on area steps. Doors stood open to the sun, showing glimpses of carpeted hallways, antique gilt lamp brackets, fine paintings, ship models in glass cases. Window sashes, too, were open: affluent, unashamed. And the parked cars that lined the vacuum-cleaned pavements flashed spotless green and crimson, purple and metallic blue. For this was 1986, my children, and the falls of Moondrift only two years begun. Governments were provident then, having not yet learned to trust the unfailing profligacy of their monthly benediction.

They gathered the Moondrift, therefore, every single grain. Dirt and Moondrift, plastic bottles and dog turds, for later separation, every single grain.

In this cleanliness, furthermore, at that time even the humbler areas of the city benefited handsomely ... For there *were* humbler areas, you must remember, then as now. Rich though we are, and richer though we may become, the shiftless are with us always. And the Disappearances, when all is said and done, can cause embarrassment to even the most needlessly industrious. A mansion without its mistress may slip a notch or two, a business without its boss may crumble altogether.

But in those far off, twenty-years-ago days, even the meanest of streets were clean, and their shoddy backyards also. For the Central Generating Authority, in its sweet inexperience, was actually paying for the Moondrift that fell on nonmunicipal property, and issuing plastic sacks gratis for its collection.

An age of golden innocence, therefore. A time of husbanding, of virtue. Of thanksgiving for fissionable manna. They called it Moondrift, romantically, knowing it was nothing of the sort, and were grateful.

We call it Moondrift still. But the romance is gone. And the gratitude. The Moondrift lies in our city streets and festers. While we grow richer, and more contentious.

The yellow city electric came silently up past the shining house, from the direction of the city center, moving slowly, looking for a parking space. It found a small one, ahead of a red Rolls-Peugeot, and reversed neatly in. The driver reached down for the briefcase on the floor beside him, then slid the door open and got out onto the pavement. He plugged his car in at the nearest charging point, stooped briefly to insert his embossed account card, then straightened his back and looked around. He was a man in his early thirties, his tie was decorated with the signature of its French designer, and his suit was chain-store chic, with detectably shiny elbows. His hair had been waved, but not odiously, and his shoes had the handmade look. But only, it has to be admitted, the look. And his fingernails were none too clean.

He was, in short, an insurance agent.

He produced a thick black notebook, held together with an elastic band, flipped it open, and referred to it, holding it at arm's length, farsightedly. Then he examined the numbers on the doors of the houses immediately beside him. He frowned, pushed his left sleeve up extravagantly, and glanced at his very digital watch. Then he set off up the street at a brisk pace, anxiously checking the house numbers as he went.

Number thirty-seven was almost at the top, just before the street led into a small square with plane trees and grass, and a modest stone mermaid supporting a dolphin fountain. Mothers were sitting on benches while their children scuffed the grass and didn't look at one another. Then, as now, the rich had their problems.

The door to number thirty-seven was closed, and all the windows, too. The man went youthfully, two at a time, up the six steps to the door. He rang the doorbell. Waiting, he adjusted his tie and looked again at his watch. The time was 03:12.

The door opened, revealing a woman against a background of Schönberg, almost certainly quadraphonic.

A man therefore, and now a woman … but hardly, as yet, anything in the least *unsuitable*.

The woman, however, was also in her early thirties. Promisingly. But she was neat and superior, with neat, superior hair done back in a bun at the nape of her neck, and a neat, superior dress of soft brown wool. Ceramic necklaces dangled upon her chest. Not upon her breasts, you understand, nor even upon her bust: she was too neat and superior for that. The man's hand went up to his tie again, was mentally slapped down, hovered uncertainly.

The woman took it.

'You're Mr Wallingford, from the Accident and General,' she said.

Thus placed so unerringly, Mr Wallingford could only apologize. 'I'm afraid I'm late,' he said. 'The traffic was the very devil.'

He must have liked the phrase, for he repeated it, gaining confidence. 'The very devil,' he said. 'And then I couldn't find a space and had to leave the car down at the wrong end of the street. You're Mrs Trenchard.'

Mrs Trenchard inclined her head. A Vanderbilt at least. She looked past him. There was a large empty parking space immediately outside her house.

'Won't you come in?' she said.

Mr Wallingford wiped his feet elaborately on the door mat. 'Nice place you've got here,' he said, as he stepped past her into the house.

Mrs Trenchard shut the door, then led him forward. The house, with all its closed windows, was stuffy, and totally quiet. There was a grandfather clock in the hallway, but it seemed to have stopped. Mr Wallingford noticed these things.

Mrs Trenchard touched his arm. 'In here,' she said, indicating a room on their right, where the quadraphonics were coming from.

Mr Wallingford looked, saw white hide settees, glass tables, vintage weighing machines, pictures of pinkish private parts in bright chromium frames. It was all the same to him, however – in his line of work one might assume he met all manner of person – and it will have been from purely professional reasons that he stepped back from the doorway.

'No,' he said firmly. 'Upstairs, if you don't mind, Mrs Trenchard. It's quicker in the long run. Gets things over with. Know what I mean?'

Mrs Trenchard appeared not to have heard him. 'A drink, Mr Wallingford? Gin? Whiskey? Vodka? White wine? ... Beer?'

'Business before pleasure, I always say.' He guffawed unsuitably, checked himself. 'Upstairs first, if you don't mind. Get things over with. The remains *are* in the bedroom, I presume?'

Mrs Trenchard raised her eyebrows. 'Naturally Haverstock is in his room. You wish to see him?'

'It's ... necessary.' He flicked defensively at his sleeve. 'Regulations, you know.'

'Of course. How silly of me.' She glided into the white settee room, turned off the music, then led him up the staircase, past matching studies of Arabia in Victorian aquatint. 'It happened last night ... The police doctor signed the certificate. I must say you've been very prompt. I only telephoned the Accident and General this morning.'

'We don't waste time, Mrs Trenchard.' He held his briefcase high, against his coat lapels, lest it bang the immaculate banisters. 'All part of the service.'

'He broke his neck, poor man. On these stairs. I was in the kitchen at the time. The police were perfectly satisfied.'

They reached the landing. A further staircase went on up to the second floor. Mrs Trenchard paused, turned, fixed him with unwavering amber eyes. 'That his death was accidental, I mean.'

Mr Wallingford looked away. 'Is ... is that the room?'

'Mine, Mr Wallingford. Haverstock preferred the back of the house, overlooking the garden. He liked to hear the birds in the morning. And he preferred the piquancy of separate rooms. He felt it lent excitement, impropriety even, to our fucking.'

She moved gracefully away. There was a faint smile on her lips that Mr Wallingford could not see. Possibly – if it were not too vulgar a thought – she believed she was winning.

Mr Wallingford followed her into the back bedroom. It was dim, the curtains drawn across the window. The body was on the bed, uncovered, wearing pajamas and a dressing gown. Mrs Trenchard crossed the room, opened the curtains. She stood there for a moment, her forehead against the glass, looking out. There were trees, and beyond them the backs of other tall white houses.

Mr Wallingford looked around for something on which to open his briefcase. The bed was a low, gray velvet oval. The rugs on the floor were shaggy yak. But he was confident now, the situation controllable, familiar. Rooms might differ, and also the bereaved. But a body was a body.

'Do you have a photograph of your husband, Mrs Trenchard?'

'I'm afraid not.' She stayed with her back to him, looking out of the window. 'He had this thing against photographs. Memorials to the dead moment, he called them.'

'Mr Trenchard wrote books, I believe?'

She turned then. 'But the jackets never had a picture. Never … Mr Trenchard forbade it. The word is eternal, you see – the human face, sadly, rather less so.' She clasped her hands lightly in front of her flat, flat stomach. 'I quote, of course. My husband's books were atrocious. God knows what anybody saw in them.'

Briefly Mr Wallingford was without bearings again. He saw a table for his briefcase by the fireplace. It cheered him. 'May I –?' he exclaimed, hastening to it and opening his briefcase without waiting for an answer. He began to sort documents out in piles.

Mrs Trenchard watched him.

'Please,' she said at last. 'Make yourself at home.'

'I already have,' he said, not noticing.

His documents prepared, he sat down at the table.

'Don't mind me.'

He produced a pair of spectacles from his inside pocket and put them on. He started filling in forms, fussing with the carbons, cross-referencing as he went.

For the time now that she was unobserved Mrs Trenchard's face, her entire body, underwent a subtle change. It sagged. Suddenly it was neither neat nor superior. Hairpins appeared at awkward angles in the bun at the nape of her neck. Her amber eyes blurred to uncertain brown. And her stomach, no longer flat, might almost – considered in isolation – have been friendly and snug to make sport upon. Except that the rest of her made such a notion utterly crass. For Mrs Trenchard, in toto, was unhappy. Anxious. Scared out of her wits.

'Death certificate?'

Mr Wallingford scarcely looked up, but his words braced her nevertheless. Hairpins disappeared, and that friendly stomach also. Head held high, she walked to the fireplace, removed the certificate from the frame of the Chippendale mirror above it, and handed the document to him.

'Thanks.' Immersed in forms. Forgetful of where he was. 'Let's see now … Cause of death, fracture of the … um … the …'

'Broken neck.' Too sharp. Clearly her nerves still jangled. She made an effort. 'I do so dislike doctors' double-talk, don't you?'

He glanced up, peering earnestly over the tops of his glasses. The thought had never occurred to him. 'My word, yes. How right you are. Yes indeed.' He returned to his papers.

Mrs Trenchard's gaze wandered composedly around the room, settled on the body in its striped pajamas and blanketish dressing gown. She frowned very slightly, struck perhaps by their homey incongruity on the oval, gray velvet bed. She glanced down at Mr Wallingford, seated beside her, her thought process unmistakable – would he notice? Then, she relaxed, clearly deciding that the point was too subtle, and he wouldn't.

Mr Wallingford sat back, took off his spectacles, laid them and his pen down on the table. 'Shoes now,' he told her.

'Shoes?' she echoed, smoothing one eyebrow with a calm, slim finger.

''Fraid so. Not that I don't trust you – personally, I mean. But the Accident and General has to be certain.'

'As you wish.' Resignedly, almost pityingly, she moved a few paces, reached up and pulled down a section of the blue flock-sprayed ceiling. It came easily, on counterweights, revealing a row of suits, and shoes on racks below them.

Mr Wallingford didn't quite hide his impressed surprise. He chose a pair of shoes. 'Better have a shirt as well, while we're at it,' he said. 'Just to be sure.'

Another section of ceiling supplied shirts, each in a plastic laundry bag.

'Underwear too?' Mrs Trenchard queried.

This time he caught the sarcasm. 'That won't be necessary,' he said quite snappily. 'Look, you don't have to watch if you'd rather not.'

'It really doesn't matter. My husband is dead. And you have a job to do. Of course you must do it.'

'Somebody has to, Mrs Trenchard.'

Never one to labor a point, she didn't answer.

He took one of the shoes, eased the laces, then stooped again over the body and slipped the shoe onto one cold, dead foot. It went on easily. He tightened the laces, tied them, tested for free play, joggling the leg, the whole body. One arm slipped off the bed, dangled to the floor.

Satisfied that the shoe was a convincing fit, Mr Wallingford moved to the other end of the bed, tactfully replacing the arm as he went. He slipped a tape measure expertly from his jacket pocket and threaded it around the dead man's neck. The corpse's eyes were closed, the corners of its mouth drawn back by muscular contraction into a faint smile.

Mr Wallingford removed the tape, noted the measurement where he had kept his thumb, compared it farsightedly with the collar size of the shirt. 'Good … very good,' he murmured.

He straightened his back. 'You wouldn't credit, Mrs Trenchard, what some people get up to. In the line of substitutions, I mean.' He fingered the shirt. 'No name tab, I see.'

'No.' Baldly. Daring him.

'Well, well … it really doesn't matter. Quite out of fashion, name tabs are.' He was conciliatory now. 'We'll just get your signature, and that'll be that. I can fill in the rest back at the office.'

He gave the shirt back to her, found he was holding only one shoe. 'Sorree … sorree …' With a sprightly gesture he turned to reclaim the second shoe. It stuck, then came off with an unpleasant plopping sound. 'Sorree … sorree …'

He was falling over himself, anxious to be away, ashamed that his job should have forced him to doubt this immaculate, unimpeachable lady. While she, giving nothing, waited patiently, unemotionally. No – *guardedly*. Her smile, too, was guarded as she accepted the pair of shoes, replaced it in its ceiling unit, and slid both units up and away.

Mr Wallingford sat down again at the table, put on his spectacles, tapped them up his nose. Then he selected a form, stood it on edge to square its carbons, and pushed it across the table, together with his pen. 'Your usual signature, please.' He made faint pencil crosses. 'Here. And here … and here.'

Mrs Trenchard wrote her name twice, in a clear, unostentatious hand: *Caroline Trenchard*. Then she paused. 'What exactly am I signing?'

'That the particulars on the claim form are correct. Policy number. The figure insured. The … um … your late husband's particulars. The date of his decease. The –'

'What exactly is the figure insured?'

'One hundred thousand, Mrs Trenchard.'

She nodded. 'And there'll be no further … difficulties?'

'None at all. Premiums are up to date. The Accident and General honors its commitments promptly and efficiently. You can expect our check within the week. I bring it myself, you know – just to be sure there's no mistake.'

'I am impressed, Mr Wallingford.' She signed again, at the bottom of the page, for the third and last time. 'I would not have you think me calculating, you understand. Haverstock's death has been a great shock to me. But one must –'

'Say no more, Mrs Trenchard. Not another word. Your late husband's wishes have been complied with – no more than that. Clearly, it was his wish to leave you well provided for.' Mr Wallingford began to gather together his papers. 'I'd just like to mention, Mrs Trenchard, that the Accident and General handles all sorts of business. House insurance. Personal effects. Comprehensive automobile ... And our terms are highly competitive. So if you should ever think of –'

It was then that the Singing began. The familiar, sliding, tuneless voices. And the smell, like synthetic roses, that was suddenly everywhere, faint and cloying in the contained spaces of the room.

Mrs Trenchard backed away. 'Have you any particular theories, Mr Wallingford? Any protective measures you wish to take?' Her calmness was an agony. 'Some people, I know, believe in darkness. There is a cupboard on the landing, if you'd prefer to ...'

But Mr Wallingford wasn't listening. He had leaned forward across the table, his head covered with his arms, his body shaking visibly. 'Oh God, not again,' he whispered. 'Not again. Not so soon ...'

Mrs Trenchard watched him. His weakness seemed to give her strength. 'Nothing does any good, you know. Nothing at all. One simply has to accept.'

Abruptly he lurched to his feet. He ran from the room, slamming the door behind him. His headlong flight took him across the landing, right up against the wall by one of the windows at the front of the house. Out of her presence now, the terrible weight of her exemplary behavior, he slowly grew calmer. The smell was still with him, of course, and the Singing. But he pulled himself together.

Looking out of the window, he could see along the row of houses to the sunlit square at the top of the hill. Mothers were clutching their children. Some were carrying them, seven- and eight-year-olds, as they staggered pointlessly around the gray stone fountain and in under the trees. A city electric coming up the hill braked to a halt in the middle of the roadway, and the driver got out. He was thin, with gray hair, and he stood on the clean hot asphalt, eyes closed, quite still, waiting.

Mr Wallingford took a deep breath. He removed the folded handkerchief from his breast pocket, spread it out, and mopped his face. It was a false sensation, he knew, but being in the house gave him confidence. He looked around, found himself in a woman's bedroom, presumably Mrs Trenchard's. Whole walls of mirror returned his image. He pulled at the hem of his jacket – it had a tendency to ride up at the back – and gingerly crimped his hair between straight fingers. Then he refolded his handkerchief and stuffed it back into his breast pocket. He sauntered to the door, observing the effect. He had a good saunter. And the Singing continued. She was quite right, of course. Nothing did any good.

He returned across the landing, softly opened the door to the dead man's room. At first it seemed that Mrs Trenchard was no longer there. Then he saw her, crouched in a corner, pressed tightly into the angle of the walls. So she was human after all. But the transformation touched him. He hesitated, moved toward her, one hand outstretched, then hesitated again at the impossibility of contact.

'Actuarially,' he said, 'the chances of a Disappearance are one in three point seven million against.'

Mrs Trenchard didn't move. Her voice came to him somewhat muffled. 'Statistically. You mean statistically. And that was last month. They haven't put out the figures for June yet.'

She got to her feet, turned to face him. Not a hair was out of place. But two wet trails of tears ran down her cheeks. She appeared to be unaware of them.

'Longish odds, either way,' said Mr Wallingford encouragingly.

'Are you a betting man?'

'Not me. Fool's game, I say.'

Mrs Trenchard smiled thinly, came forward out of her corner. 'We used to go to the races a lot. Collecting types, you know. Not really for the horses at all. Collecting types.'

Mr Wallingford frowned. 'I'm afraid I don't –'

'Types, Mr Wallingford. For Haverstock's books.' She left him to work it out for himself.

'Oh, *people*. You mean people.'

'Except that they weren't. Not to Haverstock. Not people – just types. Which is probably why his books were so atrocious.'

And the Singing continued. And the smell like sweet synthetic roses.

Mr Wallingford glanced uneasily at the body on the bed. 'I'm sure you're right, Mrs Trenchard …'

'You must not think I'm being disloyal. Haverstock knew very well what I thought of his work. It used to amuse him. "To my wife, I hack," he'd say. It was one of his jokes.'

Mr Wallingford was at a loss. 'I had a wife once,' he contributed.

'I'm so sorry. Was it …?'

'No. Not at all. No way. Four years ago, it was.'

'I see. They hadn't started then, of course. It's hard to remember.' She sighed. 'How long ago those days seem.'

And then, abruptly as it had started, the Singing stopped. The sliding harmonies ceased. In mid-slide.

'Thank God for that.' Suddenly Mr Wallingford seemed to have gained several centimeters. And he was laughing. 'My wife pushed off, you see. In a manner of speaking.'

Mrs Trenchard allowed a tactful moment, then went to the window, flung up the sash. 'That horrible smell,' she said, fanning the air.

It was a time for confidences. 'Between you and me, Mrs Trenchard, I rather like it. Reminds me of the fizzy stuff I used to have down by the canal when I was a kid.'

Mrs Trenchard was laughing too. 'I know just what you mean.' Which was, on the face of things, unlikely. Fizzy stuff and canals and Mrs Trenchard, at any age, just didn't go together.

'Well now,' said Mr Wallingford, 'where were we?' He sat down at the table, put on his spectacles with a flourish, studied the claim form. 'Signed and sealed, signed and sealed ...' He checked that the signatures had gone through the four carbons. 'That's it then, Mrs Trenchard. You'll be receiving our check within the week. The minimum of formalities. That's the Accident and General all over.'

Mrs Trenchard crossed to the door, opened it. They were back where they had started: he from the Accident and General, she neat again, and superior. And she was expecting him to leave.

But he lingered over the claim form, checking off boxes. So that she forgot her manners sufficiently to suggest, 'Shall I show you out, Mr Wallingford?'

'Shan't be half a mo, Mrs Trenchard. Checking. Just checking ... Aha!' He speared the form with a grubby fingernail. 'Gotcha! It says here, Mrs Trenchard, God knows why, but it says here: *Color of deceased's eyes* ... What color would that be, hm?'

She shot a brief glance in the direction of the bed. The dead man's fair hair shone yellowly on the pillow. 'Blue,' she said. 'Blue-gray, to be precise.'

Mr Wallingford's pen hovered, descended. 'That's it, then. You've been very helpful, Mrs Trenchard. Wish I could say the same for all my customers.'

He began to gather up his papers and stuff them into his briefcase. Mrs Trenchard had her hand on the doorknob. Then he paused. 'Better check, I suppose.' He sighed. 'Wouldn't be doing my job if I didn't. You don't mind?'

'Of course you must do whatever's necessary.'

He stood up and crossed to the head of the bed. Behind him, by the open door, Mrs Trenchard waited with seeming indifference. But the knuckles of her hand were white on the doorknob.

He bent over the dead man, lifted one cold, waxen eyelid. The eye stared flatly up at him. It was unmistakably brown.

'Oh dear,' said Mr Wallingford. 'Oh dearie, dearie me.'

He lowered the eyelid and turned to Mrs Trenchard, easing the doorknob gently out of her rigid grip. Then he closed the door and led her back to the table.

'I think you've been a naughty girl,' he told her.

He left Mrs Trenchard then and went to the window. Carefully he closed the sash, returned to the table, picked up the claim form she had just signed, held it out to one side, dangling, somewhat in the manner of a matador's cloak.

'Load of old cobblers, wouldn't you say? Strictly between you and I, that is?'

'You and me. Between you and me.' The correction was automatic, unthinking. It lost her whatever small chance she might have had.

'I'm afraid I don't go in for such refinements, Mrs Trenchard. Between you and I, Mrs Trenchard, you've been trying to work a con. And you bloody nearly got away with it.'

He sat down again at the table. She advanced toward him. 'You might as well tear that form up,' she said, still cool. 'I've wasted your time. I'm sorry.'

She held out her hand for the form. But he folded it, carbons and all, and tucked it carefully into his briefcase, which he then closed, snapping the lock.

'Jail's a nasty place, Mrs Trenchard. You must think I'm slow.'

'I'm afraid I don't understand you.'

'I think you do. Perjury, Mrs Trenchard?'

'So?'

'Fifty-fifty, shall we say? Fifty thousand for you, and fifty thousand for me?'

'Is this blackmail?'

'You could call it that.'

Two patches of red appeared, high up on her cheekbones. 'You unspeakable little shit,' she whispered. 'You totally unspeakable little shit ...'

Mr Wallingford and Mrs Trenchard: two people no longer strangers. But still, as yet, nothing one might term in the least *unsuitable*.

ONE

Moondrift: first reported 10/6/83. A dustlike fall, roughly monthly, of nontoxic fissionable material, foreign to the earth's composition. Each fall is to a depth of some ten centimeters over large, apparently random areas. The Moondrift remains stable for a period of forty-eight hours, and may be 'fixed' by the Macabee process. If left untreated it decays rapidly, and in its later forms constitutes an excellent, nonorganic fertilizer. Many theories have been put forward as to its origin, but none of these (as of today, September 1998) is yet proven.

Disappearances: first reported 6/11/85. Self-explanatory. Human beings of all ages and both sexes disappear abruptly, and without trace, to the accompaniment of a hallucinatory sound known as Singing, and a sweet perfume of synthetic roses. Disappearance rates vary slightly, on a seasonal basis. World figures suggest a high of something in the region of three million for the month of October. Effective preventative measures have yet to be devised.

Singing: first reported 6/11/85. See *Disappearances*, above. The sound, reminiscent of a choir of children's voices, is experienced over a sharply defined area of approximately four square miles, and lasts for a period of three to five minutes, beginning and ending sharply. Since neither it nor the concomitant scent of synthetic roses is capable of verification by objective, scientific means, it is assumed that – although universally experienced by those persons within a given area – both are of an entirely hallucinatory nature. Singings occur irregularly, but seldom more than once a day in any one place. Of those who experience a Singing, very few actually disappear.

Richard Wallingford – Dickie to his friends – was new to the Life Claims Verification business. So too, for that matter, was the Accident and General Insurance Company, in common with their fellow insurance underwriters. For this was 1986, only seven months into the beginning of the Disappearances, and ground rules had yet to be established. The best that AGIC had been able to come up with was the hurried issue of Exclusion Clauses, establishing that a Disappearance was *not*, in insurance terms, the equivalent of a death. And the transfer of men like Richard Wallingford from other departments.

Caroline Trenchard – Caro to her gone husband's friends – was new to the business also. Newest of all, in fact, for she hadn't given the matter a moment's serious thought until thirty-six hours earlier. She knew the government figures, of course, and she'd even heard, third-hand, of people who went, but never anybody in her husband's immediate circle. She might fear for herself – indeed she did, constantly – but she never imagined for an instant that Haverstock would go. Not Haverstock, of all people: his presence, his devastating personality, everything about him was so indestructibly pervasive.

And then, thirty-six hours ago, he'd gone.

They were alone at the time, preparing for bed. Haverstock was cleaning his teeth when the Singing started, and the disgusting smell. He appeared in his silk pajama bottoms at the door to her bedroom, dribbles of toothpaste foam running down his beard.

'Don't they ever sleep?' he said. 'Sweet weeping Jesus, don't our friends ever sleep?'

He stood beside the wall mirror: two pairs of gaping pajama bottoms (accidentally for once), two fleshy, hairless chests, two foam-dribbled beards, four frightened, bloodshot eyes. Then he went. Both of him. Instantly and completely. Without a sound.

And she didn't know whether to be glad or sorry.

Naturally, Richard Wallingford had sometimes wondered just what he would do if he caught someone actually trying to cover up a Disappearance. He'd be tactful, he thought, and kind. Very kind – pretend it hadn't happened. Poor sods, life was hard enough without him riding them. And besides, between you and I, he wasn't all that happy with company policy.

They had the law on their side, mind. Without a body to show, or *some* kind of firm evidence, it needed seven years before death could be assumed. And besides, who knew what happened to a man, after he'd gone? The experts couldn't help, nor the Church neither. One thing seemed certain, though – up to date, those who went had stayed went. So he reckoned he'd be tactful, kind, pretend the diddle hadn't happened. They'd have enough on their plates, poor sods, losing someone they loved in that bloody horrible way, without him riding them ...

'Another peep out of you, Mrs Trenchard,' he said, 'and I'll make it sixty-forty.'

Calling him names. Saying her gone husband's books were atrocious. White leather settees and pictures of private parts. Who did she think she was?

Caroline Trenchard wasn't sorry she'd told him what she thought of him. She recognized the type. Not that she wouldn't have been more discreet, she told herself, anxiously justifying her first genuine reaction in years, if there'd been any point. But she recognized the type: he was one of life's losers, his back to the wall. And she knew that wall well, how uncomfortable it made you, how desperate. She'd been against it for thirty-one years. They ought really to hold hands.

'Forty-sixty or fifty-fifty,' she said, 'it's not worth it. Take me to court if you must.' Which was how one treated back-to-the-wall blackmailers.

'They'll ask you where you got the substitute remains.'

'They can't make me tell them.'

'It'll go hard for you.' Tenderly he cradled his briefcase, the incriminating document safe inside. Everything was going for him. Everything ... except the street, the house, the woman, their unassailability. 'Ten years, at least. They'll make an example of you.'

'Five years. A suspended sentence. I was mad with grief. My lawyer will have a field day.'

It was the sort of manly phrase he'd understand. She seated herself calmly on the table and crossed one neat foot over the other. Her shoes were of the softest, honey-golden glace kid. And the briefcase in Mr Wallingford's lap was only half a meter away.

'You signed the form, Mrs Trenchard. That's perjury.' He took out his spectacles and put them on. He didn't like the middle-aged look they gave him. But they made him feel safer. 'And think of the scandal.'

'A writer's wife is used to scandal.'

Which wasn't, in her case, true. Try as Haverstock might, scandal had eluded him. Times were hard. She saw that Mr Wallingford's grip on his briefcase was scarcely secure. But she would not, could not, take part in an undignified scramble.

Richard got up from the table, sauntered over to the bed, taking his briefcase with him. He had a good saunter, he reckoned. 'Where *did* you get him, by the way?' He looked down at the dead body. 'And his clothes and all. They *are* his, aren't they?'

Behind him, Caroline was regretting having missed out on the briefcase. 'Delivered with the milk,' she said brightly.

'Come on,' he prompted. 'I won't tell. I'm just curious.'

'On special,' she said. 'This week only.'

Screw it, he thought, she's fireproof. Once you get them talking, it said in the spy movies, and you're home and dry.

'Tell me,' he cajoled.

'I can't.'

'Why not?'

Why indeed. 'To be honest,' she said, 'because I'm frightened. They told me I'd end up like him if I did.' She indicated the body on the bed. 'And I believed them.'

'Them? Who's them?'

'Just them, Mr Wallingford.' She folded her arms. 'I happen to want to stay alive.'

He sighed. Suddenly he felt defeated, tired out. And not very nice.

He turned back from the bed. 'Forty-sixty?' he suggested.

She stared at him, at the chain-store chic suit with the shiny elbows, at the tie with its French designer's signature. She could easily beat him down to seventy-thirty. Seventy thousand for her, thirty thousand for him. He'd think it a fortune.

'Done,' she said. 'Sixty-forty.'

And felt, disappointingly, no righteous glow.

Richard hated her. He hated everything about her. Most of all he hated what she'd made him do. He wasn't a crook – before the Disappearances he'd been an assessor in the Automobile Claims division: plenty of times there he'd been offered something on the side, just to look the other way, agree to a write-off when the bloody thing wasn't hardly dented. And he'd never gone along. It was more than his job was worth, he said. But it was more a matter of self-respect, really. Which was all he had.

And now, because of her, what he had was forty thousand, instead. It should have been a good bargain.

'Done then,' he said. 'Forty-sixty. Seeing as I'm a reasonable man.' By way of keeping his end up.

Done ...?

Caroline said, 'How do I know you won't come back for more?'

'That's easy. Once I've certified the form and handed it in at the head office, I won't have nothing on you. We'll be in it together.'

She wished he wasn't so eager to please. He was such an honest little man. And she couldn't remember when she had last been honest. But it was never too late to try.

'If that's the case, then how do you know I'll pay you?'

'Come again?'

No, she told herself, she wasn't being noble. He'd have seen the snag for himself eventually, without her prompting.

'I won't be able to pay you,' she explained, 'until I get the money from the Accident and General. And they won't pay me till they get the claim form back from you. And once you've handed in the form, you say you'll have nothing on me. So how can you be sure I'll keep my side of the bargain?'

'That's easy. D'you think I'm daft or something?' He returned to the table and sat down, and rummaged officiously in his briefcase. But his eyes were anxious, and it was clear he had no idea what came next.

'I suppose,' she suggested, 'you could always have your doubts. Even after you'd handed over the check, you could always pretend to have your doubts.

If I didn't pay up you could always say you'd forgotten to confirm the eye color. Ask for an exhumation order.'

She waited till he was looking at her, then met his gaze unwaveringly. 'Only for a few days, though. I'd be safe after that. After color confirmation was made impossible by natural deterioration.'

She had no notion of how long that took. But she had to protect her future somehow. And Mr Wallingford would surely bow to her superior knowledge – research into the decomposition rates of human bodies positively wasn't in his line.

'You took the words right out of my mouth,' he said. Not to be outdone, he returned to his rummaging, selected what she was sure was a random piece of paper, stared at it intently.

'Then again,' she said, 'how do you suggest I make the payment? After all, you won't want your bank manager asking awkward questions.'

He scowled at her. 'Why don't you stick to worrying about your end of things?' he snapped.

She didn't blame him for being annoyed. But she'd played at Ascendancies all her life. Therefore, 'You could always open a bank account somewhere else,' she told him kindly. 'Under an assumed name, of course.'

'I might at that.' Richard pushed at his spectacles. 'Then again, I might not.' And thank you for nothing, Mrs bloody Clever.

He clipped his briefcase shut, and stood up. If he didn't get away soon, he might say something he'd regret.

'That's it then, Mrs Trenchard. That's fixed. Properly understood. An agreement to our mutual benefit. You'll be seeing me again end of this week, beginning of the next ... And no monkey business, mind. Like you said, I can always get an exhumation order.'

He was taller than she. But, sitting up on the table, Mrs Trenchard met him just about eye to eye. And he was finding those few steps away to the door extraordinarily difficult. And she sat there watching him, not smiling, not moving, not helping him at all. Bloody woman.

'Which reminds me,' he said, gesturing with a vague fierceness, 'when's the funeral?'

'Tomorrow afternoon.' Still not giving an inch. 'Three thirty.'

A thought struck him. 'You wouldn't be planning a cremation, by any chance?' And she'd tried to make out he was stupid. 'Not a cremation, I hope?'

'Not a cremation, Mr Wallingford.' Her sloping, elegant shoulders rose and fell almost imperceptibly. 'The suppliers wouldn't hear of it. I cannot imagine why.'

'The suppliers?' But why ask, screw it? Why give in to her?

'The suppliers of ...' She tilted her head in the direction of the bed. 'They insisted on a proper interment. Possibly there's a financial interest somewhere.'

He narrowed his eyes. It sounded fishy. 'I think I'd better be there. Just to make certain.'

'Please yourself. There'll be quite a crowd. Haverstock's friends, you know. Saint Bartulph's necropolis. Three-thirty.'

'Right.' He shifted his feet. 'Right. I'll be there. Right.'

And still he couldn't escape from her bland, half-amused gaze. What was she laughing at? Not at him, surely? He'd just socked her for forty thousand, hadn't he? What the fuck was there to laugh at in that?

Caroline felt sad. Sad at herself, for the price she was exacting for her defeat. How much more fitting, she thought, to concede it gracefully. To be humble. To stop playing at Ascendancies and play at being humble instead … They were both of them rogues, of course, she and Mr Wallingford. But, of the two, he was certainly the more attractive. Criminality rested far less easily on his shoulders.

She made up her mind, slipped down off the table. 'Now that we're partners,' she said, 'perhaps there are things I ought to tell you. How I got the body and the clothes and things, for example.'

'I thought you wanted to stay alive.'

'But we're partners now. We have to trust each other.'

Wary still, he glanced at his watch. 'I have another call to make –'

'Oh, it won't take long.' She spoke warmly. She had a lot to make up for. 'It all started with an advertisement, you see. A small ad in *Groundswell*. I've still got it downstairs somewhere. Do let me show it to you.'

She led him, still unwilling, from the room. Almost, she took his hand. But he might mistake partnership for seduction. The Mr Wallingfords of this world did have rather basic natures.

She took him downstairs and into the living room. He sat on the edge of a chair, quite charming really, with his briefcase clutched protectively to his chest, while she hunted for the magazine. She couldn't remember where she'd put it – the hours since Haverstock's going were somewhat blurred. Understandably so. The shock and the grief … Grief? Yes, she decided, as she found the current copy of *Groundswell* tucked unobtrusively (suspiciously?) behind a cushion – what a good thing it was the police were so trusting – yes, she *had* felt grief at Haverstock's going. Grief for him. Grief for his loss of the stamping, tramping life that had meant so much to him. She could manage that at least.

She paused for a moment, her throat unexpectedly tight. And grief for herself also, that after nearly eight years that indeed was all she could manage. What a bastard he'd been. And his friends too, bastards every one. Except perhaps Humphrey.

She remembered Mr Wallingford. 'Here we are,' she said lightly, flipping through *Groundswell*'s pages. 'It's in every week. We first saw it months ago.

And wondered what it was all about.' She showed him the page. 'We never called the number to find out, of course.'

By her finger the words: *A Disappearance in the Family?*

And underneath: *Seven Years Is a Long Time to Wait. Why Not Call Our Confidential Advisory Service* NOW*?*

And then a telephone number.

Mr Wallingford took the magazine, stared at it dutifully. Then he put it on the chair arm and returned to his curiously intent study of his trouser knees. Why, she wondered, wasn't he more interested in what she was telling him?

She must speed things up a bit. She ranged about the room, testing weighing machines, staring out at the empty, sunlit street. 'Anyway, after the first shock of Haverstock's going, I remembered that ad. So I called the number. It was the middle of the night by then, but I didn't think of that. I wasn't thinking very clearly, I'm afraid.'

Mr Wallingford stirred. 'Where did you get all these pictures?' he asked.

'What?' She followed the direction of his gaze. 'Oh. Do you like them?'

'Not very much.'

Neither did she. But she wasn't going to apologize for Haverstock's taste. She didn't feel she had *that* much to make up for.

'So I called the number,' she said, 'and they answered at once. Most sympathetic. And businesslike, too – they took down all the particulars. Had I told anybody else? they asked. I said I hadn't had a chance. Then don't, they told me. Not till their representative had called. He'd be here first thing in the morning.'

Hearing her own voice, she realized that she was gabbling. And striding about. She checked herself. It was just that she still didn't know how Mr Wallingford worked. But she wasn't a snob. And it certainly wasn't his background that made him inaccessible. He was, like Haverstock – but so unlike Haverstock – simply a different animal. How many different sorts of animal were there?

'Gin?' she said. One of the weighing machines was converted for drinks. 'Whiskey? Vodka? White wine? … Beer?'

Addressed directly, Richard hit back. 'You don't seem very sorry,' he said. 'About your husband's going, I mean.'

He saw he'd got her there. Bitch. Reminded him of his wife – marriage had been all the same to her, too. Though the similarity went no further. Mostly what he remembered about Maggie was the fag ash.

'Don't you think that's rather impertinent?'

'Bloody rude, if you ask me.' He smiled. She was in retreat now, and he could meet her eyes. 'But you did say we were partners.'

He watched her think about it. 'Haverstock and I went our separate ways,' she said at last. Whatever that might mean. But she seemed pleased with it, and turned back to the drinks. 'Whiskey? Vodka? White –?'

'Whiskey.' He'd get shot, of course, turning up to his next call with booze on his breath. And he didn't care a monkey's. 'A big one.'

'Water or soda?'

'Soda, please … Well, as it comes.' Why couldn't he make up his mind? 'No, water.'

'Say when.' Laughing up her sleeve. And now she'd drowned it.

'When.'

She handed him his glass, poured herself the same. 'So I asked them,' she went on, 'exactly what the service was that they provided. Loans, they said. Seven year loans, on suitable security. So I told them to forget it. I was rather upset. But I just didn't have the security. There'd be no estate to speak of – I knew that, not the way Haverstock handled things. And you with your Exclusion Clauses.'

No use going on at him. What the hell did she expect. 'What the hell do you expect?'

'Please – I'm not blaming you.' Like hell she wasn't. Laughing up her sleeve. Mrs bloody Clever. 'Anyway, they said their representative would call all the same. And not to do anything till he did …'

He thought back, tried to remember how all this had started. *Groundswell* was still on the chair arm beside him. Trust her sort to have a Bolshie rag like that. Always knocking the system. Moondrift for the masses – as if work was a dirty word or something … But she'd started out to explain about the body upstairs. What was all this about loans, then?

'I'm afraid I don't quite –'

'Neither did I.' She sat down on the white settee, leaned back, crossed her legs at him. 'But I did as they said. Their representative arrived at six in the morning. Got me out of bed. Bright young man, very tactful and solemn. Called Cattermole, of all things. Asked me one million questions. I see now that he was sussing me out. You know the phrase?'

He nodded. But he was frankly surprised that she did. He couldn't imagine that anyone had assessed her criminal possibilities before. Stuck-up bitch.

'He had a bug detector too … Anyway, the upshot was that he must have decided I was genuine. For which read, too desperate to be overfussy. So he made his offer.'

She paused, swilled half her whiskey down in one go. Perhaps she needed it. He sipped his, didn't prompt her, began to feel better.

'The loans business,' she went on, 'was just a front. They had to be careful. In fact, they were a firm of undertakers. So I told them that since I didn't have a corpse, I didn't need an undertaker. And even if I *had* had one, I'd have called in the corpse disposal people. Haverstock hadn't been a barbarian, and neither was I. Minimum of fuss, a plastic bag, and a quick frizzle.'

She was cool as a cucumber. He refused to be shocked. It was the same with the pictures on the walls – no sense of what was right. And the husband as bad as her, by the sound of it.

'The young man smiled then,' she said, 'and told me that the corpse was part of the service. And the clothes to back it up. Which, being scarcely legal, was why he'd had to be so careful.'

Caroline finished her drink. It was obvious now, looking at Mr Wallingford, that dragging in the corpse disposal people had been a mistake. It really was quite infantile, needing to demonstrate how sensible one was. Especially when one man's sensible was so often another man's crass. And when all she should have been doing was trying to be nice.

She decided to wrap things up as quickly as possible.

'He made the delivery yesterday evening. In a carpet, I ask you – just like the Queen of Sheba. He'd called at other houses on the street first, making like a carpet salesman, so it wouldn't look odd. He'd even sold one or two, he said.'

By now she was regretting she'd ever started. She'd hoped to excite his professional interest, but he simply looked resentful. Perhaps it was the whiskey.

How difficult it was to know with people.

'The corpse was in pajamas and dressing gown. He arranged it at the foot of the stairs, said I should call the police around midnight. I didn't like to ask where it had come from.'

Mr Wallingford perked up. 'Deep freeze,' he said brightly. 'Undertakers do have them, you know.'

She was delighted to bow to his superior knowledge. 'I'm sure you're right. Mr Cattermole did mention rigor – he said they had a microwave oven treatment that worked wonders. The broken neck, by the way, was perfectly genuine, he told me.'

Mr Wallingford emptied his glass and expansively laid aside his briefcase. 'Pardon me for asking,' he said, 'but how much did all this cost?'

'Now that's the funny part of it.' At last, a community of interest. 'Around two fifty – no more than the price of the funeral. They weren't in it for the money, he said. I was touched. They simply saw themselves as righting a major social injustice.'

'Only two fifty. Well, well, well ...' Richard wondered if she was telling him the truth. There was a confused buzzing in his ears. He realized that he wasn't used to drinking in the middle of the afternoon. He tried to concentrate. 'What happens next?' he said.

'Nothing, really. The undertakers come early tomorrow morning in the usual way. Except that they take the clothes and things away with them as well. And help me down with Haverstock's real ones out of the attic.'

And all for two fifty. It seemed almost too good to be true. But why should she lie? Richard couldn't imagine. And they'd have got clean away with it, if he hadn't been too sharp for them. And if this stuck-up bitch had only done her homework. Checked up on the eyes. Still, it showed she was human, at least. Which he'd very much doubted.

Richard got carefully to his feet. 'That's all very interesting, Mrs Trenchard. And it's helped me a lot.' He wanted to be fair. 'They'll be in for a nasty shock the next time I do a Claims Verification. With my inside knowledge, they won't know what hit them.'

A picture occurred to him. A beatific succession of forty-sixties.

'But surely,' Mrs Trenchard was saying, 'you won't go on working? Not with forty thousand in the bank?'

Forty thousand in the bank … the reality of it slowly sank in. He was rich. So the next poor sod who tried anything, he'd deal with more gently. Let them off with a caution. He wasn't a greedy man.

'All the same,' he said, following this generous line of thought, 'it wouldn't do to pack things in too quickly. It might make people suspicious. No, I reckon I'll stay with the old firm for a month or two yet.'

Confidences? Suddenly Caroline felt she'd gone too far. 'I'm sorry I can't tempt you to another, Mr Wallingford.' Conceding defeat gracefully was one thing: encouraging this dreadful man to confidences was quite another. 'No?' she said quickly. 'In that case, I'll show you to the door.'

Because he *was* dreadful. By any standard, truly dreadful.

'Don't forget your briefcase.' He hadn't been going to. 'You'll be bringing the check at the end of the week, I believe.'

He caught up with her by the front door.

'And picking up my share.' He leaned intimately toward her. 'Fair exchange, no robbery, Mrs Trenchard. Eh? Eh?'

She looked studiously past him, noticed that the grandfather clock by the stairs had stopped. 'The less said about robbery the better, Mr Wallingford. On both our sides.'

He lingered on the step. 'The end of this week,' he said. 'Or the beginning of the next.'

She smiled at him, her best, most clearly insincere smile. 'I shall call your head office on Friday to confirm,' she told him.

And closed the door.

Mr Wallingford and Mrs Trenchard: two people no longer strangers. But between them, two inches of seasoned timber. And not, apparently, even the smallest possibility of anything *unsuitable*.

She turned then back to the grandfather clock, opened it, and began to wind up the weights. Friday … there'd have been several more Singings by then. Perhaps Mr Wallingford would have gone. Perhaps she'd have gone herself. Sometimes she wondered why anyone bothered. She leaned against the pretty floral wallpaper, then slid down till she was sitting on the stairs. On the second step up from the bottom. The house was empty, and very quiet. She wept.

TWO

Calcutta. 6/28/86. During a Singing in the city today, tens of thousands followed the advice of their new spiritual leader, Bannerji Latif, and indulged in an orgy of promiscuous lovemaking. According to Mr Latif, the Singings are a manifestation of the wrath of the Hindu goddess Siva, the creator and the destroyer.

The anger of the goddess, he claims, has been aroused by India's slavish dependence upon the West's surplus Moondrift revenue. The people of India, he says, need neither Western aid nor Western ideas. Principal targets of his campaign are birth control and Coca-Cola.

If the purpose of this latest demonstration was to turn away the goddess' wrath, then it was clearly unsuccessful. Nevertheless, the unusually large number of Disappearances reported in the aftermath of today's Singing is thought to be of little significance, since many opponents of Mr Latif are believed to have left the city unobtrusively, under cover of darkness.

Richard Wallingford's second call that slightly blurred afternoon was to a Mrs Pile, who lived with her three children in one of the inner-city high-rise blocks of apartments recently converted to two-story maisonettes.

Mrs Pile was no Caroline Trenchard. The previous day her husband Rodney had been returned to her in several pieces from the factory where he worked the Monday and Tuesday shift. Richard was able to inspect the pieces and read the excellent report of the factory doctor. All machinery in the factory was fitted with protective casing well in excess of government requirements, and Mr Pile had been in direct contravention of factory safety regulations when he chose to remove same protective casing for his own greater convenience. The factory management extended every sympathy to his widow, but must regretfully deny all liability.

Fortunately for Mrs Pile, her husband had taken out personal coverage with the Accident and General, and Richard had no hesitation in verifying the claim. Mrs Pile was distrait, but suitably grateful. If only her Rodney had worked the Wednesday and Thursday shift, she said, he'd have been with her still. It was the Monday men who did the maintenance. The figure insured was a round two thousand. Richard obtained her signature on the relevant documents and departed, wishing that all verification calls could be so straightforward.

The head office of the Accident and General Insurance Company stood on

Baltimore Row. AGIC House was an imposing block of reconstituted granite, its facade surmounted by one vast stainless-steel hand clasping another in an eternally helpful – and clearly inescapable – grip. Richard drove into its underground garage at ten to six, dawdling over plugging in his city electric, then hung about, chatting idly with the Tuesday attendant. His departmental head, Caldwell, was in the habit of leaving the office sharp at six, and Richard wanted to avoid meeting him until the following day. It wasn't that he was in the least afraid of Bernie Caldwell. But he wasn't yet quite ready to commit himself to booking in Mrs Trenchard's Claim Verification Form. He needed time, quietly, on his own, in which to consider her extraordinary story.

Or was it only the whiskey that had made it seem so strange?

When his watch gave him 06:04 he left the underground garage and went up in the elevator to the eleventh floor … A body delivered in a carpet? he thought. And all for two fifty? No, it didn't make sense. And what would a firm of undertakers be doing with all those clothes? No, that didn't make sense either. Complications loomed. Reefs beneath the surface of his sunny, forty thousand sea.

Mrs Trenchard herself he didn't think about. She was altogether too uncomfortable.

The elevator doors opened at the eleventh floor, revealing Bernie Caldwell, sports carryall jauntily in hand.

'Wallingford? What's this, then? It's after six. Those bastards upstairs don't pay us for overtime, you know.'

It was Mr Caldwell's way to affect a hatred for the company. Just as it was his way to appear twenty-five, and athletic.

Richard pulled in his stomach as best he could. It wasn't beer – it was all that sitting in cars. 'Laying up store in heaven, Mr Caldwell.' Since he knew for a fact that the carryall would be full of actuarial breakdowns. 'Been a busy day, Mr Caldwell.'

And regretted the words instantly, for they might just possibly remind Bernie Caldwell of the Trenchard claim. In which case he might just possibly put off his departure. The Trenchard claim was a biggie.

But Mr Caldwell swung past him into the elevator. 'Another day, another dollar,' he observed genially. 'I'm late already – good evening to you, Wallingford.'

Richard sidled gratefully out into the foyer. 'And good evening to you, Mr Caldwell.'

The doors closed behind him.

Paused.

Opened again.

'Which reminds me, Wallingford – wasn't it this afternoon you were to verify the Trenchard claim?'

The eleventh floor of AGIC House was open, a panorama of shoulder-high partitions, like a maze for midgets. Only Mr Caldwell, presiding at the still center, was glorified with a door, and walls up to the ceiling. Walls of glass, diplomatically, so that none should suspect Mr Caldwell of dozing beneath his sporty red bandanna.

'Sit down, Wallingford. Let's hear how you made out.'

Richard sat. 'I … there's still some paperwork to be seen to,' he muttered.

'Still, you must know the verdict. Hm?' Mr Caldwell perched on the corner of his desk, swung an imaginary tennis racket. 'A cool hundred thou – that'll shake the old bastards upstairs.'

'I speak as I find, Mr Caldwell. I can do no more.'

'You speak as you find?' Lob. 'This isn't just a buckled radiator situation, y'know.'

'I'm well aware of that, sir.'

'These are *people*, Wallingford.' Slice. 'Human beings, with hopes and fears.' Slam. 'And we're talking about a cool hundred thou.'

'I'm aware of that too, sir.'

'Well?' A drop-shot this time, just over the net.

Richard lunged. 'And I intend to approve the claim, sir.'

There. Done. He felt light-headed – uninvolved, strangely free. Well, bloody Caldwell shouldn't have pushed him so. Forced him to make up his mind when he wasn't really ready. Settle for the forty thousand. It was all bloody Caldwell's fault.

Thank you, bloody Caldwell.

'I beg your pardon?'

'I didn't speak, Mr Caldwell.'

'Ah … So you're approving the claim. Those bastards upstairs'll have kittens.' Winding up to serve again. 'No sign of a suicide situation, I suppose?'

'It's always *possible* that Mr Trenchard threw himself down the stairs, sir. But we'd never be able to prove it.'

'Wouldn't want to try. Mean-spirited in a corporation of our standing.' A let, apparently. 'Are you sure his wife didn't push him?'

'The police seem satisfied. There's to be an inquest, of course. Tomorrow. But she's not expecting any trouble.'

'So the swine just fell. I wonder why …' Mr Caldwell paused in mid-swing. 'Had he been drinking?'

'No mention of alcohol in the police doctor's report.'

Mr Caldwell frowned, and lowered his arm. 'So the swine just fell. Sensible chap. And those bastards upstairs'll just have to pay up and look happy.' He left the serving line, moved around his desk, sat at it. 'You checked his age, I hope?'

'Thirty-five in the policy, sir. Mid-thirties, according to the police doctor.'

'Excellent. Make the bastards pay.' Fingers drumming on his blotter. 'Mind you, we caught a substitution only last week. Young Deakin spotted it. Bad dye-job on the hair. Marked the pillow. Case comes up end of the month.'

Richard felt a moment's anxiety. 'Any luck tracing the … er, the supplier, sir?'

'Saved the firm thousands … No luck at all, so far. The client just isn't telling. Swine. They're all swine, you know, Wallingford. One way or another.'

'I'm afraid you're right, Mr Caldwell.' Swine? Mrs Trenchard? Oh, *yes* …

Mr Caldwell got to his feet. 'I'll be off, then. You won't see a scrap of overtime, not in this dump. They're getting a three-day week out of me, as it is. Let me have the papers in the morning.'

Giving Richard time. Still time for second thoughts. Time to discover a mistake in the papers and ask for a second visit.

Mr Caldwell moved past him to the door. Half out, he paused. 'Swine's eyes?'

Richard leaned down, untied his shoelace. 'I'm afraid I didn't quite catch …?'

'The eye color, man. Hardest of all to fake.'

Richard tied the lace again. Cleared his throat. 'Blue, sir,' he said. 'Gray-blue, to be exact.'

And thank you again, bloody Caldwell.

Later, at his own desk, he got out the Trenchard forms and stared at them. There was no going back now. Not that Mrs Trenchard need know that. But he'd have to watch her.

Forty thousand in the bank … Mind, he wouldn't do anything silly. He'd stay with the Accident and General, just treat himself to a few little extras. After all, he liked the work. And he didn't even mind the three-day week they sometimes asked of him too – it was the other four that got on his nerves a bit. No, stay on with AGIC, and treat himself to a few little extras. The sort people wouldn't notice.

Forty thousand in the bank … Christ, it was like being two meters tall, with a cock like Casanova's.

He checked the Trenchard papers, stapled them together, and dropped them gently into his out-tray for the messenger in the morning. Mrs Pile's too, not letting himself forget his duty to the underprivileged. From now on it was up to others, the messenger girl, Bernie Caldwell, the chief accountant who signed Mrs Trenchard's check … it was nice to think of all those miserable sods helping him on his way.

He got up from his desk, beige plastic integral with the partitions, and threaded his way to the elevator. There were a few of the girls and boys still working. Friends of his. Colleagues. Fellow slaves in the salt mines. But he didn't stop to chat. How could he? Not any more. He'd left them far behind. All in the one day.

He drove up out of the underground garage, turned for home. Hit the northbound rush hour which, in these Utopian, Moondrift days, was made worse by the construction work everywhere, two-tiers going up to cope with the increase in traffic that had followed the new Moondrift power stations. So now there was talk of banning all electrics in the city – and that scarcely a year after the introduction of the Fetherlite Battery Cell.

Utopian … that was a laugh.

Richard changed lanes, leaning on his horn. Governments were like that – never happier than when they were banning things. No vision. And it wasn't as if they didn't have the money these days. Industrial production up twelve percent, oil imports down seventy percent, fancy new schools, hospitals, universities, rehousing schemes, leisure centers. And here they were still building two-tiers, obsolete before they were even finished.

Leisure centers … they were another laugh. Sardine tins, more like. If you wanted room to breathe you'd far better try the inner city. In armed groups of not less than four, of course.

He saw a gap, beat two contenders, found himself boxed in behind an elderly diesel belching fumes. Bloody diesels – there ought to be a law. He turned on the radio, filled his car with savage, reassuring sounds.

It wasn't until nearly two hours later, just as he was turning into his own avenue, that Richard realized he could have stayed in town – with his financial prospects he could have had a slap-up dinner, gone to the theater afterwards. Still, it was too late now, and he wasn't all that sorry. He liked his home. And there was still enough daylight for him to get on with the extension sun parlor he was building out at the back. If Rose-Ann wasn't in – she seldom was these days – he'd microwave himself a quick supper, and then get started.

He left his car on charge in the garage and went through into the house. No sign of Rose-Ann, of course. Bloody woman. He didn't ask much of her – just a bit of movement about the place. Clumping up and down the stairs, watching the telly, flushing the toilet. It wasn't much to ask.

He turned on the TV himself, carried it through into the kitchen, and then went to look in the freezer. And it was then, undecided as he was between goulash and chow mein, that the Singing started. And with it the god-awful stink. Synthetic roses. Why the fucking hell had he ever said he liked it?

He leaned his head on the open freezer lid. His second Singing that day – it wasn't bloody fair. At least if you stayed in one place you didn't get them that often. How long could a man be expected to go on like this? Mostly you did the best you could. You forgot the last and didn't think about the next. And you comforted yourself with the odds against. Which were no bloody comfort at all.

Haverstock Trenchard – had he comforted himself with the odds against?

Richard didn't want to go. More than ever before since the Singings had started, he didn't want to go. And it wasn't the two meters tall bit either. It was

Maggie – having been reminded of Maggie, of the way things had been before she quit. You kept on because you believed that sometime, somehow, things would be that way again. Not the fag ash, that didn't matter a damn. No, it was the … the *fullness* that you hoped for. The fullness of your days.

And now, more than ever before since Maggie quit, he'd had hopes.

You couldn't buy it – he wasn't that daft. But forty thousand in the bank was a start. At least it would earn you a second glance, something to work on, something with a bit more future than just Rose-Ann. So he mustn't go now. Not now, please God. Not after four long years of simply keeping on.

Whimpering faintly, he stooped down into the freezer and began to fling frozen parcels doggedly over his shoulder. Peas, chips, TV dinners, cream and strawberry flans. The thing was to make activity. And noise. Any sort of activity, any sort of noise. While out on the thruway at the bottom of his avenue the law-abiding drew in to the side, and the maniacs pressed on regardless. Making, like him, their own activity, their own noise.

And went, it had already been established, neither more nor less frequently than everybody else.

By the time the Singing ended his freezer was just about empty, he'd cracked the face of the clock on the kitchen wall behind him with a half-leg of lamb, and the floor was ankle-deep in whitish frozen lumps. It took him nearly half an hour to pack them all back in again. The sun parlor would have to wait. He was breaking up, he thought. Next time he must get a grip on himself. Except that next time was a long way off. And might never happen.

He hesitated a moment, then decided on chow mein. The TV on the draining board behind him was showing a program all about Bessarabian macaws.

Caroline Trenchard was on the telephone. The Singing over the northern parts of the city had missed her by several miles, and she'd been calling Haverstock's friends more or less continuously since shortly after Mr Wallingford's departure. With brief intervals to refill her glass.

'Caro? Caro darling, how *are* you?'

'I'm still here.'

'But of course you are, darling. June is the month when the Heavenly Choirs are only auditioning castrati. I have it on the best authority.'

'I –'

'Which lets out the Beast as well, wouldn't you say? Nudge-nudge, wink-wink … How is Haverstock, by the way?'

'That's what I'm calling you about. Haverstock's –'

'Because we're longing for you both to come to this *fest*-thing we're throwing for Thingummy.'

'I do wish you wouldn't interrupt. It's Haverstock, you see. He's –'

'Don't spoil it, duck. You're supposed to say, "Who's Thingummy?" And then I say, "Whose thingummy do you fancy?"'

'Anything to oblige … Who's Thingummy?'

'Look, Caro – are you all right?'

'Of course I'm not all right.'

'Because you sound completely pissed to me.'

'I wish I was.'

'That's all right, then. Look – why don't you put the Beast himself on? Or better still, call again tomorrow when you've both sobered up.'

'But Haverstock's dead, you stupid shit.'

'Naughty, naughty. Dead? You don't mean *dead* dead?'

'What other sort of dead is there?'

'What? Oh, you poor thing. Poor little Caro. Poor duck … Look, don't move. Don't do a thing. I'm on my way. I'll be there in two shakes of a bee's bottom.'

'No.'

'But I insist.'

'No, I tell you.'

'And the Beast's really dead? You really mean it?'

'I've already announced it in the paper. Funeral's tomorrow. Saint Bartulph's necropolis. Three thirty.'

'Funeral? Now I know you're joking.'

'I'm not.'

'But *funeral*, darling. How impossibly quaint.'

'Quaint, yes. Impossibly, no. I … I want it.'

'Look, Caro – let's get this straight. You say Haverstock's dead, but you don't say how. You don't mean he's gone, do you?'

'He fell downstairs. Last night. Broke his neck.'

'I don't believe it.'

'The inquest's tomorrow morning. Central coroner's court. Eleven fifteen.'

'I do believe it. What *are* you going to do?'

'I told you. Have a funeral. Tomorrow afternoon. Three-thirty.'

'You poor thing. No wonder you're pissed.'

'No flowers. Did I say that? No flowers, by request. Donations instead to the Society for the Installation of Elevators in Dissolute Authors' Houses.'

'I'm coming over.'

'You're not.'

'You shouldn't be drinking alone, duck.'

'I've got my mother.'

'I thought she lived in Dar es Salaam.'

'That's my other mother.'

'Well … if you're sure you're all right –'

'I've never been righter.'

'Brave little woman. Look – I tell you what. This *fest*-thing I mentioned. There really is one. Tomorrow night. If you'd like to come alone, you'd be ever so welcome. Round off the funeral – Beauty without her Beast and all that. And there really is a Thingummy, too. Chap name of Prancing. Or was it Lancing? Anyway, I'm publishing his book. It's quite super. Well, *quite* super … Main thing is, the paperbackers love it. To the tune of trillions of millions. Which accounts for the *fest*-thing, of course. And he's a splendid fellow. Dancing, I mean. Or Glancing, or whatever his idiotic name is …'

Gently Caroline lowered the telephone receiver and replaced it on the cradle. She smiled a sharp little three-cornered smile. Humphrey hadn't sounded very sorry, neither about Haverstock nor about her. None of them had. She ought to feel piqued – not for herself, but for Haverstock. He had counted on his friends. Therefore, it was her wifely duty to feel piqued on his behalf. And it was better than the faint sense of triumph she might otherwise have felt.

She flicked on through their book of telephone numbers. As the names and figures blurred in front of her eyes, she thought how tired she must be. Hardly three hours' sleep, what with Haverstock going and the arrival at crack of dawn of the helpful Mr Cattermole. She drifted back into the living room, topped up her glass with the last of the whiskey. It was dusk now and the street lamp outside the house cast four precise oblongs of light on the living room carpet. She sat down tidily on her folded-up legs on the white hide sofa, and stared at the oblongs. If there had been nine of them she could have played ticktacktoe. But not on her own. You always won if you played ticktacktoe on your own.

If it had not been for the body upstairs that was not Haverstock, she would have let one of Haverstock's friends come around and play with her. Most of them had offered. But she'd known she couldn't risk it – they'd have gone all ethnic on her and wanted to view the body … Not that they'd have blamed her for taking steps. This *pitiful* government, my dear. I'd have done the same myself. But they'd have dined out on her steps for weeks.

She ought, she supposed, to be making plans. But it was only nine o'clock.

What a pity it was that she hadn't let Haverstock land her with children. Children were, by definition, plans. Just start them up, and they made themselves. Her father was in Australia, and her mother almost equally distant. The funeral wouldn't have brought her – but then again, it might have. Another risk Caroline wasn't prepared to take. She'd send a telegram afterwards.

It would probably be better if she seriously grieved for Haverstock's going. Then at least she'd know where she stood. She'd have been good at grief. It would have become her.

She unfolded her legs, went back to the whiskey bottle, found it empty. And Haverstock had always told her you got drunk if you switched to gin or vodka, so she decided to go out instead.

Driving down to the city, the multitude of lights confused her. She stopped the car outside a stack of cinemas, wandered up and down the pavement for a while with its cable. Then she gave up looking and reeled it in – there wasn't a charging point anywhere around. They did that, she knew, to discourage parking. A man in a mauve dress suit came out of the stack of cinemas and started shouting at her. She walked quickly away beneath the confusion of signs and street lamps.

Suddenly dimness. An area of trees in tapered concrete pots, and benches on hexagonal paving stones, and strung-out colored lights against a nothing sky. Music stamped out by the running meter. And people. Caroline kept on walking. But she felt better.

A woman fell into step beside her. 'You look lonely,' the woman said.

It was a revelation. Caroline nodded. But she kept on walking.

'So am I,' the woman told her.

Caroline frowned – the woman had no right to be lonely too – and kept on walking. Through the colored lights and the music.

'I was married once,' the woman said next. 'To a man, in the ordinary way of things. But it didn't work out.'

Caroline turned her head. 'D'you know something?' she said. 'I'd have been good at grief. It would have become me.'

The woman took her arm. '*Men* …' she said derisively. 'What you need is cheering up, my dear.'

'Loneliness isn't the same as grief, you see.' Caroline sighed. Walked. 'It's so much one's own fault. Looked at objectively, I mean. I mean, one can't really blame people for not being friends with one. Whereas grief …'

'My place is just round the corner,' the woman said.

'It's not that one wants people's sympathy.' Caroline paused. 'That's the last thing one wants.'

'Don't I know it, my dear. They can stuff their sympathy. And their understanding. Their bloody understanding.'

The woman's hand tightened on Caroline's arm, kneading the muscles like trumpet keys. She smelled of tutti-frutti chewing gum.

'Whereas grief,' Caroline murmured, 'is its own protection. Take Mr Wallingford.' She wanted to be fair to the man. 'He's not a monster. He wouldn't have taken advantage. It was my own fault, really. But I couldn't pretend. So disgusting, to pretend. People do it all the time. Everybody I know, they do it all the time.'

'What you need, my dear, is a nice lie-down.'

'Except Mr Wallingford. He doesn't pretend. I will say that for him.'

'You've had a hard time. Anybody can see that.'

Now the hand was hurting her arm. 'You're hurting my arm.'

The woman released her, and Caroline started walking again.

'We turn left here,' the woman said.

'Sometimes self-respect is all one has,' Caroline told her. 'And that's disgusting too, in a way ... If one can afford the disgusting luxury of disgust, of course. And such a poor substitute for people.' She kept on walking straight ahead. 'Don't you agree?'

But the woman was no longer there.

Caroline wondered what she was doing, there beneath the trees and the lights and the music. She thought of turning back to find the woman. It was, after all, the first time she had received an open homosexual advance. Perhaps she should have played along. Wasn't that what one was supposed to do? For emptiness' sake, for the sake of here today and gone tomorrow, shouldn't she have played along? But not, sweet weeping Jesus, with tutti-frutti.

Which was, taking things all in all, a great relief.

She came to a restaurant spilling tables out onto the hexagonal paving. There was a low picket fence around the tables, with strangulated cypresses in wooden tubs at the corners, and an untidy array of placards on sticks piled against the fence. And people at the tables inside the fence, placard people, ageless, evangelical, hanging loose. And the placards seemed to be covered with large black O's.

Caroline went in through a gap in the fence and sat down at a vacant table near to the people.

'It's not just the inaction,' she heard. 'It's the lying in high places.'

'Ostriches have to lie, George. It's built in to their posture.'

'Seven hundred and thirty-six this week, on the south coast alone. Make a note of that, Wilfred. Seven-three-six so far this week.'

'Official?'

'That's just the point. They're only admitting to five. But Barry's seen the return sheet.'

'They'll say the balance are Double-D's, of course.'

'But that's balls, man. Two-three-six Diplomatics? You must be joking.'

'*I* know it's balls, George, and so do you. But –'

A man's figure, indistinct, had arrived at Caroline's table. Black suit, white shirt. A waiter.

'Yes?'

She picked up the menu. 'A cup of coffee, please.'

'And?'

'That will be all, thank you.'

'Is after nine P.M. Now minimum charge one-fifty.'

The waiter pointed to a line of printing at the top of the menu. It read: After nine P.M., minimum charge one-fifty.

Caroline sat back and crossed her legs. 'I don't seem to have brought my purse.'

The waiter developed a face. He looked happy. Probably for the first time that day.

'Rule of the establishment. Is after nine P.M. Now minimum charge one-fifty.'

'I haven't got one-fifty.'

'With respect, you don't got nothing. Madam.'

'True.'

'So out.'

'Ridiculous.'

'You want I call the manager?'

'Yes.' She clasped her hands lightly on the table top.

'Is rule of the establishment.'

'If you touch me, I shall scream.'

'Scream is nothing.'

'Mine is, I promise you.'

Another voice. 'Can't you see the young lady's with us?' Wilfred. And about time too. She was running out of flak. 'Just bring her what she wants, there's a good fellow.'

The waiter considered arguing, then reluctantly went away. Caroline moved her chair closer to Wilfred's.

'That's really very kind of you.'

'Think nothing of it, ma'am.'

So he *had* spotted the wedding ring on her lightly clasped hands. And he'd believed it. Good old Wilfred.

'I'm afraid I was being rather naughty.'

'Guys like that ask for it. My name's Wilfred.'

'Mine's Ethel.'

Ethel? Why *Ethel*, for God's sake?

'Nice to know you, Ethel. See here – this is Barry.'

'Evening, Ethel.'

'Black one here's George. Reading from left to right, Kevin, Jane, Annabel, Jim, Latvian Jane, Bill ...'

The predictable, unimportant names drifted by. And the faces, too. The predictable, unimportant faces.

Until suddenly, peering at them, she came to her senses. She felt the cool, sobering evening air on her face and saw for the first time each individual bulb of the colored lights. And realized that for some long while now, right up to that very moment, she'd been seriously in need of care and attention. She and Ethel together, pissed clean out of their minds.

'Ethel? Ethel, ma'am – you all right there?'

She frowned, feeling horribly ashamed. Who was she to use words like unimportance, or predictability? She remembered walking. And before that, making telephone calls. And before that the bottle of whiskey in her living room.

'I … I haven't been very well,' she said. She touched the bun at the nape of her neck. 'But I'm fine now.'

'You sure of that? You know, for a moment, Ethel, you had me worried.'

That terrible name. He would keep saying that terrible name. 'No really – I'm fine. Fine …'

'That's OK, then.' Wilfred sat back, laid large gentle hands on his corduroy knees.

There was a pause, filled by the waiter's grudging arrival with her coffee. Wilfred accepted it on her behalf, paid the man, replaced his hands on his knees.

'We were discussing our tactics for tomorrow. You coming?'

Caroline sipped the coffee. It was spectacularly foul. She hoped the waiter felt better for it. 'Coming?' she said. 'I'm afraid I don't –'

'To the demo. They're hoping for a hundred thousand. We're the south coast delegation.'

'I see.'

But she didn't. And it showed.

'Where you been, Ethel?' The black man – George, was it? – leaned across the table toward her. 'Don't you care what happens? Don't they have Disappearances in your parts?'

'Of course they do.' Yes, they really did.

'And you leave it at that? You're happy to leave it at that?'

She groped. Distantly, and uncertainly, a penny dropped. 'You're the Ostriches Out people,' she said.

'Put it there, Ethel.' They shook hands. 'You've seen the present lot – they're head-in-the-sanders, every one. And liars, too.'

She smiled now, on familiar ground. 'An occupational disease,' she said comfortably. 'Of politicians, I mean.'

'And that's supposed to be an excuse?'

His anger jolted her. Something was wrong. Possibly she'd learned her radicalism in the wrong school. 'Not an excuse, George. Just the way things are.'

Wilfred was filling a large meerschaum pipe. 'They do lie to us, you know, Ethel. It's part of their policy of playing down the true scale of the emergency. And their failure to do anything about it.'

It was like talking to a page from *Groundswell*. 'Isn't there an all-party commission?'

'Shit.' George pounded the table. 'And have you seen its budget apportionment? No, ma'am – they'd much rather put themselves up as the folks that gave us Moondrift. I tell you, shit, if they put half as much into stopping the

Disappearances as they pour into developing cut-rate electricity, the Fetherlite Cell, their goddamned oil-free environment, then we'd have –'

But his words had jogged her memory. 'Oh, my car,' she cried. Her car. She'd driven it down into the city. She'd actually driven it. 'I'm sorry,' she said. 'But I don't know where I've put my car. It's a blue city electric.'

George spread his arms, turned to his companions. 'The lady don't know where she put her blue city electric. Stop the world, you people – she's lost her blue city electric.'

Wilfred stirred. 'That's a mite rough, George. She only –'

'No, man, I mean it. Maybe what she needs is a Disappearance of her own. Like Annabel here, and a mother gone. Or Barry and his two sisters – two, like, in one week. Or –'

'It doesn't matter.' Caroline got up abruptly, knocking over her chair. 'I can perfectly well buy myself another.' Which was childish. But if she couldn't join them, then – 'And Annabel and Barry can go stuff themselves. Do you think a Disappearance makes them saints, or something?'

Some have sainthood thrust upon them. But not her. Haverstock was irrelevant. She walked away from the table then, calmly and wisely.

She walked away, retracing her steps through the trees and the music, and the slow, drifting people. At once she lost her way. But her head was perfectly clear, and at least she knew why she'd come there, to the colored lights, and the music. She knew what they were all about, the colored lights and the music. And the tutti-frutti woman, any woman, any man, could have used her. If she'd only been drunk enough, even the tutti-frutti woman. Whom she'd never even seen.

She stopped walking, leaned against a tapered concrete pot. In the aftermath, tired and calm and self-compassionate, she waited.

Oddly enough it wasn't George who came after her, acting out of character because the Georges of this world always did. It was a girl who came after her. Possibly Latvian Jane. She put an arm around Caroline's waist.

'Was it your husband?' she said softly.

But the moment came and went. Came and, so dangerous, went.

'I think I remember a stack of cinemas,' Caroline told her. 'And a man in a mauve dress suit.'

After which it was only a matter of minutes before they found Caroline's blue city electric and Latvian Jane could pat her hand, and kiss her cheek, and go back to her friends.

THREE

Addis Ababa. 6/29/86. Following the worldwide pattern, Ethiopian health authorities announce a drastic improvement in their country's nutritional standards. Three years of Moondrift have transformed windswept, impoverished hillsides into verdant pastures. Irrigation plans are well advanced, and grain production is rising steadily. The entire nation is experiencing an unprecedented period of prosperity. Infant mortality is already down by an impressive 300%.

Richard and Caroline met again at the funeral. The day was fine, and Haverstock Trenchard's friends had turned out in force, theatrically somber as they waited by the open grave. The spectacle of it and them deterred Richard, who chose to loiter unobtrusively at the gate to the necropolis, thinking that there were several other ways in which he might have been more profitably employed.

There was, for example, a Mr Mandelbaum still in his daybook, whose wife had reportedly fainted in front of a mobile electric crane. Richard had the names and addresses of forty-seven witnesses, and the whole case sounded fairly straightforward. But one never knew.

He might also have spent the afternoon downtown, sorting out Rose-Ann. She needed it. Last night they'd had a flaming row. He couldn't remember what it had been about – he seldom could – but it had left him curiously unexhilarated. It hadn't been made up in bed, either. And five minutes after he'd moved through onto the divan in the spare room, he'd heard Rose-Ann snoring. *Snoring* … He should never have given her that lift in the first place. Eight or nine months ago, and he'd been stuck with her ever since. And who needed it? With forty thousand almost in the bank, who needed it?

Five days a week at least she worked in that lousy Pizza Parlor. Two above the legal maximum, saying she'd be lost without it. What sort of a woman was that, for God's sake? No, he'd have been far better off spending the afternoon downtown, sorting out Rose-Ann.

But he was a man of his word. He'd told Mrs Trenchard he'd be at the funeral, so here he was. Or more or less. Loitering in a black tie, bought specially, at the gate to the necropolis.

Besides, he had an investment to protect.

At three thirty sharp the cortege arrived: one unimpressive black limo and the hearse. Obviously they weren't straining themselves for Mrs Trenchard's two fifty. But then, why should they, when the whole thing was a bloody charade anyway?

The limo door was opened, and Mrs Trenchard got out. No, alighted. And such was her alighting that in an instant he forgot the moment's falseness, and the brown-eyes corpse of the blue-eyed Haverstock Trenchard that was being shunted out of the hearse at that very minute. So poised and dignified and elegant. And her gaze so discreetly downcast. And her soft gray dress so bewitchingly feminine. He could have wept for her.

Caroline looked about her. She was rattled. They'd taken the body early, and its clothes, and then there'd been the inquest. No hitches there. But then, after lunch, they'd kept her waiting far too long in the car outside their premises for the hearse to be ready. She felt herself to be all angles and pins. If there was one thing above all others that she'd fought against all through her life with Haverstock, it was unpunctuality. Yet even now, from beyond the Singing, or wherever he was, he had managed to inconvenience her. Admittedly, they'd made up the time on the way to the necropolis. But that wasn't the point.

She looked about her, saw in the distance Haverstock's friends. Twenty of them, at least. *A funeral, my dear – how impossibly quaint*. She lowered her gaze again and began to walk, very slowly, up the gravel path toward them. A penny for the peep show. She'd make them regret such a reckless expenditure.

She arrived at the graveside and stood, opposite Haverstock's friends, quite motionless. Knowing that the coffin being taken out of the hearse had nothing to do with Haverstock made her pose easier, her grief more real. The poor dead, brown-eyed young man had seemed so innocent. For the first time, she wondered how he'd come to break his poor neck. And what his poor relatives were doing without him. Surely he'd been deeply loved …

The coffin was carried past her and shuffled into position. She risked a glance, a gentle, grateful smile across it. Humphrey was there. And Jonno and Paul. And Runcorn and Fritzie and Jason and Clogs. And the women: Bathsheba, Jewel and Celia, Edwina and Meg. And further back, Henry, Mirabelle, Harriet, Damien, James … A funeral, my dear – how impossibly quaint.

Jonno caught her eye, and fluttered perky fingers. Celia nudged him. The gesture froze.

The vicar – out of the two fifty a measly ten – began to read the service. She bent her head over the coffin and tried not to listen to his words. *In sure and certain knowledge of the Resurrec* – dear God, what in this sad improvisation of a life was sure (except death or Disappearance) and certain?

But then the memory of the poor, brown-eyed young man came to her. This was *his* funeral. And his certainties had assuredly not been hers. So perhaps the words were true after all. In sure and certain knowledge of the Resurrection. His truth. And not merely an archaic, despairing gesture of defiance.

She began to cry. And sensed Haverstock's friends, for all the wrong reasons, shifting their feet. And felt lonely. Lonelier even than before.

When the time came she took the offered trowel, scattered ritual soil. It didn't matter that the undertaker's man who gave her the trowel must know the facts, thinking her therefore the hammiest actress since Jeanette MacDonald. It was the brown-eyed young man's truth. Or if not his, then *somebody's.*

Richard had sidled closer. His tie, if nothing else, gave him the right. And he was intrigued. Moved, also. When his parents had bought theirs at eighty on the thruway there'd been the Golden Gateway Chorale in Enfolding Quadraphonics. He'd been moved then too, but differently. And his sister whispering all the time about the caterers' men and the buffet for after.

Mrs Trenchard, he could see quite well, had other, finer things on her mind. Not that he hadn't come down off his cloud and seen her performance for the sham it was. But she still had style. He'd known it from the start. And admired it. And hated it.

Suddenly the business around the grave appeared to be over. And Mrs Trenchard's friends, a sickly gang of all sorts, were moving forward. But Mrs Trenchard herself had turned in his direction.

'Mr Wallingford,' she called, coming down the path toward him. 'How good of you to come.'

Good of him? When she knew bloody well he had his investment to protect?

She took his hand. 'You must have another name?' she murmured softly.

He was disconcerted. 'It's Richard,' he said. 'Dickie to my friends.'

'And you may call me Caroline.' She retained his hand, leaned forward and placed her lips against his cheek. Then she drew him back with her into the circle of her terrifying friends.

'Caro darling – quite choke-making. I'm positively overcome.'

'A stroke of genius, duck. Pure genius – how Haverstock would have *loved* it.'

'The most marvelous touch – our dearly beloved Beast going out in a blaze of Judeo-Christian splendor.'

Caroline experienced a moment's regret, presenting herself to Mr Wallingford in such a context. But he might well be impressed, poor man. And she'd needed a friend. Of her own. Of her very own, a friend.

'Celia pet, this is Richard. Humphrey, this is Richard. Richard Wallingford.'

She watched them sizing him up. Their surprise at this unexplained stranger. This intruder, rather.

'Greetings … Greetings, Richard Wallingford.'

She knew his suit was wrong. And his genteel, 'Charmed, I'm sure,' was wrong also. But she didn't care. Their opinion of him, of the two of them, was of no concern to her whatsoever.

For the moment, anyway, they took him in their stride, moved quickly on. They'd come back to him later.

'Caro, poppet, condolences, con*do*lences.' Jonno first. 'I'm shattered, my dear. Absolutely shattered. I mean, poor dear Haverstock …'

'It was a surprise to me too, Jonno.'

'You poor dear thing, of *course* it was.'

Paul's turn. 'We come to bury Caesar, not to praise him.'

'Flattery, Paul, will get you nowhere.'

Now Humphrey. 'I truly grieve. But then, I was his publisher.'

'We both were, Humphrey.'

The effort was wearing her down. Even her. She disengaged her hand. 'The vicar,' she said abruptly. 'I must just go and have a word with the vicar.'

She walked away, leaving them. And, at their mercy, poor, wrong Mr Wallingford. But just then, if she'd stayed, she'd have burst into tears. Or flailed about her with the machete she didn't have.

'I'm grateful, Vicar,' she said. 'I really am.'

He'd been waiting for her. 'Poetry, Mrs Trenchard. It weaves its own magic.'

'No,' she said earnestly. 'More than that.'

'Belief?' He smiled. 'I think not, Mrs Trenchard.'

She met his placid gaze. 'Then what the hell are you here for?'

'My belief – your magic. It sometimes helps.'

'Your magic too, I hope.'

'There is that.'

'And "sometimes helps" seems hardly enough.'

'Some would find it a becoming modesty.'

She was disappointed. 'Anyway, I just wanted to say thank you.'

'We might talk, Mrs Trenchard. You might come and see me.'

'I don't think so.'

'No. So I'm keeping you from … from those people.'

He might have said 'your friends.'

'More than magic,' she said, 'but less than belief. Is that possible?'

'The mistake, Mrs Trenchard, is to underrate magic. Good day, ma'am.'

Out of the two fifty, a measly ten. She fumbled in her purse. 'For the widows and orphans?' she suggested.

'Post it to me tomorrow.'

'Tomorrow I shall have forgotten.'

'Very well then. For the widows and orphans.'

She went slowly back to Haverstock's friends. A sane man, the vicar. And confession, so they claimed, was good for the soul. Possibly she *did* underrate magic. She went slowly back to Mr Wallingford.

'Er … not for very long. Not for very long at all, really.' Richard saw Mrs Trenchard coming, turned to her gratefully. How long had they known each other – he didn't know what she wanted him to say. Nor what he wanted to say. Nor, under the present scrutiny, lacking her style, how to say it.

'You're back,' he muttered. Thank God. And fingered his tie, specially bought.

'Richard. You must forgive me.' She touched his arm lightly, faced her claustrophobic friends. 'We met yesterday. Richard works for the Accident and General Insurance Company.'

He dwindled. But she was quite right – it was bound to come out, sooner or later. And there was nothing to be ashamed of, really, in working for AGIC. In the field of personal insurance they were outstanding.

'How absolutely fascinating. You're a useful man to know, Ricardo.'

'I … I do my best.'

'What a refreshing thought. These days most people seem to do their worst.'

Mrs Trenchard stared at him. 'What a shit you are, James.'

James, in faded jeans, gave her two fingers. Richard would have liked to punch him.

'Children, children …' The balding gent this, with bifocals, in a baggy business suit that must have cost three hundred. 'Let us not bicker, my children. Let us not bicker.'

'At Haverstock's going-away party, old man? Perish the thought. Sweetness and light. We all know what a fellow Hav was for sweetness and light.'

And Mrs Trenchard kept her style. 'If this were really my husband's party,' she said briskly, 'he'd be asking you all back to the house for a booze-up. But it's not, and I'm not.'

The words lay there. The sickly gang of all sorts stared at them.

Then, from Humphrey of the bifocals. 'Bless you, duck, of course you're not. Drinks are *chez moi*. You can drown your sorrows back at my place.'

'What sorrows are those, Humphrey?'

'We shall ignore that, Caro. You aren't yourself.' His gaze shifted. 'Don't you agree, Ricardo?'

Richard felt his face grow hot. 'If you want my opinion,' he said, 'I don't know why any of you ever came to this funeral at all.'

There was more he wanted to say, much more, but the words refused to come. Silence ensued, filled only with the scrape of shovels.

Then, from James, 'Out of the mouths of babes and truck drivers.'

Which earned Humphrey's instant, 'Take him away, will you, Edwina?' Lightened quickly to, 'Put him back under his stone.'

Richard watched, his fists clenched behind his back, aware that in some obscure way he had been insulted, and Mrs Trenchard too, as the fattish, youngish woman led James off down the path. Lucky thing they were on hallowed ground – he'd have clobbered the little git otherwise.

And he would have.

Caroline smoothed one eyebrow. She wondered if she should try explaining to Humphrey that there was a difference between feeling no identifiable sorrow at the loss of her husband and actually denying the whole of their years together. Her trap had not been of Haverstock's making. She was no freer now than she had ever been.

But the moment was wrong. And the company. And Humphrey would have recognized his error by now. It was just that he'd been trying too hard to keep up. Which perhaps was what they all did.

No, she thought coldly, looking around. Not all.

'I suppose it's a question of reverence,' she told him. The word wasn't right, but she let it go. Nostalgia would have been wrong too. 'And wakes aren't possible any more. But it was kind of you, Hump, to ask me.'

'Think nothing of it, duck.' He patted her arm – what she wouldn't have done, dear God, for a father – and turned to the others. 'The offer still stands, though, for all you scabrous lot. My place, as soon as you can make it.'

She looked around for Mr Wallingford. He was, unsensed, close by her side. For exhibition purposes only. Poor Mr Wallingford. While Humphrey went out among Haverstock's friends, murmuring discreetly.

Would even a Singing unite them? She very much doubted it.

She smiled at Mr Wallingford. 'Satisfied?' she said spitefully.

He jumped. 'Pardon?'

Richard looked away. All this prancing and posturing – he'd forgotten what he was really there for. And he couldn't make her out. She'd called him Richard, introduced him as her friend. So why remind him now?

'Course I'm satisfied,' he said.

'And the check?'

'Mr Caldwell's promised it for tomorrow.' The name enlarged him, his scope, his power. 'Mr Caldwell's my departmental manager.'

'Bully for Mr Caldwell.'

'But I can still stop the check, mind.' A lie. But if she could put in the needle, then so could he. 'Any time, you know. I can still stop it.'

'And I thought you were my friend.'

'Me, Mrs Trenchard? You must be joking.'

Mr Wallingford and Mrs Trenchard: no longer strangers. Yet hardly more. And certainly nothing *unsuitable*.

The man she called Hump came drifting back. Richard noticed scurf on his rucked-up, expensive collar. He spoke to Mrs Trenchard. 'Does this embargo on wakes extend to the *fest*-thing I mentioned over the phone?'

She frowned. 'It ought to.'

'What a pity … I need hardly say, duck, that the invitation includes Ricardo. Couldn't you see your way?'

'Not if you persist in calling him that.'

'Too late, alas. He is named. Identified. Nay, immortalized.'

Richard stirred. Did they think he was deaf, or something? 'Look here,' he began.

'Would you like to come?' Mrs Trenchard asked him. 'To Humphrey's *fest*-thing?'

Humphrey turned in his toes, looked modestly down at them. 'It's not really mine, you know. It's the author's. And his name isn't Glancing after all. My secretary tells me it's Fulch.'

But Mrs Trenchard took no notice. 'Would you like to come to Humphrey's *fest*-thing?' she insisted.

'I might,' Richard said loudly, 'if I knew what it bloody was.'

And the sun shone brightly down on the well-mown necropolis. And the gravediggers were patting the last of the dry, sandy soil onto the narrow mound above the coffin of the man who was not Haverstock Trenchard. And Humphrey was genuinely apologetic.

'My dear fellow, forgive me. A foolish affectation … a horror of the commonplace … two words where one would do … There is a party planned, Ricardo. This evening at eight, on a riverboat. A party to celebrate the publication of a book. I am the book's publisher, you see, and I would be pleased if you and dear Caro here could come and help us enjoy ourselves.'

A party on a riverboat? Another life, a different league. A new, forty thousand in the bank, future. Richard was filled with passionate desire.

'What would I have to wear?' He'd hire it. Anything. Rush off to the shops now, before they closed.

'Wear what you like, old chap. Absolutely what you like. The things you've got on now would do very nicely.'

Hardly. Not for a party on a riverboat. Not for another life, another league. He remembered his blue velvet, double-breasted smoking jacket.

'I've got a blue velvet, double-breasted smoking jacket.'

'Super. Just the thing. You'll come, then?'

Oh, *yes*. 'I don't mind.'

Besides, it was Mrs Trenchard's decision, really.

'What do *you* think?'

'I think we should go, Richard.'

'She thinks you should go, Ricardo.'

'Sounds all right.'

'I think it would do me good, Richard.'

'She thinks it would –'

'Can't do any harm.'

'Then you'll come?'

'I don't mind.'

Which was, Caroline realized, the maximum graciousness she'd ever get out of him. Though he was clearly delighted. She could have wrung his neck.

So why did she bother? He certainly wasn't her truck driver – heaven forbid – and never would be. She left that to other, sexier ladies. But she had no objection at all to people thinking he was. That way she'd get some peace. Her truck driver. Poor Mr Wallingford.

They were drifting away in threes and fours, Haverstock's friends, still camping it, here and there, up. But disconsolately. And the curious thing was that, now she had annexed Mr Wallingford, she didn't want to have hurt them. So she excused herself and hurried after them, moving gracefully from one group to the next. Haverstock's friends, but no longer – in the absence of Haverstock – her own enemies. Indeed, she would probably never see any of them again. So she moved among them, spreading her contrition, and sent them, liking her after all, away.

It couldn't be wrong, she thought, when it cost so little.

Humphrey was explaining how to find the riverboat. Richard did his best to pay attention. But he'd remembered Mr Mandelbaum's wife, run over by the mobile electric crane, and he was trying to fit her in to his afternoon's new timetable. The party on the riverboat began at eight, and he had to get home to have a bath and change his clothes. Three hours at least for the journey there and back. And Mr Mandelbaum lived an hour or so in the opposite direction. And the time was now well after four. So it couldn't be done. Not possibly.

'… upstream of the bridge,' Humphrey was explaining. 'First on the left on the road to the yacht club. Fisher's Moorings. You really can't miss it.'

'Fisher's Moorings,' Richard said blankly. 'No, that's fine.'

Perhaps he could phone Mr Mandelbaum, get the particulars, fill in the forms, catch the six o'clock mail with them. Then Mr Mandelbaum could sign them first thing in the morning and mail them back. After all, if he checked with a couple of the witnesses, he didn't see how he could go far wrong. Screw company regulations. He'd get the signed papers back the day after tomorrow. Bernie Caldwell would never know. And the case was completely straightforward.

'Fisher's Moorings,' he said again. 'First on the left, on the road to the yacht club.'

'Super, old man. You really can't miss it.'

But *which* yacht club, for fuck's sake?

Mrs Trenchard was returning from saying goodbye to her friends. He saw her reach the graveside and stand quietly beside it. Humphrey departed. The hearse had long ago driven off, and now the vicar and the gravediggers were following it. Richard waited in the sun. He thought Mrs Trenchard would probably know the way to the riverboat.

She lifted her gaze, smiled at him, and approached across the neat turf of the necropolis. 'Did you listen to the service?' she asked him.

It seemed such a long time ago. He tried to remember.

'*I* did,' she said.

She seemed to be expecting something. Cheering up? He remembered her smart-talking friends. And, for once, a quotation. He hoisted his trousers. 'Ashes to ashes and dust to dust – if the women don't get you the whiskey must …'

There was a long pause. Behind them, down on the road, a car hooted.

Finally she moved. 'Something like that,' she said, and began to walk back to the waiting limo. She seemed not to have liked his quotation.

He went after her. 'This party, Mrs Trenchard. I'll pick you up at seven.'

'I thought we'd agreed the name was Caroline.'

'Oh.' He was embarrassed. 'I thought … well, wasn't that just in front of your friends?'

'Don't you think I owe you?'

'Owe me?' The idea was novel. Unacceptable. He wanted her forty thousand, nothing more.

She stopped walking, met his gaze, held it in that upsetting way she had. 'All right,' she said gently, 'so I don't owe you. But if we're going to this party you'd better get used to calling me Caroline. For I shall certainly call you Richard.'

He looked in vain for a trace of the glad eye. But neither was she mocking him. 'About this party,' he mumbled. 'What say I pick you up at seven?'

She considered. 'Better make it seven thirty. We don't want to get there early, and it's forty minutes at the most to Fisher's Moorings.'

So she hadn't failed him. She'd been there before, and he should have been grateful. But he wasn't. It seemed to him that she'd been everywhere before.

'There's something I've been meaning to ask you,' he said. 'What was all that about babes and truck drivers?'

For the briefest of moments her face was defensively, uniquely blank. Then she recovered. 'It's a very long story,' she said, and walked on toward the limo.

He pursued her. 'And?'

'And I'll tell you some other time.'

'Tell me now.'

'No, Richard.'

The limo's chauffeur leaped out, opened the rear door, stood at funereal attention.

'Tell me.'

But Mrs Trenchard was thanking the chauffeur. 'Thank you so much,' she was saying.

She climbed in, and the chauffeur closed the limo door. Richard stood on the gravel drive, watching her. She was cheating him, he knew. And for the first time. Using the occasion, the obligations due to widowhood, playing by rules other than her own. He would never be able to trust her again. It was the most astonishing thought that he ever had.

As the chauffeur got in behind the wheel she wound down her window. 'It's their thick, hairy arms,' she said. 'All rather complicated. Please can it wait till later?'

Which was a cheat again. Shifting the responsibility. He addressed the heavens. 'Thick hairy arms?' he cried.

The limo glided forward, humming softly as it circled the grassy island and moved away down the drive. 'This evening,' Mrs Trenchard called from its window. 'I promise I'll explain this evening.'

Richard turned to the surrounding monuments. 'Don't bother,' he told them. 'Don't bloody bother.'

But he was going to the party, thick hairy arms or no thick hairy arms. And he had some telephoning to do first. So he ran to where he'd left his car, on the road outside the neat necropolis.

On Caroline's way home, just at the bottom of her street, there was a Singing. She slid back the glass partition. 'Please drive on,' she begged.

But the chauffeur pulled in to the side. 'It's more than my job's worth, madam.'

They waited in the Singing at the bottom of the hill up to her house. She'd have got out and run if she hadn't needed to set an example. And if there'd been anyone for her when she got there.

'That sort of thing gets back,' the chauffeur told her, his voice unnecessarily loud. 'I'm leaving end of the month, and I need the reference.'

On the sidewalks others ran. And a city electric went by, lurching improbably. Caroline leaned carefully back against the simulated hide upholstery.

'Leaving?' she asked.

'Getting out, madam. Out into the country. It's worse in the towns, you know.'

It wasn't, but she didn't argue. And the familiar sliding, tuneless voices filled the limo. And the smell of sweet synthetic roses. And they could easily go, either of them, at any second.

The chauffeur began to pound on the horn. 'It's against nature,' he shouted. 'These cars are air-conditioned, I tell you. It's against sodding nature.'

While Caroline, busy with her leaning back against the simulated hide upholstery, could think only of the limo's darkened interior corners, the exact conjunctions of side and roof and rear, and beckoning angles, their childish comfort. She would *not* seek it. She would *not* crouch and whimper. She would *not*.

The chauffeur, *sauve qui peut*, leaned his arms on the horn and kept them there. And the Singing rose above its blare, harmonies that moved and climbed and changed, shifting endlessly yet remaining endlessly the same.

Somewhere Caroline had read that they couldn't be recorded, that the finest acoustical equipment detected only silence. A nice refinement. But why, she wondered, should anyone have tried? And turned her face steadfastly away from the corners.

In due course the Singing stopped. Distressingly later the chauffeur released the horn. In a house close by children were screaming. Slowly the sweet smell of roses faded. The chauffeur wiped his face on a grubby white linen handkerchief.

'Why don't they do something?' he said. 'That's what we put them there for, isn't it? They ought to *do* something.'

One survived. If one was Caroline one made the gestures one thought important. No corners. Rationality. And marveled afterwards at such sad vainglory.

'May we go on now?' she asked.

The house's emptiness struck her in the face. She turned on the doorstep and waved to the chauffeur, but he was already driving away. She went in, closing the door behind herself. The emptiness was her own, no longer to be Haverstock's wife, whatever that might have meant. His widow, instead? Only, dear God, as a last resort.

She wandered from room to room – from Haverstock's room to Haverstock's room. His name, the sheer size of it, said everything. Big, like his books and his behavior. And, like his books and his behavior, deafening. Haverstock's wife – what *had* it meant? Effort. Composure. Smiling. Punctuality. Everything he hadn't wanted, because everything *she* hadn't wanted had been he. Irreproachable spite. It might not be why they had married – so long ago, submerged by years, the reason too foolish, forgotten – but it was why she'd stayed that way: the satisfactions of being irreproachably spiteful. But all that effort and composure, all that smiling punctuality, it took it out of one.

So what now instead? The chauffeur had said he was leaving the city. The vicar had suggested she might care to talk. And then there were the Disappearances. Surviving them was in itself quite an occupation.

She took a bath.

Then she dressed in her brightest, summeriest clothes, and went out for a walk up past the square to the High Park.

Then it was almost time to eat.

The High Park had been packed. Seething. Only two years ago, on a Wednesday, it would have been almost deserted. The Age of Moondrift. Riches. What the gods gave with one hand they took away with the other. And tipped Disappearances onto the scale for good measure. Perhaps, Caroline thought, she should get a job. Keep quiet about her sixty thousand coming from Mr Wallingford and join the laboring masses. She'd never had a job and – her social consciousness going so far and no further – she allowed the idea to intrigue her. With her English degree perhaps she should go into journalism. Journalists, for one thing, were exempt from the three-day work rule.

She dined early, just after six, in the Trattoria on Park Street that Haverstock had always avoided. But not, she told herself, for that reason.

Mr Wallingford. Richard. Over flatulent pasta (Haverstock had been quite right) she considered Mr Wallingford. Richard. Like the idea of the job, he intrigued her. Anthropologically he was quite a find. It diminished him – and herself, of course – to regard him so. But she truly couldn't help it. Like Haverstock, but so unlike Haverstock, he was such a different animal. She'd thought that before, she remembered. But defensively. Now, taking him to Humphrey's *fest*-thing, objectivity was possible. The sad, sad game of Ascendancies had been played and won. And tomorrow, after they'd exchanged checks, she'd never see him again.

She ordered a lemon water ice. It was within her power, naturally, to prolong the association. She could even see him in some manner taking Haverstock's place as the butt for her irreproachable spite. Which he probably wouldn't notice.

But *she* would.

She pushed the water ice away, untasted. It was gray. And Haverstock's going had given her the chance to make a new start. She could easily, for example, not be ready for Richard when he arrived at seven thirty. Be feminine and inferior. And thus patronize the poor man into one of Pavlov's dogs.

She refused coffee, got up and paid the excessive bill. Were new starts possible? she wondered. And the coffee would certainly have been disgusting.

Richard sweated as he hunched forward over the wheel of his yellow city electric. All the way around the Fairthorpe Two-tier the traffic lights had been against him. Mr Mandelbaum, too, had been against him. And even the witnesses. Not to mention Rose-Ann.

The witnesses first. They hadn't been at home. Eleven calls it had taken, just to talk to two. But at least those two had confirmed the facts as they appeared on the claim form. Then Mr Mandelbaum: he'd been old, and muddled, and rather deaf. Half an hour's shouting, simply to elicit the necessary particulars. Even then, Richard wasn't sure he'd understood about signing the form and immediately returning it. Followed by Rose-Ann, about whom the less said the better. And now the traffic lights. They shouldn't even have been there, not if the two-tier had been designed properly in the first place.

On the amber he accelerated away. Accelerated? In one of these electrics? That was a laugh. Still, he did his best. Thick hairy arms or no thick hairy arms, he wasn't going to keep Mrs Trenchard waiting. Men didn't. He mightn't know much, but he knew that for a fact. He turned up the radio. Its frenzy heartened him.

At last he was leaving the two-tier, skirting the High Park, driving down past the square with the modest stone mermaid. Suddenly he was filled with apprehension. Since quitting the necropolis he'd done nothing except fight the sheer perversities of fortune. Certainly he'd had no time to dread his coming transubstantiation. Not until this uncomfortable moment, drawing up outside Mrs Trenchard's house, at twenty-nine minutes past seven, in his blue velvet, double-breasted smoking jacket, with a white carnation in its buttonhole out of his own back garden. The perfect finishing touch, for all that Rose-Ann had taken it so badly. But now, sitting in his car outside Mrs Trenchard's house, suddenly the scale of his coming ordeal bore in upon him. Not least of which was the simple act of getting out of the car, and going up the steps, and ringing Mrs Trenchard's doorbell. When he didn't know who he was supposed to be.

He'd been introduced as Mr Wallingford of the Accident and General. A sufficient, and not unworthy, identity. Then Richard. Later, to her friends, he had become Ricardo. She'd invited him to the party, and he must call her Caroline. So what the hell were they? Friends? Business partners? Or simply, facing facts, blackmailer and victim?

Or was it just that she fancied him and had a bloody funny way of showing it?

She appeared in the doorway to her house, came obligingly down the steps he'd been dreading, leaned in at the car window.

'That carnation's all wrong,' she said.

Business partners, therefore. Damn it.

'You don't mind my telling you these things, I hope?'

'Of course not.' Bloody woman.

'On its own, you see, the jacket's fine. But the carnation makes it frankly overdone. I *do* hope you don't mind my mentioning it.'

'Not at all.' Stuck-up bitch. Who the hell did she think she was?

Angrily he snatched at his buttonhole. Then he checked himself. Another life, a different league – perhaps he'd better bow to her superior knowledge. The cunt.

'I bow to your superior knowledge,' he said, removing the carnation with great care and laying it down on the shelf above the dashboard. 'Shall we go now?'

He leaned across, opened the car door, and she got in beside him. She was wearing a dress of some roughly woven, gray-green silky stuff, her hair was loose, curving in elegantly just above her shoulders, and she brought with her a musky perfume, utterly entrancing. She was a stunner.

He jerked the car away from the curb. 'You were going to tell me about thick hairy arms,' he said fiercely.

She sat without speaking for so long that he thought she'd decided to ignore him. His resentment grew. They came to a junction; he asked her which way, and she pointed to the right. He was unappeased.

'It's an in-group thing,' she said at last. 'Really very stupid. You won't like it.'

He drove on grimly. A promise was a promise.

Mrs Trenchard sighed. 'A couple of years ago,' she said, 'one of Haverstock's friends was a girl called Lesley. She's not around any more – moved up north last September …'

She tailed off. Richard waited, not helping.

Suddenly she seemed to make up her mind. 'The joke,' she said crisply, 'was that Lesley had a passion for truck drivers. As lovers, you understand. They never lasted more than a week or two. But she could always pick up another. As long as they had thick hairy arms, she said, she wasn't fussy. And she gave them hell. The whole group did, one way or another. Christ, how they must have hated us.'

Richard was hot behind the ears. He gripped the wheel tightly, possessed by torrid visions of Lesley, and the vicarious joys of thick hairy arms about her body. His body. No, *her* body. And closed his eyes briefly in hasty revulsion.

'So?' he asked, his voice husky, but keeping to the point at issue.

Mrs Trenchard folded her hands in her lap. 'James's suggestion was that you were my truck driver.' She seemed to think this sufficient.

'But I don't have thick hairy arms.'

'The metaphor, Richard, is one of social and intellectual differences. Lesley is a Doctor of Philosophy. She's teaching now in one of the northern universities.'

Richard thought about it. The thick hairy arms. 'But you're not a Doctor of Philosophy.' He knew that much from the company file.

'James's suggestion,' she said impatiently, 'was that I had picked up a nasty dumb little man and was obliging him to fuck me.'

The car's wheel jerked, nearly sending them off the road. He fought it. He was disgusted. Half blind with fury. Nasty dumb little man – so that was how Mrs Trenchard thought of him. And bad language, too. Not even Rose-Ann, if she wasn't in one of her moods, called it that. He shifted his foot to the brake, preparing to stop the car so that he could throw the bloody bitch out.

'I'm truly sorry, Richard.' She touched his arm. 'James meant it as a joke, I think.'

'Very funny.'

'No, Richard. Not funny at all.'

Her voice was soft. He hestitated. Thick hairy arms. Revolting.

'What really matters, Richard, is that we both know it's nonsense.'

But what about the others? Her fancy friends – would they know it was nonsense? Would they know he wouldn't be caught dead doing that to her, not with a barge pole?

'And we won't be seeing him again, Richard. Not if I can help it.'

'But I'd like to,' he muttered, driving on. 'I'd like to see him again very much.' He balled his fist and pounded the wheel. Pictured what he would do.

Caroline relaxed, sat back, quietly watched his anger. She believed the violence he threatened. Indeed, it was for his anger's brightness that she'd let herself be cornered into spelling things out. A salutary contrast to her own indifference. She needed anger, its heat and spontaneity.

But was James worth it? Were any of them? The outrage, after all, was quite as much hers as poor Mr Wallingford's. And could she honestly say it merited the indignity, the inconvenience, of anger? Not for her own sake, perhaps. But certainly, thank God, for Mr Wallingford's, her different animal.

Presumably it was on account of this that she'd promised continuity. *We won't be seeing him again*, she'd said. Tomorrow and tomorrow and tomorrow ... She hoped Mr Wallingford hadn't noticed. But *she* had. After the event, admittedly, but she must have meant it unconsciously, even back when she'd said it.

She leaned forward, touched his arm again. 'Left here,' she said. 'Just after the railway bridge.'

For the sake of his anger? Yes. Its heat. Its spontaneity.

They drove on in silence for a while. She wondered what he was thinking. She should have known.

'Won't this James character be at the party?' he said.

She shook her head. 'Not a chance. Hump keeps his life in neat compartments. James belongs in the slummy one.' Which remark had implications. 'So do all today's lot, I suppose.'

She pondered this sad fact. 'But Haverstock was business as well,' she concluded cheerfully. 'And Humphrey's a great one for business.'

'So what about me?'

'You?'

'What compartment do *I* belong in?'

He could surprise her, after all. 'You're my friend,' she told him. 'And I'm not business. Not any more. I never was, really.' She hoped.

Several miles went by. They were getting near the river.

Suddenly Mr Wallingford bared his heart. 'What it boils down to is this,' he said. 'It's up to me what compartment I belong in.'

She didn't contradict him. She couldn't bring herself to. Even though – *vide* heat and spontaneity – she knew he was quite mistaken.

FOUR

La Scala, Milan. 6/30/86. Last night's audience at the Opera House was witness to a shocking tragedy, the Disappearance of Myfanwy Evans whose artistry in the taxing role of the Queen of the Night in *Die Zauberflöte* has been one of this season's principal attractions.

The Singing took place shortly after the beginning of the second act and, as is usual in this theater, Maestro Cantini interrupted the performance for its duration. Sadly, at the end of the Singing, it was discovered that Miss Evans had gone. (See obituary on p. 12.)

The performance was continued, however, the part of the Queen of the Night being taken at a moment's notice by the distinguished German soprano, Hilda Gerdheim. At the final curtain Miss Gerdheim received a standing ovation. There were flowers also, ribboned in black, for the gone Miss Evans.

Complimented on the efficiency of La Scala's arrangements, Maestro Cantini told reporters, 'I must not say that we have expected such a melancholy occurrence. But we have contingency plans. A complete second cast is always in attendance at the theater.'

Miss Gerdheim, a close personal friend of Myfanwy Evans, was not available for comment.

They met in the elevator, going up.

'Morning, Wallingford. Good God, man, you look rough.'

'A small celebration, Mr Caldwell.'

'And not so small either, by the look of it.'

Richard smirked. He wore his hangover with pride.

'Anyway, Wallingford, today's Thursday. You shouldn't be here. If the union men get to hear of this they'll have me shot.'

Thursday marked the beginning of Richard's five-day weekend. Normally he'd have lain in bed till nine or ten, dozing away the undesirable hours.

'Mrs Trenchard's check, sir. I thought I should deliver it.'

'A man for the cheap thrill then, are you?'

'A hundred thousand, Mr Caldwell. It doesn't often happen.'

'Too true. Those bastards upstairs – it's broken their hearts.' The elevator opened its doors at the eleventh floor. 'Then you're not really here, I take it.'

'Just dropping in, sir, to pass the time of day.'

'I thought as much. Union trouble I can do without.'

The hurdle, small though it was, appeared to have been surmounted. There had always been the slight possibility that Bernie Caldwell would insist on taking the check himself. It wouldn't have mattered very much, not with Mrs Trenchard believing he could still have second thoughts and demand an exhumation. But Richard was glad not to have to use that lie again. Not to Mrs Trenchard. Not now. Not after what had happened last night, at the party.

He followed Bernie Caldwell through into his office. The Thursday people looked up from their desks. He knew hardly any of their faces.

'Shan't keep you a moment,' Bernie Caldwell said. 'I'll just ring through for the Trenchard check.'

Richard propped himself in the doorway. He was glad he wouldn't have to lie to Mrs Trenchard. After last night they were almost friends … Taking her forty thousand, of course, was something else again. Sort of magnificent. Awe-inspiring. Certainly, when he dared believe in it, he found it so. To be honest, it scared him stiff.

Mr Caldwell finished on the telephone. 'By the way,' he said, punching the air, 'any snags with that swine Mandelbaum?'

Richard met his eye. 'Not that I could find, sir.'

'You checked the wife's body?'

'Frankly, sir, I wish I hadn't.' A nice touch that, to remember the mobile crane. Richard relaxed. Sometimes he surprised himself.

Mr Caldwell nodded understandingly, delivered a right cross followed by a left to the body. Today, it seemed, he was Muhammad Ali. 'And the witnesses?'

'I checked with two, sir.' Safe ground, this. 'Their evidence agreed in every substantive detail.'

Mr Caldwell paused. 'That's unusual.'

'They were watching the construction work, Mr Caldwell. Then the crane arrived. It had their full attention.'

Work always did. Mr Caldwell knew this, and was satisfied. He lowered his chin guard and sat down at his desk. 'Strictly between you and me, Wallingford,' he said neutrally, 'I have to tell you that we lost Deakin yesterday.'

'Gone, sir?'

'Out there, on this very floor. Working at his desk. One of our very best men.'

Richard remembered Deakin. A nice chap. A bit of a sex fiend, but a nice chap.

'I'm very sorry to hear it, Mr Caldwell.'

'So was I, Wallingford. It upset the girls terribly. Had to send most of them home …'

'You'll be seeing to his wife and kids, sir.'

Mr Caldwell looked sharply up at him. 'I already have. Company doctor owes me a favor or two. He's fixed it. Coronary thrombosis situation, brought on by overwork – and the whole floor as witness.' He bared his teeth in a smile that was more a snarl. 'And those bastards upstairs can think what they like. One of my own men … They'll pay, though. They'll pay.'

This was more than the usual, half-joking vindictiveness. This was real. Bernie Caldwell had heart, and guts, too. He'd never get another job if a thing like this got out.

Richard cleared his throat. 'You've done right, Mr Caldwell,' he said.

Thinking: and what have *I* done? The bastards upstairs would pay Mrs Trenchard, too. But it was hardly *her* welfare he'd risked his job for. And he'd never imagined that the day would come when Bernie Caldwell, of all people, would make him feel bad.

There was a movement behind him. He turned, stepped to one side to let the messenger come through the door. She laid an envelope on Mr Caldwell's desk, beside Mr Caldwell's gilt-and-onyx presentation clock. Presentation for exactly what Richard had never got close enough to read.

'Compliments of the chief accountant,' the messenger said.

Mr Caldwell picked up the envelope, opened it. The girl was leaving, but he called her back. 'Here, what's-your-name, have a look at this.' He held out Mrs Trenchard's check. 'You won't often see the like of that, my dear. Not in *this* office.'

The girl took the check, and read the figures on it. 'Flipping heck –'

'Quite so, my dear. And all for one wealthy widder woman … You *would* say the swine was wealthy, wouldn't you, Wallingford?'

Richard jumped. 'Mrs Trenchard? Er … wealthy?'

'Upper-income bracket. I mean, you've met the swine. Been to her house. The only one of us who's had that privilege.'

'I … er, I don't really think Mrs Trenchard's a swine, sir.' The least he could do. 'And not really all that wealthy.'

'They all are, Wallingford. Swines, every one.' He turned back to the girl. 'Don't you agree, my dear?'

She put the check down on his desk, as if it were suddenly very hot. 'I –'

'Only to be outdone in their swinishness, in fact, by us insurance fellers. Don't you agree, my dear? Don't you agree?'

It wasn't right, Richard thought, taking out his frustration on the wretched messenger. 'I suppose you could call Mrs Trenchard wealthy,' he put in quickly. 'She'd have to have been, to have kept up the premiums.'

'Point taken, Wallingford. Point taken.' Bernie Caldwell smiled charmingly at the messenger. 'Run along then, what's-your-name. Run along …'

The girl, mystified, ran obediently along.

'My mistake, Wallingford, is to care. Like, you know, *care*.'

'Yes, sir ...' Caring was double-edged. In some contexts, positively dangerous. 'May I take the check now, Mr Caldwell?'

'Be my guest, old man.' He replaced the check in its envelope and handed it across the desk. 'And for God's sake get a receipt.'

Going down in the elevator Richard found time to be grateful for Mr Caldwell's outburst. It had shouted down the uncomfortable murmurings of his own conscience. He'd taken the check without a second thought. But anyway, after last night, he was bound to Mrs Trenchard by more than just a shared interest in life insurance.

Caroline, too, in her high white, wealthy house, was remembering the previous night's party. At half past nine she was still dawdling over her breakfast – not because she felt in the least unwell (she was, unlike Richard, far too inured to pot and alcohol for that), but because breakfast, even when one served it to oneself, was a meal meant for dawdling over. The breakfast room, floors, walls, ceiling and curtains all in the same pretty pattern of pale spring flowers, looked delightfully out onto the terrace and the electrically heated garden beyond. Admittedly the table, decoratively laid, bore principally a bowl containing half a grapefruit, a meager rack of dietary rusk, and a tub of sugar-free marmalade. Which was how one kept one's self-respect. But – augmented by an ample coffeepot, the newspaper, and the morning's mail – breakfast was still a meal meant for dawdling over.

Caroline had slit each of the many envelopes open with her pearl-handled paper knife. Only when every one was opened had she laid down the knife and looked at their contents. For Haverstock: a letter from his Japanese publisher, fan mail from his tax inspector, bills, a reminder that his three-day work rule exemption permit ran out at the end of the month, and a circular offering a miracle copper bracelet guaranteed to protect its wearer from Disappearances for a period of not less than twelve calendar months.

Too late, alas. Too late.

For herself: innumerable condolences, mostly from people she couldn't remember (like Haverstock's family), a small Central Generating Authority payment voucher for Moondrift collected, a letter from Haverstock's agent, and an identical bracelet offer.

The guarantee intrigued her. How, she wondered, did one ever invoke it?

The letter from Haverstock's agent she left till last. It seemed, distressingly, that she was Haverstock's literary executor. She didn't want to be. Books she was sick of. Books – Haverstock's in particular, but any books at all, really – she wanted nothing whatever to do with them, to do with the writing, editing, publishing, or marketing of them. Even the reading of books, she thought, could probably wait a year or two. Especially after last night.

She laid down the agent's letter. Last night's party on the riverboat had begun like any other literary *fest*-thing. It had gone on that way, too. Rival authors, agents, publishers, and a smattering of media men, all sharpening their knives and ignoring totally the ten million copies of Fulch's book laid out on every available horizontal surface. And, at the center of it all, totally unignorable, alas, in a scarlet boiler suit, the egregious author himself. Fulch. Fulch by name and Fulch by nature. Belonging, Caroline saw at once, at the slummiest end of the slummiest of Humphrey's compartments. If he hadn't, for that one night alone, been business. He and most of his fellow guests with him.

Mr Wallingford, however, had enjoyed himself enormously. On arrival he had been offered what she truly believed had been his very first joint, and his resultant very first high had made him fireproof. Proof against humiliating party games. Proof against the shattering patronage, of Haverstock's widow's friend, of the media men. Proof against the riverboat's pseudo-Edwardian decor. Proof even against the heavy, lustful mockery of the girl who had eventually taken him, and his blue velvet, double-breasted smoking jacket, off to a private cabin and the doubtful pleasure of her thighs.

Caroline, too, against all the odds, had enjoyed herself. Four bright young publishers had sung barbershop harmonies on a platform in the main saloon. Humphrey, sticking to gin, had become almost human and had discussed Haverstock with her, as if he too had been almost human. 'It really used to hurt,' Humphrey drunkenly told her, 'seeing how lonely the two of you were.'

But then the sound of the Singing began.

The party froze, remained for an instant ice-still, then shattered into untidy fragments. Became just people. People: noisy people, quiet people, people half-gone, people (like Mr Wallingford) half-come, fierce people, frightened people, people taken in laughter, and people taken in weeping. Caroline saw hot Mr Wallingford appear in the door of his private cabin and stand, cooling visibly, by no means decent in shirt and socks, staring blankly up at the beams of the deck overhead. While up on the stage at the far end of the saloon the four bright young publishers, silent now and tipsily wise, linked arms in a solemn line and danced, snapping their fingers.

As the sound of the Singing continued the commotion, in general, died down. People crouched, glancing uneasily upward. A pregnant woman cleared a space for herself and lay supine on the floor beneath a night-black skylight, challenging the dark with the hugeness of her belly. 'Take us,' she cried. 'Take us if you dare.'

How interesting it was, Caroline thought. *I shall lift up mine eyes unto the hills, from whence cometh my help …* And from whence, apparently, came the source of the Disappearances, also. *Look down on me, oh Lord …* How interesting it was, Caroline thought, from the innocent, delusory refuge of her corner.

Until there was a shout from out on deck, and some man had stepped overboard, and enough of the party found communality enough to throw ropes, and climb down into the skiff, and even to dive in after him. All of which lusty effort, while unsuccessful in rescuing the wretched suicide, was quite sufficient to obscure completely the anxious cry of 'Where's Fulch?' from within the saloon behind them, delivered by some loyal Fulch supporter.

'Where's Fulch?' he bleated. 'My God, he's gone …'

And again, 'Fulch? Fulch – where are you? Oh God, oh God, he's gone, I say …'

It was a fine, passionate award-winning performance. But only Caroline, in her corner, heard it, and Mr Wallingford without his trousers, and possibly two or three others similarly deficient in communality.

So that when, finally, the sound of the Singing ended, and the people out on deck trooped back into the saloon, and the conversation was of poor George's suicide – or was it Henry's? One couldn't be sure – there was nothing left for poor not-gone-at-all Fulch to do but crawl out from under his table and own up. The Singing, he admitted, had been a put-on. A joke. He'd been planning it for weeks. Since a true Singing couldn't be recorded, Fulch had synthesized one onto a stereo cassette which he'd brought to the party in the hip pocket of his scarlet boiler suit. He'd smuggled in a pair of bellows, too, impregnated with cheap rose scent. These, for some reason, had not worked. But the cassette had worked – so well, in fact, that nobody had noticed the absence of roses. It had worked so well that poor George – or was it Henry? – had actually killed himself.

The point of the joke, now unfortunately lost, had been for Fulch to pretend to go, and hide under the table, and listen to what people said about him after they thought he'd gone, and then jump hilariously out to embarrass them. Instead, when they returned to the saloon, they'd been far more interested in poor George. Or was it Henry?

By that time Mr Wallingford had put his trousers on. But he still wasn't back at his sharpest. He strode up to Fulch, still struggling with his zip. 'Do you mean to say,' he asked, 'that you staged this show for *fun?*'

And when Fulch agreed, not altogether happily, that he had, Mr Wallingford abandoned the zip at half-mast and started hitting him. Blackly, and in deadly earnest. So that Fulch, taken by surprise, and not quite without shame, and anyway not accustomed to that sort of thing, fell down and could be kicked instead.

Caroline noticed that nobody, not Humphrey, not the loyal Fulch supporter, not even the four bright young publishers, interfered.

Afterwards though, when Mr Wallingford had stopped his kicking, they didn't choose to speak to him. Except Humphrey, and the erstwhile loyal Fulch supporter, and the four bright young barbershop publishers. Which pleased Caroline more than she could say.

She didn't concern herself with Mr Wallingford's motives. For all she cared he might have plowed into Fulch simply because the phoney Singing had interrupted him at the very moment of getting his rocks off. But *someone* had needed to teach Fulch a lesson, and – if Mr Wallingford hadn't been there – nobody would have, and Humphrey appreciated this, and the four bright young barbershop publishers, and even the Fulch supporter, vociferous now in his overdue apostasy. And Caroline was pleased because, at this late hour, after a long and painful day, she found she cared what people thought. What people not just business thought. Of Mr Wallingford. And therefore, by extension (an unprecedented concept) of her.

But Mr Wallingford, alas, had mistaken localized gratitude for generalized acceptance. On the way home in his car he'd said as much. 'I went down all right,' he'd said. 'Don't you reckon I went down all right?'

So, 'Of course, Richard. Of course you went down all right,' she'd answered, knowing in her heart that he'd gone down all wrong. Even without his carnation, he'd gone down all wrong …

Sitting now at her breakfast table, staring at Haverstock's agent's letter and remembering poor Mr Wallingford, she suddenly thought – and genuinely for the first time since their conversation at Haverstock's funeral – of the check, of the hundred thousand he'd soon be bringing her. And of the forty thousand she'd be giving him back.

Theirs was an interesting relationship. She should by rights have despised him, hated him. And he should by rights have been simply using her. But things between them weren't like that. If anything (for she had few illusions) they were the other way around.

And even that was a simplification.

Using him for what? Certainly there was the void left by Haverstock's going, but she liked Mr Wallingford too much to use him to fill it. And this in itself was a further mystery, since there was nothing even remotely likable about Mr Wallingford … except perhaps his anger. And surely poor Mr Wallingford was more than just his anger?

Who, then, was using whom? For *someone*, of a surety, was using *someone*.

Caroline believed herself to be an intelligent, imaginative young woman. She tried, therefore, to exercise these gifts by putting herself in Mr Wallingford's place. What did he think of her? How insensitive, really, was he? What were his dreams and aspirations? In short, once the exchange of checks had been effected, would she be seeing him again?

A reversion from his place rapidly to her own that Caroline, frowning thoughtfully at her breakfast table, quite failed to catch.

Richard sat in his car in the basement of AGIC House and stared at Mrs Trenchard's check. Reaction had set in now, and his hand was trembling so much that he could scarcely read the figures. One hundred thousand … the zeros jostled and blurred till they might well have been a million. Still, it didn't do to be greedy. One hundred thousand was quite enough: shared forty-sixty, the beginning of a beautiful friendship. Especially after last night.

He'd gone down all right. He hadn't shamed her. Pot-smoking, rude games with balloons, chatting up classy birds, he might have been at it all his life. And the bird he'd finally almost made it with – would have done, but for that bloody Fulch – she'd been bowled over by the size of him. She'd actually said so. His muscles and the size of him. His wit, too – she'd even commented on his witty conversation. No, he was sure he hadn't shamed Mrs Trenchard. Even the punch-up had gone down a treat.

He put the check back into its envelope with the receipt. The beginning of a beautiful friendship … Unless of course – nasty thought – unless of course it was really Mrs Trenchard he should have taken into that private cabin, impressed with his wit, his muscles and the size of him. Perhaps it was expected. She hadn't *said* anything, mind – but then, she wouldn't. A proud woman, Mrs Trenchard.

But he couldn't have. Not *her*. Of all the birds in the world, not her. It wouldn't have seemed right. For God's sake, he didn't even want to. Bloody woman. Stuck-up bitch.

Suddenly he was no longer eager to deliver Mrs Trenchard's check. The end, maybe, and not the beginning at all. Not that he cared. Bloody woman. But he decided to go and see Mr Mandelbaum instead. Remembering Bernie Caldwell's anxious questions.

Stuck-up bitch. Why couldn't she be normal, and bowled over, like other women?

What, he wondered, had been that classy bird's name? He didn't, to be honest, remember asking her.

Mr Mandelbaum lived in a glass and blue tile condominium. It looked several sizes grander than Mr Mandelbaum had sounded over the telephone. Grander, too, than Mr Mandelbaum in the flesh, bedroom-slippered and dusty, ushering Richard into his oyster lounge with its gold brocade suite.

'The TV's there, young man. Four hundred for it since three months. And now just blue. I do not pay four hundred for just blue. My neighbor tells me the tube is shot to hell. Is that right, young man? Is that fair practice?'

Small brown feathers were clinging to Mr Mandelbaum's creased alpaca jacket. Richard explained who he was. Mr Mandelbaum sighed, and took yellow pills from an antique silver snuffbox.

'The forms I have ready,' he said, pointing sadly to a small gilt table. 'My neighbor carry them to the post office after lunch.'

Richard explained that this was no longer necessary, he would take the forms himself.

'My neighbor is a good man. In this terrible wicked world a really good man, I tell you.'

Richard explained that he'd like to look over the forms before he took them, just to make sure they were in order. And look over the remains of the late Mrs Mandelbaum, too, while he was on the premises. Just to make sure.

Mr Mandelbaum crouched over the TV, turned it on with stubby, mittened fingers. The program, by the sound of it, concerned Bessarabian macaws. But the screen, as he had claimed, was uniformly blue.

'You're too late, young man,' he said. 'They come last night. I am in my nightshirt, I tell you.'

Richard explained again that he wanted to look over the remains of the late Mrs Mandelbaum. It was part of his job, he said. While he was on the premises. Just to make sure.

Mr Mandelbaum turned up his dusty collar. 'Berthe is not here, I say. They take her away last night. I am in my nightshirt, but she is needed. And it is part of the deal.'

Richard stiffened. 'What deal?'

'No deal. I do not say that. They tell me I do not say that.'

Richard leaned forward, switched off the TV. 'What deal, Mr Mandelbaum?'

'Do not ask it.' Tears shone painfully in Mr Mandelbaum's eyes. 'There is always need for more bodies, they tell me. Young bodies, old bodies, always need for more bodies.'

Gently Richard took his arm. 'How much did they pay you, sir?'

'Not enough. Nothing. They pay me nothing. A private matter. You do not ask. One hundred.'

Mentally Richard doubled that. Then remembered how little Mrs Trenchard had paid for her end of the service, and halved it again. The organization had to make a profit somewhere.

'How did you know to send for them, Mr Mandelbaum?'

'Them? There is nobody. You do not ask. And I do not send. They come.'

'Undertakers?'

'No. Yes. And I do not send. They come.'

Richard stared at him. Undertakers. It made sense – presumably the same lot that Mrs Trenchard had dealt with. And if he'd done his job properly, and called yesterday, before they'd collected the remains, he'd have been none the wiser. Neither he nor anybody else. He sat down by the small gilt table, put on his glasses, and checked Mr Mandelbaum's forms. Every clause, every box, every heretofore was meticulously dealt with. Obviously Mr Mandelbaum was no slouch when it came to dealing with forms. But how had the undertakers known to come, if the old man had not sent for them? Via the ambulance service? The *police?*

Mr Mandelbaum dried his eyes. 'I break no law. What is mine I sell. The TV now, a fine thing that is. You think I pay four hundred, just for blue?'

'Is there to be a funeral, Mr Mandelbaum?'

'Naturally there is a funeral. A good, fine funeral. My Berthe would wish it.'

Richard stuffed the forms back into their envelope. 'Please tell me, Mr Mandelbaum, how you can have a funeral without a body?'

'And I tell you, young man, go away. Do not insult an old man. Stones. They give me stones. Take your forms now. Go away.'

'You'll receive our check within seven days, sir.' Richard stood up. He believed the old man. 'I'll be on my way now, Mr Mandelbaum.'

He retraced his steps to the door, Mr Mandelbaum shuffling after. By rights, without a body to show, the Accident and General need pay nothing. But Richard wasn't a finicky man. Not any more. And what the corporation eye did not see, the corporation heart would not grieve over.

On the doorstep Mr Mandelbaum leaned after him. 'I am an old man, you say to yourself. And I lose my Berthe. So what is there to worry? But life is life. So please, young man, I tell you nothing?'

Richard looked down at him, saw the pleading in his lined, shabby face. Whoever it was, they'd properly put the frighteners on him. As they had on Mrs Trenchard. But she, unlike Mr Mandelbaum, had had good reason to accept the deal.

'You're a rich man,' Richard said, looking past him at the chandelier and the purple flock wallpaper. 'Why did you do it? Just for a hundred, why did you do it?'

'A rich man? What is a rich man? Today, I tell you, all the world is a rich man. But not I. Not I. I am not a rich man.'

Richard frowned. The point, one of differentials, eluded him. He saw greed instead. And could not but sympathize.

'You told me nothing, Mr Mandelbaum. You have my word. You told me nothing.'

As much, however, as he needed to know. He removed his spectacles, walked briskly away down the expensive path. Somewhere a messy road accident was being set up. Cover for some old woman's untimely going, her place being taken by the damaged Mrs Mandelbaum. About which, although whoever it was would be mad to involve AGIC for a second time, it was his duty to report back to head office.

But life, even old Mr Mandelbaum's, was life. And so, because such an elaborate organization would have long ears, and because he believed in the sincerity of the warning given to the old man, he'd report back nothing at all. He couldn't anyway, without invalidating Mr Mandelbaum's claim which, not a rich man, not he, would be doubly cruel.

It made you think, though. They were very thorough. You had to hand it to them ... It was bad law that did it, of course. Made criminals of even the most harmless citizens. The law should be changed. Once you'd gone, you'd gone. You didn't come back. In all but name you were fucking well dead.

He'd plugged in his car to the condominium's multiple charging point. Now he reeled up the cable, replaced the cap, got into his car, arranged himself behind the wheel, put the envelope containing Mr Mandelbaum's forms on the seat beside him, arranged himself again behind the wheel, sat ... Suddenly there was no further excuse he could think of to delay taking Mrs Trenchard her check. The beginning – or probably the end, he'd soon know – of a beautiful friendship. He sighed, then drove slowly away. At least he'd do his best. Bloody woman.

Ever since she'd remembered about the check, Caroline had been anxious. Which was both vulgar and unnecessary. Mr Wallingford, of all people, knew what was good for him. Of course he'd bring it. Which perhaps was the true reason for her anxiety, since with the check, he must inevitably bring himself. And with himself, possibly – no, probably – unignorable confirmation of his unignorable dreadfulness. A friend of her own. Of her very own, a friend.

She'd put her breakfast things in the dishwasher, dressed, and done her hair. She'd made her bed, and vacuumed the hall. She'd fetched her stainless-steel spade, and gone into the garden, and dug extra Moondrift in around the electrically heated roots of her roses. They couldn't get enough of it, the experts said. Her hair, her bed, her spade – none of these had ever been Haverstock's. But it was a distinction, she'd realized, of rapidly dwindling significance. After only four days. Then she'd sat in the sun on the terrace and gazed blankly at the pages of the newspaper, wishing that he'd just come and get it over with.

Mr Wallingford and Mrs Trenchard: no longer strangers. The one moving toward the other, the other toward the one. But not, as yet, anything at all *unsuitable*.

'I've been waiting for you,' Caroline admitted.

'Afraid I wouldn't come, eh?'

'Not really.' Afraid he would, really.

'Well, I'm here.'

And he was. 'Yes, of course. Please come in.' She took him into Haverstock's study. On his first visit he hadn't seemed to like the living room. Hadn't been amused. 'Please sit down.'

'Thanks.' He sat, opposite Haverstock's steel and leather desk. 'This where your husband did his writing?'

'Most of it.'

'Wonderful, really ... where they get their ideas from, I mean.'

The study had been a mistake. An invitation to banality. 'We all have ideas, Richard. The thing is to spot the useful ones.'

But he hadn't heard. 'I mean, chap like me. I could write a book. Easy … I mean, I've seen enough, done enough. It's just the ideas.'

'We can't all be writers.' Careful now. Don't snap. Don't even want to.

The time, she realized, was after twelve. And she was determined not to be the first to mention the check. 'Sherry, Richard?'

'I don't mind.'

Ignore it. Keep a sense of proportion. Such things weren't important. She thought of offering him sweet or dry, then decided to credit him with dry. 'You're feeling all right, I hope.' Handing him the glass. 'After last night's party.'

'Super.'

She smiled at the allusion. 'Dear old Humphrey.'

'You what?'

'It doesn't matter.' No allusion. But at least he was doing his best.

'Oh … Humphrey. Yes, he seems a good chap.'

'I think so. Not like the others, the ones at the funeral.' And why shouldn't she disassociate herself? 'I can't think why they bothered to come.'

'That's what I told them.'

'So you did.' She'd forgotten. The whole morning. On purpose. Remembering it threw her. 'I see it's a lovely day again.'

'Supe – very nice. Lovely.'

Maneuvering. Like two dogs, sniffing behinds. How juvenile it was. Perhaps between friends, he'd appreciate a little frankness. 'I take it you've brought the check, Mr Wallingford.'

'I'm a man of my word, Mrs Trenchard.'

She gave up. No doubt he thought in received phrases too. And they were back on surname terms.

'For the full amount?' she said coldly.

'For the full amount, Mrs Trenchard.'

Chalk and cheese, my dear. 'Then I'll write you yours.'

There was a checkbook in Haverstock's desk. She wrote the figure four, followed by a zero, a comma, and then three more zeros. It was surprisingly easy. Even now, friendless again, she felt no resentment. Numbers on a piece of paper, in exchange for which he would give her even bigger numbers.

'I'll have to postdate this check,' she said. 'I must allow time for the other to be cleared.'

'I'm not worried, Mrs Trenchard. You won't put a stop on it. You don't want trouble.'

Of course she didn't. But he needn't have reminded her.

'The name, Mr Wallingford. Whom shall I make the check out to?'

He gaped. 'Carson Bandbridge.'

It came out convulsively, clearly unprepared. Idly she wondered what lightning subliminal could have produced such an aberration. *Carson Bandbridge* … it looked like a newspaper headline: CARS ON BANNED BRIDGE. Perhaps it *was* a newspaper headline.

'I've dated it July fifth,' she said.

'I can wait.' He put on his spectacles and jauntily flicked the check from her outstretched hand.

It was an impossible moment for both of them. Out of the few available options, she didn't altogether blame him for choosing to be jaunty. At least it kept things light.

He glanced at his check, then produced an envelope with a flourish from his inside breast pocket. 'Compliments of the Accident and General.' He held it out to her. 'Fair exchange no robbery, Mrs T.'

Which, so obviously untrue, and coupled to the odious 'Mrs T.,' the epitome of all the things she so much didn't like about him, was more than she could bear. And she'd tried so hard. But he was a man who didn't learn. He'd used the same words to her once before, and ended up with egg on his face. He was a man who didn't learn.

She accepted the check. *'Robbery?'* she said. 'Personally, Mr Wallingford, I'd say that *blackmail* was the word we were avoiding'.

Which, so bloody uncalled-for, so fucking bitchy, the epitome of all the things he so much didn't like about her, was more than he could bear. And he'd tried so hard. But what did she expect? Serving him gnat's piss sherry, *It's a lovely day again*, legs crossed and tits tucked in, butter wouldn't melt in her mouth Mrs bloody Trenchard, what did she expect?

He got to his feet. 'Up yours, too,' he said. 'Madam.'

He mightn't have quite her style, perhaps. But he said what he meant.

Unhurriedly he folded his check, pocketed it, bowed stiffly, then turned and walked from the room. Mrs Trenchard called after him, 'I'll see you out,' but he kept on going. His ears were hot and there was an uncomfortable prickling behind his eyes. Bloody woman. What did she know about him, his life, what did she care about his hopes and fears? If he'd had an ounce of guts he'd have flung the check right back in her face …

Caroline had risen. Now she sank down again at Haverstock's desk, listened to Mr Wallingford struggle with the front door latch, open it, go out, close it decently behind him. Resting her elbows on the desk close beside the envelope containing the Accident and General's check, she lowered her chin wearily onto her hands.

'Damn, damn, damn,' she said.

FIVE

Princeton University. 7/1/86. At a press conference today Dr Jason Macabee, head of the national Moondrift research team and Nobel Laureate for his work on the first Moondrift reactor, gave an interim report on the findings of his team's five-year research program. Already, he said, second generation reactors had reached the construction stage, promising a 40 percent increase in operational efficiency. On the subject of the utilization of Moondrift as an explosive medium, he went on to say that the unusual stability of the fission material had been found to render this totally impracticable. At this point the meeting was abruptly terminated, following a disturbance in the hall. Several shots were fired in Dr Macabee's direction, but he escaped unhurt. Three arrests were made, one of them reportedly of a senior United States government official.

That night, Thursday night, there was a fall of Moondrift. A precipitation ten centimeters thick, give or take a centimeter. Silently, out of a cloudless sky, it dusted down over woods and fields, over lakes and rivers, over valleys and hills, and over the bright, unsleeping cities in its path. Wildlife faltered, coughed a little, flapped or scuffled, and occasionally died. Citylife too, when supine beneath the stars, rapturous and/or sodden, occasionally found death rather sooner than it might otherwise have done. Natural selection, people said, sighing comfortably.

Where the Moondrift came from, nobody knew. Tonight, as it happened, out of a cloudless sky. Though the heaviest rain-bearing cumulus had been proved to be no impediment. Out of a windless sky, also. Though the only effect wind might have had would have been to heap the stuff inconveniently against doors and windows. Out of a cloudless, windless sky this Moondrift, dulling the stars briefly, unthreateningly, as it dusted softly down. A belt two hundred miles wide, moving slowly across the land. And blessing it.

It blessed the sea also, dusting down to linger on the surface for a while in a scummy gray blanket. Then it absorbed the moisture and sank. Became, apparently, food for fishes. An amphibious beneficence. Manna from heaven, people said, nodding comfortably.

And saw no conflict.

Anyway, if not from heaven, then from whence? Why shouldn't Someone-Out-There love them? It was a pretty thought. A mystical thought, too, causing people to think variously on their souls. Certainly a thought far preferable to the Random Space Detritus theory, which seemed to be the only respectable alternative.

And the Disappearances, what of them? Someone-Out-There giveth, Someone-Out-There taketh away, blessed be the name of Someone-Out-There? Surely not. Surely no Someone-Out-There would be so cruel. No, the Disappearances were quite a different kettle of fish. The Russians, perhaps, or the fiendish Chinese … And never mind that the Russians and the Chinese claimed to go quite as often as we. They'd be bound to say something of the sort, just to cover themselves. And never mind the Random Space Absorption theory either. Who cared if scientists said the Disappearances were otherwise impossible, against natural law, matter being fundamentally indissoluble. Negative thinking got you nowhere.

So, come to that, did thinking.

Gather ye Moondrift while ye may. Moondrift and roses.

On Friday morning Richard Wallingford slept defensively late. But when he woke, Rose-Ann was still there. He saw her standing by the window, the curtains drawn back on another sunny day.

'That sodding dust's here again,' she said.

Behind her the leaves of the ornamental flowering plum in the front garden were dappled gray. And the tiles on the roof of the house opposite.

'Sodding nuisance,' she said. 'Treading in all over the carpet.'

The last thing Richard thought he wanted was a row. Nevertheless, 'It's never bothered you before,' he said. 'I'm the one who likes the place clean.'

'Poor Dickie. It's you I'm thinking of.'

'What's this, then?' Richard peered at the date aperture on his watch. 'It's not my birthday, is it?'

'Don't be like that, pet.'

'Anyway, why aren't you at work? Doesn't the Pizza Parlor need you?'

Rose-Ann scratched behind one ear. 'Thought I'd skip it for once. Don't want Bert taking me for granted.'

'Heaven forbid anyone should take anyone for granted.'

'That's what I said when I called him.'

'Good for you.'

No row, then. Richard thought he was relieved, reached for his robe, got out of bed. 'I'll put the kettle on for some tea.'

'Tea's made.'

He frowned. It was no use, he wasn't relieved. So he tried again. 'Then I'll heat up the frying pan.'

'Eggs and sausages ready on the stove.' Rose-Ann examined the tip of her scratching finger, nibbled what she found there. 'Hot cereal, too, if you want it.'

He pinched her bottom. Hard. 'You're a winner,' he said.

Feeling profoundly angry, he went downstairs. Never had she made the tea. Or cooked breakfast. Or thought about the carpets. It was he who did all those virtuous things, while she slopped around in her tatty jeans. He was the good one, she the bad. And the eggs would've gone hard, anyway, sitting there on the stove.

He scooped out hot cereal into a bowl. She'd put the cream ready. He ate slowly, searching for lumps. There weren't any. Trust her, though, to cook the eggs same time as the hot cereal – they'd be sure to be hard by the time he got to them.

She didn't come down till he was well into his third sausage. The eggs, ruinously overcooked, he'd left ostentatiously in the pan. He was feeling more kindly disposed.

She leaned in the kitchen doorway. 'I've been making the bed,' she said.

What *was* she up to? 'Well done you.'

'Breakfast all right?'

'Marvelous. Smashing.'

She hadn't noticed the eggs. 'You're not happy,' she said, looking concernedly down at him.

'Who's not happy? Of course I'm happy.'

'You're not, you know.' She drifted across to the cooker, poured herself a cup of tea. 'I can tell.'

'Nonsense … Anyway, what about *your* breakfast?'

'Had mine hours ago. Couldn't sleep.'

… Happy? Of course he wasn't happy. How could he be? Last night, in front of the TV, just when he'd been congratulating himself for having got rid of Mrs Trenchard once and for all, he'd remembered something. The receipt. The bloody receipt for a hundred bloody thousand that bloody Caldwell was going to want on bloody Tuesday. And he couldn't face her. Not again, not after *Up yours, too. Madam*. He bloody couldn't.

Rose-Ann perched on the edge of the sink. 'You got me worried, Dickie. You know that?'

He flung down his knife and fork. 'Honest to God, Rose-Ann, I don't know what you're talking about.'

'Look at that.' Her attention had wandered. 'Sodding Moondrift on me panties.'

He swiveled in his chair. Triangles of nylon, liberally coated with gray dust, were hanging on the line outside the kitchen window. He felt kindly disposed again. 'I'm always telling you, Rose-Ann, to bring in your washing at night.'

'Sodding Moondrift.'

'Never mind, pet. It'll shake off. Never mind.'

'Still be itchy.'

'Rubbish.'

'It's not rubbish. You wouldn't know.'

'Then I'll do them for you again myself.' Poor old Rose-Ann. She wasn't so bad. 'I'll do them now. Put me in the mood, it will.'

'I'm dressed.'

'When did that ever stop us?'

Rose-Ann finished her tea, poured herself another cup. 'You're not happy,' she said. 'I can tell.'

Screw her, then. So much for the lovey-dovey bit. 'What makes you think I'm not happy?'

'Things.' She gestured with her teaspoon. 'Last night … things …'

She certainly was a whiz at expressing herself. 'What sort of things?'

'All sorts … I've known you a long time, Dickie. And it wasn't only last night. Couple of days at least. You've not been yourself.'

He decided to counterattack. 'Look here, Rose-Ann, if you're talking about that bloody carnation, then you can –'

'I was wrong there. It's up to you whether you wear a stupid sodding carnation or not.'

Concessions? Now she had him really worried. 'What, then?'

'I'd like to help. That's all.'

Her sweater, hand-knit, reached down to her knees and her hair was a mess. But she'd put on her eye shadow, and she wanted to help. Suddenly he was touched. She'd known him a long time. Flushing the toilet, going up and down stairs, filling up the place. He was touched.

'You're a winner, old girl. You know that?'

'I mean it, Dickie. I'd like to help.'

'There's nothing. Honest to God, there's nothing.'

She put down her teacup. He watched her in silence, warily, as she went out into the garden, took down her washing, flapped each item dejectedly, then brought the clothes in and dropped them in the sink. Gray footprints followed her on the pink vinyl floor covering.

She ran hot water, sprinkled detergent, stirred with one finger. 'You're in love,' she said loudly. 'And it bloody ain't with me.'

She stood with her back to him, slopping her panties from side to side in the water. Suddenly he hated her. Eye shadow? Wanting to help? Slopping her panties from side to side – Christ, she called that doing the washing. Fuck her, then.

As it happened, Rose-Ann was wrong. Richard wasn't in the least in love – not in the way she meant, and certainly not with Caroline Trenchard. In love with what Caroline stood for, perhaps … but that would have been playing with words, and Rose-Ann never played with words. Possibly it was on account of this that they so seldom did what she wanted them to.

Fuck her then, the slummock. But he wasn't worried: he'd thought of a way to get his own back.

'If you really wanted to help,' he said, 'then you could do a little job for me.'

She slopped on, not answering.

'You could just go on over to this customer of mine. Pick up a piece of paper. A receipt. Just ask for this receipt. Nothing to it.' Which was his most brilliant idea in weeks. The answer to all his difficulties. Two birds with one stone – and a joke there, if he worked on it. 'Will you go?'

Slop-slop, slop-slop. 'I don't mind.'

'That's no bloody answer.' He banged the table. 'Will you go?'

She turned to face him. 'This customer of yours – she wouldn't use Chantel *No. 6* by any chance, would she?'

And that, honest to God, was just about the final bloody straw.

'Don't go, then,' he shouted.

She shrugged. 'Ask a silly question and you get a silly answer.'

Anyway, the girl was imagining things. Must be. When, he wanted to know, had he ever got near enough to Mrs Trenchard for her to come off on him? Even if he'd wanted to, which he hadn't, when had he ever?

Rose-Ann turned back to the sink. 'I put your car away last night,' she told it. 'Stank like a cathouse.'

'Don't go then, I said.'

'Of course I'll go.'

'Don't bother.'

'It's no bother.' She drained the water away, started back toward the kitchen door with her hands full of wet washing. 'I said I wanted to help, didn't I?'

'You can't hang that lot out.'

'Who says?'

'I says. You haven't rinsed out the soap.'

'It's detergent.'

'You haven't rinsed out the detergent.'

She smiled at him. 'No more I have,' she said kindly.

Then she went out into the garden.

His anger grew as he watched her hang up her dripping panties one by one. And she'd tried to tell him *Moondrift* made her itchy … All that not-rinsed-out detergent – eczema of the fanny she'd get, and good luck to her. Bloody woman. That's what they all were. Bloody women.

Behind him in the hall the telephone began to ring. He let it. He hadn't yet finished with Rose-bloody-Ann.

She returned. 'This customer of yours – what's the address?'

'I'll go myself.'

'Telephone's ringing.'

'You surprise me. I thought it was the Salvation Army band.'

'There's clever. What's the address, then?'

'I'm on my bloody way.'

'Please yourself, of course.' She paused, then timidly touched the sleeve of his robe. 'Dickie love – don't let's quarrel.'

And Richard, being only human, but sometimes more so and sometimes less, stared up at her and felt suddenly ashamed. Her life wasn't much, without him going on at her. Poor little sod. Out in the hall the telephone stopped ringing. And who the hell did he think he was, trying to tell her what to do with her own personal private panties? Childish, it was. He ought to know better.

Gently he took her damp hand from his sleeve and held it against his cheek. 'Thanks, love,' he said. 'But I really ought to go myself …'

In love? Letting her words sink in at last, he thought confusedly that perhaps he was. In love with a stuck-up bitch. He must be crazy.

'I'll go myself, pet. Sending you wouldn't be right.'

Not right. No matter how you looked at it, not right at all.

Caroline, calling from Haverstock's study, lifted her finger from the receiver cradle and began to dial again. He *had* to be at home. Her hand was trembling so much that perhaps last time she'd dialed a wrong number. So early on a Friday morning he *had* to be home. She needed him.

She'd needed the bank manager, too. Yesterday afternoon, after *Up yours, too. Madam*, inept and alone, taking in her check for a hundred thousand, she'd needed his respect. Even, considering the check's size, his admiration.

In the event, though, she'd received rather less than either.

'My sincerest condolences, Mrs Trenchard.'

'Always pleased to do business with you, Mrs Trenchard.'

'A sad loss indeed, Mrs Trenchard.'

'Would you do me the honor of having dinner with me, Mrs Trenchard?'

'What a beautiful dress, Mrs Trenchard.'

'Oysters, Mrs Trenchard?'

'Let me fill your glass, Mrs Trenchard.'

'My wife doesn't understand me, Mrs Trenchard.'

At which point she should have left the restaurant, of course, before it was too late. But she couldn't really believe it.

'Your husband told me all about the parties, Mrs Trenchard.'

'What parties were those, Mr Rogg?'

'The parties at your house, Mrs Trenchard.'

'The parties at my house, Mr Rogg?'

'The fun you all had, Mrs Trenchard.'

'What fun was that, Mr Rogg?'

'You don't have to pretend with me, Mrs Trenchard.'

'I wouldn't dream of pretending, Mr Rogg.'

'I'm a man of the world, Mrs Trenchard.'

'You're a sod, Mr Rogg.'

He and garrulous, showing-off Haverstock, sods both. And the parties, which she'd tried to forget, not worth the Vaseline they'd puddled in. So she'd demanded a taxi home, a taxi for one, and got it. And now she'd have to change her bank.

But that wasn't why, or not only why, she was calling Mr Wallingford today. Nor why her hand was trembling so much that perhaps last time she'd dialed a wrong number. He *had* to be at home. She needed him.

This time, thank God, he answered. She told him something unexpected had happened. He asked her what. She begged him to come. He said he was coming anyway. She said she hoped he'd be quick. He said he'd do his best.

She rang off, leaned her arms on Haverstock's desk, still trembling. *Something unexpected* ... she was proud now of the understatement. Something horrible, in fact: intrusive, distasteful, nauseating.

He was at her door in scarcely an hour. They went into the living room. Calmly, incredibly, she offered him a drink. He refused, saying something about it not yet being eleven. She helped herself. Suddenly she didn't want to begin.

'You first,' she said. 'What was it you wanted to see me for?'

'A receipt, Mrs Trenchard. I forgot to get a receipt for the hundred thou.'

She'd asked the question, yet hadn't heard the answer. She was crying into her whiskey. 'They know, Richard.'

'No? What d'you mean, no? Head office needs the official receipt. It was in the envelope with the check.'

'They know the truth about Haverstock.'

'Who knows? How could they know?'

'A girl – she said my greed had been my downfall. It was like a bad play. She said my poor husband deserved better of me.'

'Don't cry, Mrs Trenchard.'

'I tried to tell her ... Haverstock wasn't like that ... he'd understand ... I tried to explain.'

'Who to? What did you try to explain?'

'The girl said I was to call her Irene. *Irene*, of all things ... I tried to explain that if Haverstock knew he would only laugh. But it's no excuse, of course.'

'Excuse for what?' He was kind. He was patting her shoulder.

'Excuse for lies, for being so squalid. She made me feel grubby. I hadn't thought anyone could make me feel grubby.'

'Cheer up, Mrs Trenchard. Nothing's as bad as it looks.'

She mopped her eyes. He was taking the situation surprisingly well.

Perhaps he understood her, after all. Her shame. 'I don't expect her name's really Irene,' she said. 'I mean, people like that always work with an alias.'

'People like what?'

She didn't want to make him feel awkward, saying the word. And anyway, the remark was nonsense – *he*, although undeniably in the same line of business, hadn't worked with an alias. But then, of course, coming from AGIC he couldn't have.

'I told her I'd give AGIC back the money. But she said things had gone too far for that. The police, the coroner's court, the funeral …'

'Give back the money?' Suddenly he wasn't patting her any more. 'You can't possibly do that.'

She sighed. His sharpness of tone had penetrated. She was thinking straighter now. For the first time since that horrible phone call she was ordering her thoughts. Was that, dear God, what the simple presence of balls in the house did for a woman? She hoped not. But either way, her disintegration – therapeutic as it had been – was over.

And of course Mr Wallingford didn't want her to give back the money. He was worried for his forty thousand.

She finished her whiskey. 'It's all right,' she said, 'I won't be giving it back. The chances are I'll need every penny, just to pay off that girl.'

'I'm afraid I'm not with you, Mrs Trenchard.'

He hadn't been listening. Begin at the beginning again. Words of one syllable. 'A girl phoned me. She said she knew the truth about Haverstock, the substitute body, the clothes. She threatened to go to my insurance company with the story.'

Richard was appalled. Why hadn't she said so straight off? He moved distractedly away to the window. Outside in the street a Central Generating Authority team had arrived, with brooms and a vacuum truck. He watched them laying out the hoses.

'This girl – did she mention me?'

'Only to say you must have been a fool to let me pull the wool over your eyes so easily.'

He breathed again. A small price to pay, some girl thinking him a fool, which he wasn't, if it left him in the clear.

'She wanted money?'

'A thousand. Just for the moment.'

Just for the moment … frank, at least. 'Are you going to pay?'

'She's ringing again. I haven't made up my mind.'

Out in the street the Moondrift billowed as the CGA team began dusting down the overnight cars. And all the girl's attempts to make Mrs Trenchard feel ashamed had simply been to soften her up.

'What else can you do?'

'It all depends … I've been thinking, you see. The girl knows so much – where could she have got it from except from the undertakers themselves?'

Who cared, for God's sake, *where* she'd got it from? 'So?'

'So she can't expose me without exposing them. And if she turns out to be in league with them, then the whole thing's a bluff. They're hoping to get more than just the two fifty out of me.'

He had to hand it to her – Mrs Trenchard was a thinker all right. 'But this girl might easily have got it from someone else,' he said.

'Who else knew? Only you, and –'

'It wasn't me. I can tell you that for nothing.'

'Of course not. So it has to be the undertakers.'

Who cared, anyway? It wasn't his problem. 'You're going to tell her to go to hell, then?'

'I don't think I dare, Richard. Not till I'm certain.'

The CGA team was moving on. They worked well, leaving the street spotless behind them, even the spaces between the railings. And a couple of plastic bags stuffed into each front mailbox.

'You'll need to sweep your steps,' he said. 'I'll give you a hand, if you like. And what about the back garden?'

'I've got to be certain, Richard, that she's in league with the undertakers.'

'Of course she is. It's how they make a profit.' Especially in view of the hundred Mrs Mandelbaum had cost. 'I always thought two fifty was peanuts.'

'But I've got to be certain. I can't take risks. You must see that.'

Who cared, anyway? It wasn't his problem. Serve her right, stuck-up bitch. And he knew quite well what she was getting at. He hadn't been born yesterday.

He turned back from the window, 'All right,' he said gently. 'What do you want me to do?'

Caroline averted her gaze. She'd felt guilty, using those *Richards* when all that really united them was his fear for his forty thousand and hers for her sixty. But one did what one could.

'You might perhaps follow her,' she said. 'I mean, she'll have to pick up the thousand. You might perhaps follow her, see where she goes.'

He didn't answer.

'Please, Richard? It's not just the money – truly it's not.'

'What is it, then?'

A harsh question. But reasonable. 'Pride? I suppose that's what it is. Can you understand that? Her intolerable self-righteousness – she shouldn't be allowed to get away with it. Do you see? My grubbiness. And her power. No, not her power, the way she uses it. I lied and cheated, I know that. But, my God, she's nothing more than a common little blackmailer.'

He opened his mouth to say something bitter. But she was prepared. 'Not any more,' she said. 'You never were, really.'

Prepared though she had been, it still sounded false. Opportunist. Though it was in fact neither. Therefore she let it stand. And hoped.

He turned away, went quickly to the open door. In his dreadful weekend leisure wear. He paused, his back still to her. He clenched his fists.

'Rose-Ann says I'm in love with you.'

The words were like a douche of cold water in her face. She weathered them. Must this also be what happened when a woman had balls in the house?

'Rose-Ann,' she said carefully, 'must be a very old-fashioned girl. You and I know better.'

He didn't move. 'She's … someone I met.'

'But she hasn't met us.' Careful. Enough, perilously judged. So very careful.

Minutely he shifted his weight. 'I just thought I ought to mention it.'

'I'm glad you did.' And she was. And now, the crisis past, 'There's something I didn't tell you.' Hurrying on. 'That girl, Irene, she asked me if I'd counted the stones in the coffin.'

He swung around. 'But there weren't any stones.' Aware of, surely, yet accepting the studied change of subject.

Caroline uncurled. 'That's what I told her. She only laughed. "You think they'd waste a perfectly good body?" she said. And then something about a "conservation of resources policy."'

But Richard felt free now, as if relieved of a terrible burden. And Mrs Trenchard was right – Rose-Ann hadn't even met them. 'It makes sense,' he said. And so it did. There was always, remembering Mr Mandelbaum, a need for bodies. 'But was there time to do the swap?'

How relaxed Mrs Trenchard was, leaning back on the white hide settee. 'They took the body early,' she said, 'then kept me waiting outside their place. There was plenty of time.'

'Which proves,' because now, free, he was bright as a button, 'which proves that the girl is in with them. Else she wouldn't have known. You didn't. And,' because he couldn't resist it, 'neither did I.'

Mrs Trenchard smiled sadly. 'But she might have been making it up. The stones might be entirely her invention. Short of raiding the grave, we'll never know.'

So it really proved nothing at all. As he should have spotted.

'When's she calling again, this Irene?' To cover.

'She didn't say. I expect it's part of the plan – keeping me on tenterhooks.'

'You don't look on tenterhooks to me, Mrs Trenchard.' And re-cover.

'Thank you, Mr Wallingford. Are you ready for that drink now?'

They had a generous whiskey each, and then another. He told her, because they were truly partners now, and the favor on his side, all about Mr Mandelbaum, and the hundred paid for Mrs Mandelbaum, and the mysterious way *they* had known all about her. From the ambulance men, perhaps, or the police … They and the girl Irene, both with their convenient sources. It made you think.

He felt expansive. He hadn't formally agreed to help Mrs Trenchard. He'd asked her what she wanted him to do, but he hadn't said he'd do it. An understanding – that was what they'd come to. The sort of thing old-fashioned Rose-Ann wouldn't know about. Nothing to do with love. Like the party when he'd clobbered Fulch. She wouldn't know about that either. Part of his past, Rose-Ann was. And he was really quite fond of her.

Mrs Trenchard played tapes, long-haired stuff, but not bad. They'd have gone for a walk around the square in the sun if they hadn't been waiting for the telephone. Lunchtime came. Mrs Trenchard served a big cold tart, full of egg and cheese and black olives. And wine from the fridge, white, in a glass jug.

And then, when they were sitting out on the terrace in white wicker chairs, and he'd crossed his legs and pulled up his trouser knee to show his hose with the nifty yellow clocks, there was a Singing. They just sat there.

And waited.

But it was a long one.

'Don't worry, old dear,' he told her. 'As my dad used to say, you never hear the one that's got your number on it.'

She tried to smile. 'That was bombs. I don't think it applies to Singings.'

'It didn't to bombs either.'

The Singing went on and on. And the smell of sweet synthetic roses.

'Did you like your dad?'

'Works foreman in a candy factory. Always had his pockets full of peppermints.'

'But did you *like* him?'

'I suppose so.' What a question. 'Tell you one thing, though. Still can't stand the sight of peppermints.'

'I wish this horrible noise would stop.'

'It will, old dear.'

'I don't think I can stand much more.'

'It'll stop. You'll see.'

And, finally, it did.

But things on the terrace weren't the same. A certain graciousness had gone out of the proceedings. And the alcohol, that before had made them fit, now bred a chilly unease instead. So that they were glad when, behind them in the house, the telephone rang. Irene.

It had been arranged that Caroline should take it in the living room, while Mr Wallingford listened in on the extension in Haverstock's study. She didn't rush. Let the girl wait. And she was trembling again.

'Irene?'

'How *did* you guess?'

'Don't let's be clever with one another.'

'I expect you're right. You've decided to buy me?'

'How do you want the money?'

'Sensible woman. Incidentally, I'm more expensive now. Two thousand, I thought. Just for the moment.'

Caroline closed her eyes. 'Look – you know how much the insurance was. Why not just ask for the lot, and be done with it?'

'Consumer resistance. It's less painful this way. For both of us.'

'You mean you want to spin it out. You like making me squirm.'

'I mean you'll pay the odd thousand or so without too much trouble. While you think of a way to get rid of me … Besides, I'm not a monster. Once I've set up my reconstitution center, I'll quit.'

'Your *what?*'

'Never mind. Anyway, I'm negotiating with Rent-a-Corpse as well.'

'Is that what they're called?'

'Of course it's not. But they've got more to lose than you. Theirs is an ongoing business.'

'So you're saying that if you get enough out of them you'll leave me alone.'

'I might.' There was a pause. 'Two thousand, then?'

Caroline reached for the whiskey bottle, changed her mind. There'd been no further talk of shame. She didn't need it. 'In old notes? Tens and twenties?'

'Don't try to upstage me, Mrs Trenchard. And we don't want the bank asking questions. Take it in hundreds, as it comes.'

Honestly, she hadn't thought of things from the bank's point of view. 'How do I get it to you?'

'I'll be in touch again, after five. Make sure you're ready.'

'What could you do if I weren't?'

'Punish you. Double up on the ante. Till five then, Mrs Trenchard. And I hope you had a nice Singing. I know I did.'

She broke the connection. Slowly Caroline replaced her receiver. What the hell was a reconstitution center? And why the chat about the Singing? Possibly, because the girl seemed to do nothing without a reason, she was announcing that she lived no more than two or three miles away, otherwise she wouldn't have known of it. Caroline thought of the dozens of streets and the hundreds of houses within a three-mile radius, and wondered why the girl had bothered.

Mr Wallingford joined her. 'Rent-a-Corpse,' he said. 'I like it.'

'You would,' she snapped.

He wilted slightly. But not for long. 'So she's putting the screws on them as well,' he said. 'We must be wrong. She's getting her information from somewhere else.'

Caroline shrugged sourly. 'She could just as well be lying. I've seen them, you know, and they're a tough lot. She'd be mad to try blackmail on them.'

How innocent he was, this Mr Wallingford with a dad he'd not thought of not liking. Her own father was a famous anthropologist, currently married – so she'd heard – to a twelve-year-old Bushman girl somewhere in Australia.

She glanced at her watch – the time was after three, and the banks would soon be closing. That girl had rattled her. She tried to remember where she'd left her purse and checkbook.

'I must go to the bank. Can you stay till five?'

Grandly he rearranged his weekend polo neck. 'My pleasure, Mrs T.'

Which was beyond all endurance. *My pleasure, Mrs T.* – would he never learn? Dear God, what an intolerably stupid, innocent, dreadful man he was.

'What about Rose-Ann?' she asked him coldly.

Silence. His blank gaze.

Then, 'That's between me and her,' he said.

And it was. Of course it was.

'Of course it is. Forgive me.' Christ, what a bitch she could be when disappointed. 'I shouldn't have said that. It's good of you to stay, and I'm truly grateful.'

'Think nothing of it.' He was overhearty now, and she couldn't blame him. 'I'll just make myself comfy, then. Unless you'd like me to come with you – all that money, I mean.'

'You're very kind. But I'd better go alone. We don't want that girl to see you, and she might be watching for me at the bank.'

Caroline knew of one person who positively would not be watching for her at the bank. Mr Rogg. Unless it was to keep out of her way. So that every cloud indeed had its silver lining. After all, with the AGIC check not yet cleared, there wasn't a chance that her current account held as much as two thousand. But he'd let it go through. Anything rather than share with her so soon, by the cold light of day, the knowledge that his wife didn't understand him …

When Mrs Trenchard had gone, Richard returned to the terrace. He saw that she must have been out there early, sweeping up the Moondrift. There wasn't a trace of it anywhere, even on the lawn. Just a pair of fat plastic bags standing by the wall and a shiny shovel and a broom leaning beside them.

There was a little wine left in the glass jug. He drank it. So he was to play the private detective. The part appealed to him, otherwise he'd never have taken it on. Bloody woman. In love with her? Never. Stuck-up bitch. Jealous, too … well, they were all jealous. But Rose-Ann had nothing to do with anything. He looked around the terrace, the white wicker furniture, the neatly swept lawn, the remains of the tart on a red-and-gold plate. He was fond of her, mind. But she couldn't even wash out a pair of panties proper.

He dozed off. And when he woke it was to the same thought, so that he didn't know he had been sleeping. He was fond of her, mind. But she couldn't even wash out a pair of panties proper.

Behind him French windows stood open. The house was empty. His. Mrs Trenchard trusted him. She'd left him in charge. All those rooms, all those secrets. Her cupboards, the mysterious details of her life. Her husband's study, his life too. Letters on tables. Documents. How her sort passed their days and nights. And the house was empty. *His.*

But Mrs Trenchard trusted him.

All those rooms. The one upstairs with wardrobes in its ceiling. The dining room all flowers. That fancy lounge, those pictures, the crazy weighing machines … Those pictures? With a guilty quickening of his pulse he thought of the lounge and its pictures. Well, they were up there on public show, weren't they? And if her sort considered them all right, then who was he to argue? No harm, no harm at all. So he went, on tiptoe, pink and sweating, to have another look.

Another, closer look.

There were lots of them, more than he remembered. By the time he'd finished he'd almost finished. And felt quite ill with it. And stole upstairs, breathing heavily, guiltier than ever, to remedy the situation with a quick jack-off in Mrs Trenchard's bathroom. A devil-may-care gesture. Or ninety-nine or a hundred.

He smiled sneakily, began opening doors on the landing.

But Mrs Trenchard's bathroom, when he found it, killed the prep-school joke stone dead. Between its shaggy chocolate-brown walls, beneath its mirrored ceiling, he no longer felt inclined even to unzip. Shame had dwindled him to next-to-nothing. A sunken bathtub big enough for two, a sinister chaise longue, and rows of jars of unnamed milky lotions … Guilt he could enjoy, but shame was something else again. Such blatancy – there ought to be a law. If these were the sort of goings-on the Mrs Trenchards of this world openly admitted to, then he'd stick with old-fashioned Rose-Ann.

And jumped almost out of his senses at the sound of Mrs Trenchard's key in the front door below.

Hastily he backed out of the bathroom and eased its door shut, Though there was by now palpably no need, he adjusted his dress. Even so, descending the stairs to meet Mrs Trenchard, he didn't know where to look. Lotions indeed … Spit did Rose-Ann. And the battery vibrator in their bedside cupboard was bust.

Mrs Trenchard stood in the hall, her handbag in her hand, staring up at him. He smiled at the grandfather clock behind her.

'Everything all right?' he said, grinning glassily.

'No trouble at all. I've got the money.' She hung up her coat. 'Were you looking for the loo?'

'Not really.' But if not, then why go upstairs? 'Well, as a matter of fact … well, yes … the toilet?'

But what he'd seen, the shame of it all, was stamped on his face. He knew it.

Yet she simply smiled. 'My fault – I should have shown you around.' She pointed amiably. 'First door on the right. But I'm surprised you missed it.'

He didn't answer.

When he came out of the downstairs toilet his pulse was almost back to normal. Mrs Trenchard had her handbag open on her husband's desk. He looked over her shoulder.

'It's a lot of money,' he said, clearing his throat. 'I've never seen two thousand before.'

'Bits of paper.' She shrugged. 'Not even very pretty.'

'But it's *money*.' He was nettled. Post-bathroom lotions. Brave. 'I didn't see you being so grand about AGIC's hundred thousand.'

'I was owed that. Eight years with Haverstock, and an overdraft to show at the end of it. Eight years – don't you think I was owed something?'

'But –'

'And besides, money's a catching habit. Anyway, what's it to AGIC? Figures on a balance sheet.'

He was shocked. 'It's easy to see you've never worked for the stuff.'

'Since Moondrift, who does? A few hours here and there – it's not the same.'

'You say that. But –'

'Be honest. People are virtually paid to stay at home these days.'

He fingered the notes. Perhaps she was right. His dad would have agreed with her – he'd worked a proper five-day week, and been proud of it.

'I still think money means work to most people,' he insisted.

She sighed. 'A useful social delusion, Mr Wallingford.'

'You what?'

'Forgive me.' She smiled wanly, then moved away from the desk. 'I'm in a bad mood. Don't take any notice.'

Looking at her now, so neat, and so low in spirits, the bathroom must have been her gone husband's.

'Cheer up,' he said. 'We'll fix that girl, that Irene. She won't get away with it.'

'Does it matter?'

'Of course it matters.'

'But it all seems so squalid.' She paused by the TV set, ran a finger along the top of the frame surrounding the screen. 'This money – it's not even mine. Why don't I just give it to the wretched girl and be done with it?'

'But it's not hers either.' The idea horrified him.

'My share, I meant. Your forty thousand's safe, whatever happens.'

He hadn't been worried. He'd known what she meant. 'But why give it to the girl when it's not hers either?'

'A way of washing my hands, Mr Wallingford?' She met his eyes briefly, then stooped and switched on the TV.

It had sounded like a question, but he didn't think she expected an answer. He stared reverently at the bank notes lying on the desk. 'I was looking forward to fixing her,' he said. 'Following her and that.'

The TV brightened, showed clips of a demonstration, placards waving and people shouting *'Ostriches Out.'*

Mrs Trenchard raised her voice. 'All right,' she said. 'You've talked me into it.'

They stood for a while in her gone husband's study, watching the TV.

'And it'll help pass the time,' she added.

The film clips ended, and they were back in the studio. Behind them in the hall the grandfather clock struck five. On the screen there was a glazed interviewer, wearing a glazed safari jacket.

'Assuming that the demonstrators were to get their way, Mr Hawkridge, what steps would you expect any new administration to take concerning the Disappearances?'

'I'm glad you asked me that.' Mr Hawkridge was relaxed, wearing a relaxed bow tie. 'The devising of adequate protective measures should be given top priority. The shielding properties of lead, for example, should be fully investigated.'

'Then you are recommending a piecemeal approach, Mr Hawkridge? The symptoms rather than the root cause?'

'That too, of course. The field is wide open. No theory, no matter how far-fetched, should be discarded without the most thorough investigation.'

'What theories had you in mind, Mr Hawkridge?'

'I'd prefer not to be too specific.'

'Afraid of making a fool of yourself?'

'Not at all. But I'd prefer not to pre-empt the findings of whatever responsible investigative body the new administration might set up.'

'Do you in fact know of one single theory concerning the root cause of the Disappearances that you feel would merit serious scientific investigation?'

'The difficulties are enormous. Principally the random nature of the phenomenon. How, for example, can one assess the efficiency of a shielding agent when one is dealing with a probability factor in the region of ten thousand to one?'

'I don't think you answered my question, Mr Hawkridge.'

'I was coming to that. The difficulties, as I said, are enormous. A Singing may result in the going of one person, or three people, or no people at all. While statistical averages can of course be computed, sampling techniques are –'

'Then what you're saying, Mr Hawkridge, is that any new administration would be unlikely to develop better protective measures than the present one.'

'If you'd just let me finish. It's all a question of priorities. Take the current Commission of Inquiry – its budgetary apportionment is less than half of one percent of –'

'But, Mr Hawkridge –'

'Please? … Thank you. Government figures demonstrate that we as a nation are spending on Disappearances Research a smaller percentage of our Gross National Product than any other in the Free World. And those are official government figures.'

'On the other hand, Mr Hawkridge, am I not right in thinking that in its provision for the dependants of Disappearance victims our current administration leads the –'

'Thumb in the dike tactics, sir. Would we not be better employed building a stronger dike?'

'Yet if I understood you correctly, Mr Hawkridge, you have just finished telling us that –'

The front doorbell rang, then rang again. Mrs Trenchard glanced at her watch.

'Damn,' she said, 'I wasn't expecting anybody.' She moved away to the study door. 'If the telephone rings you'd better leave it. We don't want that girl to know you're here.' She went out into the hall. 'I'll get rid of whoever it is as quickly as I can.'

Through the half-open study door Richard heard her fumble with the front door latch. On the screen Mr Hawkridge was as relaxed as ever. 'I was coming to that,' he said.

But he needn't, as far as Richard was concerned, have bothered. For Richard's attention was firmly elsewhere. On Mrs Trenchard's unwelcoming, 'Yes?'

And on the cheerful young voice that answered her. 'You must be Caroline. I'm Irene.'

SIX

London. 7/1/86. Trading in the City was suspended at 11 A.M. today, following widespread uncertainty arising out of the absence from his place of business of Sir Maxwell Hough, chairman of Maxichem Conglomerates. Rumors of an abrupt and unexplained journey abroad were ended, however, when Lady Hough named her husband in an officially notarized Declaration of Disappearance. Trading was resumed ten minutes later, at 2:25 P.M., and found the market in a bullish frame of mind. Maxichem Conglomerates steadied, finishing the day three points up, at 170.56.

Caroline stepped back politely to let her visitor enter. She didn't know what she had expected, but hardly this pretty little thing, charmingly dressed in the ingenuous fashions of ten years ago: brown flowery smock and enormous, pink-tinted sunglasses. And of the current season's gold safety pins, massed in rows, not a single one. With her patchwork shoulder bag and long, straight hair tucked lightly behind her ears, she might – save for a weaselly sharpness of glance behind the sunglasses – she might have been the quaintest, dreamiest, most innocent young woman imaginable. And she walked with innocence too, back on her sandaled heels, head held high, unafraid.

Only then, watching the girl, did Caroline realize just how furtive people had become since the beginning of the Disappearances, scurrying from here to there, staring at the ground.

'Won't you come in?' she said.

The girl smiled, showing small, unpredatory teeth. 'I already have.'

Casually, Caroline allowed her gaze to include the far end of the entrance hall – the door to Haverstock's study stood half-closed. A corner of the desk was visible, some bookcases, nothing of Mr Wallingford. No sound could be heard from the television set. She led the girl into the living room. Closed the door. Lingered by it.

The girl sat down, comfortably spreading the soft brown folds of her smock. 'You expected me to telephone.'

'So you decided to come instead.'

The girl smiled again. 'I know that game.'

'I beg your pardon?'

'It's called Ascendancies. I've been playing it all my life.'

And, thought Caroline, with such an air of innocence as yours, probably rather better.

She crossed to the window. 'I won't offer you a drink,' she said.

The girl let that one lie for a full minute. Clearly, it wasn't worth bothering with.

'You're just what I expected,' she said.

'I'm so glad.'

'Under siege. You've been under siege for years.'

Caroline returned to the door. 'I'll get the money.'

'It simplifies things. It means you know what to expect. In fact, you probably welcome it.'

'Spare me the slot-machine analysis.'

Was she right, though? Was she?

'We're going to get on. I can feel it. You must call me Irene.'

'You told me that on the telephone.'

'It's my name, you see. And I shall call you Caroline. We can snipe across the ramparts. But I promise I'll never try to come in.'

Caroline clasped her hands at her waist, to stop them shaking. If the girl were so willing to talk, then she might give something away. About her sources. Though she didn't really believe it.

All the same, 'You got on to me very quickly.' Hm?

'It's called striking while the iron is hot.'

'You speak as if you'd had plenty of experience.' Hm again?

'I've lived for twenty-six years.'

'But surely not in the same line of business.' And again?

'You mean blackmail?' The girl laughed decoratively. 'If you can say that then you don't know much about children.'

Caroline turned away. 'I'll get the money,' she said.

The hall was deserted, the study also. She picked up the two thousand. On her way back to the living room she noticed that the front door, which she had closed, was now on the latch. So Mr Wallingford, that admirable person, had got out while he could. The door could be opened silently, but he'd wisely not tried to shut it. He'd be somewhere out in the street now, waiting to pick up the girl when she left. Admirable.

Letting the front door stay as it was, Caroline returned to the living room.

'Two thousand,' she said, handing it civilly to the girl. 'I wonder how long it'll be before you're back for more?'

The girl took the money and put it, uncounted, into her patchwork bag. 'Maybe never. Rent-a-Corpse seem prepared to be generous.'

Remembering them, Caroline rather doubted it. 'You're brave,' she said lightly. 'Even coming here was brave. Blackmailers are terribly vulnerable.'

'Not me.' The girl got up, briskly hefting her bag. 'Nobody touches me. I've been through hell and out the other side.'

'Indeed?'

'Indeed. I went, you see.'

'You went?' A mistake, such innocent incredulity. 'You mean you Disappeared?'

'It's called electronic molecular deconstitution. EMD for short. The TV companies do it all the time.'

Caroline smiled. She supposed she'd asked for it. 'I'll show you to the door.'

'You needn't pretend. Nobody knows about it – only me.' The girl perched calmly on the sofa arm. 'The Singing – it's the resonance wavelength of their high-gain generators. Given out by the aerials. The same TV aerials that channel us away after molecular deconstitution.'

Something out of a bad SF spectacular. Yet delivered with the same easy conviction as the rest of the girl's pronouncements. Caroline called her hand.

'Should you be telling me all this?'

'Not really. But I've got to tell someone ... And besides, you're money in the bank, so I'd like you to stay around.'

'I see.'

'You don't, of course. You think it's a put-on.' She dipped into her bag, brought out a small gray plastic box. Then she fiddled with it till it gave out a prolonged, ear-piercing shriek. She switched it off. 'The TV people need our psychic energies. You must have seen them, Caroline. You must have sensed that there's nothing behind the eyes.'

If it wasn't a put-on, then it was pure paranoia. 'And that box thing interferes with the wavelength?' Caroline asked, safe now, willing to oblige.

'More or less. That's a simplification, of course.' The girl put the box on the glass coffee table. 'I was one of the first to go. Back in November. They used me for Theo Rawsthorne.'

Caroline had to smile. There was something so right about it – Rawsthorne, after seven years of Evenings With, was a millionaire zombie.

'Laugh, if you like. You don't have to believe me.'

'No.' Caroline straightened her face. 'Please go on.'

'There's not much more. When I was done with they tried to dump me. Usually that's the end. But I wouldn't let go. Theo finished up in hospital. I wouldn't let go, you see.'

Caroline wasn't sure, but she thought she did remember a month or two without Rawsthorne. Something to do with a virus infection, she thought.

'It's as simple as that. I had the strength, you see. So they had to arrange electronic molecular reconstitution. I went through hell in that hospital. So did Theo. It can't happen again, of course. They've reinforced the termination process.'

She'd thought it through. How adroit were the ravings of a true paranoid. Was it kind to expose them?

'Forgive me,' said Caroline, feeling not in the least kind. 'Forgive me, but don't they have Disappearances in places like India? Where there aren't any television aerials?'

'After Moondrift? You must be joking. The vultures make their nests in them.' The girl stood up again. 'That's what I want the money for. To set up reconstitution centers. They're very expensive.'

She went to the door, head held high, walking on her heels, innocent as ever.

Caroline called after her. 'You've forgotten your plastic box.'

'It's a dephaser. And I don't need it. They'll never take me again.' She turned in the open doorway and smiled, showing small, unpredatory teeth. 'Keep it, my dear. You're money in the bank, Caroline. I'd like you to stay around.'

'Wouldn't it be cheaper,' said my dear, said Caroline, 'to spend the money on more boxes? Then the reconstitution centers wouldn't be necessary.'

'Much better. Except that if there were a lot of my dephasers around then the TV companies would find out. And all they'd have to do then would be to keep changing the wavelength. I'm not a fool, you know.'

No, not a fool. Only a lunatic.

Caroline dodged around her (and a lunatic with an eye for just that sort of detail) to reach the front door first. She opened it.

The girl was leaving now, and her sources as much a mystery as they had ever been. Lunatics have such careful minds. Too careful, surely, to be in league with such as Rent-a-Corpse? Though the promise of a reconstitution center or two might well work wonders …

'Don't look so worried, Caroline. I'll be in touch.'

'That's what I'm afraid of.'

The girl patted her arm. 'Well done. Corny, but dead on cue. Spoken like a real old stager.'

Me? thought Caroline. Indeed, yes. Utterly, dismally, a real old stager.

But, by way of rearguard, 'And what about the smell of roses? You haven't explained the smell of roses.'

Her visitor looked earnestly, anxiously up into her face. 'That's because I can't. It's a complete mystery to me.'

Which, Caroline realized, was the most distressing part of the entire unhappy episode.

Sitting in his car, some distance away down the street, Richard saw Mrs Trenchard's door at long last open and a girl come out, closely followed by Mrs Trenchard. He watched, crouched down behind the wheel. They stood together on the top step for a moment, then the girl ran lightly down into the street, waving goodbye as she went. Richard marked the cheerfulness of the wave, and the jaunty swing of the patchwork shoulder bag. Could that really be the sinister Irene? he wondered.

Then he marked Mrs Trenchard's lack of answering wave, and the defeated sag of her shoulders, and decided that it could.

Poor Mrs Trenchard. There goes two thousand. Bloody woman – for all her scornful talk about pretty bits of paper it must still have hurt when the crunch came. It was still hurting now. He could see it hurting.

The girl was walking away from him, up the street. He craned his neck, waiting to see if she had a car. She did. A city electric, the same yellow as his own. He started up at once and moved away from the curb. By the time she'd got going, if she caught sight of him in her mirror he'd appear to be simply coming up the hill behind her. He drove slowly, letting her pull out a good way ahead of him. The sun was in his eyes – it would be shining on his windshield, he thought, creating a glare. He was pleased with the way he'd worked things out.

She drove up the hill, around the square with the modest stone mermaid, and on. There was a sticker on her rear window: *Moondrift Is Bad for You*. He followed her as far behind as he dared, wishing for a bit more traffic. She came to traffic lights, turned left. He closed the gap, crossing his fingers. The lights stayed green for him, and he turned down after her.

Suddenly she whisked into a tiny parking space and stopped. He had no alternative but to drive on past. In his mirror he had a brief glimpse of her getting out of her car. Then the road curved and he could see nothing. He stood on his brakes. Another car came down the hill, swerved past him, hooting. He gave its driver two fingers, cursing under his breath. He'd surely lost her. What did Mrs bloody Trenchard expect? A reliable tail called for two of you at least. One man handed on to the next – everybody knew that.

The road had cars parked down both its sides. Turning in it, on the corner, was hell. By the time he got back to where the girl had parked there was, of course, no sign of her. He cruised on up to the traffic lights, turned again, and was lucky enough to find himself a parking space not very far away from hers, on the opposite side of the road.

What now? If he stayed in his car, and she happened to be looking out of her window, then she'd think it odd. But if he got out, and she happened to be looking out of her window, then she'd have a proper sight of him. And he didn't want that ... He decided to stay where he was. Who, for God's sake, looked out of their windows at streets as boring as this?

If not though, then perhaps he should get out after all, and try to make a guess at which house she might have gone into. He could see the rows of bells by the front doors, and the tacked-up name cards. Perhaps hers was on one of them. And perhaps it wasn't ... He sat there, frozen. He wasn't, he thought, cut out to be a private detective.

The street was humbler than Mrs Trenchard's, similar old tall houses, but narrower, with cracking plaster, and divided up into flats, bed-sitting-rooms, studios for Swedish models. No matter how rich a city got there were always streets like this, threatened with demolition, pounced on eagerly by people threatened with demolition also. They brought their last year's cars with them, and their year-before-last's dishwashers. And the CGA's black plastic bags stuffed into the letter boxes would remain unfilled …

Caroline had had an inspiration. She was ringing the number in *Groundswell* again. How simple it would be if they'd admit to being blackmailed, or deny it. And if, either way, she'd feel she could believe them. Certainly there was no harm in trying, seeing what they said. Far better than to wander around the house, in the aftermath of Irene, doing nothing.

'Good afternoon. Disappearances Advisory Service.'

She took a deep breath. 'My name is Trenchard. Mrs Caroline Trenchard. You … well, a few days ago you were able to help me.'

'Help you, Mrs Blanchard?'

'Trenchard.' Already her hand on the receiver was sweating. 'Yes. You were able to supply me with certain … with certain useful items.' It was for herself, this obliqueness. She couldn't bear to say the words. 'Do you understand me?'

'Not entirely, Mrs Trenchard.'

'Yes. Well …' The poor, nice young man, he'd have to be wary. 'It *is* Mr Cattermole, isn't it?'

'Are you sure you have the right number, Mrs Trenchard?'

But it was he. She knew it was. 'Well, the thing is, I'm being blackmailed. And I was wondering if –'

'Did you say *blackmailed*, Mrs Trenchard?'

'I'm afraid I did. And I was wondering if you could tell me if you too were –'

The phone went dead. And, when all was said and done, what else could she possibly have expected?

She could always try ringing again, but she'd only make herself even more ridiculous. So she replaced the receiver instead, got a tissue and cologne out of her purse on the desk, and carefully wiped her sweaty hand. Inconsequentially she stared at the blank television screen, smiled to herself. The glazed interviewer in his glazed safari jacket – how well he supported Irene's mad story. And now she had nothing to do but wait to hear from Mr Wallingford.

She went out into the hall. Mr Wallingford … Richard … her different animal. She didn't deserve him. Of course he disappointed her. Who, in all her thirty-one years, hadn't? But at least her spite, when directed at him, had been far from irreproachable. Which put him in another, much healthier class than Haverstock.

She turned left into the living room. The telephone rang, far too soon for

Mr Wallingford, but she snatched eagerly all the same. People. Even Haverstock's friends. And mostly she was at her best, which admittedly wasn't much, on the telephone.

'Mrs Trenchard?'

'Speaking.'

'Disappearances Advisory Service. I believe you rang our branch office.'

People indeed. And not even Haverstock's friends. 'That's right.'

'We've been checking our records, Mrs Trenchard.' A different sort of voice, this. Crisper. Senior management. Mr Rent-a-Corpse himself? 'And I have to tell you that we can find no trace of any transactions whatsoever in your name.'

Which, as a preliminary gambit, was only to be expected also.

So, 'You're sure you've got it right? *Trench* as in the 1914 war? *Ard* as in "aardvark never did nobody no harm"?'

'No Trenchard on our books, ma'am.'

Nary a smile. Haverstock's jokes were like that.

But why, if he was going to pretend he hadn't heard of her, had Mr Rent-a-Corpse bothered to call?

Perhaps she should help him along. 'There's a coffin in Saint Bartulph's necropolis, Mr Rent-a-Corpse, that must have –'

'The name's Fitzhenry, Mrs Trenchard.'

A likely one. But she wasn't to be put off. 'There's a coffin in Saint Bartulph's necropolis, Mr Fitzhenry, that must have come from somewhere. I'm sure it could easily be traced back to your premises'.

'Exhumations are surprisingly difficult to arrange, Mrs Trenchard.'

'Not if I tell the authorities that I think you stole my husband's body and weighted the coffin with stones instead.'

There was a long pause. Behind it, with a suitably graveyard chime, a clock began to strike six. Caroline felt victory within her grasp.

'Shouldn't I have been told about the stones?' she said sweetly.

'I don't think you were.'

'But I truly was, Mr Fitzhenry.'

'I think not.'

Seldom in the field of human conflict had so much been conveyed by so little.

'Is that a threat, Mr Fitzhenry?'

'You are not on our books, Mrs Trenchard.'

Of course it was a threat. But sometimes even the Mr Fitzhenrys of this world could be too clever.

'If that's the case, Mr Fitzhenry, then I'm in the clear. And bless you.'

'I don't think I quite follow.'

'It's really very simple.' Victory. 'You see, if I'm not on your books, then I'm not on anybody's. And with stones in the coffin I can tell Irene to go fuck herself.'

'Not knowing Irene, Mrs Trenchard, I can't advise you.'

'No advice at all?'

'Except to be careful. Always assuming that there *are* stones.'

Which, very much knowing Irene, there might very well not be.

'It would seem to me,' Mr Fitzhenry went on, 'that you are in a devil and the deep blue sea situation, Mrs Trenchard.'

Sentiments, but not the graceless expression of them, with which she was forced to agree. So that somewhere along the line, she realized, victory had eluded her.

'You're probably right.' With determined serenity. 'So sorry I troubled you.'

'The trouble is entirely yours, Mrs Trenchard.'

She rang off then, quickly, before he could be clever – but not after all *too* clever – again.

Far better, she thought, to have wandered about the house, in the aftermath of Irene, doing nothing. What, for heaven's sake, had they really been talking about? Certainly not what she'd intended to talk about. Unless of course they had been, but at several cunning removes. How nice it was, then, to have come across someone with whom she could have a truly intelligent conversation.

Her basic mistake, clearly, had been to think of him as Mr Rent-a-Corpse, a cosy, slightly comic, undangerous fellow. Which he wasn't at all.

Richard sat in his car, waiting for Irene on the street that was humbler than Mrs Trenchard's. Humbler? Hardly. Poorer, dirtier, shabbier, but not in the least humbler … Suddenly, Irene reappeared. She ran lightly down from a dazzle-painted front door a few houses down on the opposite side.

Richard watched her pad away down the street. She was carrying her shoulder bag again. Perhaps it still had the money in it. Perhaps she was off to make contact with her mysterious sources. He sighed. It had been nice, sitting in the car, feeling useful. Now he'd have to get out and follow her.

He got out and followed her.

He should, he knew, have plugged in first. But there wasn't time. And he couldn't have, anyway – the charging point had been prized open and stuffed full of plastic holly.

He closed the distance between them, feeling horribly conspicuous. On such a street his dog-tooth flares and his polo neck stuck out like a sore thumb. But he'd dressed that morning for Mrs Trenchard, not for layaboutsville. Still, the girl wasn't going to look around – she was almost dancing now as she went happily down the street. Not that he blamed her. He'd be dancing too, if he'd just picked up a buckshee two thousand …

Except that he wasn't. And he'd picked up forty – the check was at home in the pocket of his Italian suit. And he wasn't dancing. But then, he never had. Not like that. Not that he could remember.

At the bottom of the street there was a row of shops. Car accessories, DIY, holidays abroad, cameras, hi-fi, car accessories, DIY, holidays abroad, cameras, hi-fi … and a supermarket. She went into the supermarket. He waited outside, peering around the special offer stickers. Then he remembered that supermarkets often had back exits. So he went in after her.

She was choosing a pineapple. He dodged behind jams and preserves. She passed him on the way to herbs and spices, where she took down a packet of curry powder. He browsed among the hams and bacon. The next time he spotted her she was waiting at the checkout. Grabbing the first thing that came to hand, a jar of maraschino cherries, he hurried after her.

At the only other vacant till the cashier was picking her teeth with a hairpin. She didn't look up. He bounced his purchase impatiently up and down on the little black conveyor belt. She wiped her hairpin on her sleeve.

'Ayfiffy,' she told him spitefully. 'Plus sevnytex.'

He couldn't believe it. '*Eight-fifty?*'

She smiled. 'Plus sevnytex.'

And he didn't even like the bloody things. And she tried him with change for a ten when he'd given her a twenty.

By the time he got out into the street the girl had a good three hundred meters start on him. He lengthened his stride. She appeared to be making for a phone booth on the far corner. He broke into a run, tightly clutching his jar of cherries. In a movie once the detective had worked out the number being called from the sound of the dialing.

Abruptly the girl stopped, turned. He didn't quite bump into her.

'Are you following me?' she said.

What the hell did she think he was doing? And if she connected him with Mrs Trenchard then he was done for anyway. Therefore, in the circumstances, there was nothing for it but his most disarming smile.

'It's a weakness I have.'

She matched his smile. 'Why don't I kick you in the crotch?' she asked him.

So he knew he was all right. 'Because I'd kick you back.'

'Charming.'

'Why don't we talk about it instead?'

'Talk about what?'

But they weren't yet ready for that. He'd met her sort before, and they didn't like being hurried. There were necessary stages. Repartee. He nodded toward a bar at the end of the row of shops.

'You could always buy me a drink,' he said.

'Why should I?'

'Following girls is thirsty work.'

She took off her sunglasses, peered at him closely. 'My God,' she said.

'I know.' He hoisted his flares. 'But I can't help it.'

'Ten minutes, then.' She replaced her sunglasses and set off in the direction of the bar. 'I can spare you ten minutes.'

He trotted after her. It was the repartee that got them, every time.

'Carry your bag, miss?' he suggested.

'No thank you.'

But it proved nothing. She might just be protecting her pineapple. And anyway, it wasn't the money he wanted, it was her mysterious sources.

They entered the bar. Neon lit in red and green, with a barman, three Indians, and the TV on. She perched on a stool. He stood his jar of cherries on the counter.

'What'll you have?' she said.

'I didn't mean it.'

'I did.'

He ordered beer, and she joined him. Things were going well. He was interested to see if she'd pay with one of Mrs Trenchard's hundreds. She didn't.

'Well?' she said. 'What now?'

'We talk.'

She lifted her glass. 'Don't you ever get sick,' she said, 'of moving your lips and making noises?'

Christ. Now he knew why he'd never really liked this sort of girl. They were pretty enough, and they came on a treat. But you just couldn't depend on them. And he'd run out of funny answers.

She leaned forward, patted his arm. 'Don't cry,' she said. 'Faint heart never won fair lady.'

He stood up. He didn't have to stay there and be made a fool of. Except that he did.

'Why don't you get stuffed?' he said. Her and Mrs bloody Trenchard, the both of them.

The girl frowned. 'I'm Irene,' she said. 'Who are you?'

Who was he? 'Carson Bandbridge.' Quick as a flash.

'That's nice. Well now, Carson Bandbridge, what does a man like you do with himself all day?'

What did he do? And this time no flashes. 'Oh, this and that ...'

'I mean when you're not making like work.'

He breathed again. No doubt most of the people she knew did this and that.

'I'm ... building a sun parlor out behind my house.'

'That sounds married.'

'Not really.'

'And – don't tell me – you've got gladioli in your front garden.'

He didn't correct her, though they were in fact petunias. He wasn't a fool, he knew the way her sort mocked at sounding married, and houses, and front gardens. They mocked at everything, really.

She finished her beer. 'It'll have to be my place, then.'

Not with him it wouldn't. Not in a million years. He reached for his cherries. 'You'll be lucky,' he said.

'I seldom am. But I keep trying.'

And once, a very long time ago indeed, he'd thought that things were going well.

'You haven't asked me,' she said, 'what a girl like me does with herself all day.'

'So why don't you tell me?'

'All right.' She folded her arms. 'I'm a professional blackmailer.'

He knew what she was up to. Telling the truth, thinking she wouldn't be believed, playing a game, hoping to shock him. While all she'd really done was make things easy.

'Enterprising girl.' He settled himself back on his stool. 'Want an assistant?'

'Not really.'

Now for it. 'Who's your boss?'

'I'm a free lance.'

'Pull the other one.'

'I'd rather not.'

But not even a come-on like that could distract him. 'Blackmailers have to know things. How would a nice girl like you get to know things?'

She sighed. 'I really shouldn't be telling you this,' she said, 'but I've got to tell someone.'

'Of course you have.'

'All right, then. It's like this.'

A walkover. So it was, after all, the repartee that got them.

She removed her sunglasses, stood them carefully on the bar. 'I've been through hell, you see, and out the other side.'

The directness of her gaze was disconcerting. What on earth was she talking about? 'Me too,' he temporized. 'It's called Majorca.'

But she wasn't listening. 'I went, Carson Bandbridge. I *went*.'

'Went?' Which would teach him to count his chickens. 'You mean you Disappeared?'

'I suffered electronic molecular deconstitution. EMD for short. The TV companies do it all the time.'

Ask a silly question … 'I thought we were talking about –'

'The Singings – they're the resonance wavelength of the high-gain generators.'

'– talking about how a nice girl like you got to –'

'It's given out by the TV aerials. The same aerials that channel us away after deconstitution.'

'– got to know things.'

'The TV people need our psychic energies. You must have seen them, Carson Bandbridge. You must have sensed there's nothing behind the eyes.'

He gave up trying. 'Tell me about it,' he said.

And she did.

Her gray plastic box upset the three Indians. They protested, very civilly, that they couldn't hear the TV. She put the box back into her patchwork shoulder bag.

'They used me for Theo Rawsthorne,' she said.

And later, 'I wouldn't let go, you see.'

And later still, 'So they had to arrange electronic molecular reconstitution.'

And later again, 'I went through hell in that hospital.'

He wasn't surprised. The only thing that did astonish him was that they'd ever let her out.

She stared at him coldly. 'Please yourself,' she said.

'What d'you mean?'

'You think it's a put-on.'

'No I don't.' It wasn't worth it.

'A lot of people do, you know. They think I'm crazy.'

In fact, oddly enough, she didn't seem at all crazy. She didn't shout, or wave her arms about, or dribble. Her manner was calm, her tone convincingly matter-of-fact. What had she called it? Electronic molecular deconstitution? It sounded possible. Well, almost …

'Let me buy you a beer,' he said. 'And tell me again about that plastic box.'

She let him buy her several. And told him again about her gray plastic box. It was a dephaser.

'It interferes with the resonance wavelength of the high-gain generators. Then they can't lock in on the EMD frequency.'

He liked that. 'And it really works?'

'I've never had a failure yet.'

'Why don't you market them?' A hole in her story, screw it. 'If they're as good as you say, you'd make a fortune.'

'Except that if the TV companies got to hear of it they'd keep changing the wavelength.'

It made sense. And hundreds of people, mind, had thought that Einstein was crazy.

'Let me buy you another beer.' And her mysterious sources could wait.

'You're very kind.'

'And you say these dephasers really work?'

'Cross my heart. The bloke downstairs makes them up for me. He used to be a computer man. He's writing a novel now. And he's into Bed-Rock.'

That too. She was quite a girl. All Richard knew about Bed-Rock was that radio and TV still banned it. And he hadn't liked to go into a record shop and actually ask for one.

And so it was that when the time came, what with Irene's dephaser, and the man downstairs' Bed-Rock (and, of course, all that he hadn't yet found out about her mysterious sources), he went back with her to her place. It couldn't, after all, do any harm.

The hallway beyond the dazzle-painted front door was narrow, and smelled of dirty socks. And even coming up the front steps he'd heard the Bed-Rock. Now, as he stumbled up the stairs behind Irene, he could understand why the media wouldn't allow it. Too many of their customers, according to the surveys, were over sixty. It wouldn't do to have them keeling over.

Irene's room was up on the top floor, close under the roof, with a sloping ceiling. Most of the room, that wasn't filled with mattress, was filled with TVs. Fifteen of them at least, maybe twenty. There was an electric cooker and a sink out on the landing, and a toilet down on the next floor. Irene turned on the light, a single overhead bulb, dark red. Then she went around switching on the TVs. They were tuned to different programs. She took his jar of cherries from him, left it on one of them. Then she pushed him down onto the mattress.

Later, not nearly enough later, he leaned up on one elbow. The TVs were going flat out. And the insatiable Bed-Rock, taunting his inadequacy, was making the floorboards buzz from three storeys down.

'You're mad,' he shouted. 'You're stark, staring crazy.'

But she didn't hear him.

And wasn't he crazy too? This crazy bad actor, stuck with this crazy bad script? Like: *It's a weakness I have.* And: *You could always buy me a drink.* Right through without stopping to this moment. And all for Mrs bloody Trenchard's sake.

The girl had turned her back to him. Poor crazy thing. How often was this going to happen to her, he wondered, before she'd learn? He lowered his mouth till it was against her ear.

'Does he always play this stuff?' he shouted.

She twisted around. 'He's writing a novel.'

'So?'

'It helps him concentrate.'

Even from three stories down the music was louder than all the TVs put together. But she wasn't joking. Like him, she'd long ago run out of jokes. He got up off the bed, went out onto the landing to wash. The water was cold, and the only towel was full of tea leaves. He rummaged for another. Pushing aside the moldy cornflakes packets in the cupboard under the sink, he found money instead. Bank notes filling the entire length of the cupboard, half a meter deep, stuffed in like old newspapers, thousands and thousands of them.

Now he knew she was crazy.

He stayed for a while, simply staring. Then he closed the cupboard doors and got up off his knees. He was dry enough now not to need a towel anyway. When he went back into the girl's room he found she hadn't moved. He crossed to the edge of the mattress, past the busy TVs, and stooped over her.

'Shall I see you again?' he shouted.

She shrugged her naked shoulder.

'Tomorrow?'

She shook her head.

He didn't give up. 'Sunday, then?'

She shrugged again.

'Fine. We'll make it Sunday. Around two o'clock.'

There was a long pause. Then she nodded.

'Fine.' His voice was getting hoarse. 'See you.'

He backed away from the mattress, reached the door, went out, closed it. He really did want to see her again. They hadn't got around to his borrowing one of her dephasers, but that wasn't why. They hadn't talked about her mysterious sources, but that – to be honest – wasn't why either. He wanted to see her again because ... well, because she needed him. For God's sake, she needed *somebody*. He knew it, and so did she. He wouldn't have been there at all if she hadn't needed *somebody*.

She was crazy, of course. Stark, staring crazy. But it was a crazy world, wasn't it? And anyway, he'd forgotten his jar of cherries.

He went downstairs, past the computer man who was writing a novel, and out to his car. He drove off, his mind still on the girl, and her terrible room, and her towel full of tea leaves, and all her money. He hadn't touched it, hadn't wanted to. But it showed that Mrs Trenchard was far from being her first victim. There must have been dozens of them. And all for what? Bundles of bank notes, stuffed in like old newspapers, going moldy along with the cornflakes ...

He was making for the Fairthorpe Two-tier and home. Suddenly he realized that Mrs Trenchard would be waiting to hear how he'd made out. He thought of turning back. It wasn't far to number thirty-seven. But he couldn't face her. Not in person. Not so soon after the girl.

Caroline was getting ready for bed when he called. It was the second call in the last ten minutes. She took it on the bathroom extension. He sounded depressed, and frankly she wasn't surprised.

'I've found out where she lives, Mrs Trenchard.'

'I know you have.'

'I followed her down to a supermarket.' He hadn't heard. Perhaps the line was bad. 'It's no distance – just on past the square and turn right. And she's –'

She could have let him run on. But she didn't want to discover what sort of half-truths, what sort of lies, he'd tell.

'She rang me, Richard. Irene rang me. Not ten minutes ago.'

'What for, for God's sake?'

'She rang because she knows you came from me.'

'She *what?*'

Poor Richard. 'She said if you hadn't wanted to be spotted you should have used a car that was a less noticeable color.' She'd said other, more intimate things, also. 'I'm afraid she was rather angry, Richard.'

She listened to the loss he was at.

Until, 'She's crazy, I tell you. You should see the way she lives. And –'

'It can't be helped, my dear. It really wasn't your fault.'

'She's a tramp, you know. And I didn't lay a bloody finger on her.'

So unnecessary. After her generosity, her *my dear*. Well, she too could be unnecessary.

'I don't suppose you found out anything about her sources?'

'She hasn't any. Not in the way we thought.'

It sounded like a snap decision. Caroline raised her eyebrows, caught sight of herself in the overhead mirror, raising her eyebrows. Really, she thought, she was an unusually attractive young woman.

'Why do you say that, Richard?'

'She's got money stashed away. Thousands and thousands. Far too much for her to be sharing it with Rent-a-Corpse.'

'Not Rent-a-Corpse, Richard. The name's Fitzhenry.' A private joke, daring to say the horrible man's name.

'You what?'

'I said you still can't be sure, Richard. Suppose they split it half-and-half. That way it really wouldn't take her long to put together –'

'All going moldy. She's crazy, Mrs Trenchard.'

'I know, Richard.' Also that he didn't, for some reason, want to believe in Irene's wider complicity.

'Fifteen TVs, all going at once. And then there's the Bed-Rock …'

'You're tired, Richard. It's been a long day. I'll talk to you in the morning.'

He became calmer. 'I'm sorry I screwed things up, Mrs Trenchard.'

'It doesn't matter. The whole thing was a stupid idea, anyway. I'll see you in the morning. Sleep well.'

See him? For generosity's sake. What else?

She rang off. She hadn't even told him what the girl's anger was going to cost her. Another two thousand, first thing Monday morning, as soon as the banks were open. And she was lucky, the girl said, to get off so lightly.

Richard, however, was even luckier – so far the girl seemed unaware that she wasn't the first to play at socking Mrs Trenchard. Caroline sighed, looked up at herself looking up at herself, and sighed again. Poor Richard. She really didn't deserve him.

Richard left the phone booth and went back to his car. It was dark now, the sky ahead silvery bright from the shimmering lamps of the Fairthorpe Two-tier. He was shaking with fury. He rested his forehead on the steering wheel and closed his eyes. *I'm sorry I screwed things up* – why the fuck had he apologized? That girl, that bloody Irene … he'd thought she needed him while all the time she was pissing on him from a great height. Stringing him along. Right from the very first moment, pissing on everything about him. And then running off to tell Mrs bloody Trenchard. Christ, he must hardly have been out of the house before she'd called her. Not that he was worried. The way things stood, he was well rid of the both of them.

Who needed them? Who needed style, who needed another league? Who needed, for fuck's sake, to be needed? Forty thousand in the bank. Two meters tall, with a cock like Casanova's. The time he'd have. The things he'd do, all the things he'd always wanted to. All those things that made life really worth living.

His fury passed. Comforted, he sat up straight, switched on, wiped his eyes, and drove off up onto the Fairthorpe Two-tier. On which, half a mile further on, his city electric faltered, picked up briefly, then coasted to a halt.

Its headlights died to a yellow glimmer. He turned them off, pounded the battery gauge with his fist. Not a glimmer. It must have been on the red for miles, and he'd just not noticed. All day without a top-up. First outside Mrs Trenchard's, because for once he'd forgotten, and then outside the girl's because the charging point had been stuffed full of plastic holly. As if he hadn't enough on his mind without that. And he was too tired now even to swear properly.

He got out and started walking. There'd be an emergency phone within the next half-mile or so. And it was a fine night.

But the two-tier was creepy. Up there in the merciless electric moonlight he could see for miles. The city glowed, street upon street upon street below him. Street upon street and tower upon tower, diminishing structures of light, deathless, hung against the void, out to the rim of the earth and beyond. He looked away, walking narrowly on the curb by the retaining wall. He was quite alone. Cars rushed toward him on the far side of the divider, from nowhere to nowhere, dazzling him, dazzling him, dazzling him.

He began to run.

Beneath him the rooftops were dark with Moondrift, waiting for the next good breeze, or the next shower of rain. He was scuffing in Moondrift too, where the vacuum plows had missed. Ahead of him the two-tier curved to the right. Suddenly he realized that his side of the expressway was empty.

Since he'd left his city electric, not one single car had passed him. He paused, leaned on the wall, looked around, glad of the excuse for a breather.

The cars coming toward him were thinning out. A gap, then what seemed to be the last of them. Until it was overtaken at speed by a police car, red light flashing, that turned abruptly, savagely, across in front of it. Metal tore noisily against stone as the driver of the first car fought to avoid a collision. Instinctively Richard cowered down, waited for the crash.

The ugly sound of ripping bodywork intensified. Then it stopped. Brakes protested as the police car came to a halt also. Cautiously Richard raised his head. Beyond the divider he could see men getting out of the police car, walking back. He stayed where he was. Now the far expressway was as deserted as his own. He didn't like it.

The policemen reached the wrecked car. It was tilted up on the curb, locked against the stones of the retaining wall. They opened the door. There was a brief consultation, then they dragged the driver out. He appeared to have been alone. They flung him down on the road where he lay, not moving. One of the policemen turned him over with a foot. In the relentless brilliance of the street lamps Richard saw the dark, unpleasant mess where the man's face had been. The policemen seemed satisfied. One of them took the man's shoulders, and another his feet, and they carried him back to their car while the third carefully closed the door of the wreck. Then he took out his handkerchief and wiped its door handle.

Meanwhile the other two policemen were putting the dead man in the back of the car. One of them brought out a large plastic bag and tucked it over the dead man's head. Now they were joined by the third and they went back together to stare at the road surface, apparently looking for tire marks. Again, they seemed satisfied. Richard strained his ears, heard nothing but a low murmuring, then quiet laughter.

They returned to the police car, got in, and drove briskly away.

Richard stood up. For a moment he stared at the wrecked car, empty now and silent. Then he set off, running again, back in the direction of his own city electric. He understood very well what he had just seen. And it was vital that he shouldn't have.

He reached his city electric just in time, was leaning with theatrical dejection on its open door when the police car drove up alongside him. Soon his side of the expressway would be busy again. It had taken them perhaps six minutes to drive back to the end of the two-tier, remove the Road Closed signs, and return to where he was stranded, a quarter of a mile or so from the scene of the 'accident.' The police car stopped. Police car? Well, it was painted up like one, and fitted with a flashing light. The occupant on the near side leaned out. His uniform was good too.

'Bit of trouble, sir?'

Richard shrugged. 'Battery flat.'

'Sure it's not a faulty gauge?'

'I'd be home by now if it were.'

The man in police uniform stared suspiciously up at him, then got out, pushed past, settled into Richard's driving seat, and switched on. Richard watched him. A hundred it had cost Rent-a-Corpse to get hold of Mrs Mandelbaum. He wondered how much this little caper was hitting them for. Business must be booming.

The man looked out. 'You're right,' he said. 'Not a flicker. How come?'

'Charging point was bust. I thought I could make it home.'

'Where's home?'

Richard told him. He climbed out, asked to see Richard's driver's license, insurance certificate, charging point account card. Richard gave them to him. He checked them carefully.

'You've a good way to go.'

'It's been one of those days.'

'How long have you been here?'

'Not long. Maybe five minutes.' One wrong word, the slightest hint that he knew too much, and he'd end up in the back of the other car, along with the plastic bag. A bit more difficult to explain away, but they'd surely think of something. Two Disappearances, so close together? It had been known. 'I was just going to start walking back when you turned up.'

'Walking back?'

The 'accident' was ahead. Back was away from it.

'To the beginning of the two-tier. Or the nearest emergency phone. Whichever comes first.'

The man returned his papers. 'On your way, then,' he said.

Richard lingered. 'Couldn't you give me a lift?' he asked, making like an innocent citizen.

But the man in the police uniform wisely didn't hear him. He returned to his car. 'And if I were you, sir, next time I'd find a charging point that wasn't bust.'

He opened the door and got in. Richard saw that the car's courtesy light had been disconnected. Its interior remained prudently dark. He waited. The car waited also. He started to walk away, back along the two-tier. Still the car waited. Even though they'd be in a hurry to get to the next intersection, to remove the Road Closed sign by the traffic lights on the other expressway before too many questions were asked, they still weren't taking any chances with him. Finally, when he'd gone perhaps three hundred meters, the car, Rent-a-Corpse's car, drove off. Fast.

One should have guessed, of course, that in an expanding market the obliging ones, the already dead, the Mrs Mandelbaums, would be insufficient.

And that the moment demand began to exceed supply, alternative measures would have to be taken. Alternative measures. Bloody murder. But in a manner calculated to produce reusable remains. And to look, more or less, like a Disappearance. As long as there'd been a Singing in these parts fairly recently. All this one should have guessed.

Richard, however, like one, had been a bit slow. He knew now, though, what he should have known right from the beginning – that Rent-a-Corpse weren't playing games. And therefore that the girl Irene, whether she was in league with them or not, was bad news. Curiosity killed more than just cats. Get noticed, asked questions, and he could all too easily end up reusable remains. When was he supposed to be seeing her again? Sunday afternoon? That was out, for a start.

And what of Mrs Trenchard? His stride faltered. At least, after the girl's latest phone call, she wouldn't be expecting him to go on tailing her. So what next? Go on paying up and looking pretty? Why not? After all, according to Mrs Trenchard, it was only money.

Poor Mrs Trenchard. Caroline. They'd come a long way together, him and her. Only a few days, but they'd come a long way. Mind you, she was a bit of a puzzle. Had he been hearing things, or had she really said Fitzhenry? Perhaps she was breaking up. And he couldn't just dump her. Not if she was breaking up.

Thoughtfully he shielded his eyes against the first of the oncoming headlights. Life was funny. You couldn't just take your forty thousand and push off. You had responsibilities. Even if you weren't in love, you still had responsibilities. She was expecting him in the morning. She'd said so. And the bathroom had definitely been her gone husband's.

No, she couldn't be allowed to just go on paying up. He must think of something. Perhaps they could hide, go away to some place where that crazy girl wouldn't find them. Leave the country. Go abroad. He'd never much liked the idea of abroad, but with money in the bank you needn't hardly notice. That was it, they'd leave the country …

Mr Wallingford and Mrs Trenchard: two people no longer strangers. And still, so lost were they, nothing even remotely *unsuitable*.

His mind made up, Richard started back along the two-tier again. And his stride, for a man who was going to have to wait around for hours before the van with a replacement battery arrived, and who suddenly remembered that he hadn't eaten since a couple of slices of cheese-and-egg tart with black olives at lunch time, was strangely buoyant.

SEVEN

London. 7/2/86. In the House of Lords today, at the end of an eighteen month legal battle, judgment was finally given in the case of Smallbones *v* the South Wotton Parish Council. Mr Harold Smallbones, a Berkshire farmer owning grazing rights on South Wotton Common, has been claiming that the Ancient Statutory Extension of these rights to include the gathering of fallen timber for winter fuel entitled him to gather Moondrift also. South Wotton Parish Council's contention had been that, under the terms of the Statute, Moondrift constituted a mineral resource, and was therefore outside whatever Common Rights might be enjoyed by neighboring landowners. In a two-hour judgment, their Lordships gave it as their unanimous opinion that, whereas Moondrift is undeniably neither animal nor vegetable, its unique composition and extraterrestrial origin make it uncertain whether it could rightly be termed mineral either, within the framework of the Statute. They therefore found in favor of Mr Smallbones.

Mr Wallingford was on Caroline's doorstep at five to ten. She wasn't, honestly, quite sure what to make of such enthusiasm. For the first time, briefly, she wondered about the woman (girl?) called Rose-Ann. Someone he'd met, he said. It covered a multitude of sins. She decided, because it would be so like him, that he lived with her and wished he didn't. Foolishly. For someone had to iron those horrible shirts he wore.

She'd been sitting in the kitchen making a shopping list when the doorbell rang, so she took him through to there. It made a change. The living room, Haverstock's study, the terrace … those so many paces were what her life was made of. The house, its geometry, was her world. Even when Haverstock had been around, she'd paced remotely from living room to study to terrace. Except for the occasional, unapproachable walk in the High Park. And except for Saturdays, when she did all the shopping that couldn't be done by telephone. Fresh vegetables, for example – she liked to see what she was buying. The girl had spotted it. 'You're under siege,' she'd said.

Hence, today being Saturday, the snatched breakfast and the shopping list. Haverstock's funeral didn't count. Nor Humphrey's party. It had been an exceptional, hateful week.

'I'm thinking of going away,' she said. Though until that moment she hadn't been at all.

He didn't seem pleased. 'I suppose you mean abroad.'

'I don't think so. Somewhere out in the country, I thought.'

He cheered up. 'You'll never get a permit,' he said.

'What d'you mean?'

'You have to have essential work. Or compassionate grounds. Far too many people can afford to live in the country these days. If they did, there wouldn't be any.'

She'd forgotten the permit. Or somehow thought it didn't apply to her. Haverstock's wife, Haverstock's widow – lots of things didn't.

He leaned toward her belligerently. 'And that crazy girl'd be sure to find you.'

She'd forgotten Irene too – it was nice how she'd managed to unremember her. Her and Mr Fitzhenry. Certainly neither of them had had anything to do with her sudden decision to go away. The living room, Haverstock's study, the terrace … and now the kitchen, these had decided her to go away.

'Coffee, Richard?'

'I don't mind.'

She told herself it was her own fault. She'd asked him to come, hadn't she?

He sat down at the table. His elbow scuffed her shopping list onto the floor, and he didn't notice. 'My idea,' he said proudly, 'is that we should go abroad.'

She heard the *we*. 'Abroad?' she queried. 'What sort of abroad?'

'Anywhere you like. Somewhere hot. We've plenty of money.'

Obviously he'd got it all worked out. She pictured a lifetime of *I don't minds*. There were worse fates.

'I don't think I'd like that, Richard.' And he'd never, not once, called her Caroline. 'Rich expatriates, soaking up the sun. It sounds so vulgar.' Writers did it all the time. But she wasn't, thank God, a writer.

'Vulgar?' He was nonplussed. 'We could try a cold place if you'd rather.'

Another man, she knew, wouldn't have let her get away with such affected nonsense. There were advantages to her different animal. No, snags.

'I don't really want to go abroad, Richard. It would mean leaving all my friends.' What friends?

But, in his innocence, 'You'd soon make new ones.'

Anyway, *why* didn't she want to go abroad? Because the Saturday vegetables were really her limit, and even the country was straining things?

'I haven't got a passport.' But she could always get one.

'You could always get one.'

'I like it here.'

'And what about that girl?'

'It's time I went shopping.'

'But what about that girl?'

'We'll think of something.' She picked up her purse and went to the door. 'Are you coming?'

He came. And took the hint. They walked together down the hill to the shops, talking about the Hawkridge interview they'd seen some of on TV. What did *he* think the government ought to do about the Disappearances? That Hawkridge man was a fool, he said. Of course he was, she said. There were always people wanting to knock things down, he said. But they never have anything to put in their place, she said. Quite right, he said. So that, for a while, walking together down the hill to the shops, they were delightful Saturday morning people.

It lasted while they shopped. She chose things, and he carried the plastic bags. The sexual stereotype, but it made sense. He was stronger than she.

They stopped in at a coffee bar, sat up at the counter drinking bad coffee and eating soggy doughnuts. She told him about the hat she'd seen in a window by the vegetable shop, and he said it sounded as if it'd suit her. After they'd finished their coffee and doughnuts they went out and bought it. It didn't suit her. Then they went next door and bought him a summer jacket that didn't suit him either. Then they walked together back up the hill to their home.

Her home.

Not even that.

He noticed the change in her. Must have. 'Talking about the Disappearances,' he said, though they hadn't been for a couple of hours. Could the shopping, then, only have been a game? For her it had been real. 'That girl Irene,' he went on, 'has this crazy theory.'

Caroline walked faster. She didn't want to hear.

'She says the TV people do them. Something about needing our psychic entities.'

'Energies. Psychic energies. I know.'

'And she has this thing she calls a dephaser. It makes the most bloody awful noise, and she –'

'I know, Richard. She gave me one.'

'Gave you one?' He missed a lot of things, but not that, of course. 'You mean you've still got it?'

'That's right.'

She slowed again. They walked on in silence while he thought.

'Are you going to use it?' he said. If not, transparently wanting it for himself.

'Talking about Rose-Ann,' she said, though they hadn't been for a couple of days. Bitch, bitch, bitch – and she didn't even wish to know. 'Is she the girl you live with?'

Around all his plastic bags Mr Wallingford essayed a light gesture. 'The things you say. I thought we were talking about Irene's dephaser.'

'Is she?'

'Depends what you mean by "live with." '

The evasion stopped her dead, infuriated, standing on the hill up to her house. 'Do the two of you fuck?'

He met her gaze. 'What's that to you?'

'Nothing, really.' And it wasn't. Not Rose-Ann, nor the girl at the party, nor crazy Irene. Perhaps that was what was wrong with her. Was something wrong with her? 'I just wondered.'

'And I don't like women who use bad language.'

'You don't?'

'There's something that really *is* vulgar.'

What a long memory he had. Did he remember, she wondered, that she'd used the same word the very first time they'd met? In connection with Haverstock. *A piquancy to our fucking …* He hadn't objected then. So they'd come a long way.

'I'm sorry, Richard. It's a crude word, and I used it crudely. I'm sorry.'

He started to walk again, accepting, around his plastic bags, her apology. 'Rose-Ann's all right,' he said. 'A bit limited, but that's not her fault.'

Talking her talk. He was learning fast after all, poor man.

Caroline said, 'I'm sure she's very good to you.'

'She was out on the thruway, and I gave her a lift. Oh, eight or nine months ago. Then I asked her in, and she sort of stayed.'

'Eight or nine months – that's a long time.' For a relationship, she meant, not for sort of staying.

Richard fell silent again, adding up the months. Rose-Ann, he realized, had in fact been with him for more than a year. He'd been on the point of sorting her out dozens of times, but he'd never had the heart. Without him there'd just be Bert at the Pizza Parlor.

He'd been being honest when he'd said that Rose-Ann was all right. He wouldn't want to be disloyal – they'd got on very well, considering. And she filled up the place. But she wasn't Mrs Trenchard. A man had to take his chances – she'd do the same if someone she fancied a bit more came along. Of course she would.

Also, he took it as significant that Mrs Trenchard had raised the subject of his former life. He looked for words to reassure her. 'We take things as they come,' he said. 'She works a lot. On the quiet, I mean. Five or six days a week, sometimes.' He didn't, generously, say where. 'We're pretty free and easy. Ships that pass in the night and all that.'

Then, but only because he thought the question of Rose-Ann was just about used up, 'Did that crazy Irene really give you one of her dephasers?'

'It's back at the house.'

'And are you going to use it?'

'She said I was money in the bank. That's why she gave it to me.'

Which was the second time she'd avoided answering. But if she'd left the thing back at the house, then she wasn't taking it too seriously. Himself, he'd decided it was as crazy as the rest of Irene. And he wasn't pleased with himself for having almost believed in it.

'And she told you about the TV people and their high-game generators?'

'High gain. And the hell she went through in the hospital.'

He nodded broad-mindedly. 'What surprises me is that they ever let her out.'

'Must we talk about Irene?'

Snippy. 'Not if you don't want to.'

'I was doing my best to forget her.'

He could understand that. But Irene wouldn't just go away if she wasn't talked about. Still, neither would Rent-a-Corpse with their fake police car, and he wasn't talking about them either. And for the same reason. Plus not wanting to upset Mrs Trenchard. It wouldn't help her, knowing that he'd not be seeing Irene again because he was scared shitless.

Anyway, they'd reached the house now.

Mrs Trenchard unlocked the door, and they went in. He carried the shopping through to the kitchen. It was a long time since he'd done the shopping. Mostly Rose-Ann saw to it on the way home from work.

They unpacked it together, and Mrs Trenchard showed him where things went. When the groceries were put away he took his new summer jacket upstairs and tried it on in front of the wall of mirrors in her bedroom. It really suited him. But it was slightly tight under the arms, on account of his polo neck, and he wished he'd worn a leisure shirt instead. He took off the polo neck and put the jacket on again. It fit perfectly.

Mrs Trenchard arrived in the doorway.

He revolved, looking in the mirror. 'I don't suppose one of your husband's shirts would fit me.'

She said, 'No.'

Just like that.

Not sharply, but with a sort of desperation. He didn't press it. In fact, he respected her. Christ, the man had only been gone four days … Suddenly, taking off the summer jacket, standing there bare-chested, he became aware of himself and Mrs Trenchard. And of the bed behind them. Pictures came into his mind. Sighs. Sensations. They shocked him. But he picked up his polo neck only very slowly.

'This living in the country,' he said. 'We must think about it very seriously.'

His voice seemed to come from a great way off. Hers too. 'But it's no good,' she said, 'if I can't get a permit.'

He drifted back into the room, still bare-chested, still trailing his polo neck, letting happen what must happen. He sat on the bed. 'It's easier for a man,' he said. 'The jobs are there, if you know how to find them.'

She came toward him, unafraid. 'What sort of jobs?'

'I might wangle a transfer. Farmers need insurance like anyone else.'

'And Irene?'

'She'd never find us if we went far enough away.'

Mrs Trenchard stooped in front of him. 'You're trembling,' she said. 'Here, let me help you.'

She took the polo neck from him. He held his breath.

'You must be cold,' she said.

And helped him put it on.

He let her. She really didn't know. That was what did it. He sat there like a clumsy child, letting her guide his arms into the sleeves. She really didn't know.

'Me,' she said mildly. 'It's me Irene wouldn't find if I went far enough away.'

But he missed the gentle correction, still thinking about how she didn't know. And why should she? A decent, stylish woman like her, why should she? Christ, the man had only been gone four days …

She stepped back to let him stand up. 'That's better, Richard. You'll soon get warm.'

Then she went out onto the landing and down the stairs. 'Time for lunch, I think,' she called.

The wall of mirrors told him he was coarse, unworthy. A one-track mind, all cock and balls. But that wasn't true. He'd never thought of Mrs Trenchard in that way before, and he wouldn't again. He knew, mostly, how to behave. Today had been an exception, what with the shopping and him bare-chested and this and that, but he wouldn't let it happen again. Not that she wasn't a proper woman, but there were other things more important. What happened to style, for God's sake, stark-naked, banging away?

People did it. Stylish as you like. Obviously. But only when they knew where they were, And he wasn't a fool – he didn't need telling he was a long way from that.

He put his summer jacket back into its bag and followed her downstairs. He left the bag on a chair in the hall. She didn't know – he clung to that as if it were a rock in a stormy sea.

'I'm making a bean-sprout salad,' she said. Little white things, and chopped nuts. Then, very nicely, 'It's kind of you to worry about me, Richard. But you must think of yourself, too. You've no need to hide. You can quite well stay in the city. Irene thinks you're just a friend of mine.'

He went to the window, looked out over the terrace. 'I hope I *am* a friend.'

'Of course you are.'

Well, he'd better get it over with. He braced himself, turned. 'I socked you for forty thousand.'

'But what about me?' She was smiling. 'I socked the Accident and General for a hundred.'

'That's not the point.'

'I suppose it isn't.' Her hands were neat, neatly tossing crisp lettuce leaves. 'You deserve an explanation, Richard, and I'm afraid I can't give you one. But please believe me – I really don't resent you.'

'You must do.'

'I don't.'

It was a way she had: two or three words, said so calmly, with such calm assurance that they meant more than other people's great long speeches. A couple of lettuce leaves had fallen on the brown-tiled floor. He picked them up, washed them under the tap, shook them dry, and handed them to her. She tucked them into the big wooden bowl.

'Anyway,' she said, 'all that was ages ago.'

And it was. Only four days, but ages. He thought of agreeing with her, then decided it wasn't necessary. With Mrs Trenchard a lot of things weren't necessary.

He dried his hands on a tile-brown towel. Her handbag was lying on top of the dishwasher, where she'd put it when she came in. It was a soft leather thing, and it lay on the dishwasher so that inside it he could clearly see the shape of one of Irene's plastic boxes. He looked away. Irene's dephaser – 'It's back at the house.' Like him, she clearly wasn't pleased with herself for almost believing in it.

He hung up the towel. 'We'll eat on the terrace.' And corrected himself. 'Shall we eat on the terrace?'

Caroline let him carry out the salad, and tongue and salami, and lager from the fridge. She sat opposite him, rested her elbows on the table.

'Do you realize,' she said fondly, 'that since we met the sun has shone every single day?'

She didn't mind that it was part of the romantic myth that the sun always shone on lovers. Even when it was pouring with rain, the sun always shone on lovers. It was part of the romantic myth. And she'd let herself say it all the same. Even if he caught the connotation, poor obtuse Richard, she wasn't worried. He must, as she had said, think of himself. They were her own gentler feelings she was playing with, not his.

Thus the previous instructional twenty minutes. It was sad that they should have been necessary, but one's limitations could only be extended so far. It became a man to be proprietorial. Just as it became him, tactfully, to offer sex. Just as it became a woman, equally tactfully, to discourage the one and postpone the other.

Discourage … postpone … what cold, cowardly words they were. *Lovers*, though incongruous, was bolder. Far more mythological. While one played with one's gentler feelings. Hoping all the time that one had them.

In case of which, it was the moment that counted. Between two friends, two nonlovers, between two people the past and the future were nothing. It was the moment, and its honesty, that counted. Above all, its honesty.

A satisfactory, exonerating illusion.

They were talking grooming talk, about the TV interview they'd seen some of, about her garden, about his, about the sun parlor he was building out at the back. She cut in. 'I'm not sure, Richard, that you should come with me to the country.'

He tipped back his glass, emptied it. 'Who said I wanted to?'

'You did, Richard.'

'I did?'

In the name of honesty. 'You've been saying nothing else ever since I suggested it.'

He conceded the point. 'And you've been letting me.'

'I wasn't sure.' For once she didn't apologize. People, even though friends, nonlovers, shouldn't. 'I didn't know for certain.'

'And now you do.'

In the silence that followed she heard some thrush singing to its heart's content in the beech tree at the bottom of her garden. She wanted to cry. On account, for God's sake, of some poor hackneyed thrush?

'I'd be useful,' Richard said at last.

Which minimality she wouldn't let him get away with. 'But we've been through this before. There's more to living together than just being useful.'

'Oh. That …' He uncrossed his legs, crossed them again. 'There needn't be.'

'And I don't mean sex.' They were grown-up, weren't they? 'I meant love.'

The exonerations of honesty were all very well. But she'd ended up sounding as if she were angling for a declaration.

'We haven't known each other long enough.' Quickly sparing him. Herself. No, him.

He stood up. She was afraid he'd throw her *ages* back in her face, to which, because she had meant it and because it exposed the thinness of her evasion, she wouldn't have had an answer. Part of the romantic myth, her *ages*, but she'd meant it. They really did seem to have known each other for ages.

And he didn't, bless him, say a word. He walked away across the lawn, not saying a word.

She watched him sadly. He fingered her roses. And when he came back he'd made up his mind.

'You must put in for your permit. To live in the country, I mean. And we'll wait and see what happens.'

'Thank you.'

'What for?'

'Just thank you.'

He frowned, pleased, and sat down again. She wouldn't go, anyway. Not anywhere. She'd stay where she was, under siege. Irene had been right; she preferred knowing what to expect. So they talked about her garden, his garden, the sun parlor he was building out at the back, and gradually things got better. Until, from the house behind them, came the sound of the doorbell. Uneasily their eyes met.

He chewed his lip. 'Irene?'

'I doubt it.'

'She's crazy enough.'

'No.' She hadn't yet told him about the extra two thousand. 'Not so soon.'

'Shall I go and see?'

'I think I'd better.'

She rose, under siege, and went back into the house. The two of them there, and everyone else outside. Nonlovers, but friends all the same. The everyone else in particular turning out to be Humphrey, wearing his publisher's spotted tie, standing in the sun on her doorstep.

'Greetings, Caro. I know I should have phoned, but then you'd have put me off. Happy Saturday.'

It could easily have been an everyone worse.

'Happy Saturday,' she said, and led him through into the garden. The living room, Haverstock's study, the terrace …

He didn't falter for an instant when he saw who was already there. 'Ricardo … how nice. Now I can apologize for that terrible party.'

Richard stood up. 'It was fine. We had a fine time. Honestly.'

Caroline noted the inclusion. The two of them there, and everyone else outside. So he felt it too. But not, like her, with appendices.

The two men shook hands.

'Sit down,' she said. 'We're drinking beer. Can I get you one?'

From the kitchen she heard the faint murmur of their conversation. So Richard had forgiven her – certainly for all the wrong things, for her belated honesty, but his forgiveness seemed to stretch to all the right ones. She took a lager six-pack from the fridge and put it on the tray, and a glass for Humphrey. Love? What a gilded requirement. There hadn't been love before, with Haverstock, so why was she being so fussy? She hoped it was altruistic, for Richard's own good. With all his innocent dreadfulness, he didn't deserve her, with all her uninnocent dreadfulness. But she carried the tray out onto the terrace knowing this to be a shoddy attempt at self-delusion. The reasons for her fussiness were really quite other. Realism. Fear. Appendices.

'Humphrey's been telling me about these friends of his with a pheasant farm.'

'A pheasant farm?' She put the tray on the table. 'What's that?'

'Like a chicken farm. Only it's for pheasants. And when they're grown they let them loose in the woods for shooting.'

'Poor pheasants.' She was standing behind him. Impulsively, with Humphrey watching, she stooped and leaned her arms on his shoulders, letting her hands rest lightly across his chest. So that Humphrey, who had already added what he saw as two and two, should know that she was unashamed. And might therefore imagine that she was also without fear, or realism, or appendices.

'Poor?' Humphrey snapped open three beer cans. 'A pretty good life, I'd say. Six months living off the fat of the land, and then – bingo.'

'Personally I can't stand Bingo.'

'Ah, but then you, my dear Caro, are nobody's fool.' He filled her glass and gave it to her. She held it in both her hands, against Richard's chest. 'If you were a pheasant you'd make it your business to find out the rules.'

'What rules are those?'

'That sitting birds don't get shot. So you'd stay sitting.'

She laughed and straightened up, the point now safely made. 'That depends on how cross the dog was that they sent to flush me out.' But she left one unashamed hand on Richard's shoulder. It was easy, really, touching people. In front, that is, of other people.

'He wouldn't do a thing, if you just sat still enough. He's trained not to.'

'What a stupid conversation this is.'

It *was* stupid, wasn't it? She moved away, flung herself down in a chair. It would be just like Humphrey, trying to tell her something about herself and the man he thought of as her truck driver. Was he advising her to stay put? Or was he suggesting that she rose up and risked getting shot?

Or was he saying something else altogether?

'Are there really rules?' she said. 'So that if we could only discover them we'd be all right?'

'Dearest Caro, of course there are rules. And of course if we could only discover them we'd be all right.'

Perhaps in fact he was laughing at her. One never knew with Humphrey. 'I didn't think you believed in God, Humphrey.'

'I don't. God is for children. Which blessed state eluded me eons ago.'

Now at last she knew he was just being clever. And saw that Richard had been silent ever since her arms on his shoulders. She and Humphrey, both being clever, basically at his expense.

'Richard, love ...' But she didn't touch him again. 'Why don't you tell us we're talking arty nonsense?'

He jumped. 'The fact is,' he said, 'I was thinking about children. Humphrey mentioned them. And I was wondering why you and Mr Trenchard never had any.'

She had to believe that he was simply interested. Not vicious, not merciless, simply interested. Out of the mouths of babes and truck drivers indeed.

Humphrey reached for another lager, rescued her. 'You never met Haverstock. He was Caro's child. There wouldn't have been room for another.'

Neat enough. But it was less than the truth, an easy answer, too easy for the serious innocence of the question. Caroline closed her eyes to concentrate. 'I suppose I was never wholehearted enough,' she said.

'Caro darling – how hard you are on yourself.'

'It's true, though.' She opened her eyes, leaned forward. Humphrey, dear though he was, didn't matter. Richard did. 'With children you've got to be wholehearted. And I've never in my life been wholehearted about anything.'

The thrush in the beech tree at the bottom of her garden had flown away. The silence was completed instead by somebody's electric mower.

'Goodness me,' Humphrey murmured. 'Haven't we gone serious.' He went so far as to straighten his publisher's spotted tie. She'd discommoded him.

But not Richard. 'There's plenty of time,' he told her. 'I shouldn't let it worry you.'

Plenty of time to be wholehearted. Plenty of time, with or without him, to have children. His words were totally, magnificently, without innuendo. Almost, then, she loved him. Almost.

They sat in the sun.

'Anyway,' he went on, 'that's not what we were talking about.'

'I've quite forgotten.' She felt suddenly gay. 'What *were* we talking about?'

'About Humphrey's friends' pheasant farm. He says he's heard that they might want to take on an assistant.'

Friends in high places – it sounded far too opportune. And anyway, she had her house, her ramparts. 'An assistant?'

'Don't tell me you're interested, Caro darling.'

'What sort of an assistant?'

'There's a positive shooting mania just at the moment. Everybody and his wife is going shooting. It's this new prosperity – they pay the most fantastic sums. Suddenly every farmer with a covert on his land can make money.'

'So?'

'So there's this insatiable demand for pheasants. Thousands and thousands and thousands of them. It sounds mad, but it's true.'

Anyway, she had her house. 'I couldn't possibly raise pheasants.'

'I never thought you could, darling. I was only talking. All this' – he gestured at the garden, the terrace, the house – 'why should you?'

So that, thank God, was that.

'I can't see as it'd be all that difficult,' Richard said.

'And besides,' said Humphrey, shifting in his seat, 'there's nothing definite. Lots of people think of taking on assistants. I've done it myself.'

Richard eyed him fiercely. 'Thought about it? Or done it?'

'Well … both, actually. She's an absolute pet. But publishing's different. My dear Ricardo, how literal-minded you are.'

'Different? Publishing's just another business – how is it different?'

Gratefully Humphrey escaped into a conceit. 'Perhaps it isn't. What a nice idea – putting up birds to be shot at. I think you're right – that's *just* what I do.'

Only to be promptly recaptured. 'Mrs Trenchard wants to leave the city. I told her, without a job you can't get a permit.'

'But, my dear fellow, I was only talking.'

'So now you can *do*, instead.'

He could be horribly abrupt. On her behalf, man-to-man, downright rude. On what he thought of as her behalf. She twitched her shoulders. She'd been happy to watch them argue, discussing her future between themselves with flattering enthusiasm. But they were wasting their time.

'I couldn't possibly raise pheasants,' she said again.

Richard frowned briefly. 'What's your friends' address?' he asked Humphrey.

'My dear Ricardo, I –'

'At least you could let Mrs Trenchard have their address.' She wished he wouldn't call her that. It said all the wrong things. 'I'm not asking you to get involved or anything,' he went on. 'Just the address – that's all.'

Which Humphrey, being meek enough to be hurt by the sarcasm, felt obliged to go one better than. He turned to her. 'I'll give them a ring. Mind if I use your phone?'

'Of course Mrs Trenchard doesn't mind.'

Humphrey waited a moment for her to refute this, or even to notice it, then got up and went into the house. Caroline couldn't believe herself. She found she was welcoming Richard's takeover.

Distantly the mower mowed. 'I couldn't possibly raise pheasants,' she said, by way of disownment, for a third time.

Richard didn't directly answer. 'That girl Irene,' he said. 'I went to bed with her.'

She stared at him, disconcerted, seeking a connection. And was suddenly angry, believing she had found one. She asked, offensively, 'Was she good?'

That too was vulgar. But he didn't say so.

'I lied to you on the phone. It's worried me.'

And still she believed complicatedly that he was making one last appeal, through confession, for her love. 'I don't really care what the bloody hell you did.'

He looked away. 'I know,' he said.

And he did know. Mrs Trenchard really didn't care. Why should she? But *he* cared – he cared very much. Not about the bed, but about the lie. He had to care about the lie because, unlike the bed, it was between him and her.

Even though he knew all that was now over. He wouldn't want her finding out about it later, from that crazy girl.

'Of course you could raise pheasants,' he told her. 'Any fool could.'

He'd said *I know*, and looked away. Now, when he looked back, all her anger had gone. He didn't know why, but that was Mrs Trenchard all over.

'I suppose I could.'

She reached over to pat his hand which, not being done like the arms as a show-off in front of that prissy publisher, puzzled him again. But that was Mrs Trenchard all over.

Humphrey came out of the house. 'They'd love to see you.'

He stood beside the table, beaming down at them like Mr bloody Fixit himself, as if the whole bloody thing had been his own bloody idea.

'Where is it, then?' Richard demanded. 'This bloody pheasant farm, where is it?'

'Not far.' Humphrey rubbed his hands. 'Sixty miles or so. Just outside Stemborough.'

Richard glanced across at Mrs Trenchard. It certainly wasn't very far. But sixty was probably as good as six hundred, if that crazy Irene didn't even know where to start looking. 'When'll you go?' he said.

'You're rushing me.' She laughed.

'Somebody has to.'

'Will you come with me?'

The laughter remained, so that he took it as lightly as it appeared to be meant. 'If I've nothing else on.'

Behind the table Humphrey fidgeted, looked from one to the other, started to say something, changed his mind, said something else. 'I shouldn't leave it too long. They're in more of a hurry than I thought.'

Mrs Trenchard spread her arms. 'What's wrong with tomorrow?'

Richard checked. Tomorrow was Sunday. Sunday was when he'd decided he was too scared to go and see Irene. What with Rent-a-Corpse and so on, Irene was bad news. 'I can't make Sunday,' he said. 'I've got a prior engagement.'

They arranged to go on Monday instead, leaving – at Mrs Trenchard's suggestion – shortly after eleven. She didn't ask him about his prior engagement, and he was glad, for he wouldn't have told her. Now that things were finished between them, it was no longer her business. But, bad news or no, he owed it to *himself* to go and see Irene. Just one more time. He could deal with her more openly now, knowing that she knew that he knew that she knew about him and Mrs Trenchard. Perhaps he could shut her up, buy her off. Possibly, if he was tough enough, and he felt like being tough, he could even frighten her.

They sat on the terrace. He knew that he should go, but he didn't want to. And he remembered that he hadn't yet asked Mrs Trenchard about Fitzhenry, and it might be important, so he stayed. Humphrey stayed also, watching the two of them, smiling like a Cheshire cat. Richard felt like kicking his teeth in. He knew what it looked like, his being there and all. And Mrs Trenchard hadn't helped, mooning over his shoulder. Still, it had meant she was choosing sides, which was nice, so he'd weathered it, just as he'd weathered being there in the first place, and Humphrey could think what he liked. The truth was that he'd socked her for forty thousand. A secret like that made up for a lot.

The afternoon wore on. They talked of Mrs Trenchard's garden, and Humphrey's garden, and the conservatory Humphrey had a marvelous little man building on for him at the back. Until finally Richard could stick it no longer.

Mrs Trenchard went with him to the front door. 'I was precipitate,' she said.

He paused, half out of the door. 'You what?'

'And you took it so nicely.'

'Took what?'

'Humphrey too. His turning up. You took it all so nicely.'

'Well …'

'I was afraid, Richard. I still am.'

He thought he'd caught on. 'Oh, the *job*. There'll be nothing to it. You'll see.'

'I meant what I said about never having been wholehearted. Not since I can't remember when.'

He went out onto the step. If she didn't want him to understand her, then that was her affair.

'You've forgotten your summer jacket,' she said, fetching it for him.

He took it. 'You talked about someone called Fitzhenry. Who's Fitzhenry?'

'It doesn't matter. He's the man who runs Rent-a-Corpse. I called him up.'

'What did he say?'

'He pretended he hadn't heard of me. He said the trouble was all mine.'

Richard gave up, made an all-purpose wry face. 'Bastard. Let's hope the pheasants work out … Monday, then?' He held out his hand, for the very first time, and she shook it. 'Around eleven?'

As he went down the steps she called after him, something about precipices again, and he waved reassuringly. That was Mrs Trenchard all over. Then he hurried off down the street to where his yellow city electric was waiting, carefully plugged in to the nearest available charging point.

Rose-Ann was out when he got home, still at the Pizza Parlor, making up for not having let herself be taken for granted the day before. He was relieved. He'd had time, on his way around the Fairthorpe Two-tier, to think about things. He felt little resentment that Mrs Trenchard had dumped him, only a vague, almost luxurious sadness. Of course they didn't love each other. Not because she was stuck-up – he couldn't think of her so, not after today – but rather because he was coarse and unworthy. He'd worked that out, though not in so many words, on his walk down her lawn to look at her roses. He knew it, even if she didn't. Then Humphrey's arrival had proved the point. Humphrey was coarse and unworthy too.

Yet he was still relieved not to have to face Rose-Ann the moment he got home. He wanted to feel his new freedom. Mrs Trenchard had dumped him, and he had forty thousand in the bank. Or he soon would have. Two meters tall, and a cock like Casanova's. The time he'd have. The things he'd do, all the things he'd always wanted to. All the things that made life really worth living … And Rose-Ann meant complications. What would, should, could he tell her? How and when?

She came in while he was microwaving up a carton of goulash for supper. They hadn't, in fact, been talking all that much since yesterday, what with the time he'd got in the night before and her expecting him just to pick up a receipt and be straight back for lunch. She'd waited around for him all day – or so she'd said.

'Hullo, pet.' He looked up from setting the kitchen table. 'How's things?'

'Mustn't grumble.' She put down her bulging blue string bag. She'd stopped in at the shops on her way home. 'Who's Carson Bandbridge?'

He concentrated on the knives and forks. 'You what?'

'I meant to ask you last night. Who's Carson Bandbridge?'

'If you'd stayed in you could have asked me this morning.'

It was fair enough. He'd been up by nine. She needn't really have been in such a hurry to get off to that lousy Pizza Parlor. 'There's a check in your Italian suit. Forty thousand. Made out to this bloke called Carson Bandbridge.'

'Do you always go through my pockets?'

'It needed to go to the cleaners. I've put the check on the bedroom mantelpiece. Who's Carson Bandbridge?'

And he'd had time now to think up an answer. 'A client. Lucky sod. His wife died on him.'

'Charming.' She slopped Coca-Cola into a mug. 'Shouldn't you give him the check?'

'I will. On Tuesday. I'm not like you – I value my leisure.'

'Where does he live, this Carson Bandbridge?'

'South of the river.' Thinking of Mr Mandelbaum. 'In a classy condominium. Why the sudden interest?'

'Your work … that sort of thing … it's nice to know.'

She'd never concerned herself with his work before. But then of course she'd never seen a check for forty thousand before. And at that moment the microwave pinged, and it was time for supper.

He did his best to be friendly. He talked about her day. Eighty pizzas

Neapolitana, she told him, and a hundred and twenty-three alla Romana. More than half of them jumbo. And the pistachio ice cream wasn't moving the way Bert would have liked. And he'd been in one of his moods. Hardly a word, except to say get a move on.

Richard tipped the last of the goulash carton onto her plate.

'Poor Rosy,' he said.

They watched television. All about Bessarabian macaws.

And he still didn't know what to do about her.

That night, when they were in bed and nearly asleep, there was a Singing. Complete with sweet synthetic roses. They lay, folded very close, and waited for it to stop.

'Sodding heavenly choirs,' she said.

He stroked her hair. 'Sodding things,' he agreed.

He could feel her heart beating, strong and steady. And the familiar, lumpy shape of her. He was asleep before the Singing ended.

EIGHT

Jerusalem. 7/3/86. Speaking yesterday at the official opening of the new American-supplied Israeli Moondrift power station in the Gaza Strip, Energy Minister Cohen told his distinguished audience, 'This fine example of peaceful cooperation heralds a new era of understanding between our great nations. The OPEC states should look to their laurels. No longer can they hold the Western World to ransom. Drastic realignments, political and territorial, are inevitable.' (See Editorial on p. 18.)

Caroline was having her morning bath. And in it she was loving herself. *Loving herself* ... a phrase she had chosen on her own as a twelve-year-old, in understandable preference to the cheerful technicalities of her parents. An intuitive child, she had found it a helpful way of looking at things. But in no sense a euphemism – it was simply that, since when people did it to each other it was called love, then it should be called the same when she did it to herself.

Loving herself, giving pleasure to herself ... possibly not rationalized so until many years later, but if she didn't then who would?

She had learned to be good at it. Lying in the bath, two soft, warm, busy fingers, while her left hand stroked her breasts, looking up at herself looking up at herself. Lingering. Tenderly spinning it out, to the very brink and then slowly back. Those few moments in her life when she could exist without thought, and thus allow herself simple affection.

Sunday morning – the better the day, the better the deed. And her climax, when she half-regretfully granted it, so much grander, so much more entire, than others had ever been able to conjure for her. A private, invisible, precious joy, between herself and herself, shared only with the elegant, unashamed woman in the mirror above, into whose eyes alone she dared gaze.

They relaxed, her reflection and she, slipping peacefully down into the water. They reached out toes to turn on hot taps. They folded hands across the pale islands of their bellies. It was a drowsy time, a time for gathering in. They breathed the steamy, scented air. The mirror clouded. They closed their eyes.

Later, boiled crimson, she heaved herself up out of the bath and onto the tiles. She reached for a towel. To have the bathroom to herself was a luxury she wasn't yet used to. Haverstock had been very manly about their bathroom, striding hairily in and out, liable to push-ups. When he wasn't flinging himself in with her and splashing water all over the floor. She dried herself, languorously, taking all the time in the world.

Poor Haverstock. Such a pervasive person – so unlike Mr Wallingford, who could easily have been taught to tiptoe through her life. But it had been Haverstock's pervasiveness of course, in the beginning, that had appealed to her. Replacing that of her parents who, when she was twenty, had departed thankfully, their duty done, and gone their separate, highly enterprising ways. Three years she had existed, in a chaos of competing personalities, her own and other people's, until Haverstock had hurtled into view, literally, and shouted them all down. They'd met in a car accident, his fault entirely, in Nantes. And the volume of his swearing, and of his yellow shirt, had convinced her that with him she would be safe forever.

And so she would have been. But for the Singing's intervention she'd have been safe down all the years of her life and into her dotage, for he would certainly have outlived her. And, within the marriage framework as interpreted by Haverstock, he'd never have failed her. All the modern advantages and none of the old-fashioned disadvantages – he was strongly in favor of the marriage framework.

Safe, therefore … She dried, thoughtfully, between her toes. Gerbils, she decided, dutifully pedaling their wheel with the family tom sitting on top of their cage, were *safe*. Possibly they didn't mind the day-and-night presence of family tom, or the claws that occasionally hooked down at them. But even gerbils had been known to rattle their bars and twitter.

Hence the irreproachable spite.

She frowned. It was an untidy, self-justificatory image, but she couldn't think of a better one. She wandered into her bedroom. She didn't need images. She had exchanged a sort of safety for the luxury of a bathroom to herself. A house to herself. A life to herself. It wasn't an exchange she had chosen, so regretting it – even if she had wanted to – was irrelevant. Certainly it was far too soon to try giving herself up to a new sort of safety. A Mr Wallingford sort of safety.

Anyway, what she'd told him was quite fair, they hadn't known each other anything like long enough. On the doorstep she'd told him about her appendices, too. But only in words that he couldn't possibly understand.

She put on underwear. Then she opened the wardrobe with her summer clothes in it and got out a soft, green-brown dress. It was Thai silk, very simple, with wide sleeves gathered in at the cuffs, and a long, loose belt. She liked the oriental silks: they never cluttered her. She put the dress on, unpinned her hair from its bath-time topknot, and sat down at the mirror. Nobody would be coming today. She was preparing herself for herself. Her house, her life. She began brushing her hair.

The doorbell rang.

Slowly she laid down her hairbrush. It was the function of doorbells, she told her calm reflection, that people should ring them. Just as it was the function of doors that people should want to come through them. The pity was that one need possess either.

She looked at the French enamel clock by her bed. Her bed. Her house, too. She need admit nobody she didn't want to. The time was nearly half past ten. She went downstairs, bare-legged, barefooted, her hair swinging freely in the slight breeze of her descent. She opened the door, one of the functions of which was to be opened.

An unfamiliar young woman, frowsy, stood on the step, pulling at the hem of a pink, knee-length sweater. 'You're Mrs Trenchard,' she said.

Irene's sister? All sorts of impossible possibilities came to mind. 'I am.'

'I reckon you've heard of me.' She was stooping now, and the sweater was anxiously down to her shins. 'I'm Rose-Ann Spiller.'

Caroline tilted her head. She should have guessed. 'Yes?'

'I wanted a word.'

'A word?'

'You going to leave me standing here?'

Her bed. Her house, too. She need admit nobody she didn't want to. A charming smile. 'Do please come in.'

Rose-Ann straightened and came. They eyed each other in the hall.

'I was just going to have some breakfast,' Caroline said. 'Would you care to join me?'

'I've et.'

'Then you'll just have to watch me, my dear. Because I'm afraid I haven't.'

Behavior patterns. Defensive. Food to hide behind. Also 'my dear.' But she wasn't, just then, even aware of them. They went into the kitchen. The coffee had perked while she was having her bath, and was keeping hot. She cut a grapefruit in half and put one half in a bowl. Then she put the bowl and the coffeepot on the tray, together with a cup and saucer, a plate, silverware, a rack of dietary rusk, and a tub of sugar-free marmalade, and carried them through into the breakfast room. She rested the tray on the Dutch dresser while she shook out a clean white cloth and spread it on the table. Then she transferred the things from the tray to the table and sat down. Rose-Ann watched her through all this in silence.

Now, 'I wanted a word,' she said again.

But the domestic interlude had given Caroline time to censor. And it was Mr Wallingford she was disappointed in, not Rose-Ann. So a little common courtesy would do nobody any harm.

Encouragingly, 'Sit down, then.' And, offering the coffeepot even though there wasn't a second cup and saucer, 'Changed your mind?'

'No, ta.'

Rose-Ann sat down. Silence.

They spoke together. { 'It's a lovely day again ...'
'I got your address from ...'

Caroline laughed. 'After you.'

'It wasn't nothing.'

'No – please.'

Rose-Ann scratched her leg. 'Dickie doesn't know I'm here. I got your address from the telephone directory.'

Caroline hadn't thought he would have chosen for the compartments of his life to overlap. 'Why *are* you here?' *Hands off, he's mine?* Surely not.

'I didn't even know your name. Not till I saw it on that check.'

That check. To the account of Mr and Mrs Haverstock Trenchard ... So Richard had been bad at keeping even his own guilty secrets. Poor Richard. And now, quite possibly, poor her also. This Rose-Ann was nothing if not an unknown quantity.

'A check, Miss Spiller?'

'It was a big one. And he said it was from the Accident and General, his firm like, but it wasn't. It was from you.'

'I write a lot of checks, Miss Spiller.' Prevarication to the point of imbecility. But one had to know where one stood.

Silence.

Until Rose-Ann hoisted up her feet, rested her heels on the front edge of the rush-bottomed, breakfast-room chair, and hugged her knees. From behind her knees she said, quite casually, 'Has he done something bad, Mrs Trenchard?'

Caroline supposed he had. 'It depends what you mean by "bad."'

'Something he could get into trouble for?'

A definition that Caroline sympathized with, and could answer truthfully. 'No, Miss Spiller. Nothing he could get into trouble for.'

'You're sure?'

Of course she was. As long as she held her tongue Richard was safe. 'I'm sure.'

'I'll be on my way, then.' Lowering her no longer necessary knees. Telling Caroline, if she had ever seriously been uncertain, where she stood.

'Couldn't we talk a bit?'

'Bert's expecting me.'

Bert? 'Bert can wait.'

'Well ... Sod it, I'm late already. Bert can go hang.'

'And you're sure you won't have some coffee?'

'I don't mind.'

Caroline got up, and went through to the kitchen for another cup and saucer. She wanted to talk. Rose-Ann, too, wanted to talk. They both wanted to talk about Mr Wallingford. Richard. Dickie.

Though there was also, from Caroline's point of view, the helpful suggestion to be made that Rose-Ann stop concerning herself with the check. For Richard's sake, discretion being the better part of any relationship.

Caroline returned to the breakfast room with a cup and saucer, and – because she had seen how Rose-Ann bulged unmindfully out of her clothes – milk and sugar.

'Bert's your boss?'

'That's right. Don't mean he can take me for granted, though.'

'Of course not.'

'That's what Dickie says. He says I mustn't let myself get took for granted.'

'He's quite right.' Pouring coffee. 'Help yourself to milk and sugar.'

Rose-Ann did.

'You've known Mr Wallingford a long time?'

'Long enough.'

'He's helped me a lot. He came to see me on an insurance matter. My husband went, you know.'

'Dickie gets a lot of Disappearances work these days.'

'Have you lost anyone that way?'

Rose-Ann shook her head and held up two crossed fingers.

Caroline took a rusk out of the toast rack. 'It's a terrible shock when it happens.'

'I bet.'

Suddenly Caroline realized what she was doing. She was pussyfooting around, trying to find out, for heaven's sake, how Rose-Ann would feel if she lost Richard. And not in the Disappearances, either. Trying to find out something that – now she had met this girl, this old-fashioned girl, this girl who had told Richard he was in love – she already knew. Something, furthermore, that – on account of her appendices – was no longer of any great interest to her.

'About that check, Miss Spiller – I really shouldn't let it worry you.'

'I'm not the worrying sort.'

'I asked Mr Wallingford to deliver it to a friend of mine.'

'This Carson Bandbridge.'

'That's it. A sort of goodbye present … You know what I mean?' Hoping that, to Rose-Ann, women in Mrs Trenchard's world might indeed pay off lovers with forty thousand. And that, anyway, there were indeed none so credulous as those who wouldn't doubt. 'I asked Mr Wallingford not to say anything to anybody about it. That'll be why he pretended to you it was from the Accident and General.'

Rose-Ann shrugged. 'Thing is, Dickie's a bloody bad liar.'

So am I, thought Caroline. 'Nice men always are.'

'You've a point there.'

But I, thought Caroline, am a *good* liar. I get believed. And liars who get believed are not nice at all. 'You're lucky to have him, Miss Spiller.'

'Me? Have him? You must be joking.'

'I'm not.'

'Well, you're wrong. Ships that pass in the night, that's us.'

A familiar response. Learned. Poor Rose-Ann – how often had he told her that? But there were also none so doubting as those who wouldn't believe … Damn all those psychoanalysts and their double-, triple-, quadruple-thinks. The conversation was getting her nowhere. It was humiliating, too.

'… What's he doing today?'

'Working on his sun parlor. He's building on this sun parlor out at the back.'

'Pity you couldn't stay at home and help him.'

'He's got this kit of parts.' The idea had never occurred to her. 'It keeps him busy.'

Not that Caroline was interested, not even remembering his Sunday prior engagement. She couldn't expect to monopolize his every single hour. And would *she* have been out at the back, helping him?

The answer appeared to be yes, her appendices notwithstanding, and her humiliation complete.

She rearranged her legs minutely. 'Well …' she said.

Rose-Ann wasn't slow. 'Thanks for the coffee.' She stood up. 'And the chat. I best be on my way.'

Caroline stood also, and took her to the front door. Rose-Ann admired the grandfather clock. Caroline opened the front door, because that was one of its functions, and showed her guest out onto the front doorstep, which was there for that purpose. 'You have a car?'

'That's right.' Rose-Ann pointed. 'The beat-up blue one.' But she didn't go to it.

Caroline drew back. Frequently, according to doctors, it wasn't until a patient was going that she told you the real reason for her visit.

Thus, 'Yesterday a man came into the Parlor. Asking about Dickie.'

'The parlor?'

'The Pizza Parlor. Asking about Dickie. Said he was a copper.'

'Asking what?'

'The presents he bought me. That sort of thing. Said he was a copper.'

'Why are you telling me this?'

'Said he was a copper. I didn't let on that I didn't believe him.'

'Why didn't you believe him?'

'You get to know coppers. In the Pizza Parlor.'

'What did Mr Wallingford say when you told him?'

'I didn't. Thought I'd see what you said first.'

'You thought it was something to do with the check?'

'It might of been.'

'Now you know it can't have been.' With emphasis. But not too much.

'Wouldn't go away. Has Dickie been buying things.'

'And has he?'

'Only the sun parlor kit. And that was weeks ago.'

'Did he give you his name?'

'Said he'd be back. Name of Fitzhenry.'

Caroline closed her eyes and leaned against the edge of the open door. It was a curious question, and she didn't know why she'd asked it. She wished she hadn't. Mr Fitzhenry got about far too much for her comfort ... She wondered, again, why Rose-Ann was telling her this. Exposing her lie about the check? She wouldn't have thought Rose-Ann capable of such deviousness.

'I expect you're right, Rose-Ann. He probably isn't a policeman. If I were you I wouldn't tell him anything at all.'

'That's what I thought. A nasty piece of work, Mr Fitzhenry. But I wanted to ask you all the same. Being a friend of Dickie's and that.'

Only a friend? Caroline checked herself. The uncertainty, she realized, was hers alone. Rose-Ann was telling her this because she had already decided the extent of their 'friendship.' And was turning innocently to her in her superior position as someone with a superior position. Lord preserve us all.

But she meant Dickie well. They both meant Mr Wallingford well.

'You stick to your guns, Rose-Ann. He's probably a crook, trying to find out if you're worth robbing. If he comes again, don't tell him anything at all.'

'That's what I thought. But I wanted to ask you all the same.'

Rose-Ann went down the steps. A young woman who, unaware of such things as limitations, yet operated faultlessly within them. She thought what she needed to think, understood what she needed to understand, knew what she needed to know. 'Goodbye, Mrs Trenchard,' she called. 'You've set my mind at rest a treat.'

From which comprehensive accolade Caroline turned humbly away, and went back into her house, and closed her door. Because, after all, that was one of the functions of doors. She went back to her breakfast also, in her house, behind her door, wearing her Thai silk dress, looking out onto her garden. They were all still hers, and they still – in spite of Mr Wallingford, in spite of Rose-Ann, in spite of the dangerous Mr Fitzhenry – maintained their relevance. But she wished sincerely that they didn't.

Sharp at two o'clock Richard descended off the Fairthorpe Two-tier and drove down past the High Park. In five short days it had become a route not only touchingly familiar but also Pavlovian in the responses it elicited. Southbound, a steady heightening of awareness, a lightness of spirit, a sense of unnamed, joyful expectation: northbound, a home-going, dreamlike languor. So that, turning that afternoon not right at the traffic lights but driving straight on down the hill, he experienced a sudden coldness, a jolt, unpleasant, akin to a mental amputation. It was Irene at the end of his journey. Not Mrs Trenchard. Not Mrs Trenchard's high, white house, but Irene's attic hovel. Crazy Irene. Unshakeable Mrs Trenchard.

He'd worked hard on his sun parlor the whole morning, breaking only to wave goodbye to Rose-Ann, off to the Pizza Parlor even though it was Sunday, filling his mind with the kit's precise, logical clips and slots and sockets. There was an excluding pleasure in the manageable conjunctions of panel and bearer, soffit and architrave. So that now, backing into a parking space with a miraculously unvandalized charging point, he was no nearer to a strategy for dealing with Irene than he had been the previous day on Mrs Trenchard's terrace. Then he had felt like being tough. Now he wasn't so sure.

He approached the dazzle-painted front door, half-hoping it would be locked, and no one at home. It was on the latch. A dank, cavelike silence pervaded the house – at least the Bed-Rock had made the place *sound* as if it were alive and well. Richard pushed open the door and reluctantly went in, up the stairs past the room of the novelist who had been a computer man. Faint wooden creakings could be heard through the door, as if of a rocking chair on bare boards. Richard continued on, up and up, till he came to Irene's landing. There was an open umbrella resting ferrule-down in the sink, full of scrumpled bits of torn paper. Suddenly apprehensive, Richard turned some of them over with one finger. For some obscure reason they were slightly wet. But they weren't, thank God, money.

The landing, like the rest of the house, was ominously silent. The door to Irene's room stood ajar. Bracing himself, Richard knocked, got no answer, peered warily around it. Irene was sitting up in bed, apparently making flowers out of wire and crepe paper. She didn't look up.

'Can you cook?' she said.

Well, he'd known she was crazy. 'Not much.'

'Well, I'm bloody awful. You can't be as bad as me.'

'What needs cooking?'

'The kitchen's behind you. Why don't you look?'

Trying tough. 'Why don't *you?*'

'I'm busy.'

The sheer improbability of her bore him down. He went back out onto the landing. 'There's an umbrella in the sink,' he called.

'You're cooking, aren't you? Not washing up.'

The umbrella, however, took up nearly half the width of the landing. He lifted it, looked vainly around for somewhere to put it. Finally he had a brainwave, folded it up on its soggy contents, and propped it against the side of the electric cooker.

Half of Irene's supermarket pineapple stood on the drain board. Moldy cornflakes were in the cupboard under the sink, and the shelves above carried various pots and pans and crockery, a jar of instant coffee, and her tin of supermarket curry powder. 'There's only pineapple, instant coffee, and curry powder,' he called.

'I hate instant coffee. What's wrong with curried pineapple?'

He went back into her room. 'You're crazy,' he said.

'Don't you dare call me that. I was only seeing how far I could push you.'

Tough now, and meaning it. 'Now look here –'

She held up one finger. Listened. 'That bloody tap. It kept me awake till nearly four.'

Behind him there was the clear sound of water dripping into the sink. He added two and two. 'Why the crumpled-up paper?' he asked.

'Without it the water formed a puddle, then dripped into the puddle.'

Maybe she wasn't so crazy after all.

'Now look here,' he said, 'me and you must have a serious talk.'

'You and I.'

He controlled himself. 'Are you *trying* to annoy me?'

'Yes.'

So he went to one of the television sets and kicked the screen in. Splinters showered satisfactorily onto the floor. Irene continued wrapping wire around scraps of mauve crepe paper. 'Two thousand one hundred,' she said.

He strode to the mattress, stood over her. 'Two thousand one hundred *what?*' Stooping ready to dump her out onto the floor. 'Are you talking about money?'

'Mrs Trenchard's already coughing up another two thousand. Tomorrow morning. Now there's the TV to pay for as well.'

He checked. 'Tomorrow morning?'

'Didn't she tell you?'

'Of course she told me.' But he felt defused. 'At least we know what's what,' he shouted. 'You're nothing but a cheap little blackmailer.'

'Expensive. And I told you that on Friday.'

And besides, the word had a recoil. He thought of the check for forty thousand, now safely in the pocket of his second-best suit in the bedroom closet. 'We … can't go on like this,' he said.

She smiled up at him. 'Be a dear and go and see to that tap. It's getting on my nerves.'

Out on the landing he opened the umbrella again and put it back in the sink. The drips fell silently onto the soggy paper. The whole house was like that: soggy and silent. He wanted to leave. But he went back to Irene.

'Thank you,' she said. 'Do you like my pretty flowers?'

'Not much.'

'I do. I learnt to make them in the hospital. I went through hell in that hospital.'

'Making flowers? Sounds to me as if you had a bloody good time.'

She laid down her wire cutters. 'You're theirs,' she said. 'That's all you know. All they tell you. And they can make you into anything they like.'

Gray words. They settled grayly over him. Repartee would have had it that the hospital had obviously failed – they couldn't possibly like what they'd made *her* into. But it wasn't repartee time, somehow.

Her expression changed. Suddenly she was on top again. 'But that, of course, was only the reconstitution process. I wouldn't let go, you see. So they had to arrange electronic molecular reconstitution. EMR for short.' She reached for the reel of wire. 'They used me for Theo Rawsthorne. Did I tell you that?'

'Yes.'

Richard moved away through the TVs to the window. Through its gray net curtain he had a view of the street five stories below. He could see his car. There were children playing in the street now, but so far only with other people's. He knew he shouldn't stay much longer. 'You can't go on socking Mrs Trenchard,' he said.

Irene snipped off a length of wire. 'The TV people need our psychic energies. You must have seen them, Carson Bandbridge. You must have sensed there's nothing behind the eyes.'

Not crazy at all. And he'd get nowhere. Unless, 'Did Mr Fitzhenry put you up to this?'

'Mr Fitzhenry?' Her face softened. 'Now there's a real friend. I wouldn't be here if it wasn't for Mr Fitzhenry. He got me out of that hospital, you see.'

'Was it him,' turning from the window, trying to hide his excitement, 'was it him who told you about Mrs Trenchard?'

'I owe everything to Mr Fitzhenry. He's a real friend. He got me out of that hospital.'

Another tack then. 'Does he work for Rent-a-Corpse?'

'You don't often find, Carson Bandbridge, someone who really *cares*. Someone who sees the injustices of this world and tries to right them.'

'That's true enough. But –'

'*You* don't, for one. You don't give a damn about the injustices.'

Aha. 'Isn't what you're doing to Mrs Trenchard an injustice?'

'She can afford it.'

'That's not the point.'

'Yes it is. She's greedy. Don't you hate greedy people?'

Again his forty thousand. And what about the money under Irene's sink? There was nothing to be gained, he felt, from mentioning either. 'Does Mr Fitzhenry think she's greedy?' Now he had her.

But she frowned. 'Don't try to be clever with me, Carson Bandbridge. I'm smarter than you. I'm smarter than most people. That's why Mr Fitzhenry got me out of that hospital. He really cares, you see.'

Richard turned back to the window. Possibly it was enough simply to have established the connection with Mr Fitzhenry. It was far too neat to be just a coincidence. In which case, Mrs Trenchard was off the hook ... Idly he watched as an ambulance double-parked in the street below. People who lived in places like this were all the same – lot of malingerers, always suffering from something, more trouble than they were worth.

'I'm hungry,' Irene said behind him. 'Haven't eaten since yesterday lunch.'

He returned through the TVs. 'Don't look at me,' he said. Then, meanly, 'If he cares so much, why not call up your precious Mr Fitzhenry?'

'I might at that. But he doesn't know about you. And he won't be pleased.'

'Don't tell him then.' Positively not. About Carson Bandbridge, not a bloody word.

'Casual relationships. He doesn't approve of casual relationships.'

Richard moved away toward the door. Neither, on the present showing, did he. 'I'll see what I can do,' he said. 'There's bound to be a shop open somewhere.'

He paused. By the sound of it there was someone out on the landing. He turned back to Irene. 'Were you expecting guests?' he asked.

And before she could answer the door behind him was flung open. He spun around, saw two dark-suited men standing in the doorway. They stayed, warily frozen, their eyes flicking around the room. Then a woman in a bright summer dress, taller than they, and thinner, pushed her way in between them.

She pointed at Irene. 'That's her,' she said.

Irene started screaming. She was standing on the mattress now, spread-eagled against the wall, her eyes rolling. In one hand she still held the wire cutters. And she was stark-naked. She'd been lying in the bed stark-naked.

The two men began to advance toward her. Richard stepped forward. 'Now look here,' he began.

The nearest man caught hold of his arm and flung him casually back among the TVs. His arm felt broken. By the time he'd sorted himself out from the TVs the two men were closing in on Irene. The woman was standing over him. Irene was waving the wire cutters and screaming steadily.

'The less we hear from you,' the woman said, between Irene's screams, 'consorting with a known paranoid, the better.'

Richard got slowly to his feet. He remembered the ambulance. One of the men was gripping Irene's arm. The face of the other was bleeding where the wire cutters had bashed it. There was spittle trailing from Irene's mouth. Somehow she wrenched herself free and started away across the room to the door. The man with blood on his face caught up with her. They fell to the floor in an ugly tangle of flailing limbs. The first man circled them, watching.

Suddenly the man on the floor swore savagely and broke away, doubled over his crotch. Irene was up again, crouching, her hair in wild strands, still screaming with all the breath in her body. Bruises showed on her naked breasts.

The woman stood beside Richard, quite still, one hand lightly on his arm, restraining him. While in his head a futile, irrelevant apology revolved: *I knew she was crazy but. How could I know she was paranoid? I knew she was crazy but. How could I know she was paranoid?*

Irene lunged upwards at the first man with her wire cutters. He trapped her arm expertly and twisted it up behind her back. The wire cutters fell to the floor. Bent forward, she kicked at him with her bare heels. Shards of broken TV screen dangled from her thighs, bloody now, and scattering crimson drops with every kick. Richard stared with horrible fascination at the dark fur triangle between her legs.

I knew she was crazy but. How could I know she was paranoid?

The second man was on his feet again, panting. He fished for Irene's other arm, and caught it. Abruptly the screaming stopped and she went limp. The two men looked around the room, smiling quietly. Blood ran slowly down the face of one, and down Irene's legs. The men appeared to be waiting for something. The violent convulsion, quite without warning, as Irene flung herself down, and from side to side, her head wrenched around and her jaws snapping as she tried to bite, her feet groping and prizing between the men's legs as she tried to break their iron immobility. And she grunted now, softly, earnestly, a sound far more hateful then her screams.

The men stood without movement, hardly seeming to notice, merely adjusting their feet on the glass-strewn floorboards, until the spasm passed. Then the woman left Richard's side and stepped forward. She produced a hypodermic syringe from the pocket of her bright summer dress. Richard would have looked away, but could not. Over her shoulder he saw Irene's face, the staring terror in her eyes. He saw her writhe, and the moment's enforced stillness, the two men stretching her as if on a rack. Then the woman stepped to one side. 'She'll be all right now,' she said.

All right? It seemed, even to Richard, a curious choice of words.

For perhaps a minute longer Irene remained rigidly upright, defiant, her terror gone. Her gaze sought Richard's, but he avoided it. Its reproach. *I knew she was paranoid but.* He was afraid she would speak, but she didn't. Then her eyes closed and the strength went out of her. She was just a naked girl, unconscious, probably drunk, between two men in dark, disheveled suits.

The woman lifted Irene's head, looked under one eyelid. 'She's not shamming,' she said. 'You can take her downstairs.'

One of the men heaved a sheet from the bed and wrapped it inadequately around Irene's body.

Belatedly Richard cleared his throat. 'What about her clothes?'

'She won't be needing clothes,' the woman told him.

The man who hadn't fetched the sheet stooped, and with a quick movement slung Irene over his shoulder. Her hands trailed behind him, almost down to his knees. The two men left the room, and Richard heard them going downstairs. He realized that, except when one of them had cursed, they had not spoken during the entire obscene episode.

The woman walked away toward the open door. But he couldn't let her go. He couldn't just be left, not like that. 'I … I thought they always wore white coats,' he said.

The woman stopped, turned. 'Not any more. It attracts attention.'

'For Christ's sake, doesn't the screaming attract attention?'

'There's always the hope that they'll come with us quietly.'

Richard leaned on the TV he'd kicked in. 'You do a lot of this sort of thing?'

'Too much. The Disappearances are very hard on people. Now, if you'll excuse me …'

'Please don't go.'

'I must.' But she returned a few paces across the glass-littered floor. Apart from that, and the ruined bed, the room looked as if nothing had happened. 'I'd sit down for a bit if I were you,' she said.

'There's nothing to sit on.'

The woman took his arm. 'Have you known her long?'

'No time at all. Since yesterday. No – the day before.'

'She's been in before, you know. She's profoundly disturbed.'

'But … well, I'd have thought … I mean, not *dangerous?*'

'I can't go into that. It's not for me to say, you understand. She was out on license. A certain gentleman made her his responsibility.'

'A certain gentleman?'

'We thought she was in his care. He … rang the hospital this morning. The whole thing's been a bit of a mess, I'm afraid.'

'What certain gentleman?'

'I really can't tell you that. Now, if you'll excuse me …'

'She … she said she was hungry. Just before you came she said she was hungry.'

'We'll feed her, Mr …'

He saw it as a test, and he failed it. He didn't give the woman his name. Not even Carson Bandbridge. Neither did he ask the name of the hospital. He followed the woman to the door. They stood together, looking around at all the TVs. On one of them lay Irene's patchwork shoulder bag.

'I really ought to lock the door,' the woman said. 'Do you know if there's a key?'

He didn't. And they couldn't find one.

The woman disapproved. 'We'll just have to close the door and hope. Someone will be along from the hospital later.'

Richard considered mentioning the bank notes moldering under the sink. But they weren't important. A nice surprise for someone from the hospital.

They went downstairs, past the door of the novelist who had been a computer man. Faint wooden creakings could be heard, as if of a rocking chair on bare boards. Out in the street the ambulance was waiting.

The woman shook his hand. 'I'm sorry you had to see all that. Sometimes it's a help if they have someone there they know.'

Richard thought of Mr Fitzhenry, without a doubt Irene's friend, her certain gentleman. 'I'm afraid I didn't know her well enough,' he said.

The woman left him on the step and went out to the waiting ambulance. It drove away. Richard didn't wave. He should have given her his name. A short distance up the street the children were kicking at his hubcaps. All right, so Irene was a nut. And she'd been making Mrs Trenchard's life a misery. But at least he should have given the woman his name.

NINE

Frankfurt. 7/4/86. According to today's special press release, German wine growers are becoming seriously concerned for the future quality of Rhine wines. The particular character of these wines, they claim, has been attributable to the barren, shaley soils in which their grapes have for centuries been grown. The unprecedented fertility brought about by regular falls of Moondrift, they warn, spells the end of the fine *Qualitätswein mit Prädikat* as the world has hitherto known it. Pre-Moondrift bottlings, our wine correspondent reports, are already commanding record prices.

Caroline was waiting outside her bank on Monday morning when it opened. She had an appointment with Irene at ten. She waited calmly. And who should actually insert the keys and unlock the door of the bank but misunderstood Mr Rogg? Seeing her, he turned quickly away.

'Good morning, Mr Rogg,' she called cheerfully.

'Good morning, Mrs Trenchard.' Over his shoulder, scuttling back into his inner office.

It made her day. Which was, with her coming visit with Richard to the pheasant farm, made already.

She went to the counter, drew out Irene's two thousand, and a hundred for herself. She asked the teller if her check from the Accident and General had been cleared, and he told her it had. After doing a sum on the back of her checkbook, deducting Richard's forty and Irene's four, and leaving a bit in hand, she opened a savings account for forty-two thousand. It occurred to her that she ought to ask someone about investments. Mr Rogg? It was an amusing thought. But not today – today her mind was on other, higher things. There were pamphlets on the counter advertising Moondrift Bonds: *Invest in Tomorrow Today*. She took one and left the bank.

At the time it had seemed no more than reasonable, asking Richard to go with her to Stemborough. They were sensible grown-up people – they could be friends, surely, and simply enjoy a day out in the country together? But it was a meretricious reasonableness. Yesterday morning with Rose-Ann had shown her that. And yesterday afternoon, aimlessly walking the High Park. And yesterday evening, ringing up Humphrey, just for someone to talk to. Love? What did she know about being in love? Except that Richard, with all his unignorable dreadfulness, could never be a friend. Yet she felt lost without him.

Mr Wallingford and Mrs Trenchard: two people no longer strangers. Yet still, despite a great deal of mutual confusion, nothing that could possibly be termed *unsuitable*.

'Caro darling. How sweet of you to call.'

'I just wanted to say thank you, Humphrey. For all your help.'

'You thanked me beautifully, pet. Dinner *à deux*. I positively warmed my hands on your radiance.'

Had she really been radiant? Having sorted things out with herself on the doorstep, *I meant what I said about never having been wholehearted*, perhaps she had. Wholeheartedness didn't come easily. But at least for a few hours the possibility had existed. They hadn't talked, *à deux*, of Mr Wallingford. Humphrey being far too discreet, and she herself far too afraid of the fragile possibility.

'Well, Humphrey?' The silly girl she'd never been. 'What do you think of him?'

'A perfect poppet. And I'm flattered you should ask.'

'He's *not* a poppet, Humphrey. He's a perfectly ordinary, rather uncomfortable human being.'

'He's direct, I grant you. But I find that so refreshing.'

'Oh, *Humphrey* …'

'Well, what do you want me to say?'

'I don't know. Something genuine … That he's an oaf. A boor. That you can't think what I see in him.'

'He's a boor, Caro. And I can't think what you see in him.'

'Do you mean that?'

'Of course I don't. I know very well what you see in him.'

'What?'

'You won't like this.'

'I'm ready.'

'You don't see Haverstock.'

'Oh … Is that all?'

O wad some Pow'r the giftie gie us, to see oursels as others see us … No thank you.

'It … seems a bit negative.'

'Now you're hurt. I knew you would be. He's a lovely man, Caro darling. And I'm sure he's absolutely marvelous in bed.'

'I'm afraid I haven't yet tried.' She *was* – she was actually apologizing.

'Poor Beauty.'

'I'm *not* poor.' Then, reminded of the Beast, 'My real fear, Humphrey, is that he's just like Haverstock, only different.'

'Darling – Haverstock was a monster.'

'And you're sure Mr Wallingford isn't?'

'Of course I'm sure. If you'll pardon the phrase, my pet, your Mr Wallingford is one of nature's gentlemen.'

Oh God. 'Then you think I'm mad.'

'I think you're on the rebound.'

Which was what friends were for. 'I've told him he can't come to live with me in the country.'

'That's a pity.'

'I'd have thought you'd be cheering.'

'The job is for a couple, you see. I nearly mentioned it on Saturday. Then I thought you might feel I was rushing things.'

She wished he had. Then as meretriciously reasonable as ever, she wouldn't have followed it up. 'I'm glad you didn't. Things between us are … rather delicate.'

'Rebounds often work, my dear.'

'You really believe that?'

'Not really. But they might. With someone like you, they might.'

Which was also what friends were for. And sufficient to send her to bed, in spite of everything, precariously hopeful.

On the way home from the bank Caroline stopped in at the garage to change cars. Sixty miles in her city electric was quite feasible, and the people in Stemborough would be sure to have a charging point. But then one had to stay for at least the minimum thirty minutes on full boost. And anyway she preferred the Maserati. Richard would prefer it, too.

The job was for a couple. She still wanted it. Rebounds often worked. Might work. Would work.

She parked the Maserati outside her house and went in to wait for Irene. There'd been a letter in the mail that morning from Haverstock's agent. Something about a big foreign film sale. So she could probably go on affording Irene for a good while yet. Still, as she'd said to Richard, showing off, and later wished she hadn't, money was a catching habit. Perhaps she really would be able to hide in Stemborough.

She waited for Irene.

Irene didn't come.

Half past ten. Eleven. Ten past eleven. And Richard.

'I should have called you. They've taken Irene away. Back to the loony bin. That bloody man Fitzhenry.'

They sat in Haverstock's study and she listened to his story. The attic room, the doctor in her bright summer dress, he made the scene come alive.

'It was horrible.'

'Poor Richard.'

'Poor Irene.'

They agreed that Mr Fitzhenry was a dangerous bastard. She didn't have to tell him about Rose-Ann's visit to be able to do that. Apparently Rose-Ann hadn't told him either, or he'd surely have mentioned it. Suddenly he jumped to his feet.

'Irene's dephaser. She gave you a dephaser. Where is it?'

'I'm … not quite sure. Somewhere around.'

'I want it.'

She got Irene's dephaser from her handbag in the kitchen and gave it to him. He pounded it on the steel corner of Haverstock's desk. Eventually the plastic case burst open, a battery fell out, a loudspeaker dangled, and colored wires. He tore them off and flung the pieces, case and all, into the fireplace.

'A man downstairs made them for her. He was in his room all the time. Rocking. But he must have heard …' There were tears in Richard's eyes. At last, in front of her, he could care.

'You should have called me.'

'I tried.'

She'd been up in the High Park. 'You should have tried again.'

'I couldn't.' Not if by then he'd begun to shut it out. 'Rose-Ann knew something was the matter. But I didn't tell her.'

'Poor Richard.'

Poor Rose-Ann.

Caroline packed a picnic. The sun was shining again. When Richard had recovered she took him out to the Maserati.

'It's not paid for,' she said. 'Without AGIC's check I'd have had to give it back.'

A distraction? A bag of candy? Why not – they were all only children, really. But principally something he'd understand. A reason why money was a catching habit. For all their days were today, and her past words preyed on her mind.

He walked the whole way around the Maserati. 'I saw it on my way in. But I never dreamed it was yours.'

'Haverstock's really. It terrifies me. Would you drive, please?'

The ultimate in gone man's shoes. But Richard didn't seem to mind. He put down the picnic basket and opened the Maserati's door. Scents of leather wafted out. Caroline picked up the basket, carried it around, and put it in the back.

He turned to her. 'That receipt,' he said.

It came from nowhere. 'What receipt?'

'AGIC's receipt for the hundred thousand. I'd better have it now. Then I won't have to come in when we get back.'

She stared at him. Was he fishing? Even if he was, she didn't care – he was going to come in anyway. The possibility of whole-heartedness did exist. She'd made up her mind. She was going to let him in. But she couldn't tell him so. Not yet.

'I'll get it,' she said, and went back into the house.

Richard leaned savoringly on the Maserati's open door. The day had a last-day-of-the-holidays feel about it. Tomorrow he'd be back at work, back in the real world. Which was why he'd asked for the bloody receipt. Bloody Caldwell would have a bloody fit if he didn't bloody get it.

He lowered himself into the driving seat. And immediately forgot Bernie Caldwell. Mrs Trenchard came swinging down the steps from her house. Swinging ... her beautiful hair, her beautiful skirt about her beautiful legs. She got in beside him, gave him the envelope with the receipt. Then she reached forward to the white leather glove compartment.

'Let's go,' she said. 'I'll map-read.'

He pulled away from the curb. To drive that car was like a symphony, a whole rock opera, like making music. More than that, so subtle and complete were the connections, it was like *being* music. A touch, hardly more than a thought, and it began. Exquisite images flashed in shop windows. He strode the world, commanded the universe.

'Left at the traffic lights, and out under the two-tier.'

Must she? He supposed she must.

They drove out through the suburbs, blasting them into deserved insignificance. He found she was talking about Mr Fitzhenry and Irene, and he tried to listen.

'... but why? I'd have thought she was doing a marvelous job.'

He caught at the word, repeated it. 'Marvelous.'

'So why send her back to the hospital? Unless she wasn't passing on his share.'

'Of course not.' Mmm?

'Always assuming that she *was* working for him. Which I think we have to.'

'Have to.' The music faded.

'It's far too much of a coincidence otherwise. I mean, she'd be the perfect person for his purposes. So what on earth must she have done to make him send her back to the hospital?'

'The stones.'

'What? Richard, I don't think you've heard a word I said.'

'Yes, I have. She told you about the stones in the coffin. She shouldn't have. They let you off the hook. It proved he couldn't rely on her.'

'Richard, you're brilliant. Next on the right and up onto the thruway ... No, that won't do. How would he know she'd mentioned the stones?'

'You telephoned him. Perhaps you told him.'

'You're right – I did ... Oh Christ, Richard, then the whole thing's my fault.'

'Not a chance. It's her own fault. No – his. There must have been some kinder way of shutting her up.'

'But I wish I hadn't told him.'

'Of course you do.' The car made him generous. To himself, too. He reached out and patted her leg. 'But you really couldn't have known.'

She covered his hand with hers. 'The man's a monster.'

They drove on along the thruway, communicating thus, for several miles. Then his hand got moved in a casual rearrangement.

'Do you think he'll put someone else onto me, Richard?'

'He'll have to find someone first. Unless he's got a team. And anyway, he must know by now that you've smelled a rat. If you ask me, he'll stay well out of it.'

'And what will happen to the girl?'

Richard considered. It seemed to him probable that the two men in dark suits, or others like them, would happen to Irene. But, 'They taught her to make paper flowers last time.'

'Paper flowers?'

'That's right. She told me all about it. You bend this bit of wire around this bit of crepe paper. She enjoyed doing it. So I shouldn't worry.'

She seemed satisfied. It wasn't often, he thought, that you could tell Mrs Trenchard a story like that and get away with it.

The car and Mrs Trenchard. He wanted the journey to go on forever. Even talking about monstrous Mr Fitzhenry, he wanted the journey to go on forever. And they weren't now, not any more. She was telling him for some reason about a motor accident in a place called Nantes, and her voice went agreeably on, and he didn't have to listen. The car and Mrs Trenchard. The last day of the holidays. Music. Forever.

They left the thruway at the fourteenth exit, descended onto a plain of rich meadows and heavy, summer-green trees with horses standing in their shadows. Houses in softly weathered brick, with tall, white-framed windows, stood among cedars at the ends of wide graveled drives. Farms, red roofs, red walls, ancient, clustered, their barns and cowsheds in the folds of gentle hillsides. Cottages, oak-framed beneath centuries' accumulations of thatch, joined with the winding hedgerows, confirming some inborn logic of footpath and byway.

They stopped by a gate and unloaded the picnic. A meter or so inside the gate stood a stiff, dusty wall of barley, thigh-high and silent, dotted with scarlet poppies. They climbed the gate and went a short distance along the back of the hedge. They stumbled frequently, for the earth had been churned up by tractors and then allowed to grass over. They found a fairly level place and laid out the picnic.

The grass was long and dry and coarse, and not particularly comfortable. They reclined like lords and ladies. Richard reached forward and broke off, with some difficulty, a single rattling stalk of barley. He wasn't a countryman. He didn't even know that it was barley. He separated the grains one by one till he had a small handful, then gave them to Caroline. She gave him one back. He broke it carefully between his teeth, was surprised at how milky and good it was. He lay back, chewing the barley straw. High overhead, invisible against the white-blue sky, little birds twittered ceaselessly. He didn't even know they were skylarks.

It was hot in the narrow depression between the hedge and the wall of barley. To his right it stretched away, seen from that low level, to infinity. On his left it ended after only a few meters, in the corner by the gate. Insects buzzed. He flapped at them idly. The wall of barley in front, the hedge behind. And Mrs Trenchard at his side.

She'd brought a bottle of wine. He leaned up on one elbow and opened it. She held out glasses which he filled. They drank to nothing in particular. To everything.

They stayed for an hour, possibly more, between the hedge and the wall of barley. They didn't talk much, finding it perfectly satisfactory to listen. Once a car came slowly along the lane on the other side of the hedge. But it didn't stop. Another time a bicycle, only audible when its rider started whistling number one on the hit parade. And it didn't stop either. They ate their picnic. A hawklike bird, Mrs Trenchard thought it was a buzzard, flew over quite low down. For a while they watched the place where they'd last seen it. And when they finally got up, they comfortably went their separate, uncommented-on ways to pee.

Caroline knew she'd been right. Meretricious only in her reasonableness. But *right*. Give an inch, and you got back a hundred miles. She couldn't remember when she'd ever been so happy.

They reached Stemborough shortly after three. They asked the way to the pheasant farm at the post office. It was another ten minutes on, past a small conifer forest. Ahead of them was a long, flat-topped ridge, not very high, gray-green, with a single, straight-sided clump of trees breaking the skyline and flowing briefly down the forward face of the ridge. Caroline thought there'd be wind always in those high trees.

The pheasant farm lay to the right of the lane: a big field divided into tall, wire-netted pens, with feeding and watering troughs, and shelters of conifer branches in each. Adjoining them were long wooden sheds like broiler houses. And the birds themselves, the size of scraggy moorhens, shifted and scuttled in restless, brown-speckled waves across the balding grass.

The house stood close beside the lane, converted from a row of old, red-brick cottages. Richard drove in through an open, five-barred gate, and parked the Maserati in the cobbled yard behind the house, alongside a smart electric Landrover. Low tile-hung outbuildings flanked two sides of the yard, and an apple orchard filled the third, behind a white picket fence. A golden Labrador got up from the shade of a large stone trough filled with geraniums and ambled over to inspect them.

Caroline got out, lingered by the car. Suddenly she felt awkward. She hadn't yet told Richard the job was for a couple. He didn't like having his decisions taken for him. Now, therefore, just before Humphrey's friends appeared, when he could hardly make a scene, say no, drive away without her, was obviously the best moment to mention it. A cowardly way to handle things. But today, poised on any number of brinks, she was a coward.

She joined him at the rear of the car. 'I … I called Humphrey last night,' she told him. 'He said the job was for a couple. Two people.' She gestured vaguely. 'A … a couple.'

Richard stared at her. His scalp shifted and his eyebrows puckered. He flushed. He seemed not angry but unreasonably amazed. 'Two people? You mean us?'

'If we suit.'

'But you said … you said we hadn't known each other long enough.'

'But I took all that back.' Now she was the one who was angry. 'Didn't you hear me?'

'You never.'

'On the doorstep. I said –' She broke off. The door of the house had opened and a young woman, enormously pregnant, came padding out. Caroline smiled at her, waved, glanced sideways. 'Will you come?' she whispered. 'If we suit, will you come?'

The answer was clear in his face.

The pregnant woman approached. 'I'm Madge,' she said. 'I forget your names, but you're Humphrey's friends.' Her vowels were faintly rural, her face scrubbed and embarrassingly healthy.

It was Caroline who introduced herself and Richard. In front of Madge she felt horribly etiolated and barren.

'Jerry's under the sink,' Madge said. 'He'll be out in a minute. You found us all right?'

'We asked at the post office.'

'Then Bessie's got her teeth back. I'm glad to hear it.' Madge started back toward the house. 'Her husband trod on them, you know. We say he did it on purpose. Though it didn't stop her talking. You just couldn't understand a word she said.'

The door opened into a large untidy kitchen, scrubbed pine table, double-oven range. A thin, anxious man in purple corduroys was on his knees amid an assortment of buckets and Ajax tins in front of the sink.

'D'you know about S-bends?' he said. 'My spectacles keep falling off. I can't see a bloody thing.'

Richard wandered over. 'The name's Wallingford. Pleased to meet you.'

'Jerry Pascoe.' The man wiped one hand on his shirt and held it up. Richard shook it. 'Bloody thing's bunged up. And I can't seem to shift the bloody nut.'

Caroline, trying not to watch, to care, saw Richard's momentary hesitation for his trousers' sake. Then he was down on his knees beside Jerry Pascoe, and the two men were peering into the cupboard.

Richard said, 'Got a flashlight?'

The other man clambered to his feet. 'Good idea.' And he went to get one.

Thank God for men, Caroline thought, and the easy camaraderie of S-bends.

Madge had perched herself on the edge of the table. She hooked a chair out with one foot. 'Make yourself comfortable, Mrs Trenchard. I don't sit down much. Not for the next few weeks.' She patted the improbable shelf of her belly.

'Please – call me Caroline.' She sat self-consciously on the chair.

'Not Carrie?'

Carrie? No one had ever called her that before. A new name for a new, wholehearted lady? 'Carrie will do very nicely.'

'Good. Marvelous.' Madge folded her arms. 'Well now, Carrie, what d'you want me to tell you about us?'

The abruptness of the question put Caroline, Carrie, at a loss. Usually, she imagined, job interviews went the other way around.

But Madge was already gesturing around at the mess. 'We aren't always like this, you know. Well – most of the time, but not always. Anyway, you'll have your own place, so it won't have to bother you.'

'I … like a bit of a mess.' And, almost, she did.

Just then Madge's husband returned with a rusty bicycle light. He was frowning and banging it.

Richard looked up over his shoulder. 'Which way were you turning the nut?'

'Right to left, I think. Or was it left to right?' The bicycle light produced a faint glimmer. 'Thank God for that.'

He got down on his knees beside Richard.

'Best thing is,' said Madge, 'if I show you your quarters. They're not much, mind, after what I reckon you've been used to.' She stood heavily. 'This place used to be four cottages. We've got two-and-a-half now – the rest is yours. If you decide to take it.'

Caroline stood also, followed her back to the door. 'Oh, I'm sure we'll –'

'Don't be too hasty. Own front door mind. And all the garden you want. But it's still not much.'

They went out into the cobbled yard and along the back of the house. Who was interviewing whom? Caroline decided to find out. 'You talk as if the job is ours for the taking.'

Forthrightness worked. 'And so it is. You should have heard the characters Humphrey gave you.'

Dear Humphrey. 'But what about the pheasants?'

'They're nothing. Bit of common sense, nothing more. If we can do it, so can you. Main thing at this stage is to stop them jugging out.'

The Labrador had tagged on behind, trailing some long piece of blue material in his jaws. Madge led the way to a white stable door, opened the top half, reached in for the latch to the bottom section.

'They're poults now, by the way. Best get the jargon right. Chicks first, then poults. They only become pheasants after they've been hardened off ... One kitchen.'

She stepped back to let Caroline in, then thrust cheerfully past her. 'One kitchen, one dining room, one sitting room, one bathroom. Bathroom downstairs on account of the plumbing. Upstairs two bedrooms and a sort of large sloping closet we haven't got a name for. You won't be planning for a child's room, I expect.'

'Not ... really.' Would she be planning for a child's room? Not ... really.

'Thank God for that. Too many kids in the world as it is.'

She led Caroline through the cottage. Neat little white-washed rooms, with open brick fireplaces downstairs, and a minimum of furniture. Already Caroline was seeing some smaller pieces from her city house in position. But *jugging out* ... and *poults* ... and getting *hardened off* ...

'Madge – Madge, I really think we ought to talk about what's involved in looking after the pheasants.'

They were standing in the sitting room. Someone, presumably Madge, had put an earthenware pitcher full of big yellow daisies on the windowsill.

'The pheasants, Carrie? Bloody things. Anyone can do it. Leave 'em to the men.'

'If it's so easy, then why take on Richard and me?'

'Good point. Well, you can see how I'm situated. Popping on the twenty-fourth, if I've got my dates right, please God. So I'll have my hands full ... And as for Jerry – well, Jerry's the inventive sort. He's got this scheme for home-brewed cider. And miniature cats – there's a fortune to be made if we can breed them small enough. And mushrooms in the old stables. And mink up in the barn. He's a great believer in diversification.'

It was worrying, however, thought Caroline, that the diversive Jerry couldn't manage a simple S-bend.

Madge, it seemed, had spotted Caroline's uncertainty. She perched herself on the back of a chintz covered arm chair. 'Anyway,' she said, 'we're both bone idle. And Jerry made a pile with a book on Moondrift right at the beginning – *Manna from Heaven: the Bible Was Right*, you know the sort of thing. So we don't really have to bother. He's your complete atheist, by the way. Humphrey published it. That's how we got to know him.'

The proposition improved. Caroline wandered around the room, stooped to look out of the window. There was a view of apple trees and a wide sweep of meadow beyond. And the daisies smelled sharp and clean.

'What happens in the winter?' she said.

'Oh, the winter's no problem. You can help with the mink. And there's always the tax returns to see to. And ordering in the starter crumbs.'

Whatever starter crumbs might be, it still didn't seem exactly an action-packed winter. Perhaps she could join the Women's Institute.

'On the subject of salary,' Madge said, 'I'm leaving that to Jerry. It's the freedom we're after, mostly. A place like this is a bloody drain, when there's just the two of you.'

Out in the yard the Labrador was waiting for them, still wetly mumbling the piece of blue material. Caroline stooped to pat him. The material seemed familiar. Suddenly she recognized it as her Givenchy scarf. She must have dropped it getting out of the car. Unobtrusively she disengaged it from the dog's amiable smile and hurried after Madge. It was damp, and only slightly shredded.

Back in Madge's kitchen the two men were sitting at the table, drinking beer. Neither stood. 'He's fixed it,' Jerry said. 'Bloody marvelous.'

Caroline leaned on Richard's shoulder. 'Most nuts unscrew right to left, don't they?' She wasn't really being unkind. But she wanted to be needed, too.

'Depends how you look at them,' Richard said tolerantly. 'Upside down or right side up. Not always easy to tell.'

Wise man. Preserving the mystique and at the same time excusing his future employer. She put her scarf on, damp end down the back. 'I've been hearing about the pheasants,' she said.

'So have I.' Richard leaned back, his hands behind his head. 'Main thing is to get them in at night. The fools would rather roost in the pens – it's called jugging out – but then the foxes get them. And there's hawks in the daytime, which is why every pen has its shelter of branches. It'd be safer and easier to keep them in all day of course, like broilers, but then their feathers don't grow properly, don't harden off. Then when they're put to covert the poor little buggers can't stand the cold.'

He was showing off abominably. But he was also doing his best to get the job. And where did that leave her? Sort of glorified home help to a woman with a new baby? Well, she didn't mind. It would all be useful experience for when … if … no, *when* she had one herself.

'Beer?' said Jerry.

She sat down, had a beer. Madge propped herself against the range, drank milk. Just for the moment beer made her puke, she said.

Richard emptied his glass. 'Another job,' he went on, 'is cutting their beaks to stop feather-picking. There's fifteen thousand, so it's quite a production … As to food, by now the poults are nearly four weeks old and on to turkey crumbs. With a little kibbled wheat, of course. But –'

Enough, however, was enough. *Kibbled wheat*, for God's sayke … 'I've been looking at the cottage,' Caroline said. 'I think it will do very well.'

Richard smiled. 'If you say so, old dear, then I'm sure it will.'

Roleplaying, too, was all very well. But even in this deferring to her he seemed to imply that there'd be hell to pay if she turned out to be wrong. No tiptoeing through her life, then. She felt a sudden chill. Another Haverstock? Another Beast? Humphrey didn't think so. And anyway, what new, wholehearted lady wanted a tiptoeing gentleman?

All the same, though, Richard's present performance disturbed her. It lacked … she knew what it lacked, it lacked dignity. And Richard, although failing in so many things, had always managed dignity. Yet what he was doing now was all theater. Salesmanship. Which was hardly surprising in a man who had earned his living as a salesman.

'Don't you really want to see for yourself where you're going to live?' she said.

The sharpness of her tone brought an alien specificness into the untidy kitchen. Jerry glanced at his wife. In the pause that followed neither of them spoke. Then, slowly, Richard sat up straight and put his two feet squarely on the brick floor.

'There's no need,' he said. 'I trust you.'

Not heavily. But not lightly either. Simply, 'I trust you.' So that she knew her fears were nonsense. Always he could be pulled back. Which Haverstock never could be. Rebounds worked. They'd be safe together.

The moment passed. Jerry took off his spectacles and began cleaning them on his shirttail. 'You'll take the job then, will you?'

Caroline didn't hesitate. If ever she was to live wholeheartedly, then now was the time to start. Of course they'd take the job.

But Richard got in before her. 'We'll have to talk it over, of course. We'll let you know tomorrow. But I'm pretty sure the answer'll be yes. And thank you both very much.'

'Yes indeed,' Caroline said. 'Thank you both very much.'

Richard was going to be good for her.

Before they left they were shown over the farm, the storerooms, the pens, the rearing sheds, the bottled gas heating system. And the packing section where hundreds of crates were stacked up to the ceiling. There was the barn being fitted with cages ready for the arrival of six breeding pairs of mink. And among the cages a spitting family of farm cats, unusually small animals, which had given Jerry the idea of trying to produce a true miniature. There was a fortune to be made out of a true miniature, he said.

Caroline walked at the tail of the party, touching things, imagining the farm as her home. The woods, the lane beside the house, the long, calm line of the hill above them. Already her days in the city seemed like a dream. What would she be giving up? The Saturday morning walk to the shops. Humphrey. And, of course, her house … from living room to Haverstock's study to terrace … and back again. Her house, her lousy, half- assed life. She reached for Richard's hand and held it tight.

Back in the yard again Madge leaned against the Maserati. 'That's it, then,' she said. 'And what I want to know is, what's in it for you?'

Jerry said, 'Now, Madge.'

'No, I mean it.' The afternoon was very warm, and Madge pulled out the top of her dress and blew down inside it. 'This car and all – it's obvious that you're not short for the odd penny. So why us? There's no three-day week here, you know. And if you *do* come, can we depend on you to stay? Or will you suddenly take it into your heads to run off to the south of France?'

Jerry started to say 'Now, Madge' again, but Richard interrupted him. While all Caroline, Carrie, could do was regret having brought the Maserati.

'It's a fair question,' Richard said. 'And as to staying, if we come, we'll stay.' He turned to her. 'Isn't that right?'

'Of course we'll stay.' Never before had Caroline pleaded. 'Because if we come it'll be because we want to. It'll be a new chance for both of us, and we'll be too proud to give it up. For myself, I'll stay because it's time I made a success of *something* in my life. And as for Richard –'

'We'll stay. I've already said it.'

Not a man for reasons. But a commitment all the same. To each other, Caroline realized, quite as much as to the job. And Irene, thank God, nothing whatever to do with it. Poor Irene.

'We have Disappearances here too, you know,' said Madge. 'Only last week Mr Haskins down in the village went.'

'They know that, Madge,' her husband said.

'Just so long as it's understood. There's a lot of nonsense talked about life in the country.'

It was understood. Richard held the car door for her, and Caroline got in. He went around the hood, shook hands with Jerry and Madge. Then he got in too. The Labrador put his paws up on the door and tried to lick Richard's face through the open window. They backed up, turned, and drove out into the lane. If they came, they'd stay. If they came … Jerry and Madge stood in the open gateway, waving. The picture left in Caroline's mind was of Jerry, his arm around his wife, and Madge, one hand on the shelf of her belly, and the long calm line of the hill behind them.

They drove through Stemborough and on. For a long while neither of them spoke. Then Richard said, 'Did you mean it?'

'Mean what?'

'It. All of it.'

And she did. But, 'Why did you say we had to talk it over?'

He shrugged. 'It's what people say. Anyway, don't we?'

'I suppose we do. They seem a nice, easygoing couple.'

'He's all right. She's a bit on the bossy side.'

'At least one knows where one stands with her.'

They drove on.

'Richard – I did mean it.'

'I wasn't sure.'

They passed a village pond, decorated with muddy white ducks.

'That cottage bit – you seemed pretty snippy.'

'I'm sorry.' And she was supposed to be letting him in. 'I'm sorry, Richard.'

'Not to worry, old dear.'

They came to a junction without a signpost, between high hedges, and took a chance on the lane to the right.

'How much will they pay us, Richard?'

'Hundred a week, and the cottage for nothing.'

She had no real idea what she spent, living in the city. But a hundred a week sounded a lot. 'That sounds a lot.'

'It's not. But it'll do us … Then you think you can live with that Madge?'

'I can *work* with her. It's you I'll be living with.'

'Then you think you can live with me?'

Again. Again he dared demand such simple, impossible things. Her newest, most tenuous convictions in terms of yes and no. Yes, I can live with you, Richard. Its deterring banality. And besides, she'd said it already a dozen times, in other, less embarrassing ways.

'Doesn't that look to you like a farmyard ahead, Richard?' Providential. 'We must have taken the wrong road back at the fork.'

They turned in the farmyard, drove back to the junction, and took the left-hand lane instead.

'Lucky we're not in a rush,' Richard said. 'You've nothing on this evening, have you?'

This evening. 'Yes, I can live with you, Richard.'

'You're a funny one.'

He drew the car in to the side of the road, stopped, and twisted around to face her. For a moment she was afraid he'd kiss her. He kissed her. He was kindly, expert. And he stopped before it could become anything more than kindly and expert. So that it remained a pleasant acknowledgment of mutuality.

They drove on again.

'When d'you think we can move, Richard?'

'Any time you like.'

'They want us there before Madge has her baby. D'you think we can manage it?'

'I don't see why not.' He smiled at her. 'Are you happy?'

Oh God. Not again. But this time, if with effort, 'Yes, Richard. I'm very happy.'

Just before the thruway they stopped for tea. Not because either of them wanted tea, but because they wanted the journey not to be almost over. They had toasted buns with homemade strawberry jam. They talked about Jerry and Madge. And about buying themselves a dog – a Dalmatian, Caroline thought – and whether it would get on with Jerry and Madge's Labrador. And about trading in the Maserati for something more suitable – a Volvo estate car, Richard thought. And about taking up, of all things, beekeeping. Life in the country. They felt sure there'd be room on the farm somewhere for two or three hives. As long as the bees didn't get in and sting Madge's baby.

Finally, reluctantly, they got up, paid the bill, and left the restaurant. And then, just as they were walking across the parking lot to the car, there was a Singing.

Caroline stood very still, quite, quite still, Richard beside her. The Singing slithered like knives. And the sickly smell of synthetic roses drifted on gently suffocating waves. She closed her eyes, staggered. When she opened them again, Richard was a short distance off, staring back at the red-tiled roof of the restaurant.

She stretched out a hand toward him. 'Tell me about your dad, Richard.'

'I've told you about my dad.'

'Tell me again.'

'What?'

'Help me, Richard.'

He frowned. Her hand stayed disregarded. 'You don't really think the TV companies do it?' he said.

'Of course I don't think the TV companies do it.'

'Because there *is* an aerial. Up there on the roof. There *is* an aerial.'

The Singing climbed, shifted, climbed, stayed always the same. It pinned her, there in the brilliant sunlight on the parking lot outside the restaurant. She was horribly afraid. Near to losing herself totally in the drawn-out agony of her fear. She didn't want to go. Dear God, sweet God, she didn't want to go.

'Please help me, Richard.'

'That girl's crazy. Of course it's not the aerials.'

'Please – help me.'

'You what?'

'*Help me.*'

'I can't even help myself, old dear.'

Of course he couldn't.

Poor man, of course he couldn't. She wept. She'd been a fool to ask.

The Singing went on.

And there were no corners.

She stood, helplessly weeping, pinned in the brilliant sunlight on the parking lot outside the restaurant. She didn't want to go.

Haverstock hadn't helped her either. Nobody had helped her. And now this Mr Wallingford, this nature's gentleman, this different animal who was in fact so very much the same …

Richard waited, staring now up at the cloudless summer sky above the restaurant. It was the best he could manage, not to run and scream and kick things. In the annihilating presence of the Singing, it was the best he could manage. And the smell, like the fizzy stuff he'd had down by the canal when he was a kid. All he could manage was to wait for the nightmare to pass.

His gaze shifted briefly, then returned to the sky. Mrs Trenchard was crying. Even her, poor soul. But that was the Singings for you. Even the King of England must look pretty silly, with one of them rattling his chandeliers. He wished he could have helped her. He really did. But what did she expect? It's a bird, it's a plane, it's *Superman?*

Oh Christ, he thought, if this goes on much longer my brains'll burst.

It stopped. As always, abruptly, quite without warning, the Singing stopped. And he was still there. He hadn't gone. Neither had she.

'Well, well, well …' He laughed and stamped his feet, asserting his retained substantiality. 'That was a nasty one. They might have spared us that, I reckon.'

He held out his hand to lead her over to the car. But she had already turned and was going on ahead. He let her. She was drying her tears.

He got into the car beside her and drove away from the restaurant, up onto the thruway. They hadn't gone. But she didn't seem to want to talk. He'd always known she was a funny one. This job for a couple, just when he thought he'd been given the old heave-ho. Coarse and unworthy … it just went to show that you never could tell. God alone knew what she saw in him. But then, what did any woman ever see in any man, all thumbs and hairy nostrils. And now she'd let him kiss her.

They'd have a good life. He'd see to that.

He glanced at her sideways. 'Are you happy?' he said.

She looked down, tugging her skirt over her knees. 'I think I've worked it out,' she said. 'That question means *you* are.'

'Are what?'

'Happy.'

He turned back to the road. 'You bet I am.'

They passed a car, driverless, abandoned on the median strip. A Disappearance? Or had Rent-a-Corpse, he wondered, been at it again? Though it could, of course, be a perfectly ordinary, old-fashioned road accident.

She interrupted his thoughts. 'Richard –'

'Hmmm?'

'Oh – nothing.'

'Go on. Tell us.'

'It doesn't matter. Really.'

'Then why not say it?'

'Well …' Suddenly she relaxed. 'I was only wondering if we couldn't do something for Irene.'

'She'll be all right. Making her paper flowers and all. Irene'll be all right.'

She was looking at the map now, and only grunted. Because it wasn't, Richard had a strong suspicion, the question she'd meant to ask at all.

After that they talked very little. Richard didn't mind – he was driving the Maserati, living its music, its effortless precisions. And if that wasn't enough, he had the future to think of, the future with Mrs Trenchard, simple, real, clean. No more Bernie Caldwell. No more Life Claims Verifications. No more grubby peering at remains. Forty thousand in the bank, and a new life. In the country, with Mrs Trenchard. Home when the day's work was done to a cosy farmhouse kitchen. And Mrs Trenchard. The wind in his hair and honest dirt beneath his fingernails.

'I tell you one thing,' she said abruptly, 'if the insurance companies insisted on dental charts for all their customers they'd save themselves a lot of trouble. *And* put Mr Fitzhenry out of business.'

A cosy farmhouse kitchen … He dragged himself back. 'You're right,' he said. 'You can't fake teeth, no matter what.'

'I'm surprised nobody's thought of it. Why don't you tell them?'

'Maybe I will.'

But he didn't think he'd bother. What he owed bloody AGIC would be lost on a pinhead. And besides, he wouldn't be working for them much longer.

They came to the end of the thruway, hit a traffic jam, crawled through endless suburban streets. He turned on the radio.

'I'm sorry, Richard. But I've got a bit of a headache.'

'It'll be the sun, old dear. Not to worry.'

He turned it off again. The wind in his hair and honest dirt beneath his fingernails. He couldn't wait.

Finally they dipped under the Fairthorpe Two-tier, turned right at the traffic lights, drove around the square with the modest stone mermaid, and pulled up outside her house. The sun was just above its roof, dark red and huge. Tomorrow was going to be another fine day. They climbed out of the Maserati. His legs were stiff.

'It's been marvelous,' Mrs Trenchard said. 'Thank you so much for coming with me.'

'My pleasure. Think nothing of it.' He began to walk away toward his yellow city electric.

'Richard –' Her voice was suddenly urgent, and he paused. Was she going to ask him in? But the tension had passed as she went on, 'Did I give you that receipt?'

'You did.' He patted his inside pocket. 'Want any help with the picnic things?'

'No thanks. I can manage.'

'OK then. See you tomorrow.'

'See you tomorrow. And Richard –' Their eyes met. 'I really don't deserve you.'

He knew he was blushing. 'Balls to that,' he began. But she had already hurried away up the steps to her front door and was fitting the key in the lock. She went in without looking back.

He stood for a moment, staring up at the blank windows of her high white house. Then he turned, walked on to his city electric's charging point, and began reeling in the cable. He was glad, really, that she hadn't asked him in. He was still in the country. She'd have sat him down and made him a fancy city supper. And he was still in the country. The country him, new and worthy. And the country her, new and – what was her word? – wholehearted. He only wished he understood half the time what she was going on about. But the job was for a couple, and that meant the two of them. She'd said it, so it had to be true. And asking him in to a fancy city supper would have spoiled it.

It wasn't until he was getting into his yellow city electric that he remembered Rose-Ann. He felt suddenly sick. He was going to have to tell her, and he dreaded it. Not because she'd make a fuss – Rose-Ann wasn't like that. But because she *wouldn't* make a fuss. And that was far, far worse.

TEN

Leeds, England. 7/5/86. In the city's Commodore Hotel last night members of the *Solar Heating Society* and *Why Windmills*, onetime bitter rivals, met together on the sad occasion of the joint winding-up of their two organizations. Stirring farewell speeches were made, followed by a dinner dance and disco for the younger members. 'The world hasn't heard the last of us,' emphasized Pamela Ambrosini, chairperson of *Why Windmills*. 'We look on Moondrift as a purely temporary aberration. It won't go on forever. And when it ends, governments will turn in desperation to us for solutions to their present, shortsighted policies. With that day in mind my colleagues and I will be keeping our armor bright.' After Ms Ambrosini's speech a collection was made, to be put toward future expenses … Metal polish?

On the eleventh floor of AGIC House Richard was sitting at his desk, going through his papers, arranging them in piles. The time was ten to nine. He'd left home earlier than usual that morning. Breakfast with Rose-Ann had been bloody horrible, the air heavy with what he hadn't told her. And the thing was, she'd noticed it, just as she'd noticed it the night before.

'Cheer up, Dickie. It mayn't never happen.'

Christ, how lousy life was. Because it *would* happen, Mrs Trenchard had said so, and then what'd become of poor bloody Rose-Ann? Half a dozen times he'd tried to tell her. *Rose-Ann, old girl, I'm pushing off* … Or the roundabout approach: *We've been together a long time now, Rose-Ann* … Or the philosophical: *The fact is, Rose-Ann, that people grow out of each other* … Each one was true. But each one needed a stronger man than he to say it.

He'd hoped for a chance in bed, with the lights out. But she'd gone to sleep instantly. She'd never been the worrying sort. And her snoring was so much what Mrs Trenchard would never do, and he hated himself for that thought even more. And he lay there, hating the snoring and himself, until – quite suddenly – it was morning.

People got hurt. It was a fact of life. Movement, progress of any kind, and someone got hurt. Sons left mothers, thruways tramped on back gardens. It was an undeniable fact. And anyway, he'd stuck the knife in days ago, really. At least he should be man enough to admit it.

But what could he do? In the face of her hand on his cheek and her 'Cheer up, Dickie. It mayn't never happen,' what could he do?

And then, toward the end of breakfast, maybe all that heaviness of what she wasn't being told got too much for her. Or maybe she was stirring the pot. Either way, it was a great relief. A proper row, if nothing else.

'I went to see your Mrs Trenchard,' she said.

'You what?'

'Sunday morning. While you was on your sun parlor. I went to see your Mrs Trenchard.'

'How dare you?'

'She was nice. She gave me coffee.'

'Bothering AGIC customers. How dare you?'

'We had a nice talk. She's awfully grand, Dickie.'

'Grand? She's a woman, isn't she? What d'you mean, "grand"?'

'I don't think she'll have you.'

'For Christ's sake. She's an AGIC customer. She doesn't have to have me. Anyway, how did you find out where she lived?'

'Her name was on that check. I looked her up in the telephone book.'

'How dare you? Bothering AGIC customers. And what for? Because if you were checking up on me, then –'

'I wasn't checking up on you. Not in the way you mean. I was worried about that check for her lover.'

'Her *lover?*'

'That Carson Bandbridge. She told me all about him.'

'Bothering a lady like that. How dare you?'

'I don't know how I dared, Dickie. But I did.'

'You were checking up on me. That's how. Bloody women – they're all the same. Once they get their claws into a bloke they –'

'Dickie love – I don't think she'll have you.'

' – they don't let go. He can't call his soul his own. It's all –'

'I said I don't think she'll have you.'

He didn't either. He'd had the night to sleep on it, and he didn't think so either.

He kicked himself up from the kitchen table. 'I'm going,' he said.

Which was only kind. Another man would have flung it in her face: I was with her all day yesterday. We're going to live in the country. It's her idea. She took me down there in her Maserati. It's her idea. And she's not the sort of woman to say a thing like that and then go back on it. She's got style. Really got style. And the whole thing's *her idea* … Another man would have said all that. And who could blame him? It was true, wasn't it, every word?

'I'm going,' Richard said. 'And be sure to give my love to Bert at the Parlor.'

And now he was sitting at his desk on the eleventh floor of AGIC House, going through his papers, sorting them into piles. At least Rose-Ann had got him out of the house. But he was going to have to face her sooner or later. And proving her wrong about Mrs Trenchard would have little joy in it.

At three minutes to nine, punctual as ever, Bernie Caldwell arrived in the elevator. He wove his way through the maze for midgets, bouncing one hand cheerfully along the tops of the partitions. Richard half rose, his knees braced against the underside of his plastic desk.

'Good morning, Mr Caldwell. I've got the Trenchard receipt, Mr Caldwell.' And up yours, Mr Caldwell.

From where Mr Caldwell was standing, Richard's disembodied head might have been floating on a sea of partition tops. Mr Caldwell beamed. 'On the green in one, Wallingford. I'm delighted to hear it.'

Other heads, among other partitions, bobbed and disappeared.

'Shall I bring it to you now, Mr Caldwell?'

'Truly, Wallingford, the internal mail is hardly momentous enough for such a unique document.'

Richard took that to mean yes. He and Mr Caldwell met, by devious means, at the door to Mr Caldwell's office.

'After you, sir.'

'Thank you, Wallingford. Thank you ...'

Mr Caldwell slung his sports carryall onto a chair. He paused to chop a short number eleven shot into the area behind his filing cabinet, then bounded in. The onyx presentation clock on his desk began to strike nine, a lugubrious, churchyard chime, strangely out of keeping with its jazzy, gilt-and-green case. He stiffened for a moment, looked rememberingly from it to Richard and back again. Then, as if at some private joke, he smiled.

'So, Wallingford ...' He held out his hand and Richard gave him the envelope containing the receipt. 'So Superswine has scooped up the boodle, has she?'

'Mrs Trenchard has accepted our settlement of her claim, sir.'

Mr Caldwell swung his invisible number eleven. The envelope fluttered. 'A trifle on the defensive this morning, are we? I don't detect an *involvement*, do I?'

Carefully Richard closed Mr Caldwell's door. 'It's just that Mrs Trenchard seems to me, sir, like quite a pleasant person.' And even that was traitorous. But he was saving his limited supply of courage for later, more daunting matters.

'A pleasant person ... I'd be pleasant too, Wallingford, if I'd just rooked the Accident and General for a cool hundred thou.'

'*Rooked*, Mr Caldwell?'

'A figure of speech, nothing more. Don't look so guilty, man.'

He didn't look guilty. He could have sworn he didn't look guilty.

'I ... I've brought the Mandelbaum papers in as well, sir. They'll be on your desk within the hour.'

'And was Mandelbaum also a pleasant person?'

'He thought I'd come to mend his TV. The screen was all blue.' There was safety in Mr Mandelbaum. 'He kept on telling me how much it had cost him. He's an old man. But we got the Claim Form filled in all right.'

Mr Caldwell sat down, opened Mrs Trenchard's envelope and took out the receipt. 'A pleasant person … certainly she has a pleasant signature. I can actually read it.'

Which required, thank God, no comment. But Richard wished he would get off the subject of Mrs Trenchard. He would prefer a decent, discreet separation between cause and effect, between her and the bombshell he was screwing himself up to deliver. His resignation from the Accident and General.

'This particular pleasant person, Wallingford – will you be seeing her again?'

'To interest her in further insurance, sir?' One of his quicker flashes. He was proud of that.

'What else, man? We are in an insurance situation, are we not?'

'But the Handbook recommends tact in such matters, sir. Pressurization of the bereaved is scarcely accepted practice.'

'Which is why I asked if you were seeing her again.'

A natural lead-in to his announcement that he wouldn't be seeing *anybody* again, not in an insurance situation. But too soon, and too close. In fact, Richard had begun to wonder if he mightn't be wiser to make his announcement some time later in the week.

'I … haven't arranged an appointment, sir.'

Mr Caldwell was holding the receipt up to the light, almost as if he suspected it of being a forgery. 'Frankly, Wallingford, I'd stay away from Superswine if I were you.'

And still Richard kept his nerve. 'If you say so, Mr Caldwell.'

'I do say so. She seems to be one of life's lucky ones. If she insured her home today, well above its market value, it would burn down tomorrow. If she insured the diamonds she doesn't really want, they'd be stolen the very next week. One of life's lucky ones is Superswine. I've learned to spot 'em, Wallingford. And I've learned to avoid 'em like the plague.'

Richard cleared his throat. 'On the subject of insurance in general, sir.' In desperation. If bloody Caldwell wouldn't change the subject then Richard would have to change it for himself. 'I've been thinking – if AGIC insisted on dental charts for every Life Policy holder, then we'd cut out all chance of substitutions.'

Silence descended in Mr Caldwell's office. From outside, through the ceiling-high glass walls, the faint sound of typewriters became audible, and computer terminals, and the ringing of telephones. Richard waited, shifting his feet, wondering what he'd done. He hadn't, he realized, been asked to sit down yet.

Finally, silkily, 'Don't you like your job, Wallingford?'

'It's not that, sir.' A cue, all the same. 'Although, as a matter of fact I –'

'On whose side are you? On the side of those bastards upstairs?'

'On nobody's side, sir. I just thought that if –'

'And you're perfectly right.' Slowly, Mr Caldwell leaned back in his chair, smiled a particularly open and charming smile. 'Dental charts are a marvelous idea. The answer to all our Life Claims problems. Introduce them, though, and you put yourself out of a job. That's all.'

'As far as that's concerned, Mr Caldwell, I –'

'Leave it with me, will you? I'll put it to the directors. All credit to you, though. I've been wondering for some time when someone would come up with it.'

Richard was disconcerted. 'You mean you –'

'I jest, Wallingford. I jest.' The entire conversation, indeed, seemed to Richard to be some ill-conceived sort of jest. 'I should have thought of it myself, of course. Dental charts … and an end to the substitution business. But don't worry – I'll see you get the credit.'

'There's really no need, Mr Caldwell.' At last, via generosity, hopefully disarming, a safer way in. 'There's really no need.'

'But I insist. Those bastards upstairs'll give you a gold-plated watch, like as not.'

'But you see, sir, I … I won't be working for AGIC much longer.'

There. The step was taken. And the whole quitting thing was her idea. She'd really got style: she'd never say a thing like that and go back on it.

Of all the reactions Richard had expected, laughter was not one of them. Suspicion, anger, incredulity … but not *laughter*. Yet Mr Caldwell had thrown his head back and was laughing uproariously. It stung Richard to even greater heights of valor. 'In fact, sir, I would like to leave as soon as possible.'

Mr Caldwell mopped his eyes. 'On full pay, I suppose, to the end of the year?'

'Not at all.' Richard was shocked. What right had he to expect anything of the sort? 'Though I did hope, sir, that in the circumstances the usual month's notice might be dispensed with.'

Mr Caldwell stopped laughing. 'What circumstances were those?'

Shut up, Wallingford. 'No circumstances, sir. None at all … My long service with the company perhaps. My … my good record.'

'In exchange for which I may pass off your dental chart as my own? Are you bribing me, Wallingford?'

With Mr Caldwell, with bosses in general, many of Richard's antennae were inactive. But he thought he knew when he was being played with.

'With a gold-plated watch, sir? I don't think so.'

Mr Caldwell leaned toward him, head on one side, forearms flat on the desk. 'Only the watch, lad? Nothing more?' He spoke in sadness. 'Oh, Wallingford, Wallingford ... What an *honest* man you are.'

The bat was bloody Caldwell's. And the ball. A doubtful position of power, however, when the other man didn't really want to play. So Richard, bewildered, held his peace.

Mr Caldwell sighed. 'Run along, then, man. Tidy up your desk, and then push off.'

'Now?' Still wary. 'You mean *now?*'

'Certainly I mean now. I like you, Wallingford. I really do. And I'll miss your happy smiling face. But you're not really cut out for an insurance situation.'

Which got Richard, in spite of himself, nettled. Being told he could go was all very well. But, 'When I was with Car Claims Assessment, Mr Caldwell, the department did the best figures in nearly –'

'See Pay Section on your way out. I'll ring them.' Mr Caldwell smiled his charming smile again. 'And be sure to give them any expense account items you have lying around. I'll see they're attended to. And your salary to the end of the month.'

'Thank you very much, sir.' Richard hesitated. Everything was coming up roses, and he should have felt like a million. But bloody Caldwell ought to be being bloody. He didn't like it. He walked the two paces to the door, turned. 'And what about my outstanding calls, sir?'

'Deakin's replacement will see to them. He's a keen young man. And dependable. But he's not honest like you, Wallingford.'

Richard liked it even less. The thing was, bloody Caldwell wasn't joking. Not any more. And honesty, knowing what Richard did, came as bitter praise. Inexplicable, too. In Bernie Caldwell's book no man was *honest.*

'And Wallingford –' Richard paused, the door half open. 'Good luck, man. Try not to get eaten alive.'

'Thank you, sir.' What for?

Richard returned to his desk. His papers were already in order: Mrs Pile and Mr Mandelbaum, and the week's list of new calls. He felt a moment's nostalgia – it had been a good job, and he'd been good at it. When he'd been with Car Claims Assessment the department had done the best figures in nearly twenty years. He felt puzzled, also: bloody Caldwell ought to have been being bloody. Perhaps, in his own bloody way, he was. What, for example, was all that about not getting eaten alive? By whom, for God's sake?

But the future beckoned. The future with Mrs Trenchard. She'd never say a thing like that and then go back on it.

Pay Section was down on the seventh floor. He emptied his desk drawer, stared at the assortment of travel brochures and headache pills and elastic bands and contraceptives, and dumped the lot into his wastepaper bin. Then, stooping guiltily, he retrieved the contraceptives and put them in his wallet.

People got judged by their rubbish. He didn't go in search of Deakin's replacement. Like Deakin, he wouldn't be a Tuesday man. And anyway, Richard would rather not meet the bloke who'd be taking over his job. He revolved one last time in his plastic swivel chair, ritually, then went down in the elevator to Pay Section on the seventh floor.

The street up to Mrs Trenchard's high white house was clean and quiet. Doors stood open to the sun and cats basked on area steps. Richard adjusted the sleeve of his second-best suit and glanced at his digital watch: 10:37. He had traveled this street for the very first time, he realized, only a week before.

He found a small parking place, ahead of a red Rolls-Peugeot, and reversed neatly in. He was a good way down the hill from number thirty-seven, and he could probably have found a space much higher up, close to the square with the modest stone mermaid. But he wasn't, suddenly, in all that much of a hurry.

He walked up the hill, paused briefly outside Mrs Trenchard's house, then climbed the steps to the front door. It was, as it had been on all previous occasions, closed. Not the only closed door on the street, but almost. And the significance of this, if there was one, would have escaped him even if his mind had not been on other matters. He wasn't, taking all in all, a great one for significances. He rang the doorbell.

It was a long time before the door opened. And when it did, Mrs Trenchard looked distrait, still in her dressing gown which, although undeniably handsome, gave her none of the style he was used to.

'Come in,' she said.

As if otherwise he mightn't have.

Significances or no significances, her dressing gown and her *Come in*, as if otherwise he mightn't have, told him something was wrong.

Caroline, unusually, had had a terrible night. Not, of course, because she reproached herself. Self-reproach was a waste of time and nervous energy. How often, for God's sake, did a day pass when one might not reproach oneself? Certainly she should have told Richard the truth. Certainly she should not have let him go away believing what he did. But that was over and done with. For various unworthy reasons – no, for one unworthy reason: cowardice – she'd tried to tell him several times, and failed. And no amount of self-reproach would ameliorate her failure. So that, obviously, was over and done with.

Her terrible night, therefore, must have been due to something else, equally a waste of time and nervous energy: dread. Dread of the moment when telling him could no longer be postponed. Yet his judgment of her could never approach in severity her judgment of herself. So, obviously, there was nothing really to dread.

At four o'clock in the morning she had sat up in bed, racked with painful laughter. She was having her terrible night on account of self-reproaches she didn't believe in, and dread that was without cause. So she pulled herself together, lay down again, and firmly went to sleep. And she stayed asleep, firmly, till after ten. These things could be done, if only one were firm enough.

Now she leaned, still in her dressing gown, on the inside of the closed front door. Richard was standing in the hall, by the grandfather clock, looking like death. The time was ten forty-two. Only once since buying the clock, on the day after Haverstock's going, had she omitted to wind it.

'I'm afraid you can't come with me,' she said.

He stared at her. He should have been surprised, pathetic, angry … He should have been *something.*

'To the country, Richard. I don't want you to come with me.'

Not even her use of his name sparked any reaction.

'Us. It's all off. I suppose it was never really on.'

At last, a movement. Toward her. 'It was, you know. It bloody was.'

Toward her. And, with her back to the door, she had nowhere to go. 'You may have thought it was.' The words were holding him off. 'For myself, I was only playing.'

'No. It was on. It bloody was.'

'Have it your own way.' He was right, of course. She hadn't been playing. 'Anyway, it's off now.'

Her indifference worked. He turned and went into the living room. She followed him, stood in the doorway. Allowed herself, 'I'm sorry, Richard.'

'Why?'

She misunderstood him. On purpose. 'Because I don't like disappointing people.'

But it didn't work, not even the insulting understatement. 'Why is it off?' he said patiently.

'Because I'm the sort of person I am, Richard.' She wasn't going to blame him. At least there had to be *some* dignity in the proceedings. 'Because I disappoint people all the time.'

'For Christ's sake –'

'Please don't swear at me, Richard.' Surprised … pathetic … but please not *angry.*

He moved about the room. He was wearing a different suit, rather less dreadful than the other. But his shirt and tie were comfortingly just as bad as ever.

'I take it you've had your breakfast, Richard. I'm ashamed to say I overslept. I wonder if you'd mind if I …?'

'Do what you like.' He paused in his moving about. 'Bloody weighing machines …'

She watched him poise himself aggressively, one knee raised. Her eyes widened, and she bit her lower lip. If there was one thing she hated, it was violence.

He saw she was watching him, and relaxed. 'I thought you were going to have your breakfast.'

'I'll have my breakfast when I choose.'

'You're just like Irene. You know that?'

'Hardly, Richard. Irene is a paranoid schizophrenic.'

'Irene wanted me to kick her TV in. I kicked it in. Irene was pleased.'

Fury washed over her. 'On the contrary, Richard. If there's one thing I hate, it's violence.'

'See what I mean?'

He pointed at her, at her hands. She looked down – they were shaking.

'Let us not quarrel, Richard.' She folded her arms carefully across her chest. 'There's no point at all in quarreling.'

'You're bloody right there's not.' He stared around the room. 'I like your pictures, Mrs Trenchard.'

'They were Haverstock's idea, really. But they have a certain charm.'

'The bathroom upstairs – was that Haverstock's idea, too?'

'We designed it together. I find the overhead mirror a useful aid to masturbation.'

He was still then, suddenly, not moving a muscle. So she'd got to him. It was a pity, she thought, that there was nothing in her life she wouldn't use.

'You didn't seem very surprised, Richard, when I said you couldn't come with me.'

'Surprised? I quit my job this morning on account of us. That shows how surprised I am.'

'I'm sorry.' She really was. 'But I expect you could get it back.'

'Maybe.'

'And anyway, you won't need it. Not with my forty thousand.'

She waited.

For him to go and leave her in peace.

But, 'Maybe,' he said again.

So, 'Did you tell Rose-Ann, too? About us?'

'Of course I told her.'

'It's no use trying to make me feel guilty.'

'All right – I didn't tell her.'

'I said from the very beginning that we hadn't known each other long enough.'

'I didn't tell her.'

'Less than a week, Richard – I mean, what did you expect?'

'I said I didn't tell her. Stuck-up bitch.'

He pushed out past her into the hall. She heard his voice fading in the direction of Haverstock's study. 'Stuck-up bitch, stuck-up bitch …' Of course he hadn't told Rose-Ann. Rose-Ann who, unaware of her limitations, yet operated faultlessly within them. She followed him to Haverstock's study, stood in that doorway instead.

Richard was leaning on Haverstock's steel-and-leather desk, his head lowered. The remains of Irene's dephaser were still in Haverstock's fireplace.

'Am I the stuck-up bitch, Richard? Or is Rose-Ann?'

He didn't lift his head. 'What are you going to do about the pheasant job?'

'It's for a couple.'

'I know that.'

'So I'm going to have to call them and tell them it's off.'

'You haven't yet?'

There'd not been time. 'I'll do it now.' There'd been plenty.

'And what then?'

'I don't know what you mean.'

'Without the job, what'll you do then?'

'I've a lovely house. I'll stay in it.'

He looked up. 'I've a nice house, too.'

'I'm sure you have.'

'With a sun parlor out back. It's not like this, of course. But I'm not complaining.'

He sat down at Haverstock's desk. Half time, she thought. And caught herself thinking it. Now she really wanted him to go.

'Yesterday was all right,' he said.

For the sake of accuracy, 'Some of it.'

'Some of it.' He nodded. 'Most of it.' He ran a fingernail to and fro along the join in the leather desk top. 'It was the Singing that did it.'

'No!' But he'd cut her open.

He shrugged his shoulders, looked at the dirt his nail had gathered from the join in the leather desk top. She took a deep breath, went forward into the room, and picked up the telephone.

'I'll call Jerry and Madge.' Bleeding.

Abruptly he got to his feet. 'You'll find me in the garden when you've done.'

She waited till he had gone, then dialed the number Humphrey had jotted down on the blotter. After a long, unendurable time Jerry answered.

'Good morning,' she said. 'This is Mrs Trenchard speaking.'

She told him they wouldn't be taking the job. He said he was sorry to hear it. She said there were personal reasons. He said he quite understood.

After she had hung up, she leaned for a while against the steel edge of Haverstock's desk. Then she went out to Richard. He was sitting in one of the white wicker chairs on the terrace. The living room, Haverstock's study, the terrace …

It broke her. All of it. Suddenly it broke her.

'You bastard,' she said. 'I only wanted you to hold my hand. And you wouldn't even do that.'

She was weeping.

He looked away. 'Not much use holding hands, old dear. Not with a Singing.'

'Old dear? *Old dear?* Is that all you have to say to me?'

'You wait for them to stop. That's all.'

'But I was frightened.'

He jumped to his feet. 'You think I wasn't?'

'I didn't want to go, Richard.'

'Go?' He was shouting now. 'How could you go when you'd never bloody come?'

She was close to him then, close enough to slap his face. With all her strength, jerking his head sideways.

He raised his arm. 'Stuck-up bitch.'

'Coward.'

'Bitch.'

He hit her then, openhanded, just as she'd hit him.

'I'll kick your balls in.'

'Try it.'

'Coward.'

'Fucking bitch.'

They circled, watched for an opening. Suddenly he laughed. 'Just look at us,' he said.

He, not she.

And still she didn't join him. 'You let me down,' she said.

'What did you expect? It's a bird, it's a plane, it's Superman?'

'No. Just –'

'I knew what you expected. I … just couldn't make it.'

Their eyes met. She touched his arm. 'No one could,' she said.

But that wasn't true. Not Richard, perhaps: not Humphrey's nature's gentleman, her own different animal. The terms alone were a barrier no man could have climbed over, certainly not with solely a last minute wholeheartedness to help him. But there were others who might. Given time, and a steadfast belief in the possibility, there were others who might. Richard, unignorable dreadfulness and all, had shown her that.

The garden was very quiet. If there'd been a thrush in her beech tree, it had been frightened away by their shouting long ago. And it was too early in the day for electric mowers.

He led her around, and sat her down in one of the white wicker chairs. He stood behind her. 'You still haven't had your breakfast,' he said.

She smiled. There was security in non sequiturs that weren't. 'It wasn't fair of you to say I haven't come,' she told him. 'I have – hundreds of times.'

'I didn't mean that.'

'Of course you didn't.'

'And you know I don't like dirty talk.'

'I'm sorry.' She'd planned it as the lead-in to something else. 'You see, Richard, I –'

She stopped. There'd been something else she wanted to say. But not, after all, to him. To herself, really. And she no longer needed, if she ever had, to vocalize her most important discoveries.

No, she never had. Not even to herself … She stared at the brushed green grass of her lawn. But wasn't that what her new, steadfast belief was all about? That she might, just once, dare have them understand each other? She and herself, herself and Richard?

The only truly difficult thing she'd ever have accomplished.

'I did come, Richard. To you. That *was* what you meant, wasn't it? For a time yesterday, I did come to you.'

He tried to interrupt, but she held up her hand.

'You thought I was playing a game. Because I thought I was, too. So you went along with me.' Simple, laborious words. 'And when the Singing happened, and I asked for something more than the game, you moved out. Of course you did. It looked as if I'd changed the rules without telling you, so you moved out.'

Simple, laborious … An unsmart prosiness, but not, please God, a talking-down for his sake. A necessity, rather, if one was to dare to – no, if *she* was to dare to have them understand each other. No longer the cowardly impersonal. She and herself, herself and Richard.

'But I hadn't changed the rules, Richard. I'd discovered, instead, that it wasn't a game. I really had come to you.'

He stood behind her. 'Now she tells me.'

'Because I want us to understand.' She'd lived from joke to joke herself. But not now. She twisted around now, while it wasn't too late, and faced him. 'I loved you, Richard.'

Instantly, too instantly, 'And what about me, for Christ's sake?'

'No.' She stared up at him, asking him to match her honesty.

He stood, with his suit that was not as dreadful as the other, and his shirt and tie that were as bad as ever, and his fake handmade shoes, and his hair that was detectably waved, and his fingernails that were slightly grubby, looking down at her. She had no idea what he saw. The question, for once, never even entered her head.

'No,' he said finally. And again, 'No.'

He found himself smiling, though at what he wasn't quite certain. And as for her, she was grinning like that bloody Labrador down on the pheasant farm. He thought for the second time how crazy they must seem: first screaming at each other like fishwives (whatever fishwives were), and now laughing together like a couple of kids. And all over what? A lousy job that neither of them really wanted.

That, and who loved who. Which people always went on about. Either you did, or you didn't. So he was the man who'd socked her for forty thousand. So she was the woman who'd led him up the garden path, then spat in his eye. Maybe that made them quits. Either way, nobody had to come any more, and nobody had to go.

'I'll see you again?' he said.

'I don't expect so.'

'Why not?'

'We'll both be too busy.'

Which was a relief, because he suddenly didn't think he wanted to. 'What now?' he said.

'It's eleven o'clock. If I don't have breakfast soon it'll be time for lunch.'

She held out her hand and he helped her up. They went into the house. As it closed about them he realized how much he hated it.

'Don't you hate all this?' he said.

She seemed astonished. 'Oh, I won't be staying. I don't know what I'll do, but I won't be staying.'

'You'll be all right, though?'

'I'll be all right, Richard.'

She turned left into the kitchen. He followed her, watched her fill the coffeepot and stuff some cardboardy bits of biscuit into a toast rack. He ought to be on his way.

'Looks like a boring old breakfast,' he said.

She laughed. 'It's no use, Richard, throwing the baby out with the bath water.'

Christ, she was at it again. 'You should hear yourself, Caroline. Half the things you say don't make bloody sense.'

She laughed again. 'You called me Caroline.'

'You said I was to. It's your name, isn't it?'

'Of course I did.' She fetched marmalade. 'It's a boring old breakfast, but will you have some?'

'I ought to be on my way.'

She stood by the coffeepot, waited till it started perking. But she didn't try to persuade him. 'I'll come with you to the door,' she said.

They walked through the house. He remembered how he'd nearly bust up her lounge. But he'd been caught that way once before, with Irene.

'You really are a bit like Irene,' he said.

'The nice bits, I hope.'

'No. The nasty bits.'

'Then I'll have to watch it.'

If she'd seemed upset, he'd have said something more. About her nice bits being so much nicer, perhaps. But she didn't seem at all upset. He stood on the front doorstep, shading his eyes against the sun.

She said, 'Shall you try to get your old job back?'

He shrugged. 'In cars, maybe. There won't be any Life Claims Verification if your dental chart idea catches on. I like cars. I'm good at cars.'

'That's you fixed, then.'

He looked at her sideways. 'Think of me, will you, when the Maserati comes up for renewal?'

'Won't we be too busy?'

'Business is business.'

'I doubt if I'll be keeping the Maserati.'

'Whatever you get instead. Just think of me.' He hunted in his wallet. 'My card.'

She took it, studied it solemnly. '*Richard Wallingford, Esq* … I'll think of you, Richard Wallingford, Esq.'

'Good.' He hurried away down the steps. 'You mind you do.' At the bottom he turned and waved. 'You mind you do.'

Then he saw that he needn't have hurried away, that there was nothing to hurry away from, a beautiful, stylish woman standing in the sun, nothing to hurry away from, so he climbed the steps again and hugged her.

'You mind you do, Mrs Trenchard,' he said.

Mr Wallingford and Mrs Trenchard: two people no longer strangers. And now, alas for lubricity, without the remotest need for anything *unsuitable*.

Later, sitting in his yellow city electric after she'd hugged him back and he'd gone away again, but slowly this time, decently, down the steps and all the way down the street to where he'd parked it, he felt a stiffness in his pocket where he'd just replaced his wallet. He drew out Carson Bandbridge's check and tore it into small pieces. He put the pieces on the seat next to him, ready to dump in the first litter basket he came to. He'd never honestly believed in Carson Bandbridge. And neither, he suspected, had Rose-Ann.

EXTRODUCTION

On the eleventh floor of AGIC House a man was dialing a telephone number in an office with glass walls up to the ceiling. It wasn't a very fine office, even by the naïve standards of 1986. It was possibly three meters square, with a desk, and a filing cabinet, and a plastic wastepaper basket, and two chairs. It was, in fact, a departmental manager's office, at a time when departmental managers were still rather more, but also rather less, than silicone chips.

The departmental manager within the office, however, was very fine indeed. His clothes were exquisite, his haircut superb, and he put it about that he'd recently inherited a great deal of money from a maiden aunt. And, being after all a departmental manager, he was believed. Departmental managers were.

He was fine, also, in the confident way he dialed his telephone, a number he knew by heart, clearly assuming without question that he would instantly obtain the connection he required. He was obviously a man accustomed to obtaining instantly the connections, and everything else, that he required. Of lean, athletic build, he looked considerably younger than his forty-seven years, for he kept himself painstakingly in shape: during the summer he played tennis, in the winter, golf, and he sparred all the year around in a gymnasium not far from his place of work. On his desk there was a clock in green onyx, with gilt pillars, and a neat brass plaque: *Bernard Caldwell. From his friends in the Waverley Squash Club*. He had retired from squash five years before, Club Champion at forty-two.

He finished dialing the number. Instantly, a young man's voice, crisp and helpful, answered.

'Good afternoon. Disappearances Advisory Service.'

The man in the office leaned back and put his feet up on the desk. The connection, inevitably, was the one he required.

'Fitzhenry here,' he said.

'Sir?'

'How are you, Cattermole?'

'In the pink, thank you. And you, sir?'

'Fine. Fine … I thought you ought to know, Cattermole. I've dispensed with your branch collector.'

'I'm sorry to hear it, Mr Fitzhenry.'

'She proved unreliable.'

'There was always that chance, sir. Though she was in many ways ideal. A ... *financial* unreliability?'

'Not at all. She observed the split meticulously. But someone had told her about our conservation of resources policy.'

'It was not I, Mr Fitzhenry.'

'I'm sure it wasn't. But she passed the information on to a customer.'

'You couldn't have that, sir.'

'No. Any more than I can have people in the branches shooting their mouths off.'

There was a long pause. The man in the office turned up his toes and watched the creases come and go in the expensive leather of his shoes.

At last Cattermole spoke. He had evidently decided to change the subject.

'Shall we be taking her into stock, sir?'

'Certainly not. I sent her back where she came from.'

'Very magnanimous, if I may say so, Mr Fitzhenry.'

'Don't crawl.'

There was another pause.

'Will we be getting a replacement, sir?'

'I'm not sure. There's been a development. I may have dealt with it, but I'm not sure. It could put us out of business.'

'Dental charts, sir?'

'We always knew it couldn't last, Cattermole.'

'But there is a saying, Mr Fitzhenry, concerning the making of hay. Stocks are very good at the moment. And we had a call only twenty minutes ago. A very promising estate. Battersby's checking it out.'

'Tell him to cancel. Tell him we haven't a collector.'

'We could always up the initial fee, sir. Just to tide us over.'

The man in the office frowned, took his feet off his desk.

'We're selling a social service, Cattermole. The fee must be low. That's how we get cooperation.'

'That, and the heavy mob, sir.'

'Heavy mobs cost money. A back where we started situation. Tell Battersby to cancel.'

'Anything you say, Mr Fitzhenry.'

Cattermole, in an office even less fine, a small, shabby room on the second floor of an undertaker's premises, eased his neck in his sparkling white collar. Mr Fitzhenry pretended he didn't like yes-men, but really he loved them.

'We always knew it wouldn't last, Mr Fitzhenry.'

'Also, there may be trouble with the Trenchard widow.'

'She rated as a Class A risk, sir. Contingency plans are available.'

'Reuse might be difficult. I gather she's not a very common type. I'd rather we didn't take her into stock.'

'Contingency plans are available, sir.' The heavy mob. And cheap at the price.

'I'm glad to hear it. And, Cattermole … why did you tell your branch collector about our conservation of resources policy?'

'I, Mr Fitzhenry?'

'You, Cattermole.'

Cattermole, at bay, stared wildly around his small, shabby office. In an unguarded moment he had indeed told his branch collector about their conservation of resources policy. Stones in the coffins. He'd hoped it might make her laugh: it had.

'Not I, Mr Fitzhenry.'

'Not you, Cattermole?'

'No, sir.'

'Cattermole, you're sacked.'

It was a euphemism. Nobody in Disappearances Advisory Service was sacked. They knew too much.

'But, Mr Fitzhenry –'

Cattermole expected to be interrupted. Ominously he wasn't.

'But, Mr Fitzhenry, I swear it was not I who told her. Battersby – why could it not have been Battersby?'

There appeared to be interference on the line. He tried again. 'Or one of the men down in the Refrigeration Annex? I always said it was a mistake, having the collector come here with cash deliveries. My recommendation was for neutral ground to be chosen – I even put it in a branch memo.'

Memo or not, he was wasting his time. Contingency plans were available. Alternatively, he could just as easily be taken into stock. He was, he decided sadly, a *very* common type.

But, 'I swear it was not I who told her, Mr Fitzhenry.'

He was sweating. The telephone receiver was slippery in his hand. He pressed it more firmly to his ear.

'Mr Fitzhenry? *Please*, Mr Fitzhenry …'

Mr Fitzhenry didn't answer. And it wasn't interference on the line. What came over it was a loud, unpleasant singing sound. And now, although Cattermole knew it to be impossible, a sickly smell of synthetic roses.

Thoughtfully Cattermole replaced the telephone receiver. He stared at it. Could it be possible, he wondered, that Mr Fitzhenry himself had been taken into stock? Someone else's? He stood up, tiptoed across his small, shabby office, out through the door, and down the stairs. Once out on the street on which the undertaker's premises were situated, he began to run. There was no need to, really, but he ran all the same. And he didn't look back.

Sometimes, my children, even for a poor silly pheasant who didn't know the rules, just sometimes the going was good.

If you've enjoyed these books and would like to read more, you'll find literally thousands of classic Science Fiction & Fantasy titles through the **SF Gateway**

✶

For the new home of Science Fiction & Fantasy . . .

✶

For the most comprehensive collection of classic SF on the internet . . .

✶

Visit the SF Gateway

www.sfgateway.com

D. G. Compton (1930–)

David Guy Compton was born in London in 1930. His early works were crime novels published under 'Guy Compton', but he began producing SF as 'D. G. Compton' in 1965 with *The Quality of Mercy*. His 1970 novel *The Steel Crocodile* received a Nebula nomination, but it was 1974's *The Continuous Catherine Mortenhoe* that made his reputation. Eerily predictive of the 21st century's obsessions with media voyeurism and 'reality television', it was filmed as *Death Watch* in 1980. Although he spent many years in the United States, D. G. Compton now lives in the Southwest of England.